Her Christmas Prince

HEIDI BETTS
BRENDA HARLEN
CATHERINE MANN

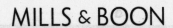

MIX
Paper from
responsible sources
FSC C007454

This book is produced from independently certified FSC™
paper to ensure responsible forest management.

For more information visit: www.harpercollins.co.uk/green

Printed and bound in Spain
by CPI, Barcelona

MILLS & BOON

First Published in Great Britain 2019
by Mills & Boon, an imprint of HarperCollins*Publishers*
1 London Bridge Street, London, SE1 9GF

HER CHRISTMAS PRINCE © 2019 Harlequin Books S. A.

Christmas in His Royal Bed © 2007 Heidi Betts
Royal Holiday Bride © 2011 Brenda Harlen
Yuletide Baby Surprise © 2013 Catherine Mann

ISBN: 978-0-263-27945-0

1119

SALLY WORBOYES

Banished from Bow

Harriet was abandoned as a child in nineteenth-century London's East End. Ragged and terrified, she was forced to scavenge for her food until Mary Dean found her and took her to a smart house in Bow where she was brought up as a sister to Mary and her younger brother Arthur.

But 17 years later, Harriet and Arthur have fallen in love, and Harriet is pregnant. Driven out of Bow by neighbours who spit at them and call them heathens, they seek refuge in two rented rooms in Stepney.

Eking out a meagre but free existence, they are happy, but then Arthur, like so many others working as railway delivery-men, is caught pilfering and faces a prison sentence. However this is soon to be the least of their worries. Harriet has kept a diary she stole as a child, the diary of the perpetrator of the Whitechapel killings. The Jack the Ripper murders. And now the owner of the diary has returned to the East End in search of Harriet and the diary – and will stop at nothing to get it back . . .

CORONET BOOKS
Hodder & Stoughton

SALLY WORBOYES

Girl from Brick Lane

Not all is as it seems at Number 10 Beaumont Square. The apparently perfect marriage of Tobias and Grace Wellington is fractured when a dark secret emerges. But to the public eye, nothing changes.

However twenty years later Tobias' past catches up with him. Flora Brown and her daughter Beanie are employed below stairs as cook and scullery maid. Beanie is the illegitimate daughter Flora conceived with Tobias all those years ago. Tobias fears that she will talk if he sacks her, so he has no choice but to let them stay: him above the stairs and them below.

The Wellingtons' offspring, Sarah and Herbert, have no idea that the scullery maid is their half-sister. Sarah and Beanie become great friends; Herbert, however, is a class snob and dislikes Beanie intensely. In the meantime Grace finds that she likes and trusts her cook: they are both suffragettes. During a few sherries one night the truth about Beanie comes out. After tears and apologies, the two women become even closer and vow never to tell the children that they share the same father.

However, secrets are hard to keep and inevitably the wrong person gets hold of the right information.

CORONET BOOKS
Hodder & Stoughton

SALLY WORBOYES

Wild Hops

It is 1959 and emotions are running high in the Kent hop fields, where the harvest is traditionally picked by East Enders on their summer break. Picking by hand is becoming a thing of the past as mechanisation takes over. The Armstrong family – Jack, Laura and their daughter, Kay – are devastated by the news. Far from the bustle of Stepney, the hop fields offer hard work but fresh clean air and lively social gatherings around the campfires.

While Jack leads the protest against the machines, Laura Armstrong is otherwise preoccupied: will this mean the end of her seasonal love affair with the farm owner, Richard Wright? And what of Kay who, on the brink of womanhood, craves adventure and creates turmoil when she and the handsome gypsy lad, Zacchi, meet in secret?

As tensions grow between the East Enders and the local Romanies, it becomes clear that this summer will change lives forever . . .

WILD HOPS is a vibrant tale of illicit love, firm friendships and the indomitable character of the East Enders.

'Sizzles with passion' *Guardian*

CORONET BOOKS
Hodder & Stoughton

SALLY WORBOYES

Over Bethnal Green

Jessie Smith's hope of a blissful married life is dashed when her husband Tom is called up for army training. She had been looking forward to living with him and baby Billy in their small terraced house in Bethnal Green, even though Tom's irresponsible behaviour sometimes borders on the downright criminal. But there is more to fear – the horror of a new world war.

When Tom is sent abroad and the Blitz begins, Jessie is left to cope with the baby alone. Her twin, Hannah, has been recruited to the secret establishment Station X at Bletchley Park. Immersed in her work decoding German messages, Hannah has no idea of Jessie's desperation. And when Tom does a runner and goes AWOL, things get rapidly worse . . .

In OVER BETHNAL GREEN, Sally Worboyes once again captures the vibrant spirit of the East End during the forties, and the resilience and character of those who lived there.

CORONET BOOKS
Hodder & Stoughton

SALLY WORBOYES

Down Stepney Way

Docker's Daughter

CORONET BOOKS
Hodder & Stoughton

Down Stepney Way copyright © 1999 by Sally Worboyes
Docker's Daughter copyright © 1995 by Sally Worboyes

Down Stepney Way first published in Great Britain in 1999
by Hodder & Stoughton

Docker's Daughter first published in Great Britain in 1995
by Headline Book Publishing

This omnibus edition published in 2003 by Hodder & Stoughton
A division of Hodder Headline

A Coronet Paperback
10 9 8 7 6 5 4 3 2 1

A CIP catalogue record for this title is available
from the British Library

ISBN 0 340 83079 4

Typeset by Palimpsest Book Production Limited,
Polmont, Stirlingshire

Printed and bound in Great Britain by
Mackays of Chatham PLC, Chatham, Kent

Hodder and Stoughton
A division of Hodder Headline
338 Euston Road
London NW1 3BH

Down Stepney Way

For Mum
My thanks to Kirsty Fowkes and Jane Heller

Chapter One

1936
In the clear October morning, clusters of people from around the East End were gathering in Cable Street with one aim in mind – to stop the Blackshirts from marching through Stepney. Some were filling their pockets with stones from ready-made piles while others armed themselves with pieces of splintered wood and bottles. The sombre mood changed to one of unease when a local lad arrived, excited and out of breath, to announce that the march had begun. The Jewish Party and the Communists were joining forces to make it clear that the Fascists would *not* get through.

Oswald Mosley had originally planned to meet his legion at Royal Mint Street, march on to Aldgate, along Commercial Road and into Salmon Lane in Limehouse, where a big outdoor meeting was to be held, but the route had been changed. He was in fact leading the Blackshirts along the Highway by the docks towards Cable Street.

The police were out in force, there to see the procession through without trouble, but men, women and children were ready to rebel against authority and had come out to make their voices heard and to show their outrage. Along the route barricades had been built of beds, chairs, and anything else that the people could lay their hands on. Prepared for the worst,

the Jewish Party had set up a first-aid post in Aldgate, near the Whitechapel library, and a team of cyclist messengers had been organised between main points and headquarters. Another team was ready to rally those still inside their homes and urge them to come out and help stop the march of the Fascists.

Suddenly another young messenger climbed onto a make-shift platform and yelled, 'They're coming! They're coming! The Blackshirts are coming!'

There was a roar of protest and then the brass band began to play. Soon the streets were filled with patriotic song: 'Rule, Britannia, Britannia rules the waves, Britons never never never Shall be slaves . . .'

Jessie Warner gripped her younger brothers' hands and pulled them through the seething mob. Pushing and dragging the boys, she wove her way through as best she could, cursing herself for taking this route home from the Tower of London.

'Is it a war, Jessie? Is it?' Stephen, the seven-year-old, was too frightened to cry.

'No, Stephen, but we shouldn't be here! There's going to be a fight!'

'Why, Jessie? Why are they going to fight? They're grown-ups . . .'

'Just don't let go of my hand,' she ordered.

'It's the Blackshirt march, Stephen!' screeched Alfie, fired up and doing his utmost to pull away from his sister. 'We can watch from a side road!'

'No! Keep moving!' Jessie kept a tight hold on both of them but the sudden jerking as thirteen-year-old Alfie stopped in his tracks caused her to lose her balance and twist her ankle. Her scream shot through the noise of the mob but was ignored. She limped across the pavement to sit on the windowsill of an old terraced house.

'You shouldn't have done that, Alfie,' said Jessie, wincing in pain. 'You could have brought the three of us down.'

Alfie wasn't listening; stretched to full height and craning

his neck, he was desperate to get a view through the ever growing assembly. 'I'm gonna make my way up the Highway to watch 'em march!'

'You are not! You stay right where you are until this pain eases, then we'll go home, *together*.'

'Come out of your houses!' a young Jewish lad flew by, yelling at top voice. 'They're on their way. Come out and fight!' He was waving a red flag. 'The police are there as well! The police are coming!'

'It *is* a war, Jessie,' murmured Stephen, tears now rolling down his cheeks. 'They're going to blow us up. I want to go home.'

'We will, sweetheart. We will. Just give me a minute.' She pulled the silk scarf from her neck and tied it round her ankle.

'Ready now then, Jess?' asked Stephen, gripping her hand.

'Nearly.' Jessie removed her combs which had come loose, pulled her long wavy hair back and secured it. 'Now we'll go. We'll stop off at Grandfather's and—'

'The police are on horseback!' Alfie was beside himself. 'They've got batons and guns!'

Within seconds, stones and bottles were being thrown in the direction of the mounted police. Shouted insults followed. More stones. More bottles. The sound of breaking glass and yells of abuse were terrifying. 'Surrender!' yelled one man. 'They shall not pass! *They shall not pass!*' Others joined in with the chant and more groups arrived carrying banners. The noise reached a crescendo and Cable Street was packed with an army of civilians ripe for confrontation.

Alfie cheered loudly. 'They're pulling up railings and paving stones!' he said excitedly.

'We should go *now*, Jessie,' said Stephen, trying to be brave.

'Yes, we should.' Grabbing Alfie by the collar, Jessie hauled him away, defying the sickening pain shooting through her ankle.

3

Alfie half-heartedly struggled against her but deep down he, too, was frightened. The oncoming clatter of hooves on cobblestones and sound of breaking glass urged Jessie on and gave her the strength of two people. She pushed through the mob, her ears ringing with the roar of the protesters: 'Down with the Fascists! Fuck off to Germany! Sod off to Spain! Go and live in Italy! Get out of England!'

When the three of them reached their grandfather's house in Broom Court, Jessie was trembling. Stephen had stopped crying but the occasional sob still escaped as his mind filled with what he had seen and heard. Alfie was moody with himself because secretly he had wanted to leave the frightening scene. But he could always blame his big sister – it was she, after all, who had forced him away. Still, he was angry at missing an opportunity to throw stones at the police.

'It's not fair,' he grumbled. 'There were lots of kids there who were younger than me. I shouldn't 'ave took any notice of you, Jessie. If it wasn't for you hurting your ankle, I wouldn't 'ave come away.'

'Shut up, Alfie, and don't you *dare* cheek Grandmother Blake this time.' Instead of knocking respectfully on the door, as she would normally, Jessie found herself banging the knocker with some urgency. Grandmother Blake appeared looking very stern and disdainful.

'I'm sorry,' said Jessie, shrinking, 'we were in Cable Street and—'

'You've woken your grandfather,' came the terse reply. 'You shouldn't be knocking at all, never mind nearly smashing the door down. What do you want?'

'If we could just come in ... I've sprained my ankle and—'

'If you could walk from Cable Street to here, you can walk home. Let your mother see to you.' Her unyielding expression showed no sign of weakening as she began to close the door.

'I'm very thirsty,' said the brave Stephen, 'and Jessie's ankle is very, very swollen!'

Glancing dispassionately at Jessie's leg, Grandmother Blake raised her eyes and sighed. 'That's nothing. Tell your mother to put a cold flannel on it.'

'If we can just come into the passage for a tiny while,' pleaded Jessie. Her ankle was throbbing badly. 'I need to sit down on the stairs and if Stephen could have a glass of water—'

'No. Your grandfather's resting. He needs the quiet.' The door was slowly closing between them when Jessie heard the familiar quiet cough of her grandfather in the passage.

'That's all right,' came the softer voice of the man she loved. 'Let them come in for a minute.'

'Please yourself,' said Grandmother Blake, turning away. 'They can wait in the hall. I'll fetch a glass of water.'

'You shouldn't bang on the door like that,' said Willy, as his grandchildren filed in. 'What's the matter?' He looked from the boys to Jessie. 'Did someone hurt you?'

Alfie peered up at him. 'What's a Fascist?'

Quietly chuckling, Willy pulled on his braces. 'Someone who's not a Jew. Why?'

'There's a battle going on in Cable Street and—'

'Blackshirts and Reds,' sighed Willy, rolling his eyes. 'I might have guessed. Go on down into the scullery, you can wrap a wet cloth round that ankle, Jessie. I'll get Grandmother Blake to make a pot of weak tea to warm your bellies, then be off home.' Gazing into Jessie's frightened face he tried to comfort her with one of his infrequent smiles. 'Gang warfare, that's all it is. Give it a month and it'll be forgotten.'

'I'm sorry we didn't go straight home, Grandfather, but my ankle – I could hardly walk another step.'

'That's all right,' he said, 'you did the right thing, but don't stay too long. You know your grandmother likes her quiet.'

That was the last time Jessie saw her grandfather alive. A few

5

weeks later, Willy returned from a day's work at his cobbler shop, sat down by the fire and slept his last sleep. He had told no one about the severe pains in his chest that had been troubling him of late.

Jessie took his death very badly, crying into her pillow nightly and asking the same question of God over and over. Why? Why him? Why was her grandfather dead when there were so many wicked people walking about in the streets?

Unlike Willy's other grandchildren, Jessie had been a regular visitor to 10 Broom Court since she was old enough to walk there on her own. Sometimes when she'd banged the iron knocker of the dark green door, one of her uncles would appear in the doorway, frowning. He'd put a finger to his lips and whisper in warning, 'Grandfather's in a mood.'

Shrugging, Jessie would slip past, along the narrow passageway and down the staircase to the basement where she knew he would be sitting in his armchair, looking into the glowing coals of the fire. Willy Blake had spent most of his leisure time thinking or reading. When he was absorbed in a book, Jessie would tiptoe across the room, lower herself into the other armchair by the fire and keep quiet until spoken to.

She loved the small, quiet room, with just the sound of the hissing coals, the rustle of a page as he turned it, and the breathing of his black mongrel dog, Peggy, who lay quietly at his feet. It was here that she discovered the reward of patience. When in the right mood, her grandfather would draw her into his private world, arousing her interest and curiosity. Then, he would tell her fascinating stories of times gone by. Other times, not one single word passed between them. He would end the visit by closing his book and giving her a nod or she would leave of her own accord, sensing his mood, and quietly pull the door shut behind her until she heard the brass catch drop.

When arrangements were being made for his funeral, Jessie was mortified to hear that even though she was sixteen, a

working girl and the eldest of her brothers and sister, she was still considered too young to attend his funeral.

'It's not an occasion for young people, Jessie,' explained her mother, Rose. 'Stop fussing now and be more like your brothers and sister. They don't want to go.'

But Jessie did want to go, very much. There had been a special bond between her and her grandfather. She had inherited his Germanic looks, hair so blonde it was almost white and blue eyes, and was the only grandchild to have done so. She knew she was closer to him than any of the others.

On the day he was buried, Jessie stood with her arms woven through the black railings outside his house in Broom Court, watching with the neighbours as the hearse slowly pulled away. The sound of the horses' hooves echoing on the flagstones reminded her of the last day she saw him alive, the day of the Cable Street battle.

An occasional shake of the head and pursing of lips were the only movements from onlookers. To the people who lived in the courtyard, he was an ordinary man, of few words, who'd always return a smile and doff his hat or cap and who kept himself to himself. A silver-haired gentleman, no more, no less.

Jessie often thought about his last comforting words to her after the riot in Cable Street. *Give it a month and it'll be forgotten.* But he had been wrong. People were still talking about it. Communists were boasting that they had won the biggest fight in working-class history and the Blackshirts were angry because their march had been stopped. Insulting slogans against Jews were still appearing on walls in Jessie's neighbourhood.

Much to the family's dismay, Grandmother Blake soon married. Her new husband was a man with whom she had been having a secret affair. The grandchildren were told to call him Uncle. It was then that Jessie stopped going to the house. The mood there changed – the parties had begun. The piano in the best room, where Willy used to sit and play soft tunes, was used to accompany bawdy songs of the day, sung by the

gathering of boozy friends. Laughter and ribald conversation filled the place, forcing out any trace of Willy's presence as master of the house.

On her last visit and before the new 'uncle' moved in, Jessie asked permission to tidy the locked cupboard to the left of the fireplace where her grandfather used to sit. It was his private cupboard and no one had been allowed to pry into it. Grandmother Blake grudgingly let her, though it was clear the contents of the cupboard didn't interest her much. Jessie hadn't got far in her search for something that would remind her of him when she found a small worn family album. She didn't recognise anyone in any of the faded photographs except for the one of her grandfather, which was loose and at the back of the album. Younger though he was, his eyes and high cheekbones placed him. He was standing with one hand resting on the hood of a large, old-fashioned pram, and in the pram, cramped together in a space for one, were two baby girls, sitting up and smiling.

Before closing the album, Jessie found, tucked inside its leather cover, a marriage certificate — between William Ernest Gunter and Ingrid Weiss. She held her breath and stared at it, knowing it was important but not understanding why. Then, for the first time in her life Jessie stole something. She stole the certificate and the loose photograph, stuffing them quickly into her boot, half afraid Grandmother Blake would burst in and catch her. For some reason she felt that the two were connected and that the piece of paper belonged to Willy, even though the surname wasn't the one she knew him by. The name of the woman he'd married, according to the certificate, was a mystery too, because it wasn't the name of her grandmother, or at least not the name of the person she had believed to be her grandmother. Was it possible that the cold, unfeeling woman known to her as Grandmother Blake was not kin after all? *She's Willy's daughter, all right,* is what Jessie had heard said about her own mother, Rose, but she couldn't remember anyone saying that she was the daughter of Grandmother Blake.

With the marriage certificate and photo safely hidden inside her ankle boot, Jessie left that special room for the last time. Heart pounding, she took the stairs two at a time, terrified that she might be found out. Once outside in the street, she made her way home to Stepney Green, and in the privacy of the bedroom she shared with her sister, Dolly, she pulled the crinkled document from her boot and read it again. William Ernest Gunter, occupation shoemaker. Her grandfather's Christian names were William Ernest and he had been a shoemaker but the surname was wrong. His name, so everyone had been led to believe, was Blake, and the woman thought to be his wife was hardly German, and her name was not Ingrid.

Jessie glanced around her bedroom for a secure place to hide her finds. She fixed on the air vent which had a metal cover. She climbed onto a chair and slipped both the certificate and photograph inside, safe in the knowledge that she could reach in and take it out whenever she wanted. Happier, she lay down on her bed, feeling as if she still had a very special part of her grandfather to herself. She wondered if Ingrid Gunter might still be his wife and her own real grandmother. She must have died – it seemed the only explanation. Jessie allowed herself a brief dream that the old woman was alive and lived nearby.

Jessie felt a mixture of hope and warmth at the thought. Maybe the strange feeling that had come and gone all through her life could now be explained. The feeling that something or someone was missing from her world. She decided then that somehow she would find out the truth and perhaps discover her real grandmother.

On Christmas Eve, following Willy's death, Jessie woke to the sound of her father, Robert, coughing in the passage. His footsteps on the lino had seemed to be part of her dream, but from the thin stream of light shining through the gap under the bedroom door she could make out her surroundings and was relieved to realise that she was in her room and out of the

bad dream which had gripped her. Shadowy, evil men had been chasing her and her grandfather through dark woods. She had been having recurring nightmares since her grandfather died.

Safe and secure, she glanced at her sister Dolly, fast asleep in her bed a few feet away. Dolly, at the age of fifteen, slept as soundly as a baby. Alfie and little Stephen shared the bedroom next door and above them were the two attic rooms where the lodgers Mr and Mrs McCarthy lived.

Lying in her warm bed, with the sound of muted voices below, Jessie looked forward to the beginning of this special day, her seventeenth birthday. Hearing the mantel clock strike six, she did as she always did and drew her feather eiderdown round her, making the most of it. The room was freezing cold and condensation had iced on the inside of the window. She would wait until she heard the sound of the street door close behind her father as he went out into the frosty morning, on his way to the docks where he worked as a crane driver. Much as she wanted to see him before he went out, she knew he wouldn't have time to see her open her presents.

A few minutes after the street door closed behind him, she got up, wrapped her grey blanket round her and crept out of the room, only to find that her brother Alfie was in the passage, ready himself to creep downstairs.

'Where do you think you're going, Alfie?' said Jessie, all-knowing.

'To get a glass of water. I'm gasping.'

'Well, just you go back to bed and I'll fetch it up.' This wasn't the first time that Alfie had tried to creep downstairs on Christmas Eve before her.

'I can get it myself,' he barked. 'I'm not a cripple.'

Smiling at him, Jessie slowly shook her head. 'It won't work, you know. It's *my* birthday and you know that you're not allowed to go down before me. The same as none of us are allowed to go down before you on your birthday.'

'That was when we were kids,' he said. 'You're seventeen

now, and I'm nearly thirteen. I can't be bothered with all of that baby stuff.' He turned towards the staircase, but Jessie was too quick for him. She grabbed the corded waist of his pyjamas and would not let go.

'You're not too old for a clip round the ear,' she said. 'Now get back to bed and I'll bring you a glass of water up, and don't start arguing or you'll wake the lodgers. If they leave, Mum loses the rent and that means no pocket money for you and Stephen.'

'What do I care about pocket money? I'll be going to work soon.' He pulled away from her and slouched back to his room.

'Alfie, haven't you forgotten something?'

'No. Oh, yeah. Happy birthday,' he mumbled grudgingly.

She couldn't blame him, thought Jessie, going downstairs; it was, after all, Christmas Eve and as grown-up as Alfie liked to act, he was still a boy, especially at this time of year. More excited than little Stephen at times.

In the kitchen, after a birthday kiss and greeting from Rose, Jessie sat by the warm cooking range, her bare feet close to the glowing coals, and watched her mother lay the table. As well as the two best cups and saucers and small china plate of tea biscuits, Rose had spread the special lace-edged cloth the way she always did on her birthday and for some reason Jessie was reminded of the Christmas Eve morning when she was thirteen. Dolly had been given a new doll with arms and legs which were double-jointed, Alfie had got his train set and little Stephen, after months of pleading, was rewarded with something which was a strange request for a boy – a plain doll's house, made by their father, in which he'd placed quite a few of his lead soldiers.

Jessie had been given a red patent-leather box handbag and matching shoes, the first time she'd not been given a toy of some sort for Christmas. It was also the first time she had given Dolly one of her prize possessions. She gave her sister her bassinet pram for her new doll.

'I hope those boys are not going to come bounding down yet,' said Rose, breaking into her thoughts. 'There's a lot to do before I feed them.'

'I don't think they will.' Jessie's mind turned to her grandfather. She would miss the family visit made to him each year on Christmas morning, when he would be spruced up in his best clothes, with a small present for each of them piled up next to the fire. The few words that he repeated every year went through her mind. *It wasn't cheap so look after it.*

Gripped by a sudden need to touch and look at his photograph, she slipped out of the kitchen and went quietly to her bedroom. Standing on a chair, her hand inside the air vent, feeling for the secret document and photograph, she was appalled to find they had gone.

Rose's quiet voice behind her made her jump. 'I had a feeling you'd be digging around for those. You'd best come downstairs, Jessie.'

Jessie looked across to Dolly, worried.

'Don't fret about lazy bones,' said Rose. 'The house could fall in and she'd still sleep on. I dare say she's dreaming about Christmas time in the days of old.' Only one subject had interested the rebellious Dolly during her schooldays – the history of London from the time of the Romans who had named it Londinium. A casual reference to 'the twin-hilled City of the South ... girt about by fen and marshes' by her teacher had caught her imagination. From that day onwards, when she was no more than nine years old, Dolly had read and listened and questioned and bored to death even those who *were* interested in her chosen subject – and most were not.

Back in the kitchen, Rose, a little shaky, poured them both a cup of tea. 'I suppose your seventeenth birthday is as good a time as any to tell you a bit of home truth,' she said.

Ashamed, Jessie felt herself blush. 'I shouldn't have hidden Grandfather's things like that but, well, I wasn't sure what to do about them once I'd taken them and time just went on and—'

'It doesn't matter about that. I noticed that the metal cover on the air vent wasn't on properly. That's how I found your secret. The marriage certificate's safe now in my document box. Best we don't say anything to Dolly or the boys just yet.'

Flattered that her mother was speaking to her as an equal, Jessie rose to the occasion. 'I know you don't like me to be disrespectful but I've never really warmed to Grandmother Blake.'

'I know, but that's to be expected. She's not exactly put herself out for you, has she? She's not interested in any of my children, or me, for that matter, and I think you've worked out for yourself the reason why.' Rose sipped her tea, and waited.

'I'm not really sure, Mum, but I think I can guess.' Feeling as if she was treading on eggshells, Jessie went on, 'It was the name Gunter . . . and, well, I did happen to see your birth certificate once and on that you're down as Gunter as well. Rose Maud Gunter. I wasn't spying, it's just that—'

'You were curious. You don't have to feel bad about it. I'd be disappointed if you didn't care less. Grandmother Blake is *not* my mother. What's more, and this you must keep to yourself, she and your grandfather were never married. He never married her because he never divorced his first wife – my real mother. You can work out what that makes my half-brothers and that's why we have to keep the skeleton locked in the cupboard. They don't know about it.'

Mystified by the casual way Rose was revealing family secrets to her, Jessie did her best to look and sound normal and to keep it going. 'So . . . your real mother couldn't have married again either.'

'No.' Rose lowered her eyes. 'I really don't want to say much more than that, Jessie. It's enough that you've brought things to the surface. I *shall* tell you about it, but not now. Not today. Let's keep today a happy one. It's Christmas Eve and it's your birthday.' She looked at Jessie pensively. 'We'll keep the lid on it for now. It's a sad can of worms, I'm afraid.' Pulling herself out of her mood, Rose brightened. 'I've got a present

for you which belonged to my mother. I was keeping it for your twenty-first when I thought I'd be ready to tell you everything about my past, but you may as well have it now. Now that you know.' Rose handed Jessie a small wrapped packet. 'It's a bit old-fashioned, so you don't *have* to wear it if you don't want to.' Wanting her daughter to open the present before Dolly or the boys came down, Rose urged her on, reminding Jessie that they had to make a start on the bird and plucking it in the back yard was out of the question. It had turned much colder in the night and the water barrel outside had a layer of ice on it. 'Look after it and keep it safe,' Rose went on. 'I'd like to think that you'll pass it on to your own daughter, one day.'

Untying the ribbon, Jessie slowly unwrapped the paper, savouring this time alone with her mother. She wasn't really expecting it to be anything more than something a bit special, but she was wrong. She could tell by the beautiful, small, red velvet box with domed lid that there was something really lovely inside.

Pushing open the lid with the tip of her thumb, she gazed at the delicate gold and pearl brooch. It wasn't a child's brooch, it was proper jewellery. For a second she thought her mother must have given her the wrong box.

'You clip it on to the collar or neckline of a dress,' Rose told her.

Touching the smooth reddish gold with the tip of her finger, Jessie couldn't find the right words to express herself. It was beautiful.

'My mother gave it to me when ... when I was very young,' said Rose, casting her eyes down. 'She used to wear it all the time. That much I do remember. That and her sweet smell.' She drew a trembling breath and pushed back her shoulders. Composure was all-important to Rose. 'I've got something put by for Dolly as well. A locket. Apart from a ruby and diamond ring, those two pieces of jewellery were all my mother possessed.' Again, Jessie saw Rose summon her willpower as she quietly coughed

and swallowed the lump in her throat. 'She was more of a plain woman than a fancy one when it came to dressing herself.'

Sorry now that she had caused painful memories to surface, Jessie remained quiet. Rose had always lived according to her own Victorian upbringing – that children should keep no secrets – yet here she was, confiding one to her daughter.

'I don't really understand,' Jessie murmured at last, longing to know more.

'You will in time.' Rose locked her fingers together and straightened. 'Now that you know about Granny Blake you'll understand why she's never shown any of you affection. Although to give her her due, she treated me much the same as her sons, more or less. Your grandfather made up for it when he could. I believe he loved me more than he loved my half-brothers, and he loved you, Jessie. He just wasn't very good at expressing himself.'

'He didn't have to show it. I knew.'

'Yes, I suppose you must have. You did spend a lot of time with him. I was pleased about that. It meant a lot to me.' Rose turned away then, saying, 'Maybe I'll be able to talk about my mother in years to come, Jess, but not yet . . . and not so soon after your grandfather passing away. So, wear the brooch for high days and holy days and put it somewhere safe the rest of the time.' She added, 'You'll find that life will start changing from now on. Take it as it comes and ask me whatever you have to. I can't promise to answer all of your questions but I'll be disappointed if you go to others for answers.'

Jessie thought of the photograph that had been with the certificate. 'What about the photo of grandfather and the babies in the pram? Who were they?'

'I don't know. I expect it came loose in the album.' Rose turned her face away, hiding her guilt. 'I don't recognise it.' Quickly she changed the subject to the day's work and told Jessie she was to make the porridge while she herself got on with other things. 'No doubt those boys'll be down any minute,' she

sighed, emptying her cup. 'I expect Dolly will sleep on until I drag her out of bed.'

Five minutes later she was busy with her chores, quieter than usual, but clearly the day would continue as normal, as if nothing had changed.

That night, before she turned off the gas mantle above her bed, Jessie wrote a few lines in her notebook: '24 December 1936 – Mum's told me a secret which I must keep from Dolly and the boys and it has to do with the mysterious marriage certificate. There are three million unemployed and we are very lucky that Dad has work. In November, Mum became the official owner of Grandfather's cobbler shop.'

It was a good Christmas, despite their recent bereavement. They all loved their presents and were allowed to stuff themselves full of chocolate, oranges and nuts, once they'd eaten their modest Christmas dinner. On 31 December, Jessie wrote in her diary: 'The most important things that happened this year were – on 20 January King George V died. On 10 December King Edward VIII abdicated from the throne. On 4 November William Ernest Gunter died.'

Very soon into the new year of 1937, the country saw a rise in trade and by the end of March Rose took on a cobbler full time. Jessie continued her employment in the offices of a soap factory in Hackney and Dolly started work as a waitress in a gentlemen's club, so small extra treats could be afforded.

The Warner family had been one of the luckier ones in the East End. Not only had Rose made a few pounds each week during the bad times but her husband, Robert, had always managed to get work in the docks, due to his size and hard-working nature. With so many unemployed, ordinary folk hadn't been able to afford to have their footwear soled and heeled but now that things were improving, Rose was considering selling new boots as well as repairing old ones. Spring brought a new feeling of hope to the working classes.

Sadly, though, the Jewish problem had rekindled and Fascist slogans were appearing on walls and hoardings again. No matter how many times the insulting remarks were scrubbed off the wall at the top of Jessie's turning, it did nothing to deter the culprits from slipping out after dark and re-chalking DOWN WITH THE JEWS!

Jessie, deep in thought, was trying to fathom the thinking behind it. The early evening May sunshine streamed in through the scullery window where she was sitting. She had also been remembering that dreadful day when she and the boys had walked innocently into the centre of the battle in Cable Street.

It wasn't just because Max, her boyfriend of two years, was Jewish that she was worried. Having seen the ugly mood of the anti-Facists as well as the menacing behaviour of Blackshirts, she was in fear of what might happen next. After Cable Street and all the publicity that followed, the Blackshirt movement had gone quiet, it was true, but during the past few months it had all started up again.

Shaking herself out of her sombre mood, Jessie got up and washed the pine table with soda water, cursing her sister Dolly for managing, yet again, to duck out of helping in the kitchen. Not that she wanted her around, with her endless chatter about Fred, her boyfriend. When she'd done the table, Jessie took off her apron and slipped into the parlour.

Dolly wasn't sewing the hem of her skirt as she had said but copying another poem from an ancient poetry book she'd found in a second-hand shop in Aldgate and which she would tell Fred she'd written herself – especially for him. She glanced up, her face full of innocence. She was wearing her best orange and black frock.

'If you think you're going to sneak out to see Fred, Dolly, you're out of luck.' Jessie glared at her sister.

Dolly turned a page of her book and sighed, as if she was sick of the sight of Jessie. Adding insult to injury, she then asked in her usual offhand way if she could borrow two shillings. 'It's

Friday, pay day, so I know you've got it, Jess. Fred's taking me to the pictures and paying for my seat but I need the bus fare there and back.'

Sometimes Dolly really did push her luck. The new frock she was wearing had cost her an entire week's wages and was one which Jessie had seen in the window of Pearls Fashions in Mile End Road and told Dolly about. Dolly knew full well that she'd set her heart on buying it and had got in first. That was Dolly.

'No, I won't lend you the money,' said Jessie. 'And what's more, you're not allowed to be by yourself with Fred till you're sixteen and that's nearly a year away.'

'If you tell on me,' said Dolly smugly, 'I'll tell on you. I saw what you were doing with Max on the doorstep last night. He had his hand up your skirt and you're not meant to be doing that, seventeen or not.'

'Your mouth needs to be washed with carbolic. Max isn't like your dirty boyfriends. He respects me.'

Closing her book with a snap, Dolly began to laugh. 'Miss High and Mighty. If you could only see yourself. Acting as if you're over twenty-one. You'll die a spinster, the way you go on. A stuffy, dried-up old maid.'

Hearing their parents coming down the stairs, Jessie bit her tongue. They were going to Hammersmith to visit some of Robert's family, the uppity Warners who had always believed that he had married beneath himself because Rose was a girl from the East End. Jessie was to look after the boys and see to it that Dolly didn't creep out. In truth she was glad that her sister was in a rebellious mood. She wanted her out of the house. Max was coming round.

Jessie leaned towards her sister and spoke in a quiet voice. 'I'm not lending you one penny.' She said this knowing full well that she would pay up, just to see the back of Dolly.

'Are you in there, girls?' Rose's voice drifted in from the passageway.

Dolly answered for them. 'Yes, Mum. I'm just about to do my sewing and Jessie's borrowing my poetry book for a read.' There was a sly smile on her face.

Popping her head round the door, Rose looked pleased. 'Good girls. See the boys go to bed at their proper time, Jessie, and you put away the dishes, Dolly. We'll be in later than usual. You can both stay up till ten o clock and listen to the wireless.'

'Thanks, Ma,' cooed Dolly, adding, 'If I clean all the windows inside and out tomorrow, would you treat me to half-a-crown? I thought I'd pop down to Riley's and buy some coconut ice, for all of us.'

'Take a shilling out of the lodgers' rent tin,' said Rose, straightening her hat, 'and learn a lesson from your reckless ways, spending all that money on a dress and leaving yourself with nothing. You should be ashamed of yourself. And don't think you'll get out of paying double keep next week, because you won't. You'll be just as hard up as you are now because you'll have your borrows to pay back as well. Bus fares to work and the like.' With that Rose disappeared and Robert looked round the door.

'If those boys play up you can send them to bed early, and no arguing, you two. I'll hear it from Alfie if a row breaks out.' He winked at his daughters and left.

Following him to the front door, Jessie asked her father if it would be all right for her to march with him the next day.

He rubbed his chin thoughtfully. 'Well, I don't think anyone else's daughters'll be on the dockers' march, but then not many are like my Jessie, are they? I didn't think it would take long before you took an interest in politics. All right. You can come.'

When they'd gone, Jessie turned her thoughts to Max. Dolly had been lying when she said she'd seen them on the doorstep. It wasn't possible to see the front step from any of the windows. She'd guessed right though, Max had put his hand up her skirt

and not for the first time. Little did Dolly know that they'd
gone much further than that.

'I heard you talking to Dad, Jessie. You needn't have crept
to the front door to ask if you could go with him tomorrow.
We all know you're his favourite and can wind him round your
little finger. Dockers' march? What are you after then?'

'I'm not after anything. I feel like going on a march with
lots of handsome dockers, that's all. Don't worry, I'll tell them
I've got a young sister at home who can't wait for it.'

'Speak for yourself,' said Dolly tartly. 'Won't catch me with
my knickers down.' She tilted her head to one side and recited,
'"Jessie this and Jessie that and Jessie wouldn't pee on the new
doormat." If Dad only knew what his beloved Jessie got up to
with Max on the door*step*.'

'I don't s'pose for one minute that you've thought any more
about our grandmother?' said Jessie, changing the subject which
might have led to a scratching session. 'Our *real* grandmother.
Because if you haven't, I think it's time you did.'

Dolly looked away, feigning interest in something she'd seen
though the window. 'No, Jessie, I 'aven't. Mum's not bothered so
why should I be? She's probably dead anyway.' She went back to
her copying of other people's thoughts.

'You surprise me. Isn't history what you live and die for?
Apart from boys.'

'My interest goes back one thousand seven hundred years,
Jessie. You can keep this century and the one before it.
I'm only—'

'Yeah, all right, Dolly. No lecture, thank you. As for our
grandmother, you've known since February, your birthday, and
you love the gold locket Mum gave you, which was *hers*. For all
we know she might be living in poverty somewhere, all by herself,
wondering if she's got any grandchildren, wondering what her
own daughter looks like. She could be a lonely old—'

'Well, whoever she was and wherever she is, she can't be
all that 'ard up – she had some nice jewellery so she must've

had a few bob. That brooch you collared must be worth something.'

'Three bits of jewellery aren't exactly the crown jewels. For all we know, what she's given us might 'ave been all of her precious belongings.'

Dolly raised her eyes to the ceiling and sighed theatrically. 'I see poor lonely old women every day. You only 'ave to walk down Whitechapel. There are plenty of war widows to take pity on if that's what you want to do with your time. You should join the Salvation Army, the uniform'd suit you.'

Refusing to rise to her sister's bait, Jessie satisfied herself with the fact that Dolly would soon be out of the house and the boys in bed. She had stopped off and bought them a comic each on the way home from work, the *Eagle* and the *Dandy*, which she'd promised they could read by gaslight, ensuring that she and Max would be undisturbed in the sitting room.

Pouring herself a glass of water, Jessie thought about the next day and the real reason for wanting to go on the dockers' march. She wanted to have some time alone with her dad. She would ask him if her real grandmother was still alive and where she was living. He had always listened to her in the past when she had other questions and he'd always answered as best he could – they were close, which made Dolly jealous. Not that Robert showed favour but Dolly loved to be the centre of attention and resented her sister getting some of it.

Jessie opened the tiny iron fire door to the copper boiler and checked to see if the fire needed stoking. The weekend hock of bacon in the simmering water, according to Rose's instructions, had to be taken out at eight o'clock. She was relieved to see that most of the coals were bright orange since the coal bucket was low and the last thing she wanted was to have to go into the dark, damp coal cupboard to fill it. The heat from the boiler didn't do much for her complexion; it was hot enough to redden her pale cheeks and once that happened no amount of face powder would

tone them down. She didn't want to look a sight when Max arrived.

She straightened, pushed the fire door shut with the tip of her shoe and went to the window, pressing one side of her face against the cool pane and then the other. Sudden loud banging on the front door startled her.

She hurried to open it. When she saw their neighbour, old Bob Jennings, on the doorstep Jessie knew instantly why he was there. His wife had been very ill, and Jessie guessed she had just passed away and the old man wanted Rose to lay her out. In Tanner Street, it was Rose Warner that people turned to when someone died.

Cap in hand, eyes red-rimmed and too distressed to speak, Bob's grief was all too evident. He and his wife had been married for sixty-two years.

'Mum's not in, Bob,' Jessie said gently.

'Oh,' was his choked reply, 'that's a pity. Do you know what time she'll be back?'

'About half past ten.' Jessie stood to one side and invited him into the passage but he raised a trembling hand.

'I must get back. She's on 'er own – not that she knows much about it.'

'Shall I tell Mum to come over once—'

'No,' he cut in. 'I dare say that'll be too late ... I don't know. What do you think, Jessie? Should I try and get one of the other neighbours?'

She squeezed his arm affectionately, telling him that her parents were walking to Stepney Green station and if she ran she would get to the station before they went through the barrier. Slowly nodding, the old man pushed a hand deep into his trouser pocket and pulled out a shilling, telling her to get a cab. For him to offer her a shilling out of his meagre earnings as warehouse porter meant that it was Rose Warner he wanted to see to his wife, and no one else. Jessie assured him it wasn't necessary to take a cab and that she would be able to catch them up.

Rapidly telling Dolly to see Max into the sitting room when he arrived, Jessie rushed out of the house and hurried through the back streets of Stepney Green, taking every short cut and forcing herself to remember the times when Bob's wife had been full of life. The couple had no children of their own and had made up for it by keeping open house where the children of neighbours were concerned.

Before she fell ill, Mrs Jennings would take in washing each week and sometimes Jessie, as a child, would help out by putting it through the mangle and folding it before carrying neatly ironed piles along the street to the owners. For this she sometimes received sixpence. Sixpence, a mug of cocoa and a biscuit.

As she neared the station, Jessie saw her parents chatting to friends outside the barrier, obviously in no great hurry. Relieved that she'd caught them, she hurried towards them. It was Robert who saw her first and he guessed immediately that something was wrong. His smile dissolved. His first thoughts were for Dolly, Alfie and Stephen.

'It's Betty Jennings,' said Jessie quickly. 'Bob came over ...'

Rose understood at once. 'Oh dear, I'd better get back.'

'Bob's waiting for you,' said Jessie. 'He's really upset. You go on. I'll catch my breath and follow.'

Robert kissed the top of her head. 'We'll wait while you pull yourself together.'

Jessie shook her head, telling him that she would rather stop there for a minute or two. 'Five minutes, that's all, Dad.' She wanted to be by herself. Leaning against the brick wall of Stepney Green station, she waited until they had gone before she shed a tear. Covering her face, she tried to block out the echoing sound of people talking and laughing in the entrance to the station. Not all of them were there to catch a train; it was a meeting place. Ben the bookie, a familiar figure, small and skinny, was taking bets as usual, eyes darting everywhere, on the look-out for the local bobby.

'You all right, love?' Jessie looked up to see a tall, good-looking man with lovely green eyes smiling at her. 'You ain't asleep, are you?'

'I'm catching my breath if you must know.' Embarrassed, she pulled her handkerchief from her sleeve and blotted her face.

'That's funny, 'cos I'm catching mine as well,' he chuckled.

'Why, is someone chasing you?'

'The law. Some bugger pinched my cap so I pinched someone else's.' He flicked the peak of his cap and winked. 'Best quality as well.'

'I could tell by your voice that you was a tea leaf.'

'And I could tell by your face that you'd have lovely blue eyes – once you opened 'em. Fancy a drink?' He nodded towards the pub on the corner.

'No thanks.' She stepped away, not really wanting to turn down the offer. She would have loved to have had the courage to say yes and go with him, but it didn't seem right.

'I'm sure I know you from somewhere.' He took her arm, as bold as brass. 'What school did you go to?'

Easing her arm away, Jessie asked him the same question. 'Which school did *you* go to?'

'Be fair,' he grinned, flirting with her. 'I asked first.'

'Please yourself,' she said, feigning boredom.

'Cephas Street,' he confessed, shrugging.

'I might have guessed.' He was obviously a show-off and probably from a rough family if the school he'd attended was anything to go by; just another tall, good-looking charmer, she thought, turning away.

'Tom! What are you doing here?' A woman in her sixties, nicely rounded with a friendly face, was hurrying towards them. 'You promised me you'd help your dad get the dinner ready!'

'Give me a break, Mum. I was just helping this young lady.' The tone of his voice had changed and now he was touching her with anxious concern.

The woman rolled her eyes and turned to Jessie, her

face relaxing into a warm smile. 'Not in any trouble, are you, love?'

'No. I've just had some sad news, that's all.'

'I can see you've been shedding a tear or two. All right now, are we?'

'Yes, thank you,' she said.

'Where d'yer work then?' Tom asked her.

'Hackney soap factory — in the offices,' she said, and turned to walk away. She reproached herself for telling him where she worked and then questioned her reason for doing it.

'The name's Tom. What do they call you?'

'Everything under the sun!' she called back, smiling to herself. There was something about Tom and his good-natured mother that seemed familiar, but she couldn't put her finger on what it was. She hadn't met either of them before and yet she felt as if she might know them.

Tom was thinking the very same thing as he walked home with his mother Emmie.

'You were a bit shy with that one, Tom. Was it my imagination or were you blushing?' she asked, watching his expression.

'Course I wasn't blushing, Mother. She seemed all right, though, bit of a snob but there you go.' Tom shrugged.

'So, my son, a knight in shining armour. Whatever next?'

'Talk sense. I cheered her up a bit, that's all, Anyway, mind your own business, nosy cow.'

Emmie quietly laughed at his cheek, but he was right, when it came to her three lads, she did want to know all the ins and outs.

'Nice girl, though,' murmured Tom. 'She reminded me of someone.'

'Oh yeah?' Emmie wasn't really interested; Tom fell in and out of love more times than he had hot dinners.

'Didn't remind you of anyone then?' he asked.

'No, Tom, I can't say she did.'

'Same colour hair, I s'pose.'

'As?'

'Hannah.'

'There must be hundreds of natural blondes living in the East End, son.'

'I know, I know, she just reminds me of her, that's all.'

'If only Hannah was part of a decent family, the way that young lady likely is. At least Hannah's got you to look out for her. She values your friendship more than you realise.'

'Friendship? What are you on about? She's more like a sister than a mate.'

'That's true. Oh dear,' Emmie paused for a rest, 'my poor old pins. I've been on my feet all day long, serving snooty customers in Wickham's and then seeing to those poor sods down the home. I think I'm gonna 'ave to give up my charity work, Tom.'

'Oh yeah? Pull the other leg. Anyway, about Hannah . . .'

'What about her?' said Emmie, putting her weight on his strong arm and resuming her slow pace.

Tom looked at his mother sideways. 'You should have adopted her years ago. I doubt that Gerta the German would have cared, there's no love lost between mother and daughter there.'

Emmie didn't want to get into this topic, she'd kept a tight secret for many years and idle chitchat wasn't going to catch her out. 'Lumbago's a terrible thing, you know,' she said, changing the subject. 'One of my old ladies has got it real bad. I hope to God that when I go it'll be a quick death, a good strong heart attack while I'm in my bed. Let's hope our Johnnie'll do what he promises and get to be a millionaire, then I can have private nurses looking after me.'

'Johnnie,' chuckled Tom, 'my elder brother the entrepreneur. Anyway, be no need to pay out for a private nurse, will there? Not if you go quick, in your sleep.'

Johnnie's latest venture was to sell threepenny coupons outside Millwall, West Ham and Arsenal football grounds.

Emmie's youngest, Stanley, was a different kettle of fish, regular as clockwork and never missed a day's work down at the bell foundry. Tom, content with his earnings from the docks and a little bit on the side from his perks, didn't have the same ambitions as Johnnie. He was a romantic, through and through. Emmie hoped that when he did finally settle down, he would stay in the East End — which, as far as she was concerned, wasn't a bad place to be. Besides which, she would miss him if he left.

They reached the turning where they lived. Emmie couldn't wait to get inside her house and put her feet up. 'I'm gasping for a cup of tea, Tom,' she said.

'So am I. Let's hope Hannah's still there, with the kettle on the stove.' Tom pushed his hand through the letter box and pulled at the key-on-a-string. He opened the door and followed Emmie inside.

'Hello,' smiled Hannah as they came into the kitchen. 'I was just about to give up on you, Tom, and go home. Charlie's gone down to the pub, Emmie, he got fed up waiting too. Your dinner's in the oven.'

'Fed up with waiting? Do me a favour, he's casseroled the lamb chops instead of frying 'em just so that he could go down the pub. It's dominoes night. Trust my husband not to miss that.' Dropping into a kitchen chair, Emmie kicked off her shoes, glancing sideways at Hannah's face — at her swollen eye. 'Who did that to you?'

'It's not as bad as it looks. One of the Reds slapped me with the back of his hand, outside the Blackshirts' club, and caught me with his ring. I slipped out early before my mother got on the platform to give *another* of her long and well-rehearsed talks.'

Emmie chuckled gently. 'You've got to be more careful, Hannah. The chief librarian won't take kindly to you turning up for work looking like that. Don't forget, you're a public

servant in a respectable place, you have to look the part. I take it no one there knows that you're a Blackshirt?'

'Don't call me that, Emmie. You know why I go. If I refuse my mother will get into one of her spiteful moods.'

'You've got to learn to stand up to her, love. She's just a silly, ignorant woman. Your father going off didn't help matters, but there we are.'

There was a silence from Hannah which was to be expected. Emmie had criticised Hannah's dad, Jack, and that was a mistake. His memory was all that the girl had to cling on to. Jack and Gerta had planned to emigrate to New Zealand when Hannah was just a baby but for some unknown reason, Jack had gone alone leaving Gerta, a German, with Hannah. If Jack had taken her with him, Hannah would be out there living the good life instead of having to put up with Bethnal Green and three miserable rooms above a tobacconist's shop. But she was a survivor and had learned very early in life that it was better to be servile where Gerta was concerned. Maybe Jack would come back for her one day. It was Hannah's dream that he would, a dream that had kept her going. He had loved her more than life itself and he was the one who took her to the zoo and carried her on his shoulders to Bethnal Green gardens and to the fairgrounds. In his letters to her, Jack always made a point of writing about New Zealand and how healthier the life was there, but the worst of it was, Gerta cut his address out of the letters so that Hannah couldn't write back.

Tom looked at Hannah's face and frowned. 'I've told you before, Hannah, it's your own fault getting involved with that lot.'

'I don't want to talk about it,' she said dismissively. 'Oh, and by the way, my mother was expecting to see you this evening, Tom. She had another newspaper clipping to show you about her hero Mosley. Because you didn't come round she got at me. You shouldn't tell her something and then not do it.'

'That eye looks like a monkey's arse,' he said, which brought

a smile to both Hannah and Emmie's face. He handed his mother a cup of tea.

'She's determined to get you to join, Tom,' Hannah persisted.

'Over my dead body!' said Emmie. 'She'll have me to answer to soon if she goes on at him for much longer. You tell me, Hannah. You tell me if she does keep on at him, because as sure as I'm sitting here, he won't let on. I'll wring her skinny neck, so help me. A son of mine a Blackshirt? I don't think so! It's bad enough she's dragged *you* into it.' The Blackshirt movement was growing in the East End and Gerta Blake was an ardent member. She had forced poor Hannah to join up too, though Hannah had deep misgivings, Gerta, however, brooked no resistance.

'She's been trying to find a way to persuade Tom for years. She knows I warn him against it and that makes her angry.' There was a smile on the girl's face which gave Emmie hope; perhaps Hannah *was* beginning to fight back. 'Last week she managed to get him to herself in her room,' Hannah continued. 'Tom lit a cigarette just like I told him to. She hates the smell so she asked him to leave. My plan worked.' Her blue eyes could go from mournful to sparkling in a moment, swollen and bruised or not. She pushed her hand through her short curly blonde hair and laughed.

'If it hadn't, you would have eavesdropped and got caught,' said Tom, sipping his tea. He looked at Emmie. 'She's done that before. She gets me to leave the door ajar and raise my voice so she can hear what's going on but Gerta clocked it. Sharp as a razor.'

'Tom pretends to be deaf in one ear,' said Hannah. 'He used to do that at school when he was poking fun at the headmaster.'

'It's a wonder they didn't expel the little sod, he played truant enough times.' Emmie poured herself another cup of tea and listened to their banter. Hannah would be all right, she was

growing up at last. Seventeen and only just beginning to think for herself. Gerta had been worse than just strict with the girl, never allowing her to read fashion journals or listen to what she wanted on the wireless.

'Gerta's a character, Hannah, I'll say that for 'er.' Finishing his tea, Tom stood up. 'A very strange woman.'

'She believes she's won you over, Tom, that she's got you interested.'

'She *thinks* she's won me over – there's a difference. You know I can't be bothered with all that palaver. Your mother bores the bloody life out of me. Mosley this and Mosley that. The bloke's trying to be another Mussolini. I see it every day, down the docks, men with nothing in their lives so they start preaching. If it's not politics it's religion. Bore you to death and know they're doing it but does it stop 'em? Hitler's Gerta's hero, silly cow. She ain't got a clue. How old is she? Forty-two? Forty-three? Yet to listen to 'er you'd think she'd turned fifty. I bet she's not had a man since your dad ran off.'

'Don't be disgusting, Tom!' said Emmie. 'You're not down the docks now, thank you.'

'Sorry, Mum.' He stretched and announced that he was going to have a wash and shave before his dinner and then go down to the pub to have a pint with his dad. 'I might have a bath by the fire when I get back – if the water's hot in the copper. I've been running about all day, some bugger nicked my cap.'

'Well, how comes you were wearing one when we came home?' asked Emmie.

'That was someone's else's. That's why I've been running. Silly bastard would 'ave called a copper as well if he'd seen one, all over a cap. That's all I needed, a pocket full of easy-come fountain pens and I get pinched for nicking a cap. I can hear my mates laughing now.'

Emmie stopped herself from chastising him; he was nineteen, after all, and in any case it would have been a waste of time. Her

son had been stealing bits and bobs since he was six years old and no number of whippings had stopped him. 'I wonder what it's like in prison?' she murmured instead, trying a different tactic, hoping the thought of being locked up might at least make him think.

'I don't intend to find out. I'd jump on a ship to Australia if there was any danger of that.' He grinned and went into the scullery for his wash and brush up.

'My mother said something quite odd the other day.' Hannah had slipped into a reflective mood and sounded as if she was miles away. 'She asked me if Tom intended to marry me.'

'She did *what*?' laughed Tom. The scullery door opened and he stood grinning in the doorway, in his vest with his braces dangling. 'Whatever gave her that idea?'

'I don't dream about you either, Tom, but I don't find the idea that ridiculous.' Hannah couldn't help looking a little hurt at Tom's disbelief.

'But I'm your mate, Hannah! We've never been—'

'I'm not asking you to marry me! I'm just telling you what she said.'

'But we've never been like that together. She must have seen—'

'Oh, for God's sake! I only mentioned it because I thought she wanted to talk you into joining the party not the family,' Hannah said, exasperation in her voice.

'What did you tell her?'

'I said that I loved you but not in that way, and that you love me but not in that way.'

'Oh. So that's all right then.' He closed the door between them again.

'Fancy her asking a thing like that,' said Emmie, puzzled.

'She was in one of her tormenting moods, said that I would probably end up being a spinster in any case.'

'You should tell her that you've got dozens of men on the

end of string and that you plan to take 'em all back home, one at a time, to try 'em out. See what she makes of that.'

Hannah smiled. 'Maybe I will — one day. One thing's for certain, as much as I care about your daft son, I wouldn't want to be his wife.'

'Just as well!' called Tom, ''cos I think I might 'ave met the love of my life today. She wouldn't tell me her name but I know where she works.' There was the robust sound of splashing water from the scullery.

'Well, Tom,' Hannah called back, 'that's the first time I've heard you mention a girl without using an expletive to describe her qualities.'

'Cheeky cow! She reminded me of you, funnily enough. Don't know why. Same white wavy hair, that's all. Longer than yours, though. She's a bit of a toffee nose as well. Nice though, I liked her. Could be love at first sight.'

'Again?' said Emmie, stopping him before he got too carried away. 'I'm ready for my dinner and bed. It don't look like Tom's stopping in to play cards, Hannah love. Will you be going to the pub with him?'

'No. My eye's beginning to throb again. I'm not in the mood for cards anyway. I'll call round tomorrow after the dockers' march — it is tomorrow, isn't it, when Tom's marching?'

'I think so, child, yes. Try and keep away from the Blackshirts, there's a good girl. That eye'll get worse before it gets better.'

'The club's running down in any case, the numbers have steadily been falling. Only the strong Fascists are still members now, and those who've started romances and use the club to meet up, without wives and husbands realising what actually goes on there.'

'Yeah, but all it takes is just one well-planned speech from Mosely to get them all going again,' said Emmie, concerned. 'It's been quiet for a while so you can bet your life something's on the boil somewhere.'

Returning to the room, Tom put an arm round his mother's shoulders. 'Couldn't lend me five bob, could you, Mum?' He'd lost at cards again.

'Playing in your lunch break at the docks again,' grouched Emmie, reaching for her purse. 'You'll never learn, will you? And I want it back! You get away with blue murder.'

'Well, you will keep opening your purse, Emmie,' said Hannah. 'I'll see you tomorrow evening,' she added as she left.

'I put some money on a greyhound, Mum — a tip and a dead cert. I wanted to buy that new hat you've been going on about.'

'The trouble with you, Tom, is that you spend money before you've got it in your pocket. You'll end up in the debtor prison if you're not careful.'

'And you can fetch in a cake and a file. You'd love that, you know you would.'

'It's not funny, you've got to start acting more responsible, Tom.'

'I was unlucky, Mother, that's all. It should 'ave won!' Tom leaned forward and towel-rubbed his hair.

'What's tomorrow's dockers' march in aid of this time?' asked Emmie, pleased that he was at least accountable when it came to the union.

'More money, less hours, better conditions.' With that he went upstairs to put on a clean shirt and tie, leaving Emmie to think about what Gerta had said, about him marrying Hannah. What would happen when Tom did meet the right girl? How would Hannah fit into that little scene? The two of them had been as thick as thieves since they were very young.

Opening the door leading to the flat above the shop, Hannah did her utmost to be quiet. She had almost managed to creep past the door of Gerta's sitting room when she heard her moving about. Hoping her mother wasn't going to appear, Hannah tiptoed towards her bedroom. There was the sound

of the doorknob slowly turning and then the telltale creaking of the door.

'Why must you creep about like a *fluchtling*! If I don't hear you come in, I smell you.' Gerta was standing in the doorway scowling at her.

'I wasn't creeping, I was going quietly, in case you were having a nap.'

Gerta narrowed her eyes. 'You went out looking like this? You didn't cover that eye? It isn't something to look at. Do you feel proud of it? Is that the reason? You want people to stop and ask what happened?' Her heavily accented voice was shrill and cross.

'The patch made it feel worse. I thought it best to let the air get to it and anyway I was only going round to play cards with Tom and I knew he wouldn't mind seeing me looking like this.'

'Tom? But he was supposed to be coming here, to see me.'

'He forgot.'

'Ha! *Ich glaube nicht*.' Gerta moved closer to Hannah and examined the eye. 'You said you were going to the market.'

'I changed my mind.' She tried to look forcefully at her mother and hide her longing to get to her room.

'Was that after or before you left the flat? Because if it was before, you lied to me then, and if it was after, you are lying now.'

'I had the pad on when I went out. It irritated so I took it off and then decided to go to Tom's instead.'

'You think I don't see through your lies?' sneered Gerta, her face too close for comfort. 'Why would you want him to see that ugly eye? He is a man. Doesn't it bother you? At your age I did something special with my hair. If I had been cursed with white hair I would have coloured it by now, and if my face looked like that, I would choose not to be seen by a man.' She leaned to one side and studied Hannah's blushing face. 'I don't recall you having a crush on a boy. Isn't that a little odd? You don't like men — is that it?'

'My eye's throbbing,' murmured Hannah. 'I'm going to have a wash and lie down.'

'*Wasche?* Ha! You spend time in there just *looking* at yourself. Or are you in the wash room scrubbing your body over and over? Because if that is so, let me remind you that it is God who may cleanse the soul. Soap and water will not do his work.'

Hannah knew that her mother was a bitter and twisted woman but she still couldn't brush off her spitefulness. All her self-doubts, ironed out by Tom or Emmie, returned within minutes of being back in her company. A few selected words from Gerta and Hannah withdrew, back into her shell.

'I don't feel hungry this evening so I won't have any supper. After my wash I'll go to bed and—'

'Haven't you forgotten something? Or do you want free food now as well as free service?'

'I haven't opened my pay packet yet,' said Hannah, her voice quivering. 'I've never once missed giving you my keep.'

'There is always a first time. I would like to think I could trust you but you have already turned into a liar. Cheating people is never far behind.'

Taking her pay packet from her handbag, Hannah opened the small manila envelope and withdrew a pound note. Hiding her contempt, she placed the money on the side table in the hallway.

'You can ill afford to pull faces, Hannah,' snapped Gerta, sweeping up the note. 'There is cold pork and red cabbage in the kitchen. Cucumber salad is in a side dish. If you don't eat it this evening it will save me bothering tomorrow.'

In her bedroom, Hannah vowed that soon she would find herself somewhere else to live, far away from her mother. Feeling very much alone, she switched on the bedside lamp, sat on the small wooden chair and tried to imagine herself in different surroundings, anywhere but in this silent, lonely room.

Chapter Two

On Sunday morning, to the sound of the church bells in the background, Jessie was enjoying her favourite hobby, helping out in the back yard, or garden as her dad preferred to call it. Leaving him to prune the climbing rose on the back wall, she snipped at the dead tulips and placed them in her basket. Her thoughts were on the handsome Tom whom she had met once again on the dockers' march. Worried that she had agreed to go on a date with him, she toyed with the idea of asking Max if he would mind. She had surprised herself by agreeing so readily to meet up with Tom but more surprising was her reaction at seeing him again — she had, without a shred of doubt, been more than pleased. Seeing him the very next day after their first meeting was certainly an odd coincidence, but even more strange was that she felt as if she had known him for a while — and from the way they had chatted, anyone could have been forgiven for thinking the same. Tom was the exact opposite of Max who was the quiet, serious type with a more gentle humour.

'I think we'll have a lovely show of roses this year, Jess,' said Robert, cutting through her thoughts.

'We always do, Dad. I've missed the tulips again. I wanted to press the petals but they've had it — all limp and falling apart.'

'Never mind, wait for the roses to come out in summer

and press those instead. So,' Robert wiped the sweat from his brow, 'what did you think of yesterday, Jessie? Your first dockers' march.'

'It was good, and I wasn't the only female there, was I? Some of the wives came out, and in good voice. I liked Tom. He seemed nice.'

'He's all right. Pass me that sack, Jess. I'll put the cuttings in there for now, till they've dried out, then we can have a small bonfire.'

Handing him the damp sack, Jessie probed a little further. 'You don't know much about him then?'

'Tom? No. But if first impressions are anything to go by, he's ... like I said, all right. But I wouldn't set my sights on him, Jess, he's not the settling down kind. If he was a sailor he'd have a girl in every port, I reckon.'

'It won't hurt to go out with him just the once, though, will it? You don't think Max would be upset if he found out?'

Robert drew breath and raised an eyebrow. 'I wouldn't like it if your mother had done that to me, but as you say, it will only be the once and you say it's a foursome so it can't do no harm. But best you don't mention it to Max for now.'

'I'll tell him afterwards — once a few weeks have gone by.' Jessie smiled broadly which did not go unnoticed by Robert. 'It's funny really,' she said, 'my meeting him a second time like that, within twenty-four hours. Does he work in your wharf?'

'He goes from one to another. Tall, strong lads like Tom will always get work.' Robert looked at his daughter sideways as he worked. 'How is Max these days? Haven't seen him to talk to for a while. Not going off the boil, is it?'

'Course not. He's worried about the Blackshirts though, spends more time at the Jewish Club, at meetings, discussing the troubles and that.' Jessie paused and then said lightly, 'So, you think that Tom's a bit of a wide boy then?'

'I never said that. He's a bit free-spirited, that's all.' Lighting his pipe, Robert went back to examine his climbing rose. 'I think

that'll do for now. I don't know about you, Jess, but I'm ready for a nice cup of tea. Come on, we'll take a break.'

Following him in through the back door, she said, 'So you think it's all right, if I go on the foursome?'

'It's up to you, Jessie. I'm not going to interfere one way or another, you're old enough to make up your own mind. Just don't go two-timing Max, that's all I'm saying.'

He was right, thought Jessie, but then she had no intention of two-timing Max. She fancied a bit of fun, that was all, and Max at best wasn't full of joy. She loved him, or at least she supposed she did. Why else had they been courting for two years or so? And it wasn't surprising he was a bit serious these days, with the anti-Jewish undercurrents that were all around and seemed to be swelling. 'You won't say anything to Mum, will you?' she added as they arrived in the kitchen.

'Not until a few weeks have gone by,' he chuckled, echoing what she had said. 'Now let that be the end of it.'

Pleased that her dad had, in his own way, given her the thumbs up, Jessie felt more settled about it. She knew she could rely on him to make her feel right about things, he always did. She couldn't imagine life without him. She loved Rose just as much but they weren't as close as she and her dad were – and, on the other hand, there had been times when she envied the way Dolly and her mother chatted together, so that evened things up.

Washing her hands under the cold tap, Jessie found herself thinking about Tom again, wondering if he would behave himself when they were in the picture palace. Being a foursome made it feel less like a proper date and for that she admired Tom for suggesting it. Maybe he was just as shy about going out with her as she was with him? Perhaps he'd heard she was already courting. She remembered the way he and his mother, Emmie, got on so naturally and warmed to them both.

Once Emmie had seen her husband Charlie off to Brick Lane

that same Sunday morning, she enjoyed a quiet cup of tea by herself. Charlie wouldn't be back for hours. After he'd spent time rummaging through boxes of spare bits for his old crystal set collection, he would go on to Petticoat Lane where he'd meet up with his fellow wireless enthusiasts in their favourite pub. She wouldn't see him until three in the afternoon when he would want his Sunday roast, and that suited her fine. Emmie was ready for her favourite pastime – baking tarts and cakes for the week. She looked at the four wirelesses sitting on the sideboard and hoped Charlie wouldn't come back with more clutter.

Tom, still dreamy from his chance meeting with Jessie the day before on the dockers' march, drifted into the kitchen and sat down. Emmie listened as he poured out his heart for ten long minutes. He was in love again and waiting for her to say, 'Bring her home then, son' – though his brothers and dad would crucify him in front of the girl if he didn't leave a gap between her and his last girlfriend. Emmie had counted seven loves of his life so far this year and the month of May wasn't out yet. God help me through June, she thought, with its silvery moon.

She finished her tea, took her rolling pin from the drawer and went to work on the pastry she'd prepared for a steak and kidney for the next day's dinner. With her husband working in the fruit market and her three sons in full-time employment, the neighbours believed she was rich. She had always wanted strapping sons who would take after their father and that's what she'd got, but strapping sons have big appetites and hers ate her out of house and home. Tom continued to bend her ear, as she worked and she kept one ear open to his chatter.

'It's different this time, Mum. I've never met anyone like her.' Sitting in his father's old Lincolnshire chair, he reminded her of Charlie when she was first married to him. He and Tom were like two peas in a pod. 'She does work in the offices of the soap factory like she said, and as luck would have it, so does Ron's new girlfriend Sally. She knows Jess and likes her.'

Ron, Tom's best mate, was just as bad, in and out of love

all the time. 'I thought he was gonna marry the last one,' Emmie said innocently, having a dig at both lads.

'Changed his mind – just in the nick of time. She wasn't all the ticket,' Tom said firmly.

'Couldn't have been if she thought she could tie Ron down.'

'Jessie lives over Stepney Green, in one of the nice streets. Her old man's a crane driver – East India Docks. Probably earns twice as much as Dad. Nice bloke though, from an educated family over in Hammersmith. He reckons he's the black sheep.'

'Didn't take you long to find out the family history, did it? You might've done better chatting up the girl instead of her dad. What was she doing while the pair of you was chewing the fat?'

'Walking next to us, all quiet and thoughtful. I couldn't believe my luck when I saw 'er. I meet 'er by chance on Friday and then the next day she appears out of the blue in a bloody dockers' march, of all things. I was straight in, talking to her old man, putting my best foot forward.'

'How old is she?'

'Dunno. Seventeen, eighteen. What difference does it make?' He was challenging his mother to criticise this newfound angel of his. 'She is a cracker, though, ain't she? A natural blonde with lovely blue eyes.' His gaze was unfocused as he indulged his fantasy. Emmie had seen it all before. 'And she's clever with it ... Works in the manager's office ...'

'What's her father's name?' She wasn't really interested, concentrating more on rolling out her pastry. 'I might know the family.'

'Robert Warner. You won't know him. I told you, he's from Hammersmith way and if Jessie's anything to go by, her mother'll be from somewhere nice as well. Christ knows what they're doing in the East End.' His head still in the clouds, he didn't notice his mother's reaction to what he'd just said.

Emmie was stunned. She pulled up her kitchen chair and sat down heavily, dusting off her hands. Of all the girls that he could have met up with, it had to be Jessie Warner. There weren't many miles between Bethnal Green and Stepney Green, but it hadn't crossed her mind that their paths would cross and neither had it occurred to her that the girl at Stepney Green station could be the baby she had once held in her arms. It might have been funny if it didn't spell trouble.

Emmie took a deep breath and said sharply, 'Pretty blondes are ten a penny and you've hardly spoken two words to the girl.' Abruptly she stood up and poked the hot coals of the cooking range. 'Anyway, enough of this. I've the beds to make.'

'The beds? You're in the middle of making a pie!' Tom looked at her in surprise.

'I can finish it later. I think I might have one of my headaches coming on, I might lie down for a bit to save it getting worse. Cover everything with a clean tea towel for me, there's a good lad.' She wanted to be by herself. There was some serious thinking to do. She would have to be very careful how she handled this new situation. Very careful indeed. 'Did you arrange to see this blonde of yours again then?' she asked, dreading the answer.

'Yep. In a foursome. We're going to the pictures next week – that's if she turns up.'

Let's hope she doesn't, son, thought Emmie, let's hope she doesn't turn up.

Up in her bedroom she weighed up the pros and cons of paying Rose Warner a visit and then cursed Tom for spoiling her Sunday. She would now have to break their unspoken rule of years gone by and meet up with her old friend.

The following morning, after a restless night tossing and turning, Emmie decided that she would not put off until tomorrow what could be done today. Tom had, without knowing it, brought chickens home to roost.

When she had fed and seen the men off to work, Emmie

dressed in her pink and green flower-patterned frock with matching bolero and her favourite straw hat and left the house to visit her old friend, Rose Warner. Making a note to give her doorstep a going-over with red cardinal polish and her windows and paintwork a good spring clean, she closed the door behind her and enjoyed the May sunshine on her face.

Walking along by Charrington's brewery, she thought back to the days when she was employed there as a bottle filler. The smell of beer brought back those heady days when she and the other women had larks with the lads, way back, before the last war. Blushing at the thought of it, she nodded and showed a hand to the chaps in the loading bay and remembered Charlie as a young man, when he worked there.

Emmie and Rose went back a very long way and their parents had also been good friends in the past. If she was honest with herself, Emmie would have been the first to admit that she would much rather turn round and go home, but Rose had suffered terribly in the past and if she could save her from more heartache now, she would.

'You're as pretty as a picture today, Emmie,' Jim of Jim's Bird Cage Shop called from his shop doorway. 'Where you off to?' The man had always made her smile; short and skinny, always chirpy, he reminded her of the birds he sold. Just as well he couldn't sing like a canary, she thought, because if he could, he would have, right there and then.

'I'm making the most of the May sunshine, Jim, and with a bit of luck I'll manage to persuade a friend of mine out of her cobbler shop for five minutes. I fancy an afternoon cuppa in the tea rooms.'

'Well, ducks, if she's too busy, you can always take me!' Jim laughed heartily, still managing to keep his tiny, hand-rolled cigarette tucked in the corner of his mouth. 'What d'yer think of my new sign then? Painted that m'self.'

Emmie drew back and read aloud, '"Budgies boarded during your holidays." You've always boarded birds, Jim, 'aven't

you?' She tried to get round having to pass comment on his sign-writing which was, to say the least, uneven. 'It's a bit early in the year – no one I know goes away till midsummer or hop-picking time.'

'Well, I thought a nice brightly painted sign would cheer people up. I found an old tin of yellow paint and mixed it with a bit of red. Work of art that.' He gazed at it with an air of satisfaction, puffing on his cigarette

'Well, it's bright, I'll give you that.' Emmie grinned at him.

'What about a nice yellow canary then, in a golden cage?' He waved a hand at the various cages hanging outside his shop. 'I could let you have that little brass one cheap. Look at the way it's gleaming in the sun. Just polished it. I'll throw the bird in for threepence, seeing as it's you.'

Once a tout always a tout, thought Emmie. From the time Jim could walk he had worked alongside his father selling his fine feathered friends, as he called them. Formerly the proud owner of a battered stall in Club Row, Bethnal Green, he was now his own boss with a successful little business, hardly a rich man but certainly better off than when his arse hung out of his trousers.

'I daren't, Jim. I would love that little cage and I would love my very own bird.'

'I'll 'ave a word with your Charlie when *he* next passes, tell him how you've been yearning after that little cage. A canary, was it?'

Laughing at him, Emmie wished him the best of luck and went on her way. Monday was her day off from Wickham's department store and usually the day when she would catch up on everything: washing, ironing, the lot. Not this Monday, though. This Monday she had other more important things to think about. Tom, with his good looks and an eye for a pretty girl, was more trouble than he could imagine.

Turning into Hayfields Passage, Stepney Green, Emmie

imagined herself in bygone days living in one of the grand Georgian houses which surrounded the old village green. Cherry trees, now in full bloom, surrounded the square where she and Charlie had gone one night when they'd had a few too many – before they were married. She liked to think that that was where her eldest son, Johnnie, was conceived. Under the cherry blossom trees.

Not many people could afford the luxury of living in these towering houses now, and those who could had moved on to pastures new. What a shame, thought Emmie, that it stopped being fashionable for the well-to-do to live in Stepney Green. When she was a nipper, running around in bare feet in the 1890s, she'd often helped her dad deliver flowers from Covent Garden to the very house she stood in front of now. She had loved sitting up on the cart beside him, sipping hot tea from a tin flask while he drove the old carthorses.

Pausing below the marble steps leading up to the oak and glass-panelled door of the Craft School, an elegant Queen Anne terraced mansion, she remembered the days when she would go in there with her dad. They had never been further than the entrance hall, but that had been enough. At that time, a very grand family lived there, with housemaids, a butler, and a cook-in-charge, a rounded woman with a permanent smile who wore a big white apron. Emmie remembered her well. She also remembered the freshly baked buns and biscuits the cook had pressed into her hands while her dad brought in the blooms.

How proud she and others in that neck of the woods had felt, having the gentry as neighbours. Sighing, she allowed herself an impossible dream – there but for fortune go you, me and the boys, Charlie. And a suite for Hannah.

At the Broadway, Emmie pushed open the familiar door to Rose's cobbler shop. She was pleased to see that Rose was there, placing small tins of black shoe polish on a shelf.

'Stuck in 'ere on a lovely spring day, Rose?'

The look of surprised delight on her friend's face as she

turned round was a tonic. 'Emmie Smith! Well, well, well. My goodness.' Rose shook her head, beaming. 'This is a surprise! You look so well, Emmie. Flourishing like the blossom.'

'You're looking well yourself, Rose. You 'aven't aged a day.' Emmie smiled affectionately.

'Come on out to the back. Cobbler George'll look after the shop for me.'

The old man, tapping nails into the sole of a boot in the corner of the shop, nodded and smiled. 'If you're putting the kettle on, Rose . . .'

The women made their way through to the back quietly laughing. Stepping carefully around piles of shoes, some waiting for repair and others ready for customers, Emmie nodded to the apprentice lad who was giving a pair of shoes a spit and polish. To one side of him was a neat row of boots and shoes he had already shone and to the other a pile awaiting attention. He looked tired, bored and gloomy.

'You won't be sorry, son,' said Emmie. 'It's a good trade to be in and what you're doing is all part of your training. You'll soon be elbowing Cobbler George out the way.'

'Right an' all,' said the old boy, chucking. 'Right an' all.' The fourteen-year-old apprentice didn't look so sure about it.

As they went into the little room at the back, Emmie said, 'Oh, I do love the smell of freshly cut leather and shoe polish, Rose. You've got plenty of work, by the look of things.'

'Sign of the times, Emmie. A bit more work for everyone, thank goodness. Let's hope it lasts right up and into the forties.' A familiar faraway look that Emmie had once teased her about swept across Rose's face. 'Let's just thank our blessings and not fear tomorrow. None of us knows what lies in store, do we? The shoes and boots that are coming through now are fit for repair but a year or so ago we were lucky if there was any heel or sole left on them to be mended. We did our best but the work took twice as long and we couldn't charge a penny more. But there, I suppose you had your fair share of having to make

ends meet.' Rose filled the kettle as Emmie sat down at the scrubbed wood table.

'It wasn't a bed of flowers, no. But all my men are in work now so I mustn't grumble. I expect you're wondering why I've turned up like this, out of the blue?'

Rose lit the gas ring beneath the kettle. 'It's lovely to see you, that much I do know. You should pop in more often when you're out shopping. I expect you usually go down the Bethnal Green market but you must wander up here to the Broadway sometimes.'

'I don't, to be truthful. Don't have the time. It's a good twenty-minute walk from my place to your shop. Anyway I'm here now and I'm pleased to see you looking so well.'

Rose eased the lid off a biscuit tin. 'You're a sight for sore eyes, I must say. I was ready for a break and it's lovely to share it with you.'

'You couldn't swing a bloody cat in here, Rose,' said Emmie, looking around, 'now you've put a bit of furniture in. It must be lovely to have a little back room like this. You can shut yourself away for ten minutes. We all need to escape sometimes, don't we?'

'It does get hectic, I must admit. I sometimes wonder if I'm coming or going.' Rose looked through the doorway to check that the shop hadn't filled and then closed the door. She was genuinely pleased to see Emmie and it showed. The difference in their ages hadn't mattered all those years back and it didn't matter now that she was in her forties and Emmie in her fifties.

While she piled a plate with biscuits, the kettle boiled and Rose filled the pot, set out the cups and sat down opposite her friend. 'How are those sons of yours, Emmie? Still hanging on to your apron strings?'

'That they are, all three of the bleeders.'

'You've always mollycoddled them, don't deny it,' Rose chuckled quietly and poured out the tea. 'No wonder they're in no hurry to go.'

'What about your two lads and those girls of yours, Jessie and Dolly?'

'Much the same as ever,' said Rose, passing Emmie a cup of tea. 'Alfie's still a naughty boy, Stephen's as soft as ever, Dolly as lazy and for ever going on about the early days of London, and Jessie — well, she's turning into a very inquisitive young lady. Always questioning things. Questions, questions, questions.'

'And some you can't answer?'

'Some I'm not ready to answer. We never did need to say much to each other to get our message across, did we?'

'Which is how it should be. Who are Jessie's questions to do with?'

Rose shrugged, sipped her tea and then shrugged again. 'My mother. I don't want to have to think about all of that.'

'No, I don't expect you do. Jessie obviously takes after you. At her age and before it, you was full of bloody questions as well.'

'Was I? I can't say I remember.' A glazed expression crossed Rose's face. 'Jessie was very fond of her grandfather, and very upset when he died. She went through his things soon afterwards, looking for a keepsake. Found his marriage certificate, of all things. She'd hidden it well but I found it in the air vent in her bedroom. So I had to tell her that Grandmother Blake wasn't my real mother.'

'Perhaps it was for the best. Maybe you should have told your children before now, all of them. Keeping secrets for too long can cause a lot of problems — the webs we weave and all of that?'

'Maybe. I've told Dolly too now, about Grandmother Blake, nothing else, and she doesn't seem bothered. But like I say, my Jessie's the prying type, has to know everything. She'll want to find my mother next. She may well be led to an unmarked grave.'

'Now then, Rose, that's not like you. Your mother can't be

much more than seventy and that's no age. I take it you couldn't be persuaded to find out more about her?'

'No. As far as I'm concerned, she's gone from my life.' Rose's face showed no sign of emotion as she looked directly at her old friend. 'How's Charlie these days? Got plenty of work?'

Rose clearly wanted to change the subject, but, impatient to get to the point, Emmie answered in a tone to end that line of conversation. 'Charlie's all right. Still only a porter down Covent Garden but he's well known there and well liked. Earns an extra bob here and there.' Then, taking a deep breath and blowing caution to the wind, Emmie got to the heart of the matter. 'Rose, I'm afraid that something's cropped up, right out of the blue. I think we've got a little problem and to tell you the truth I don't know which way to go about solving it.'

'By "we" I take it you mean *us* — not you and Charlie.' Rose looked wary.

'I do. I suppose you guessed something was up the minute I walked in your shop.'

'Your face gives you away, Emmie. Out with it then. What have you got to tell me?'

'It's to do with Hannah.'

'I thought as much. Go on.' Rose was expressionless but she sat extremely still.

'My Tom's still as thick as thieves with her — mates though, not sweethearts.'

'She's gone away to New Zealand, hasn't she? That's what you've come to tell me.'

'No, Rose, she's still here, in Bethnal Green, and she's all right, all things considered. It's just that my Tom and your Jessie have—'

Rose cut her off with a laugh of disbelief. 'Your *Tom*? My *Jessie*? Don't be so daft, Emmie. Jessie's courting Max Cohen, Leo and Ginny's son from the shop next door. They plan to be engaged. Jessie doesn't even know Tom. She's hardly ever over your way and when she does go out it's usually with Max

or . . .' Pressing her fingers against her lips, Rose closed her eyes. 'Please, Emmie, please don't tell me that she and Hannah have met up.'

'Pull yourself together, Rose! I didn't say that. Now for goodness' sake just listen to what I've got to say.' Emmie put her cup down forcefully.

'I'm sorry, Emmie, but deep down inside it's something I've always dreaded.'

'Jessie and *Tom* have met up. Don't ask me how it could have happened, it just has and he's walking around like a lovesick puppy.'

'Does he know?' Rose leaned forward anxiously.

'Not yet. But I'll have to tell him if he mentions her again, before things go too far and he wants to fetch Jessie home to show her off to his brothers. He's a good boy and he'll listen to me. I'll ask him not to see her and I shall tell him to keep it to himself. There's no risk of him telling Hannah, he's not like that. He'll be sworn to secrecy – as I've had to be all these years.'

A deep sigh escaped from Rose. 'Oh dear. Well, you have shaken me, Emmie. And there I was this morning, thinking how things were on the up. There's nothing to say that he won't go against your wishes. You know what they're like, young people these days. Tell them not to do something and they'll be all the more determined.'

'If I can't sway him, no one can. He can be a bit self-centred at times and there's not much I can do about that. We can't get inside our children, can we? We can't make them do what we think is right. We've got to let them make their mistakes and—'

'But this is too *serious*, Emmie. You mustn't allow him to make a mistake; but there, he'll see that, once you've told him, of course he will. At least I should hope so. Mind you, he used to be a little sod if my memory serves me right. Caused you to have sleepless nights many a time.'

'High-spirited, that's all.'

'Well, that's one way of putting it, I suppose.'

Emmie bristled. 'That's quite enough of that, Rose! Don't come the high and mighty, not with me. I know your beginnings, don't forget, and to give my son his due, he's no pansy. He has strong opinions about some things and I can't say that doesn't please me.' Emmie drew breath; this wasn't the way she wanted it to go. Softening her voice, she leaned closer to her friend. 'Neither of us'll come out in a very good light over this, Rose. He'll say we should have told Hannah much earlier on, and he'll have a point, but there, what's done is done, we have to think of a way round it.'

'He could cause so much trouble by meddling and not realise until it's too late.' Rose pursed her lips and shook her head. 'If you can't put a stop to Tom seeing Jessie then I shall have to do something. I'll find a way, even if I have to lie to her, say that I've heard things about Tom which aren't nice.'

'Well, you must do as you think best.' Emmie was disappointed. She had never thought that she would let someone threaten to defile her son's good name, especially not her old friend Rose Warner.

'Yes,' Rose went on, as if she was barely aware of Emmie's presence 'that's what I shall do. Tom won't know so it can't hurt him. There's no saying it'll work, Jessie has a mind of her own too, but we've got to try and put a stop to it now, before it gets out of hand.'

Straightening her hat, Emmie stood up. 'If I don't go now I'm afraid this will break into a row, Rose, and I don't want that. I don't think you're being very fair on my son, none of this is his fault.'

'Well, it's not mine, Emmie, and I'm sure my Jessie hasn't got thoughts on your Tom. Like I say, she's—'

'Courting Max Cohen,' Emmie finished angrily. 'Be warned, Rose, if we do try and keep our children apart, it might well have the opposite effect. Young people stand up for their rights more these days.'

'*Your* children might, Emmie, but mine wouldn't dare. I've brought Jessie up differently from that.'

'I wouldn't be so sure of yourself if I were you. You're living a cosy life now, and good luck to you, I say, but don't ever suppose that things'll drift on without trouble. Anything can happen to any one of us, at any time. Anyway, enough of all that. Once you've had time to take in what I've told you, you might want to hear what Hannah's been going through with that German bitch, Gerta. What she's still going through. The poor child's never had any friends except for Tom. The only children who were let into Gerta's home to play with Hannah came with their parents, Fascist party members or the like.' Emmie was deliberately laying it on, hoping to weaken her friend and touch the soft spot she remembered so well. 'Tom managed to cross Gerta's barrier,' she continued, 'but only because she sees him as useful, a potential Blackshirt, a steward.'

'Time's running on, Emmie,' said Rose, rising. 'I've a lot of work on. A great deal to do.' She locked her fingers. She was struggling to keep her composure. She didn't want to hear what a terrible time Hannah had had, and she certainly didn't want the word Blackshirt spoken in her shop. As far as she was concerned, there was nothing she could do now with regard to Hannah to make amends, it was too late for all of that, but Emmie was not easily stopped.

'Tom and I often laugh at Gerta. Whenever her hero, Mosley, is in Bethnal Green, Stepney or Shoreditch, she'll be there at the front, applauding him.'

'Well, let's hope that Tom and Hannah's friendship continues,' said Rose. 'We don't want to ruin something like that over a silly five-minute romance, do we?'

'Hannah and Tom's friendship is important, I'll grant you,' said Emmie, tight-lipped. 'He thinks the world of her.' She smiled at her friend once more and lowered her voice. 'She's turned out lovely, Rose. You can be very proud—'

The crockery jumped as Rose slammed her fist onto the

table. 'I have just *two* daughters, not three! Jessie and Dolly! And that's all! I *won't* have you stirring up the past. How could you, Emmie? Coming here and telling me all this. Just tell your son to keep away from my Jessie! Tell him she's promised to another man.' Rose took a deep breath to compose herself and then quietly asked Emmie to leave. 'Close the door behind you, there's a good friend. I need time in here on my own.'

'Drop me a line if you want,' said Emmie, choked. 'No one else will see the letter. I'll burn it once I've read it. You know my address.' With her head high, she walked through the shop, hoping this wouldn't be the last time.

She smiled at the young apprentice and then at Cobbler George in the corner, wondering if they had heard the heated conversation. She paused inside the shop door and was weighing up whether to go back and comfort Rose when a sudden rumpus outside startled her.

'Stinking Jews. Yids!' The sound of breaking glass followed.

Emmie shuddered. A lad no older than one of her own had thrown a brick through the grocery shop window next door. She threw open Rose's shop door and went outside, ready to give someone the sharp end of her tongue. She was pulled up short by the sight of Mr and Mrs Cohen standing helpless as one of the hooligans gripped the end of their egg stall and heaved it up, tipping the whole thing over and sending hundreds of eggs smashing to the ground.

'*Why?*' cried Mrs Cohen. 'Why are you doing this? We've always been here. You all know us. Ginny and Leo *Cohen*! Why? What have we done?'

'You're fucking *Jews*, ain't yer? Taking over our fucking shops and jobs! Get back to where you came from!' The last of the hooligans ran off, laughing.

'Come inside, Ginny, come in.' Mr Cohen, white as a sheet, was trembling. He turned to the bystanders, shocked and confused. What could he say?

'Bastards,' muttered an old man. 'Cowards. They want stringing up.'

'This is it then,' said another, 'they're back in business. It's started up again and this is just the beginning of more to come.'

'Beginning?' barked a third. 'Where've you bin 'iding out? You wanna walk along Whitechapel, see the windows that've been smashed there. Mosley's stirring things up again. Clever bastard. We might not 'ave 'ad the man's education but we know what he's up to!'

Emmie turned away. All she wanted was to be back in her kitchen having a drop of something in peace.

'Emmie! Come inside.' Rose's voice rang out above the gathering of angry people. It sounded like a headmistress issuing orders and it put Emmie's back up. First Rose had ordered her away and now she was ordering her back inside.

'I'm sorry but time's run on, Rose,' she said curtly. 'I should be elsewhere.'

Rose stepped towards Emmie and forced a smile. Squeezing her arm, she put her mouth to her ear and whispered an apology.

'There's no need,' said Emmie, drawing away. She had had enough.

'Don't let it all get churned up now, not after all this time, Emmie, please. Jessie will be deeply hurt if she finds out from someone else.'

'And so will Hannah. Perhaps you had best say something yourself before Jessie *does* hear it from other quarters. And maybe I should speak to Hannah. You can't keep this kind of thing bottled for ever. It's a sorry and sad thing if you can't speak straight to your own, Rose Warner.'

'But Emmie,' Rose gripped her friend's arm and Emmie could feel her trembling, 'we can't tell her, it wouldn't be fair or right, not after all this time. Think of my other children, Emmie.'

'I am, Rose, I am.'

'It's too late. Surely you can see that.'

'I shan't do anything, Rose,' Emmie said. 'The ball's in your court now. I've my own life to lead and three sons to think of.'

'We've got enough on our plates already,' said Rose, 'trouble coming in from outside.' She waved a hand at Mr Cohen's smashed window. 'We can't afford to cause grief between our own.'

'Bang on, Rose, and that's exactly why you should see to it that your own house is in order.' Emmie pulled her arm away. 'I shall tell my Tom in my own good time. I just thought you'd want to be aware that a storm may well be brewing. You can please yourself whether you act on it or not.' She turned and walked away, leaving Rose to stare after her.

It hadn't been easy but Emmie had done as she would be done by, and once the feeling of upset had gone, she would sleep easier for it. But the time between leaving Rose and clearing the dinner table that evening was very difficult. Trying to behave as if there was nothing playing on her mind had brought on a headache. While Charlie and the boys discussed boxing, Emmie mulled over how she might handle the problem of Tom, Hannah and Jessie. After much deliberation, she decided her only course of action was to tell Tom everything and persuade him not to see Jessie again.

Knowing that two of her sons and Charlie were going to listen to an important boxing match on the wireless, she pretended that her back was playing up and asked Tom to help her wash and wipe the dishes — he wasn't interested in boxing.

Rolling a cigarette, Tom compromised. 'I'm not wiping up and I'm definitely not wearing a pinny. I'll wash, you wipe.' Charlie, Stan and Johnnie left the kitchen very quickly, before they were roped into helping too.

Once they were by themselves, Emmie told her favourite son to sit down, she wanted to talk to him.

'Go on then,' he said, lighting his roll-up. 'I'm all ears. What's the matter?'

Nervously rearranging fruit in the bowl on the table, she began, 'It's about Jessie. Jessie Warner.'

'Oh yeah?' Tom's face brightened at the mention of Jessie's name.

'I know you won't want to hear this, Tom, but I shouldn't waste your time with that one. I heard something when I was down the market.' She was suddenly breaking the promise to herself to be truthful. In fact, she was being as bad as Rose Warner had planned to be, slandering an innocent.

'I don't *believe* this! You've been snooping around, checking up.' Tom shook his head defiantly. 'You go too far, Mother.'

'Her name cropped up, Tom, right out of the blue,' Emmie persisted. 'She's a do-gooder. Nice-to-everyone type, and she's broken many a heart. They say she leads the lads on and then drops them cold.'

'You don't know the first thing about Jessie. Gossip, that's all you know.' Tom pushed his chair back to leave but Emmie grabbed his wrist and looked him straight in the eye.

'Yes, I do. I know quite a bit more than I've let on and now it's time to put you in the picture, whether I want to or not. I admit I wasn't telling the truth about her just now. I did make it up, but still you mustn't see her again.' She leaned back and waited for his response. He said nothing, just raised an eyebrow and waited. 'I know the family,' she continued, 'and I know the family history and that's not because I'm a nosy old cow.'

'Go on then. What's wrong with the family?'

'Nothing. There's nothing wrong with her family, not really. As it happens, Jessie's mother is a very old friend of mine. I can't tell you what a bombshell you dropped when you told me the family name.'

'So what's the problem?' He was making it obvious that his patience was being stretched.

'It's to do with Hannah. With Hannah and with Jessie. I'm afraid that you're piggy in the middle on this one. It was a one in a million chance that you and Jessie should meet and become friends. Not so with Hannah, that wasn't fate, that was prearranged. I was keeping an eye out for her, even before you brought her home. This isn't easy for me, Tom, so don't you start shouting and swearing, just sit there and listen, and trust that I know what I'm talking about.'

'I'm all ears.' He smoked his cigarette, waiting.

'Hannah and Jessie are sisters.' The stunned silence from Tom was something Emmie had not experienced before. She wasn't surprised at his quiet laughter a moment later; in fact, she was relieved by it. This was more like her Tom.

'Tch. The things you come out with, Mother.'

'You'll have to drop the idea of seeing Jessie, son, unless you never see Hannah again, and for the life of me I can't see how that'll come about. I can't cut her off and as sure as I'm sitting here I won't cut you off.' Emmie had to make Tom understand the seriousness of the situation.

'Well, that's something, I s'pose,' he said, smiling and leaning back. 'But you can't expect me to believe Hannah and Jessie are . . . sisters.'

'It goes back, right back, to nineteen eighteen.'

'Oh, not the war, please.'

'Your dad fought alongside Robert Warner, Jessie and Hannah's dad, in northern France. Back here, me and Rose Blake, as she was known then, worked side by side at the sugar refinery. Rose and Robert were engaged at the time and if she hadn't fallen pregnant with the twins I think they'd have carried on with their plans to secure good positions before they married. Robert wanted to put a deposit down on a little semi in the suburbs and Rose wanted that too.'

'What did you just say?' Tom's voice sounded different, almost as if he really did have something stuck in his throat.

'Oh, for goodness sake, Tom. Listen and I won't have to repeat myself. Your dad fought alongside—'

'Not that!' His jaw clenched and he looked as if he was ready to hit someone. 'You know what I mean. You said *twins*.'

'That's right, son. Twins. Non-identical twins. Hannah and Jessie.' Giving time for it to soak in, Emmie went quiet.

'Oh, Mother,' he said, shaking his head. 'I hope you've got it wrong.' He glared at her and she just gazed back at him with a look in her eyes that said it all. No, she hadn't got it wrong.

'A shotgun wedding followed. Rose didn't carry well, which wasn't surprising, the young couple were living hand to mouth in one tiny room in a house which'd already been marked unfit to live in. Rose was a worker, scrubbed that room from top to bottom while Robert fixed and repaired windows, cupboards and doors, borrowing tools from your dad and using scraps of timber from the local yard.'

Tom eased himself forward, elbows on the table, and pushed his face close up to Emmie's. 'Are you really telling me that Hannah is Jessie's twin sister?'

'Robert was studying to be an architect,' Emmie carried on. 'He got work wherever he could, repairing and decorating, labouring backstage in the theatres, anything. In the end he had to give up his ambitions and get regular work down the docks. Eventually he went from being a labourer to a crane driver. So times got a bit easier for them but that was after they'd given up Hannah. Those times were very hard. You'd be surprised how much heartache people of our sort had to bear—'

'I'll get the violin out in a minute.' Tom's face was hard.

'You see, coming from a middle-class family, Robert had no skilled trade and unlike the rest of his kin, he wasn't cut out for the police force and had no intentions of joining the rank of city gentlemen. They was poor – too poor to support two babies and that was the simple truth of it. They had a hard choice to make

and it nearly broke Rose's heart but in the end they decided one of the girls would have to be adopted. It would be best for both of 'em, the only way to give 'em both a decent future.'

Tom held up a hand to stop her. 'What has all of this got to do with my seeing Jessie?'

'You'll be bringing together twins who were parted before they were a year old.'

He slowly shook his head. 'Well, if it's true, Hannah'll be pleased as punch to find out that Gerta the witch isn't her mother.'

Emmie sighed sadly. 'No, son, it's not quite like that. What a lovely fairy story that would make. The parents don't want Hannah back, they don't want the girls to find out that they've been kept apart all these years, that one of them was given away. Things are not as cut and dried as you like to think.'

'Well, they're gonna find out. One way or another. I'll tell 'em if you don't.'

'As I said, things are never that easy. Jack Blake, the man Hannah believes is her father, is really her uncle, Rose's half-brother. Jack Blake and his wife – Gerta – couldn't have their own kids, and they was planning to emigrate to New Zealand. It seemed the perfect solution – to pass Hannah to her own flesh and blood and send her off to a new future in a new land.' Emmie shook her head. 'It didn't work out like that, though. Jack and Gerta had an almighty bust up and he went off to New Zealand without her.' She looked sharply at Tom. 'But she loves that man more than anyone. Don't you think that that bit of news on its own would destroy her? Finding out after all this time that Jack's not really her dad?'

Tom glared at her, his face taut. 'They gave Hannah away and no one, *no one*, saw fit to tell her once she was old enough? No one told her she'd been adopted or that she had a *twin* sister? That her father was really her uncle? It stinks, Mother. It . . . *stinks*.'

'Yes, it does, but it was their wish and with something like this you have to abide by those wishes.'

'Bollocks to that. What about Jessie's dad, Robert? He seems a decent enough bloke. Didn't he want to make arrangements to see Hannah?'

'That was the idea at the time, but Gerta soon put a stop to it. Once they'd handed over the baby, new rules started to crop up until Gerta had managed to banish Rose and Robert altogether. Rose accepted it for the sake of the girls and I promised to keep an eye out for Hannah. When you brought her home that day after you'd had a fight in the playground and wanted me to clean her up before she faced Gerta, I felt as if God was at work, and that's why I swept her up as if she was an Orphan Annie. You and your brothers thought she was a replacement for the daughter I never had and that was fine by me.'

'But you knew what Hannah was going through, living with that dried-up bitch,' said Tom angrily. 'You should have said something *years* ago, you should 'ave refused to be part of it. It's not right!'

'No, Tom, it's not. But I'm not stepping in and neither are you! Leave it be. Hannah's come through and no doubt she'll find herself a nice young feller and go off and get married. Then she can make her own family.'

'She's only *seventeen*.'

'And so is Jessie! But I s'pose you're going to say that's different.'

'*Hannah's* different,' Tom said. 'Never wears lipstick and powder. Dresses more like a boy than a girl. She won't be in any hurry to get married. Family of her own? Now *you're* trying to turn a grim tale into a fairy story.' Tom ground out his cigarette furiously.

'Hannah dresses the way she does because Gerta's been too bloody mean to ever allow the poor girl to spend money on a nice frock or lipsticks. You've seen the way Jessie presents herself. Put Hannah in the same clothes and make-up and she's even prettier than her twin! If Rose could have had her wish, she and Robert

would have been able to raise both babies. It broke their hearts at the time and I *won't* see them go through any more grief! I won't! The secret is our burden too, and it must go with us to our graves.'

'Like hell it will,' Tom snapped.

'What's that supposed to mean?' said Emmie.

'It means that one of us is going to talk to Hannah – you can choose which one. And if I do start courting Jessie, I'll fetch her home to meet Dad and the boys. I'm not gonna add to things by keeping *her* hidden away.'

'And you don't think that's a bit thoughtless? A bit on the selfish side, to turn their lives upside down just because you've taken a fancy to Jessie?'

'No, I don't. You lot can't run our lives the way you ran your own.' Tom narrowed his eyes and glared at Emmie and she saw something she had never seen before. She saw loathing.

'I'm nineteen, not nine,' Tom went on. 'If I'd known earlier about Hannah, I would 'ave told her. As it is, you've put me right in the middle. You're just as bad as that German bitch she's had to put up with all these years.'

Emmie was deeply wounded, both by his words and by his anger. 'I'm gonna forget you said that, son. Let's put it down to reaction. You've had a bit of a shock and this is your way of—'

'Don't gimme all that toffee, Mother! I'm not a kid.' The expression on his face was unyielding, and Emmie could see that, right then, he despised her, that she was no longer his wonderful mum but an interfering old cow.

'I think you should sort out your loyalties, Tom.' Emmie moved towards the door; she needed to be by herself. It wasn't easy, being despised by her own son.

'And maybe you should sort out your loyalties,' Tom shot back. 'Stop trying to rule everyone's lives, and that includes Dad's. He's been under your thumb for too long.' He reached out for his tobacco tin. 'If you think you're gonna rule me as

well, you're mistaken. If I want to see Jessie, I will. If I want to introduce her to Hannah, I will. It's my business now and if you don't like it, next time keep your secrets to yourself!'

Emmie felt sure this outburst wasn't coming out of the moment, but was an opinion of her that he must have held for some time. She wondered miserably if her other sons saw her in the same light; perhaps she had been living in cloud cuckoo land, all that fetching and carrying and baking . . . Maybe they'd all been taking the rise behind her back.

She turned to look at Tom, sitting at the kitchen table, his head nestled in his hands. 'Did you mean all of that?'

'Mum, please. Go and have a lie-down or something. I want to be by myself for a minute. You can stop worrying, I won't go on the foursome, I'll send a mate in my place, but that's not to say I'm leaving it there. I'll get Sally to put in a good word for me and keep Jessie sweet till I've decided what's for the best.'

Emmie felt a strong urge to go to him, to hold him close, but it wasn't the right time. She had seen him go from one courtship to another but this time he really did look like a man in love. Sod's law, she thought. Sod's law.

Chapter Three

When Sally Brown slipped Jessie a note from Tom in the factory canteen, her first reaction was to tear it up but she thought better of it. She didn't know Sally that well and she might report everything back to Tom. Why should she let the rotter believe he had got under her skin? Feigning airy indifference, Jessie pushed the note into her cardigan pocket to read again in private and went back to her office. She had gone like a lamb to the slaughter that night, turning up outside the Odeon, wearing her best clothes, waiting like an idiot in the drizzling rain. When Sally, Ron and a complete stranger arrived, she had wanted the ground to open up. The pathetic excuse given by Sally's boyfriend, Ron, was that Tom had sprained his ankle. In the note that Sally had given her, he'd written that he had put his back out playing football.

At her desk, Jessie took the envelope from her pocket and read it again before tearing it into small pieces and throwing it in the bin. Tom had had the gall to write that he would like to see her again, one day. She had taken a big risk going on that date behind Max's back; had he found out, she might well have lost him and deservedly so.

Preoccupied with her thoughts, she didn't hear the door open or Sally come into the office.

'What did he say?' Sally whispered from behind.

'Tell him to drop dead when you see him and say that I wouldn't go out with him if he was the last man alive and sound as if I mean it because I do,' snapped Jessie.

'I *knew* he wanted to see you. I knew it!'

'Well, you needn't sound so pleased, Sally, because I don't want to see him, so there won't be another foursome arranged, not with me there leastways.'

'Oh yeah, pull the other one,' teased Sally. 'You know you fancy going out with him.'

Jessie spun round to face her. 'I do mean it, actually. I'm only sorry I said yes in the first place. I am courting, you know.'

A loud, deliberate clearing of the throat came from behind the frosted glass partition; Jessie's boss, Mr Reed, was making it clear he didn't want Sally in there. 'You'd best go, I've got loads of work.'

'Miserable old sod. He needs a seeing to. I'll send Betty the bust from talcum powder round. *My* office manager never minds if one of the girls comes in for a quick natter.' Sally deliberately raised her voice. 'Anyone'd think we was in *prison!*'

'I'm trying to concentrate, Jessie. Would you please ask your friend to leave?' Mr Reed spoke in a quiet, controlled voice.

'I'll see you later and you can tell me exactly what was in that note,' chirped Sally. 'Tom's a right cracker and he's got it bad for you – lucky cow.' There was another, louder, clearing of the throat from behind the screen.

'She's just going, Mr Reed. Sorry about that.' Angry, Jessie waved Sally away and out of the office. If Tom really had thought anything of her, he wouldn't have stood her up. Sally was good fun but not very bright. She grinned at the impatient Jessie and hovered by the door.

'Can I ask you a question, Mr Reed?' said Sally in her best voice, the one she sometimes used when sitting on the switchboard in the post room.

'Very well. Just one.'

'Thanks. Well, we all know what's gonna happen on

the twelfth, don't we?' There was a touch of excitement in her voice.

'Get to the point, Sally.'

'Well, the point is, Mr Reed, I thought it would be nice if we could get up a charabanc and all go together to watch the procession from Buckingham Palace, after the coronation. They're 'aving street parties round our way but I'd much prefer to go to Buckingham Palace, wouldn't you, Mr Reed?'

'I shall be going, as a matter of fact, with my family.' His tone had changed, he sounded relaxed and friendly. 'My children are very excited about it. I'm pleased to see you take an interest in our current history.'

'Current 'istory?' Sally looked at Jessie and pulled a face. 'The King and Queen are getting crowned! Course I'm interested. Wouldn't miss it for the world.' This conversation between Mr Reed and Sally was being carried out through the frosted glass partition; neither of them could see the other. 'Them princesses are lucky cows, ain't they? Elizabeth and Margaret. You seen them frocks they wear, tch, all silk and satin and velvet. Still, there you go, they are royal, ain't they? They're bound to dress like that. I would if my dad was a king.'

Jessie was worried that Mr Reed would lose his patience with her. 'You'd best go now,' she whispered. 'I'm going with Mum, Dolly and the boys. You can come with us if you like.'

'It's unfortunate,' said Mr Reed reflectively from behind his screen, 'that the Duke of Windsor abdicated. A king of England, getting involved with an American divorcee. Scandalous. It'll be a blot on the history books I'm afraid.'

Sally smiled, a soppy expression on her face. 'Ah well ... he loves 'er, don't he? Must do. To give up a kingdom. Romantic, I think.'

'Mmm. That'll be all then, Sally,' said Mr Reed, ending the conversation with a tone of finality.

Sally looked at Jessie and curled her top lip in a comical fashion. 'Oh right, I'll be off then.' She turned to leave but was

struck by another thought. 'I tell you what will be a blot on the 'istory books, Mr Reed.'

'What's that, Sally?'

'Old Blue Eyes the Duke being mates with Adolf Hitler. I mean, that Hitler's not a very nice man is he, all the trouble he keeps causing to the Jews and that. You wouldn't fink someone who was once King of England would be mates with someone like that.'

'We don't know that they're friends, Sally. People in high places often have to mix with others in high places. It's the way of things. 'Now, enough chat, Sally. Be on your way.'

'Oh right . . . if you say so, Mr Reed, if you say so. You bosses know best.' Sally backed out of the office, whispering, 'Fancy a coffee after work, Jess?'

Warming to Sally again, Jessie slowly shook her head, disappointed. 'Can't. Max is meeting me outside the gates.'

'Ne'er mind. Tomorrow, yeah?'

'All right. Tomorrow.'

Later, Jessie sat opposite Max, enjoying his treat of a cup of coffee and cake in Joe Lyons. He was unusually quiet, his dark eyes troubled and Jessie could tell there was something on his mind. There was no point in pressing it, he would tell her in his own good time. 'You do know that the Vicky park fair opens tonight, Max?' she said hopefully.

'It'll be there for two weeks, Jessie. We can go on Saturday,' Max replied in a flat voice.

'I thought it would be nice to go on the first night. It's where we first met,' she said, 'remember?'

'That was over two years ago,' he said dismissively.

'True.' Obviously sentimentality wasn't going to work, she thought.

'It was a nice idea.'

'But?' said Jessie, annoyed.

'But what?'

'But you don't want to go.' She waited for an answer.

It didn't come. 'You don't seem very happy, Max, bloody miserable, in fact. I know you're not one for smiling for nothing but you're giving me the blues as well.'

'I'm not very happy, Jessie, no. You seem chirpy enough, though.'

'Well, I would, wouldn't I? I'm sitting here with you, enjoying coffee and cake, and you know this is my favourite place ...'

'Times are bad,' he said, shaking his head, 'really bad.' Max didn't look up, just slowly stirred his coffee.

'I thought that trade had picked up. That your mum and dad's shop was doing quite well. Mum's shoe menders is up on last year.' Jessie tried to jolly him with her optimistic tone.

'I'm not talking about trade, although in a sense that has something to do with it. Blackshirts.' Max pushed his hands across his face and ran his fingers through his dark hair. 'It's getting worse. The more successful we Jews are, the more they see us as fair game.'

'It'll pass. Street warfare, that's all it is, at least that's what you've been saying over the past couple of years. They haven't been back since the egg smashing, have they?'

'No, but my parents are really frightened. It's why I wanted us to meet up now instead of later.' He looked at her earnestly.

Jessie couldn't remember ever having seen Max so serious and worried. 'Why? What's happening later?'

'There's a meeting at Harry Zeid's house, one of our members. We're keeping it quiet though.'

'Why? Why do you have to keep it a secret?' She didn't like the sound of it.

'Well, whenever we've met at the club just recently, things have gone wrong. Hymie comes with good information as to where the Blackshirts are going to hold a meeting or which hoarding they plan to stick their posters on, and it doesn't happen. We go to the venues — and nothing. We check the

hoarding, ready to tear down the propaganda — nothing. Then we hear that meetings were held elsewhere and we see the bloody posters on hoardings we didn't know about.'

'There's a spy in the camp,' she said, teasing him. She couldn't help feeling this was all nothing serious, just boys enjoying their games, pretending it was all real.

'It's no laughing matter,' Max said, frowning. 'Anyway, there'll be just a dozen of us. If it happens again, that narrows the odds of finding out who it is. We can't rely on Communists or the Labour Party or the Liberals. If we're to avoid a repeat of what's happening in Germany and what happened in Austria, we've got to be more organised. The Jewish Party needs to change and become more disciplined. East End Jews have been singled out deliberately. The press focuses on the Fascism against Jews in the East End which keeps attention off other towns, where it's probably just as bad. More publicity means more trouble here, in Whitechapel. The Blackshirts are being seen as heroes, and the pack grows by the day.'

'And because of that, we can't go to the fair, kind sir?' she said, trying to lighten things.

'I wouldn't have gone in any case, not with the mood as it is. The thugs are out there hungry for blood. Jewish blood.'

'Show them you don't care. Brazen it out.' Jessie sipped her coffee, while Max stared at her with concern in his eyes.

'But I do care, Jessie. I care about my parents, my aunts and uncles . . . Grandpa . . .'

'Now you *are* being daft. Remember Cable Street? Just about everyone came out against the Fascists. A policeman even surrendered to your lot and Mosley was turned back, the march cancelled. You *won* that demonstration, and there'll never be another as well-planned. Come on, Max, you remember, everyone came forward against them, it was a triumph. The streets were packed with people doing whatever they could to stop Mosley getting through. Dockers, shopkeepers, housewives, kids even.'

'But that show's over, Jessie. You can't do something like that a second time. We Jews are passive by nature—'

'Until you're under threat! Even I remember the bricks and coshes, Max. Your lot are just as bad if not worse than the Blackshirts when push comes to shove.' Easing off one shoe, Jessie stroked his calf with her toe. 'Don't go to the meeting tonight. Let's go back to your house and play a nice record on the gramophone. We can turn the lights down low, lie on the sofa . . .'

Smiling at her, Max shook his head. 'I can't. I promised.' By the look in his big, soft brown eyes, she thought she might just win him over.

'Please. Just this once. Miss the meeting for me just this one time. I want to show you how much I love you. I'm wearing your favourite . . .' she waited for him to finish the sentence.

'Perfume?' He was beginning to weaken.

'Nooo . . .'

'Stockings?'

'Close, Max. Very close.'

'Well, the meeting's not until eight . . .' He reached across the small table and squeezed her hand. 'And as it happens my parents are out. We'll have the place to ourselves.'

Outside, Jessie impulsively guided him towards Violet Alley, where it was dark except for the dim street lamp. She slid her hands across his broad shoulders and caressed his neck, her soft blue eyes gazing into his. 'Do you love me, Max?'

'Of course I do. I've said so, haven't I?' He nuzzled her neck and murmured, 'It's a waste of my time telling you, Jessie, if you don't believe me.'

She smiled, moved closer and kissed him on the mouth. She would shake him out of his dour mood. Kissing him with passion, she slipped her hand inside his jacket, pulled at his shirt, then eased both her hands inside onto the warm flesh of his back. Within seconds Max's hands were everywhere, his breathing heavy and hot. Once aroused, Max never wasted time.

Lifting her skirt above her waist, he pulled the loose leg of her silk knickers to one side and pushed himself deep into her soft, fleshy crevice.

'Oh God, darling . . . you're adorable,' he moaned, his voice deep and husky. 'Who needs music . . .' He kissed her again and before she could answer he was affording himself protection against fatherhood. Thrusting himself back inside, as if there wasn't a second to lose, he quickly reached the heights of his passion. Once again she was left wondering if this was all there was to lovemaking. The earth did not move for her the way it did for Max.

Coming out of Violet Alley, arms round each other, they bumped into one of Max's friends and before she knew it, Jessie was being guided back into the coffee house, with his comrade in tow. There she listened patiently to Max and David for more than an hour until she was bored to death with their conversation. 'Well,' she said at last, 'it's all been very interesting, but I'm going to leave you to it, boys.'

'I'm sorry, I'm sorry.' Max splayed his hands. 'Not another political word, I promise.'

'You can't blame us, Jessie,' said David, nudging his loose glasses up and back into place, 'and we're not the only ones, you know. Quite a few of our friends are going to Spain to fight for what we see as the struggle against Fascism.'

'Pity they don't stop *here* and fight against it, then you and Max wouldn't be so concerned about being outnumbered by Blackshirts, David.' Jessie leaned over the table, smiled at him and then tapped his wristwatch. 'You've been going on about Spain for twenty minutes. Before that it was Hungary, and before that, Berlin.'

'Well,' said David, 'these are very worrying times, Jessie. Very worrying.'

'Yes, well, the debate's over for me. I'm going home. You can go on reasoning for and against joining or not joining the group leaving for Spain. If you want to link up with the International

Brigade in the revolutionary fight against the Fascists in Madrid, *do it.*' She pulled on her blue felt hat and pushed up the brim. 'But if you ask me, I don't think that either of you will leave England — but talk it over for another couple of hours, why don't you?' Leaving Max to his companion she stalked out of the coffee shop.

By the autumn, Max and David had still gone no further than London, other than in their dreams, but Jessie had to admit that more and more Fascist and anti-Fascist slogans were appearing in the streets, and Max had been right about one thing — the mood was worsening. People huddled in clusters, talking earnestly, their discussions sombre as the days got shorter and the nights colder.

Pushing the key into the lock of the front door after a refreshing walk home from work, Jessie wondered if her earlier damp mood had been brought on by some of the men at work going on about the atrocities abroad. As far as she was concerned, it would do more good if the British people focused more on the good things that were being reported on the wireless and in the newspapers. Industry was soaring and factories were booming with the demand for electrical appliances. Chain stores such as Boots and Marks and Spencer were opening dozens of new branches, and hire purchase was making things affordable to working-class families such as hers and Max's.

Inside the house, the familiar sounds of Stephen and Alfie playing Lotto and Rose moving around in the kitchen eased some of the tension Jessie felt, though she couldn't get rid of her nagging worry about her brother, Alfie.

Just recently, when tidying the boys' bedroom, she had discovered a packet of Woodbines and two cigarette stubs under Alfie's bed. Inside the cigarette packet was half-a-crown and to her horror she also found a sheath knife. She knew that Alfie had been hanging around with older lads of fifteen and she'd heard him using very bad language once or twice. More

worrying than the smoking or the foul swearing was where the money was coming from to buy the cigarettes. If Alfie'd been dipping into Rose's shop till, as Jessie suspected, it would really shake her. She'd always had a tendency to think that her children were above serious wrongdoing. And what of the knife? Where had he got that from?

Going to her room, Jessie promised herself that she would at least mention the smoking when the time was right. Relaxing on her bed, she thought about Max and wondered if he would ever pop the question and if so whether she would accept. Lately he seemed to talk about nothing but politics or money. He was now working for a small accountancy firm and was never happier than when faced with columns of figures and difficult calculations.

She loved Max no less than when they first started to go out together and she still found everything about him attractive – the way he dressed, his sometimes dry sense of humour, his handsome face and thick black hair. Why then did she still not melt the way he did when they were locked together in passion? Max would never know it, but apart from enjoying his kisses, she really did the rest to please him; she got her pleasure from that. But did other girls do it for the same reason?

She was deep in thought as to how she might broach the subject with Sally when the bedroom door opened. She was surprised to see young Stephen in the doorway. He was tearful and pathetic. His lips and cheeks had been reddened with one of Dolly's lipsticks and their mother's hairnet was on his head. Worse still, he was wearing nothing but a brassiere and a pair of Dolly's crepe knickers. She heard laughter from the boys' bedroom, not just from Alfie but from Dolly too.

'They ... made ... me ...' He could hardly get the words out and he was shivering with cold. Jessie was off the bed and beside him in a flash, pulling him close and telling him to take no notice of them. Slamming the door shut she leaned on it so they couldn't come in.

'Take everything off, Stephen. Take off the knickers and rip them up. That'll teach Dolly a lesson. They're her best ones.'

Stephen just stood there, quietly sobbing and shaking his head. 'They'll ... tell ... everyone.'

Jessie knelt in front of him and looked into his face, smiling. 'No they won't, sweetheart, because I know things about Dolly – and Alfie too.' She pulled off the hairnet and wrapped her grey blanket round him, covering his skinny white body. 'They've got nothing up here, Stephen,' she tapped the side of her head. 'Their skulls are filled with cold porridge and hard-boiled eggs.'

A smile spread across his tear-stained face. 'That's why Dolly's always farting. Hard-boiled eggs do that to you. So do porridge oats.'

'Well, there you are then,' she laughed. 'They're full of wind.'

'They need a dose of syrup of figs.'

'Or caster oil?' said Jessie, egging him on.

'Or both?' He threw back his head and laughed. 'Let's give them both.'

'Yeah, let's do that,' she said, clasping his shoulders. 'Let's give it to them on Sunday. They won't 'ave a clue what they're scoffing when they eat trifle at tea time on Sunday.'

'Yes! Yes!' He jumped up and down, his eyes bright and shining again. 'And I'll get to the lavatory before they do. I'll lock myself in and before I come out I'll hide every bit of bottom newspaper up my jumper.' If only the other two would give Stephen half a chance, thought Jessie, he'd brighten up their days with his sense of humour. 'And it won't just be their vest bottoms that'll be yellow,' he added, giggling.

'Shush, Stephen, keep your voice down. They'll hear you and—'

A short sharp rap on the door stopped her mid-sentence. Jessie knew it was her father because he was the only one who knocked on the bedroom door.

'What's going on in there?'

'Nothing, Dad. It's just me and Stephen having a giggle.' Knowing he'd want to come in, and seeing the frightened look on her brother's face, she told her father she was in her underwear and that Stephen was taking the mickey out of her bloomers.

'Well, keep your voices down, your mother's listening to the wireless.' There was a pause but they knew he was still out there. 'Stephen, the lads have arranged a game of street football for tomorrow afternoon, after school. Why don't—'

'Good idea, Dad!' he called back, quick off the mark. 'I'll score a goal and show 'em.' Both Jessie and Stephen had to cover their mouths to stop him from realising that they were taking the rise.

'That's the ticket, son. That's the ticket.' Robert went downstairs a happier man.

Stephen stood in front of Jessie, bending both arms and flexing muscles which were as flat as fried eggs. She dropped onto her bed and buried her face in the pillow. Taking a sly glance at what he was up to next, Jessie roared with laughter – he was playing to his audience of one, striding around the room mimicking the strong man who broke out of chains outside the Tower of London. In that moment, Jessie knew that it didn't matter about him dressing up or being a skinny waif; one day her Stephen would be in the limelight, on stage, accepting rapturous applause with all the confidence in the world.

Sunday soon came round. Stephen had reminded Jessie three times what they were going to do with the syrup of figs. Making her way to the kitchen and looking forward to turning a boring sweet into something else, Jessie overheard her parents talking and was thankful that Stephen wasn't with her.

'Well, if you hadn't mollycoddled him from the start, Rose, he might well be out there now, with the other kids.'

'Oh, stop going on about it, Robert. If the truth be known it's only your own pride that bothers you. You always wanted he-men for sons.'

'Don't be silly. I just wish he was more like Alfie, that's all.'

That rankled, and before Jessie could stop herself, she was in there, surprising them with her sudden arrival. 'I don't think you'd say that if you knew what I found under Alfie's bed.'

They turned and looked at her, waiting.

'He's been smoking. I found a packet of Woodbines when I pulled his comics out from underneath.'

Instead of anger she saw her father's expression relax and then turn into a smile before he burst out laughing. 'So that's where he keeps 'em – the crafty little bastard.'

'Robert!' Rose slammed down the tea towel and stood with hands on hips. 'You just *swore*.' She spoke as if she truly couldn't believe it. 'And in front of our Jessie *and* on a Sunday!' Jessie wondered which her mother felt most protective towards, her or Sunday.

'I never swore,' he said, a touch defensive. 'The word's in the dictionary, Rose.'

'That's right, and with a clear definition, so now tell me that Alfie's a bastard.'

Jessie could hardly believe her ears; never, not once in her entire life had she heard either of them use that word. Twice in one day was unthinkable.

'I came to make the trifles,' she murmured, reminding them that she was there. 'I asked Stephen if he'd give me a hand, if that's all right.' They noticed her nervousness and did their best to relax back into a Sunday mood.

'Of course it's all right,' said Rose, 'and if you don't want to do it this week, Jessie, ask Dad to help Stephen. It won't be the first time he's made the trifles for me.' She eyed Robert, daring him to say that their younger son should be anywhere but in the kitchen – the woman's place.

'Twice. I've made the trifles twice, Rose. Once when you were laid up with tonsillitis and once when you were in bed nursing your baby.' He looked at Jessie and winked. 'Our little

Alfie. She gave me a strapping son — a ten-pound baby boy. I cooked the roast that day as well. I was so proud, I would've baked a cake if your mother had wanted it.'

Jessie glanced at Rose to see that she was blushing and was obviously flattered.

'Oh, go on up for your nap,' she said, giving Robert a warm smile. 'I'll be there shortly.'

'So what about Alfie smoking?' Jessie was puzzled by their indifference, she'd expected them to go through the roof.

Robert stepped towards the kitchen door and squeezed her shoulder. 'Boys will be boys, Jessie. But don't you worry, we know all about it, we've got a card up our sleeve. We'll offer him one of his own Woodbines and get him to smoke a whole one in front of us. I guarantee he'll be sick afterwards and won't be able to look at another one, let alone put it to his lips.'

When Jessie was alone with her mother, she decided to take the opportunity to ask her a question that had been on her mind for some time. She had been too wary of her mother's displeasure to ask before but over the last few months her curiosity had grown so much she could barely contain it. It was time to take the plunge and ask. 'Mum,' she said hesitantly, hoping her mother's good mood would last, 'why did Grandfather change his and your name?'

Rose slowly turned round, her smile gone and a haunted look on her face. 'Why do you ask that, Jessie, and right out of the blue? You are a strange girl.'

'Because I don't understand it. It keeps on coming back into my mind. There must be a simple explanation.'

'It's not a puzzle. I expect it was just something he did to please Granny Blake, used her name instead of his own because he already had a wife. I don't know and to be honest I wish you'd stop thinking about my parents.' Rose closed her eyes and sighed and Jessie could see the pain on her mother's face.

'I'm sorry, I shouldn't have asked.' Jessie moved towards her mother but Rose put up a hand to stop her.

'I don't really know why he changed his name, Jessie, but I can see you're not going to rest until you know as much as I do.' She turned her face away. 'Tomorrow. I'll tell you tomorrow, when we're by ourselves. Now let's leave it at that.' She walked out of the kitchen, leaving Jessie frustrated and wondering why her mother always put off telling her things.

'We gonna make the trifles then?'

She spun around to find that Stephen was in the doorway. His innocent, smiling face warmed her.

'Come here, funny face.' She held out her arms and he wrapped his skinny self round her waist. Hugging him, she kissed the top of his head. 'I love you, do you know that?'

'I love you too, Jess,' he said, adding, 'Did you find the syrup of figs?'

'No, but I found the caster oil.' She reached for custard powder and a packet of jelly. 'But we mustn't go too heavy, Stephen, just a drop in each of their glass dishes. Enough to teach them a lesson, that's all. It won't happen straightaway, you know. It takes hours to work, overnight even.'

'Not if you put twice as much in.'

'No, I'm not doing that. You'll have to be patient. You'll get your own back, don't worry,' she said, tousling his hair.

'If it hasn't worked by the time I go to bed I won't be able to sleep.'

'Stop trying to blackmail me. Anyway, you'll probably be gassed in the night by Alfie farting – that'll send you off.'

The following morning, Jessie woke out of a strange dream and knew there was something she had to remember. It came in a flash and she was out of bed and on her way downstairs in no time, wrapped in her favourite grey blanket.

'You're up early, Jessie. Your dad's only just left for work. Did the front door closing wake you?' asked Rose.

'No. I didn't hear him go.'

'Well, since you're down you might as well have a cup of

tea, there's one in the pot. And here, put these on your feet. They're your dad's old ones. You'll catch pneumonia walking about barefoot.'

'I woke up thinking about you this morning,' said Jessie, pulling on the thick hand-knitted socks. 'I was wondering what it must have been like all these years, not seeing or knowing where your own mum was. Did you ever try to find her?'

'I hardly knew my mother, you're making too much of it.' Rose joined Jessie at the table. 'It doesn't bother Dolly so why does it bother you so much?'

'I don't know. I just feel as if a part of our family is missing, that's all. I can't help it. I can't stop my mind from thinking about it.' Jessie considered. 'Maybe it's because Max's family, his heritage, is so important to him.'

'A part of our family missing? And you think that's because you never knew your grandmother?'

'It must be, mustn't it? Why else would I feel like this? Dolly's different from me, she can shrug things off. I can't help the way I am. I've tried to be more like her. God knows why.'

'All right, Jessie, I'll tell you all there is to know since I've promised and that'll be the end of it.'

Rose related everything in a passive voice, as if she was reeling off someone else's life story. She had been eight years old when she was put into a children's home, and she hadn't seen her mother since but could remember her. Her father had appeared at the home one day and taken her away to live with him and the strange woman she was to look upon as her new mother – Grandmother Blake. Her half-brothers were born over the next five years and although she got on with them, she never really felt she was as much a part of the family as they were.

Willy had dismissed any questions Rose had asked about her real mother until she stopped bothering to ask, and all she could remember about those times was that Willy had stopped smiling and laughing the way he used to. She could vaguely remember the house they'd once lived in but had no idea where it was.

Only when she described her tiny bedroom did Rose show any emotion, and even then she covered it well.

She went on to say that her real mother had spoken with an accent, which she realised now had been German. That much she could remember. She knew that her mother had been born in Germany and that her father, Willy, was half Polish, half German, but unlike her mother he had been born and bred in England, and that was why he didn't have a German or Polish accent.

'So there you have it,' said Rose, ending her story, though for Jessie it was only the beginning. 'Not such a mystery after all, is it, Jess? And not all that interesting. I should have your wash-down now, the water in the copper's just about the right temperature. Thank goodness we'll soon be on electricity, and with a bit of luck, by this time next year, your dad will have converted the back room into a bathroom. Isn't *that* something to look forward to?'

Rose went about her work, preparing breakfast and packed lunches as usual. In the scullery, Jessie filled the big blue and white jug with water from the copper and poured it into the china bowl, her mind on her grandfather and why he had changed his name.

'There must have been another reason for him to change his name,' she said to herself but loud enough to catch her mother's ear. 'It couldn't have been just to please Grandmother Blake surely.'

'Maybe it was all down to the war,' said Rose from the kitchen. 'Several Germans living over here then did the same thing. Your great-grandfather's shoe mender shop was burned down because he was a German. He opened another one later, once the war was over, which is the one we've got now. He was a clever man.' Rose's voice took on a worried tone. 'He always warned that it wasn't finished and that there'd be another break-out in the thirties or forties . . .'

'People at work are saying they can see another war coming.

They say Hitler won't lie down,' Jessie said, coming back into the kitchen.

'It's a wonder no one's shot that man in the back,' said Rose sharply, 'the amount of degradation he's causing to people he thinks inferior. I dread to think what those poor Jews and gypsies are going through in Austria. I don't know where it will all end. This Blackshirt business should have died out by now but it hasn't. Hitler's probably behind that as well, making chums with Mosley who's too slow to see he's being used. If I had my way we'd move out of the East End tomorrow, to the countryside, away from all the troubles.'

'Where there's no work,' said Jessie.

'Where there's no work,' agreed Rose.

'Did Grandfather fight in the war? He never spoke about it.'

'No. They needed people like him back here. He was the finest bootmaker around. Many Home Guards wore boots that your grandfather or his apprentice made. It's a pity none of my half-brothers wanted to learn the trade. I think that's why I took an interest in the shop, if truth be known. But I don't understand why people, women as well as men, are joining the Blackshirts, Jessie. I suppose they're frightened that unemployment will get worse again. They've had enough of having to watch their children go hungry and cold in the past. Now that things are better they want it to stay that way.'

Dolly stormed into the kitchen. 'There must have been something wrong with that trifle you made, Jessie. I had to get up in the night and use the chamber pot. I bet Stephen never washed his hands before helping you!'

'Yes he did. I hope you've emptied and washed the pot if you 'ave used it. I never heard you go out to the back yard.'

'Well, you wouldn't, Jessie, would you? Fast asleep and snoring while I was out there with a torch, freezing to death!' Dolly, looking rather paler than usual, turned to Rose. 'Her

and Stephen put something in my trifle, I know they did, to get back at me.'

'Back at you for what, Dolly?' asked Jessie, smiling. She knew her sister would never openly admit what she and Alfie had done to Stephen. 'I don't know what you're going on about. I thought the trifle was smashing.'

'It was very good', said Rose. 'I expect you ate too much and too quickly, Dolly.'

Stephen and Alfie appeared next, and Alfie, too, looked a sorry sight. His face was bright red with embarrassment; he had his bed sheet rolled into a ball. 'This is for washing,' he said. 'I shit the bed.'

'Alfie!' Rose was taken aback more by his language than the state of his bedding. 'Don't you dare use that word again, my lad!'

'It wasn't my fault that it happened.' His pride really had taken a bashing. 'I thought it was a fart—'

'That's enough!' snapped Rose. 'We haven't even had breakfast yet!'

Jessie winked at Stephen who hid a grin.

'What shall I do with it then?' Alfie asked, backing away.

'Oh, put it outside in the yard, in the tin bath, and turn the tap on it.' His face went from bright red to off-white and Rose wondered if both he and Dolly were going down with something. 'Once you've done that,' she said, 'go on back to bed. You can have the day off school.'

'I don't want the day off, just the afternoon. I'm playing in the football match in the morning and—'

'You go for the day or not at all,' said Rose, 'and no more of your bargaining. Go back to bed or get washed and dressed. Suit yourself.' She sat down, shaking her head. 'I'm beginning to wish none of you had grown up, it was easier when you were small. Now you've all got minds of your own.'

'Ah, but we are still children at heart, Mum,' said Jessie. 'We've just got bigger, that's all.'

'Mmm,' murmured Rose, unconvinced.

'I haven't got bigger,' said Stephen. 'I'm under average – nurse at school said so.' The remark warmed Rose. She held out an arm to him and Stephen was in there like a shot, on her lap and cuddling up, gazing longingly at his thumb.

'Don't you dare,' said Rose. 'You might be under average but you're not a baby.'

Later that day, after work, Jessie slipped into her bedroom and lay on her bed, thrilled by what she had found out during her extended lunch break. Mr Reed had asked her if there was anything preying on her mind as she seemed preoccupied. His question surprised her, he almost had her feeling like an equal.

In actual fact his concern was for himself. Jessie was a good and reliable employee and he was worried about losing her. He had been wondering if she was toying with the idea of taking a position elsewhere. When she explained that she wanted to find her real grandmother but wasn't sure how to go about it, he became interested and she was surprised to discover that for some years he had been researching his own family line. He now had a family tree going right back to the seventeenth century and was not going to stop there. Mr Reed told her to go to Somerset House in the City and explained in detail how to go about tracing her grandmother in the records.

Jessie had thanked him from the bottom of her heart and Mr Reed had clearly been moved by her sincerity. He suggested she make a start by taking an extended lunch break which she could make up on another day. She did as he suggested and having followed to the letter the advice he had given her, she found what she was looking for at Somerset House. An entry in the records. Her grandmother was alive and living not so far away, by Victoria Park.

In her room, brushing her long wavy hair, Jessie was going over the fabricated story she would tell her parents as to where she was going this evening, when Dolly appeared.

'Mum needs a hand with the washing up, Jessie – if you

can pull yourself away from that mirror. I would help but I'm off to the Sally Army.'

Turning to look at Dolly, Jessie grinned at her. 'Pull the other leg. Sally Army? You?'

'They're meeting up outside the Salmon and Ball pub, on the corner of Cambridge Heath Road, and—'

'I know where it is, Dolly. Since when were you interested in the Salvation Army?'

'I'm not. It's one of the band players I'm interested in, a tall, dark, handsome musician,' she said, admiring herself in the mirrored wardrobe. 'He plays the tuba. It's why he joined the corps, so he could be part of a band. He wants to be a professional and one day play with the big bands.'

'So you're going to join up,' said Jessie, smiling, 'wear the uniform and do all that goes with it, are you?'

'If I have to. It's what musicians' girlfriends do. He's broke, of course, like all performers before they get their big break. He's a road sweeper at the moment and loves his old work horse — that's why he took the job. If he's not playing his tuba he's in old man Lipka's stable, brushing down that old mare. He'll have a stallion of his own one day and canter along country lanes.'

'And Fred?' Jessie wondered what had become of Dolly's old boyfriend.

'Too childish and he's got no ambition. He'll be a foundry worker all his life. Where's your rose-red lipstick?' Dolly rummaged through the side drawer of the dressing table.

'And Mum's pleased, is she — that you're showing an interest?'

'Course she is, she reckons that you should join as well, said it would be right down your street. I didn't agree. I said you'd take it all too seriously.'

'Really? And what did she say to that?'

'Never uttered a word, went straight into her quiet mood. She knows I'm right.'

'I would sooner you didn't use my lipsticks, Dolly,' said Jessie, watching her sister stroke her best one across her lips.

'Don't be selfish. I don't mind if you borrow mine. I've said so.' She hadn't, but there was no point in arguing with her, she would only insist she had.

'Yours are too bright and too cheap. You go out with well-shaped lips and come home with a big red smudge.'

'Do I now? Well, we can't all afford the best, can we, Jessie?'

'You could if you bought one or two good ones and made 'em last.'

'Said the old woman to the girl. I'm gonna have to have a word with Max, you need a good bit of the other to bring you alive.'

Jessie smiled to herself. Dolly believed she was a virgin.

Her mother's footsteps sounded on the stairs, and a moment after Dolly left the bedroom, Rose appeared in the doorway.

'You needn't help in the kitchen, Jessie,' she said. 'I'm making Alfie do the drying for a change, a punishment for being cheeky at school. They sent a note home.'

'That's good, because I'm going out soon, to the Whitechapel Art Gallery to listen to a talk on the designer, William Morris.' Jessie extended her lie, saying that after the talk there was to be a demonstration on weaving, embroidery, and tapestry.

'I s'pose Dolly's told you where *she's* off to.' Rose was obviously relieved to think that her wayward daughter was showing signs of reforming. William Booth, the founder of the Salvation Army in the mid-eighteen hundreds, was Rose's hero. She'd often recited one of his lines: 'Some men's ambition is art, some men's ambition is fame, some men's ambition is gold. My ambition is the souls of men.'

'Maybe she's turning over a new leaf at last,' said Jessie.

'Oh, I shouldn't be so lofty about her. She's a bit strong-willed but in your own way you're no different, Jessie. I just wish she wouldn't wear so much lipstick and powder. I see that

Vaseline's no longer the mode, she's using mascara and eyebrow pencil now. What time does the lecture begin?'

'Seven o'clock sharp. I'd best get my skates on. I'll jump on the bus and—'

'So,' she looked directly at Jessie, 'you're not being like your sister and secretly meeting a new boyfriend.'

Jessie knew she was referring to Tom. Even though it had been months since Jessie had seen him last, and then been stood up, she still thought about him. Rose, who must have been told the story by Robert, sometimes mentioned 'a new boyfriend' with a strange look in her eye as though she was trying to catch Jessie out. This wasn't the first time that her mother had probed her about him.

'I wouldn't two-time Max.' Another lie. In truth she was beginning to tire of Max's sombre moods and their joyless dates. The girls at work always seemed to be going out and having fun and she was jealous. The truth hit home one day when Sally cracked one of her jokes and the sound of her own laughter made Jessie realise how little she had done that lately. She couldn't remember exactly when she and Max had stopped laughing together.

'Well, don't hang around afterwards,' said Rose, her voice cutting through Jessie's thoughts. 'You know what it's like out there at the moment.'

'We're not Jewish, Mum,' she said, fed up with hearing about it. 'It's those poor sods who're trembling in their boots.'

'Oh, I don't know so much. One of the lads along the road got a terrible beating from a group of Jewish lads – and just for chalking on the wall.'

'I can't say I'm surprised. You must 'ave seen what they write.'

'All the same, that's no reason to break his nose.'

'I don't know any more,' murmured Jessie. 'The more I hear about it, the more confused I get.' She swung her legs off the bed and slipped on her shoes. 'Anyway, I'll be all right, don't worry.'

'The chap on the wireless said that the fog was going to get worse tonight, pea soup time again. Remember to take a torch just in case and take your smog scarf or you'll be sneezing black tonight.'

When Rose had gone, Jessie clenched her hands and gritted her teeth. Why oh why did her mother say the same thing every time she went out in the evening when winter was on its way? Surely she realised that anyone would want to wrap up against the bitter weather.

On her way out, Jessie looked in on Robert, reading his newspaper in the parlour. 'I won't be late home, Dad,' she said. 'Keep the fire burning.'

'Ah, Jessie. I wanted to have a quiet word.'

'Oh. Must it be now?'

'I've been thinking,' he said, his brow furrowed, 'about you and Max.' He locked his fingers together and sucked on his teeth, something he was inclined to do when giving his children advice. 'I think it might be best if you weren't seen out together for a while.'

Jessie couldn't believe her ears. He was the last person she thought would say that. 'But if we all stop mixing with our Jewish friends in public, that'd mean Mosley was winning surely.'

'I'm not saying you shouldn't see him, just don't go walking out together till things calm down. Max can come round here sometimes and you go to his house. The nights are drawing in and you don't know who'll be lurking in alleyways armed with coshes, and in the present mood girls like you will be tarred with the same brush, in a manner of speaking. I'm not saying this just because Max is Jewish — he's a Red as well.'

'No he's *not*. Max might go on about it but a Communist? He's not that political, Dad. What made you think that?'

'It's what they're saying down the docks, Jessie, about the majority of the Jews, that they've united with the Communists for strength. Be careful, that's all I'm saying, and get Max to stay in the background for a while.' Robert turned back to his paper.

On her way to the bus stop, Jessie had to admit that her father had a point. There was an atmosphere of pending trouble. She'd passed four pubs on her way and although they were lit up, there wasn't much noise of talking or singing coming from them and she hadn't heard anyone playing the piano. And it wasn't just the men who were standing on street corners in groups, everyone seemed to be out that evening, street walkers, tram and bus drivers, conductors, cabbies. It was as if the East End was a place waiting for something to happen. Expecting it.

Crossing the Mile End Road she saw several more groups of people standing around, so she paused for a moment to properly observe what was going on. Couples were strolling hand in hand, small groups of men, small groups of women, all going in the same direction − towards the People's Palace.

There were no placards or patriotic flags, so it couldn't be a demonstration. Since she was going that way, catching a bus which would take her from the Mile End, down Grove Road and on to Victoria Park, Jessie slowed down. There was a different and strange mood in the air. A mood of defence rather than attack, of intrigue rather than fear, and it all seemed calm and controlled as more people arrived from side streets. A clock above a pawnbroker's showed it had just turned seven.

Debating whether to go on walking with the crowd or wait at the stop for her bus, Jessie caught a glimpse of a figure she thought she recognized. It was Tom. Unlike other couples who were enjoying each other's company, he didn't have his arm round the girl he was walking with and he wasn't holding her hand; they were simply strolling along together. Throwing back his head and laughing, Tom glanced behind him at another couple who were enjoying a quip and in that split second his and Jessie's eyes met.

His first reaction was disbelief, but then, with some hesitation, he waved her over. Surprising herself, Jessie made her way through the crowds towards him. As she drew near, a cloud of

concern swept across his face as he looked from the girl beside him to Jessie.

'Hello, Jessie,' he said, greeting her as if they were old chums. 'This is my friend Hannah. Hannah, this is the girl I was telling you about. The one I met outside Stepney Green station in the summer.'

'Late spring,' said Jessie, correcting him, 'after you'd just pinched someone's cap.' She smiled to suit her mood. She felt very pleased to see him and ready to put him firmly in his place.

'I'm glad to meet you.' Hannah held out her hand, which came as a surprise. East End girls didn't shake hands, but Jessie responded as if it was the most natural thing in the world.

'Tom stopped talking about you,' said Hannah, smiling, 'so I presumed it had fizzled out.'

'There was nothing to fizzle, Hannah. Tom's manners aren't as good as yours. He stood me up. Sent someone else in his place – on a date, a foursome. A gentleman he is not!'

With a knowing smile, Hannah glanced at Tom and shook her head. 'You coward.'

'Coward?' said Jessie, unsure if she'd just been insulted. 'What makes you say that?'

'Tom believed it was love at first sight – you must have scared the life out of him.'

'All right, Hannah. That's enough,' said Tom, taking command.

'Why don't you walk with us?' Hannah glanced over Jessie's shoulder. 'Or are you with someone?'

'No. I'm by myself and just happened to be passing. What's going on?' Jessie looked at the crowds.

'You mean you don't know? And you really were just passing?'

'I'm on my way to somewhere else, to see a relative. Is it a demonstration?' Jessie sensed Tom's eyes burning into her and could feel herself blushing.

'I suppose you could say it's a demonstration, yes,' said Hannah, who was only too pleased to fill Jessie in on the details. It had been rumoured that Oswald Mosley would speak at the People's Palace, he would explain what his intentions were and had always been, and tell the Jewish community that he was not out for their blood as some of the press would have them believe. 'It's just another bit of Fascist propaganda to gain more members,' said Hannah.

'Come on, Hannah,' urged Tom. 'If we don't get moving we'll end up at the back of the crowd.'

'Tom thought it would be nice to go for a stroll on this crisp October evening, and I thought he meant just that. We were going to walk all the way to the Tower and have a drink in his favourite pub. I put on my best red hat for the occasion.'

Jessie was quite struck with Hannah; she seemed very natural and Jessie felt easy in her company. Glancing at her not-so-fashionable grey coat, Jessie saw that she was wearing a small clip-on brooch very similar to the one that Rose had given to her.

At the People's Palace, Jessie and Hannah chatted on while Tom kept himself to himself, looking around, hoping to catch a glimpse of the infamous Mosley. He was surprised at the number of people who had turned out. Hannah suddenly let out a low, despairing groan. 'Of course *she* would be here. I should have known. She said she was going to see a friend – she doesn't have friends, she has comrades.'

'Who?' asked Jessie.

'My mother. Her over there, in black. She tells people she wears that colour because she is still in mourning for my father – who is not dead.' There was a pause as Jessie tried to take in her strange remark. 'She is so conniving,' Hannah went on. 'She didn't tell me about Mosley coming because she wanted Tom to be here and knew I would try and stop him. But Tom is the one being tricked here.'

Tom scowled. 'Shut up for five minutes, Hannah. You can talk some things to death, you know.'

Quietly laughing at him she said, 'Mosley's not going to be here, she just wanted you to come and listen to one of his lapdogs. She tricked you.'

'And how would you know that?'

'Because, Tom, it would have made front-page news.'

'You're wrong there. Why do you think this many have turned out? Because there are no police around, that's why. He kept it a secret from the press. Let it be known by word of mouth.'

Again Hannah laughed at him. 'I told you it was more propaganda.' She pulled his jacket sleeve. 'Come on, we'll make our way to the Tower through the back streets. I don't want to get involved in this.'

'Don't be a silly girl, Hannah. It's a free country, we'll walk where we want. I want to take *this* route to the Tower and have a drink in my favourite pub on the way.'

'We can do that on the way back! They'll be gone by then. Please, Tom, I'm sick to death of listening to them. I know that's who it will be on the platform, one of Mosley's puppets.'

'According to some of the newspapers,' said Tom, distracted, 'Mosley's not as anti-Semitic as you've had me believe. He wants a great future for Britain, that's all.'

'Ah. So she finally got through to you then?' Hannah sighed. 'I knew she would, in the end.'

'Like I said, some of the news reports—'

'From *some* of the newspapers,' Jessie chimed in, to remind them she was there. 'It depends which newspaper you read.'

'You tricked me into coming out for this walk,' said Hannah. 'Why, Tom? Why do you need me by your side?'

'I never tricked you. I fancied a walk to the Tower and, yes, Gerta did mention this was scheduled and I thought I might find it interesting. So, yeah, I'm blacking my nose. Nothing wrong with that, is there? Hannah? Oh, for Christ's sake. *Now* what?' Hannah was staring past him at the platform.

'I was wrong, Tom.' She had spotted the banner, the

bodyguards and the man. Mosley *was* making a brief appearance. 'You will see the man in the flesh after all.'

Before either Tom or Jessie could get a good view of him, Mosley was off the platform again and into his chauffeur-driven limousine which was standing by with its engine running. All they saw of the man was the back of his head as the car sped away.

'Well, you could hardly call that an appearance.' Hannah was laughing again. 'He was here long enough for his publicity agents to take photographs of him with the crowd. Now can we go?'

'Be quiet for five minutes, Hannah,' Tom said, irritated. The rapturous applause mixed with catcalls and whistling was deafening as one of Mosley's men stepped up onto the platform to give a speech, his henchmen surrounding him.

'Come on, Tom, we can cut through the back doubles to Commercial Road.' Hannah looked and sounded nervous. 'We'll make our way to the Tower from there, or make our way back home. There's going to be trouble this evening, I can smell it in the air.'

'Don't talk daft. You go back if you're that worried. I want to have a butchers at the man. Take Jessie with you ...' He rubbed his chin thoughtfully and then pushed his hand through his hair, worried. 'No, on second thoughts, didn't you say you were going somewhere else, Jess?'

'Yes. I am, when I'm good and ready. Don't worry, I won't be hanging around here for much longer. This is not my idea of an evening out.'

'If you're really this interested, Tom,' said Hannah, 'I promise to let you know another time when Mosley actually is going to give a talk. I promise. This is not a good time.' Hannah's anxiety began to make Jessie feel edgy too.

'I want to stay and listen to the speech, that's all. Just listen to what this man's got to say. I'm not gullible, if I think he's talking a load of rot, I'll say so.' Tom grinned and winked at Jessie. 'Free speech. Mine. He should admire that.'

Resigned, Hannah linked arms with him. 'It'll look better if we appear to be a friendly threesome just passing by. Take his other arm, Jessie.'

Jessie did so, for the fun of it and to annoy him, but Tom wasn't annoyed, his sideways glance at her showed his interest in her. Squeezing her hand, he said, 'Stop worrying, you've got a bodyguard.'

'I can't stay long,' said Jessie, warming to him. 'I've got a date.'

Tom laughed quietly. 'So you said, with a relative. An old grandma?' He couldn't have known how right he was.

'Not one Communist,' murmured Hannah, studying the crowd for familiar faces. 'This spells trouble. They must have gathered elsewhere, ready to make a grand entrance. I wonder which route they'll take.'

'Stop *worrying*,' said Tom.

'Well, I'm going home. I don't think you should hang around either, Jessie, I really don't.' Hannah turned to leave but Tom was too quick for her and grabbed her round her waist.

'You're not going anywhere. I need you to tell me who's who.' With his arm firmly gripping her, Tom pleaded, 'Ten minutes, that's all, then you can go.'

The man on the platform began to speak and Tom lifted himself to full height and listened intently while Hannah continually looked around for the first sign of trouble.

'Soon the others will come,' she murmured, 'like small opposing armies. The Reds, the Jews and an army of Blackshirts, dressed to intimidate. Those already here are mostly sight-seers and people like you, Tom, on the brink of joining up.'

Jessie looked from Tom's serious, attentive face to the speaker who was dressed in a light-coloured suit, with black shirt and black tie. Tall, broad and erect, he was an attraction for the women, and there were several young women in the crowd. Mosley's men, like himself, had become heroes and heart-throbs

to some as Rudolph Valentino and Clark Gable had to others, and this speaker was on good form:

'Sir Oswald Mosley counts it a privilege to live in an age when England demands that great things shall be done! A privilege to be of the generation which learns to say what we can give instead of what can we take! For thus our generation learns there are greater things than slothful ease; greater things than safety; more terrible things than death.

'Hold high the head of England; lift strong the voice of Empire! Let us to Europe and to the world proclaim that the heart of this great people is undaunted and invincible. This flag still challenges the winds of destiny! This flame still burns! This glory shall not die. The soul of Empire is alive, and England again dares to be great!'

'Oh yeah?' The voice of an old East Ender filled the calculated silence. 'Once you've kicked out the Jews and anyone not pretty enough to be at your party!' This brought laughter.

'Sir, anti-Semitism was never our policy! We never attacked the Jews as a people. We never attack any man on account of race or religion, and we never shall. From the very outset we have preserved the principle of no racial or religious persecution. The fact that Jews enjoy an excessive influence in British—'

'So what do you want then?' yelled another. 'What is it you're getting at? 'Cos I'm blowed if I understand your fancy talk. Speak as you find, sir. I'm a plain man. So give me some plain talk – if you can.'

'I will do my best, sir. Firstly, Blackshirts were hired for one reason and one reason only, to protect meetings from Communists and the Jews who attacked our Olympia meeting and have often been responsible for groundless assaults upon our members—'

'Yeah, yeah, we know all that! We wanna know why you're 'ere and what you want. What d'you want to do for this country and for us? What're you about, sir?'

'A fair question. We ask those who join us to march

with us in a great and hazardous adventure. We ask them to dedicate their lives to building in this country a movement of the modern age, which by its British expression shall transcend, as often before in our history, every precursor of the continent in conception and in constructive achievement. We ask—'

'Waffle!' yelled one of the crowd. 'The man was asking for answers, not claptrap. Tell us what's needed and what you intend to do!' There were both favourable and unfavourable responses from the crowd. Hannah felt sure there were people planted among the crowd to provoke conflict.

'What d'yer want the British people to do? And tell us why we should do it!' shouted a younger man.

'We must strive to continue to reduce unemployment figures! Improve economic conditions and social conditions! Deter a party controlled by Communists! Communism destroys all honour and trust among men, even within its own party.' The speaker paused for a few seconds to allow that thought to soak into the people's minds.

'The tactics are always the same,' said Hannah. 'I've seen this act so many times it makes my stomach turn. It's a well-planned speech.'

Jessie leaned forward and whispered in her ear, 'Are *you* a Blackshirt, Hannah?'

She whispered back, 'Yes. I have a tyrant for a mother. She forced me to join. Talk to Tom. Do what you can to persuade him to leave here now, before the trouble starts.'

Jessie studied Tom's face, he was hanging on every word the man was saying so what could she possibly do to make him leave? She would wait five minutes more and then slip away. She had, after all, another more important meeting to attend. She was going to find her grandmother. Her thoughts drifted away from the immediate scene as the speaker's voice rang out into the October evening.

'Many of the typically English characters among the Communists have come over to us. And for good reason, one being

that the Blackshirt movement is the only guarantee of free speech in Britain—'

'Never mind about free speech! Tell us 'ow you aim to reduce unemployment so we can have some grub on the table! Because that's why most of us are giving you our time of day! You gonna ship out all the foreigners back to their own countries and make this a British Britain? 'Cos if you are, and you're prepared to say so in public, I'll wear the uniform of the Blackshirt! Enough's enough!

'The foreigners are getting all the fucking work! The Jews eat chicken while our families are making do on bread and fucking lard!'

'Come on, Tom,' Hannah pulled at his sleeve. 'He's finished, he's just given the stewards a nod. The seed's been planted and now they'll leave the crowd angry.'

'He's not going anywhere before he answers my questions – let's see if he'll admit that Mosley's an ally of Hitler.'

'He won't answer, he'll just smile. He's waiting for someone like you to take the bait, I've seen it all before.'

Jessie saw that an army of men were approaching, silently marching, with not one banner or flag to be seen. She nudged Hannah and nodded in their direction.

'I knew it. It's the Communists!' She jerked her hand from Tom's arm, turning quickly to look behind her, and sure enough another lot from the other direction was coming their way. 'And now we have the Jews,' she said.

Jessie thought about Max and the mood he and his friends had been in lately. They could very easily be part of the mob striding towards them. Jessie realised they were sandwiched between Communists and Jews who no doubt believed that all those gathered here were ardent Fascists.

'This is very organised,' murmured Hannah. 'They've got together over this one and no doubt there will be other small splinter groups coming too. Let's hope that the Blackshirts do turn up or we might well be the target here.' She stepped

backwards, a very frightened look on her face. 'Tom. We have to get away from here. *Now.*'

'He's gone — the speaker's bloody well legged it!' Tom was furious. 'I've never seen anyone move so quick!'

'That's because he's seen there's going to be trouble!' snapped Hannah. 'He's no different from any other human being, Tom, except that just like his teacher, Mosley, he's an excellent showman.'

'Mosley's always been for his country though, Hannah, he never changed his spots on that issue. I've been doing my homework.'

'Listening to my mother, you mean. She's *hypnotised* you.'

'Nuts! I can work things out for myself. What that speaker had to say made sense. I—'

A milk bottle flew through the air and just missed Tom's head. Within seconds there were more sounds of smashing glass and shouts of abuse as well as screams from the women present, and both the Communists and the Jews were storming towards them.

'Where is the army of Blackshirts to protect us now?' said Hannah. 'I told you, this was a calculated plan to show the Reds and the Jews in a very bad light. The press will have a field day.'

Above the noise of the crowd came the voice of a young Jewish man who was no more than a couple of feet away. 'Bastard Blackshirts!' Turning to confront him, Tom was met by a heavy fist which sent him reeling backwards and down onto the pavement, bleeding and shocked.

His immediate response was to scream at the girls to run, but they were too stunned to move. Forcing himself to his knees, the blood pouring from his mouth, he shouted, 'Run, Jessie, run!'

Too terrified to react, she just stood there as if in a daze. It was Hannah who reached out and grabbed her arm, wrenching her away and yelling at her to run fast. Her heart pounding as

if it would burst, Jessie felt the same fear as she had in Cable Street with her brothers.

They pushed and shoved their way through the angry fighting crowds. They sped through the back streets, under arches and through alleyways. They ran until they had to stop. Leaning on the wall of a local school, not one word passed between them until their breathing became more normal and their hearts stopped thumping as if they would burst.

'I have such a stitch in my side, Jessie,' gasped Hannah.

'Me too.'

'We needn't have run this far, we could have walked once we were out of danger.'

'No. I wasn't going to stop running until I had to. Where do you live, Hannah? Is it far from here?'

'No. A five-minute walk, if that.' Hannah pressed her hand to her side and doubled forward. 'My mother won't be in so you can come back if you would like to.'

Jessie took long, slow breaths of air. 'I would love a cup of tea ... after a glass of water.'

'Me too. Come on. We can walk now.' Hannah held out her hands. They were trembling. 'I've seen what can happen when there's a clash. People will be hurt and I wouldn't be surprised if someone isn't killed. Did you see any police there?'

'No.'

'Precisely. No Blackshirts. No police. This time they even managed to outsmart the law.'

'Who?'

'The Union of Fascists.'

Safe in the flat in Hannah's small kitchen, Jessie took in her surroundings. It was all so clinical, cream and light-green paint, everything scrubbed and not one ornament around to collect dust. Everything had its place, in a cupboard or behind closed doors. This was not a homely kitchen and Jessie couldn't imagine cakes being baked here, ever.

'I hope Tom's all right,' said Hannah, pouring boiling water

into the teapot. 'The people who'd gone to listen were totally outnumbered. Most of them were just ordinary folk, not there for the politics but simply to sightsee and catch a glimpse of Mosley. They were being used like pawns in a chess game. Maybe now Tom will drop any thoughts of joining the Blackshirts and my mother's work will have been a waste of time. She's been trying for years to get him to join up, telling him that it's not the Blackshirts who cause the trouble.'

'Well, he's hardly going to drop it now, is he, Hannah? You said yourself that the Blackshirts didn't turn out, so he'll blame the other factions.' Jessie took a steaming cup of tea gratefully.

'Yes,' Hannah sipped her tea, 'you're right, and the more I tell him the way it really was, the more he'll argue with me. He can be single-minded at times and I'm only a *female*, what do *I* know about anything?'

'More than anyone at that gathering, by the sound of it,' said Jessie, checking her watch. 'I have to go. I'd love to stay longer and find out more about . . . well, about everything.'

'Meaning Tom?'

Jessie couldn't help smiling. 'Are you a mind-reader as well, Hannah?'

'I knew what *you* were thinking,' she said, triumphant. 'Jessie, why don't we meet up sometime for a coffee, or a drink?'

'Good idea, let's do that. I work at the soap factory, in the offices. Give me a pen and paper and I'll write down the phone number. Ask for the wages department, my boss shouldn't mind one call coming in for me.'

'Do you really mean it?' said Hannah, a touch of disbelief in her voice.

'Of course I do. Why shouldn't I?' The girls looked into each other's light blue eyes and a sense of familiarity swept through them both.

'I don't usually make friends this easily,' smiled Hannah.

'Well, it's high time you did.' Jessie leaned back and held her gaze. 'I like you, Hannah. I like you a lot.'

Chapter Four

Jessie tried to push all thoughts of the frightening attack from her mind but she felt that the People's Palace would never be the same again. Stepping down from the bus at Victoria Park, she shuddered against the cold mist in the air which enhanced the aroma of smouldering wood from a garden fire somewhere nearby.

It was eight thirty and the rising full moon broke the darkness, casting shadows behind the trees and catching small leaves as they floated down, adding to the carpet of rust-coloured foliage, not yet raked from the park. Crisp leaves on the wide pavement rustled under her footsteps as she peered at street doors, trying to make out the numbers. Somewhere along this road lived her grandmother.

Her steps slowed as she began to lose her confidence. A voice deep inside her told her that this mission could go badly wrong. Maybe Ingrid Gunter preferred to forget the past, like her daughter Rose. She might find this visit intrusive and upsetting.

Jessie found herself in front of wide steps leading to the front door of the house she was looking for. Without thinking, she brushed her fingers across the face of a rundown, life-size statue of a lion, one of a pair, sitting either side of the dilapidated wrought-iron entrance gate which had not been closed for several

years. Wedged into the earth with its hinges rusting away, it was ready for the rubbish dump. The building itself had been neglected too and was in need of restoration and repair; paint was peeling and there were cracks in the plaster on the lower half of the façade.

Taking a brave, deep breath, Jessie climbed the steps and pulled on the old-fashioned brass bell. Twelve tenants were registered as residents here, some single, some married and some with children, and Jessie felt sure that one of them must be in. The wait seemed like an eternity.

The boy who eventually struggled to open the heavy door was a ten-year-old who looked as if he could do with a good bath and a hot dinner. He peered up at Jessie and narrowed his eyes as if he was seeing light for the first time.

'I'm looking for a Mrs Gunter,' said Jessie, hesitant. 'She's quite old and—'

'The owd German tart that lives dahn the airy?' The boy closed one eye and curled his top lip.

'Well, that might be her . . . unless there's another old lady here, living on her own.'

'Nar, there ain't.' He sniffed and wiped his runny nose with the back of his hand and rubbed it down the side of his oversized trousers. 'You want the old gal in the pit. She ain't a witch, is she?'

'I don't think so,' said Jessie, half smiling. 'Why do you ask?'

'Dunno.' He lifted one leg off the floor and broke wind. 'Go dahn an' bang on the door. The bell don't work and she's a bit mutt and jeff.' He slammed the door in her face and shouted from behind it, 'Now fuck off!'

Jessie went down the worn steps that led to the basement flat, half expecting a mouse to run across her feet. Some litter had blown or been thrown into the airy but other than that it was all quite clean. Bracing herself, she knocked on the door and waited. The door opened before she had time to think about changing

her mind. It opened soundlessly, no eerie creaking, no stale dank smell, no dark passage, no bent, witch-like old woman. Instead she looked into the fresh and intelligent face of someone she almost recognised. Ingrid Gunter had similar features to Rose and the same searching eyes.

'Yes? What do you want?' Although to the point, Ingrid had a soft, quiet voice and Jessie could detect the German inflection. She stood erect, her chin pushed forward, her eyes alert and not full of misery as Jessie had imagined. Her silver hair was pulled back into a neat bun and her clothes, dark and simple, had no creases. The lace-edged collar on her grey dress was snow-white and Jessie could smell the faint aroma of lavender. The woman didn't look as if she belonged in a basement flat in Hackney but in a thatched cottage in the country surrounded by orchards and rose gardens.

'I'm Jessie,' she said, smiling nervously. 'Jessie Warner.' She looked into her grandmother's face and saw her changing expression. 'I don't suppose the name means anything—'

'It means nothing to me.' Jessie was sure Ingrid Gunter knew exactly who she was, she had answered too quickly. 'You have the wrong house.' Ingrid stepped back and began to close the door but Jessie put the flat of her hand against it.

'Please, let me come in. I can tell that you know who I am. I won't stay long and I won't ask too many questions, I promise. Just give me a few minutes of your time, that's all I want.'

The old woman looked at her with a piercing gaze. 'Did she *die*? Is that why you've come? To tell me she's dead?'

'No. My mother doesn't know anything about this, no one knows. I did it of my own accord. I wanted to find you.'

'Why?'

'I don't know.' Jessie waited as the seconds ticked by and the old woman decided whether or not to let her in.

'And *nobody* knows you are here?'

'Nobody. Cross my heart.'

Ingrid's tension seemed to dissolve. She nodded and stood

to one side. 'Go through.' She possessed a quiet dignity. 'All the way to the end of the corridor and into the sitting room.'

In the small, comfortable room, Jessie at once felt easy. Memories of her grandfather washed over her. There was a dark, polished, carved sideboard, a small feather-cushioned settee and two old, comfortable-looking armchairs. There was nothing modern in the room except for a Clarice Cliff tea set and an orange, red and black vase filled with fresh flowers. A few patchwork cushions were scattered on the settee and there was a new cream Bakelite wireless under the wall lights which had lovely pale green and cranberry glass shades.

A small coal fire burned in the fireplace, and on the black iron trivet sat a kettle of water, from which steam was wisping out of the spout. The apartment, unlike Jessie's home, had already been wired for electricity, yet Ingrid Gunter still used the fire to boil the kettle. The walls had old-fashioned fading wallpaper on which hung some framed photographs and a collection of miniature paintings. The scent of beeswax polish reminded Jessie of home and there was a delicious smell of baking coming from the kitchen.

'Please, take a seat.' Ingrid waited until Jessie lowered herself into an armchair before she herself sat down in the chair opposite. 'You are young and will want to ask questions. I am old and will not want to answer them. Say what you have come to say and then you must go.'

Her forthright manner reminded Jessie of Dolly. 'I found out where you were living, through the records office.'

'Why? Why should you want to find me? I am not a part of your mother's family now or your life so why should you come here?'

'You're my grandmother.'

'Ha. It could be said.' She picked up a polished brass poker and prodded the glowing coals in the fire. 'I suppose your curiosity was aroused when your grandfather died. Something was said and you latched on to it. Too young to be wise. It must

have been fun to discover you had a grandmother who had been kept in the dark. It gave you something to do. Dig up a bit of the past. Well, I hope your thirst for intrigue has been quenched. I'm not dead. What will you do now for a pastime?'

Whether she meant to or not, she was fuelling Jessie's passion, she wanted to know more. 'How did you know he'd died?'

Her grandmother paused, as though wondering how much she should reveal. Then she said slowly, 'The authorities. He was still my husband, according to the law. As far as I was concerned he died years ago.' There was a short pause as the clock ticked loudly. 'What if I tell you that I don't like callers?'

'I'm not a caller, I'm your flesh and blood. Did you have any more children?'

'No.' She turned away from Jessie's searching eyes and gazed at the floor. 'No. The love a mother has for her child is almost too much. Once is enough.' She went quiet again. 'My brother had beautiful children and now he has beautiful grandchildren. I see them often. They are my family.'

'That cake in the oven smells lovely,' said Jessie. It sounded cheeky but she was actually trying to remind Ingrid of it because there was a slight smell of burning coming from the kitchen.

'Yes. The cake.' The old woman pulled herself up from the armchair and went into the small kitchen. 'Would you prefer tea to coffee?'

'I don't mind,' Jessie called back, surprised at the offer.

'Perhaps you wouldn't mind giving me a hand.' A second invitation, and from someone who didn't want to spend much time with her.

'The cake did not burn. I've left the oven door just open. In a moment, perhaps you would lift it out for me while I grind the coffee beans.'

Jessie glanced around the small, neat kitchen. Everything was in its place, pretty cups and saucers were displayed on a small kitchen dresser and on the white enamel surface, in a corner,

sat two of everything from a plain blue dinner service – her everyday crockery. One set for herself and one set should she have a visitor. There were lace curtains at the kitchen window and across the back door which opened on to the garden. The floor was covered with bright blue linoleum with small red squares.

Jessie watched fascinated as the graceful woman spooned coffee beans into her iron grinder. 'I don't think I've tasted real coffee, we always have Camp. I'm not sure about Joe Lyons, the coffee there does taste different but—'

'I doubt that Joe Lyons has time to grind the beans himself but I'm sure he would use good coffee and charge for it.'

Jessie lifted the fruit cake out of the oven and placed it on the draining board to cool. 'This looks delicious.'

'The sugar bowl is in that cupboard. It's dark brown sugar, you may not like it but I don't use white.'

'I love dark brown sugar, we always have it at Christmas time. Mum lets us scoop out the flesh from an orange and fill it with sugar. Once it's been sitting for a week she lets us eat some of it, before we chop up the peel for the puddings.'

Ingrid spooned ground coffee into her percolator. 'I suppose you will boast to your mother that you have found out about me and where I live.'

'Not if you don't want me to.'

'If *I* don't want? Since when did what *I* want matter? How much do you know about Mr Gunter and myself?'

'That he left you and it made him sad, that my grandfather, who I loved *very much*, was besotted by *her* until he realised his mistake and missed someone. You.'

'You seem to have known him well. Did you despise him for what he did to me?'

'No. I could never despise him, we were quite close.'

'You must have been special to have managed that. Here,' she handed Jessie an oven glove, 'bring in the kettle of boiled water from off the fire – and try not to scald yourself.'

Obeying her instructions, Jessie carried on talking, raising

her voice a little. 'He never mentioned you or said anything about what had happened, but once I found out, after he died, I realised he must have sometimes been thinking about you when I was there.'

'And how could you know what he was thinking?' she said, taking the kettle from Jessie. 'You would have to be very smart to have seen inside Mr Gunter's mind.'

'I was the only one in the family who sat with him. Sometimes we'd talk but mostly we'd sit and be quiet. He would have told me to go home if he hadn't wanted me there. He was like that.'

Ingrid asked Jessie to carry the tray, laden with coffee and warm cake, into the sitting room. 'From what age did you visit him?'

'Always, right from when I was a scruffy urchin.' Jessie set the tray down on the small occasional table and watched as her grandmother cut two slices of cake.

'I doubt you were ever scruffy or an urchin.'

'Do you know what he mostly ate?' said Jessie, enjoying the memory. 'Slices of sharp cooking apple, a piece of cheese—'

'And raw onion,' the old woman finished for her. 'I can't pretend that I'm not pleased now that I've got over the shock of seeing you on my doorstep but don't take my hospitality to mean that I want you to come and go when it takes your fancy.'

'I wouldn't do that. My parents taught us to have good manners, not that Dolly or Alfie always practise it but at least they *know* when they're being bad-mannered. Grandfather wouldn't have stood for my coming and going either.'

Ingrid tensed at another mention of him. 'We'll drink our coffee and eat cake together and then I would like you to leave. Meanwhile I would prefer it if there was no further talk of that man. Willy Gunter has much to answer for. He did wrong and God would not have forgiven him — and he will have known that, which is why he had the worried look you refer to.'

'I didn't say worried, I said sad.'

'He had his Maker to face and I don't envy his last few minutes before death. He knew he had wronged me. I was a good, hard-working, faithful wife, and doting mother. I did not deserve what he gave me in return, the pain and the loneliness, the worst kind of suffering for someone who has lost her family. It's not good to love too deeply. Once, he did love me, yes, but not after he met the Gypsy whore. You shouldn't make excuses for him or try to justify what he did. Leave me something at least. I was the victim so I may curse him. Hating is easier than loving.'

Jessie sipped her coffee and found the silence strange; it was as if everything had been said and yet there were so many things to discover about her grandmother. She wanted to ask about Rose and what she was like as a small child, but that would have to wait until another visit.

'You should eat the cake while it's still quite warm, that way you will taste the fruit.'

'Mum always makes us wait until it's cooled down. She says it's not good for the digestion if—'

'That's because she's had English housewives to listen to instead of her own mother, and for that you may thank your beloved grandfather.'

'I know it's not much help now,' Jessie broke off a small piece of her cake, 'but I'm sure he regretted what he'd done and I know he wasn't happy with Grandmother Blake. He wasn't in his grave five minutes before she had another man move in.'

'He got what he deserved. When he left me I had no money and a child to bring up. He changed his name so that I could not trace him. I had no choice but to put my daughter into the orphans' home. I could have found him if I wanted, but I would not beg, I would never beg. I managed by myself, scrubbing thick grease from kitchen floors, always with the thought that I would one day get back my little girl. Then I discovered he'd taken her away from the home and I gave up. He had taken everything. When he took my child he left me with nothing.'

'I thought he changed his name because of the resentment in the East End – against Germans,' murmured Jessie, ashamed of what she was hearing.

'So that was his story? Ah well, it made my life easier not having to worry about my child's welfare. I trusted the Romany to look after her.' She raised her eyes and looked straight at Jessie. 'Was she a good mother?'

'Mum was fed and clothed, but I don't think she was loved. She grew up thinking that her real mother didn't want her.'

'Well, well. Aren't you a glowing light. I will sleep much better knowing that. What I could never understand ... is why your mother repeated what had happened to herself. She gave away your sister. Times were hard for her, of course they were, but—'

'She never gave away my sister! Dolly lives with us. She's always lived with us. Mum wouldn't give one of us away. Who told you that?'

Ingrid's eyes clouded over and her face showed her remorse. 'My brother has been bringing me tales for years, he doesn't live far from where you are and thinks it his duty to bring me news. As usual he got it wrong and I apologise.' She looked very uncomfortable. 'I'm weary now, you have tired me with your questions.'

'It's time I was getting back home anyway, they forecast fog, and there's been a lot of trouble round our way between gangs.'

Rising, Ingrid shook her head. 'Mosley is a foolish man who is causing trouble which could have a devastating affect on this country.'

At the front door, she said, 'Please try to understand that I am better off being left in peace. I've put the past behind me. Don't tell your mother that you came. As far as I am concerned I have no family and that is how I prefer it.'

Jessie found that very hard to believe. 'Surely you'd like to

see your only daughter again. She'd come, I know she would, once I explained what—'

'After thirty-three years? I don't think so. You are young and fanciful and I'm sorry to dash your romantic notions. Had she have wanted to, like you, she could have tracked me down a very long time ago.' Ingrid looked up at the sky and frowned. 'I think the forecast is right. Be home before that blanket of fog begins to fall.'

Jessie didn't want to leave things there, it seemed too final. 'How come you know so much about us if you weren't interested?'

'My brother keeps me informed whether I like it or not.' She nodded her goodbye and the expression on her face forbade Jessie to ask anything else. Then Ingrid smiled weakly and closed the door.

Jessie leaned against the wall to collect her thoughts. Her grandmother had not shed one tear. Did she really not care? Jessie didn't believe it.

The sound of a man's voice from inside startled her. 'You were very hard on her, Ingrid! Too hard. She is just an innocent child!' It must be Ingrid Gunter's brother; he had presumably decided to keep out of the way until she left.

'I don't want to *hear* it!' Jessie flinched at the misery in Ingrid's voice. 'You hated my husband for what he did to me, so hate his offspring ... *and* his offspring's children! That girl is nothing to us. *Nothing!* We must forget she ever came!' Ingrid's voice dropped to a pitiful tone. 'We must forget. I've lived without them, I will die without them.'

There was a quiet moment and then Ingrid spoke again. She sounded like a different woman. 'He did love me, you know ...'

'I know, Ingrid, I know. Try to remember the good times.'

'My only child, Wilhelm, my only baby. We could have brought her up, we could have managed between us. Do you

see what happened? She repeated the actions of her own mother. Do you see, Wilhelm? Do you *see*?'

'Shush. You have my family, Ingrid. My children adore you, you know they do. You have a family with us. We'll forget she ever came.'

Jessie arrived home exhausted and ready for her bed; too much had happened in one day. Hoping her parents were too involved with a programme on the wireless to start asking questions about the William Morris exhibition, Jessie went into the house very quietly. She'd had enough for one day and wasn't in the mood for trumping up a pack of lies about the Whitechapel Art Gallery and the exhibition. It would be much easier to deal with it in the morning over breakfast when everyone was in too much of a hurry to show interest.

Creeping along the passage, Jessie was surprised to hear laughter and conversation coming from the sitting room and recognised the voice of one of her uncles, her father's brother — the family orator. The family bore. She also recognised another uncle and an aunt. The Warners had paid a surprise visit.

Since Dolly was out and the boys were asleep in bed, she would have to go in for a few minutes and make polite conversation — it would be expected. Jessie knew the form. She ran the usual questions through in her mind: how was life treating her; had she received promotion at work yet; was there an engagement in the air; which author was she reading these days ...

Slipping quietly into the sitting room, she sat on a low stool, thankful that they were engrossed, or at least pretending to be interested in what her dad had to say. Glancing at the detached expressions on their faces, Jessie felt sorry for her parents; the Warners had never been interested in their lives or what happened at the docks.

Her eyes rested on Rose, who was sitting in the upright green velvet chair doing her best to look the part expected of

her. Jessie longed to tell her where she had been and who she had found; she wanted her to know that she looked just like her own mother and she wanted to hold her very close and tell her what a lovely woman Ingrid Gunter was, a lovely old lady with as much pride as her daughter.

Sensing Jessie's eyes on her, Rose looked across at her, a puzzled expression on her face, her eyes full of questions. It was as if she knew what Jessie was thinking and where she had been.

'So I'll be testing it tomorrow,' Robert's voice broke through Jessie's thoughts. 'I don't think my crane'll take it and I've said as much, but I'll do it.'

'Testing what, Dad?' said Jessie.

'My crane. They think they know best. Extra load? It's asking for trouble, but that's the way it's going now. They want us to do more work in less time, Jessie.'

'You can refuse though, can't you?'

'Refuse? I should think not. There are too many men ready to slip into my driving seat. No. I'll do as I'm told and we'll just have to see who's right.' He tapped his pipe on the edge of the black iron grate in the fireplace and smiled at her. Turning to Rose he winked. 'If anything should go wrong, I just want red roses and don't go in black.' Polite laughter greeted this and Jessie excused herself, saying she had to be up extra early in the morning.

Closing the door behind her and allowing a long relieved sigh to escape, she was surprised to see Stephen sitting on the stairs, elbows resting on knees, hands under chin. Her heart went out to him – he looked lonely. 'Stephen? You should be asleep by now. What's the matter?' She sat down with him and kissed the top of his head. 'Who's upset you this time?'

'No one. There's nothing the matter.'

'Yes there is. I can tell. Come on, silly, out with it.'

'They keep taking the mickey out of me at school, call- ing me names.' He stared out, as if he was in a world of

his own. 'Now I've been put at the back of the class and it's worse.'

'What kind of names?'

'Daffadown Dilly, Simple Simon, Silly Boy Blue . . .'

'But you're not simple, Stephen, far from it. You're much cleverer than Alfie and he's older than you. Come to that, you've got more up top than Dolly.'

'I know that. She lives in the past and never finks about the future. Mum said so.'

'Lives for the minute, more like. Well then what is it? Are you being lazy at school? Not learning your tables or spellings? Is that what it is?'

'No. I can't see what's written on the blackboard and now I've been put at the back with the dunce so it's worse.'

'Ah well, it sounds like you might need specs.'

'No! That'll make things worse. More names. I'd rather drown myself then wear those things, or cut my throat on Dad's razor, or put my head in the gas oven. Or—'

'Yeah, all right, you've made your point.' She tried not to laugh at him and tousled his hair, keeping a serious tone to her voice. 'Well, we'll just have to get Mum to have a quiet word with your teacher. Then she'll move you down the front and no one need know why you've been put there. Now stop fretting over that and listen. I've got a secret that I shouldn't tell.'

'A real secret or somefing and nothing?'

'A real secret and you're not to tell a soul. Promise me you won't.'

'God's honour,' he said.

'Come on then, into my room. I take it Alfie's asleep in bed.'

'No. He's gone out. Through the bedroom window. He'll get killed if Mum or Dad finds out. He's put stuff under the quilt to make it look like he's under the covers, asleep.'

'Oh God. Don't you ever think of copying Alfie, will you?

He's heading for trouble, make no mistake. Do you know where he's gone?'

'Yep.' Pleased with himself Stephen bounced up the stairs and into the girls' bedroom and lay on Jessie's bed, hands behind his head, skinny legs crossed. 'He's gone to chalk words on a wall with his mates.'

Her heart sank. 'What words?' As if she didn't know.

'Down with the Jews. 'Im and his mates are getting sixpence each for doing it, a man's paying 'em. Don't know who he is though. Fancy getting a tanner for chalking on the wall. It's the same man who gave Alfie a knife to look after.'

A wave of dread shot through Jessie. My God, she thought, it's as if we're all leading double lives.

'It's all right, Jess, isn't it . . . about the knife?'

'Course it is. I dare say Alfie bought it with his ill-gotten cash but fobbed you off with that story about a man. Unless there's more that you're not telling me?'

'Not really,' he said, sorry to disappoint her — and himself.

'Good. I tell you what, Stephen, on Friday, pay day, I'll give you sixpence for not chalking on the wall. And don't ever mention this to Max — about Alfie. He'd be really hurt.'

'You won't tell Dad, will you? Alfie'd kill me. So would his mates.'

Jessie smiled. 'No, sweetheart, I won't tell, but let me know when he's going again and I'll follow him, pretend I just happened to be out for a walk, then I'll clip him round the ear and his friends too.'

'But you won't call a copper?'

'No, I won't do that. No need. I've a feeling Alfie will draw their attention soon enough. Now then, wait till you hear this. Grandmother Blake is not our real grandmother.'

'So?'

'Oh. It doesn't bother you then?'

'No. She don't like me anyway. Never smiles or anything.'

'Fair enough. So what about our real grandmother? What if

I told you that that's where I've been. What if I told you that I've found where she lives and Mum doesn't even know that and what's more Mum doesn't even know if she's alive but I do. She's really nice. A proper granny.'

'What, with a silver bun and that?'

'Yep. With silvery-grey hair and soft blue eyes, just like Mum's.'

'Did she give you any presents to bring back?'

'No. She's a granny not a fairy godmother. She lives really close to Victoria Park, near the boating lake.'

'Has she got her own boat?' Stephen asked.

'Tch, she's not rich, Stephen, she's—'

'Poor?'

'No! She's just *normal*. Like us.'

'The kids at school say we're rich 'cos Mum's got a shop and Dad's got a job.'

'Well, I suppose we are, compared to most. Not rich, but not poor. Do you want to come with me next time, to see her?' Jessie looked at him eagerly.

'Dunno.' He looked doubtful.

'Oh, right. I'll take Alfie instead.'

That decided him. 'All right then, I'll come. When we going? Tomorrow?'

'No. In a few weeks' time.'

'A few weeks! That's ages away. Why did you tell me now? Now I'll have to wait. I can't wait all that time.'

'In *two* weeks then. We'll give her time to get over the shock of this visit. She didn't know who I was at first, she lives on her own but her brother visits. Just think, Stephen, she's our mum's mum, her *real* mum. Don't you think it's good that we've found her?'

'Dunno.'

Pulling her pillow from under his head, Jessie playfully hit him with it. 'You don't know nuffink, do you?'

'Nope.'

Within seconds Jessie and Stephen were thoroughly enjoying a hardened pillow fight, laughing and shrieking as each of them received blows. The childish fun banished Jessie's worries. Tomorrow was another day and another day meant facing up to all the troubles going on around them, but for now, all that was forgotten and she was happy. Very happy.

Arriving at her desk the next morning five minutes early and still in a good mood, Jessie found Mr Reed keen to know how she had got on in her search. She had hardly had time to take off her coat when he was firing questions at her.

'It's a very long story, Mr Reed,' she chuckled, 'but to cut it short, I went to the address and I found my long lost grandmother.'

'Wonderful, Jessie!' he exclaimed, excited. 'Wonderful! I wish I'd been there to see it. Do you think they'll get together now?'

'I don't know, we'll just have to wait and see.'

Chuffed that he had been of help, Mr Reed got carried away, telling her all about his own family history. 'It's a passion, I suppose. Once you make a start, you just have to go on and on. I wouldn't be the least bit surprised if you're not back there soon, Jessie, digging further into the secrets of your family.' He shook his head at the wonder of it. 'Fascinating . . .'

Thankfully, she managed to change the subject at an appropriate pause. A memo, which Jessie had seen on her way into the building, was her excuse. It was pinned to the notice board and had been signed by all three directors. The wording was careful but the message was clear: anyone discovered to have any involvement with the Blackshirt movement risked losing their job. There were quite a few Jewish people working in the factory and in the offices, not to mention the sales reps.

Mr Reed didn't have an opinion, but then, as he openly admitted, he wasn't the least bit interested in politics. 'Each to their own,' he said, 'each to their own.'

'There was trouble again last night, outside the People's Palace,' said Jessie, remembering the ugly scene.

'Exactly my point. Religion and politics, the cause of all ill.'

On her way home from work, smiling to herself, Jessie imagined Mr Reed taking his family on a tour of the Tower of London and behaving like a guide. The smile faded from her face when she saw yet another insult to Jews chalked on the wall at the top of the turning. It was time to have a word with Alfie about this man who had been paying him money to do his dirty work and giving him knives to look after.

Searching through her handbag for her door key, she hadn't noticed anything out of the ordinary and it wasn't until she pushed the key into the lock that Jessie realised the Venetian blinds were down. She stared at the windows and felt strangely aware of being watched. She turned round and saw one of the neighbours opposite, leaning against her front door, arms folded and looking very sad. She caught Jessie's eyes and lowered her head.

Crossing the cobblestone road, Jessie asked what had happened and why there was an eerie silence in the street. 'Our blinds are down, Mrs Adams, and your front room curtains are drawn. What's happened?'

The woman couldn't answer; she turned away and went into her house, leaving Jessie to find out for herself. Looking back at the drawn blinds of her house, she knew that something was wrong at home, that something very bad had happened. Walking slowly across the street she knocked on her front door instead of using her key, as a fear stronger than anything she had experienced rose from the pit of her stomach.

It was Dolly who answered the door, Dolly with a red, tear-stained face who stared at Jessie as if she was a stranger and then spoke in a monotone.

'Dad's been killed.'

Jessie stood paralysed, staring back at her sister, waiting.

Waiting for her to smile and say it was only a joke. But it wasn't April Fool's Day and not even Dolly would make such a joke. Jessie opened her mouth to say something but no words came. At last she spoke her sister's name. 'Dolly?'

'Dad's been killed,' she repeated. The house was still and silent, with no sign of movement. 'He's dead, Jessie. Daddy's dead.' She turned and drifted along the passage, away from her, as if she was only a dream.

Jessie went inside and lowered herself onto the fourth stair and sat gazing out at nothing, Dolly's words floating through her mind. *'He's dead, Jessie. Dad's been killed. He's dead, Jessie.'*

The crane. The heavy load.

Her face got colder and tighter by the second as a strange wailing sound rose from deep within her, growing louder and louder until she was screaming. 'No-ooooo! No! No! No!' She punched the stairs over and over and it didn't hurt; she couldn't feel a thing as she went on punching and screaming and punching, until she finally exhausted herself.

Raising her head, she stared at the front door. It hadn't closed properly. She would wait and see for herself whether he came home from work or not, see if Dolly was right. Soon he would come in, smiling and winking at her. She didn't move, just sat, silent and staring.

Nobody came. Nobody touched her. Through her flood of tears she could see the lodgers, standing on the stairs above her, watching. They never moved. They never said a word.

As if in a dream, she walked down to the basement and looked for her mother in the kitchen. She wasn't there. She glanced out of the window into the back garden and there was Rose, wearing the same dress she'd had on that morning and hanging out the washing. Jessie's mother was hanging washing on the line. Her mother was hanging washing on the line and her dad was dead.

Chapter Five

On the morning after the tragedy, the house had an exceptionally tranquil atmosphere. Rose had been up all night and the girls had been drifting about since the crack of dawn. When Dolly had slipped into bed beside Jessie during the night, she had welcomed it. Neither of them had said a word, they just huddled together as if it was the most natural thing in the world.

All three of them coasted silently through the house as if they were in church and slowly got themselves ready to face their first day without Robert. The boys, who had been crying on and off all night, were fast asleep, exhausted.

Rose, pale and red-eyed, made the porridge as usual but none of them ate a morsel, as if eating food was too normal. Several pots of tea had been brewed and this they did drink, sipping endless cups in silence. None of them mentioned Robert or the accident and when Jessie arrived at work, she could hardly remember having walked to the bus stop or getting on the bus. She had simply arrived here.

As she went into the building, one of the men from the loading bay met her on the stairs. His eyes were downcast as he murmured, 'Never mind, Jessie. We'll all rally round. All of us.'

It was those few kind words which brought reality and

she felt herself go icy-cold again. As he moved past her, she turned to him and whispered, 'Rally round?' Had more time gone by than she'd realised? Wasn't it just yesterday that it had happened. 'My dad?' she murmured, looking into his face. 'You know about that?'

'Bad news travels fast, love. We're all deeply shocked. I never, not in a thousand years, would have expected you to come in today. You didn't have to, you know.'

Nodding and smiling weakly, she backed away up the staircase. George was about the same age as Robert and she thought how like her dad he was. She hadn't noticed before. 'I might go home, George. I don't know.'

'Well, you just get the word through to me and I'll see to it that one of our drivers takes you. One of the women can go with you as well, for the company. You're not on your own with this one, Jessie, we're all behind you.'

'Does everyone know?' she asked, her voice sounding as if it was coming from somewhere else.

'If they don't yet, they will soon. There's a piece in the early editions. There'll be more before the day's out. I should think all the papers will cover it, Jessie, it's an outrage.' He doffed his cap and walked away, shoulders hunched.

The sincerity in his voice and his kind words had touched Jessie but not enough to draw tears. She hadn't cried since Dolly had first told her. Maybe other people were absorbing the grief and anger instead of her. She didn't feel angry. She didn't feel anything. Just numb. It wasn't a bad feeling. It wasn't really a feeling at all.

In the office she was mystified to see a small gathering round Mr Reed's desk. Was it his birthday and he hadn't told her? The conversation stopped the moment she stepped into the room and they all looked at her. A quiet word from Mr Reed and they began to leave, nodding and squeezing her arm as they went.

Once they'd gone, her boss walked slowly towards her, his

arms reaching out. 'You shouldn't have come in, Jessie.' He laid a hand on her shoulders, put a finger under her chin and smiled fondly at her. 'We'll see you get home. Would you like to go back in a cab with your friend Sally? Or shall I arrange for Mr Brady's chauffeur to take you home in the company car?'

'That'd be something, wouldn't it?' she said. 'Me in a Bentley.'

'OK. I'll see to it, and Sally can go with you.'

'I was only joking, Mr Reed. Why would they chauffeur *me* around. Anyway, George Brown from the loading bay said he'd get someone to take me in one of the vans.'

'If that's what you'd prefer, Jessie.'

'It doesn't really matter. I wasn't expecting to go home. Today's our busy day. All the dockets and wages—'

'Van or Bentley,' he spoke in a fatherly fashion, 'or a cab. You choose.'

The thought of her and Sally in a chauffeur-driven car should have made Jessie smile, but it didn't. 'The Bentley,' she said, shrugging.

'The Bentley it is. But first things first. Sit yourself down and I'll ring through to the kitchen for a breakfast tray. Would you like tea or coffee?'

'Coffee. Nothing to eat.'

The crashing of the door as Sally barged in startled them both. She had a newspaper in one hand and she was crying. 'Jess! They said you'd come in! I'm sorry, Jessie. I'm so sorry! It's terrible. It's the worst thing I've ever known!'

Jessie took the newspaper from her hand. It had been folded back to a page showing a news flash: DOCKER TRAPPED INSIDE RAGING INFERNO AS CRANE PLUNGES INTO THE THAMES.

'Silly thing. That wasn't my dad. That's not what happened to him. This is someone else. They overloaded his crane and—'

'But it mentions him by name, Jessie. That's *terrible* if they've made a mistake. Is your dad alive then?'

'No. He was killed yesterday. Dolly told me ...' She suddenly felt very sick. White stars were shooting through her head. 'I don't know. Do you think so? I don't know. We went to bed.' The feeling of nausea was overwhelming. 'Mr Reed?' The flashing white stars surged forward until everything was flashing white and then it went black.

Jessie didn't really appreciate the ride in the chauffeur-driven Bentley; she was fully conscious but it was as if she was drifting through time. She'd asked Sally not to go with her. She just wanted to be by herself until she was with her family. All she wanted was her mother, her sister, and her brothers.

The boys and Dolly were at home but Jessie was horrified to see that the sitting room was crammed with people, mostly men, her father's work mates from the docks, some of whom had witnessed the horror. Her uncles were also there as well as Grandmother Blake. Jessie thought of the scene in the sitting room the night before it happened, when they didn't show the least bit of interest in what her dad was saying. Jessie had never much liked them; now she felt that they were partly responsible. If they had listened, had reacted, had told him not to be a fool, maybe he would have paid attention and would be in his favourite chair now instead of in the morgue.

The more his smiling face as he explained about the heavy load and the crane came to mind, the more she believed that he had been waiting for his brothers to tell him not to drive it. But neither of them had, and they probably had no idea that he had been hoping for an excuse not to risk his life.

Jessie looked from them to officials from the National Workers Movement, who were having a quiet word with her mother. The conversation was low and their expressions serious. Jessie overheard one of them insist that it was management's fault and those responsible would be brought to justice and made to answer. Compensation was mentioned but Rose broke into tears at that point and the conversation stopped.

Dolly was earnestly telling a young reporter how she had

always wanted to be a writer herself, how she loved to read poems and early history. Sadly for her, he wasn't interested. All he wanted was a quote from a distressed member of the family.

'I bet no one around this way knows that Chaucer used to live in Aldgate,' Dolly told him, 'and that his dad owned twenty-four shops in Whitechapel. I don't expect you knew that either.'

'No, I didn't. How fascinating, Miss Warner. Now, about your father's accident——'

'Whitechapel was no more than a village then of course, same as Stepney and Bethnal Green——'

'It must have been a terrible shock,' he said, his pencil poised over his notebook. 'What were your first thoughts when you heard about it?'

'A shock? Oh no, it's an everyday occurrence round these parts. Men go crashing into the Thames every day. Of course it was a shock! I've told two reporters that already! We don't really want to keep on being reminded! It only happened *yesterday*.'

'Well, it's my job to let the public know ... and it will help your mother——'

'No it won't. It can't bring Dad back and that's the only help she wants.' Dolly went quiet and glanced around her. 'I think everyone should go now.'

'Of course, I understand how you must feel, but if I could just ask you one question. What do you think of the London Dock Management now?'

Dolly looked sideways at him and sighed heavily. 'I don't think about 'em, never have done.'

'Ah.' There was a glimmer of hope from the reporter, 'So you've always been against your father working in the docks, worried for his safety, cranes being somewhat antiquated.'

'No. I love the docks. Dad used to take us there sometimes to see the ships. The London docks are not that old, you know.' Now she was side-tracking to annoy him. 'St Katherine's was

only built a hundred and fifty years ago. It was the Romans who started it really, they built Londinium on the banks of the River Thames and—'

'I, er, I see another young lady's arrived. Would she be your sister, Jessie?'

'Yeah, that's our Jess. She looks too upset to talk to you though.' Leaving the journalist to himself and without a quote, Dolly went over to Jessie and squeezed her arm. 'You all right?'

'Not really. I'm going up to our room. Can you cope with this lot?'

'I'm about to throw 'em all out.'

'No, you mustn't do that, Doll, as much as I'd love you to. You'll embarrass Mum.'

'She doesn't want them here, Jess. Look at her face, she's drained. Don't worry,' she whispered, 'I'll be as polite as I can.'

In the quiet of her room, Jessie lay on her bed and brought her dad's face to mind. His kind face and brown wavy hair, the way he was relaxed and smiling when he joked that if the worst should happen they were to send red roses and not go in black. The worst had happened, and Jessie could not take it in. How could he be dead? She thought about red roses. Imagined her bedroom full of them, deep red and scented. 'Don't go away, Dad,' she whispered. 'Stay with us.' She turned on her side, curled up her knees, hugged her pillow and cried herself to sleep.

Both Jessie and Dolly had been given a week off work with pay and the boys a week off school to allow them to mourn their father. When Robert's body was brought back to the house in the coffin, the atmosphere seemed to change and each of them found they were pleased to have him back and looking so peaceful, as if he was asleep. Fortunately, Robert hadn't been badly burned. Some of the newspapers had exaggerated

the story or jumped the gun before proper press releases had been given out. The engine of the crane had been overstrained and a fire had been the result, but the neck of the crane had given way under the heavy load before the flames really took hold, plunging into the River Thames, where Robert died from drowning, not from burns or fumes.

On the eve of the funeral, relatives and friends arrived to see him for the last time before the coffin was closed for ever. Jessie was fetching and carrying sandwiches from the kitchen when she overheard one of her father's friends having a quiet word with Rose. Intrigued by the secretive tone of his voice, she listened outside the door.

'No, Rose, it's nothing to do with the compensation, I promise. I've something else to tell you.' The family friend sounded as if he was about to make a confession. 'It's about Robert.'

'Not now, Bert. Later,' said Rose, tired. 'Wait until everything's settled down a bit. I don't want to talk about the wrongdoing of the dock board for the time being. Maybe later when—'

'It's not about that, Rose. It's more private . . . personal. Robert asked me to pass on a message to you if anything went wrong. I don't really think he believed anything would go wrong but, just in case it did, he wanted me to . . . well, to say . . .'

'Come on then, Bert, out with it. I must give Jessie a hand upstairs. What was the message?'

'He said I was to ask you to, well, to . . . to bring the girls together and not to leave it for too long. I know what he meant, Rose, because he told me all about it, way back. It's not for me to offer an opinion, I'm just passing on his wishes.'

'I see. Thanks for telling me, Bert, and for keeping it to yourself. I'll give it some serious thought and I'd appreciate it if you could push it from your mind.'

'I will, Rose, don't you worry. As far as I'm concerned,

what he told me will go with him to his grave and with me to mine.'

They continued to speak in a whisper. Jessie slowly backed away, running the words through her mind. Think seriously about bringing the girls together? What had he meant by it?

Upstairs, Jessie was glad to see that Max had turned up. She hadn't given him much thought but he was a comforting sight and when he put his arm round her she realised just how much she needed him, needed that deep feeling of trust, warmth and loyalty.

That night, once everyone had gone and Rose was resting on her bed, Jessie and Max sat on the front step and talked in a way they had not done before, mostly about their childhood and their parents. When he pushed his hand through her hair and said he loved her, she started to cry.

'That's it, Jess,' he said. 'Let all the grief out, cry away the sadness, because one day you will smile and be happy again, I promise you. My Jessie will laugh again.' He kissed the tip of her nose and brushed strands of loose hair from her face. 'I'll always be here for you. Always.'

'I know you will, Max.'

Taking her hand he suggested they go for a slow walk, there was something he wanted to show her, something that might cheer her up a little.

Strolling along the Broadway, Jessie confided to Max what she'd overhead that day, the message from her dad delivered by one of his best friends. Max shrugged it off, saying that people got very emotional and sometimes carried away when there was a death in the family. He suggested she forget it. Jessie went on to tell him about her visit to her real grandmother. The accident had happened the very next morning so she hadn't had the chance or the inclination to talk to anyone about it. Other than Stephen and Mr Reed, no one else knew.

Max was pleased for her but in his usual, sensible way, he advised that she be very careful about mentioning it to Rose.

He told her to let it lie for a couple of weeks and although Jessie said she agreed with him, she had already decided that she would bring them together as soon as she could, before her grandmother died and it was too late. She had learned a very important lesson from her dad's death, *his* lesson, which he'd often repeated: put off nothing till the morrow if it can be done the day.

'Well, here we are,' said Max, stopping outside a small pawnbroker and jewellery shop. 'This is it what I wanted you to see.' He pointed to the jewellery display in the window. 'Can you see that tray in the corner, between the grid ...'

'The ring tray? The diamond ring tray?'

'Engagement ring tray, Jessie. Look at the ring third from the left, top row. The solitaire.'

'Yeah, I'm looking.'

'Well, that's the one I've been paying off for. I was keeping it a surprise. Your dad knew about it, he was the only one I told.' Max placed his hand on Jessie's face and looked into her blue eyes. 'Will you be my fiancée, Jessie Warner?'

'Max, would you have been paying off on that beautiful ring if you thought for one minute that I would say no?'

'You do like it then.'

'Like it?' She looked from him to the ring, the sparkling diamond ring. 'It's beautiful. Of all the others, that's the one I would have chosen. I love it.'

'It's not the biggest though.'

'It is to me.' She wrapped her arms round him. 'I'm really, really pleased you told Dad. I feel as if he's here, giving his blessing. He thought a lot of you.'

Choked, Max lowered his eyes. 'I know.'

'It will be all right, won't it? Tomorrow. The funeral. Me and Mum and Dolly ... and the boys. We'll get through tomorrow, won't we?'

'You'll get through it, Jessie. People always do. One way

or another.' Max gave her another long, comforting hug and they walked slowly home together.

And indeed they did get through it. The procession, the church, the heartrending service. When the guests had returned to the cars to make the short journey from the church back to the house, Rose, Jessie, and Dolly and the boys were left by Robert's grave to say their private goodbyes. Holding a beautiful wreath of red roses, they carefully lowered it onto the coffin and prayed together. Opening her eyes after saying a few silent words to her dad, Jessie glanced up to see that Rose's attention was elsewhere and that her face showed uncertainty. She was peering at a woman standing beneath an overgrown tree who was looking over at them.

Jessie looked from the strange woman to Rose and whispered, 'Who is she, Mum?'

'No one to concern ourselves over. You and Dolly take your brothers and see if your uncles have sorted out who's to go back to the house in which cars, there's good girls. I just want a few minutes by myself.'

Pressing a single rose in her hand, Jessie brought it to her lips and then dropped it into the grave. 'Goodbye, Dad,' she murmured and walked away, arm in arm with Dolly, towards the cemetery gates.

Rose moved towards the woman. She felt she should know her, there was something familiar about her. Something *very* familiar. She quickened her pace, hardly able to believe her eyes. She hadn't seen Gerta in a very, very long time. Why she should turn up at Robert's funeral was beyond her.

'I trust the service went well,' said Gerta when Rose came up to her. 'I was sorry to read about the tragedy. It was quite shocking.'

'Thank you'. Rose managed a tight smile. 'If I had known you were here I would have asked you to join us. How are you?'

'Struggling. But I'm used to it. Your brother, Jack, has

much to answer for. He left me a broken woman.' Gerta showed no sign of compassion. 'Why do you not ask about Hannah? About her welfare? Or have you completely wiped that daughter from your mind?'

'Of course I haven't. I think about you both. Don't forget it was *you* who insisted that Robert and I should have nothing to do with her, Gerta. Don't tell me you've changed your mind after all this time.' Rose felt her stomach turn. Was Gerta here to cause trouble?

'I am here for one reason and one reason only. To remind you that your late husband had five children, not four. I would like you to set the record straight, with your solicitor.' There was a chilling smile on Gerta's face.

How she has changed, thought Rose. 'Why would I want to do that, Gerta?'

'I doubt you would want to do it, but needs be.'

'Needs be? Get to the point, please. I've guests to attend to.'

'All I want is fair play. According to the newspapers you're likely to get a handsome sum in compensation for the way Robert died. I want my share. I'll settle for fifty per cent of your claim since I took on fifty per cent of your responsibilities those years back.' Gerta glanced over Rose's shoulder and saw that Jessie was by the gates, watching them. 'Maybe I should beckon Hannah's twin to come over so we might explain.'

'No. I've heard what you have to say and yes, I will speak to my solicitor if the claim is successful. But I warn you, these things take time, and I want your word that you will keep the secret.'

'I have nothing to gain by giving it away, though the loss to you would be heavy. Twins should never be parted and yours would not forgive you for it. Your daughter is on her way over. She looks very much like Hannah, doesn't she? Except for the way she presents herself to the public. I would have expected you to see that your girls would dress more plainly. It looks

as if I am about to meet her. What would you like me to say? Who shall I pretend to be?' Gerta's cold eyes were livened with something like amusement.

Rose spun round. Jessie was too close for comfort. 'I'll be in touch as soon as I can,' said Rose, wanting to leave.

'Good. Because if you don't, you'll have the newspapers to deal with and you can be sure that the picture they paint of you won't be a pretty one.' The evil smile was back.

'If you talk to a reporter I'll see to it that you get nothing. I don't care about other people and what they think of me, I'm only concerned for my children. Robert and I did what we thought was for the best at the time. Now I see that we were wrong. Keep away from my family, Gerta, I warn you.'

'How can I do that when I have one of them in my loving care?'

Turning on her heels, Rose strode towards Jessie, linked arms with her and walked her out of the church grounds.

'Who is she?' asked Jessie. 'What did she want?'

'Never mind. We shan't be seeing her again. Let's get this funeral over and out of the way. I've had enough of people and false pleasantries. All I want is to be at home with my children by my side, and no one else.'

Later, when the last of the visitors had left the house, Rose, the boys, and Jessie enjoyed a cool glass of lemonade in the kitchen, exhausted from having to talk to so many people. Taking them all by surprise, Dolly appeared, made up to the nines. She'd taken off her smart funeral suit, put on one of her bright frocks and was wearing more make-up than usual. Her eyebrows had been pencilled black, her face powder was heavy and her rouge almost as bright as her lipstick. To top it all, her light auburn hair was brushed out and lacquered stiff. Even the boys were shocked into silence.

'And where do you think you're going, looking like that?' There was a slight tremble to Rose's voice, whether from the trauma of the day or the sight of Dolly, it was difficult to say.

'I'm meeting all my mates at the Tavern,' she said. 'It's free drinks! They want to cheer me up, they've arranged a whip-round. A shilling from each of them to pay for my drinks. There's gonna be about a dozen girls from work there, we might even go back to Ivy's house for a bit of a do. Her mum and dad said we could.'

'Well, you can just go and wash that muck off your face and take off that dress.' Rose's voice was unbelievably calm. 'We're in mourning for your father, in case you've forgotten.'

'I know, but we don't have to sit around and be miserable. Eileen at work is Catholic and they always sing and dance after a funeral. They're doing this for me. *Especially* for me!'

'Dolly, I can understand if you need to be with your friends for an hour,' said Rose, 'but you are not to go out looking like that. You know how your father felt about heavy make-up — and Eileen's family do things differently from us.'

'But Dad's not here to see me, is he? So he can't get into a temper over how I look. I can wear what I want now that Dad's not around.' She dabbed a little Evening in Paris scent behind her ears. 'I'll be sixteen soon, don't forget.' Having shocked them into silence yet again, Dolly flounced out of the room, telling them not to wait up. The slamming of the street door sent a shudder through them all.

Gripping the back of a chair, Rose used every bit of willpower not to break down. Her face showed her torment. Torment and fear. There were four children to bring through and she had to do it by herself.

Jessie beckoned her brothers away, into the passage, where she gave them a hug and told them to read their comics, on their beds, until she went up. They both started to cry, and it seemed to Jessie that her world, their world, was falling apart. The loud banging at the door snapped her out of her silence. 'Up you go, boys. I'll just see who that is.'

Jessie opened the front door to find her friend Sally on the step, holding a lovely bouquet of bright flowers, orange, red

and yellow dahlias. 'These are from me, Ron and Tom. Tom suggested it. He thought they might cheer you up a bit.'

Jessie didn't know what to make of it. *Tom* had suggested they send some flowers? 'That's really kind, Sally, but you shouldn't have come out on such a damp night. Do you want to come in for a minute? We can go in my bedroom, Mum's not really up to seeing anyone.'

'I'm not surprised. I wasn't expecting to be asked in, Jess, I only came to deliver the flowers and say how sorry we all are.' She pushed the bouquet into Jessie's arms. 'And Tom sends his best wishes and love.'

Confused by the word love, Jessie waved Sally into the passage. 'My bedroom's the first door on the left, after the second small flight of stairs. Wait in there for me. I'll be up in a minute.'

Taking the flowers downstairs into the kitchen, she saw that the boys hadn't gone up to bed but were huddled close to Rose, Stephen by her side and Alfie on her favourite padded footstool, snuggled up, with his head on her lap.

'I was just saying to the boys that a day out would do us all the world of good. We could go to Chessington Zoo. What do you think, Jessie?' Rose's voice was thin and strained. 'It would brighten us all up.'

Moved by the small family scene, Jessie nodded and said she thought it was a lovely idea. Then she excused herself and went to her room, wondering if her mother would be able to pull herself through the next few weeks. She had always relied on their dad for companionship in the same way that he had relied on her. Now Rose was alone.

'I'm really pleased you came round, Sally,' said Jessie. 'How's everyone at work?'

'As if you care,' Sally said, eyeing her friend. 'You don't have to pretend with me, Jess. We're mates.' She pulled an envelope from her pocket. 'Tom asked me to give you this card and say how sorry he was about everything.'

Jessie took the envelope and put it in her drawer. 'I thought he might have been with the other dockers, outside the gates. The hearse stopped at the docks especially so they could say their goodbyes. I looked out for him, but he wasn't there.'

'Well, he wouldn't be, would he? He's still in the London.'

Jessie's eyes widened. 'The London Hospital?'

'Yep. Broken bones and a few stitches here and there. Luckily that handsome face of 'is wasn't marked — except for a busted lip and black eye. He's been in there for a week, Jessie. I thought you knew.'

'The attack at the People's Palace. I haven't given it a thought. I was there ...'

'I know, he told me. He knows you got away safely though, Hannah told him.' Sally went quiet and thoughtful. 'I don't know what to make of this Hannah, they seem really close. I can't help thinking that they're sweethearts. Tom insists she's more like a sister but I'm not sure. What did you make of it?'

'I liked her,' Jessie said, her mind still on Tom. 'I should go and visit him ...'

'Ron reckons that Tom's gonna join the Blackshirts over that night. Get his own back.'

Jessie ignored that. 'How long's he in for?'

'Another week or so. Would have been out tomorrow but the bone specialist was worried about his fractured arm. I won't go into the gory details but they might 'ave to break and reset it again in a couple of days' time. You must have read about it in the local.'

'No ... I've not been in the mood to read about people trying to kill each other. I'll go and see him.'

'What's your boyfriend gonna think about that, Jess? You visiting a handsome feller in bed? Won't Max be jealous?'

'No. Max isn't like that. Besides, we're getting engaged. He's paying off for a ring.'

'Oh, right. So you're not interested in Tom then?'

'Not in the way you think. I suppose he sees me the same as he does Hannah — a friend.'

'If you say so, Jess. If you say so.' There was a wry smile on Sally's face.

Jessie's first day back at work after the tragedy wasn't as difficult as she had imagined. Once those who knew her had inquired about her and her family's welfare, life in the offices and the factory continued as normal — busy.

Making a snap decision to go and see Tom after work, Jessie wished away the butterflies which were playing havoc with her stomach. She felt nervous about seeing him again, as if she was doing something wrong. Sally's question as to whether Max would be jealous had touched a chord and worried her, so to avoid unnecessary upset she decided she wouldn't tell Max about the visit. What the head doesn't know the heart can't grieve over.

At the hospital, by Tom's bedside, in the long, clinical, hospital ward, Jessie searched for the right words and felt a complete fool. Seeing him lying there, bruised but as handsome as ever, she also felt shy. 'I'm sorry I haven't brought anything. The shops were closed by the time I left work and—'

'That's all right, Jessie,' he said, pulling himself up into a sitting position and wincing in pain. 'Mother sees that my cupboards are full — look at that fruit bowl. She fusses around as if I'm a six-year-old.'

'Are you an only child then?'

He raised an eyebrow. 'Hardly. So, Jessie Warner, you've pardoned me then, at last.'

'Pardoned you? I'm still waiting for an apology! Standing me up was one thing, but sending some poor sod to do your dirty work . . . And as for your messages, sprained ankle? Hurt your back? You sure it wasn't a sprained wrist?' Jessie sat down by the bed.

'Good,' said Tom, straightening his pillow, 'that's that out of the way. You gonna ask how I am then?'

'I can see how you are. They'll be turning you out in a couple of days.'

'I wish. It's the nurses. They're doing their best to keep me here for as long as they can. They love me.'

'I bet they do.'

'Anyway, never mind me, how's your mum?'

'Not too bad. Oh, and thanks for the flowers — and the card. I appreciated that. Does it hurt?'

'Course it hurts ...' he placed a hand on hers, 'knowing you'll walk out of here soon and I won't see you again.'

She withdrew her hand. 'Why did you do that to me, Tom? Being stood up in front of Sally was really embarrassing.'

'I had my reasons. Anyway, I sent a good-looking bloke, someone who'd treat you like a lady. He was all right, wasn't he? Treated you with respect?'

'Tch. Respect. It was meant to be a date not an appointment. Anyhow, that's all behind us now. I must be mad coming in to see you but there you are. I'll probably kick myself for it.'

'No you won't. And I'm glad you came, I've not stopped thinking about that night when I could have been with you at the Odeon, sitting in the back seat. I'm sorry for what happened but I had no choice — I *thought* I had no choice.' Glancing past Jessie, his expression turned serious. Hannah was approaching.

Jessie followed his gaze. 'Ah ... I'd best be going, mustn't play gooseberry twice. Besides, I'm meeting my chap.'

'Oh, right, yeah, mustn't keep *him* waiting. Mind how you go, Jessie.'

'You as well, Tom.' She smiled at him.

'Tom, you look so much better,' exclaimed Hannah. 'I can't believe it. Your cheeks are *glowing* with health. Doesn't he look fine, Jessie?'

'He's all right. You can have him all to yourself now.' Jessie stood up as if to leave.

'I don't want him all to myself, thanks very much,' she smiled, 'so you needn't go on my account.' She looked at Jessie and showed sympathy. 'I was sorry to hear about your father. Very sorry. I wanted to come and see you but I don't know where you live.'

'Thanks.' Jessie was grateful for the simple, natural and sincere sympathy Hannah offered. 'It was a shock and none of us are over it yet. It's gonna take a very long time to get back to normal. It did cross my mind to call on you, as it happens, but I don't think I went outside our house all of last week, except to run down to the shop.'

'Well, you know where I live and you may knock on the door whenever you want. If my mother should answer, take no notice of her manner, she's not the friendliest of people.' Hannah looked from Jessie to Tom. 'He hasn't stopped mooning over you, you know.' She grinned and gave him a peck on the cheek. 'I said you would see her again.'

'Jessie's trying to leave, Hannah.' Tom was uneasy at the way the girls were getting on, they were a little too close for comfort. 'She's late for her date. I don't want her boyfriend coming in and breaking my other arm.'

'Pay him no attention, Jessie. You take the chair and I'll sit on the edge of his bed. Matron has just gone off duty and—'

'Hannah, she's got to go.' Tom sank his head into his pillow. 'I'm in a hospital bed, not a deck chair on the beach, enjoying the sun and air. I'm supposed to be resting. One of you go, for Christ's sake. Two of you at once is one too many.'

'You make us sound like a matching pair.' Jessie turned to Hannah. 'He doesn't exactly give out gentle hints, does he? I hope the nurses do what you want them to, Tom. 'Bye, Hannah.' Head down, she walked slowly away without turning back.

'Jessie!' Tom called after her. 'Thanks for coming! I'll return the visit once I'm out of here.' His shout was met with shushing from other visitors and hospital staff.

Jessie had to admit that she'd wanted to see him again, if only to find out why he had stood her up, though she was still none the wiser. This had been the third time she'd seen him and each time she had been left with a desire to see him again. Stupid cow, she thought. Stupid blind fool! Lost in her thoughts, she collided with a visitor.

'I'm so sorry,' she apologised. She began to perspire, inwardly blaming the heating system, it was very hot in the hospital. 'It was my fault and I'm really sorry.' She helped the woman pick up the bag of oranges which had scattered. 'I should have been looking—'

'That's all right, love, no harm done. But you should slow down a bit ... Jessie Warner. You'll get to wherever you're going a lot quicker if you do. What's my Tom done to upset you then?'

Jessie stared at her. She looked vaguely familiar but she couldn't place her.

'Don't recognise me, do you?' smiled Emmie. 'We met outside Stepney Green station. I'm Tom's mother.' She squeezed Jessie's arm. 'My condolences over the terrible tragedy. I was very, very sorry to read about it.'

'Thank you,' said Jessie, backing away. 'I came in to see Tom because I was there when it happened, at the People's Palace. I met up with him and Hannah and ... well ... I just wanted to come and see how he was.' Blushing, Jessie hurried away, anxious to be outside in the cool, fresh air and away from all of them.

'Poor kid,' said Emmie, pulling up a chair next to Tom's bed, 'losing her dad at such a fragile age. It doesn't bear thinking about.'

'It was good of her to come and see me,' said Tom, wishing Jessie hadn't left. 'I never expected that. I'll drop her a line

while I'm in here,' he said, rubbing his chin. 'It'll kill a bit of time.'

Emmie checked the fruit in his bowl. 'I wonder how she knew you was in hospital.'

'Sally told her.'

'Oh, right. I thought perhaps you'd written her a letter or something.'

Ignoring that, he turned to Hannah. 'She never believes a word I say, I may as well talk to the brick wall.'

'She's a friendly girl, isn't she?' said Hannah to Emmie. 'I met her that evening when Tom was beaten up. We got on really well. She came back with me for a cup of tea. I feel as if I've known her all my life.'

There was a moment's silence as Emmie and Tom exchanged worried glances.

'Move your chair, Hannah,' said Emmie, inching hers closer to his bed. 'My bloody feet are killing me. I'm going to ease off my shoes.'

Tom rolled his eyes. 'Don't mind me. Make yourself at home. I can handle pain without the need for a bit of sympathy.'

'Go on,' said Emmie, enjoying herself. 'I would never 'ave guessed it.' She pushed her face close to his and examined his eye. 'That's coming along nicely. Have you opened your bowels today?'

'Bloody hell,' he moaned. 'If you ever embarrass me while Jessie's here . . .'

'Oh, she's coming again then?'

'I never said that, what I meant was, don't embarrass me in front of . . . strangers.'

'Oh dear. So she's a stranger now?'

'I don't think so, Emmie,' said Hannah, enjoying the banter between mother and son. 'You should have seen the way he brightened up when Jessie was here. You know what I think? That she was a little jealous of my coming during her cosy

visit. She's as mad about him as he is about her. This time I think Tom was right about fate playing a hand.'

Emmie ignored that. She could act her way through this hospital visit but deep down she was very worried. The twins had met up sooner than she imagined. She wanted Hannah to go so she could find out from Tom what exactly was going on.

'Look at him,' chuckled Hannah. 'Doesn't he look like the dog who just let the bone go?'

'Listen, Hannah. I am in a bit of pain as it happens, my arm's throbbing and I'm tired—'

'She'll be back, Tom, stop sulking. Anyhow, I only came in to give you my good news. I'm looking for a flat,' she said, looking very pleased with herself.

'Good for you,' said Emmie. 'It's just about the right time for you make a move, but don't go rushing into anything. Let me have a look before you take one on, you don't want to make a mistake and have to go running back home to your mother, not once you've flown the nest.'

'Of course I'll want you and Tom to see it first. I'm going to take my time. I want two spacious rooms with plenty of light and it must be sunny and with a view. A beautiful view of a garden or a lake.'

'Around this way? You'll be lucky,' laughed Tom.

'Maybe not around this way, Tom. Maybe in Essex, Walthamstow. The chief librarian was telling me that his daughter found a small self-contained flat there which is very reasonable and has its own tiny garden. He thinks there's another one up for rent which is just a fifteen-minute walk from the railway station.'

Emmie couldn't remember seeing Hannah looking so radiant, she really was beginning to bloom at last. 'I can't say I know too much about the place, love, but one of our cleaners at work has a daughter who's marrying someone from

Walthamstow, as it happens. I'll get a bit more information from her if you like.'

'You see. Twice in one week – fate?'

'Can't see you living in the country, Hannah,' said Tom.

'Walthamstow's hardly the country, son,' Emmie answered for her, 'but it's out of the East End. Just don't bite off more than you can chew, Hannah, and take things one step at a time.'

'Don't worry, I will.' She leaned forward and kissed Tom on the cheek. 'Get Sally to write down Jessie's address for me. I would like to call on her. I think she wants to be friends as much as I do.'

Once she'd gone, Tom and Emmie looked at each other and cleared their throats. 'See what I mean, Mother? The pair of them met by accident and got on like a house on fire. Who's gonna be the one to break the news?'

'Well, I can't break a promise. I don't really see what I can do about it. I haven't got an idea in my head over this one.'

'Hannah hasn't stopped talking about her since they met,' he said.

'That's no surprise. You can't even count Hannah's friends on two fingers. She's bound to latch on to someone like Jessie, even if they wasn't twins.'

'My thoughts entirely, Mother,' he said, throwing her an accusing look.

On her way home, Emmie found herself thinking about the unhappy time, way back, when Jessie and Hannah were parted. Full of self-reproach, she wished things had been different. On reflection, she felt she might have done more at the time to help Rose and Robert to keep both babies. But she was younger then, she hadn't learned to deal with life the way she did later. She had gained power to the elbow with time and would speak out when right was right and wrong was wrong. No more than a couple of years back, she could have taken the reins and laid down the law, telling Rose what she must

do and seeing that she did it. Not any more, though. She was feeling her age.

The thirty-minute walk home from the hospital tired her. The house was very quiet when she let herself in. She hung up her coat and hat and went into the kitchen. On the old pine table the flour was ready, the peeled and sliced apples marinating in brown sugar and cloves. Catching sight of her reflection in the small mirror above the butler sink she peered more closely at her face. She hadn't always looked like everyone's mother. She'd once had an hourglass figure and took pride in her looks, her good looks. She'd had the best head of hair in her time, thick, long, curly red hair. Her hazel eyes had been bright and clear. Now they were dull, with deep lines spreading outwards. In days gone by, she would have taken the time to put on make-up, brush and style her hair; she was fifty-six years old and she could have been taken for seventy. She pulled the lapel of her blouse forward and smelt her body. Instead of Lily of the Valley talcum powder, there was a tinge of perspiration mixed with the scent of Lifebuoy soap.

'What *have* you done, Em? Where's that lovely slim woman you once were?' She lowered herself into her chair, knowing exactly what she'd done; she'd given up what she once was in order to be the best mother and the wife of all wives. She'd been doing that for so long that she hadn't noticed the change or when it had come about. 'Emmie,' she murmured, 'Emmie, where are you?' She swept the back of her hand across her face and brushed away her tears.

The light of the moon shining through the kitchen window warmed her. It was as if a familiar old friend had come out to comfort her, a familiar and reliable friend who returned as regularly as clockwork, season after season.

Without thinking she reached out and took an apple from the fruit bowl, a lovely crisp, green and red apple with a nice smell. She bit into it and the juice ran down the corner of her mouth. When she was a nipper the only time she ate an

apple was when she'd pinched one off the back of a market stall, way back when she wore no socks in the summer and second-hand boots in the winter. Through all of those hard times she couldn't remember being miserable. She'd come from a big happy family who made the most of everything. Emmie wondered right then if she would ever get back that 'couldn't care less' feeling.

The house seemed so quiet. Johnnie and Stanley were out and her husband, Charlie, had gone to bed. But Emmie enjoyed the time by herself. In the silence she could hear the call of an owl in the distance and thinking of nothing in particular she began to hum the tune of a song she used to sing along to at the local music hall, when she was no more than fifteen or sixteen. Before she realised it, she was quietly singing:

All the girls in our town ... they lead a happy life,
Except for just the serious one, who wants to be a wife.
A wife she shall be ...
According to who she goes with;
Along with a certain naval boy,
Who gave her a little bundle of joy;
A wife she shall be ...

As memories of those heady days came flooding back, she thought about her satin pouch containing her lipstick and powder, tucked away in one of her cupboards. Maybe she would bring it out of the dark, maybe she would put on her favourite rose-red hat and navy coat, maybe she would go down the local and join her sons for a drink. She was beginning to feel a little more like she had in the old days, when she would sit with the women in their corner of the local and start them off in song.

One hour later, Emmie was on the sofa with her feet up. She had remembered that she'd promised to take Tom a piece

of that apple pie in the morning, on her way to work, and Johnnie and Stanley would be looking forward to a piece as well, after their bread and cheese supper. A couple of beers always gave them an appetite. She drank in the lovely smell of baking pies coming from the kitchen, sank her head into a feather cushion and closed her eyes for ten minutes. Her friend Rose would be all right. She'd get used to being a widow . . . in time. They would all get used to the idea that there would now only be a space where Robert used to be. Robert Warner, a kind and gentle man as well as a good husband and father. Emmie could hear her Charlie snoring from above and for once in her life she welcomed the sound.

Chapter Six

During the months that followed, the Warner family pulled together and did their best to get on with their lives. Dolly's strange reaction to her father's sudden death continued for a couple of weeks — she went out every night, dressed to kill. Fifteen- and sixteen-year-old lads were continually knocking on the door until she herself began to tire of it. Wisely, Rose said nothing to her daughter and waited for it all to fade away.

Christmas came and went with as little fuss as necessary. Rose just wanted to get it over with. On New Year's Eve, she flatly refused to share it with anyone except her children. She didn't want to have to see out that year with people trying to cheer her up and neither did she want to reminisce. When she woke on New Year's Day, she saw that it had snowed heavily in the night and would have been happy if it had gone on snowing until it reached halfway up their front door, blocking out the world.

In February there was more upheaval in the house as at last the electricity was put in. When the workmen had gone, all of them took delight in running around the house playing with the switches, thrilled by the instant and much brighter lights. For Rose's birthday in early March, Jessie and Dolly clubbed together and bought her a small bedside lamp from the Co-op, and as a really special treat, Jessie coerced Dolly into agreeing

to paying off weekly for a small one-bar electric fire for Rose's bedroom.

The case of negligence over Robert's death dragged on, but the family solicitor was hopeful that the claim for compensation would soon result in a substantial sum being paid to Rose and the children.

Slowly Rose tried to pick up the broken pieces of her life and get back into her old routine of running the cobbler shop as well as the household. But her heart wasn't in it and she became quiet and subdued. Jessie found it difficult sometimes not to be sharp with her, but Max was a tower of strength, giving her advice, calming her when she was angry, lighting her up when she was down. He reckoned that by the following month, July, he would have paid for the engagement ring in full and it would be in its proper place, on the third finger of Jessie's left hand.

Alfie still had the occasional secret smoke and continued to slip out through his bedroom window when he was supposed to be turning in, but there had been no more sign of the knife under his bed. Stephen was still withdrawn but both Rose and Jessie agreed that he was gradually getting back to his old self. He still clung to Rose, and Jessie often discovered them enjoying a cuddle in the big armchair in the sitting room. Whether it was right for Stephen or not, Jessie wasn't sure, but to see them getting so much comfort from each other warmed her heart.

There had been a change in tenants and now, living at the top of the house, was a young Scottish couple, newly married. They, like the tenants before them, kept themselves to themselves and were always polite and friendly when they paid their rent. Since the tragedy, Dolly had had several jobs. She hadn't returned to the gentlemen's club where she'd been a waitress, even though they'd given her a week's leave with pay after Robert's accident. From the gentlemen's club she'd gone to a handbag factory in Leman Street and then on to waitressing in coffee houses and tea rooms; back to the handbag factory, on to a shoe factory and then finally to a toy factory in the Roman Road, Bow, where

she had just met with a minor accident. A spring on one of the clockwork toys she had been assembling had skittered out and caught her eye. Walking around the house like an invalid, with the injured eye bandaged, she looked a sorry sight. Only Alfie had been brave enough to poke fun at her, which had been met by a thump on the shoulder. She was now on her bed nursing her eyes and sulking.

In the kitchen, impatient for the iron to heat, Jessie turned the gas flame higher; she was about to press her favourite dress to wear that evening. Leaning on the kitchen wall, she thought how easier things would be once the compensation came through. Her mother would be able to go shopping for modern electrical appliances, and an iron was at the top of the list.

Jessie wrapped a linen pad round the handle and lifted the iron off the gas flame, licked her finger and checked the heat and then pressed away the creases from the green, red and black patterned skirt of her frock. Max was taking her to the steak and chip restaurant at London Bridge.

'Watch your brothers out there for me, would you, Jess?' said Rose from the doorway. 'They're messing around with the hose pipe. I don't mind them playing with it so long as they've got their bathing trunks on but I don't want them annoying the neighbours again. They squirted water over Mr Brody's son, Rodney, yesterday and he wasn't amused. He'd been working so hard out there in the yard, mucking out that filthy chicken run. That lad's a saint — he loves those chickens.'

'I know. Stephen told me.' Jessie tried not to smile. Little did Rose know that she and Rodney chatted over the garden fence from time to time and she knew that he hated the birds and the run; more than anything he hated the smell. He did it for the weekly payment of a shilling and nothing else.

'I'm going to the Broadway to do a bit of shopping,' Rose went on, a little preoccupied. 'Get Dolly to peel the vegetables for me. Bad eye or not, she should be able to manage that.'

'I'd rather she stayed where she is, to tell the truth,' said

Jessie. 'Her face is as long as a kite and she's in a rotten mood. Max is coming round so he can peel the spuds.'

'I shouldn't think so. Men don't like to do kitchen chores.'

'Max is different, the men in his family muck in. I suppose that's got something to do with them being Jewish – I don't know. They're different from us.'

'I'm not saying it's a bad thing, Jess. All I'm saying is that you don't want to give him the wrong impression, that you won't make a good housewife. That's all I was thinking.' She picked up her handbag and left.

The fact that Rose hadn't taken her shopping bag or her basket didn't surprise Jessie. Her mother had been surreptitious of late and she had a feeling it had something to do with the strange woman at the cemetery. Whenever she broached the subject, Rose dismissed it, but this morning she seemed particularly worried and agitated. She hadn't even mentioned popping into the cobbler shop to check on how the Saturday help was coping. Saturday was now Rose's day off as well as Sunday; since Robert's death she had wanted to be at home when her boys were there.

Once Rose had left the house, Jessie tapped on the yard window to draw her brothers' attention and beckoned them in. Knowing Rose would be out nearly all afternoon and Dolly would more than likely sleep through most of the day, she wanted to spend some time with Max in the house without there always being one or the other of them coming or going. Alfie came to the kitchen to see what Jessie wanted. He stood in the doorway, tall and skinny, dripping water.

'How would you and Stephen like to go to the pictures this afternoon? They're showing a Mickey Mouse film at the Foresters. *Steamboat Willie*. Plus a cowboy film.'

'What, you gonna treat us?'

'Yeah, I'll treat you, Alfie. I would treat you more if I thought you was a good boy.'

'I'm not a boy, Jessie. I'll be going to work next year.'

'I know, but that doesn't make you a man either. You know that Dad knew about your smoking, don't you? He promised Mum that you were only experimenting and it would soon stop.'

'I only 'ave one now and then!'

'Yes, but one thing can lead to another and another and—'

'So you want us to go out,' said Alfie, stopping her flow, 'so you and Max can do it in the living room.'

'Do what in the living room?' Jessie couldn't believe that he meant what he was saying.

'A do. You know, up against the wall.'

'Alfie! That's disgusting! Me and Max wouldn't dream of such a thing!'

'Oh,' he said, disappointed. 'Dolly said you did it all the time.'

'Did she now? Well, Dolly doesn't know what she's talking about, and neither do you. If you realised what you'd just said—'

'I know what it means! I'm not a kid any more, Jess.'

'Oh, silly me! I forgot. You're a young man soon to be leaving school. Maybe you'd rather not go to the pictures with your *kid* brother.'

'I don't mind looking after him,' he said, sniffing.

'Nope, you're right. You are too old for all of that.'

'I *said*, I don't mind!'

'Well, if you're *really* sure, Alfie. Oh, and Mum left a bob on the table for fish and chips for the pair of you.'

'Blimey. Two treats in one day.' Alfie grinned.

'You know it wouldn't hurt you to offer to help in the shop on Saturdays. Mum works there all week and she only takes Saturday off so she can catch up here and go shopping. She has to pay someone to cover for her and Saturday's one of the busiest days.'

'Would she pay me?'

'Tch. I expect she'll let you earn some pocket money. Go on. Get out of my sight and tell Stephen to dry himself properly. Oh, and Alfie,' Jessie called as Alfie scampered off.

'What now? I can't do everything, you know.'

'A neighbour had a word with me the other day. I'm not saying who it was, because I promised I wouldn't. You've been seen chalking Fascist slogans on walls and you know that's wrong. Wrong *and* dangerous. If Mum gets to hear, you'll cop it, not to mention what Max'll think of you if he finds out. He'd be really hurt.'

Avoiding her probing look, Alfie turned away. 'I wasn't gonna do it no more anyway,' he muttered. 'I forgot that Max is Jewish.'

'And what about Max's mum and dad? Mr and Mrs Cohen? How would you like them to find out that you're one of the bully boys? They've had a brick through their window, don't forget.'

'I didn't *know* they were Jewish! I only did it for the tanner. I couldn't care less about anything else.'

'Good. Now come here and give me a cuddle. You're not too old for a hug – and neither am I.'

'I'm not cuddling you!' There was a telltale crack in his voice and he was pressing his lips tightly together.

'You're not gonna cry, are you? It's all right, Max doesn't know about the chalking, if that's what you're upset about. Alfie?'

'I miss my dad,' he said, screwing up his face, desperate to hold back tears. 'I want to see him again, Jessie, just one more time, that's all, so I can say things to 'im.'

Her own eyes filled and Jessie pulled him close and stroked his back. 'You *can* see him, whenever you want, Alfie. You can look at his photograph or just keep on remembering the good times together. It will help, Alfie. I do it all the time. I tell you what, in a couple of days' time, you and me are going to have a little talk. I've got something very special to tell you. Something which'll change all of our lives for the better. Especially Mum's.'

'Tell me now, Jess, tell me now,' he said, his head burrowed into her neck. 'Is it to do with Dad?'

'No, sweetheart, it's not. But you'll like it, I know you will.' Jessie led him to a chair, sat him down and held his hands. 'It's a long, complicated story and I'm not going into it all right now, but I will tell you this and you must promise not to go on at me until I've the time to explain it properly. Granny Blake isn't our real grandmother.'

Wiping his face with the back of his hand, he sniffed again. 'I've never liked the old cow anyway.'

'She's all right really. It's just that we're not blood relatives so she couldn't take to Mum nor us the way she might have. Anyway, we may have lost our dad, Alfie, but we're going to gain a grandmother and Mum will have her own mum back again, after nearly a lifetime of being without her. Last year, just before Dad was killed, the very day before, I found our real gran. Mum doesn't know and she might be cross with me for going behind her back, so you mustn't say anything. Promise you won't.'

He nodded and wiped away the last tear with his sleeve. 'What's she like? Where does she live? Why hasn't she come to see us?'

'I knew you'd do this to me. Just accept that better times are to come and leave it at that. Promise me you won't mention it again until I bring it up. Promise.'

'So long as you don't leave it for months and months.'

'Oh, I won't do that. I'll pluck up the courage soon and tell her.'

'I'll keep the secret then. I won't even say anything to Stephen – or Dolly.'

It was the wrong time to tell him that she had already told Stephen. 'Good.' He was out of the chair in a flash and away, happier than Jessie had seen him in a while. That little talk had done her the world of good too. It seemed to her that Ingrid Gunter, a real grandmother, would be a way of helping

to heal the painful wound the family had suffered when they lost her father.

When she had the house to herself, apart from Dolly hiding away upstairs, Jessie washed and brushed her hair, put on some make-up and the freshly ironed frock and waited for Max. She didn't have to wait long. Unfortunately, though, he wasn't in the same frame of mind as she was. He'd arrived once again in one of his heavy moods. She thought she'd win him round with a kiss and a cuddle, but she was wrong. She had got him in the parlour, on the sofa, but she hadn't got him going – hot sunny day or not.

'It's true,' Max said, preoccupied, 'the BUF did weaken but—'

'The what? What are you talking about, Max?'

'The BUF.' He looked surprised, as if he was seeing her for the first time. 'You don't know what BUF stands for?'

'No. I can guess though. Blackshirts – United – Fascists?' She was making it clear that she couldn't really care less what it stood for.

'British Union of Fascists,' he said, shaking his head despairingly.

'I'm sick of trying to work them all out. What, for instance, does CPGB stand for?'

'Communist Party of Great Britain.'

'ILP?'

'Independent Labour Party, now replaced by the Socialist League.'

Jessie racked her brain but couldn't think of any more.

Max reeled them off for her. 'NUWM – National Unemployed Workers Movement. UAB – Unemployment Assistance Board. PLP – Parliamentary Labour Party. TUC – Trade Union—'

'ILU?' she said, interrupting his flow.

'There isn't one.'

'Yes there is.'

'No there isn't.'

'Think about it, Max. I L U?'

He shrugged, splayed his hands. 'Sorry, Jess, but there isn't.'

'I Love You.'

'Oh, and I thought for the minute you were really interested in what I was saying. Anyway, my party is easy for you to remember – I'm a Socialist. Coming back to you, is it?'

'Ah, but are you so sure about that, Max?'

'Of course I'm sure about it. I've always voted Labour. My family vote Labour. My grandparents—'

'Dad was worried that you might have become a Communist.'

'That's crazy, Jessie. Your dad was pulling your leg.'

'No he wasn't. It's what he'd heard down the docks. That your lot were joining with the Communists against Mosley and his Blackshirts. In fact he wanted us to stop walking out together for a while, until things calmed down.'

'Exactly. Which is why the Fascists put that about. The docks have always been a good grapevine, your dad should have known better than to be taken in by propaganda.' His expression as he looked at Jessie changed. 'I'm sorry. I didn't mean that.' He pushed his hands through his hair. 'It's getting to everyone. My sister said something similar, as it happens. She thought that we should ease off seeing each other for a while. Of course I said we—'

'Which sister?' Jessie asked.

'Moira.'

'I thought as much, she doesn't like me. She's never been keen on us going out together. She wants you to marry a nice Jewish girl. Nathan looked down on me and now she does as well. First of all she was just a bit unfriendly, now she's cold. Deliberately cold.'

'No she isn't, Jessie, you're overreacting. Moira and Nathan are not like that. My sister, like Nathan, just doesn't happen to

believe in mixed religion marriages, that's all. If you were just a friend, she'd be different. Besides, what can you expect? She's bound to be concerned given all the anti-Jewish slogans that keep appearing.'

'That isn't my fault, Max.' All this talk about Moira and Nathan not believing in mixed marriages was news to Jessie. She hadn't actually thought much about Max's sister or her husband and she hardly saw the couple; when she did, Moira's snobbery drove her mad. 'What will she say when we get engaged, I wonder.'

'She's already said it. She thinks it's a mistake. She's been giving me lectures ever since I mentioned it.' Max's expression was wry.

'Oh, so you've told her our secret, that's nice. I've not even mentioned it to Mum, but Moira has to be told, mustn't leave Moira out of it.' Jessie knew she was sounding childish but she couldn't help it.

'I was just paving the way. I thought that by letting her in on it first, she might see things differently, but she didn't. She was shocked, in fact.'

'Moira was shocked? Tch. Oh dear.' Jessie was getting more and more upset, and she was infuriated that Max seemed oblivious of how he was making her feel. 'Well, maybe we should call the whole thing off then.'

'Don't be silly. I think the two of you should sit down and talk about it. She's got nothing against you personally, Jessie, she likes you. She likes you a lot, but . . .'

'But what, Max? What are you trying to say?'

'I'm not *trying* to say anything, I couldn't care less one way or the other, but she and my mother think—'

'Oh, *right*, so there's been a family discussion.'

'Let me finish. She and my mother wondered if you might like to think about converting. They would be willing to help with your Bible studies and—'

'Stop it, Max. You know full well that we're Church of

England. If Mum heard you saying such a thing she'd be offended and hurt.' Jessie went quiet and waited to hear his reaction but there wasn't one. Not one word.

'All right,' she said finally, 'I'll sit down with your mum and your sister and we'll talk about it. They can talk Judaism to me and I'll listen, but they've got to do the same and listen to *hear* what I have to say about Christianity.'

'Would you do that?'

'I've just said I would.'

He slipped off his chair and down onto his knees, laying his head in her lap. 'I love you so much, Jessie. I've been worried because I knew there would be a problem and I was frightened.' He eased her down onto the floor, onto the rag mat in front of the fireplace. 'I don't want religion to come between us, Jess.' He looked up at her with those doleful brown eyes. 'It won't, will it?'

'I hope not, Max. To be honest, I've not really thought about it. I've not considered what *my* family and friends might think about my marrying a Jew – it's not exactly an everyday occurrence, is it?' She kissed his puzzled expression away and then kissed him as she'd never kissed before. It was different this time because she was angry and her anger caused her to feel more passionate.

'I take it,' said Max, his voice husky, 'that your mother's not likely to come back and—'

'Catch you with your trousers down?' Jessie laughed quietly. 'Wouldn't that be something?'

Rose tapped lightly on Emmie's front door, hoping that her friend would be alone. If Hannah was there, she would turn round and go back home before her daughter saw her.

Emmie opened the door. 'Gracious me,' she said in surprise, 'you're the last one I thought it would be, Rose. What a turn-up for the books,' she smiled, '*you* slumming in Bethnal Green.'

'Don't be ridiculous, Emmie. Slumming indeed. Am I to stand on your doorstep then?'

Laughing, Emmie waved her in. 'I was only joking. It's lovely to see you at my door, I must say. Come in and take the weight off your feet.'

Rose followed Emmie through into the kitchen. 'You keep the place as nice as ever, Em. What lovely bright walls — very cheerful.'

'Your timing could have been disastrous, Rose,' she said, placing the kettle on the gas stove. 'It can't have been less than fifteen minutes since Hannah was here. Lucky for us, it was one of her flying visits. She's gone to view some lodgings — a one-bedroom flat.'

'It did cross my mind once I was at your front door but—'

'Well, there's no spilt milk to cry over, is there? She's gone. To be honest I don't really think she's that serious about moving away, it's enough for her to have the vision of one day escaping from Gerta. She's viewing places out of her reach and then reports back how lovely or how unsuitable they are. She's having a smashing time of it. God love her.' Emmie slipped one of her headache pills into her mouth and washed it down with a glass of water. 'You're lucky to have caught me in, Rose. I'm usually at Wickham's of a Saturday and if it hadn't been for my migraine attack earlier on, I wouldn't be here now.'

'I should have realised that as well,' murmured Rose.

Leaving the kettle to come to the boil, Emmie and Rose went into the front room where a small coal fire burned in the polished brass grate. 'You look as if you could do with a break yourself, Rose, you've lost a bit of weight. A holiday by the sea would do you the world of good.'

'I've too many things on my mind to think about that yet, Emmie, which is one of the reasons I'm here. It's to do with Gerta. She turned up at the funeral.' The sound of the whistling kettle filled the house.

Ignoring the high-pitched noise, Emmie's eyes narrowed as she stared disbelievingly at her friend. 'Gerta? At the funeral? No. You must 'ave been mistaken, Rose, surely.'

Rose waved a hand towards the kitchen. 'See to the kettle, Emmie.'

'Gracious me, I hope she didn't go to your house as well.'

'No. She was at the cemetery, hiding in the shadows, under a tree, waiting to get my attention. Emmie, please. That whistling is going right through my head.'

Emmie went into the kitchen, set the tray and returned to the sitting room, forgetting to put any biscuits out. 'The tea needs to brew for a couple of minutes,' she said, sitting opposite her friend. 'I can't for the life of me think why she would have turned up, Rose. Surely you're not going to tell me it was from compassion.'

'No. Greed. She wants a share of any compensation that's paid to me and the children, and she wants power of attorney over Hannah's finances. She has no understanding of the way these things work. I confided in my solicitor that there was another child to be considered and that's slowed things down even more. I don't think she believes me. It's why I came to see you, Emmie. I need someone to talk to. I'm at my wits' end in case Gerta shows up at my door.'

'Well, I never did,' said Emmie, shocked.

'I haven't seen her for nigh on sixteen years and, my goodness me, how she's changed.' Rose shook her head. 'She seemed such a decent woman all those years back. Quiet and reserved. She accused me of neglect, implying that once my brother had deserted her and gone back to New Zealand, we should have sent money to support Hannah. I know full well that Jack was sending her an allowance and still is. We may not write to each other much but we do keep in touch.'

'Well, it doesn't surprise me. The woman's a cold, conniving bitch. So what will you do about this? I know what I'd like to do.'

'I agreed to sort something out for the sake of Hannah but I feel as if I'm being blackmailed and I don't like it. It's a horrible feeling, and I can't shift it from the pit of my stomach.'

'You must be careful, Rose. You'll be making a rod for your back. That woman will always have something over you. I think you know what my advice would be.'

'I *can't* tell Jessie. How can I after all this time? I had to go outside, into the back yard, when Gerta chose which of my twin girls she would take. It nearly killed me. I don't want all of that dragged up again.' Rose shuddered. 'Goodness knows what it would do to the girls, never mind my other children.'

'It is blackmail,' said Emmie, pouring out the tea, 'and that's a criminal offence. I hope you told her so.'

'I don't know what I said in the end, to be honest. All I wanted was to get away from her. I do believe there is a streak of evil in the woman. She's within her rights to ask for compensation for Hannah, she is Robert's child and I know it's what he would want, but how do I go about it without Hannah knowing where the money's come from?'

'We can get round that, Rose. Gerta won't go to the authorities – she wouldn't have a leg to stand on. Your brother's been sending an allowance for her and officially Hannah was adopted, so I can't see—'

'That's just it,' Rose cut in. 'She wasn't legally adopted. We just put her into their care. Don't forget, it was fif- teen years ago. There were fewer regulations then. If Gerta's not satisfied, she could really go to town and likely get more than she deserves in any case. All she has to do is say that we dumped a baby on her doorstep and she took pity on it.'

'No, Rose, you're worrying too much. I'm sure if we sit here long enough and look at all the options we'll find a way through this.' Emmie felt sure there must be a way.

'I feel very uncomfortable with her having the upper hand like this. She can do what she likes, whenever she likes. She's

very bitter about my brother leaving her and blames us, blames all of his family, for messing up her life.'

'Poppycock. She messed up Hannah's life, more like. She's got no feelings for that poor girl, Rose. None. I'm sorry if you don't want to hear it, but it's the truth.'

Rose let out a deep sigh. 'I've let Hannah down badly, haven't I?'

'Never mind that now. We have to think of the present and what's for the best.'

Sipping their tea, neither said a word for a while. There was nothing uncomfortable about it, no embarrassment, they were just two friends mulling over a shared problem.

Glancing out of the window, Rose saw that there was some pink and white blossom on the trees in Emmie's back garden. 'Sometimes I can see a light at the end of the tunnel, Emmie. Sometimes,' whispered Rose, distracted.

'Of course you can, now that the winter and those harsh March winds are behind us. We all need the sunshine. You'll pick up and have the strength of two to deal with that woman, I'm sure of it.'

'I hope so. I don't seem to have the heart to go into the shop and deal with the business any more. I've lost interest in cooking and I've still got Robert's clothes to sort out. They're hanging in his wardrobe and sitting on his shelves, as if he was still there.'

'Well, I can't help you with the shop, Rose, but I can see that Robert's clothes go to a very good cause. I've done it before, more than once. My neighbours rely on me for that sort of thing, and you can imagine what it's like down at the old people's home. Always someone popping off. Why don't I sort it all out for you on Monday? You go into the shop as usual while I'm at your house packing things away. It's got to be done and it's best that you're not there. It won't take me more than a few hours.' Emmie poured them some more tea. 'To tell you the truth, Rose, I'm very pleased that you came to me for advice.'

'I wish I'd come sooner,' was her tired reply.

'Never mind. What we've got to do now is get you back on the road again, because if Robert can see you, from wherever he is, that's what he'd want to see – you on your feet again, getting stronger by the day. Then we'll get you out there socialising again as well. I wouldn't mind getting out of the house myself, now and then. Wouldn't it be lovely if we were to join Sister Esther's sewing circle at Bromley-by-Bow. We always said we would one day, didn't we? You remember, way back, when the war was on?'

'Dear Emmie,' said Rose, drying her eyes, 'you do have a way of bringing back the good memories. We did have our dreams, didn't we?'

'We did that, and who knows where it might lead us? That space above your cobbler shop would make lovely needlework rooms. The light coming in through those big windows would be a joy to work by. I wouldn't mind betting those rooms are full of junk which should have been thrown out years ago.'

Quietly laughing, Rose agreed. 'They always said that you had second sight. How you could know what those rooms look like I've no idea.'

'Just imagine it, Rose,' said Emmie, carried away, 'a dozen of us women up there using the finest of fabrics to make up lovely evening gowns and day frocks.'

Rose smiled at the thought of it. Her friend was dreaming but, yes, Rose had to admit to herself that it was a lovely vision and Emmie was right, the rooms should be put to a good use and so should her wayward daughter, Dolly. The one thing she'd been very good at when she was at school was needlework. Yes, Dolly could sew a fine seam and had made quite a few of her own clothes, without a pattern. It was food for thought.

'So,' said Emmie, bringing them both back to reality, 'Gerta. The sooner we get started on her, the better. She's a touch scared of me, if the truth be known. I'll challenge her to go public about Hannah and Jessie and I'll defy her to try and squeeze a penny

more out of you than your other children will have. We'll keep it all nice and fair and then a bit later on, once the finances have been dealt with, you and I will have a talk as to what move we make next – with regard to Hannah and Jessie.'

'Not that again, Emmie, please. The girls mustn't meet up.'

Rose was wishing for the impossible. Where Hannah and Jessie were concerned, thought Emmie, there was a hand much stronger than theirs at work. Emmie had a feeling Rose feared losing Jessie's love if she ever discovered what had happened. She toyed with the idea of telling Rose that the girls had already met up but decided that her friend had enough on her plate for the time being; the wretched woman looked as if she had all the troubles of the world on her shoulders. As for Jessie and Tom, their destiny was anyone's guess.

Jessie had enjoyed a long soak in the bath while the house was quiet. Max had gone to a meeting with the promise that he would be back later to take her out for supper at London Bridge, as arranged. Pouring the last remains of water out of the tin bath and into the outside drain, Jessie looked sadly at Robert's vegetable patch. The new season's potatoes he'd planted in early autumn were ready for pulling and the broad bean plants looked in good shape. Strolling to the back wall, she checked the climbing roses. They were already in bud and would hopefully be flowering before the pink japonica and orange burgeris had finished flowering.

Robert had loved his garden and spent several hours out there, working his tiny bit of land, which Rose still referred to as the back yard. Between the small shrubs Jessie saw that the weeds were taking hold.

Against the side of the brick lavatory was the wooden trough which Robert had made and in which he would normally have planted trailing lobelia and a mix of other flowers. This summer they would not have the pleasure of his display. Hooking the

tin bath onto its place on the back wall, Jessie heard someone knocking on the front door and her heart sank. She was enjoying her solitude.

With a towel wrapped round her freshly washed hair, she opened the door a little and peered through the gap, astonished to see her grandmother Ingrid Gunter standing on the doorstep.

'May I come inside?' she said matter of factly. Jessie nodded and opened the door properly. 'You seem very shocked to see me. You think me too old to catch a bus or pay you a visit?'

'Mum's not in – no one's here except me and Dolly and she's asleep.' Swallowing, she was caught with an irritating cough.

'Show me where the kitchen is,' said Ingrid. 'You need a glass of water.'

Leading the way, Jessie went downstairs, still coughing. She sipped some cool water. 'It's a bit of a jolt, seeing you here,' she finally managed to say. After all her plans to visit Ingrid, now here she was.

'Well, you could offer me a chair. Maybe a cup of tea?'

'Of course, I'm sorry.' Jessie pulled a chair out from under the pine table. 'I'll put the kettle on, Mum should be back soon.' She felt herself go rigid. 'She doesn't even know that I went to see you.'

'You kept your promise. That makes me very happy. So, we have trust between us. Very important.' Ingrid looked around the kitchen. 'I like it here, there is a something about it that reminds me of the house I shared with your grandfather before he ran off. We had a back-to-back, two up, two down, it was smaller than this house, but yes, it had a similar feel. I was very sorry to have to give it up.'

'Mum could come in any minute,' said Jessie, nervous of what would happen if she did.

'I hope she does. After your visit, I thought about it, thought about what you said. It's time we met. I read about the tragedy and bided my time. Two shocks close together

might have been too much for your mother to take. How is she?'

'Sad for most of the time but pushing on. We're all pushing on, not much choice really.'

'No. Sometimes one doesn't have a choice. I hear footsteps on the stairs. Someone is creeping about.'

'That'll be my sister, Dolly. She's been in bed all day with a sore eye.' Jessie glanced anxiously towards the door.

'Ah. And now she is in for a surprise. Why don't you go and speak to her in private? She may react against me if—'

'Why?' Dolly appeared in the doorway. 'Who are you?'

'I'm your grandmother,' said Ingrid smoothly. 'I was keeping myself to myself but your sister came in search of me and turned my world upside down. Why don't you join us? Jessie is going to pour us some tea when she gets round to it.'

'Oh. So you're not dead then?'

'Should I be?'

'You might as well have been.' Dolly pulled off the lid of the biscuit tin. 'We've never seen hide nor hair of you. Where 'ave you been all this time? Why haven't you come round before now? Grandmothers do that, you know. They bring presents at Christmas and birthdays.'

'Don't mind her,' said Jessie, giving her sister a black look. 'She's in a bad mood because she can't go out tonight. Well, she could but she won't, not with that bandage wrapped round her head.'

'I couldn't care less about the *bandage*. I can't wash my hair!'

The sound of the street door opening and slamming shut startled Ingrid. The girls were used to it. The boys had arrived.

'This'll test you, *Grandma*,' said Dolly. 'They'll fire hundreds of questions.'

Ingrid wasn't ruffled by Dolly. 'Then don't tell them who I am. Say I'm an old friend of your grandfather's.'

The boys rushed into the kitchen and raced to the biscuit tin. They seemed happy enough.

'Good film, was it?' asked Jessie.

'Champion. Is there any cake left?'

'There is, Stephen, but you can't have any yet, not until you remember your manners. We have a visitor, in case you hadn't noticed.'

Munching a chocolate biscuit, Alfie peered at Ingrid and gave a quick nod. 'Hello.'

'I'm very well, thank you. And you are?'

'Alfie.'

Ingrid held out her hand. Bemused, Alfie shook it. 'I am Mrs Gunter. A very old friend of the family. How do you do.'

'I'm all right. What country d'yer come from?'

'I was born in Germany but spent most of my life here, in England.'

Alfie regarded her for a moment then said, 'Oh. Come on, Stephen. They're playing Tin Can Tommy. Be back in an hour!'

Grabbing a couple of biscuits, Stephen followed his brother out of the kitchen and bounded up the stairs behind him. Then came the loud slamming of the street door as the boys ran outside.

'Well, that just leaves my daughter to be faced,' said Ingrid. 'I think it might be better if you girls were to go up to your rooms once she arrives. I have some explaining to do after all these years and so does she.'

'Don't you think I should say something first?' said Jessie, worried.

'That is entirely up to you but I wouldn't recommend it. You needn't worry. What I have to say will not make her angry, she may even forgive an old woman for not having more willpower when she was younger and stronger than she is now.'

'Well,' said Dolly bluntly, 'you don't have time to argue the toss. That's her coming in now.'

'Ah.' Ingrid breathed in, straightened, and then pushed her shoulders back.

'This doesn't feel right,' said Dolly uneasily. 'I don't think this is a very good idea. It's making my eye throb.' Ingrid found herself smiling at Dolly.

When Rose walked into the kitchen she was met with silence. She glanced at Ingrid and then at Jessie. 'What's going on?' she said, puzzled.

'Hello, Rose.' Ingrid's voice was quiet but there was no sign of worry on her face. 'I hope you don't mind but I asked the girls if they would be so kind as to leave us alone when you arrived.'

Rose stiffened and took a step backwards and then another until she felt the kitchen wall behind her and could lean against it. Beckoning to Dolly, Jessie slipped out of the kitchen. As quiet as lambs they went upstairs, hardly daring to breathe. They heard the kitchen door close.

'This doesn't feel right, Jessie,' said Dolly again.

'I know. We didn't have much choice though, did we? We couldn't throw her out. Should we listen on the stairs? What do you think?'

'Not me. I'm going up to our room. I don't want to take the blame for this. This is all your fault. You should have kept your nose out of it.' Dolly slowly climbed the stairs. 'It's too quiet down there. This is the calm before the storm. I'm going under the bed covers ...' Her words trailed off as she made her escape.

'Thanks, Dolly. Thanks very much.'

Creeping back down the stairs, careful to avoid the creaky ones, Jessie trod carefully towards the kitchen door and listened. It was quiet. Too quiet. Neither of them was saying anything. She put her ear very close to the door in case they were whispering. Nothing. She decided to go in.

'Have you seen today's paper, Mum? I can't find it anywhere.' This seemed an appropriate excuse.

'It's in the parlour,' said Rose distractedly, 'where it usually is.'

'Speaking of newspapers,' said Ingrid, 'what did it feel like having your name spread across the pages?' She seemed to be suggesting that that was how she knew where her estranged daughter lived.

'We got used to it,' said Jessie. 'One article was much the same as another. The nice thing about it was that they made Dad out as a hero. He would have had a laugh at that. Max says the publicity will help our compensation case.' Jessie looked from Rose to Ingrid. 'So. Am I in the black books then?' Neither of them said a word. 'Oh, come on, this is silly. You're together now so you may as well—'

'Mind your manners, Jessie, please,' snapped Rose.

'Manners? We're family, not strangers.' She turned to Ingrid, trying her best to make light of it. 'All we need is your mother as well. Still, for all we know, she may well be in this room with us, in spirit.'

'If you are talking about the afterworld, she is not there. My mother is still alive. Ninety-six and going strong. She lives in Düsseldorf. I went to visit her a year ago with my brother and his wife and she was in good spirits. We went by boat and train, and two trams – three if you count the tram at this end.'

Still Rose remained silent.

'Would you like another cup of tea ... Grandma?' said Jessie, chancing her luck.

'Thank you, no. Please call me Ingrid. I'm not used to such a grand title.'

'I'll try.'

The silence stretched, until finally Rose broke it.

'It's a pity you never met Robert. Just like Jessie, he wanted to know more about you, and why you had to put me into a home.' Her cold tone covered the hurt and confusion she felt at being confronted without warning by her long-vanished mother. Jessie meant well but she could have

no idea of the conflicting emotions that were bubbling up inside Rose.

'And you? Weren't you curious? Didn't you want to find out why I had to do it? Maybe you were too ashamed of your father to face me.' Ingrid's voice was gentle and soothing.

'Or maybe I was waiting for you to find out more about me?' said Rose.

'I knew all there was to know about you. My brother gave me regular reports, he fancies himself as a detective. From the very day I placed you in the home, he kept check. I had every intention of getting you back once I had found somewhere for us to live, somewhere decent. A place that would not only provide a roof over our heads but give me employment as well. I was searching for a position as resident housemaid in one of the big houses or boarding schools.' It seemed that once Ingrid opened up, there was no stopping her. 'I found just the right place, but by then it was too late. Your father had you under his wing.'

'You could have come to see me!' Rose's hurt was fast changing to resentment.

'It would have confused you. Madam Blake had taken over my role and you seemed to be well cared for. I once saw you leave the house with them, a hand in each of theirs. They took you to the park and I followed to watch you on the swings. Mr Gunter was pushing you and you were laughing. I took that to mean that you were happy. I, on the other hand, was not. I walked away and vowed that I would not interfere. Decades later, a persistent granddaughter turns up for a cup of coffee.'

'I might have guessed she would go in search of you,' said Rose. There was the merest hint of a smile on her face but it faded within seconds. 'I suppose it couldn't have been a happy time for you either.'

'No, it wasn't, but I've not been miserable all of my life. I have some good friends, a nice home, a lovely family, my brother's family. Some of my old friends have passed on — Emmie Smith's mother, for instance. That did upset me very

much. She was an old and loyal friend, before and after Madam Blake came on the scene. Her daughter Emmie takes after her; she, too, is a good family woman and she has done well by both you and me. I see her from time to time and she keeps me up to date.'

There was another frosty silence. Jessie knew she should leave but she wanted desperately to stay and find out more.

'Well now, isn't Emmie the dark horse,' said Rose tightly.

Ingrid pulled herself up from the chair. 'Now that you know where I live, maybe you will come to see me, once in a while. I hope, I very much hope you can find it in your heart to forgive me.'

'I don't know where you live.' Rose spoke as if she didn't care one way or the other.

'Ask your inquisitive daughter. Maybe she will bring you with her on her next visit.' With that, Ingrid gave a graceful nod and waited for Jessie to show her out of the house, leaving Rose to herself.

'How long has all this been going on, Jessie?' asked Rose when her daughter returned.

Jessie related the story from the beginning and ended by telling her mother that Ingrid, underneath her resentment, had been sad and lonely and upset by her visit and that she doubted she would ever forgive Mr Gunter, as she called him, for betraying her so badly. Rose listened patiently, looking thoughtful and a little sorry.

'Well, some of this is news to me, Jessie, and I must say I do feel some shame at what your grandfather did to her. I can hardly believe it, but then Grandmother Blake is a very strong-willed woman, not to say very beautiful when she was younger.'

'It was brave of her to come,' said Jessie, rubbing her hair with the towel. She realized it had been ridiculous to think there would a fairytale reunion between her mother and grandmother. There was too much pain involved – but she hoped time would soften it.

'Was it? I don't know. I'm a bit thunderstruck, to tell the truth. I had no idea that she'd been keeping watch from afar — and for so long.'

'She gets a bit muddled, though. When I went to see her she blamed herself for you giving away a daughter. As if you'd do a thing like that. I hope I don't get muddled when I'm her age.'

This off-the-cuff remark struck like lightning. Rose held her breath, wondering what would come next.

'I told her that Dolly lived with us. Then she blamed her brother for getting his facts wrong. She went all quiet after that.'

Relieved and thankful that her mother had not revealed anything, Rose asked Jessie where she lived.

'Over by Victoria Park. I'll write the address down and leave it on the dresser.' Pulling her hair back, Jessie pushed in a comb. 'Do you think you might visit her then?'

'I don't know. It's been a bit of a shock, one way and another.'

'Yes, but will you go?'

'*Yes*, Jessie. I will go. When I'm good and ready.' Rose refused to say another word on the subject.

Chapter Seven

When the day came for Jessie to go and see Max's mother and sister, there was a worried knot inside her stomach. Why had she agreed to this farce? She had no intention of changing religion and her original reason for saying she would go was to find out exactly what was on Moira's mind. As far as Jessie was concerned, Moira was at the bottom of this sudden problem which had little to do with her being a Christian and Max a Jew. Moira's sights were set higher for her brother.

Turning into the street where Max lived, Jessie braced herself for a confrontation and hoped that she was wrong and that they *were* thinking of her and Max's welfare and whether they would be able to adjust to the trials and tribulations of a mixed marriage, as Max had said. She rang the doorbell and was disappointed that it was 28-year-old Moira who answered the door and not her mother. Jessie liked Mrs Cohen, they had always got on from the time she was small and used to pop in to what was then her grandfather's shoe menders, to help polish boots.

'You're early, Jessie. I've only just got here,' said Moira brightly. 'Come in, come in.' Jessie checked her wristwatch; it was five to ten in the morning, she was just five minutes early.

With her hair set and lacquered, her make-up perfect, Moira looked glamorous next to Jessie, who had her hair tied back and

apart from a smear of lipstick was wearing no make-up. Gliding through the passage and into the small back room where Max's parents spent most of their time, Moira pulled out a chair from under the small gate-leg table. In her bright orange and green frock and chiffon neckerchief, she looked as if she was ready to go to the theatre, but this was nothing unusual because she always looked smart and dressy.

Since it was Saturday Jessie was wearing slacks and a puff-sleeved blouse; she shouldn't have felt too casually dressed for the occasion, but she did. Before sitting down, she made a quick check of her nails to make sure her clear varnish hadn't chipped. Her confidence had begun to wane.

'I'm sorry if I'm too early, Moira. I must have walked too quickly,' she said. 'I meant to get here on the dot.'

'Not to worry, darling. I'll put the kettle on, but if you don't mind my passing on a bit of friendly advice, it's better to arrive five minutes late than five minutes early. I don't mind, of course, but you never know how your hostess might react. Some people might think it impolite.'

Settling herself in the newly decorated room, Jessie admired the pale pink and green flowery wallpaper. 'It's very quiet, Moira,' she said. 'Where's your mum?'

'My mother's had to go and see Auntie Becky,' she said. 'Auntie Becky gets headaches when she feels like it and has us all running round after her.'

Glancing at the spread on the table, Jessie thought it didn't look as if Moira had just arrived. A try was set with two bone china cups and saucers and there were smoked salmon bagels on a plate. Jessie could smell cigarette smoke in the air and more than one had been smoked if the glass and chrome ashtry was anything to go by. Neither Max nor his parents were smokers.

'My father's at the synagogue, Jessie, before you ask. He spends most of Saturday there.' Scooping up the ashtray, she went through into the adjoining kitchen and tipped the evidence into a small cream pedal bin. Jessie knew Moira's secret. They

all knew Moira's secret and she knew they all knew but liked to pretend that she didn't know they all knew. That was Moira.

She put the kettle on and came back into the room.

'And Max is keeping out of the way while you and I argue religion' said Jessie.

'I hope that isn't what my brother said, Jessie. He knows I wouldn't dream of such a thing. Arguing over religion? I don't think so.'

'I was only joking, Moira, trying to lighten things, before we start discussing it.'

'Oh?' Moira raised an inquiring eyebrow.

'I'm sure God must have had a sense of humour. He would have had to, wouldn't he, if he really *can* see each and every one of us every second of the day — and what we get up to.'

'Yes, dear, if you say so, although I don't think your priest would think much of—'

'Vicar. Catholics have priests. We have vicars.'

'Of course, of course,' she said, shrugging it off in typical Moira style. She never admitted she was wrong.

'I wonder what Jesus would have made of Mosley and his little army of Blackshirts. I suppose in a way the Fascists could be seen in the same light as the Roman army. They wanted to change the world as well.' Moira's confidence and self-possession always made Jessie react by showing off — she couldn't help it.

Moira frowned. 'We don't mention that name in this house.'

Jessie wasn't sure if she was referring to Mosley or Jesus. 'Sorry. I wasn't thinking. How's your hubby then?' she said, trying to warm her future sister-in-law.

'Nathan is very well, thank you. He's just been promoted, as a matter of fact. Area manager. We're very pleased. Very proud. The company he works for are enjoying a boom year.'

'That's nice. It couldn't have been much fun for him, going round knocking on people's doors, trying to get blood out of

a stone. The tally man's not that popular round this way. Not when it comes to paying out.'

'Nathan wasn't a tally man, dear,' said Moira. 'He was a debt collector. But you're right, he's much happier and far more suited to an office. He had to do the street rounds first – ground work. It's company policy to begin at the grass roots. Now he's got a beautiful desk to sit behind. Antique. He's very keen on antiques.' Moira got up to get the kettle. 'Personally I prefer Art and Craft. Our flat in Stamford Hill looks very different from this house. Not that my parents have antiques, of course. What do you think of the decorating? Nathan paid good decorators to come in once the house was wired for electricity. Does your house still have gas lighting, dear?'

'No, not any more.' Jessie bristled under Moira's air of superiority.

'That's nice. So ...' Moira poured boiling water from the kettle into the coffee pot. 'I hear that you want to marry into our family, Jessie. Is that right?'

'I thought that was why you wanted to see me. I thought you knew that Max has been paying off for an engagement ring. His idea, not mine. He'd like us to get married early next year, which is why I don't think our little talk about my changing religion will have much point. It takes years of studying and practice, from what I've heard.'

'You surprise me, Jessie.' Moira sat down and placed a cup of tea in front of Jessie. 'Help yourself to milk and sugar. The milk is fresh.'

'Why do I surprise you?'

'Well,' Moira laid the flat of her hand against her breast, 'you know what they're like.' She flapped her hand. 'Men and their hearts. My brother was always one for the girls but I would have expected him to have grown out of that if he did have marriage on his mind. Seriously on his mind, that is.'

'So you don't think he has then? Grown out of it?' Jessie said, frowning.

'No, darling, I don't. He thinks the world of you, sure, but Max, settling down? I don't think so. Not for a few years in any case.'

This conversation was not what Jessie had been expecting. 'But if he's not ready for marriage why would he be buying me a diamond engagement ring?'

'Zircon, dear. I'm sure it's a lovely dress ring. Beautiful. But a diamond? Max isn't earning a fortune — yet.'

'It is a diamond, Moira. He pointed it out to me and said it was a diamond. He's not a liar, your brother. You must know that.'

Moira shrugged and lowered her eyelids. 'So he has dreams bigger than his wallet. Most young men do these days. In many ways Max is immature, although I wouldn't want him to know I said that. I worship the ground he walks on. He's a prince among men as far as I'm concerned. But then, I'm family.'

Determined not to be put down, Jessie straightened and looked her in the eye. 'He's been paying off for the ring for months and I don't think he's a prince among men, he's just an ordinary feller who I happen to love. And he's not immature, far from it.' Now it was Jessie's turn to sound smug, 'You can trust me on that one.' Seeing Moira's expression change from complacent superiority to discomfort was worth putting up with all her condescension.

'Of course,' said Moira, recovering herself, 'you should know best.'

'I feel bad now,' said Jessie, play-acting, 'telling you about the ring. I thought you knew.' She playfully pointed a finger. 'You crafty cow, Moira, you wormed it out of me.'

'I didn't exactly have to *prise* it out of you, Jessie. You must be very careful about bragging.'

'Anyway,' said Jessie, biting her tongue, 'what *did* you want to talk to me about? Max said it was to discuss Judaism and Christianity.' She looked into Moira's face. 'What's this all about?'

'Goodness, you have changed. You mustn't be so harsh, but then, poor darling, you have been through a very difficult time. If I may give you another little bit of advice,' she leaned forward and pulled a strange face, 'don't get bitter. It would be such a shame. You're a lovely girl.' She leaned back again and smiled benignly. 'I just wanted us to have a little chat, that's all. We never seem to see each other, and yes,' she said, lighting a cigarette, 'I have been concerned about the differences in Max's life and yours. Most of our friends are Yiddish. Everything we do is Yiddish. It's very unusual for a Jew and a Christian to become sweethearts, very unusual. We're a tight-knit community. Family and friends don't like it if one of us marries out.' She leaned forward again, resting an elbow on the table and admiring her red nail varnish.

'You're a sweetheart, Jessie, and we think the world of you, don't get me wrong. But marriage?' She reached out and opened a drawer in the table. 'Here, let me show you something.' She withdrew a few photographs. 'This one is of Cousin Harry's bar mitzvah, taken last year. I'm sure Max told you about it. This is the world you would be marrying into. We Cohens are a very traditional family. Now, can you see yourself fitting into that scene? You, with your lovely blonde hair, blue eyes and pale skin, you would stand out like a sore thumb. You see what I mean?'

This was like Hitler in reverse. 'You're saying that I wouldn't fit in because of my appearance?'

'Now you're being silly. Of course I'm not saying that. All I'm saying is that you should think seriously about it. Would you be happy? Or a fish out of water?'

Jessie studied the photograph and could see what she was getting at. 'I wouldn't *have* to go to bar mitzvahs,' she said, shrugging, 'although if I saw Max wearing a skull cap, I must admit I might laugh until I got used to it.'

'You *would*?'

'Yes, Moira, I probably would. I'm sorry if it offends you.'

'You know what I think? I think you should come to a Friday night Sabbath. Take supper with us next Friday.'

'When Max will wear a skull cap.'

Moira bowed her head, smiling. 'When Max will wear a skull cap.'

'You want me to laugh at him. In front of everyone.'

'You're sharper than you make out, Jessie, even if you are wrong. As if I would want you to laugh at my brother.' She placed a red painted fingernail on the photograph and tapped it. 'I think he looks charming.'

'Is that Max?' said Jessie, seeing him in a different light.

'Of course it is. You don't recognise him?'

'The girl next to him, the redhead, is she one of your cousins?'

'No, darling.' Moira quietly chuckled. 'No, that's Sadie and Bernard Marcovitch's daughter. The Marcovitches are very close family friends. Max has known Sarah for as long as I can remember. They practically grew up together. I would have thought he'd have mentioned her. Everyone said they would get married. Look at this picture.' She showed Jessie another and then another and another. 'Look at the two of them in this one. Dancing the Charleston as if there weren't any troubles in this crazy world of ours. Look, here's another.'

The next photograph was Moira's trump card and Jessie reacted exactly as she had hoped. It was a picture of Max kissing the very attractive redhead on the mouth, and it shocked Jessie. Shocked her to the core. It was a very recent photograph.

'Such a beautiful girl,' said Moira. 'You see what I mean? They fall at his feet, but this one he likes. As you can tell. Isn't that a lovely gown?'

'So this is what Max gets up to behind my back. Well, if that's how you lot behave, to be honest with you, Moira, I wouldn't want to marry into your family. Not for all the money in China.' Suddenly filled with rage, Jessie snatched the kissing photograph and ripped it to bits. 'Show that to Max.

Tell him that's what I think of him – and of you for going behind his back.'

Half running, Jessie left the house and made her way home, too shocked and too angry to cry. Max had been leading a double life, laughing and dancing and kissing other girls. She thought about the gifts that he'd bought for her; she would collect them together, pack them all into a shopping bag and throw them at him.

Stopping to draw breath, Jessie leaned on a lamppost, unable to believe what she had seen and what she had heard. Of course she knew about the family celebrations to which she hadn't been invited; she had understood at the time. She had never expected Max to attend a family christening with her or go to church for midnight mass on Christmas Eve or be there for the carol service, but she hadn't expected him to be trifling with other women at his family functions.

Slamming the front door shut, Jessie ran upstairs to her bedroom and banged around, opening and shutting drawers and cupboards until she'd found the gifts Max had given her. She would show him what she thought of his womanising.

She sat on the edge of her bed and remembered her lovely engagement ring, sparkling in the window. She looked at her naked finger and felt like weeping. Feeling desperately alone, she realised just how badly she missed her dad. She so wanted to hear his comforting voice telling her that it would all sort itself out and that she had overreacted to a jealous sister. She wanted her dad to tell her that Max wasn't a ladies' man but a good, loyal boyfriend, compassionate and understanding. She looked at the presents, half in, half out of the shopping bag. She glanced at his love letters on the dressing table tied with ribbon. Had they been full of romantic fantasies instead of genuine love? Then the photograph came back to her again and her anger returned. She *would* take them back. She had every right to be angry and every right to let him know that she was angry.

Grabbing the bag, she rushed downstairs and out of the

house, slamming the door behind her. She wanted her mother, Dolly, and the boys to know that she was upset and angry. She would tell them all about it later.

Rose called her name from the sitting room window and Jessie glanced up. Dolly was there too. Ignoring them both, Jessie strode off back to Max's house.

'All right, Jessie love?' A neighbour was scrubbing her doorstep. 'You look as if you've lost half-a-crown and found a penny!'

Jessie ran on, weaving and shoving her way through shoppers and those out for a Saturday browse on a sunny June day.

This time it was Max who answered the door.

'Here, you can have these back,' she snapped. 'I don't want them! Give them to the girl in the photograph. The one you were kissing! You cheat! You liar!' Furious, she threw the bag at his feet and turned away, forcing herself not to run. She would keep some dignity at least.

She had expected and hoped to hear Max calling after her, but he didn't. By the time she reached home, Jessie was more upset than angry. Finding Rose waiting for her, she burst into tears.

'What's going on Jessie? Dolly saw you rush out earlier. What's happened?'

'Max. That's what's happened! Good old trustworthy Max.'

'I thought it might have been. You've had a lovers' tiff. Come on. Come in the kitchen and tell me all about it. What's he done?'

It wasn't until she had a cup of tea in front of her that Jessie finally poured out her troubles. 'All that Max said was that his sister wanted me to go round there to discuss religion. To see if I could be persuaded to change.'

'To Jewish,' said Rose, knowingly.

'But that's *not* what it was about.' She explained what Moira had done and then waited for her mother's angry reaction.

'And that's all?' said Rose. 'That's what this is about? A photograph?'

'It was enough. Moira was trying to tell me something, something that Max couldn't bring himself to admit. I don't fit into the family. I'd be the odd man out.'

'I can't say I'm that surprised, Jessie,' said Rose quietly. 'Your dad was a bit concerned that you might have married and then had regrets. As nice as Max and his family are, they do things differently from us. I'm fond of his parents, you know I am, we've been friends for years. I couldn't have wished for nicer people to work next door to, but they have different ways to us. No better, no worse, just different.'

'But I thought you were all for it. Suddenly everyone thinks it's wrong. This is the first time it's come up. Why, all of a sudden, are me and Max not suited? Has something happened that I don't know about?' Jessie looked wretched.

'No, of course not.'

'It's all this Blackshirt business,' said Jessie. 'That's what's doing it. We're all turning against each other. We were never like this before. Did you ever know Stepney people to be like this?'

'You and Max are from different backgrounds, that's all. Very different backgrounds. I expect his sister was just letting you know what lay in store, that it wouldn't be easy for either of you.' Rose paused and then shook her head. 'Showing you a photo of Max with another woman wasn't the way to go about it. That was very hurtful.'

'I hate her for that. I do. I *hate* her. Once Max drags the truth out of her, he'll be livid. When he does come round to apologise for Moira – which should be any time now – will you let him come up to my bedroom, just this once?' Jessie pleaded, hoping her mother would understand how important this was.

'Did he say he was coming round?' asked Rose.

'No. But he will once he knows what's happened. He looked really hurt when I threw his gifts back at him. So will it be all

right then? If he comes into my bedroom? I'll leave the door open, if it bothers you.'

'You can go into the sitting room, Jessie. I'll make sure no one disturbs you. That way you can have the door shut and there'll be no risk of the boys hearing your private conversation. Your bedroom's not the place, it wouldn't be right. Once you've made up, things might get out of hand. I trust Max with you, we've always trusted him to behave properly but—'

'You don't want us doing things we shouldn't.'

'I'm not saying that you would—'

'We already have, that's what makes it worse,' Jessie blurted impulsively.

The look of shock on Rose's face brought Jessie to her senses. What was she doing? Why had she said it? There was no stopping now, she would have to go on. 'We have been courting for two years, Mum, and we did plan to marry.'

It hadn't crossed Rose's mind that her seventeen-year-old daughter might have already tasted the forbidden fruits. 'I hope you're not saying that you've let him go all the way?'

Jessie could feel her cheeks burning. 'Well, no . . . not all the way.' If there was a time to lie, thought Jessie, this was it.

'Gracious me,' said Rose, pressing a hand against her bosom and taking a deep breath. 'Thank goodness your father isn't here to listen to this.' She stood up and turned her back on Jessie. 'I think you'd best go to your room now, Jessie.'

'We've been going out together for two years! Didn't you and Dad ever think that we might have . . . well . . . you know?'

'Please, Jessie. I don't like this kind of talk. You should know that.'

'You're not being fair! I've seen your marriage certificate and I know that you were pregnant with me before you and Dad got married. That never bothered me so why should Max and me have to wait?'

There was a pause, while Rose collected herself. 'We'll talk

about it another time.' She had no intention of doing so. It had been distressing enough to hear her daughter speak so casually about her own guilty secret, her and Robert's secret. The last thing she wanted was to have her own past picked over as some sort of point of comparison.

Later, in her room, Jessie started to cry. Soon Max would come round and make her feel better, she felt sure of it. Then she would apologise to her mother who was far too strait-laced to discuss sex with anyone, even her own daughter. She had shocked Rose and now she would have to lie her way out of it and try and get things back to where they were before she made that damning confession. She would say that she was still a virgin.

After several nights of crying herself to sleep, Jessie realised that Max wasn't going to appear, he wouldn't be coming round to say that Moira was wrong and that it had all been something out of nothing. Jessie hadn't realised just how much she would miss his friendly face and comforting ways. It was as if a part of herself had been taken away.

Dolly, Alfie and Stephen were being kind to her, which made it worse. Rose knew what Jessie was going through but was helpless to do anything about it; her daughter was going to have to be brave and face facts. Max, for whatever reason, was not going to run to her and she would have to go back and apologise for her behaviour if all was to be saved.

Eventually, Jessie decided she had to stop crying. It wasn't fair. Passing her mother's bedroom, she had seen Rose sitting on the edge of the big double bed holding a pair of her father's pyjamas which she had kept back. There had been other things, too, to remind them – a letter through the post addressed to him, one of his socks turning up in the wash or under the bed.

Going into the sitting room, she found Rose sewing a patchwork cushion. 'I'm going to make a pot of tea, Mum. Do you want a cup?'

Rose looked up at her and nodded. 'That would be nice. What time is it?'

Glancing at the hall clock, Jessie told her it was half past four. 'Shall I call the boys in for a wash before tea? They're in the street playing football.'

'No, leave them for a while,' said Rose. 'Stephen's fulfilling your dad's wishes at last, we don't want to spoil that. Give them another half-hour.' She laid down her sewing and rubbed her eyes. 'I've given myself a headache with this tiny stitchwork. Pull the curtains across, would you, Jess? I'll stop in here for twenty minutes or so. I expect it'll pass once I've sipped a warm drink and closed my eyes.'

Back in her own bedroom, sitting on her bed and drinking her cup of tea, Jessie ran it all through her mind again: Moira; the photos; their talk. Perhaps her pride had made her see things in a worse light than intended. But she had thought about it every night and arrived at the same conclusion. It was over, and while Moira's methods had been underhand, she was right about the reasons. That hadn't stopped Jessie from missing Max. They had been seeing each other for so long that he really had become an important part of her life. She likened it to losing her dad. She was grieving for two men who had meant everything.

Sally had been a godsend. It was her shoulder that Jessie had cried on in the office, she who had patiently listened to the story about Moira over and over again; she who had many times heard how all Jessie's plans for a future with Max would now come to nothing.

The one thing that had struck Jessie was something that Sally had said in the canteen the day before, on Friday: 'Jess, you do realise that not once, through all of this, have you mentioned the word love.' And she'd been right. They had gone on to discuss love and what love actually was. Sally had said, 'You just *know*, Jess. There's no other way of describing it.'

Their tête-à-tête in the canteen had been the reason why Jessie had at last come out of herself. She had hidden herself

away almost every evening since she and Max had split up. Now she was back in her room again, drinking her tea alone, but for a different reason — she *wanted* to be by herself. It was as simple as that.

With her pillows propped behind her, Jessie listened to the children in the street. The boys were playing football and the girls were enjoying a game of skipping. She could hear their chant and it took her back to when she had done the very same thing out there in that same street. Lighter inside, she sang along with them:

> All come in together,
> Never mind the weather,
> When the wind begins to blow,
> We'll all go out together ...'

'Jess? Are you asleep in there?' Rose sounded timid by comparison to the woman she had once been. A wave of guilt swept over Jessie. She slipped her legs off the bed and sat up, determined to turn over a new leaf, for the sake of herself and everyone around her. She pushed her hand through her long unbrushed hair and braced herself, ready to be the person she was before she broke up with Max.

'Jessie? Your friend's downstairs. Shall I ask her to come in or would you rather I made an excuse? It's Sally from work.'

'Sally?' Jess was off the bed in a flash and opening her door. 'I'll come down,' she said, smiling.

'Oh, that's better, Jessie. Much better. You have bucked up. The boys are just in and the table's laid with sandwiches and some cake. If your friend wants to come in and—'

Jessie placed her hands on Rose's shoulders. 'Mum, it's over. I'm not going to mope around any more so you can stop worrying about me. Next week, we'll go to see a show, a really good, old-fashioned variety show. Something for all of us.'

'That would be a tonic, Jessie, I must say.' There was a genuine smile on Rose's face too.

'Good. I'll have my tea later. Will it be all right if Sally comes into my room for a short while?' Rose had never encouraged any of her children to have friends in, especially not in the bedrooms.

'I should think so. There's a bottle of lemonade downstairs, Sally might be thirsty after her walk. It's very hot and dry out there.'

Jessie went downstairs to greet her friend, feeling much lighter inside. Maybe she would go out with Sally for a drink that evening.

'Blimey, Jessikins,' exclaimed Sally, 'you look a right two and eight. I think it's time you went to the hairdressers', you need a style and set. Still, not much we can do about that now except to sweep it all up on top and put some lacquer on. Hurry up, we're going out.'

'I haven't got any lacquer, Sally. I don't use it. It's like glue.'

'I'm sure it is, but who cares so long as it does the trick. You'll have to do something with it, and you could put a bit of lipstick on.'

'Where are we going?' Jessie's spirits began to rise. Sally always cheered her up.

'Anywhere. I don't care. After our little chat yesterday, I thought it was time you had an outing. Can I come in then? Or you gonna leave me standing on the doorstep like a stray cat?'

'Of course you can come in but do we have to go out? Can't we just sit on my bed and talk?'

'No, we bleedin' well can't. We've done enough of that. You and Max are finished, it's past 'istory. Now go and do something with yerself, can't go for a drive with the chaps looking like a dog's dinner.'

A frown swept across Jessie's face. 'What chaps?'

'Tom's been driving me round the bend and up the wall.

He wants to see yer. Him and Ron 'ave bought a car between 'em, an old banger they've named Susie. They 'ave to get out and push it now and then, but it goes all right for a good few miles. They want us to go out together. Tonight. They're outside, waiting for an answer, but Tom wants to have a little chat with you first. Me and Ron'll go for stroll while you get on with it. Well, go on then. Move yerself!'

'You shouldn't have done this, Sally. You shouldn't have brought him round here. It's not clever.'

'Couldn't stop 'im. He'd found out where you lived anyway and you know how he feels about yer. Once I told him you was finished with Max,' she shrugged, 'well, there ain't no keeping him down now. His ol' green eyes lit up, they did.'

'You *shouldn't* have told him. I asked you *not* to! It's none of his business.'

'Oh, shut up and brush yer bloomin' hair. Fink yourself lucky that someone as 'andsome as Tom fancies yer. Mind you, he might not if he sees you looking like this, like something the cat dragged in.'

'Well, we'll see just how much he likes me for myself then, won't we?' Not caring about her long unbrushed hair or pale face with no rouge or lipstick, Jessie strode out of the house, leaving Sally to go inside and drive Rose mad with her incessant chatter.

Striding up to an old black car, Jessie wrenched the door open and sat on the badly worn and cracked leather seat, staring ahead, waiting to hear what Tom had to say for himself. Since Max, she trusted no man to be honest.

'What do you want, Jess?' The voice was familiar, but it wasn't Tom's. It was one of her childhood friends, Freddy Knight. 'I'm just off to pick up me girl,' he said, worried.

What could she say? There were two other motors parked further along the road. She cursed Sally. Why hadn't she described what Tom's car looked like?

'Sorry, Freddy. I've got in the wrong car,' she said. 'What's

he gonna think of me, Freddy? That must be the one, that old thing along the road. Help me out, Freddy. Drive off or something, anything.'

'Don't be silly. Get out now and tell him you needed to have a word with me. Go on, make him jealous – us blokes love it.'

'Do you?' Jessie said. 'Well, us girls don't. I broke up with Max because of something like that.'

'Well, that's a typical woman for you. Jess? You're feeling all right, ain't you?'

'Of course I'm all right, why shouldn't I be?' She didn't move. 'I didn't mean to suggest that *your* car's an old banger, by the way. I just wasn't thinking when I got in.'

'Well, you'd best start now, before he pulls away, before that little bit of jealousy turns into something else. Go on. Don't get in the black car, that belongs to Mr Allen, the credit man. He's paying his weekly visit to Merry Widow Jackson. The next one along's got two blokes in it.'

'That'll be them.'

'Right. Good. So you'll be off then? Only I've got to pick up my bird now.' He looked at his wristwatch. 'I'm already late. We're meant to be going to Epping Forest ... for a picnic.' He grinned, winking at her.

Jessie managed a smile and climbed out.

'Have a good time,' said Freddy.

Waving him off, she saw that he was laughing to himself inside the car. She couldn't blame him, it must have looked funny from where he was sitting.

She walked the few steps to Tom and Ron's car and bent down to speak to Tom through the open window of the back seat. She felt a rush of that old familiar black magic as he looked into her eyes and smiled. 'Sally said you wanted to have a word with me. Well, here I am.'

Tom blew a smoke ring, 'What did you get in that car for?'

'Freddy's a mate, I was passing on a message from another friend,' Jessie lied smoothly. 'Why?'

'Just wondered, that's all.'

Ron was out of the car in a flash. 'I'll, er, I'll take a stroll with Sally and leave the pair of you to it. All right if I knock on your door, Jessie?'

'I suppose so. But don't go in. Mum's not up to it.'

Tom looked at Jessie. 'You gonna get in then or what?'

'No. What do you want?'

Laughing quietly at them, Ron walked away. 'Ten minutes and I'll be back with Sally,' he said.

Tom cleared his throat and Jessie could see she was annoying him.

'What does Hannah think of your car, then?' she asked. 'Or wouldn't your girlfriend be seen dead in it?'

Leaning back and stretching one arm, he groaned deliberately. 'She's not my girlfriend. I like your hair like that, Jessie, it suits you. All free and easy. Pity about your charm though, that seems to have vanished. I remember the first time I saw you, outside Stepney Green station, looking sad. Then there was the dockers' march when you were smiling and lovely. How would your dad feel, I wonder, if he could see you now, acting like this? He'd be gutted, I reckon,' Tom chattered on, 'knowing his accident had changed you. His Jessie, his lovely girl, all nasty and bad-tempered. Now get in the car and do as you're told.' He moved along the seat to make room for her.

'Bloody cheek. Who d'you think you are?' she said pulling at the door and bouncing down onto the badly sprung back seat. She slammed the door shut.

'Jessie, stop play-acting. It's not clever and it don't suit you.'

'I wasn't play-acting,' she said quietly. Any mention of her father still upset her.

'Yes you were. Right,' He drew on his cigarette. 'Let's start again. I'm sorry I let you down that time, all right? I wanted to see you but I couldn't. I just couldn't get there. Don't ask me why.'

'Why?'

'Very funny,' he said, trying not to smile. 'Anyway, we're together now, in this motor and I'll say it just once, and then it's up to you. You can laugh or listen. I've not been able to get you out of my mind. Simple as that. You drive me mad, always there, when I fall asleep and when I wake up. Thank Christ I don't dream or I'd never be free of you. I knew you was getting engaged so I kept away. But once Sally told me it was off, that was it. Now if you're not interested, fair enough, just say the word and you won't hear from me again.'

Jessie looked away from him, out of the window, and went quiet. 'Don't put up much of a fight, do you?'

'I've got my pride. Anyway, I think you feel the same whether you like it or not, but if, for some reason, you want to fight it, I won't stop you. Maybe you don't think I'm good enough to meet the rest of your family. Who knows? With someone like you it could be any daft thing. And you don't have to worry about Hannah being competition, if that's what's on your mind.' He looked straight at her. 'She's a very close friend, right?'

'I'm sure. I thought my last boyfriend was honest, but I found out different.'

He raised an eyebrow. 'So can I take it that you'll go out with me?'

'Hannah could come with us, you must have plenty of friends who would jump at the chance. We could go on a foursome, couldn't we? Or would that be too much for you to bear, seeing her in another bloke's arms?'

Tom pushed his chin forward defiantly and tried to keep calm. Jessie had, after all, been through two losses, her dad and her fiancé. She was bound to be bitter. 'No, he said, thoughtfully. 'It wouldn't work. She's too much like a sister, I'd feel uncomfortable.'

'I bet you would.'

'Best forget it altogether.' He leaned across her, pushed open the door and waited for her to get out.

'Who said I was going?' She raised her eyes and saw the stony expression on his face. She knew she was pushing her luck. 'I'm sorry. You were right. I *was* acting up.'

He pulled the door shut again. 'Why?'

'I don't know. I'm a bit confused and ... I can't be sure about you and Hannah. I don't want to barge in and break something that's good. You do get on really well and I like her a lot. I mean that, I'm not just saying it.'

'I can see that. Would you sooner I went away?'

'No.' She struggled to find the right words but it wasn't easy. 'Look,' she finally said, 'something did happen between us. I don't know if it was the first time we met or on the dockers' march, and I don't want you to think I'm saying this because I'm on the rebound ...'

'Go on.' His voice had changed, he sounded more serious, older.

'Well, I have thought about you, probably more than I should have. When I saw Hannah coming into the hospital when I was visiting you, well, I was jealous. I had no right to be, but I was.'

Tom's face lit up with both relief and joy. 'Jessie, Jessie, Jessie.' He pushed his hand through his fair hair. 'I'm crazy about you! I thought you didn't care.'

'Why else would I have agreed to go out with you in the first place? I was nearly engaged, don't forget. I'm not the sort that two-times. You can imagine how I felt when you didn't turn up.'

'Good. I'm glad you're not a two-timer, because I would hate to share you with anyone.' He gently pulled her close to him. 'I think I love you, Jessie Warner,' he said, crossing a bridge he had not crossed before. He had often said he was in love but had never declared it to the girl in question.

'I don't think I know what love is, Tom.' Jessie's heart was thumping as she spoke.

'I do, now.' He kissed her softly on the lips and very, very

slowly, they moved closer together until his arms were holding her tight and their bodies were touching. Jessie responded in a way she had never responded to Max. This was different. Very different. She felt her body stir, come alive; every part of her seemed to be gently throbbing. Her breathing changed and her heart beat even faster.

Freeing his lips from hers, Tom gazed into her face. 'I'm putting my trust in you ... I hope you don't leave me a broken man.' His voice was deep and husky.

'I won't hurt you, Tom. I'm not a heart-breaker.' There was a slight tremble to her voice which was nothing compared to the way she was trembling inside. 'I don't know what's happening to me,' she said. 'You make me feel different.'

Laughing at her, Tom stroked her face, her beautiful face. 'I don't know when it happened, Jess. Maybe the first time I saw you — who cares? Who cares when it was, how it was, what it was. I've never been this scared before. You frighten the life out of me. I suppose it's happened at last — you've bowled me over.' He narrowed his green eyes and grinned at her. 'You've made me love you.'

'I made *you* love *me*? And what have you done to me? Cast your spell over me, that's what.'

'Maybe. But I'll say this much, I won't hurt you, Jessie. I'll never hurt you. I'm yours for as long as you want me. I don't know how long that'll be, maybe for ever or maybe for a while, until you go off with someone else or back to your boyfriend. You might break my heart but I'm willing to take that risk.'

'You can stop thinking that way. I've never felt like this before. You make me angry, you make me laugh, I like quarrelling with you ...'

'And I want to squeeze you to death,' he said. 'Squeeze the life out of you and keep it for ever.'

Tearing herself away from his embrace, Jessie kissed him on the cheek. 'I'd better go back inside. Sally's waiting and Mum'll be worried.'

'So shall we all meet up tonight then?'

'I don't think I can cope with it, Tom. You, me, Sally and Ron, I've been through a lot during the past couple of weeks. All I want to do is be alone and think about us. I suppose that sounds daft.'

'No. I know what you mean,' he said, taking a very deep breath. 'So, how about if I pick you up tomorrow? We can go for a drive – or we could go dancing. You name it.'

'Let's just wait and see how we feel. Come round tomorrow at seven, then we'll decide.'

'Whatever you say, Jess, whatever you say.'

They sat there for a few moments, neither saying anything, until Jessie broke the silence.

'But how would that look? Sally and Ron are expecting us to go out with them.'

'That was the idea,' he said, 'but actually I don't wanna share you with anyone right now. I wouldn't be able to take my eyes off you – or keep my hands off you, come to that. Go on, out you get. Too much too soon. And don't slam the door, it might fall off.'

Laughing, she got out and walked slowly away, knowing his eyes were on her and loving every second. *Now* she knew. Now she knew what love was.

'Is he your new boyfriend then?' She could hear Stephen's small voice but she was on another planet. 'I liked Max. He never 'ad a car but he brought us sweets and played cards with us. You never gonna go out with 'im again then? Jessie? *Jessie!*'

His penetrating voice brought her back to earth. Stephen was sitting on the front step, cupping his chin with both hands. 'Max is all right, Stephen,' she said. 'We'll still see him, he's a family friend, he's bound to come and visit ... and play cards.'

'But you won't kiss 'im on the doorstep no more?'

'No, I won't kiss him on the doorstep no more. Me and Max'll always be friends though, I hope. You know what I reckon? I reckon he's found something out. He kissed another

girl and he found something out.' She was thinking about herself and Tom and what they had just discovered.

'So he won't be sad then?'

'No, he won't be sad.'

'What did he find out?'

'That even though he liked me a lot, I wasn't the right one for him.'

'And that man in the car. Is he the right one for you?' Stephen looked sideways at Jessie. 'You gonna marry 'im?'

Laughing, she put her arm around his shoulders. 'I don't know. We'll just have to wait and see, won't we? Now then, how about you running down to Riley's and buying some twisted cough candy for all of us?'

'I've gone off it. What about if we wait for the toffee apple man? He'll be round soon.'

'All right, but how about if you nip down to Riley's first and get me tuppenny worth of snowfruits.'

'Don't mind.'

'Well, go on then. Take a shilling out of my purse. It's in my handbag on my bed, and don't go pinching any of my sweets before you get back with them.'

'Course not,' he said, rushing into the house. When he got to the stairs, he turned round. 'Can I 'ave a ride in his car one day?'

'We'll 'ave to wait and see. See how well you do at school now that you've been moved down the front of the classroom. See if it really was poor eyesight or laziness that got you bad marks.'

'It was! I do try hard!'

It would have been nice if she could have believed him, but quietly, in her own way, Jessie had been testing Stephen, without him knowing. From what she could tell, there wasn't much wrong with his eyesight. Her brother had a way of winding people round his little finger to get what he wanted. But then no one was perfect.

Catching sight of her reflection in the oval mirror in the

hall, Jessie could see that Sally had a point; she looked terrible, her hair was too long and straggly and it was out of style. She placed her hands on either side of her face to see what she might look like with short hair. She liked what she imagined, and she knew exactly where her mother's sharp scissors were.

Wasting no time, Jessie went into the sitting room and to Rose's sewing box. Lifting the heavy steel scissors, she hid them between the folds of her cotton skirt and went to her room, closing the door behind her and wedging a chair under the handle, in case she was disturbed.

Holding the scissors just above her shoulders, she cut a straight line. As the thick chunk of wavy blonde hair slid down her front to the floor, she suddenly had second thoughts. She had had long hair since she was a small child. But it was too late for regrets, and she had to work quickly, before Dolly demanded to be let in.

Using her hand mirror to cut round the back, she concentrated and kept a keen eye as she snipped away, first one side and towards the back, and then the other. The crunching sound as the blades cut through her hair gave her goosebumps. What would Rose say? Facing front again she was mortified to see that one side was much shorter than the other. She carefully snipped the longer side but still it wasn't even. She snipped again. Now it was shorter than the other side. Panic set in.

She threw the scissors onto the bed, kicked all her thick hair underneath it, cleaned up the dressing table and put on her hat. She pulled the rim down as far as it would go.

She crept down the stairs and managed to get out of the house without being seen or heard and she walked very quickly, her head down, hiding her face until she arrived at the local salon. She looked furtively through the window. The hairdressers were all busy cutting or setting, and two more customers were waiting for curlers to be taken out.

Leaning on the wall between the salon and barber shop, she wished away the past hour. What had she been been thinking?

If only she hadn't picked up those scissors! How could she go on her first date with Tom the next day looking as if rats had been at her hair?

She covered her face with her hands as she felt tears sting her eyes.

'The hat pulled down is a dead give-away, young Jessie.' It was Maurice Simons, the barber.

'I cut my own hair,' she said tearfully. 'It's a mess.'

'You're not the first. Come on in. I'll call my wife down and she'll take you upstairs to our flat. Give me fifteen minutes and I'll come up. I'll give you a short back and sides,' he joked.

'Oh, Maurice, if you could get one of the hairdressers to—'

'You should be so lucky. On a Saturday she wants a hairdo on demand. Today you will have to settle for me.'

'But you're a barber, you cut men's hair and you use a razor. I don't want short back and sides, Maurice.' She shuddered at the thought of it.

'Come with me. Upstairs – before you draw a bloody crowd.'

Ignoring the cheeky asides from the male customers in his shop, Jessie followed Maurice through a small doorway and upstairs. 'I only meant to give it a trim,' she said.

'Sarah!' Maurice called to his wife who was in the kitchen preparing the evening meal. 'You remember when our Ruth got hold of my scissors?'

'Could I ever forget!' she yelled back. 'Why aren't you cutting hair? It's a holiday all of a sudden?'

'We have a private customer!' Flapping a hand and rolling his eyes, Maurice took off Jessie's hat. 'Well, at least you haven't shorn the lot. With this I can do something. Come and see, Sarah.'

'My God. What have you done?' Sarah stood in the entrance to their flat, a hand over her mouth. 'Does your mother know about this, Jessie?'

'Leave her alone, woman. Hasn't she got enough to worry about? Of course her mother doesn't know. Rose would go potty.'

'I was trying to give myself a new look.'

-'Sit her in front of the mirror, Maurie. I'll fetch your scissors and a towel.' She went back into the kitchen, smiling to herself.

'So, madam,' he said, sitting her down and speaking to her reflection in the mirror, 'you want the new style, yes?'

She nodded and managed a faint smile. 'I'm not sure about a fringe though.'

He pushed his fingers through her hair and tousled it. 'No. Your face wouldn't suit a fringe. I think you should keep the side parting.'

'Oh, I thought the new style needed a middle parting.' She was disappointed and a touch worried. He was a barber, after all, and in his sixties. What could he know about the latest trends?

'*You* thought. Which one of us is the stylist here? I'll show you something.' He drew a comb through her hair to produce a straight right-sided parting, then combed it again to show a left-sided parting. 'As a matter of fact it would look wonderful with a left parting but then you'll say that's the boys' side, correct?'

Jessie nodded, her worry deepening.

'But you can see how the left suits you?'

She nodded again, half-heartedly.

'But you won't break the rules. What do you think, Sarah?' he said, taking the towel from her.

'For once in your life, you're right. Let him do what he wants, Jessie. You'll get the best cut and you'll start a a new rage. But I think you should have a fringe.'

'Why? Why should she be like everyone else? Look.' He combed Jessie's hair back and pushed it to the side. 'That doesn't suit her?'

'It'll fall across her eyes ...'

'Do me a favour, woman, go away.' He flicked his fingers at her. 'Go cook the supper. You think I would give her a cut that would fall where it shouldn't? She's got good, thick, strong hair. It's a joy to work with. I've never come across natural blonde hair like this before, it's normally so fine you can't do a thing with it.'

'I suppose you could be right,' said Sarah, 'but then Jessie's got such a lovely face you couldn't go far wrong.'

'I never go anywhere wrong, thank you very much. Go away.'

Sarah threw up her hands and smiled at Jessie's reflection. 'He asks my advice, I give it, he takes no notice. Why ask in the first place?'

'I'm going to give her a fringe! I'm taking your advice! But it will be a long fringe, one she can brush away from her face, not one that sits there looking like a bloody pelmet!'

'Which is what I said in the first place!' she called, going back to the kitchen.

Maurice smiled at Jessie in the mirror. 'See what I mean? She wins whatever. Now then, I'm going to dampen it, then cut it, then wash it; finish off with the scissors, a little snip here and there, then almost dry it, and then use the curling tongs on the ends. What I would like you to do is put a smile on that face because you are going to walk out of here looking like a million dollars, a model out of one of those women's journals you young girls waste your money on.'

Jessie wasn't convinced but was relieved to be hidden away and in safe hands. 'Wake me up when it's over,' she said wryly.

'Tch. Anyone would think I was a surgeon.' He continued to talk while he dampened, combed and considered. Once he began to cut, not another word escaped his lips and Jessie kept her eyes closed throughout, too frightened to watch as her hair got shorter and shorter.

'OK, young lady,' he said at last, 'but before you examine this work of art, remember, it's still damp, it hasn't been washed or tonged.'

'I know,' she said. She opened her eyes and stared at the reflection of someone she hardly recognised. Her face broke into a broad smile, showing her lovely straight white teeth. It was a perfect cut and style, level with her chin. She gazed at her new self, speechless.

'Well?' There was laughter in the old man's voice.

'I love it. I love it, Maurice, you're a genius. A real genius.'

'I know.' He winked at her, pleased as punch. 'You wait until we've finished with you. Every head will turn as you walk along the street.' He called loudly to his wife, his face filled with pride. 'Sarah! Come and show Jessie to the bathroom, she can wash her own bloody hair.' Proud of his good deed, he went down to the barber shop.

Ten minutes later he was back. The last of his customers had gone and he had closed the shop. He put the finishing touches to Jessie's hair and then admired his work over a cup of tea with her and his wife. Thanking both him and Sarah, Jessie eventually got up to leave. As they took her through to the front of the shop, she asked for the fourth time if she could pay for the cut and style, but they wouldn't hear of it. 'I loved doing it,' said Maurice, 'and I owed your father a favour – he did one for me once. Besides, when they see you, maybe the ladies will be queuing up outside my door instead of the hairdressers'.'

'You steal my customers and I'll divorce you,' said Sarah in her droll way.

'Mum will love it and I expect Dolly'll be down first thing, sitting in one of those barber chairs. I wouldn't be surprised if the girls at work . . .' Her words trailed off as she followed Sarah and Maurice's gaze. They were staring at their shop window, their faces twisted with torment. Painted across their window, in large white letters, were just two words: JEWS! YIDS!

Sickened by it, Jessie felt ashamed. There was nothing she

could say or do to help. She left them to scrub away the abuse themselves, which is what they wanted. Each of them had been living in the East End since they were very small children, immigrants from Poland, and each of them, like a thousand or so others, considered England to be their home.

Jessie was scared to think what might follow now their shop had been marked. Her thoughts turned to Alfie and she prayed that he would be at home when she got there, that he had had nothing to do with it.

'Blimey!' Alfie was the first to react when Jessie walked in with her new hairstyle. 'You look like someone else, Jess!'

Jessie had never been so pleased to see him. He obviously hadn't just come in, he looked as if he'd been there, reading his comics, since when she went out.

'Oh. Thanks very much, Jessie!' said Dolly. 'I was gonna get mine done like that next week. Now everyone'll say I've copied you. Well, they can say it. I'm still getting mine cut in that style.' She went back to her paperback.

Stephen said nothing. He just sat there gazing at Jessie, wide-eyed.

'Do you like it, Mum?'

'I do, Jessie, I do like it . . . but it's a bit of a shock. Whatever made you decide to do it?'

'I don't know. You'll never guess who cut it.'

Rose stood up and circled her. 'It's a very good cut. Wherever did you go? Not up to the West End, I hope. That would have cost a week's pay.'

'No, Mum, not up to the West End. Down the road, to Maurie Simons.'

'Maurie Simons? The barber? You went to a men's barber shop? Well, I never did, what a dark horse that man is. I hope you thanked him, Jessie.'

'Of course I thanked him.' Jessie didn't mention what had happened afterwards because her mother was smiling for a change.

'You wanted to make yourself look nice for this new boyfriend, I suppose. The one Sally brought round here. Tom, wasn't it? The one you told Dad about a while ago.'

'Yeah, Tom,' she said, with stars in her eyes. 'Tom Smith.'

'It's a bit soon after Max,' Rose said cautiously. How on earth was she going to keep Jessie from meeting Hannah if Tom really was the new love of Jessie's life? 'Be careful, Jessie. People do strange things on the rebound.'

Jessie didn't want to get into an argument but she did want her mum to accept Tom. 'It's not on the rebound,' she said, calmly but firmly. 'To tell you the truth, I was smitten by him right from the beginning.'

'Out of the frying pan and into the fire, if you ask me,' said Dolly, green with envy, having seen Tom on her way home from shopping for a new pair of shoes. 'Still, we can't tell you anything, Jessie, can we? You always know best. So where does he live then, this Tom?'

'Mind your own business,' said Jessie lightly. 'I don't want you pinching him off me, do I?' The truth was, Jessie had no idea where he lived and didn't think her mother would be too pleased about that. Little did she know that her mother could have told her where he lived.

Rose kept her knowledge to herself. She would have to warn Emmie to keep quiet too. Rose sighed. She was beginning to see that creating new secrets as well as keeping old ones was dangerous.

Chapter Eight

'That was a lovely dinner, Emmie girl, smashing,' said Charlie, giving his wife one of his special winks. The old saying was certainly true where he was concerned – the way to a man's heart is through his stomach.

'I'm off out.' Johnnie, their eldest, looked across the dinner table at Tom. 'Fancy a pint?'

'Might do. I've just got to pop round and see Jessie first. Where you drinking?'

'Blind Beggar, but I won't bother to look out for you. If you're meeting this incredible Jessie of yours, we won't be seeing you.'

'Yes you will. I won't be there more than half an hour so if you go on from the pub, don't forget to leave a message behind the bar.'

'Will do. Don't wait up, Mum.'

Emmie snorted. 'As if I would. Keep your voice down and take your shoes off when you get in. Some of us need eight hours' sleep.'

'I'll tiptoe, promise.' Johnnie turned back to Tom. 'Why don't you bring Jessie along? You've been courting the girl for a good while now. Time we had a look at the goods.'

'All in good time, Johnnie boy, all in good time. She's the right one so you'll be seeing plenty of her in the future.' Tom grinned.

'Oh yeah. Like all the others that got the elbow – or gave you the boot. Do you know what I reckon, Dad?' said Johnnie, in a baiting mood.

'Go on, what?' Charlie liked joining in his sons' banter.

'I reckon he's frightened that me or Stanley'll pinch this one from him, so she must be a looker, eh?'

Laughing, Charlie waved him off. 'Tormenting fucker,' he said. 'Go on out. Pity Tom don't take a leaf out of your book, son. Don't love 'em – just leave 'em.'

'Too right, Dad, too bleeding right,' said Johnnie, laughing. 'I've got a million to make before I settle down. Ain't that right, Mum?'

'That's right, son, yeah. A million for you and a million for me and one for the pot.'

'You wait and see. I'm the only one in this room with a bank account, so what does that tell you?'

'That you're tight,' said Charlie, 'and stashing it all away. Come the war and you'll be lucky to see any of it. They'll bomb your bank first off. Spend it while you can, son, preferably on me.'

Tom looked thoughtful. 'So the football coupons are working out then?'

'Yep. I told you it would work, but oh no, you didn't wanna come in with me. I've got a few hundred in the bank which is better than being a hundred in debt, which is what I was eighteen months ago. But the bank manager had faith; yep, a stranger had faith in me. What with that little sideline and my regular job with all that lovely overtime—'

'Oh, sod off out,' said Charlie, used to his son going on about money. 'Just don't give up your proper job, that's all. At least that's reliable money.'

'I won't, Dad, don't you worry. If there's an hour to work, I'll work it. See you.' With that, Johnnie was gone.

'Mind you, he has got a point,' said Charlie, leaning back and looking at Tom. 'Money grows more money. What's with

the black shirt then? New fashion, is it, or did your pet flea die?'

'Go to bed, Charlie,' said Emmie, 'or you'll be in a right mood first thing and blaming us for keeping you up.'

Standing up, Charlie made a business of having a good stretch. 'I was up at half past three this morning. Blooming fruit comes in from the farms earlier and earlier. Blackberries tomorrow, Em. That should please you, eh?'

Once Emmie and Tom were alone, she nodded at Tom's shirt and said, 'I hope you're not wearing that for the reason I think you're wearing it.'

'I'm going to the club, Mum, and that's all there is to it.'

'So you're not seeing Jessie then?'

'Yes I am. Before I meet up with Johnnie for a pint.'

'You're a bloody fool, getting involved with that lot. I knew this was coming. You've been thinking about joining for a long time, I know. Getting a hiding was just the excuse you'd been waiting for.'

Tom gave up the pretence. 'Dead right. I've been thinking about it long enough, now I'm doing it. They're not *all* bully boys. It's just a handful of spivs that 'ave wormed their way in, a small faction, not interested in politics. You'll always get that. We can wipe them out.'

'I won't be able to look some of my neighbours in the face if it gets out. You needn't have bought that shirt, they don't all walk around like that.'

'Course they don't. This style of shirt, in black, is all the rage. Besides, I never bought it, Johnnie gave it to me. Stop worrying. We're not all thugs. You'll be surprised to know that a lot of police officers are Blackshirts on the quiet. A hell of a lot.'

'Never! As if they'd have anything to do with it.' Emmie refused to consider it.

'It's got nothing to do with law and order, that's the point. It's politics.'

'Tell that to Hitler.'

'We're not talking about Hitler. We're not copying Germany or Italy. We just want what's best for our country. If things go on the way they are, by the time we reach the end of this century, England'll be bursting at the seams. There won't be enough houses or jobs for a quarter of the population by then unless it's controlled now. If we don't make noises now, Europe'll suck us in and you can forget what England stood for. What Britain stands for.'

'Yeah, and if we're daft enough to be taken in by Mosley, Hitler'll suck us in,' said Emmie.

'Forget Hitler', Tom said firmly. 'We'll blow him to bits in the next war – with Mosley leading the way.'

'I think you're getting your facts a bit mixed up, son. The papers say that Mosley doesn't want another war against Germany.'

'Maybe not but that's not to say he'll sit back if we're a target. I told you, he's for England, and we'll fight to keep this country the way it is, war or no war.'

'Well, it's all a bit much for me to fathom. How you know so much about it beats me. I think you've been a bit of a dark horse on the quiet. I shouldn't let your brothers hear you talk like this.'

'You'd be surprised. Ask Johnnie what he thinks about it. He's the clever one, after all, the one who's gonna be top dog living in a bloody mansion.'

'Johnnie? What's he got to do with this?'

'Take a look in his trunk. I did. He's never pushed his views but when I found out, 'cos I was nosy, he explained one or two things to me. You don't really think he's gonna spend the evening in a pub, do you? Johnnie? He's as tight as a bank manager. There's no bar in the social club that we're going to. Cups of tea only. Free cups of tea.' Smiling, Tom picked up his tobacco tin and left.

As Tom's words sunk in, Emmie could see how it all fitted. Johnnie had always been the secretive one, never too open about

his comings and goings. She had to face the fact that she'd been living in a world of her own. She wondered about her other son Stanley. But Stanley was only just sixteen, and mad on girls and dancing. He wouldn't waste his time on such things. Not Stanley.

Blackshirts. Two of her sons were Blackshirts. She should have felt angry, or at the least very disappointed with the pair of them, but she didn't. Loath though she was to admit it, secretly Emmie felt quite proud of her boys, of their patriotism, and she imagined that Tom was probably right, it was only a handful who were anti-Semitic and uninterested in politics. She wondered about her husband, Charlie. Did he know what Johnnie and Tom had got themselves into?

When she had cleared the kitchen, Emmie went into the best room and put up her feet. Her sons were old enough to know what they were doing and by the sound of it Tom wasn't joining the Blackshirts because he wanted to see the Jews leave this country but because he didn't want to see millions more foreigners coming in. No doubt Johnnie was of the same mind. She couldn't argue with that, not really.

She picked up her knitting. She was making a pullover for Charlie's next birthday; it was a very tricky Fair Isle pattern with six colours, no easy task. When the door knocker sounded she cursed. She wasn't expecting anyone and all the men were out except for Charlie, who was in bed, snoring.

She was more than surprised to see Rose on her doorstep. 'Hello, Emmie. I'm taking a bit of your advice and getting out while the evenings are still nice. So I thought I'd pop round for a visit. I'm not disturbing you, am I?'

Emmie thought that her friend's little speech had been rehearsed and her heart went out to her. Rose was probably feeling the loneliness of widowhood. 'Course you're not disturbing me. It's lovely to see you. Charlie's in bed and the boys are out so I'm by myself.'

Rose didn't stop talking as she followed Emmie into the

living room, which was unusual for her. Emmie was only half listening at first, her mind on her knitting which she would have to put away, but not before marking which row and colour she was on. When Rose mentioned Ingrid, Emmie drew breath.

'I couldn't believe my ears, Emmie, when my mother mentioned your name ...'

'Sit down, Rose, and I'll pour us both a drop of sherry. I've still got some left over from Christmas.'

'When my mother said you had been seeing her all these years, I was shocked. You never said a word about it, I felt as if I'd had my head in sand all this time.'

'I know what you mean, Rose, I've had my fair share of such feelings of late. Not very nice, I grant you.'

'Why didn't you write and tell me you'd seen her, Emmie? Why did you let me believe that my mother was dead? You'll never know the shock I had when she arrived out of the blue.'

'For a start, Rose, I was sworn to secrecy – once again. Secondly, you never believed she was dead and you know that's the truth. You might have thought she'd gone back to Germany, and I could see nothing wrong with you believing that. Had you ever shown the slightest interest in your mother, I would 'ave been in like a shot. To tell you the truth, I'm glad it's all come out.' Emmie handed Rose a glass of sherry and drank hers down in one before refilling her glass.

'She said you'd met up in Wickham's,' Rose murmured.

'That's right.' Emmie sank into her old feather-cushioned armchair. 'She came in after a hat – way back, when I was working in millinery. It was lovely to see her again. She asked me to not mention it. She spotted you once, you know, along Whitechapel, but ducked into a side street.'

'How could she recognise me after all this time, Emmie? That really is too much to believe.' Rose shook her head.

'I showed her photographs of us taken after the war,' Emmie admitted.

Rose laughed bitterly. 'Well, well. Whatever will you tell

me next? My mother knows all there is to know about me and my family while I knew nothing about her life.'

'No, and whose fault's that? Besides, there was nothing much to tell. Ingrid wanted to know how you'd fared and I told her. She invited me over to her little basement flat for coffee and I went. I love Victoria Park, you know I do. You remember us, years ago, on the boating lake? We used to shriek with laughter.'

Rose nodded. 'Of course I remember it. They were happier times.'

'Anyway, once we'd met again we kept it up, seeing each other every month or so and that way she got to hear about Hannah. I shouldn't have told her about the twins but I did, and only because she asked and I was trying to get her to go and see you. I do believe she's blamed herself all these years. In fact, I know she has. She thought that because she'd given you away, you'd done the same – history repeating itself. Silly woman. I thought it was a load of bunkum but I never said so. It wasn't my place to pass judgement, one way or the other.' Emmie looked at her friend. 'So there you have it, Rose. No more, no less. I bumped into an old family friend one day and we kept in touch.'

'But there's something else I've got to worry about isn't there?' Rose pointed out. 'Jessie and Tom. I did think you were going to have a word with your son. I would have come round sooner to broach you on the subject but I thought it had fizzled out. It seems to be going from strength to strength now.'

Emmie held up a hand. 'I did have a word when you first asked me to, Rose. And he listened. In fact, he stood Jessie up on that first date, you may remember. But once she split up with that Max feller, there was no stopping Tom – or Jessie, if you ask me.' She paused and then went on, 'And I'm afraid the girls have met up too, which was no fault of Tom's. He was out walking with Hannah and they bumped into Jessie. Apparently the girls got on like a house on fire – which is to be expected,

in my opinion. It happened some time ago.' Emmie's expression was sympathetic as she looked at her friend's stricken face. 'I did think about coming to see you about it, but what was the point? They'd met, and that was that. I do believe they've become friends. I believe it might be for the best.'

Rose's knuckles were white. 'Have they now? Well, things seem to be going from bad to worse, Emmie, and your son, Tom, always at the centre of it.'

'I'll pretend I didn't hear that, Rose.'

'Knowing how delicate the situation is, I would have thought he'd have kept away. There are plenty more fish in the sea for the young men round these parts.'

With a smile on her face, Emmie leaned forward and patted her friend's hand. 'It's about time, Rose Warner. You've been bottling your anger for too long. Maybe you should go straight round to see Gerta now – while you're fired up?'

'I had every intention of doing so . . . but I came here instead. I can't face the woman, Emmie. I've news over the compensation claim but if I go round there – I might just slap her face. That face. I can still see her expression at the funeral even after all these months. She was gloating, I'm sure of it.'

'Well then, write to her instead. I take it you've something to tell her that she'll be pleased about?'

'Yes and no. Hannah will have a fair share but it's to go in a trust where Gerta won't be able to get her hands on the funds. It will go to Hannah when she's twenty-one, which is when I shall see her and when she'll learn the truth.'

Resting back in her armchair, Emmie was pleased. 'You've done well, Rose. That's the best news I've heard in a long time.'

'I've an excellent solicitor, I will say that. But yes, I have had to think on my feet over this. I dare say Hannah could do with the money.'

'Dead right. She's still looking for a flat but I'm afraid they don't come cheap. She doesn't earn that much at the

library. It would be lovely if she didn't have to wait that long—'

Rose raised a hand. 'Enough said, Emmie. She'll *have* to wait. Of course if Gerta gets nasty over it, then things will be forced out into the open before then. I pray to God that isn't the case. I'm in no fit state to fight her or to face Jessie or Hannah should it all come out sooner than I would like. Now let's leave it there, shall we?' There was a no-nonsense tone in her voice.

Rubbing her eyes, Emmie yawned. 'Whatever you say, Rose. Whatever you say.'

'And you will have a word with Tom? I feel certain that if he were to stay away from Jessie, she and Max would get back together again, which would simplify things.'

Ignoring that, Emmie turned the conversation to Ingrid. 'I'm pleased you and your mother have got together at last. It's a pity it's taken so long. Too many wasted years, eh?'

Rose knew exactly what her friend was implying. 'Oh, I don't know so much. What you don't have you don't miss.'

'If you say so, Rose,' smiled Emmie, 'if you say so ...'

When Rose arrived home, she went into the kitchen where she found Jessie by herself, drinking a glass of freshly pressed lemon and water.

'I can hear those boys aren't asleep yet. I don't know where they get their energy from,' said Rose, taking off her light blue straw hat. 'I suppose Dolly's out dancing again.'

'No. But she's getting ready to go out,' said Jessie.

'Is she now?' Rose glanced at the clock. 'Not at this hour she's not. It's gone nine. I'll have to have a word with her. She goes too far.'

Jessie was only half listening. She was feeling nauseous. She prayed the lemon drink would make it pass before Rose noticed. Jessie's worst fear had been realised; she was pregnant. Pregnant with Tom's baby. She hadn't told him yet; she hadn't had the courage. He seemed preoccupied lately. Jessie had a strong

feeling that he had joined the Blackshirts but she couldn't think about that, she had far more important things to worry about.

The lemon drink wasn't working. Rose was going on about Dolly. Her voice sounded distorted to Jessie, as if it was coming from miles away. She recognised the sensation; it was similar to when she had passed out at work, the day after the accident at the docks. She wrapped her arms round herself. *Not now, Jessie, not now!*

'What's the matter, Jess?' said Rose suddenly. 'You've gone a terrible colour.' She placed an arm round her daughter and studied her pale face. 'What is it? Are you in pain?'

'Stars . . .' murmured Jessie weakly. She heard Rose call her name and the next thing she knew she was on the floor, her head between her knees, being propped up by Dolly.

'The . . . floor . . . hit . . . me . . . in . . . the . . . face.' She barely managed to get the words out. 'It came up . . . and hit me in the face.' Rose told her to save her strength, not to say another word, as she patted Jessie's sweat-beaded face with a wet sponge.

'She's as white as a ghost, Mum,' murmured Dolly. 'Should I run for the doctor?'

'I'm all right, Dolly,' said Jessie, recovering. 'I drank some milk earlier, the remains of the bottle, and I think it had curdled.'

Rose stroked away damp strands of hair from Jessie's face. 'Help me get your sister upstairs and into her bed, Dolly. It won't hurt you to stay with her and have an early night, you've been clocking in at work late far too many times recently.'

'I'm all right, Mum,' said Jessie, taking deep breaths of air. 'Honestly, I can manage. Let Dolly go out.' Her legs felt like jelly, but if she had to she would drag herself up those stairs.

'I'd rather not be clocking in at all,' Dolly said, helping Rose ease her sister up from the floor. 'The rest room reeks of old ashtrays.'

'Well, that's your own fault. If you'd stuck it out at the handbag factory until they put you on satin evening bags, which

you would have loved, you wouldn't be working at the toy factory, would you? You would have been very good at sewing the satin handbags and it's good wages, piecework.'

'I'm leaving the factory soon anyway.' Dolly put her weight under Jessie's arm as they helped her up the stairs. 'I might apply for a position at the Bethnal Green Museum if it's not too boring.'

'Work is work, young lady, not a daily outing to find amusement.'

Once Jessie was in her bed, Rose folded and tucked in the sheet and then felt Jessie's forehead for a temperature, and stroked her hair, telling her she would be fine by the morning. Jessie felt as if she was a small child again, being watched over and cared for.

'I'll come up later to see how you are, Jessie,' said Rose. 'Try and get some sleep.'

Try and get some sleep? It was a job trying to stay awake. She heard the bedroom door close behind Rose and Dolly before she drifted into sleep. Tom appeared in her dreams; he was standing tall, smart and handsome at the altar, waiting for her. She was wearing a beautiful trailing satin dress and long veil, with Dolly and Sally as her bridesmaids, dressed in blue. Everyone was smiling as she walked along the aisle, holding her dad's arm. Her grandfather was there too. Happy and smiling, gliding along to the sound of the organ, Jessie glanced at Rose in the front row. There was a look of horror on her face; she was staring at her daughter's stomach, which was growing by the second, bigger and bigger, and she was screaming, telling everyone to keep away from her.

'Jess! Wake up! *Jessie!*'

'It's all right, Dolly,' Jessie murmured, half asleep. 'It was only a nightmare. Where's your bouquet?' Then she sank into a deep sleep.

The following weeks weren't easy for Jessie as she tried to hide

her condition, but at least their lavatory was outside in the back garden, away from everyone. She could be sick without being heard. She still hadn't told Tom she was pregnant. She was afraid that the burden and responsibility of a baby would be too much for his free spirit. She couldn't face seeing his reaction, not yet.

Her mother would be furious, of that she had no doubt, furious and ashamed. And then there was the rest of the family, her aunts and uncles and, worst of all, Grandmother Blake. Jessie pictured her on hearing the news, a telling look on her face and that knowing smile. The neighbours would talk, and Emmie, Tom's mother, would likely think her a tramp. She and Tom had, after all, only been courting for a few months.

She had tried telling Sally on one occasion, leading up to break the news by saying that she couldn't describe the love she felt for Tom, but Sally had been in one of her frivolous moods and had ruined it by laughing at her. 'One word'll cover it, Jess. Fancy. You fancy Tom and he fancies you,' she said, 'just like me and Ron.'

So Jessie had decided to keep the secret to herself for as long as possible. Once it was out in the open, everyone would start making plans, plans that hundreds of other women who had conceived out of wedlock had made, and she didn't want that yet. She had feigned a period and would go on doing so until she could no longer hide her secret. She was eating good nutritious food but no bread or sweet pudding. She had just eaten an egg salad for lunch. She had to be healthy for the baby but she couldn't afford to put on weight too fast.

'You need fat on your bones, Jessie,' said Rose, before leaving the house to go shopping. 'It's bad enough when people are ill and lose weight through no fault of their own, without you going on a diet for the sake of vanity.' With that, she picked up her shopping bag and left the house.

Jessie asked Dolly why she hadn't gone into the factory that day. She usually worked Saturdays.

Ignoring the question, Dolly kept her back to Jessie – she was washing a blouse in the butler sink. 'You wouldn't think it, would you,' she said, 'but back in Saxon times they ate really well, beef, mutton, chicken and goose, and they ate oysters like they was peanuts. There's a girl who works in the office at the factory who's as skinny as a rake, all she ever eats is—'

'I'm not on a diet for my looks!' Jessie cut in. 'I'm just trying to stay healthy, that's all. One of the girls at work has studied nutrition and she says that we eat far too much fat – butter, lard and cheese. And it's not good for the heart ... or the blood.'

Dolly found this amusing. 'See if you say that when it's Sunday with roast beef and batter pudding for dinner, with apple pie and custard for afters.'

'You shouldn't just take a day off when you fancy,' Jessie continued, determined to get her sister's mind off food. 'You'll get the sack if—'

'I'm gonna give it up.' She gripped the sodden blouse with both hands and twisted it until she had squeezed most of the water out before she put it through the mangle. 'There's no jobs at the Bethnal Green Museum for the likes of me so I might try for a job in one of them Marks and Spencer branches that 'ave opened up.'

'You go from one job to another and if you're—'

'So?' interrupted Dolly sharply. 'What's wrong with that? Better than sticking in one boring job for nearly three years. I don't know how you can bear it, no wonder Max dumped you. Three years with having to listen to you go on about the same old people at work.'

'Max didn't dump me. Anyway, I've got Tom now and I wouldn't have him if I was still with Max.'

'Probably not, knowing you. Can't have *two* boyfriends – oh no! You're so bloody prim and proper. You want to break out of it.' Dolly twisted the mangle forcefully.

Jessie couldn't help smiling. Prim and proper. She was hardly that. If only she could have told Dolly there and then that she was

pregnant, it would have given her the shock of her life. 'So why're you thinking of leaving? I thought you didn't mind the work?'

'It's all right,' said Dolly, 'but the women are boring, except for Cook in the canteen. I love Cook, she looks after me, piles up my plate when no one's looking. I sneak off the factory floor sometimes and go and give her a hand. She has to make up the fire in the snug where Management have their coffee, bloody cheek. They take right liberties there.'

Jessie was surprised at the way Dolly was opening up. She hardly ever talked about work, only boys. 'She'll miss you if you leave then, won't she?'

Dolly threw her blouse over the airing rack and scowled. 'That bossy cow ...'

'Who?'

'The secretary. The chairman's secretary. I was stoking the fire yesterday afternoon to give Cook a five-minute sit-down and I was making the flames burn just right when she came in and shouted at me, asked what I was doing in there and not at my work bench. Smug cow. It's all her fault.'

'*What* is?' asked Jessie. Dolly seemed close to tears. 'What happened?'

'I laid the poker down for a second to try and make up an excuse why I was in there, one flipping second ... She saw the smoke and smelt the singeing before I did.'

'It burnt the carpet?'

'Course it did. I was looking at her! Trying to look sorry while she barked at me. She saw the smoke and that was that, said it would cost me my job and it did, she saw to that. I wasn't even rude to 'er and only called her a bleeding cow once I knew I was out.'

'There'll be other jobs, other nice people to work with,' Jessie said sympathetically.

'I'm not bothered. I might learn shorthand and typing, keep Mum happy. Sitting in a warm comfortable office all day doing bugger all can't be bad.'

'Don't you believe it. I'll never forget when I first started work in that typing pool at the London Electric. The manageress used to walk up and down the aisles, keeping an eye on every one of us girls as we sat there typing. She made sure we were typing all the time. We weren't allowed to talk except at tea break, in the canteen. Fifteen minutes we got, and it took half that time to get there and back. By the time we got our cup of tea we had to swallow it down. You wouldn't put up with something like that, Dolly.'

'At least you've got a career. You could get a job anywhere now, in any office. Whereas I can only work in a factory, below stairs or in a tea shop. What kind of a career's that?'

Jess was surprised by Dolly's change of attitude; up until now she'd been adamant that she would never work in a stuffy office. 'A career's not everything,' she said. 'You'll be married by the time you're twenty, I bet. Married with babies. You're pretty enough.'

'I might even go abroad to find work,' said Dolly dreamily. 'America. Don't imagine that all I want is the butler sink and boiler. If that sort of life's not for you why should it be the life for me?'

'Maybe it is for me. A little one up, one down ... a small fire burning ... dinner in the oven for when my man comes home ...' It was Jessie's turn to sound dreamy now.

'Oh yeah? And what's come over you? What's changed *your* mind? The handsome Tom? He's done this to you, has he? Made you go all soppy?'

'Maybe. It was different with Max. I did sort of think about a future with him, but it was Max who brought up the subject of marriage – and Moira who smashed it down.' She smiled to herself, pleased now that Moira had stepped in. 'I'd marry Tom tomorrow if he asked me.'

'What're his brothers like?'

'I haven't met them yet. Why?' Jessie knew why she was asking. She was hoping there might be another at home like

Tom. Dolly always opened the door when she knew Tom was coming round and would chat to him while Jessie collected her things.

'Just wondered,' said Dolly. 'So, you haven't been invited round his house and Mum's not asked you to fetch Tom in yet even though you've been courting for months now. Max was in for a cup of tea on your first date.'

Dolly had touched a raw spot. It was true, Rose hadn't shown any interest in meeting Tom and whenever Jessie mentioned him she went quiet.

'Don't forget that Max's parents own the shop next door to ours,' Jessie said. 'Mum already knew Max. She's known the family for years.'

'What about Tom's then? I bet you don't even know what his address is.'

'Of course I do.'

'Well then, why don't we pop round there and see them? It's Saturday and I'm skint. I can't go out shopping, not even for a new lipstick. We could go for a stroll, pop in to see Tom.'

'I suppose we could.' Jessie cleared the table of cups and saucers. 'It's a lovely day. The boys won't be back from the boxing club for a few hours yet.'

'Our Stephen,' laughed Dolly, 'in a boxing ring, all white and skinny with gloves bigger than his own 'ead.'

'Don't be daft, Stephen never goes into the ring. He likes to watch Alfie winning his rounds. It's better than sitting at home doing nothing.' Jessie examined her face and hair in the mirror. Since she'd had her hair cut, it always looked good, even if she said so herself. Tom had been strange about it at first, sulking because he liked long hair, but he soon came round, admitting in the end that her chic new style suited her face. Lovely was the word he used, eventually.

'Come on then,' she said. 'I'll just put a bit of lipstick on and we'll go round there, see if we can fix you up with his brother Stanley.'

'Right,' said Dolly. 'I'll go and make myself look my best then – mustn't let the side down.'

Walking down the street arm in arm, talking and laughing, Jessie realised that she and Dolly hadn't been out together like this since they were very young.

'Mum seems a lot better since Granny German came onto the scene and they see more of each other,' said Dolly, 'and you're a lot different since Tom came along. It's funny how everyone seems to have changed.'

'So you think I did the right thing, then?'

'You know you did the right thing. Max was all right but Tom's a cracker and more like us, in a manner of speaking.'

'I think Mum would have preferred me to stay with Max.'

'She'll come round, Granny German'll soon pull her up. She's all right, I like 'er. I'm glad you went and found her, Jess,' Dolly said earnestly.

'What's come over you? You didn't care tuppence before. Or was that an act?'

'Course it was an act, I'm not made of stone, you know. I felt really sorry for Mum when she told me about it and I was sad but I'm not like you, I don't dwell on morbid things. You take life too seriously.'

What a dark horse she was turning out to be, thought Jessie. She'd kept her true feelings hidden all this time. 'We're nearly there,' she said. 'Don't get all huffy if we're not invited in or I'll die of shame.'

'Tch. Of course I won't. I've got manners. I just pick and choose when to use them, that's all.'

'Well, bite your tongue if your temper gets up.'

'Temper? What temper?' said Dolly with mock innocence. 'I'll be as quiet as a mouse. What number is it?'

'Eighteen.'

'Not far then.' Dolly stopped and looked around her. 'This is nicer than I thought it would be. A few trees as well. I thought the back streets of Bethnal Green were a dump and

full of rubbish. This ain't bad, nice little corner shop ... no horse dung in the road ...'

At that moment a horse-drawn cart turned the corner. It was the fruit and veg man. The red-faced vendor tipped his cap to them as he passed and then turned into another street, leaving a pile of steaming horse manure in his wake.

Laughing, they linked arms again and walked on towards Tom's house. 'Bethnal Green's changed,' said Dolly. 'I was thinking of the old days instead of now. The Jago, near Shoreditch. That *was* the pits at one time, right up until the turn of the century. Fights went on there day and night and the women drank neat gin. Did you know that before Queen Victoria had—'

Jessie quickly cut her off before she could get into her stride. 'Dolly, please, not now. Tell me later. We're here.'

Outside Tom's front door, Jessie suddenly felt unsure of herself. Had Tom wanted her to see where he lived, he would have taken her back there by now. 'I've changed my mind, Dolly, let's go home.'

'Not likely!' Dolly pulled herself away and knocked three times before Jessie could stop her.

It was Emmie who answered the door. 'Is Tom in?' said Dolly, as bold as brass.

'He is.' Instead of a welcoming smile, there was concern on Emmie's face.

'We were just passing,' said Jessie, 'so ...'

'Ah.' Emmie had to think fast, Hannah was inside. 'Well, you'd best come in, the pair of you. I'll give him a shout.'

Dolly was the first in, eager and smiling. 'I've come to see if your other son, Stanley, is as handsome as your Tom.'

'Dolly!' hissed Jessie. She could kill her sister at times.

'Well, you're out of luck, madam, Stanley's at work, although he should be home soon. But that's not to say he won't be out again in a flash after filling his belly and having a quick spruce. You can wait in the front room and I'll—'

Laughter drifted into the passage, a girl's laughter, merging with Tom's. It was Hannah.

'Jessie! I can't believe you've called in at this very moment! I was just thinking about you. Tell her, Tom. Tell Jessie what I just said.' Hannah and Tom came out and joined them in the passage.

'Word for word?' asked Tom, sighing and slightly embarrassed by Jessie's unexpected appearance in his home.

'Word for word.' Hannah's eyes were sparkling.

'She said, "I've just had a vision of Jessie looking in at the window as if this was a baker's shop and she was choosing which cakes to buy."'

'It's true! I really did see it, and you were wearing *that* frock!'

'I wore it when I saw you in the hospital,' said Jessie, 'so you were bound to think of me in it.' She felt jealous that Hannah was here.

'But you must have lots of dresses, yet I imagined you in that one. Were you thinking about cakes, Jessie?' There was hope in her voice.

'Well, I wasn't thinking about this being a bakery or choosing cakes, but I thought I could smell a cake baking and it made me think of buns, which made me feel hungry.' Her jealousy disappeared as fast as it had come.

'You see! Thought transference.' It went very quiet as Emmie and Tom glanced at each other.

Hannah turned to Dolly, enjoying herself. 'I'd say that you are Jessie's younger sister. Now tell me I'm wrong. I bet I'm not.'

'You're right,' said Dolly dispassionately, 'we're sisters. We don't look much like each other though, so you *must* be a witch. Jessie looks more like you than she does me as—'

'I'll have no talk of witches, if you don't mind!' snapped Emmie, cutting her short. Collecting herself, she turned to Jessie. 'How are you, Jessie and how's your mother?'

'She's fine, thank you. We were just passing and—'

'You thought this was a railway station? Because that's what it looks like, everyone standing around waiting for the next train. If you'll all go into the front room I'll fetch a pot of tea and some buns, hot from the oven.' She turned to Tom. 'The cat might 'ave got your tongue but I'll have your hands. Come and take them buns out for me, my rheumatism's playing up.'

Following Hannah into the front room, Dolly said, 'Are you family then?'

'No. I'm Hannah. Tom's friend.' They all sat down.

'Oh? What's his brother like? Stanley? Only his mum's trying to fix us up.'

'What she means, Hannah,' said Jessie, 'is that she's hoping Emmie will fix them up. You have to take everything Dolly says with a pinch of salt.'

'Are *you* courting, Hannah?' asked Dolly, unfazed.

'No . . .' Hannah turned her face away. 'Actually, I've never been on a date. I have been asked but never had the courage to go. My mother always said that boys ask you out for one thing only. I've heard her say that so many times that I think I believe it.'

'So you should,' said Dolly, 'it's true. Let 'em kiss you goodnight and their hands are up your jumper or inside your blouse and in your knickers if you're not quick enough to stop 'em. Dirty sods. Are you a foreigner?'

'No. My mother's German but I was born in this country. My father's British born and bred.'

'I thought as much. Being German's all right, your lot were in the East End much earlier than most people like to think. After the collapse of Roman rule, German tribesmen took over the East End – I bet you didn't know that. *Stibba* people came to Stepney, *Bleda* to Bethnal Green and *Weappa* to Wapping. The country was re-Christianised and a small wooden church appeared in *Stibba*, that's when the church began its six-hundred-year rule in East London,' Dolly finished proudly.

'That's very interesting, Dolly.' Hannah went very quiet and then said, 'I didn't think I had an accent ...'

'I never said you did. It's the *way* you talk. You can always tell.'

'Tom'll be in soon,' said Emmie, coming into the room. 'He's just having a quick shave and change of clothes. You took him by surprise, turning up like this, Jessie. Took us all by surprise.' She placed the tray on a small side table and told the girls to help themselves. Dolly was in like a shot.

'How many sugars, Jessie?' asked Hannah.

'Give her six to fatten her up a bit, she's too skinny.'

'Just *one*, thanks, Hannah.' Jessie scowled at Dolly. She wanted her support right now, not torment. Jessie was beginning to feel she'd done the wrong thing, barging in on Tom's family like this.

'Well, I'll leave you to it, girls,' said Emmie. She was worried her tense expression would give things away. 'I've work to do in the kitchen. Give my regards to your mother, Jessie.'

'How come you know Mum?' asked Dolly.

'She doesn't, Dolly. We were in the papers, don't forget. Most people around her know about Dad's accident. Isn't that right, Emmie?'

'Yes, that's right.' She sniffed the air. 'Ah, here he comes, Brylcreem goes before 'im.' Sure enough, Tom came in a moment later, going straight to the tea table.

'It's funny you should come round, Jess, I was gonna pop round to you earlier than I said, as it happens. There's a meeting at my club that I can't miss.' He poured himself a cup of tea. 'If I do come round, I can only see you for an hour or so. Is that all right?'

'An hour? But it's Saturday night, Tom.' Jessie tried to hide her disappointment.

'I know. Can't be helped.' He sipped his tea and winked at her. 'I'll make it up to you tomorrow. We'll spend the day over

Victoria Park and I'll take you on a boat. I'll even let Mum make us a picnic up.'

'Sounds lovely to me,' said Dolly, stretching and showing her legs and leaning back in the armchair as if she was at home. 'What club is it?' she asked, thinking she might go and keep Tom company.

'Trade union. Stuff and nonsense but there you are, it's all to the good.'

'Speaking of which,' said Hannah, 'I'd best be going. I'll see you there, Tom. Try not to be late.'

'Oh, so you're going as well, are you, Hannah?' said Dolly.

'Yes. I help the secretary – take notes of the meeting, that kind of thing.' Hannah was covering up for Tom and Jessie sensed it, but she would say nothing, she could rely on Dolly to ask the questions.

'Are there many girls there then?'

'Not too many,' Hannah told her.

'So it's mostly men?'

'You could say that.'

'I wouldn't mind joining a club like that,' said Dolly, thinking about all the lads who might be there.

'You have to be a member of the union,' said Tom. 'The Workers Union.'

'Oh, that lets me out then. You must be popular, Hannah. Not much female competition.'

'Does that pot want refilling yet?' Emmie was back in the doorway, being mother.

'No more for me, thank you,' said Jessie, ready to leave. She wanted to go home, to have a chance to think things over. She did trust Tom, but she could tell he was lying about where he and Hannah were going, and she didn't like it.

'Are you a member of the trade union as well, Mrs Smith?' joked Dolly.

'Trade union? Ha, not likely.' She turned to Tom. 'Have you glanced at today's paper yet, Tom? Unemployment's set to

rise again. The docks'll be the first to be hit, you won't find so much work down there if this goes on. That's why I think you should be casting your nets for back-up wages instead of wasting time on *union meetings*.' Emmie didn't believe his story about where he was going any more than Jessie did.

Emmie sat down and looked from Tom to Jessie. 'I've come up with an idea. A bloody marvellous idea. But to see it through we'll need a bit of capital. Property investment. It's just the right time to buy and rent out, I reckon. The houses round this way will never be as cheap as they are now.'

Tom looked astonished. 'You want to buy this house, Mother? Whatever for? I know the rent went up but—'

'Not this one, no, but the rent rise is exactly the point. I'm talking about four terraced houses, the two up, two downs in Grant Street. I got the word today and I think we should move ourselves, get in quick. The landlord, like a lot of other people, believes there'll be a war and if there is, this part of London'll be hit. Well, let 'em think that way, let 'em sell up cheap and go off to Dagenham to buy rows of houses there. It'll make way for the likes of us.'

'How much are the houses?' said Jessie, holding back on her enthusiasm. A two up, two down was the very thing that she and Tom would be needing, now a baby was on the way — not that Emmie and Tom knew that.

'Three hundred pounds for each one, I heard,' Emmie continued, 'but that's way over the top. I should think the man will take a lot less than that. He's got other property to sell and he wants the cash quick to reinvest.' She breathed in as if the air was fresh off the sea. 'I've always fancied owning a bit of property.' Tom's sudden reflective mood gave her hope. She could see he was listening. 'Your dad's got a bit put by in his post office account, Tom, and Johnnie's got a few bob in the bank. You should think about it too, Hannah,' she said, without thinking.

'But I don't have any money, Emmie, you know that,' said Hannah.

'Not now ... no,' said Emmie. Quickly checking herself, she added, 'Well you know your dad's been sending money for years. I should think it's mounted up by now.'

'Yes, but my mother wouldn't give me any of that. It's hers. It's definitely hers.'

'Well, maybe she'll come round one of these days, eh?'

Jessie had slipped into a world of her own as she thought of herself and Tom owning a house. A surge of excitement rushed through her. Her hand instinctively moved across her stomach to where her baby was growing and she smiled inwardly. This was turning out to be a visit and a half. 'I've got some money coming to me,' she murmured dreamily. 'If I have a word with Mum ... she might be interested in making an investment.'

Tom chuckled quietly, and Emmie glared at him. 'You think it's funny, do you?'

'I think that you talking like a property magnate is, Mother. Hilarious. You're living with the fairies again,' he said, adding to the insult, which made Jessie see red.

'I think your mother's right, Tom.' Relaxing into the armchair, Jessie felt a strange calm come over her. 'But if there is going to be a war, would it be wise to buy houses around here, Emmie?'

'It's a risk but I think it's one worth taking. We can take out insurance, don't forget, and war or no war, in a few years that row of houses'll be worth a damn sight more than the landlord'll accept right now.'

'Could we go and see inside them today?' asked Jessie, surprising everyone.

Tom's patronising chuckle riled Jessie but she held her tongue. 'I thought you had more sense than that, Jess,' he said, 'listening to the ramblings of an old woman.'

'I would like to see them!' snapped Jessie, furious with him for the way he was patronising both her and his mother. 'Because you see, Emmie' she went on impulsively, 'I'm having your son's

baby.' There was a stunned silence in the room. 'So we'll be needing a little place of our own – or I will, at least.'

The silence continued to hang in the air.

'I hadn't meant to break the news like this,' Jessie added, 'but since those houses are coming up ...'

It was Dolly who broke the deathly hush. 'God, Jessie, Mum will do her *nut*. Phew. And you'll cop it, Tom.' Dolly sounded genuinely worried. Scared even.

'Well, well, well. There's one in the eye for all of us,' said Emmie, stunned.

'When our Jessie drops a bombshell she really drops one.' Dolly shook her head as if it was the end of the world. 'Mum'll blame you, Tom. She won't have you in our house now. You've done it now. She'll send Jess away, and once the baby's born, she'll get it adopted ... and she won't let Jessie ever see you—'

'That's enough, Dolly,' said Jessie. She looked across the room at Tom. There wasn't a flicker of movement in his face or his eyes. Then he licked his lips with his tongue, swallowed, then licked them again. He was well and truly knocked for six.

'What the bleeding hell's going on?' Charlie stood in the doorway. 'It's like a morgue in 'ere. What's 'appened? Em?'

'It's all right, Charlie,' said Emmie, as if in a trance. 'Tom's having a baby, that's all.'

There was a moment's pause while Charlie took this in. 'Fair enough,' he said, rubbing his chin. 'St Peter's. It'll have to be St Peter's. All my family have wedded there and been christened there.'

'St Dunstan's is my church,' said Jessie to Charlie. She had found an ally. A prop.

'Well, you please yourself, gel. We'd best 'ave your mother over for tea, though, to talk about it. I haven't seen Rose in years.'

'Go and check that tap in the back yard, would you, Charlie,'

said Emmie, glaring at her husband. 'I think someone might have left it running.'

'You what? Tch. Wasting bloody water,' he grumbled, turning to leave.

'Do you know Mum then?' said Dolly, mystified. 'Jessie never said anything about—'

'No, I didn't. Because I never knew,' said Jessie, looking at Tom for an explanation.

Emmie flicked her hand at Charlie, a casual signal for him to leave. He made a hasty exit. 'That was donkey years ago,' she said, covering herself. 'It's a pity the silly old sod's short-term memory is not so good. He was the one who left the tap running. So,' she said, shaking her head gravely, 'we have a little problem then.'

Turning away from Emmie's chiding eyes, Jessie braced herself for what was to come, hoping that Tom might take the lead, but it was not to be.

Emmie finally spoke. 'You have shocked me, Jessie, taken the wind out of all our sails, I should think.'

'So, shall we all go and look at those two up, two downs then?' said Jessie, desperate to avoid any debate on the matter.

'I think you might have told me when we were on our own,' said Tom, his face drawn with worry.

'I was going to but ... it just came out. I'd said it before I knew.' She bit on her bottom lip. 'I'm sorry.'

He looked away from her and drew breath. 'It would have been nice to be the first to be told.'

Charlie came back into the doorway, easing the tension. 'I'll have to give the place a coat of emulsion, Em, if there's to be a wedding. We got any more of that green paint left?'

'You've been at that bloody whisky bottle, 'aven't you?' Emmie said, bemused by his casual handling of the situation. 'I marked the label so I'll know, Charlie.'

He flapped his hand and left, making for the street door. His voice once again cut through the awkward silence. He was on the doorstep outside, calling to a neighbour. 'Harry, mate!

Come and 'ave a drink. Our Tom's just got himself engaged. Fetch Winnie and the girls. I'll send one of my lads out for a crate of beer!'

'Charlie! Come inside! You bloody fool!' Emmie turned to Jessie, apologising. 'Showing us all up like that. I'll take the rolling pin to him, so help me. Charlie! Get in here!'

'Oh, don't be like that, Em,' said Charlie, back in the doorway. 'This is a proud moment for me. We're gonna 'ave a wedding at last ... and I'm gonna be a grandfather.'

'Go upstairs and have a wash and shave. And put on a clean shirt! We'll all go round the pub once Tom and Jessie get back from ... where they're going.' She didn't want to tell him about the houses and start him off again. 'Save your invites for the wedding day, you bloody fool.' She turned to Jessie and did her best to make things easier for her. 'Well, go on then, the pair of you. Go and take a look at what we were talking about. See what you think.'

Jessie caught on. She could see the sense in not letting on to Charlie just yet.

'And that's it, Mother?' said Tom, baffled. 'No angry lectures? No excitement? Nothing?' He sounded let down by the casualness of it all. He was, after all, going to be a dad.

'It's a bit late for lectures. Save the excitement for when you get back from Grant Street. And as for nothing, don't you ever call my grandchild a nothing!'

Tom's face broke into a smile and then quiet laughter. 'She's taking over already, Jess.'

Jessie looked back at him, smiling shyly as the happiness slowly returned.

Practically pushing Tom and Jessie out of the door, Emmie said goodbye to Dolly and asked her to pass on her best to their mother. 'You'd better not let on to your mother that it's out in the open,' she said. 'We don't want her thinking I wormed it out of Jessie first. Have a drop of brandy ready, though, for both your sister and your mother. They'll need it.

She's not going to be the least bit happy about this, make no mistake.'

Outside in the street, Jessie took Tom's arm and squeezed it, whispering in his ear that she loved him and wanted to have his baby more than anything. Before he could respond, his brother Stanley yelled to him from the end of the turning.

'Tom! Hang about. Where you going?' Stanley, looking rugged and handsome in his work clothes and boots, swaggered towards them, his eye on Dolly.

'We're just off to see a man about a dog, Stan. Catch you later, boy.'

'Hold your horses, Tom. Slow down.' Arriving at Dolly's side, he gave her the once over and then winked. 'Who's this then?'

'Jessie's sister, Dolly. Jessie, meet my kid brother, Stanley.'

'Hello, Stanley,' smiled Jessie, loving his style.

'All right, Jess?' He spoke as if he'd known her for an age. He turned back to Dolly. 'Fancy coming out for a beer tonight?'

'I don't drink beer,' she said. 'Mine's a port.'

'Whoooo, the girl's got taste, Tom. I'll call for you at eight. Be ready.' Giving them a quick nod, he slipped into the house, calling to Charlie, telling him to put the kettle on.

Dolly was over the moon. 'Well, it looks like I won't be going out with my mates tonight after all,' she said with a huge smile.

Having told Stanley off for shouting in the street, Emmie went back into the sitting room. Hannah was still there, alone and looking sad. 'You should have gone with them, love. Why didn't you?'

'They didn't ask me. I wasn't part of that happy scene.' She smiled bravely. 'It's all right, Emmie, I understand. I'm not really family . . .'

'Don't talk so daft. But what about this shocking news, eh?' How Emmie longed to sit down and tell her that she was going to be an aunt.

Hannah made no response. She sat gazing at the fireplace, miles away.

'Of course you're family, Hannah,' said Emmie, patting her hand. 'Don't be upset, they'll realise you've been left behind and be more the sorry for it. Excitement got the better of them, that's all.'

'No, I don't think so. My place is with my mother whether I like it or not – until I move away, that is.' Hannah raised her eyes to Emmie's. 'Do you know what she said to me the day after Tom was beaten up, when I was in bed crying over it? "You think that lying in bed will make your friend better, Hannah? No one, *no one*, feels sorry for those who feel sorry for themselves. Get up and open the windows, let the air in. All I can smell in here is stale air and stale clothes." Why does she hate me so much, Emmie? What did I do?'

Gutted, Emmie swallowed. 'There's always the attic room, Hannah. I've told you that before. We could clear it out and make space for a single bed and a cupboard. It wouldn't be the Grand but it's better than ... living with that woman.'

'That woman. She's my mother and yet I also think of her as that woman. Why? I just don't understand. Look how you are with your sons.' She turned back to the fireplace. 'But never mind, I'll find a room somewhere soon, further away from here. I can't take much more, Emmie. I can't bear it in that place, not even in my own room. And she's the one to blame for Tom joining the Blackshirts, not me.'

'You think I don't know that? I know your mother better than you think, Hannah.'

'She tells me over and over, "You have no pluck, no mettle. I spit on you." Tell me, Emmie, tell me the truth, do other mothers talk to their children like that? Am I too sensitive, like she says?'

'You are sensitive, love, and that's no bad thing. But no, a mother doesn't usually say such things.'

'I thought that Tom wouldn't want to see me again after

he was beaten up. I didn't think I would be welcome here, but I was wrong. You've been kind to me, all of you, but it's time I sorted out a life for myself.

'It's a very strange thing, but once my mother had finished going on at me that morning, a kind of feeling of freedom passed over me. I opened the curtains in my room to let in fresh air and sunshine, and as it flooded in, quite suddenly I was filled with a sensation that someone was there, giving me love and comfort and hope. I didn't hear a voice exactly but a message ran through my brain – the very gentle voice of a man. "It's all right, Hannah," he said. "Everything is going to be all right." Does that sound foolish?'

'No, Hannah, it doesn't.' Deeply moved by what she had said, Emmie took time to settle herself. Hannah could not know that on that morning her real father, Robert, had been killed. While she was lying on her bed, he was lying dead in the River Thames.

Shuddering, Emmie collected herself. 'It's a strange world we live in, Hannah, a very strange world.'

'Do you think it's possible that my father was picking up on my misery, from all those miles away in New Zealand?'

'It's possible, love, who are we to say?'

'Emmie . . .' Hannah's eyes moistened. 'Why didn't he come back for me?'

This was all a bit too much for Emmie, this conversation. What could she say to Hannah? What could she say to make her feel worthy of herself? She didn't know why Jack hadn't come back for her. She wasn't a mind reader.

'He will come for you, Hannah. He said he would and he will. I expect he's been saving for the fare all these years, his fare over here and both fares back. That's a lot of money, love, and it would take a long time for him to save that much.' She said this having decided that as soon as Hannah left to go home, she would write to Rose's brother Jack in New Zealand. Enough was enough. It was time he got over here and sorted things

out. Rose would know his address, surely, or Grandmother Blake, if it came to that.

Once Hannah had gone home, Emmie made the most of the quiet to think about the eventful afternoon and wondered if outside forces were at work, herding Rose and herself together again and into pastures they'd visited before.

Chapter Nine

Jessie was pleased to find that Grant Street was only a five-minute walk from Tom's house. Had it been further they would have got into conversation about her condition and she didn't want that. That would come later when she and Tom were by themselves. Looking at him, she could see that he was in a daze, one minute a wry smile on his face and the next thoughtful.

'They must be the ones,' said Tom, looking across the narrow road at four houses in the terrace. There weren't any For Sale boards out but it was obvious that no one was living in any of them.

'Looks like someone's got here before you,' said Dolly, looking up at a window where a woman was staring out at them.

'Stroke of luck,' smiled Tom. 'Let's hope they've got keys to all four houses.'

They crossed the narrow cobbled road and while Jessie peered into the filthy downstairs windows, Tom knocked on the door. It wasn't long before they heard footsteps echoing on the floorboards. 'Let me do the talking, girls, all right?' he said.

'Ay ay, Captain,' said Dolly, giving a fine salute which Tom ignored. 'House ahoy!'

'Daft as a brush,' he said. 'Should go down well with Stanley.'

The door, after a couple of jerks from the inside and a nudge from Tom's foot, finally opened to reveal a man in his fifties, wearing a suit and tie.

'What can I do for yer?' he said, frowning, as if they had disturbed him.

Tom offered his hand. 'Sorry to bother you, mate, but we've just heard that these places are coming up for sale and I'm interested.'

'In all four of them?' The man eyed him suspiciously.

'Depends. Need a lot of work doing to 'em,' said Tom, stepping back and giving them the once over. 'Are you the owner or a contender?'

'I'm showing someone around. The couple's only interested in this one. I'm looking for three hundred and twenty for each one, but I'm a fair man and it's open to discussion.'

Hearing quiet conversation from the couple who had been viewing the upstairs, Tom gave Jessie and Dolly a sign to keep quiet.

'I think we've seen enough, thanks,' said the woman who looked to be in her thirties and down on her luck.

'More than enough,' said her husband, a short, squat man. 'If we can pay five shillings a week, we'll take it. Between us we can clean the rest of 'em up and caretake for yer, two years rent at five bob a week and you've got a deal.'

Ushering them out as quickly as possible, the owner told them he'd be in touch and then turned to Tom. 'Dreamers,' he said, rolling his eyes.

'All right to come in and have a butchers then?' Tom was behaving as if he had a wad of money burning a hole in his back pocket.

'Don't see why not. In you come. You as well, girls. Can't have you standing out there, can we? Someone might run off with yer. He's a lucky man, I'll say that for 'im, two women and looking to buy four houses. Can't be bad.'

'I'm his future sister-in-law, actually,' said Dolly, sweeping

past him. 'Growing mushrooms, are you, or is that damp I can smell?'

Laughing at her, the man closed the door behind them. 'You'll smell more than damp by the time you've viewed these properties, my love. If you're looking for fresh paint and lace curtains, you'd best look elsewhere.'

'Take no notice of her,' said Tom. 'She was born with a silver spoon in her mouth. Be all right once I shove a scrubbing brush and bucket of hot soda water in her hands.' He patted the passage wall. 'Trouble is, she's right. The place is damp.'

'That's why they're cheap. Mind you, it's not as bad as—'

'Cheap?' said Tom, stopping his flow. 'Who're you kidding? I do read the papers, you know. A new three-bedroom semi with garden and garage costs as much as you're asking for these slums. I wasn't born yesterday so show a bit of respect.'

Tom's audacity paid off. The man sniffed and considered. 'True,' he said finally, 'you can get a new house for what I'm asking but that's in the suburbs. Add fares or petrol onto that and—'

'How much?' said Tom, halfway amused by the charade.

'And you're after all four? Well, we landlords have to scratch each other's backs, I suppose.'

'I'm not a landlord, but I've got brothers and we might be interested if the price is right.'

'Mmm.' He sucked his teeth and slowly shook his head. 'It's one price for the dealer and one for the public, you see. We have to be fair. A dealer's got to make a profit, whereas you—'

'Six hundred for the four of 'em – if I like what I see once I've had a butchers at the insides.'

'Six hundred? You out of your mind or what? Six hundred. Oh dear, oh dear, oh dear. You are a card. Well now, let's see, *might* let them go for a grand if it's cash in hand. Can't say fairer than that.'

'Six hundred but not all in cash. There aren't many who could come up with that kind of money. Make it six and you

can have two hundred in notes.' Tom was thinking about Johnnie and his bank account.

'Well, you might as well take a look now that you've come. Rock-solid, these little houses. Built to last and only been standing for twenty-five years or so.'

'Is that right? So whoever had that date inscribed on the plaque outside was telling pork pies then.'

The man looked at Tom, his eyes narrowing. 'Outside, you say?'

'That's right. It's filthy but my eyes are good. Eighteen ninety.'

'Do you know, I've never noticed that. Well, that throws a different light on things. That was a very good year for building houses, and once you've got all the windows and the back door open, I reckons this damp'll dry out. It makes no odds to me anyway, these'll be gone by the end of next week at the price I'm asking. I hate to let them go but I've been made an offer I can't refuse – in Dagenham. Row of cottages, ten of 'em. They were gonna be demolished to make space for a factory, some kind of fashion industry.' He shrugged. 'I should get a good price for 'em once I've done them up a bit. They're more for your middle-class sort of person.'

'Is it all right if we look round then?' said Dolly, breaking up the chummy monologue.

'Course it is.' He looked at his wristwatch. 'Fifteen minutes and I'll be back. Here, take the keys so you can have a look at the others as well. One's much the same as the other but you'll still want to go over 'em. I can see you've got your wits about you. If you can raise the six hundred for all four, you'd be a fool not to grab 'em. If you are interested, I can arrange for electricity to be wired.' He tapped the side of his nose. 'You name it, I've got the contacts.'

'That's decent of you, trusting me with the keys.' Tom looked him straight in the eye and waited for the catch.

'Well, you're 'ardly gonna run off with 'em, are you? Ta ta,

girls – for now.' With a wink and a grin, he strode off down the road.

'Tom? You didn't really expect him to come down that much in price, did you?' asked Jessie.

'I'm kicking myself, Jess, I should have said five hundred. Never mind, we'll send Mother round to see him, she'll get it down to five for us, you'll see. Right then.' Tom rubbed his hands together. 'You girls check this one out while I take a look at the others. Don't forget to look at the back yard – and the lav.' Tom went straight out and into the house next door.

'Well, this is all exciting, Jess. I wonder if there's a cellar.' Without another word, Dolly was gone, in search of treasure, leaving Jessie to herself.

She placed the flat of her hand on the passage wall and checked all along it and yes, it was damp here and there, and the place did smell of dirt, but there was something appealing about it. She hadn't seen any of the rooms, but she liked the house. Leaning on the passage wall she imagined it with fresh white paint on the woodwork and delicately flowered wallpaper. Plain white nets and curtains at the window, nice lino on the floor and a couple of rugs.

Dolly returned, wiping the dust from her hands onto the skirt of her frock. 'Why does this house seem much older than ours when it's not?'

'Because it's not lived in, Dolly. What would you expect?' Jessie was already being defensive about the house, as if it was her own.

'Maybe it's because it's got a cellar and the rooms are small, but it's got a good feel about it,' said Dolly. 'It reminds me of my local history teacher. He used to live down this road when he taught at our school. He wanted the class to go on a tour of his house, which hadn't been touched, other than cleaned, since it had been built. Even the wallpaper was original, so he said. He was posh but loved the East End,' Dolly prattled on, 'especially Bethnal Green which, according to him, was the nicest of the

villages, surrounded by woods, with a small wooden church and cottages. He said the village was ruled by the Lord of the Manor in Chaucer's time. He'd go on for hours about Chaucer, where he lived, where he ate, what he did for entertainment. It is interesting, mind you,' she continued, opening a corner cupboard and flinching at the sight of a spider. 'Chaucer took lodgings in the Gate House, over the Ald Gate. The rooms had a cellar beneath and when the first bell of the day tolled, the great gates were swung open and—'

'Yeah, all right, Dolly. You do get carried away. Could you see anything in the cellar or is it too dark down there?'

'Too dark.' She turned and leaned on the wall, arms folded, still there, back in the days of Chaucer. 'Grain and dung carts would arrive from Essex, cattle being driven through, and pigs, herded onto Smith Fields.'

'You amaze me sometimes, Dolly. How you fitted so much information into your brain, I don't know. Maybe that's why you 'ave trouble taking things in now, it's all crammed with Chaucer.'

'Yeah, but just imagine it, Jess. The lowing of cattle, the creaking rattle of carts and the clip of hooves. Street vendors shouting, "*Rabbit and venison pie! Roast pork! Pheasant! Eels peppered! Saffron mackerel!*" Not to mention "*Strawberries, ripe! Strawberries ripe!*"'

'You'll end up being carted off yourself if you go on like that. Come on.'

'I've seen enough,' said Dolly. 'I'll go and find Tom and look at the others. Let's hope they haven't got rats in the back yard as well. I saw one run along the fence, just now.'

'Dolly, that's not funny!'

'It wasn't meant to be, don't get so aerated, Jessie, think of *the baby.*' Dolly grinned, pleased at the thought of becoming an auntie. 'Anyway, a single rat's nothing. One trap and it'll be dead. Clonk!'

'If it really was one then there'll be more,' said Jessie.

'I wish I hadn't mentioned it now, one single rat and you go white. There won't be another plague, don't worry. The plague bell won't toll, Jessie.'

'Dolly, stop it. Go and find Tom and drive *him* mad.'

Thankful to be in the house by herself, Jessie walked cautiously around, looking and listening for any signs of vermin. Her fears soon dissolved as she went from one small room to another and out into the back yard. She loved the place. When she caught sight of a mouse scampering around an old ruined shed, she shuddered and then smiled. At least Dolly was wrong about the rat. You won't find rats where there are mice, her mother had always insisted.

Standing in the middle of the downstairs room, Jessie admired the small old-fashioned cupboards and shelves. They gave the place a cottage feel. The scullery had an open fireplace which smelled of damp coal and there were antiquated brass oil lamps hanging in every room. In each of the fireplaces, there were gas pokers and on the windowsills burned down candles. Cobwebs were everywhere.

Above the street door there was an arched coloured-glass window, with just one small crack in one of the panes. The sun shining through cast a ray of yellow and pink light into the hallway. Jessie avoided the cellar which was small and pitch black. The two bedrooms upstairs were fine and once they had peeled off the layers of lino, she felt sure it would smell a lot better. The late afternoon sun seemed to be shining in through every window, as if it was welcoming her into this new home. She wondered what Tom was making of the other three and of Dolly's chatter.

'It's true, Tom, honest, Stepney *was* a village, with rich and poor, farmers and millers – a thriving village. And I'll tell you something else. Way back, the Duchess of Suffolk had a house in Stepenham and a marquis had a mansion just by the church.

Our part of the woods was seen as a *rural retreat*. London's back yard, more like. Still is.'

'Do me a favour, Doll, and pass me that old bit of curtain cane on the windowsill. I want to measure this room,' said Tom, paying not the slightest attention to her ramblings.

Sighing, Dolly handed him the curtain rod. 'I'm going next door, see what Jessie's up to.' She left him to it, wondering why he couldn't show just a bit of interest in the way things used to be.

'Tom's been in and out of all the other three, she said, joining Jessie in one of the bedrooms. 'I bet that brass bed'd come up a treat. Some of the bits of furniture want chucking on the bonfire but some of it's solid oak and sound. Did you see that bedside cabinet in the other bedroom? I should imagine that's an antique. Early Victorian.'

'I wouldn't want it.'

'I wasn't thinking of using any of it, Jessie. I'd clean it up, polish it, and put it in the auction rooms. My friend's dad does that – he earns out of it as well. Used to be a rag and bone man. Now he's gone upmarket.'

'You upstairs, girls?' called Tom from below.

'Yes. Come on up!'

'No need,' he called back. 'I've seen enough. I wanna get back and fetch Mum and the boys to have a look, while I've still got the keys.'

'Looks like someone's thinking of going into the property market,' said Dolly. 'We'd best get home, you've got some music to face.'

Not wishing to spoil her present carefree mood, Jessie ignored Dolly's reminder of the battle to come. 'So you like it then?' she said as they went down the stairs.

'I will once you've scrubbed it. Don't know what Mum'll think though.'

'I think she'll like it,' murmured Jessie, 'and she'll love the

idea of a Warner owning their own house. It's what she and Dad always wanted.'

'Mmm,' smiled Dolly, 'but not quite as soon as this.'

Closing the front door behind them and linking arms with Tom, Jessie was touched to see that her sister was being thoughtful and strolling ahead, giving them a chance to talk privately about buying one of the houses. 'What do you think then?' she said, hoping Tom liked what he'd seen as much as she did.

'I think you'll make the best mum in the world, Jessie Warner.' He put his arm round her waist and gently squeezed her. 'The best mum and the best wife. I'm the luckiest man alive.'

'That's not what I meant, I was talking about the house. I daren't ask how you feel about ... well, you know.'

'Shocked. Bloody shocked. But I keep seeing this tiny little version of you,' he said, his emotions stirred. 'Anyway, the house. If we can buy the four off him, we'd get a good deal. How we'll raise the money is something else but we've got to do it, it makes sense.' He grinned broadly. 'The Smiths owning property. That'll be one in the eye for some of the neighbours, I can tell you, and Mum deserves the thrill she'd get from it. She's been a grafter all her life, Jessie. So has Dad. There are four working men and one working woman at home and Johnnie's got enough cash in the bank to buy one for himself. He'll put in a word with the bank manager for the rest of us. I don't like to ask, Jess, but—'

'There'll be enough from my share of the compensation money for us to buy one. Mum says it should all be settled in a month or two.'

'No. I didn't mean that. I meant will you be able to manage? If I get one of these mortgages, well, we'd be a bit struck for cash for a while. I'll get two jobs, of course I will, but—'

'Tom I want to use the money to buy that house, there's no point in lining the bank's coffers with interest payments. If

we use my money, we can use your wages to do the place up a bit and buy some furniture – second-hand furniture that we can paint nice light colours. We don't have to move in straightaway and we needn't get married for another two months – that's if you want to get married.'

'Nah, not me, you'll have to find someone else. Sod that for a lark,' he said, sounding serious. 'I'll still buy one of them houses though, in case I find someone I do want to marry.'

'Stop it, Tom. I've been worried sick in case you wanted to get rid of me.'

'Oh, thanks. You think I'd do a thing like that, do you?'

She squeezed his hand. 'Sorry. I was just checking. Anyway, can we use my money to buy it?'

'No. That's your money, Jessie. I'm not touching that.'

'Once we're married, it'll be *our* money, Tom. I'll tell you what, I'll do a deal with you. I'll say no more about you having joined the Blackshirts, because I know you have, if you let me do what I want to do with my own funds. If your brothers and your mum manage to buy the other three, all well and good, but don't bank on it. Let's just think about us.'

'Fair enough, Jess, but if you use your money, the house'll be in your name. It's your name that goes on the deeds or nothing.'

'That sounds fair,' she said, not caring one way or the other.

'If you're really sure it's what you want ... I'll work day and night to make it like a little palace for you. I can get a bit of work down the market as well as at the docks. I'll work my fingers to the bone. I will, Jessie. I'll work till I drop.' Taking her by surprise, he let go of her hand and lifted her high in the air. 'My Jessie, having my baby. What more could a man want?'

'A two up, two down?' she said, laughing. 'Put me down, Tom. You might drop me.'

'Never in a million years would I drop you, sweetheart.' He slowly lowered her until her feet touched the ground, and kissed

her. 'I love you, Jess. I love you so much it hurts. I've driven the blokes down the docks mad, telling them how lovely my Jessie is.'

'I love you as well,' she said, brushing a kiss across his cheek, 'but I've got to get back home now, to face Mum. She's not gonna be as thrilled about this as we are.'

'Do you want me to come with you?' he said, but half-heartedly.

'No. That wouldn't go down very well. She'll want me to herself so she can vent her anger. I'm going to have to look a very sorry daughter, Tom, full of regret. No, I don't think your being there'll help, the opposite in fact.'

'Thank God for that.' He gave her a peck on the cheek. 'I was dreading you'd want me to be there. Go on then. Catch Dolly up. I've got a meeting to go to.'

A deep and worried sigh escaped from Jessie. 'I hope you haven't joined just to get your own back, Tom. It was a street brawl and you came off worse. Why can't you just leave it at that?'

'It's not revenge, Jessie. I believe in the cause. I love my country and I don't want to see it going down the pan with every Tom, Dick and Harry coming in from every bloody country. I'm not saying we should kick out all the foreigners, they're here now, but something's got to be done to stop them pouring in. Britain's not that big a place, and England's a lot smaller. It stands to reason, if you pour too much beer into a glass, what happens?'

'It spills over and makes a mess. Trust you to use beer as an example.'

'Now stop worrying over it and mind your own business.' He glanced at her stomach. 'You've got enough to think about now.'

'But they're Fascists, Tom.'

'Fascists. People say that as if it's the devil with horns they're talking about.' He shrugged. 'It's no more than a bunch of

politicians trying to do what they think is right for their country. You can't blame 'em for that, Jess, and before you even think of asking, no, I won't be chalking insults on walls or throwing bricks through windows. But I will go to the meetings, and I will march with them, and I will beat the drum. I'll beat the drum for England. Our England, Jessie. Our children's England.' Smiling at her, he brushed loose strands of hair off her face. 'I promise you one thing, if war comes, Blackshirts and Jews will fight alongside each other, the same as we live alongside each other, the same as we love to have a good punch-up now and then, and the same as we fall in love with each other. You loved Max – he was a Jew. I once courted a girl who was Jewish and she adored me. Couldn't keep her hands off!' He kissed the tip of her nose and winked. 'Stop thinking about things that don't concern you. Think about what kind of wallpaper you'd like to see in the nursery instead. I think the back bedroom'd make a smashing little nursery.'

Quietly laughing at him, Jessie shrugged off her worry. 'I don't agree but I don't care, not right now.' She did care but that could wait until they were married, then she'd change his way of thinking. 'So you liked it then? The house I was looking at?'

'I preferred one of the others which had a little lean-to out the back. We could use that for a kitchen, once I'd fixed the broken panes and that.'

'We could let that second bedroom – until baby comes along,' said Jessie, thinking of Hannah.

'That's true.' He held each side of her face and kissed her. 'See you later. Good luck with your mother.'

Stepping up her pace to catch Dolly, Jessie was filled with thoughts of the future and the last person on her mind right then was Max, but there he was, standing outside the Bancroft Hospital, chatting to Dolly. She hadn't seen him since the day she threw his gifts back at him.

'Hello, Jessie,' he said, looking sheepishly at her. 'You look well.'

'Thanks. How are you – and the family?' She could feel herself blush. 'Your mum and dad all right?'

'So so.'

The awkward silence that followed was broken by Dolly who once again was being tactful. 'Nice to see you again, Max.' She turned to Jessie and winked. 'I'll see you back at the house.'

'Don't say anything, Dolly!' Jessie called after her. Dolly didn't look back but just raised a hand.

'She's growing up at last,' said Max, smiling. 'I suppose that's because of your dad. It takes shock and grief to pull us round sometimes.'

Jessie decided to get to the point. 'Seeing a photo of you kissing another girl gave me a jolt, I can tell you, but I can see now that Moira had a point, we weren't really right for each other, not for marriage, and I think you know that, Max, deep down.'

'My family don't rule my life, you know. They couldn't see it working but that doesn't mean to say that I felt the same. You did though,' he shrugged, 'so there we are. One little lecture from Moira and you ran. I think I had more of a shock than you, Jessie.'

'Are you seeing the girl in the photograph, Max?'

'Of course I see her, I've been seeing her since I was very small. Her family and mine are very close. I've taken her out a couple of times since we broke up, yes.'

'Well, there you are then. There must be something between you and there's no way I would have put up with that.'

Max looked sad. 'But I still love you, Jessie. I'll always love you. If anything goes wrong, promise you'll come and see me, or write. Promise?'

'Do things have to go wrong then? For us to stay friends?' Jessie smiled, trying to cheer him up.

'No, we don't have to wait for that.'

'Max ...' Jessie searched for the right words. 'Max, don't wait for me and Tom to break up. It's not going to happen.

I know it's all a bit sudden but,' she clenched her hands, her fingernails digging into her flesh, 'we're going to be married, quite soon.' She reeled off the last line very quickly.

'That's absurd, Jessie, and you know it. You know nothing about each other. How could you in so short a time?'

'I love him, Max,' she said, shrugging. 'We've been together a while now. I don't need longer than that.'

He looked from her face to her stomach. 'Well, I hope it all goes right for you. Dolly said something and I guessed the rest.'

'Oh. Well, it's not a case of *having* to, if that's what you think,' Jessie said hastily.

'No, it's not a case of having to because I would marry you tomorrow. I wouldn't mind about ...' He nodded at her stomach. 'I would bring it up as my own.' He took her hand and moved closer. 'Jessie, please don't marry that man. It's too quick. Marry me instead. Please, darling, I'm begging you. Don't do it. Please don't do it.'

That man. Max had referred to Tom as *that* man. Did he know already? Had he found out more about Tom than he was letting on? 'Tom's a decent bloke, Max.'

'No, Jessie. He's not. I know what I'm talking about. I know his brother, Johnnie.'

Jessie slowly withdrew her hand and smiled weakly. 'Maybe in another life, eh?'

'This *is* our life, Jessie. We should be together.'

She was beginning to feel trapped. 'Look, let me come round to see you now and then, or let's meet up for coffee. We don't have to cut each other off. You'll find someone else to love, a nice Jewish girl, someone who'll fit in. Let's stay friends.'

He looked down at the ground. 'If that's what you want. It's better than nothing. You can phone me at the office.' He slipped his hand inside his pocket and pulled out a small wad of business cards. 'I've been promoted,' he smiled. 'Junior accountant. I get to deal with the small uncomplicated clients.'

'You deserve it.' She took the card and nodded. 'I'll have to go. I've got to break the news to Mum. Don't say anything, will you, to Moira or your mum and dad or—'

'Of course I won't say anything. Besides, you're not married to him yet.' Choked, he turned and walked away, thinking that he would make it his business to keep in touch with her, married or not. Once she learned that Tom was a Fascist, she would be shocked, he thought.

When Jessie arrived home, she found Rose in the kitchen boiling the whites. Jessie signalled for Dolly to go upstairs, so that she and their mother could be by themselves. Searching for the right words, Jessie sat on the low windowsill and glanced out at the back garden. She thought about her dad and what he would have said. No matter how hard she tried to picture his reaction, she couldn't. She couldn't even picture herself telling him.

'Mum,' she said, her voice a dead give-away, 'I've got something to tell you, something that you're not going to be pleased about.'

'Go on then,' said Rose in a tone that suggested she was expecting a confession. 'Your sister hasn't said a word out of place but I could tell that something's happened.' She paused. 'Has it got something to do with your visit to Tom's house?'

'Not really. It had already happened before I went. But Tom did ask me to marry him while I was there and I said yes.' She kept her eyes lowered. Her mother's silence told her that she had guessed – there was no need to spell it out.

'I should have realised when you fainted that morning,' said Rose, her tone resigned and dispirited. 'I should have known then. Does Max know?'

'Max? Why do you ask that?'

'Well, he is the father, isn't he? He's got every right to know. He might well want to marry you himself, and I can't say I wouldn't prefer him for a son-in-law, even though he has taken liberties with you.'

'Max isn't the father,' said Jessie, closing her eyes and waiting for the explosion.

'What do you mean?' Rose sounded appalled.

'I'm carrying *Tom's* baby, Mum. We shouldn't have made love but—'

'Good gracious . . .' Rose grabbed the back of a kitchen chair and steadied herself. 'I've never heard such talk. Where do you think you are? In a *brothel*? You bring shame on our good name. I dread to think what your father would say . . . God rest his soul.' She lowered herself into the chair. 'That things should come to this,' she murmured, her voice breaking. 'You've not been with the scoundrel for five minutes.'

'I love him. Really love him. I thought I loved Max but I didn't, I mistook what we had for love. He realises that as well, deep down, that's why he never came round. He's a smashing feller, Mum, but if I married him it wouldn't last five minutes. Either that or we'd both regret it and stay together in a third-rate marriage to keep up appearances.'

'And you think that this fly-by-night will make you happy? Because I don't. I give it a year, if that, before he's off somewhere else.'

'How can you *say* that? You don't *know* him. I'm sorry it's not Max, I know that's what you wanted, to see me off with a solid, reliable husband, but what good is that without love?'

'Rubbish! Love. You don't know what you're talking about. You've a lot to learn yet, my girl. A lot.'

'I know. I've got to learn how to be a mother.'

'There's no "got to" about it! You can have an abortion. I know a decent midwife who'll do it and keep it under wraps. I'll shame myself by going to her over this but it'll be less of a disgrace than letting everyone watch your stomach grow, and you only knowing the father for a second. It'll be all round the streets. We've never had a scandal before, never. I'll thank you not to mention it to anyone, especially my sons.' Rose couldn't know how much she was hurting Jessie with her words.

'I want to have my baby,' she said.

'Out of the question.' Rose shook her head. 'Out of the question.'

'I'm not going to kill my own flesh and blood.'

'You *are* killing your own flesh and blood! You're killing *me*! Haven't I had enough heartache? Wasn't it enough that your father put pride before his fall? He got into that crane *knowing* it was dangerous. *Knowing* he was taking a risk. He left me a widow with *four* children to take care of. Wasn't that *enough*! Did you have to add to it by acting like a whore!'

'I'm sorry. I didn't want this to happen. But it has and I'm keeping it.' Tears were running down Jessie's face.

They made no difference to Rose, she would not allow emotions to rule the day. 'Either you get rid of it or you leave this house. I'll wash my hands of you. I'll have nothing to do with weddings, births or a blighted marriage.' She brought her hand down onto the table with a crashing blow. 'I'll have *nothing* more to do with you if you have this baby! And what's more, you can't marry that man!'

'Why not?'

'You just can't, that's all! That's all there is to it. You will not marry him or see him again! Now let that be an end to it!'

Pressing her hands against her face, Jessie tried to stop crying but it was hopeless; she loved her mother and couldn't bear to hear her saying such things. She loved her father and wanted him to be there, to make everything all right.

'If you go through with this,' said Rose more calmly, 'I mean what I say. You'll have to go. You can have your share of the compensation for the death of your father to set up home. There's to be no more discussion.'

'What if I went away and had it adopted?' said Jessie desperately. 'I would do that if you'd let me go on seeing Tom. If it all works out we could marry later on, in a year or so.'

Rose shuddered and turned her back on Jessie. 'I don't want

to talk about it any more. I can't think straight. I've had a shock. Leave me be.'

Dolly came into the kitchen. Rose straightened her shoulders and lifted her chin. 'Don't creep around like that, Dolly, there's a good girl,' she said. Jessie marvelled at how quickly she could pull herself together.

'I didn't mean to creep. Granny German's arrived. She's upstairs in the sitting room. I said that you and Jessie were having a few private words. Shall I tell her to come down or to go away?'

'Of course you won't tell her to go away, child. I didn't hear the door.'

'No. I was outside, sitting on the step. I saw her coming.'

Rose stood up and brushed her hands down her skirt and pushed her hair into place. 'Make a fresh pot of tea, Dolly, and bring a tray up to the parlour.' She checked her face and hair in the small mirror over the sink. Ignoring Jessie's eyes, she left the room.

Dolly let out a low whistle. 'Rather you than me.' She looked at Jessie's tear-stained face. 'That went down a bomb, didn't it?'

'Worse than I thought it would. She wants me to have an abortion, give up Tom, go back with Max. If I go against her wishes she'll cut me dead. I'll gain a husband and lose a mum. Not a bad day so far, is it?'

'I can't say I'm surprised, you did jump into bed a bit sharpish. I know Tom's irresistible but all the same . . .'

'I'm not ashamed of myself if that's what you think. I'm just angry for not making sure Tom had a Durex.'

'Oh, that's very nice. Speak your mind, don't you?'

'You can learn from my mistake. Don't let your boyfriend have his way unless he puts one on.' Jessie wasn't in the mood for niceties, she wanted to shock someone and Dolly was as good as anyone. 'You should use a Dr Rendall as well, just in case the rubber splits.'

'Stop being so *disgusting*. It's not clever. If Tom could hear you now ... I'm glad it's you getting married and not me. I'm not gonna put up with all that mucky business. It sounds revolting.'

'Why're you smiling then? I can tell you are, Dolly. Little Miss Innocent. Don't tell me that you and Fred didn't do anything naughty.'

'Course we did, but nothing like that! He used to slip his hand inside my knickers and massage me ... and that was lovely. But he never undid his flies when he rubbed against me, I would have punched him in the face if he'd tried that.'

When Dolly had gone upstairs with the tea tray, Jessie felt very low. Upstairs her fate was being discussed. She imagined her mother and Granny German discussing the best way to hide the disgrace – send her away to the country to have the baby and then give it away, or take her to a back street in Whitechapel where she would have it ripped from her. She started to cry again. It all seemed so unfair, what she and Tom had done had happened so naturally, they loved each other in a way that no one could understand and now they were being punished for it. She thought about the little house, her two up, two down with the lean-to that would have been turned into a proper kitchen. She glanced out of the window at the flowers in her dad's garden and imagined her own little house with vases and vases of flowers, picked from her own back yard.

'Mum said will you go up.' Dolly had returned.

'What does she want?'

'How am I s'posed to know?' she said, a touch indignant. 'I don't get talked to around here, I get told.'

'What kind of mood are they in?'

'Jumping for joy. What mood do you expect them to be in?'

Jessie gave her a look of contempt. 'I don't know why I bothered to ask, you're just a kid. What would you know?' She got out of the kitchen before Dolly could answer back – she had seen the flash of anger in her eyes.

'Miss High and Mighty!' Dolly yelled up the stairs after her. 'Not so *saintly* now, are you!' Her voice rang through the house; not only would her mother and grandmother hear, the tenants in the attic would too. 'They've got names for girls like you!'

Jessie ignored the insult and went into the sitting room, bracing herself to face both mother and grandmother.

'Pay no attention to Dolly,' said Rose quietly. 'It's reaction, shock. I dare say she's as shocked as I am.'

'Sit down, Jessie,' came Ingrid's quiet, controlled voice. 'Your sister has a lot to learn about people. You are not a whore – far from it.'

Jessie smiled weakly at her. 'I've got to get used to it. It's what everyone will say, in their own way.'

'You're not a bad girl, Jess,' said Rose. 'You've been feckless but you're not bad. Sit down now, we've something else to tell you.' Her voice was so low Jessie could hardly hear her.

'I think it might be better if you closed the door first,' suggested Ingrid.

'I don't want to talk about it,' said Jessie. 'I know what you're going to say and I'll just have to accept whatever you have in mind. So do what you want with me.' She turned to leave but Rose stopped her.

'Sit *down*, you silly girl. What I have to say has nothing to do with your condition. Besides, we've been talking. Your grandmother thinks you should marry your fiancé and have the baby.' Rose shuffled in her seat, embarrassed and uncomfortable.

'Fiancé? You mean ... Max?'

'No. I mean Tom. You can wear this for now,' she said, offering Jessie a ruby and diamond ring. 'You can keep it if you want. Don't thank me for it, thank your grandmother.'

Jessie looked from Rose to Ingrid, puzzled. Her grandmother gave a nod of approval, silently telling her to accept the gesture and to go easy on her mother. 'I haven't met this young man of yours,' she said, 'this Tom, but I have heard about him from time to time from his mother, Emmie. It would seem to

me that he is a caring and thoughtful youth. Do you love him? This Tom?'

'Of course I do. But I don't understand ... you know Emmie as well?'

'Yes I do. She's a good friend.'

The memory of Ingrid's first visit washed over her. She had mentioned Emmie then, but it hadn't occurred to Jessie that she was referring to Tom's mother. 'Everyone seems to know Emmie,' she said, miles away. She turned the ruby ring in her fingers. 'Thank you for this,' she said, 'it's lovely.' There was a moment of quiet as a more relaxed atmosphere took over the room. 'Was this the one that Grandfather gave to you when you got engaged?'

'Yes,' said Ingrid. 'Your mother would like you to wear it and I think you should have it. I know you were very dear to him — as I was, once.'

Bewildered, Jessie asked if she could go to her room for a while and talk again later on. All she wanted right then was to be by herself. To think and to cry by herself.

'No, Jessie.' Rose's tone was serious. 'I've something to tell you, something very important. Once you've taken in what I have to say, I'll call Dolly up. The boys can be told later, when they're in their beds.'

Worried as well as confused now, Jessie sat down. What could be more serious than her being pregnant?

'Now,' said Rose, 'what I have to say isn't going to be easy for me, Jess, and if it wasn't for your grandmother, I wouldn't be telling you at all.' Rose glanced at Ingrid and took a deep breath. 'I've just been told off, Jessie, by *my* mother.'

Thumbing her wedding ring, she began her story. She told Jessie that when she was in the same predicament, eighteen years ago, she and Robert had been courting for over two years before they broke the rules. She told her about Armistice and how overjoyed the women were when their men came home from war. Jessie wondered if she was telling her all of

this to help make her feel better about her *condition*, but she was wrong.

'The thing is, Jessie, me and your dad were very hard up, struggling to make ends meet. We could hardly afford to feed ourselves and pay rent on our rooms, let alone feed two babies.'

'*Two* babies? But Dolly wasn't born then.'

'No, that's right, but you were and ...' Rose swallowed and turned her face away, hiding the pain, 'so was your twin,' she whispered. 'I gave birth to twins, Jessie, non-identical twin girls.'

'You can't have,' said Jessie, a nervous smile on her face, 'you would have told me.' She looked to her grandmother, but Ingrid avoided her eyes.

'I should have told you ... me and your dad should have explained when the time was right, which is what we'd promised ourselves, but the time was never right.'

Jessie felt very strange, her emotions mixed. She was a twin? She had a twin sister? That feeling of someone being missing all through her life came flooding back.

'She died ...' murmured Jessie. 'I had a twin and she died. I think I knew.' She met Rose's troubled eyes. 'I always felt as if something was missing ... missing from me. She didn't die straightaway, did she?' Then, like a flash of lightning, she remembered the photograph of the twins in a pram.

'She didn't die, Jessie. We just couldn't afford to clothe and take care of two babies ... so we had to let someone else take care of one.'

'No!' An icy sensation swept across her, she shook her head, not wanting to hear it. 'No. You wouldn't do that. Dad wouldn't have done that. You wouldn't do that to us. We loved each other. She was part of me and I was part of her ...'

Both Rose and Ingrid were stunned by what Jessie was saying. Could it be that they had somehow stirred a deep memory within her? They slowly turned to look at each other

and then at Jessie, who had a strange, faraway expression. 'My twin,' she murmured, 'my twin, you took her away from me, you took her away and it was cold.'

Rose was too upset to speak. Ingrid moved across the room, sat on the arm of Jessie's chair and gently patted her back. 'It's the hardest thing of all, child, to give away your own flesh and blood. Like me, you mother did it for the very best of reasons, she had only you and your sister's welfare at heart.'

'Did you choose?' said Jessie, gazing into Rose's face. 'Did you pick and choose which one would go and which would stay?'

'No, it wasn't like that,' said Rose quietly.

'Where is she now?' asked Jessie, in a low, controlled voice.

'Not many miles away,' said Ingrid, lifting Jessie's chin and smiling at her. 'I think that once you have got over the shock, you are in for a nice surprise.'

'It's all right, Mum,' said Rose, 'I'll tell her.' She patted her face dry, cleared her throat and took a deep breath. 'There was a reason for my not wanting to entertain Tom, Jessie. And I have to confess that his mother, Emmie, tried her best to persuade me to tell you about Hannah before you found out from someone else. But I was so scared, Jessie . . .'

'Hannah? Did you say Hannah? Tom's Hannah?' A vision of Charlie standing in the doorway of Tom's living room swept across her mind, when he had said that he hadn't seen Rose in years. And Tom's mother, Emmie . . . who had brushed it off, saying she knew Rose from way back.

She wondered about Tom, about their first date when he stood her up. Had he been warned off? Jessie turned her attention to her grandmother. Hadn't she all but told her on *their* first meeting? Hadn't she said, *your mother gave away your sister*? More importantly, why had everyone kept the truth from her? From her and from Hannah? Or did she know too? Surely not? No . . . Hannah hadn't been told, of that she felt certain.

'Yes,' said Ingrid. 'Hannah is your twin sister. So you see, she was never gone for ever, *meine liebling*. It was destined that you would come together.'

'Of course she is,' murmured Jessie, trance-like, 'of course she's my twin. I knew that ... we both knew that ...' The tears were trickling down, a slow stream of tears. 'We felt something straightaway, I think, but we didn't know what it was.'

Rising from her seat, a little unsteady, Jessie went to the window and stared out. 'Why isn't she here? Didn't she want to come?'

Concerned over her fragile state of mind, Ingrid went to her. 'She hasn't been told. She doesn't know that Gerta's not her real mother or that your uncle Jack is not her father.'

Jessie laughed bitterly. 'I never even knew she was supposed to be my cousin, let alone my twin. You weren't taking any chances, were you? All of my life I've missed her. I know you won't believe that, but I did, I missed someone and all the time it was Hannah.' She blew her nose and looked at Ingrid. 'I want to see her.'

'And so you shall. Come and sit and make it easier for your poor mother,' said Ingrid.

Allowing her grandmother to lead her back to the armchair, close to Rose, Jessie remembered the baby growing inside her. 'Maybe I'll have twins,' she murmured through her tears. She looked across at Rose. 'It's all right, Mum, I don't blame you. I don't blame anyone. I know it must 'ave been hard for you, having to tell me now.' She smiled faintly. 'I think your mum's bossier than mine.' That spontaneous quip broke the tension and lightened the heavy mood.

'You could be right there,' said Rose, smiling. 'Your dad wanted to bring you together years ago, Jessie, but I was terrified you'd hate me for splitting you up, not to mention how Hannah would feel. It's only recently, after you'd met up with Tom and I started to see Emmie more often, that I learned how unhappy

she's been, living with that wretched woman. I thought she was wanted.'

'She'll be all right,' said Jessie. 'She'll be fine ... we'll make up for it. We'll make up for everything. She can come and live with us now ...'

Rose cautioned her. 'Maybe, but we *must* tread carefully and not rush into anything. I know it'll be hard for you, but you've got to be patient ... and more importantly, you're to keep away from Hannah until we have a full family reunion.'

Jessie started. 'But why? Why can't I see her today? You've told *me* so—'

'Your uncle Jack is coming back to England and we have to wait until he's arrived. He especially requested, urged even, that we wait. Apparently he's been trying to get a transfer from the New Zealand office to London ever since he received the news that your dad had ... met with an accident. But his arrival is fairly imminent. He'll let us know once he's here and ready to face Hannah.'

'You make Hannah sound like a judge,' Jessie said.

'Well,' said Rose, 'in a way both my brother and myself will be on trial. Hannah is in for a shock and one she won't be too pleased about. We've all been lying to her since she was a baby in a pram. I don't expect her to fall into my arms – blood mother or not.'

Jessie could hardly take it in. 'Everything's happening at once.'

Ingrid nodded. 'Yes, and not before time where you and your twin are concerned, and where your mother and I are concerned. It would seem that this is the year for estranged mothers and daughters to come together.'

'Yes ... and estranged sisters ... and brothers.' Jessie imagined the expression on her brothers' faces when they learned there was another one of them. 'You can live here too ...' She spoke without looking at Ingrid. 'We can all live together.'

'There are tenants in your attic rooms who bring in rent for your mother and I have a nice flat all to myself, thank you.'

'The tenants could move into the rooms above the cobbler shop,' said Rose, tentatively. 'There's no reason for you not to come and live with us – unless you'd rather not.'

'I would rather not. I'm too set in my ways. I'll stay over by Victoria Park and you may visit me there. I don't know or care much for this part of the East End. And an invitation for Christmas would be nice. Christmas with grandchildren is how it should be. Pride has deprived me of that for too long.' Ingrid got up. 'Now I must make my way home.'

Showing Ingrid to the door, Rose thanked her, not just for the visit but for helping to sort out her mind and her life. 'Maybe now that we've cleared the air all round we can do some catching up,' she said.

'I would like that, Rose. I would like that very much. Do you know what my worst fear was? That one of us should die without us having repaired the bridge. That was my very worst fear. God does work in mysterious ways, doesn't He? The person responsible for bringing your family together is the very person who might have been the cause of pushing you and Jessie apart.'

'Tom?'

'Tom. *Auf wiedersehen.*'

Rose hugged her mother for the first time since their parting many years ago.

She went back into the sitting room filled with a sense of long-awaited relief, and was moved by the way her own child, Jessie, was curled up on the settee, still tearful but smiling. 'Well, things do have a way of working themselves out, don't they, Jess? We've got a long way to go yet. The gossips will have a good time denouncing the Warner family but, oh my Lord, how far along the road we've all come.'

Pulling her shoulders back, Rose suggested they call Dolly in to tell her about Hannah. 'Let's hope she won't be jealous,'

she said, 'or fearful that Hannah will take you away from her. Dolly's more sensitive than you think.'

'I know, but before she comes in, will you do something special for me? Will you hold me close and rock me, the way you used to when I was little?'

'Oh Jessie, what are we to do with you? One minute you're a woman and the next a baby,' said Rose, smiling and sitting next to Jessie on the settee, drawing her close. 'You don't want me to sing a lullaby as well, do you?'

'No, you can save that for when your first grandchild comes along.'

Chapter Ten

Turning out some freshly baked tarts, Charlie's favourite, Emmie was doing her best to soften up her husband who had never like meddling in other people's affairs.

'I just don't think you should get involved, Em, that's all I'm saying.' He licked a finger and turned the page of the *Betting News*. 'Leave it to the Warner family, let them sort it out. You'll get no thanks if it goes wrong or if it comes right.'

Emmie smiled to herself; her Charlie could go on at times, repeating himself over and over.

'You're like a record on the blooming gramophone with the needle stuck, Charlie,' she said. 'If that's not the fifth time you've said it today, I'm a Dutch herring.' Of course he had a point and in other circumstances, she would be the first to say leave other people's family matters alone, but the Warners' business had become her business, firstly because of Hannah and secondly because of Tom. Tom and Jessie. 'Anyway, I'm not interfering, if that's what's worrying you,' she went on. 'Rose asked me to have a word with Gerta and that's all I'm going to do, have a word. Something I should have done a while back but as it's turned out, the timing would have been wrong. Jack Blake's ship came in first thing this morning and Tom's arranged to pick him up from his hotel this evening, to take him to Rose's house.'

'So why go to Gerta's?'

'Needs be, and I owe it to Rose. Once today is over, Charlie, I'll be able to wash my hands of it and we can concentrate on putting on a nice wedding reception here.' That was her trump card. Charlie couldn't wait to have all his friends round and the neighbours in for a good old knees-up. 'I do feel sorry for poor Jack though.'

'Poor? I doubt it,' said Charlie, his nose still in his paper, as if it held more interest than what was going on in his own back yard. 'He's probably made himself a fortune out there.'

'Selling encyclopaedias? Fat chance of that.'

'Don't you be so sure, Em. How else d'yer think he can afford to come all this way? I might 'ave a word with 'im once he's sorted out his commitments. Wouldn't mind emigrating myself. I bet the rents out there are a damn sight cheaper than they are in this country.'

He had played right into her hands over another bone of contention and she was quick to take advantage. 'Very true, Charlie,' she said earnestly, 'which is all the more reason why we should think seriously of taking that loan from Johnnie's bank to buy one of them houses. We could afford to pay it back between the two of us, and we wouldn't have rent to pay then, would we?'

Hoping that Charlie's sudden silence meant that he was thinking about it, she kept quiet and waited. Tom had almost talked the subject to death, going on and on about it since the day he visited the houses and had shaken hands on a very good deal if the four went at once. Johnnie the entrepreneur was going to pay cash for his one and take a loan for another, and Tom had already marked one for himself and Jessie. So that left one and Emmie wanted it for Charlie, herself and young Stanley.

'I'd rather go to New Zealand,' said Charlie. 'Johnnie should give us the money to go, see us safely over there, out of England when the war's on. If you was thinking straight,

Emmie, you'd want the same.' He shook his head despairingly. 'Getting in debt to buy a bloody 'ouse that's gonna get blown to smithereens. Fucking stupid.'

'Don't swear, Charlie. Now that young Jessie's coming into the family you're gonna have to give it up. If you swore in front of her mother, Rose, I would die. You know how strait-laced she is.'

'Well, don't blame me if it all goes wrong, that's all,' he said. 'Just remember that I was against it and all for going across the world and away from the bombs. Just you remember that.'

Emmie felt her heart lurch. Whether Charlie knew it or not, he had just agreed to the bank loan and house purchase. She would have to be very careful and go along with his game-playing.

'The day you get off your arse, Charlie Smith, to go anywhere further than Southend is the day I'll sing for my supper.'

'Now who's swearing.' He flicked another page of his paper. 'And as for your singing, you'd do better to say your prayers and ask Him where the money's coming from for this wedding, 'cos if you think it's gonna be a ham sandwich and trifle do, you're wrong. We're doing it properly and not on a bloody shoestring.'

Happier by the minute, Emmie forced back her laughter and kept a straight face. She wanted to be on her way but she would have to bide her time, let him think he was the boss for a bit longer. To have him on her side was a good deal better than having to live with his sulks, which had been known to go on for weeks sometimes. She still hadn't won him round over her visit to Gerta.

'England beats anywhere abroad any day,' said Emmie, knowing full well that that was Charlie's true sentiment; he was a King and Country man. Mention England and he almost stood up to sing the national anthem. 'Oh, yes,' she continued, 'England's a good place, so long as you know how to work

with the system to make ends meet and pinch whatever else is needed to lighten the load.'

'Work with the system? Ha. Go and talk to all the bleeding foreigners, they'll tell you how to do that. Pouring in from every corner of the bloody world to take our jobs and 'ouses.'

'You're beginning to sound like Mosley, Charlie.'

'Give over, woman. That pompous bastard? A lot of good his claptrap's done. The man wants to try doing a full day's work. I'll have kippers for tea.' Charlie's tone made it clear that there was to be no more talk on that particular subject. 'Nice pair of kippers today instead of for Sunday breakfast.'

'So you will think about that house then? I've got my heart set on it, Charlie, a place of our own, something to leave to our grandchildren and a fresh start for us – a lovely new house.'

'New? You must be joking. It'll want a lot of bloody work done on it before it'll look halfway decent – God knows how many gallons of paint and rolls of wallpaper. Well, go on then. Sod off round to Gerta's, give me five minutes' peace.'

'What about your kippers?' she whispered, as she kissed his cheek.

'I'll have 'em when you get back, so don't be long. Tom's fetching Hannah back 'ere after the dog stadium, which should be in about an hour if I'm right ...'

'Then he'll pick up Jack from his little hotel in Aldgate and take him round Rose's place, but not before I get there with Hannah, right, Charlie?'

'Yeah, all right, I've got it. But what if I can't keep Hannah 'ere? What if she wants to go home, and walks in on you and Gerta going at it hammer and tong ...'

'That mustn't happen,' said Emmie quickly.

'Exactly. Which is why Rose and Jack are the ones who should handle this.'

'Well, you'll find a way to keep her 'ere for me, won't you, Charlie? We don't want to mess things up now.'

There was a rustle of newspaper and a grunt from Charlie.

'Good. That's that settled then,' said Emmie. She checked her face in the mirror above the fireplace and reached for her lipstick and powder, she didn't want Gerta to think she was going to seed.

'Don't let the German get the better of you,' said Charlie, as she headed for the door.

Smiling to herself, Emmie left the house. You're a funny chap, Charlie Smith, she told herself. Never show your true feelings. You're just as worried about Hannah as I am but you'd never let on.

Emmie knocked three times, on Gerta's front door, the copper's knock, as it was known in the East End. Three sharp raps. She could see then why they did it, there was a ring of authority and no-nonsense about it.

'Yes? What can I do for you?' Gerta peered from a crack between the door and the wall.

Giving the door a nudge Emmie wedged her foot between it and the door frame. 'I could tell you what I want right here if you like, Gerta, but the neighbours would have a field day because I don't intend to keep my voice down. It's up to you. Ask me in or let the world hear about your private, sordid business. Rose Warner has been to see me.'

She shrugged. 'You'd better come off the street before my neighbours think you've escaped from an asylum.' She stood to one side and jerked her head for Emmie to enter.

'This staircase could do with brightening up,' said Emmie, goading her. 'A pot of paint doesn't cost much. All these dark shades of paint and varnish ...'

'I don't bother with fashions. Why pay good money just to make other people feel better? Besides, I don't encourage visitors and this is good enough for me.'

'And Hannah?'

'Hannah? Ha! She's plainer than anyone. She would be happy living in a cell in a convent.'

'Yes,' said Emmie, 'compared to living with someone like you I should think that would be an attraction.'

Gerta showed her into the sitting room and nodded towards the chair in which she was to sit – a tall-backed wooden chair. Emmie sat down on the sofa instead. 'I'll come straight to the point, Gerta, since neither of us wants to be in the other's company for longer than necessary. Rose has come clean with the girls and let them know that Hannah is not your daughter but Rose's.'

Gerta snorted in disbelief. 'That woman would die rather than let the scandalous truth come out. What would people think of her, giving away a baby? Separating twins. You are more foolish than I thought if you believe that Rose Warner has the guts to tell the truth.'

'So wheels have been set in motion,' said Emmie, 'and steps taken to ensure you don't get a penny of Hannah's share of the compensation.'

'You may set whatever you want in motion. The authorities will take my side. I have kept the unwanted child all these years, loving and caring for her, as a blood mother might. It was hard for me, since my own husband left, and I am entitled—'

'You won't get one penny, Gerta. I wrote to Jack and he tells me he divorced you. You kept that one close to your chest, didn't you?' Emmie was feeling very much on top of things. 'He's with Rose and his family right now.' He wasn't, but Gerta wasn't to know that, and he would be with them soon. 'He's coming to see you, tomorrow, to ask about the money he's been sending Hannah, which she hasn't seen a penny of.'

The colour had drained from Gerta's face, Emmie noted with satisfaction, and she seemed dumbstruck. But not for long.

'I spit on you,' she hissed. 'I spit on the Warner family and I spit on Jack Blake. I spit—'

'Spit where you like,' Emmie cut in. 'It doesn't change anything.'

'And soon my homeland will spit bombs all over your precious England. Hitler will take this country. Then he will clean it of *all* degenerates. Britain will become his domain, Emmie Smith, and people like you and Jack Blake will be swept into the gutter.'

'I don't think so, Gerta.' Emmie wished Charlie was here, he would be roaring with laughter by now. 'The British are stronger than you think, my dear. Hitler won't stand a chance against us British, trust in that.'

'This country is not prepared for another war. It is asleep,' Gerta sneered.

'Cat-napping, Gerta, cat-napping, and whether you believe it or not, most of us can read the newspapers and listen to the news on the wireless. It would seem that your favourite cause is on the wane.'

'Really?' said Gerta spitefully. 'And how will your sons cope with that?'

'Find another social club to join, because that's all they're in it for, Gerta. The free women and the tea dances. Not many take it quiet as seriously as you do, my dear. There are Blackshirts and there are Blackshirts.'

'Oh,' said Gerta, deflated. 'So you know. You surprise me.'

'We don't believe in secrets between family, which is why Hannah is being told the truth. I've stepped in now and there's no getting rid of me. You see, my son is going to marry Jessie Warner, Hannah's twin, so it really is my business now. Don't test me on this one, Gerta. Don't even think about bringing my sons down with your vicious tongue because if you do, I'll make you wish you'd never left Germany.'

Gerta stood up abruptly and asked Emmie to leave. 'Please pass on a message to your friend. Tell her that I will settle for less than I asked but I will not settle for nothing.'

'I'll do that with pleasure. I'm sure she'll be ready to make

a small settlement ... for your troubles. She's not a greedy woman.' And with that, Emmie swept out.

At home, Emmie found Hannah in the best room enjoying a cup of tea with Charlie. The next step was to get themselves to Rose's house, before Tom arrived there with Jack. The plan was well laid but it could still go wrong.

'Charlie's been telling me about his time in the trenches during the war, Emmie. It's such a good story. What heroes he and all the other soldiers were.' There was a knowing smile on Hannah's face; she had heard the story many times and Emmie knew it.

'Well, up you get, Hannah. We've a visit to make.'

'A visit? To where?'

'It's a surprise, now be a good girl and don't spoil it for me. Come on, I may have found you a nice room with a good family.'

'A room? With a family? But I was thinking about a flat, a small place of my own.'

'I know, but you haven't found anything you like after all this time and I think this would suit you nicely. It's only a fifteen-minute walk or so, and it's a lovely evening. At least come and see it, Hannah. I've gone to a lot of trouble.'

'Well, I suppose there's no harm in looking ...'

'Course there ain't, gal,' said Charlie, his timing perfect. 'If Em's given it the thumbs-up, it can't be bad. Go on, the pair of you, and don't take too long about it. The boys'll be in soon and I'm blowed if I'm gonna start frying kippers for that lot.'

Hannah was quieter than usual as they walked through the back streets, listening more than talking. Emmie thought she had probably picked up that something was afoot, but Hannah asked no questions. What she was thinking was anyone's guess. As far as Emmie was concerned, once she'd delivered her into Rose's hands, her job was done and she would slip away.

When they turned into Rose's street, Emmie began to panic a little. How would Hannah react to suddenly finding out the truth and being thrust into the Warner family? Her insides fluttered with worry, but there was no turning back now.

'The family you're about to meet are not exactly strangers, Hannah,' she said as they reached the front door. 'This is Jessie's home. She'll be waiting to welcome you.'

'Jessie? Jessie lives here?'

'That's right. Jessie, her mother, her sister Dolly, and their two young brothers, Alfie and Stephen.' Saying no more, Emmie knocked on the door.

Hannah craned her neck. 'I can see there are attic rooms. Are they the ones to let?' Now she was smiling.

'Let's wait and see, shall we?'

It was Rose who answered the door, looking apprehensive. 'Hello, Emmie,' she said, and then turned to Hannah. 'You look in fine fettle, Hannah. Come in.'

Ignoring Hannah's quizzical look, Emmie motioned for her to go first and she did, without a word.

Jessie appeared in the hall and stood looking at her twin, not moving a muscle, hardly breathing. It all seemed to fit, the way she looked, the way they had got on when they first met. Walking slowly towards her, Jessie's instincts were to go against all that she'd been told to do, which was to stay passive. Excitement rose within her and she just wanted to lead Hannah away from everyone else and hold her tight. She gripped her arm instead and brushed a kiss across her cheek, whispering, 'Hello, Hannah. You're in for a surprise.'

Hannah looked over Jessie's shoulder at Emmie, her eyes full of questions. Jessie was still clinging to her and Hannah had the strange feeling that she was smelling her skin.

'That's enough now, Jessie,' said Rose quietly. 'You'll frighten her off.'

'Into the sitting room, is it, Rose?' prompted Emmie. Now that it came to it, she found she couldn't just slip away as she'd

intended. She had to see this thing through, she had to be there for Hannah.

'Yes. Dolly's waiting to welcome you too, Hannah. The boys are upstairs, we'll call them down once we've explained a few things.'

'I don't want to sound ungrateful,' Hannah was at a loss for words, 'but this is all a bit overwhelming. I don't understand.'

'I'm sure,' said Rose, guiding her in, 'but everything will become clear.' Rose sat down on the sofa and patted the space next to her. 'Come and sit down.'

Hannah did as Rose asked, looking very uncomfortable. Jessie and Emmie sat on chairs. Dolly was in the armchair.

'Now ...' said Rose, 'this is all going to come as a shock to you and once I've said what I've got to say, you'll no doubt wonder why I've left it so long to tell you.'

Hannah looked to Emmie for some sort explanation, but Emmie just nodded encouragingly.

'Has something happened to Tom?' she finally asked.

That one small question touched Emmie to the core, Hannah's thoughts had gone straight to her Tom.

'Tom's fine, Hannah,' she said. 'In fact, he'll be here shortly.'

Another silence followed. This time it was Dolly who stepped in.

'You're not gonna believe this, Hannah,' she said, leaning back, arms folded, 'but all that you said that day at Tom's house about you and Jessie thinking the same thing and at the same time – well, you would wouldn't you, being twins.'

The room went still, no one seemed to breathe even.

Hannah stared at Dolly. 'Say that again?'

'I know.' Dolly grinned. 'I was shocked as well when they told me. Mum and Dad had you adopted 'cos they couldn't afford to feed two babies. We're your family and we want you to come and live with us. We've got some catching up

to do.' Dolly was the only one smiling. 'They picked a right one, though, didn't they, with that bleeding German woman. From what I've heard of it, she's a bit of a loony.'

'That's enough, Dolly,' said Rose, secretly grateful for her daughter's straightforward manner. She took Hannah's hand and squeezed it. 'Dolly certainly doesn't beat about the bush, does she?'

'What did she mean? I'm nobody's twin. I don't have any brothers or sisters.' Again Hannah turned to Emmie. 'Why are they doing this? Is it some kind of a parlour game?'

Emmie, who knew her better than anyone, realised that Hannah was waiting for a simple explanation. She wasn't shocked, she wasn't upset; she was slightly indignant, that was all. Rose was going to have to open up and stop beating about the bush herself soon, before Hannah got totally confused.

'I'm sure Dolly didn't mean what she said about your foster mother, Hannah,' said Emmie, giving Rose a sharp look to prod her into speech; this was her job, after all. 'Gerta might have her strange ways but she's hardly a loony.'

'Foster mother? You mean this is serious? You think I'm Jessie's twin sister?'

Rose laid a hand on Hannah's shoulder and squeezed it. 'I know you are, my dear. It pains me to think about it, but I let Jack and his wife Gerta have one of my babies to bring up as their own. At the time, Robert and I were very, very poor and didn't have enough money to look after you, but they did, and they wanted you very much.'

'She took me in,' murmured Hannah, her eyes now fixed on the floor, 'when my own mother turned me out ... is that what you're saying? If so ... that means a great deal, doesn't it?' Again she looked to Emmie for answers. 'She saved me from Dr Barnardo's ... from going into a children's home.'

'No, Hannah!' Startling everyone, Rose stood up. 'She did no such thing. I would *never* have placed you in a home. Gerta was my sister-in-law. I trusted her. She and my brother begged

me to let them have one of my girls. I didn't want to give you up, of *course* I didn't! But we were living in one room which only just had a roof. We thought it was the best thing all round, and so it was, at the time. My brother loved you like a father would love his own child.' A strangled cry escaped from Rose. 'He cherished you.'

'So my father is not my father, he's ... my uncle? Is that what you're saying? And when he tired of me, he left me there ... with her?'

There was a heavy silence, and once again it was Dolly who broke it

'That's all over now,' she said brightly. 'You can live here with us. I think you look more like me than Jessie – except for the blonde hair.'

Hannah looked across at Jessie but did not return her twin's weak smile. 'How long have you know about this?'

'Not long. I wanted to come straight round to tell you but I was told I had to wait until now. Mind you,' she said, her cheeks flushed, 'I think I've always known something. It was as if I missed you without knowing who you were. I know that sounds daft but—'

'It doesn't. I've lived with that feeling too and it made me feel very lonely, I would rather not have had it. I know I was once very close to someone ... someone who wasn't there any more.' She turned to Rose, still no smile to light up her pretty face. 'How old was I when you did this thing?'

'Almost a year old,' said Rose, her voice heavy with remorse.

'So we would remember something, of course we would. No doubt we shared the same pram and the same cot.'

'Yes,' Rose managed to smile through her tears, 'you did.'

'Well,' said Hannah, 'I feel very sorry for myself as that baby. I think it was a cruel thing to do to a baby. I don't think that my mother, Gerta, is the wickedest one of all.'

She stood up, tall and erect, rendering them all speechless. 'If you will excuse me, I think it's time I left. Don't bother to show me out, and Emmie, don't bother to walk me home. I'd prefer to be alone.' She looked from Dolly to Rose and then to Jessie. 'And as for welcoming me into your home, I'm afraid it's too late for that. I don't belong in this family. I don't have any brothers or sisters and you are not my mother!'

This was more than Emmie could take. She stood up and faced Hannah. 'You just stay right where you are, Hannah! How *can* you condemn Rose out of hand like this? You have no idea what she has been through! You owe your mother an apology!'

'*Apology?*' Hannah's anger was frightening. Emmie hadn't bargained for this. 'I'm not bloody *apologising* for what *she* did to *me*!

'Calm down, Hannah,' said Emmie. 'Listen to what—'

'No! I've heard *enough*. Who do they think they *are*?' She turned on all of them. 'You lure me here under false pretences and then tell me that I am one of you! Strangers! That's what you are to me, *strangers*! So prim and *proper*, living in your nice big house with this fine furniture. One big happy family. You shun me for nearly eighteen years and then expect me to come smiling and grateful? Well, I don't want to be one of you. I hate the sight of everyone in this room! You can go to bloody hell! *All of you!*'

The knock on the front door was a relief; Tom had timed it perfectly.

'Do you want to tell Hannah who's at the door, Rose, or shall I?' asked Emmie.

Rose, pale and drawn, shook her head. 'I'll tell her myself, then I'll go to my bedroom. Don't be so hard on my brother, Hannah. He's come a very long way to help you through this.'

'What did you say?' Hannah's voice and expression changed

instantly. Her face and neck became taut and her soft blue eyes filled with tears. 'My father . . . is *here*? At the door?'

'Yes,' said Rose, 'he's here. I'll leave you to your reunion. I'll be in my room if I'm wanted.' A broken woman, Rose was grateful for Jessie and Dolly either side of her.

'It'll be all right, Mum,' whispered Dolly.

'It was shock, that's all,' added Jessie as they went upstairs together.

Downstairs, Emmie wearily pulled herself to her feet. 'Well, I suppose I'd better open the door. Tom can walk me home. We'll leave you alone with your father, Hannah.'

'No, Emmie! No! Please don't leave me. Please, Emmie! I'm sorry for what I said! I'm sorry, Emmie! Don't go! He might hate me too!'

'Hate you? You think they asked you here because they hate you? Is that what you think?'

'Well, perhaps not, but they do now. Stay with me!'

'All right, Hannah. I'll stay with you.'

She opened the street door.

'Hello, Emmie,' smiled Jack. 'It's good to see you again.'

Emmie did her best to return his smile. He looked older, his face lined and tanned, his hair sprinkled with grey, but he was still handsome Jack Blake. 'Hannah's in the parlour, Jack. I'm afraid it's all gone badly wrong. Maybe you can talk to her. Rose is too upset to see you, she's in her room and no doubt crying her eyes out.' She looked from him to Tom and he did exactly what any mother would want her son to do, he put his arms round her and held her close, shushing her and telling her not to be upset.

'Did you really expect Hannah to fall into their arms?' he said gently. 'I suppose she shouted the odds.'

'She was a very wicked girl, Tom. The things she said to poor Rose, and in front of those girls. I blush at the thought of it. I wish I'd let you have your way. She wouldn't have behaved like that if you'd been here. I'm sure of it.' She looked at Jack.

'Oh Jack, I am sorry. I thought it was going to be so lovely. It's what I've always dreamed might happen and it all went wrong. What *have* I done?'

Jack touched her arm comfortingly. 'Started the ball rolling, my friend. We've a long way to go but look how far we've come. Now you go on upstairs to comfort my sister, and Tom, you go and see to your sweetheart. I want to see my Hannah alone. I've waited a very long time for this moment.'

Jack went into the sitting room and closed the door behind him. He gazed at Hannah for a moment and then held out his arms to her. 'Come here, sweetheart. Come and give your old dad a hug.'

Crying, Hannah fell into his arms. 'I've missed you,' she said. 'I missed you so much it hurt.'

'I know, I know.' He stroked her lovely soft hair. 'I'm here now and I promise I'll never leave you again. Never.'

'But you'll have to go back surely,' she said, her head buried in his shoulder. 'How can you stay in England?'

'Very easily, my pet,' he said. 'I have no intention of going back. This is the day I've been saving for.' He pulled himself away from her and looked into her face. 'Now then, I know you've had a shock. A real shock. But there is more, sweetheart, and I think it's right that we get it all out of the way now. It's to do with your mother.'

'Which one?'

'Gerta.'

'I want you to know before the others, and if you don't want to tell the others, we won't. I think we should sit down.'

Jack explained briefly that Gerta wasn't all she seemed. Her role as an ardent Blackshirt was a clever double-edged cover for the fact that she was a German agent, a spy, who had been under surveillance for quite a while. He told Hannah that Gerta had insisted she get a position in the local library because the books that she brought

to and fro contained coded information for another agent to collect.

The fact that Gerta was an agent did not shock Hannah; on the contrary, it came as no surprise. If anything, it threw light on things she had often found puzzling. 'But how could you know all this?' she asked, sitting closely by Jack's side on the sofa. 'I feel as if I'll wake up soon and find myself in that room, with her reading into the small hours, if reading is what she was doing. She doesn't look like a spy.'

'Agents are usually very ordinary-looking people who don't draw attention to themselves. Gerta, in her own way, was an ordinary German, living in England, who loved the Führer.'

'Why are you telling me now? Because they're going to arrest her?'

'Yes. So you must come and stay with me in the hotel or stay here with ... with your family. You mustn't go back to the flat for a few days. Then we can return to collect your things.'

Hannah let out a low whistle. 'I can't believe all this is happening. Does Tom know about it?'

'No. But I will have a word with him in private. He and his brother have got to stop attending meetings and burn any evidence of a uniform or anything to do with the Fascist movement. It's very possible that there will be a war, Hannah. If there is, Oswald Mosley and his officers will be interned.'

'Well,' said Hannah, all self-pity gone, 'what will I find out next? Maybe they'll want to arrest me?' She looked at Jack, suddenly frightened. 'Will they?' Her hand flew to her chest as the implications sank in. 'I was passing messages in the library books I took out. Why haven't they interrogated me?'

'No need, Hannah,' he said, quietly laughing at her. 'You've been under surveillance too, and they checked you out, believe me, right down to the rubbish you throw away in the dustbin.'

'But how do you *know* all this?'

'I just do. Don't ask questions I can't answer. Just accept it, Hannah, if you can. It will take strength—'

'Oh, I think I've got that. I've had to have it. It was only the thought of you coming back for me one day that kept me going at times. You, Tom and Emmie, and dear, lovable, Charlie.'

'Shall we ask my sister Rose to come downstairs now?'

'Is she really my mother? And Jessie my twin sister?'

'Yes, Hannah, she really is. Now I suggest that we don't say a word this evening about Gerta and what's about to happen to her. There won't be a fuss, nothing in the papers about her in particular – several agents will be arrested over the next few days in and around London. My arrival in England today and not last week or next week was deliberate. I wanted to be here when it happened and I wanted you out of the flat when they took her.'

The waiting seemed like an age to Jessie as she sat with Tom and Dolly in their bedroom. She went into Rose's room to ask if it was time yet for them to go down and was pleased to see that her mother looked better for having had a chat with her close friend, Emmie.

'I should think we're all ready for a good strong cup of tea,' said Rose, smiling at Jessie. 'It's been a long day and it's not over yet.'

'I'll go and tell Dolly, Tom and the boys to come down, shall I?'

'Yes, I should think they've had enough time together now. Let's hope he's managed to bring Hannah around.'

When they all went back into the sitting room, Jessie pushed the boys in ahead of her. She thought they would be enough to bring a smile to Hannah's face if she was still upset.

'Well,' said Emmie when they were all settled and it was clear that Hannah was more like her old self, 'now that we're in the one room together, I would like to say something. Getting

everyone together like this, and giving poor Hannah not one shock of her life but two was *my* idea. I was prepared to take full blame if it had all gone wrong, as it looked as if it had at one point, but since all seems fairly well, I'll take the credit instead.' Emmie's smile was broad. She focused on Alfie who was yawning. 'So if you don't mind, I'd like a little thanks. Well, Alfie?'

'What you looking at me for?'

'You're the eldest son, head of the family.'

His expression changed instantly. 'Oh, yeah ... well, I suppose I am. Um ... thanks very much ... from all of us.' Alfie looked across at Dolly and flapped his hand. 'Pour out the tea now, will you, Dolly?'

'Cheeky bugger.'

'Will you be moving in then, Hannah?' asked Stephen, a touch nervous.

'No. I won't be moving in. It was very nice to be asked, but I'm going ahead with plans I had already made.' She looked at Jack and smiled. 'My father isn't going back to New Zealand.'

'Is that right, Jack?' Rose's face lit up.

'Yes it is. When I received Emmie's letter, I decided then that England was where I belonged and, well, what with one thing and another, the time was right. So I asked for a transfer to London and the head of department agreed. I bought a one-way ticket.'

'Well, I'm very very pleased to hear it,' said Rose. 'If you should ever want to take up my eldest son's offer, I would love to have you here. We all would. I'm sure our tenants would understand, provided we give them fair notice to leave.'

'It's a lovely offer,' said Jack, 'but one I won't take up. No disrespect. It's just that I'm not really cut out to live in attics, although I'm sure it's a great flat.' He glanced at Hannah and smiled. 'I'm happy to stay in the small hotel with my daughter and look for a nice comfortable house which suits us both.'

'In the East End?' asked Rose hopefully.

'No, my dear, I'm too used to space around me now. Epping Forest perhaps.' He checked his wristwatch, 'We should be leaving soon, Hannah. I want to pay a visit to my mother and my brothers, who you may or may not remember.'

'I don't,' said Hannah, 'not really.'

Jack's easy manner had banished all shyness from the boys and before he could leave he had to answer all their questions about his life in the bush. Dolly and Hannah took their tea to a corner of the room and sat on the low stool, chatting. Emmie and Rose sat quietly, sipping their tea, too tired to talk.

'Come on, Jess,' whispered Tom. 'Let's get out of here.'

'I'll just say goodbye to Hannah in case they've gone by the time we get back.' Weaving her way round chairs and the table, Jessie touched her twin's elbow. 'I'm just going out for a walk with Tom. You will come and see me soon, won't you?'

'What about tomorrow? I don't think I'll be going into the library,' she said. 'I'll be taking a week off – Dad said it would be good to do that.'

Jessie kissed her on the cheek, squeezed her arm and whispered, 'I'm really pleased we've found out about each other.'

Outside in the street, Jessie and Tom put their arms round each other and strolled along, happy to be alone. They talked about Hannah, Jack, and their own future. Rose had listened when Jessie told her about the house she and Tom wanted to buy and after hearing all the details, she agreed to let Jessie use her part of the compensation money to buy it.

When Jessie talked about the baby, Tom became thoughtful. 'Jess, I've got something to ask you. I want an honest answer because it's your future, our future ... or maybe just yours ... that we're planning.'

His serious tone worried her and she wondered if he was about to suggest something horrible. 'Go on then, Tom, get if off your chest.'

'I know you bumped into Max the other day,' he said,

'Dolly mentioned it. And I know you're bound to bump into him again, so I want you to be absolutely sure that it is me you want as your husband and not Max. It's best you say now, Jessie, to save messing up both our lives – and his.'

'Of course it's you I want to marry. You know I love you, and in case you've forgotten it's your baby I'm having, not Max's. I've not been seeing him while I've been seeing you, if that's what you think. Is that what you think?'

'Oh, thank Christ for that.'

She couldn't believe her ears. 'You mean you *did* think the baby might be Max's? Surely not. You wouldn't think I'd trick you over something that important?'

'No, of course not, silly. I just thought you might want a back door to slip through, that's all. I was just checking, in case you were still in love with Max ... and felt stuck with me.'

'Well, now you know. I've never been this happy, so don't spoil it. I loved you before I even knew that you'd been looking after my twin for me.' She picked a small wild rose from a hedge growing in a neighbour's front garden and pushed it into the buttonhole in his jacket. 'I don't want anything to change ... ever.'

He cupped her face and kissed her lightly on the mouth. 'You'll be all right now, Jess. You've got me to look after you.' He slipped his arm round her waist and they walked on, passing a newspaper seller. He was shouting to draw attention to his placard which read: 'Advice from Minister of Defence, *"JOIN THE TERRITORIAL ARMY – BE PREPARED FOR A SECOND WORLD WAR!"*'

'Warmongers,' said Tom, smiling. 'What they'll do to sell a newspaper.'

'I hope you're right. Some are saying that they'll be calling men up before next summer. They wouldn't do that if they weren't expecting a war, would they?'

'Stop *worrying*. Everything's on the up. Anyway, our baby's due in April. Wild horses wouldn't drag me away from my

family, neither king nor country will take me away from my Jessie and my baby girl.'

'How come you're so sure it's a girl?'

'I just know. Don't ask me how. I just do. I can see her now, long white hair, running towards her daddy, arms outstretched. My daughter. My little Emma-Rose.'

'Oh, so you've chosen a name already, have you? Don't I get a say in it?'

'You can pick the name if it's a boy.'

'Fair enough.' That suited Jessie; she couldn't lose either way, Emma-Rose was perfect.

'In April nineteen thirty-nine I'll be the proudest father of the most beautiful baby girl, you'll see.'

'And our little family of three will be living in Grant Street.'

'In our little two up, two down. So no more talk of me going off to fight the Germans. It's not gonna happen. Trust me. There won't be a World War Two.'

That night, before turning off her bedside lamp, Jessie wrote in her notebook: '13 August 1938 – Our Prime Minister, Neville Chamberlain, is to visit Hitler for a crisis talk. It's more frightening than the *The War of the Worlds* on the wireless. Mum's secretly looking forward to being a grandmother. Tom says there won't be a war. Hannah has been told she's my twin and I think – I hope – she's pleased.'

SALLY WORBOYES

OVER BETHNAL GREEN

Coming soon from Hodder & Stoughton

Sally Worboyes' fantastic East End trilogy continues . . .

Jessie Warner has married Tom Smith and their baby Billy has been born. But the newfound joy in Jessie's life is not reflected in the outside world, as the threat of war finally becomes a reality. Tom is called up almost at once, leaving Jessie to cope with the new baby alone. The Blitz over the East End begins, bringing panic and despair to the Londoners, as well as courage and hope in the face of danger. Then Tom goes AWOL and Jessie finds herself in a desperate situation. Meanwhile, Hannah, Jessie's clever twin sister, has been recruited to Bletchley Park to help crack the German communication codes . . .

Vivid and atmospheric, OVER BETHNAL GREEN captures the spirit of the East End and its indomitable people during some of the darkest days of the Second World War. Don't miss this wonderful novel in Sally Worboyes' East End trilogy, beginning with DOWN STEPNEY WAY.

Read this exclusive extract from Sally Worboyes' next book, OVER BETHNAL GREEN, continuing the story of the lives and loves of the characters in DOWN STEPNEY WAY, as they face the trials and tribulations of war time ...

Chapter One

On a sunny September morning in 1938, a group of workmen turned up in Bethnal Green Gardens and started to dig trenches. There was such an air of high spirits and so many onlookers that the mood was more comparable to children playing with their spades and buckets at a seaside beach than to preparations for the potential horrors of war. The gravity of the situation soon became clear when just a few days later the fitting and issuing of gas masks began.

Cupping her hands round her warm drink in her tiny living room, Jessie Smith, although tired and looking the worse for wear, was at least thankful that at last her six-month-old son Billy was sleeping soundly after a fretful night of teething trouble. Like most people in Britain, she and her twin sister Hannah, who was on a one-day home leave, were waiting to hear what the Prime Minister, Neville Chamberlain, had to say. In their hearts each of them knew what was coming and the room seemed to have filled with doom and gloom even though in their own way they had been willing the news not to be bad. They had deliberately avoided any talk of what might be and fantasised instead about the type of house that Hannah might one day live in should she end up married to the wealthy but boring man who had set his sights on her at Station X.

'The trouble is,' said Hannah, 'there only seem to be two types of men, rich and boring or poor and interesting.'

Jessie found it strange that her twin had not mentioned qualities which she would have named – magnetic, exciting, irresistible. 'What about my Tom? Where does he fit into your ideas about men?'

'A bastard but you can't help loving him?'

Quietly laughing at her sister's honesty, Jessie had to agree. 'Especially when he's been on a drinking binge with 'is dad and brothers.'

'Ah,' said Hannah, all-knowing. 'I remember those nights out. They were always getting up to some kind of no good, sailing on the wrong side of the law. Emmie used to wait for them with a rolling pin. She really did. And she hit them with it too. Across the bottom. She would tell me about it the next day, with a crafty smile on her face. "They pulled it off, love," she would whisper, slipping me a pound note. I hardly knew whether to take it or not.'

Recoiling from Hannah's familiarity towards Tom and his family, Jessie tried to rise above her jealousy. Her sister had, after all, known Tom for years before she herself had ever spoken to him. 'He never tells me where he gets the money to drink,' she said. 'He just winks. I don't need to know more.'

'Of course,' said Hannah, laughing. 'Another parcel falls off the back of a lorry at the dock gates and he and his dad and brothers go on the town to celebrate.'

Their diversion from reality ended when from the wireless came a hushed silence broken only by a quiet crackling. The stillness seemed deliberate, as if the BBC was preparing listeners for the worst kind of news. It was 3 September 1939.

With a ghastly dread in her stomach, Jessie quietly prayed that the country's biggest fear had not been realised. Head bowed and wishing that Tom, her husband of one year, was there by her side, she listened earnestly to Chamberlain's slow and grave delivery.

I am speaking to you from the Cabinet Room, 10 Downing Street. This morning, the British Ambassador in Berlin handed the German government the final note, stating that unless he heard from them by eleven o'clock, and they were prepared at once to withdraw their troops from Poland, a state of war would exist between us. I have to tell you now that no such undertaking has been received, and that consequently this country is at war with Germany.

Stricken by the announcement, Jessie switched off the wireless. Her mind went back to a dark day in the spring of this year, in April, two weeks before Billy was due. Tom had received his call-up papers ordering him to report to the Tower of London where he would be conscripted into the army. They had been married for just six months at the time. Until that morning post had arrived, Jessie believed that nothing could spoil her and Tom's perfect world.

'I can't say I'm all that shocked,' murmured Hannah. 'This war was on the cards.'

'I s'pose so,' replied Jessie, half wishing her twin wasn't there right then and saying such things. It made it too real too soon.

'Life is about to change, Jessie. For all of us. No more thinking the best.'

'I know. I think it hit me really when Tom's call-up papers came in April. I shook like a leaf. Couldn't stop. That poor bloody postman. I feel sorry for 'im now. He was only doing his job but he must've sensed the resentment us wives and mothers felt when he delivered them brown envelopes. Poor sod. You should 'ave seen the look on 'is face.' Jessie covered her face with her hands. She wanted Hannah to go. To explain why would be impossible. She and her twin were very close but for some strange reason she needed to be alone right now. Wanted to be by herself to think for herself.

'Thank God for Tom's mum next door. Good old Emmie,'

she said finally, trying her best. 'I expect she'll be listening in with the other women at work. Three sons to go to war. I don't know what's worse, seeing your husband go off and wondering if you'll ever see 'im again, or watching three sons walk away.'

'Well, aren't you the light at the end of a dark tunnel,' said Hannah, smiling, trying to lift her sister's spirits. 'We Brits have more backbone than that, Jessie. And Emmie's got guts for two strong women. And as for Hitler, let him try to take England. Just let him try.'

'Britain,' said Jessie. 'He won't settle for less.'

'Well then, he's in for a surprise, isn't he?'

'Let's hope so.'

'Oh, you can take it from me. If—'

'Hannah, please! I don't want to talk about it.' Jessie's tone was anguished. She glanced across the room at Billy and sighed. 'I don't really want to talk about anything. It's all too much for me.'

'Sorry, Jess. I wasn't thinking.'

With Billy asleep and the wireless switched off, the only sound in that room was the ticking of the clock and the hissing of the fire. Staring into the glowing coals, Jessie glanced at the wedding photograph of her and Tom on the mantel shelf, radiant and in love. Next to it was a group wedding picture showing her mother standing proudly between Jessie and Hannah, and their sister Dolly, with her younger brothers, Stephen, in his Boy Scout uniform, and Alfie in his very first suit. The smile on their mother Rose's face hid the disappointment she had felt. There had been no white satin lace dress for her daughter, no bridesmaids and, worst of all, Jessie had been carrying Tom's child when she went to the altar.

But Jessie had made a beautiful bride and looked radiant in her oyster satin coat with tiny coloured glass buttons and matching skirt, which now hung in the wardrobe upstairs,

waiting for another occasion when she might have the chance to wear it.

Jessie couldn't blame her mother for being cheerless at her wedding; she did, after all, have to stand alone to see her daughter married, without her late husband by her side. It had pained Jessie that her dad had not been there on her special day. She knew that her mother had not really taken to Tom and, well-mannered though she was, Rose hadn't been able to hide her feelings. His easy-go-lucky approach to life worried her.

Rose had made her views known to Jessie about her son-in-law's attitude towards the possibility of war. In her opinion, he liked the idea of being paid to train as a soldier, with board and lodging provided, while Jessie received an army pension. Jessie told her mother she was wrong and that once she got to know Tom properly she would realise he had been innocently baiting her. Rose had not been convinced.

Before his conscription in April, Tom had given up his job at the docks and taken an offer of freelance work as painter and decorator, which Rose considered reckless of him. The work had been spasmodic and he and Jessie, during those late winter months, had struggled to make ends meet.

Hannah pushed Chamberlain's speech from her mind and went into the kitchen to make them both a cup of tea while Jessie enjoyed the memory of one particular weekend when Tom had been home on leave. Standing by the butler sink, stringing some runner beans, she had been admiring the bluey-pink hydrangea bush in the garden when Tom had crept into the house and sneaked up behind her, giving her the biggest surprise of her life. It was little things like that that kept their love burning. During his periods of leave from the army, they had spent much of the time making love or fussing over their baby, Billy. On that leave Tom had seemed more worried than usual. He'd dropped hints about her being in London with all the French sailors on the lookout for a bit of romance.

'Actually they're called matelots,' she'd said innocently and in fun. It hadn't gone down well. Tom was a jealous man by nature and it was beginning to show. He had related tales he'd heard about the generosity of the French sailors who lavished presents of silk stockings, chocolates and brandy.

'Just don't go leaving our Billy and going out with 'em, that's all,' was his usual parting remark when his leave ended.

'You know,' said Hannah, coming into the room with their tea, 'Tom's very nervous about losing you.' Once again, as had happened before, the twin sisters seemed to have been thinking the same thing at the same time even though they had been in different rooms.

'What makes you say that?'

'Well,' said Hannah, sitting down, 'that time when I had a day off and came to see you when Tom was on home leave, he quizzed me on the goings-on around town.'

'Did he now?'

'It's all right. I was quick off the mark. Gave him a look that said don't even think about using me to spy on my own sister. I had, after all, come especially to tell you *my* good news.'

'That you'd been summoned for war work.'

'Yes.'

'And are you still chuffed over it, now that you're there?'

'Yep. I love my work. It's such a fantastic place. The hours are long and it's hard work, but I love being there. And you know how I enjoyed working in the library. I don't even miss being around books.'

Jessie's curiosity was piqued. 'Come on then, tell us what goes on there – or where it is at least. Don't be mean. You know I won't say anything.'

'I can't. I'm sworn to secrecy. Tom tried and failed and you know how persistent he can be,' Hannah said, smiling, hoping that would be the end of it.

'Please yourself. I just wondered what your room was like, that's all. I'm not bothered one way or the other.'

'Oh, I can tell you that. It's small but it's mine and the sun streams in through the window which looks out over the grounds. That's why I like it so much. It's heaven compared to that miserable flat over that dusty shop in Bethnal Green.'

'With a tyrant for a mother.' Jessie remembered Gerta, the woman who had made Hannah's childhood a misery.

'*Foster* mother,' Hannah corrected. 'And it's all buried in the past where it should be.'

Jessie turned the conversation back to her sister's work. 'What do you do there then? Just tell me that bit. Office work? Filing?'

'I mustn't tell you, Jess! I can't tell you what I do or where I work and live. It's secret stuff to do with the government and it was made clear that my lips must be sealed. I could get into a lot of trouble for even talking this much about it.'

The room went quiet again. Jessie didn't like the sound of it and didn't like her sister having to be away from the area, especially now. 'So now that war's been declared, will you still be able to come back now and then?'

'I hope so.' The tone of Hannah's voice made the message she was giving clear: no more talk of it. So Jessie pushed it from her mind. Very soon Emmie would be home from work and straight in to commiserate over the announcement on the wireless. They had things to discuss, that was for sure. Emmie would want to make plans straightaway, marking out every single air-raid shelter in the borough and advising Jessie to only shop close by those shelters for the sake of safety. After all, she had her grandson to think of as well as her daughter-in-law.

'I wonder how Tom's taking the news,' said Jessie, feeling worse by the minute.

'He's with men, don't forget. Soldiers. Their instincts will be to protect their territory. Knowing Tom, he'll be in a fighting mood.'

Maybe Hannah was right but on his last visit home, just a few weeks previously, Tom had still been adamant that Britain would not go to war. He had never believed that the day would come when the Prime Minister would make the announcement that Jessie had just listened to on the wireless.

'I think,' said Hannah, 'that Tom plays his cards close to his chest. All that talk about war never coming was a cover. He's not daft, Jessie. He knew.'

'Maybe.' It was becoming clear to Jessie that her twin sister knew Tom better than she did. And there was no denying that Tom knew Hannah better than all of them. But that was understandable. Jessie had only discovered the existence of her twin a year ago and Hannah had been a close friend of Tom since early schooldays. And now Jessie hardly saw anything of Hannah since she'd been posted to Buckinghamshire. What with her sister's absence and Tom having been stationed at Thetford, Jessie wanted to get out of the house sometimes and bring some fun into her life. Every other woman she knew, it seemed, was working in a factory preparing for a war and going out with friends in the evenings for a lively time. If she was honest with herself, she would have had to admit that she did sometimes feel envious. Jealous of her twin Hannah and jealous of her other sister, lively, carefree Dolly. Her own life seemed dull and lonely by comparison to theirs, even if she did have the beautiful son she adored.

'I'm going to have to go now, Jess,' said Hannah, checking the time. 'I don't want to miss my train.'

'No, you don't want to do that,' Jessie said with a touch of bitterness. They hugged and Hannah promised to come and see Jessie as soon as she could.

'It'll work out, Jess, you'll see. This time next year we'll be looking back with relief and smiling.'

Once Hannah had gone back to the centre at Bletchley Park, where enemy codes were deciphered and where Hannah's adoptive father, Jack Blake, had also been stationed months

before her, as a code breaker, Jessie felt very much alone in her two-up, two-down in Bethnal Green, which she loved. It was true that she regularly saw her in-laws who lived in the same street, and her own mother, Rose, twice a week, and sometimes her younger brother Stephen stayed overnight, but for all of that nothing filled the empty gap she felt. She missed Tom's strong arms holding her close in bed and she missed the times when she and her twin sister had sat and chatted for hours on end about everything and nothing.

Jessie's other sister Dolly, true to form, had been having a whale of a time and making the most of the pre-wartime spirit. She was always going out on dates and was very popular with the Dutch marines whose ships sometimes docked in London. The East End, it seemed, was as popular as the West End when it came to night life, the pubs and taverns full of laughter, cheerful music, and song.

On the way to the bus stop to see Tom off on his last leave home, Jessie had been mortified when he said he had thoughts of not going back. The conversation immediately changed into an argument with her telling him not to dare to do anything stupid. She told him to stick it out like the rest of the conscripts and that was when he revealed his true worry to her. He asked if she'd been seeing her old boyfriend while he was away, Max Cohen, whom she had courted for three years before meeting Tom.

The unexpected question had thrown her. Of course she hadn't been seeing Max but more importantly, why had Tom even asked? She had been faithful, unlike some other married women, and hadn't even gone out for one evening, and there he had stood, accusing her. She had refused to answer him at first, which had caused him to be even more testy. She wouldn't deny it and that, in Tom's eyes, made her look guilty. When Tom had demanded to know why she wasn't denying it, she had yelled, 'I shouldn't need to!' not caring who heard. 'Of course I haven't seen him! He's in the bloody army as well, isn't he!'

His reply had shaken her. 'No he's not! As if you didn't know! Got out of it and all because he's got two left feet. Did you know he 'ad two left feet, Jess?'

If she had not been so livid with him she would have found his remark funny. She hadn't thought about Max in a while but Tom had obviously been worrying about leaving her in London with the man she had once given herself to and said she would marry living close by. Now with the likelihood of being posted abroad, Tom would be even more anxious as to what she might be getting up to. She hadn't realised until then just how damaging jealousy could be. It had all started with a light joke from Tom but had grown and was still spreading, affecting them both for different reasons.

With Billy in her arms, awake and contented, Jessie went out into the back garden and picked a dahlia for him to play with before letting Harry out of his hutch for a run-around, which would please her son more than anything. He loved the rabbit and chuckled whenever it ran or hopped or deliberately turned its back on them. Able to crawl about now, Billy struggled to get down from Jessie's firm grip but the last thing she was going to do was let him loose in the back yard. 'You'll have to wait, Billy, till you can walk. Then you and Harry can chase each other.' From the expression on his face, she almost believed he understood every word and had a feeling that he'd do his utmost to pull himself up on to his feet when he was in the old playpen a neighbour had recently given her.

Walking around the garden, pointing out different leaves and flowers, Jessie felt as if she was in a strange kind of dream. Here she was with her adorable baby boy, her rabbit frisking around in the afternoon sun, the roses still in bloom and autumn flowers all around, and yet war had been declared. *War*. It didn't seem possible that it could happen in her country.

She recalled the day in April when Tom had been summoned into the army. It came flooding back as clear

as if it was happening right then. Jessie had wept when she saw the letter. She was in bed when Tom let himself into the house and she heard him knocking into furniture and singing, badly and out of tune, obviously very drunk.

'You were meant for me ... I was meant for you ...' he sang. 'Nature patterned you and when she was done ... Jess was all the good things rolled into one ... You're like a plaintive ... melody ...' There was a pause, then he sang loudly, 'Jessie — I've had no tea ... I ... 'm so hungry I could eat ... a horse ...'

When he found the letter propped on the table, telling him to report to the Tower, he staggered up the stairs, drunk and flabbergasted, as if it had arrived without any warning whatsoever. 'Jess. Jess ... they can't do this to me ...' he said, hardly able to end a sentence. 'I can't leave you, Jess.'

His performance irritated her. 'Tom, you'd better sober up. An' didn't you once say, you'd fight to the bitter end to keep Hitler's hands off Britain?' She tried to hold in her anger. 'Stop play-actin' and go to bed — in the box room, where you can snore as loud as you like. I need my sleep.'

But Tom had been in no mood to be quietened. 'I wasn't looking forward to going away to fight Hitler, Jess ... and I *don't* snore.' He did and he knew it.

'When you're this drunk you do. Where'd the money come from for your night out?' She wasn't going to let him off the hook.

Winking, hoping to soften her, Tom smiled and then hiccuped. 'Perks. Perks of life. A parcel fell off a lorry as it was coming out of the dock gates ... and the driver pulled away without realising.' Hunching his shoulders he sported that look of innocence he often used. 'What could I do but pick up that parcel? I've had a few beers, Jess, that's all. I was celebrating with my brother, Stanley. We sold most of the stuff.'

'And the rest?'

'We've, er, we've stored it,' he said, telling what he would

call a white lie. 'Round a mate's house.' Play-acting or not, he suddenly looked like a man in the depths of a despair as he sat on the edge of their bed. 'Not much to celebrate though, is there? I've got to leave you, Jessie, and I don't wanna do that.' Watching him waving the call-up papers in the air, she knew very well that he was deliberately being melodramatic. 'They can't mean it. I'm not a bloody soldier, I'm a decorator!' He slumped down on to their bedroom chair, a sorry sight. Looking like a frightened child, head lowered, he sobered up and became more serious and more honest. He said haltingly, 'This has really upset me.'

That got Jessie's back up. 'Upset *you*?' she snapped. 'Well, how do you think *I* felt? I saw those papers and went crying to your mother and *you* went down the pub.'

'Yeah, but . . . I hadn't seen the letter, *had* I?' he said, trying to get her sympathy. 'I wouldn't have gone out if I *had* seen it, Jess. You know that.'

It all seemed so trivial now, looking back. But Jessie still believed that it was the stress of Tom's antics and his call-up that had brought on her birth pains the very next day, two weeks before her time. For a while, it had been touch and go if she and the baby would live. Thank God it had been all right.

Pushing all of that from her mind, Jessie left her baby in his pushchair, happily watching Harry the rabbit, and went inside to make herself another cup of tea. After all, there was worse to come now. Bloodshed and killing of innocent people, men, women and children, with bombs dropping all over the world. She feared for Tom who underneath it all was a real softie at heart. He had cried his eyes out on the night Billy was born when they had very nearly lost him. It had been a close thing and they were lucky that their baby had an excellent midwife to watch out for him and Jessie. Not only had he arrived early and unexpected but when she finally gave birth, the house had gone dark. The electric meter had run out of coins. Worse still, the

umbilical cord was caught round Billy's neck and the midwife had only the light of a torch to work by.

'Never mind, Billy,' Jessie whispered, 'I won't let anything 'appen to you. No. It would 'ave to be over my dead body.' She looked up at the sky. 'Please, dear sweet Jesus, keep me safe so I can take care of my baby.'

To Jessie's surprise and joy, Tom was allowed home for an overnight visit the day after war had been declared and before he was posted abroad. When he turned up on the doorstep, she simply couldn't believe it. He was the best sight for sore eyes anyone could wish for and she didn't want to let him out of her sight. They made the most of every minute together, hardly apart, always in the same room, always with Billy – and for the first time since she had known him, Tom helped her in the kitchen, preparing food, washing up, anything so long as he was by her side and touching her. In bed, they made love for most of the night, clinging to each other as if they might never see each other again.

At the breakfast table, Tom looked terrible. His eyes red and his face drawn. 'I don't want to go, Jess,' he said, choked. 'I want to stay here with you and Billy.'

'You can't, Tom, you know that. Try not to think about it.' She was finding it all too much and her voice gave her away. Of course she didn't want him to go but what choice had they?

'Why am I going?' he said, looking like a child about to be abandoned. 'I don't wanna murder people and I don't want a bullet through my 'ead. All I want is to stay back 'ere in Bethnal Green, go to work, and come home to my family. That's not too much to ask, is it?'

'No, but you 'ave to go for the same reason as every other man. If you don't go out there and stop Hitler, he'll take this country and who knows what kind of a life we'll be facing. This is a free country, Tom. Fight to keep it

that way. For Billy, if not for us. Think of 'is future and our grandchildren.'

'I s'pose you're right,' he said, sipping his tea. 'Greedy bastard wants to own and rule the world. Territorial rights. That's what this is all about. The twentieth century and we're still thinking like cavemen.'

Jessie glanced at the clock. 'We'll 'ave to get a move on soon. You don't wanna miss your train back.'

'I won't miss it, Jess, 'cos I've no intention of catching it. I'll go back in a few days' time. Say I 'ad the flu. Doctor'll give me a sick note. He's all right. We 'ad a chat last time I was back when I met 'im in the street. He didn't know it but I was checking up on what his views were.'

Jessie laughed out loud. 'Silly bugger, Tom. Course he knew what you was up to. Don't you think that scores of other men'll be trying it on? There'll be a mile-long queue outside 'is surgery, you see if I'm wrong.'

'Well, there you are, then,' said Tom, easing a cigarette into the corner of his mouth. 'There's my excuse. I couldn't get an appointment.'

The banter continued until Jessie realised that he really had made up his mind. He wasn't going back that day and relief began to take over from worry. She would have him around for a couple more days and where was the harm in that?

They made the most of their two extra days together. Instead of Tom going down to the pub, Jessie fetched home ale in a jug and she couldn't remember a time when they had been more in love and happier.

But fate had something up its sleeve. The very morning that he had intended going back, there was a knock on the door and it had the same sound to it as what was commonly known as the 'copper's knock' in the East End. Tom was playing with Billy, jumping him up and down on his lap, his uniform ready and waiting on the back of the kitchen door. Jessie was in the kitchen frying bacon and poaching eggs. Coming into the

living room, she paled. 'Tom.' Her voice was no more than a whisper. 'Tom, I think it's the red caps.'

His mood now sombre, Tom slowly nodded, showing that he was thinking the same thing. 'Take Billy. I'll open the door.'

Dressed only in his trousers with braces dangling, Tom faced them. Neither of the two men on the doorstep said a word, they just stared into his face. 'Fair enough,' said Tom. 'I was going back today anyway.' He waved them in and closed the door. 'Fancy a bacon sandwich? I'm just frying breakfast for the wife while she feeds the baby.'

The delicious smell and sound of the sizzling bacon was tantalising and something that no ordinary man could resist and, duties aside, these two were ordinary men.

'Take a seat,' Tom offered. He winked at Jessie and went into the kitchen to take up where she had left off. They would have to do without eggs – the bacon was ready and he didn't want to keep them waiting longer in case they had second thoughts and resisted the sandwich.

'Them bloody barracks,' said Tom cheerfully, coming into the room, 'damp as you like. Thought I was in for pneumonia.' He handed each of them a sandwich. 'Felt all right when I woke up this morning though – apart from a splitting headache. I was gonna send in a sick note but you know what it's like when you're in bed sweating it out. And the doctor was too busy to come out.'

'I'm sure he was,' said one of the men, chuckling. 'You'd be surprised how many of you have gone down with this sudden epidemic which only seems to have affected blokes ready for war. Strange, that.'

Enjoying a short break from work and the unexpected pleasure of hot, crisp bacon between two slabs of baker's bread, the men kept their thoughts to themselves. And when Tom asked if there was time for him to have a quick wash and shave, they shrugged and told him to be quick about it. He left

Jessie telling the officers about baby Billy and how she feared he might have caught Tom's heavy cold on top of having just got over a chesty cough. They only half listened to her; they kept one ear on the movements of Tom upstairs.

Ten minutes later one of the men said, 'Sorry, Mrs Smith, but I'll have to ask you to fetch your husband. It's time to go.'

'Tom!' she called up the stairs but deep down she had a sickening sense he was not there. The creaking floorboards from Billy's nursery had been a dead giveaway as far as she was concerned. There was no reason for Tom to go in there unless he had decided to slip out of the upstairs back window.

Her instincts were right. Tom had gone and a neighbour hanging washing on the line had helped him by opening her yard door which led into another neighbour's garden and then to a narrow alleyway. All of this Jessie learned from her neighbour once the military police, furious and red-faced, had gone. The woman was pleased with herself and Jessie had to smile, though she really would have liked to scream.

'It was good of you to help out,' she said, 'but he'll get into more trouble for it. He should have known better.'

Laughing, the woman left Jessie to herself. She and the other women in the street knew Tom Smith quite well and it didn't surprise them one bit that he'd managed to dodge away. To them it was funny but then they didn't have to rely on him to stay put and ensure that the army paid Jessie her pension to feed and clothe herself and Billy.

Tom made his own way to Thetford, unescorted. Once again, he somehow managed to talk his way out of trouble. He wrote to Jessie, telling her that being on the run from the army and dodging the red caps was not only stimulating but easy. His casual joking about it worried her. To Tom this was no more than a prank; to Jessie it spelled trouble.

Soon after war with Germany was declared, air raid sirens

were heard all around Britain but thankfully it was a false alarm – a false alarm, but a grim reminder that during this war ordinary people, young and old, would be a target. But Britain was prepared this time, unlike during the First World War. Prepared and as ready as they could be to face the ordeal ahead.

Gas masks were issued to adults and children and trenches had been dug in readiness. Important buildings were sandbagged and public air-raid shelters, built earlier that summer, were ready and waiting. Air-raid wardens had been well trained and knew what to do when the bombs began to fall. Auxiliary firemen, too, had been drilled and tested and knew how to tackle a growing fire as well as how to extinguish an incendiary bomb with a stirrup pump. The stamp of active war was present everywhere and the atmosphere, strangely enough, was not of depression but camaraderie as people of differing class and religion were drawn together, by the threat they all faced.

Before the month of September was out, communities began to break up as women and children were evacuated and men went off to fight for king and country. Over a million Britons were evacuated from the cities but Jessie had no intention of leaving the East End and neither did her family or several of her neighbours. They, like many others, chose to stay at home and rely on the government's offer of protection to every household in the big cities – an Anderson shelter, to be erected in the garden. The corrugated iron hut was to be sunk halfway into the ground and covered with earth and sandbags as a means of shelter from the bombing.

It was a strange time for everyone. Women took their responsibilities seriously and were strong in the face of having to begin new lives without their men and keep their heads above water and hold their families together. It wasn't really until January 1940, when the government issued millions of ration books, that the grim reality of what was to come truly hit home.

Four ounces of butter and four ounces of bacon or uncooked ham a week, with just twelve ounces of sugar per adult, was a joke as far as Jessie's mother-in-law, Emmie, was concerned. She was known for her cooking abilities and she did not want to let the side down. With just herself and Charlie at home to feed, she had volunteered to prepare meals for five old folk in her turning, who would find it impossible to fend for themselves under the circumstances. She wasted no time in rooting out extra provisions via the black market. Her husband, Charlie, too old to be called up, had joined the million other men who had signed up with the Local Defence Volunteers, which proved to be an excellent grapevine as to where those extra provisions might be found or swapped.

Jessie's mother, Rose, continued to run her cobbler shop with her youngest son, Stephen. Stephen's love for the stage had led him to join a local drama group; he found his vocation early in life – and his sexual preference. His mother's inner worry over the years that there might be something different about her son was becoming a reality. Stephen was destined to remain a bachelor boy. Jessie's other brother, the rebellious Alfie who was just seventeen, had secured work in the metal foundry, hoping this would release him from having to defend his king and country should the war drag on. Alfie had other fights to fight when fledgling mobsters crossed the territorial line of his gang's patch in Stepney, where he now lived by himself in two rooms above an Italian café.

As for Jessie, she worried about her sometimes irresponsible husband and was kept on her toes by her lively baby. The happy family life that she had been looking forward to was now overtaken by the war and the restrictions it brought, including the blackout. Even the tiniest hint of light from the edge of a window at night prompted an angry shout of 'Put that light out!' And, beneath the blackout curtains, like every other household, the windows were heavily taped to prevent flying glass, and so by day as well as

by night there was a constant reminder of the country being at war.

But Jessie took the war in good heart and like others began to grow food in every part of her garden. It was the same all over the country. Allotments, gardens, back yards, even window boxes were now being used solely to grow vegetables or fruit.

There were other changes too. Trees, kerbs and lamp posts had been marked with white to help in the blackout and women were doing the work of men in factories, shipyards and railway sheds. Ironically, the war was doing far more for the women's movement than the Suffragettes had managed in earlier years.

Jessie's sister Dolly had applied for a job as a bus conductor, which she loved, it being more sociable than any other occupation she could find. Petrol rationing had been introduced with a severity that forced many people take their cars off the roads and use public transport. Men from all walks of life now came into Dolly's happy orbit and she was always full of it when visiting her sister and nephew, baby Billy.

While Dolly chatted about the latest and most handsome sailor she'd met, Jessie hid her envy. To her, it seemed an age since she had enjoyed an evening out. To walk arm in arm with one of the tall blond Dutch sailors Dolly spoke of was a dream that often comforted Jessie when she was feeling at her lowest.

'I don't know why you don't come out with us, Jess,' said Dolly, carefully repainting her fingernails. 'Mum would come and sit with Billy, you know she would. You can't stay in forever.'

'It won't be forever, Dolly,' said Jessie. 'The war'll be over soon and my Tom'll be back where he belongs.' She strapped her son into his highchair and went into the kitchen. 'Watch him for me, Doll. He's worked out how to undo the buckle on his straps. It's spam sandwich with a bit of mustard for lunch.'

'That'll do me.' Dolly cupped Billy's double chin and kissed

his smiling face, finding some of his dribble. 'Erghh, you messy little sod!'

'What's he done now?' called Jessie, pleased to have him off her hands for five minutes.

'Messed up my lipstick!' Undoing his buckle, Dolly lifted her nephew out of his highchair to squeals of laughter. 'He weighs a blooming ton, Jessie! What you been feeding him on?' She tickled Billy under the arm and chuckled with him. 'Little fat sod, ain't yer?' she said, cuddling him. 'Handsome devil. Got your dad's lovely green eyes and your mum's blonde hair. Them little girls are gonna love you.'

Billy babbled on, talking in his own language.

'Gibberish,' said Dolly, laughing at him, 'that's all you can do. Talk a load of gibberish.'

'Juish,' said Billy, demanding more attention. 'Dirsty.'

Dolly pushed her face closer to his. '*Juice* not juish. And *thirsty* not dirsty. Billy try. *Thirsty*. Go on then ... th-th-th-thirsty!'

'Dirsty!' The fourteenth-month-old laughed out loud and clapped his podgy hands together. 'Juish!'

'You little tyke. *You* know. Yes you *do*. *You* know 'ow to say it.' She tickled him again. 'I can't wait to get one of these little bundles of trouble, Jess.'

Coming into the sitting room, Jessie sighed. 'You, a mother? Tied down to the kitchen sink?'

'I'm talking about later on once the war's over and I'm ready to settle down. Have you heard from Tom this week?'

'A postcard came this morning. He's getting on all right with the French now. His landlady's come round at last.'

'Blooming cheek they've got, them frogs. I wouldn't mind, our men are out there in France for their bloody benefit, you'd think they'd be grateful.'

'Anyway, he seems all right.' Jessie took Billy from her for his afternoon nap. 'I hope he's behaving himself with all them mademoiselles, that's all.'

'That's doubtful,' said Dolly, biting into her sandwich.

'Oh, thanks! What a ray of sunshine you are,' said Jessie, taking Billy upstairs.

'Trouble with you, Jess, is that you go through life thinking nothing'll change! It's about time you livened up a bit. Come dancing with me and my mates tonight. You won't look back!'

'I'm a married woman, Dolly,' said Jessie, coming back into the room.

'So? Loads of married women whose men have gone to war go out. You can't sit in all the blooming time. Silly cow.'

Jessie dropped into an armchair, fed up. 'I don't sit in *all* the time. Once we've finished this bit of lunch I've got every intention of going out for a walk. You can wheel Billy in the pushchair for me.'

Dolly sipped her tea. 'A nice trip over the park, I s'pose.'

'Yep. And then on to visit Mum and Stephen. It's better than sitting in all day.'

'Yeah, I grant you that. It is better than that. Tch. I don't know. You're getting old before you've stopped being young.'

'And you're getting on my nerves. Be quiet for five minutes.'

That said, Jessie and Dolly sat in silence. Dolly wondered what she would wear to go out that evening and Jessie wondered whether she should hang the washing on the line or dry it by the fire. It was a crisp, bright January day but it could change to cloud and rain within minutes. 'Did you catch the weather forecast today?' she asked, miles away.

'No, funnily enough I missed it, Jess.' The last thing Dolly thought to do was listen to a weather forecast. 'If it rains we'll put our umbrella up. If it don't, we won't. It's risky but sod it, let's live dangerously on our walk, eh?'

Amused by her sister's sense of humour, Jessie snapped out of her mood. A couple of hours later she went upstairs to brush her hair and put on some lipstick and powder. Staring

at her reflection in the dressing-table mirror, she could see that Dolly had a point. She *had* turned into a dowdy housewife.

Wrapped up against the cold air, hats pulled down over their ears, with Dolly pushing the pram and Jessie by her side, they enjoyed the early January sunshine as they strolled along the Mile End Road to take Billy to visit his grandmother Rose. Turning into Whitehorse Road, they heard someone give a wolf whistle. Glancing over her shoulder to see if the admirer was worth a smile, Dolly was amused to see that it was Max, dressed smartly in a suit and unbuttoned dark overcoat.

'Well, well, well,' said Dolly, loving it, 'look who's come out of the woodwork.'

'Who?' said Jessie. 'One of your old flames?' She kept her eyes firmly fixed in front. She didn't want to be tarred with the same brush as her wayward sister. 'Or one of your new boyfriends?'

'No,' said Dolly, cockier than ever, 'one of yours.'

Max reached their side and tipped his hat. He had eyes only for Jessie. 'Mind if I walk with you?' he said, showing his row of perfect white teeth.

'Max, it's you!' Jessie, without thinking, kissed him on the cheek. She was pleased to see him and didn't mind who saw. 'Tom said you'd managed to stay in civvi street. Lucky devil.'

'It wasn't good luck, Jessie, it was bad luck. Wouldn't have me because ... apparently ... my feet wouldn't be up to all that marching.' He turned away from those blue eyes of Jessie's, which he had once adored, and paid attention to Billy who was sitting up, enjoying a Farley's rusk biscuit. 'He's a mixture of both of you, Jess,' he said, his regret showing.

'Right, well, if you'll excuse me and my nephew,' grinned Dolly, 'we'll be on our way.' Grabbing the handle of the pram again, Dolly strode off, wiggling her buttocks for Max's benefit. 'I'll see you at Mum's, Jessie!' she called back over her shoulder.

'She's a gem,' said Max with a smile. 'Come on, Jess,' he laid a hand on her arm, 'I've got masses to tell you and I want to hear how you've been coping.'

'I'm not sure, Max ... you know what people are like. If Tom should get to hear—'

'That you walked along the street with me in broad daylight? Come on, Jessie, this isn't like you. What's happened to your self-confidence?'

'I don't know about that ... but yeah, it's not as if it's nighttime, is it?'

'No. But then again, that didn't both us much once upon a time. So long as we were alone.'

'Don't, Max. Don't stir up all the memories. I'm married now and a mother as well.' She couldn't believe how shy and embarrassed she now felt in his company. 'Not that anyone would take me for anything else but a married woman. Dolly reminded me today how dowdy I was looking.' Jessie would be the first to admit that she was begging for a compliment. Max was right, her self-esteem was on the low side.

'Trust Dolly,' he said, quietly laughing. He remembered Jessie's exuberant, loud-mouthed sister well. 'She never was one for being tactful.'

'So you do think I look drab then?'

He squeezed her arm and an old familiar feeling swept through her. Nothing physical, just a nice friendly feeling. 'You look lovely, Jessie. Although your hair could do with styling. You should go and see the barber again.'

She laughed to be reminded of when she had once had her hair chopped off. Chatting about old times, they soon arrived at Joe Lyons, their previous regular meeting place. 'How's your mum and dad?' she asked, slipping on to a chair at their favoured table by the window.

'More relaxed than they were. At least the war's stopped all the other troubles. They had another brick through their shop window, you know. Blackshirts. I know what I'd like to

do if I came face to face with one.' Max looked murderous thinking of the racist attacks his family had suffered.

'Tom and his brother Johnnie walked out, you know, as soon as they realised—'

'That Mosley was likely to be interned?' Max cut in.

'No, it was before all that. They didn't know—'

'Jessie, please. Don't start making excuses for them. They were Blackshirts no matter what. I'll never forgive them. Never. No Jew would.'

Thankful when the waitress arrived with tea and cakes, Jessie took the opportunity to steer the subject back to Max's family. She hadn't heard from Mrs Cohen since she'd married and in a strange way Jessie had missed her. Only once or twice had Mrs Cohen been to visit her mother at the cobbler shop, next door to the Cohens' delicatessen. Having discussed Max's mother and father, Jessie took the bit between her teeth and mentioned Moira, his sister, the one who had been responsible for them breaking off their engagement.

'Moira's fine,' said Max soberly.

'But?'

'But she's been told she'll never have children and it's devastated her.' Max looked serious. 'She and Nathan will adopt children but not until the war's over.'

Breaking off a piece of her fruit bread and popping into her mouth, Jessie shrugged. 'Let's hope they don't adopt someone's twin.'

Max looked bemused by her off-the-cuff remark. 'What makes you say that?'

'You mean you haven't heard?'

'Heard what, Jessie?' He leaned back in his chair and listened intently as she told the incredible story. Her parents, Rose and Robert, had been young newlyweds just after the First World War and very poor, unable to feed and clothe one baby, let alone two. Rose's half-brother Jack Blake and his German wife Gerta had pleaded to adopt one of the twins since

Gerta could not herself have children. It had been a well-kept secret and had it not been for Tom introducing the twin girls much later in life, neither Hannah nor Jessie would have known anything about each other. Hannah would have continued to live in Bethnal Green with her adopted mother, Gerta, who had turned out to be a tyrant — a cold, uncaring woman and a strong supporter of the Blackshirts. Hitler was Gerta's hero and Mosley her heartthrob. Since the day the girls had discovered they were twins they had become closer than very best friends. Closer than ordinary sisters. Ending her story, Jessie said, 'I always knew something was wrong. I thought I was losing my mind at times. Missing someone who didn't exist. That I *thought* didn't exist. And then, wham bang, it's out in the open.'

'You've lost me, Jess ...' He chuckled. 'My loss, not yours. But there we are — you chose Tom.'

'Max, please. Don't.'

'I can't help it. We would have been married by now. I would have married you, Jess. I *should* have married you.'

'No. Billy wasn't your baby.'

'That wouldn't have mattered. It doesn't matter now even.'

'Maybe not but what *does* matter is that I love Tom. I love him and I'll wait for him.' She sipped her tea and looked at him over the cup. 'You're not shocked then at my having a twin sister?'

'I *am* shocked. You've shocked me. You've really shocked me, Jessie.'

'I know,' she said, enjoying the thrill of shaking the one person she thought was unshakable. 'Mum's been more relaxed since it came out. She's been wonderful, Max. She bought most of the things for the baby — the pram, pillows, blankets ...'

'Jessie,' said Max, a faraway look in his eyes, 'I can't believe you've got a twin.'

'You will once you meet her. She's more attractive than me.'

'I don't know what to say.'

'I know what you mean. It came as a shock to me as well.'

'*Your* twin. I can't wait to meet her.'

'Well, once she's back for good, I'll introduce you.'

'Back? You mean she went off again?'

'War work. For the government. Can't talk about it though.'

'Why not?'

'Because I haven't got a clue what she does. I suppose you've heard about our Alfie?'

'Alfie.' Max chuckled. 'He surprised us all, didn't he? Who would have thought that little wayward sod would have turned out to be so independent and quick off the mark.'

This attitude from Max surprised her. 'What are you talking about?'

'Well, he's employed, at the ammunition factory, he's got himself a nice little flat and he's involved in good work – selling tickets for charity in Mile End. He even helped by selling dance tickets in aid of the Boys Jewish Club. Made two pounds for us, Jessie.'

Yes, thought Jessie, two pounds for your club and four pounds for Alfie, more like. 'Oh, good. He is keeping up the good work then.' There seemed little point in spoiling her brother's good if false reputation. Maybe he would grow into it.

'Speaking of which, I should be off soon, Jess,' said Max, checking his watch. 'I'm due at the under-eighteens' boxing club. I've joined the board.' Pausing for a few seconds, he looked into her face. 'Can we do this again? Or maybe go to the pictures instead?'

'I don't know, Max. Let me have a think about it.'

Of course. Listen, I've just got to pop next door to the

tobacconist.' He stood up and Jessie felt sure he'd grown taller. 'Wait here for me. I'll be two minutes,' and he rushed out of the tearooms.

'Did you want some more tea?' The waitress's voice drifted through Jessie's thoughts.

'No thanks. I'm just waiting for my friend to come back from the shop next door and then we'll be off.'

The girl broke into a smile and looked relieved. 'I thought he'd walked out on yer.'

'No ... and he's just a friend. An old mate. Not a boyfriend. I'm already married. He's gone to buy some cigarettes.' At that moment, Max returned, carrying a large box of chocolates which brought a different expression to the waitress's face. Jessie saw it as a smile of condemnation. She wondered if she and Max had looked like lovers sitting there, talking together as if the time in between seeing each other had never passed.

'These are for you, Jess,' said Max, offering her the pretty floral box of chocolates. 'A treat.'

'Max, I can't take those.' Jessie was aghast.

'Why not?'

'Well, my mother for a start. I'm just going round there, don't forget. She'll think we're up to something.'

'Don't be silly,' he said, pushing them into her hands. 'I don't know what things are coming to if I can't buy an old flame a small gift.'

'Small? It must have been the biggest box in the shop.'

'Maybe. Anyway, take them to your mother's and tell her they're for you, her and Dolly, if that makes you feel better.'

'It does, Max. Thanks.' Jessie stood up to leave with him and was embarrassed when he took her arm. She could feel the eyes of the young waitress on her and felt guilt creeping in again. She imagined Tom looking in on the scene – he would be angry and jealous, hurt and scared. Frightened that he might be losing his wife.

'Thanks for the tea, and the chocolates. I'll see you ... some

time. When Tom's back on leave, maybe we could go for a drink together. In a foursome?'

'Maybe,' he said, tipping his hat. 'See you around.'

'Max, don't go.' Embarrassed, she smiled and shrugged. 'Well, not with that look on your face anyway.'

'What look?'

'Doom and gloom.'

Relaxing into his usual easy-going manner, he smiled. 'Jessie, listen. If anything should happen ... I mean if you need me, well, you know where I am.'

'Thanks. I'll remember that.' Exchanging a look that required no spoken word, they turned and walked away from one another.

OVER BETHNAL GREEN will be available from July 2000. Don't miss it.

Docker's Daughter

For my family
– Pete, Esther, Duncan and Robin

ACKNOWLEDGEMENTS

I am indebted to Geraldine Cooke for her vision and encouragement, Jenny Page for her patience and Divisional Commander, Phillip Hagon, Metropolitan Police Service, for his help and advice.

Chapter One

London 1962

It was two in the morning when the shrill ringing of the telephone pierced the dark silence of Kay's bedroom. Instantly awake, she was filled with panic. Why would anyone ring at such an hour? Blanking horrid thoughts from her mind, she listened for sounds from her parents' bedroom. Not afraid of the dark but of what might lie behind the phone call, she pulled herself up in bed and waited, hoping it would stop. Maybe someone had dialled a wrong number.

Three rings later she shot from her bed out of the room and along the passage, her hand sweeping the wall until it found the light switch.

'Hallo?' Kay's voice was quiet but her tone almost dared the caller to give her bad news.

'Kay . . .' It was her aunt Liz. The heavy pause that followed told her something terrible had happened to her uncle Bert. That wonderful, healthy,

1

lovable man who had just celebrated his birthday. Pushing her long blonde hair from her face, Kay composed herself before asking what was wrong.

'Get Daddy for me, there's a good girl . . .' Liz's weak voice trailed off.

Jack being a heavier sleeper than Laura moaned and turned over as Kay's urgent voice woke her mother. 'Was that the phone?' She was still half asleep.

Before Kay had a chance to say who it was, Laura was out of bed in a flash. Just awake but alert enough to realize that only grave news came at that hour, she repeated over and over to herself, *Please don't let anything have happened to Dad*. Grabbing the black receiver with one hand, she steadied herself with the other, gripping the back of the chair, feeling light-headed and giddy from getting out of bed too quickly. Her heart was thumping as the dread of hearing her ageing father ask for help swept through her. She had asked him many times to give up his cottage and move in with the three of them.

'It's Aunt Liz,' Kay whispered as she stood in the kitchen doorway waiting to hear the worst.

'Liz – what's wrong?'

'I think Bert's . . .' her voice trailed off.

Slipping on to a kitchen chair, Laura drew her feet up off the cold linoleum and tucked her thin cotton

nightdress under her toes. 'Liz, please . . . what is it?' A cold chill ran through her. 'What's happened?'

'I've phoned for an ambulance.' Liz's voice sounded thin and empty. 'He called out—' She broke into a high-pitched cry, 'I thought it was just a nightmare! I thought he'd gone off again. I went back to sleep.' Another tense pause filled the space between them.

'I went back to sleep, Laura! May God forgive me . . .' Her pained voice struggled to control the sobbing. 'I went back to sleep.'

Backing away from her mother along the narrow passage, Kay leaned against her bedroom door and tried to control her breathing. She knew that something serious had happened. Gripping the handle to the door of her room, willing her hands to stop shaking, she stared back at Laura. She didn't want to hear what was coming. She wanted her mother to smile and relax her face.

'It's your uncle Bert. I can't protect you from this, Kay. And it's going to hurt.'

At that moment, Kay knew by instinct that this was going to be a turning-point in her life. Her mother was admitting that she could not protect her from everything that life threw her way. She had no choice but to deliver the crushing blow which was hovering like a weapon between them.

'He's dead,' Laura murmured, 'gone.'

Turning away, Kay threw herself on to her bed and screamed into her pillow. 'It's not *fair*! He's my uncle, Mum! My uncle Bert!'

Liz had taken Bert's sudden death very badly, and was unable to cope with anything, especially having him laid out in her front room as was the East End custom. She had been given tranquillizers, and could only just manage to drag herself through the days leading up to his funeral. Her round, smiling face which so often lifted those around her, was now ashen and drawn as she sat in her small, quiet living room with her younger brother, Jack. Her hair seemed to have gone from grey to all white in just a couple of days and her red-rimmed eyes were swollen from crying.

'If only I hadn't gone back to sleep Bert might still be alive.' She gazed into her cup and pushed a floating tea leaf to one side.

'Stop tormenting yourself, Liz. You heard what the doctor said, it was all over in seconds. There wasn't anything you could have done about it.' Rubbing his eyes, Jack sighed heavily. 'We have to be thankful he died in his sleep.'

'The house is so quiet. I'll never get used to it.' She sipped her tea which had been laced with whiskey.

'Why don't you stay with me and Laura for a couple of weeks? Till the funeral's over and you've had a bit of time to get used to the idea of being on your own,' he said, believing she would turn him down flat.

'That'd be nice, Jack. I would like that.'

Pleased that his sister offered no resistance, Jack thought he might as well touch on the other idea he had been turning over in his mind. Finding the right words was the most difficult part.

'Lizzie, I don't quite know how to say this.' Turning his head to avoid her searching eyes, he caught sight of Bert's polished boots in a corner of the room. 'I can see why it would be too much for you to have Bert's body . . .' he took a deep breath. 'Why don't we have him laid out in my front room instead of the chapel of rest?' He reeled the words out quickly. A painful silence hung in the room.

'His mates could come and go, and—'

'Yeah,' Liz cut in, making it easier for her brother. 'I would prefer that.' She slipped one of her heart pills under her tongue to ease the pain.

'Good. That's good.' He was relieved to have got that over with. Reaching for his hand, Liz squeezed it and looked into his grief-stricken face. 'Thanks, love. I would never 'ave got through this without

you and Laura.' She gave him a weak smile. 'Laura won't mind having me there, will she?'

'What d'you think?'

'Yeah. Silly question. We're like sisters really.'

'Too right.' He leaned across and tipped a little more Irish whiskey into her cup. 'We'll soon 'ave some colour back in those cheeks of yours.'

'What about our Kay?' Liz asked sadly. 'How's she taking it?'

'She's young. Seventeen. Still a baby. She'll get over it quicker than we will.' Jack lowered his head, praying to God he was right.

Laura had hardly entered their spare room since Jack had moved out of it and back in with her. With Kay by her side, she scanned the room in silence.

'Let's make it nice and bright for aunt Liz, Mum,' Kay said.

'Yeah.' Laura swallowed hard. 'Good idea.'

'I'll make a pot of tea.' Laura felt her daughter squeeze her arm before she left the room, and was thankful for the natural warmth she gave.

Standing by the window, the daylight falling across the pale blue candlewick bedspread, Laura imagined Jack lying there all those nights by himself and wondered why they had let it go on for so long. They had spent over four years living under the

same roof but not sharing the same bed, until Kay was nearly drowned in Kent two years previously, and both she and Jack were brought sharply back to reality.

The pale blue cover was significant for another reason. This third bedroom had been intended for their second child, Baby John, who had died in his sleep when he was no more than three months old. Neither Laura nor Jack had forgiven themselves for not waking when, as they believed, their baby would have made some small noise for attention. The cot had been placed as close to their bed as possible, yet neither of them had heard a thing.

Pulling the blue cover from the bed, Laura decided she would buy a new brightly patterned one for Liz. The curtains could come down too; she would run up some more on her new electric sewing machine. It wouldn't take her long and it would be worth it for more reasons than one. She didn't want to be reminded any more of the time when her marriage had almost broken down and she had done little, if anything, to stop it happening.

Had it not been for Kay's accident, she and Jack might not be together now. They did love one another, and probably always had. Pride and other people had got in their way and almost ruined it for good.

Sighing, Laura folded the bedspread and squeezed it on to a shelf inside a cupboard. The blue lampshade would go too; and so would the multicoloured rag mat. They could all go to the charity stall at Bethnal Green market. She silently thanked Bert for giving her the courage finally to bury the saddest time of her life.

'Goodbye, Baby John,' she whispered as she unscrewed the light bulb from the lamp and lifted the soft-blue shade from the stand. 'God bless.' She closed her eyes and willed herself to be strong. After all, that tragedy had happened a long time ago.

As Laura held the shade close to her, she looked out of the window and up at the sky. The sun was just coming out from behind a grey cloud and its rays streamed in and lit up the room.

'Look after Baby John for us, Bert.' The sun was on her face now, and its warmth seemed to flow through her body. Smiling, she sat down on the edge of the single bed, trying to recognize the new sensation filling her being. If she could have given it a colour it would be pale gold. Warm comfort seemed to fill the room as if someone who loved and cared were there.

'My God,' she whispered. 'You've found him. You're with him!' Leaping up from the bed, she pulled open the bedroom door. 'Kay! Kay!'

As Kay appeared in the kitchen doorway at the end of the passage, she and Laura stared at each other.

'It's Baby John,' she finally managed to say, 'he's alive. Your brother's alive.' She waited for the pained look on Kay's face to dissolve.

'Not here, not in our world, but somewhere else,' she said reassuringly as Kay came slowly towards her. 'He's happy. He's with your uncle Bert and they're both happy.'

Kay reached out and pulled her close, burying her face in her mother's thick, sweet-smelling hair. 'It's all right, Mum, it's all right.'

Laura pulled away and gazed at her. 'Kay, something just happened.' She swallowed hard and wiped the tears that were streaming from her hazel-green eyes. 'It was wonderful. I don't know how to tell you, but I've just been allowed to see into another world.'

'Come on. You'll be all right.' Kay led her into the kitchen, hardly daring to look at her for fear she would break down too.

'But these tears ain't grief. Don't you understand?' she said, emphasizing each word, as if Kay were too young to take it in.

'I'll put a little drop of brandy in. We could both do with it.' Still Kay couldn't look at her mother.

Then Laura realized. The experience had been

meant for her and her only. It wasn't something she would be able to share. She would have to settle for that, and not go shouting it across the world.

Kay awoke to the sound of her dad sobbing in his sleep in the next room, and his tormented face sprang into her mind. She wondered whether she should go in and shake him out of the nightmare, knowing that once he stirred, he would not get back to sleep again. She decided against it. She didn't want herself or her mother to see her dad's sad eyes which had often been referred to as 'laughing blues'.

Having made up her mind to leave him, believing that dreams only lasted seconds, Kay climbed out of bed to make herself a cup of strong tea. She could always catch up on sleep.

Warming herself by the two-bar electric fire in the kitchen, she tried not to think about her uncle Bert lying so still on the other side of the wall, and started to make a mental list of the food she and her mum would need to buy for the funeral guests. It wasn't until the sound of birdsong began to break the silence that Kay felt brave enough to go into the front room and put the cut flowers in water. She caught a glimpse of her pale, freckled face in the mirror and grimaced at her red puffy eyes and lank hair. She vowed to catch up with herself soon and

pay a little more attention to the way she looked. Her own mother, her fortieth birthday approaching, still took pride in her appearance and Kay didn't want to let the side down.

As she slowly pushed the door open, the array of colourful blooms delivered courtesy of the florist brought a lump to her throat. She thought that if her uncle Bert's spirit was in that room he would be touched at the kind gesture made by their local shop. With this thought in mind, Kay took great care in arranging the flowers in glass vases.

Adding a light blue iris to red and white carnations, she felt lighter in mood as the early-morning April sun presented itself, shining through the net curtains and across Bert's open coffin. Up until then, she hadn't been able to look at him lying there so peacefully, but the sun seemed in an instant to have lifted her spirits, and Kay went over and looked down at the uncle she had loved, not caring that her tears were dropping on to the crisp white gown he was dressed in. Her dad had been annoyed about that. Jack had wanted Bert to be buried in his dark blue serge suit, but it was the last thing he had thought to tell the undertaker, and now it was too late.

When the day of the funeral finally arrived, Kay and Laura were busy all day pouring cups of tea and

forever cutting more sandwiches for the stream of relatives, friends and dockers who arrived. Numberless bottles of brandy, whisky and beer found their way into the flat. Every man brought a bottle of something, knowing how much they would all need the drink to help them through the day.

As the time drew nearer for the hearse to arrive, the noise reached a crescendo. A mixture of crying and laughter filled the flat as stories unfolded about Bert and some of the things he had unwittingly got himself into. Kay heard it all from the kitchen and smiled to herself. This was more like it. This was what uncle Bert would have wanted, everyone enjoying a good drink on his behalf.

She caught Laura's eye and smiled back at her. She had said earlier that she didn't want her seventeen-year-old daughter to wear black. Kay lowered her head and hugged herself, perched on a chair in the crowded kitchen. The sharp contrast of her long blonde hair against the little black dress she was wearing looked wrong. She was too young to be in mourning but respect had to be paid.

Weaving among the guests, Laura reached Kay and took her by the shoulders, gently guiding her out and into her bedroom. Sitting her down on the edge of her bed, she lifted Kay's chin and smiled bravely into her face. It was just a couple of weeks

ago that Laura had said how grown-up Kay was, but now the expression on her mother's face showed that she was seeing her as a baby again.

'I know it hurts, Kay,' she said gently. 'It's the first time for you . . . well, apart from your brother, but you were too young to remember that.'

She hadn't been too young. She did remember it. But this wasn't the time to say so. 'Will it ever go away, Mum, this feeling inside? This pain that doesn't hurt like a pain usually does?'

Unable to answer, Laura moved across the room and looked out of the window, anything to avoid Kay's searching blue eyes.

'BERT, BERT, I LOVE THAT SHIRT!' The suddenly booming voice of good old red-faced Harry the insurance man, and the robust laughter that followed, took them by surprise.

'Mum, how could he?'

'I knew it wouldn't be long before they'd have to say something about them white frills,' Laura chuckled through her tears.

'WHERE DID YOU GET THAT SHIRT? WHERE DID YOU GET THAT SHIRT?'

Now it was the turn of Bert's brothers, Frank and Freddie. The song resounded through the flat, and there was no doubt in Kay's mind that the entire block could hear it. Shrugging, a wan smile on

13

her lips, she joined in and encouraged her mum to do the same. Within seconds, they were singing at the tops of their voices and crying at the same time.

While the mourners braced themselves inside the flat, ready for the undertaker to arrive and screw down the lid of Bert's coffin, wreaths and tributes were arriving, and neighbours dutifully laid them outside the block of flats until the tarmac where the children usually played was covered in flowers, with only a driveway left for the funeral cars when they arrived. A wreath had even been hung over the *No Spitting* sign.

There were hearts, crosses, footballs. One arrangement was shaped like a docker's hook. It was a farewell fit for a king. Bert's family were known and liked in the East End, even by men who had connections with the underworld.

Kay watched proudly as her dad slipped his broad shoulders underneath the front of the coffin, and together with Bert's three brothers, carried it out of the flat and down the flights of stairs while the official pallbearers stayed close by, ready to move in should any of the intoxicated men give way. They need not have worried; these were strong men, full of pride, and nothing in the world would have

stopped them fulfilling their role of carrying Bert to the hearse.

'Chin up, Liz mate,' one of the neighbours called out as the women stepped into the funeral car.

'Take care of 'er, Laura!' called another.

Through her black veil, Liz's tear-stained face could only manage a weak smile as she showed a hand to the crowd that had turned out.

The procession following the family mourners seemed to go on for ever, until they had left the council estate. The funeral cortège made its way along the narrow backstreets, passing several elderly gentlemen who stood with their heads lowered, caps in hand, as the cars continued towards East India Docks, where they would pause to allow the rest of the dockers to pay their last respects.

'So when we remember our dearly departed Albert, let us not forget that God has always been there, from the moment of birth until death. And in our hearts we shall always remember that . . .' the vicar glanced down at the papers in front of him, 'that . . . Albert—'

'Bert!' Jack cut in impatiently. 'He was known as Bert!' His voice echoed around the silent church and was followed by mumbling from the rest of the congregation. Some were embarrassed by his

outburst, some agreed with Jack, others just wanted to get the whole thing over with.

'He was christened Albert, Dad,' Kay whispered.

'I know that!' Jack's angry face turned away from her and glared up at the vicar in the pulpit. 'Just get on with it, will yer! You've bin up there for twenty minutes telling us what a lovely man we're about to bury. D'yer think we don't know that?'

'Shush, Jack. Show some respect.' Laura gripped his arm. 'The man's only doing his job.'

Jack swallowed, ran his fingers through his hair and shook his head slowly at the vicar. 'You said the same things—' there was a crack in his voice, 'two years ago, when we buried Alf the Overcoat!'

Whether it was from drink or delayed shock Kay had no idea, but she found herself giggling at her dad's remark. When she heard other people trying to stop themselves laughing she let herself go. Adding insult to injury, a mourner in the back pew then relieved himself by evacuating a long, psalmodic gust of wind.

'God, that's terrible.' Kay was deeply embarrassed by the way the vicar was losing control over his drunken congregation. The service was quickly turning into a farce.

'I'm sorry, Kay,' Laura chuckled, 'but you're gonna have to get used to the idea that this lot

16

won't put up with hackneyed sermons. Especially not at a time like this.'

Turning her head to look at everyone, a faint smile appeared on Kay's lips. 'You're right,' she murmured, 'and so are they. And uncle Bert would 'ave been the first to say so.'

Kay squeezed Laura's hand, then looked from her mother up to the perplexed vicar and wondered how he would manage to conduct the rest of the service. She needn't have worried; as if by telepathy, her uncle's brothers, Frank and Freddie, were making their way towards the coffin with her dad and a family friend close behind. As they lifted it on to their broad shoulders, the vicar quickly signalled to the organist to play.

A respectful hush fell upon the church as everyone softly sang Liz's chosen hymn:

> Abide with me: fast falls the eventide;
> The darkness deepens; Lord, with me abide:
> When other helpers fail, and comforts flee,
> Help of the helpless, O abide with me.

With Liz, Kay and Laura following closely behind, the men walked in a stately manner along the aisle, carrying the much loved Bert to his final resting place.

Chapter Two

'Freelance docker? There'll be bloody murders, I'm telling yer! Once the word spreads. Then we'll see. Sly bleeders.' Jack pinched the smouldering tip of his roll-up between his thumb and finger and dropped the dog-end into an ashtray. 'Giving Bert's job to an outsider? They knew what they were doing, all right.' Pushing open the lid of his tobacco tin with his thumb, he pulled out a few strands of Golden Virginia. 'They'll get more than they bargained for, you mark my words.'

Curled up in an armchair, gazing up at the ceiling, Kay couldn't help thinking about her uncle and how his name might be used to stir up more anger and add another wharf to the growing unofficial dock strike that was spreading through London. Only two weeks out of this world and not allowed to rest in peace.

'Does it really matter, Jack?' Laura said. 'At least they took someone on. One more off the dole queue.'

Jack's light blue eyes glared back at her, his high cheek-bones flushed with anger. 'You can't see it, can you? The reason the strike started up in the first place was because they did the very same thing at another wharf! A supervisor died and they gave his job to an outside man. They've done the selfsame thing to Bert. If that's not deliberately pouring oil on the fire, I dunno what is.' He flicked the top of his Zippo and lit another roll-up.

'And now more and more cases are coming to light. Most of them casuals don't hold union cards.'

Turning his back on Laura, Jack stared out of the veranda windows and sighed. 'Six regulars applied for that job, and it goes to a casual labourer.' He turned and looked her in the face. 'How d'yer reckon Bert would 'ave felt about that, eh?' He swallowed hard and pressed his lips together, willing himself not to break down.

'Leave him out of this, Jack. You'll only upset Liz. Best she doesn't know about it—'

''Course she'll get to know about it!' he barked, not bothering that she hated to be interrupted. 'You think I'm the only one who's livid?' He stormed towards the living-room door and pulled with vengeance at the handle. Turning back to her he said, 'Our blokes'll come out now; join the other wharves on strike, and if you ask me, it's about time as well!

20

'Once Jack Dash gets the bit between his teeth, you'll see, we'll bring this government to its knees.'

The slamming of the door behind him sent a shiver down Kay's spine. In her heart she felt that her dad was right and secretly believed that the Import Trades Committee wanted to break the trade union and eventually would. As far as she could tell from listening many times to Billy, her grandfather, who had been a stevedore for a good part of his working life, some union officials were inclined to push management too far too fast, and their demands could lead to the end of the London docks.

Slipping her feet into her shoes, Laura sat upright on the sofa, where she had hoped to have a little doze on her afternoon off. Thursday was the day she looked forward to all week. A time when the flat would be empty and she could spend an hour or so thinking.

'What time d'yer think you'll be in for dinner?' she called after Jack.

'Don't know! Leave it on steam if I'm late. And if any of the men drop by – tell 'em I'll be in the Carpenter's Arms later on!'

Relieved that Jack would be out for the rest of the afternoon, she kicked off her shoes again and lay down, flinching at the sound of the front door banging behind him.

'I wish he wouldn't slam the door like that,' Laura said, closing her eyes.

'I'm going out for a walk, to the museum.' Kay kissed her mother lightly on the cheek.

'I thought you'd grown out of that,' Laura smiled as her eyes glazed over. She was remembering. 'You used to spend hours in that place, gazing at that big doll's house . . . you must know every nook and cranny.'

'I won't be long. Enjoy your catnap.'

Resting her head on a cushion, Laura closed her eyes and tried not to think about the turbulent weeks that lay ahead. For Jack to walk out of the docks as soon as he heard about Bert's job going the way it had meant that a few others would have followed him. It was just over an hour since he had thrown down his docker's hook in a temper. The entire wharf would have heard about the business and there would be pandemonium.

It was all a far cry from the dreams of tranquillity and country living she had been caught up in just over two years ago. Allowing the face of Richard, her ex-lover, to move into her imagination, she wondered if they would ever see each other again.

While Liz sadly packed her few belongings into a small suitcase, Kay sat on the edge of the bed

studying a holiday brochure. She had given up trying to persuade her aunt to stay on another week until she had had more time to get over uncle Bert. Looking up from the colourful pictures of sand, sea and sunshine, Kay studied Liz's face. She was caught up in another world.

'Why don't you come to Spain with me, aunt Liz? I'll look after you.'

A faint smile swept across the ageing face. 'I couldn't take that foreign food, Mog. I've only just got used to the idea of eating chicken chow mein. Besides, they eat horse meat over there, don't they?' She chuckled, carefully folding her mauve cardigan and laying it on top of a grey skirt.

'Dad always goes on about that, but I never know if he's kidding or what.'

'Your dad's all right about you going, then?'

Knowing how her dad had first reacted to the idea of her going away with her friends, and abroad at that, Kay knew that he wouldn't give in on this one. 'He'll come round.' She couldn't keep the touch of defiance from her voice.

'I wouldn't bank on it.'

Kay laid the brochure on top of her aunt's open suitcase. 'Look at that. He can't have anything against me going there. It looks like paradise!'

'Yeah. So do all the pictures in them magazines.'

'It beats hop-picking though, don't it?' Kay smiled, turning over the pages, hoping to impress her aunt.

Sitting on the edge of the bed next to Kay, Liz became pensive, staring at nothing. Kay knew she was thinking about uncle Bert. She had a vision of him herself, bending down by the fireplace outside the huts, setting it up ready for cooking the Sunday pot-roast.

'He was a good picker.' Liz smiled. 'Loved the smell of them 'ops; and the flavour it added to his cheese sandwiches.'

'Didn't put hops in with the cheese, did he?' Kay said, trying to lighten the atmosphere.

'No. The taste came from handling 'em.' Liz looked down at her own hands and thumbed her wedding ring. 'Poor old Bert,' she whispered, 'two years of saving up for that caravan and now he'll never get the chance—'

'But you will, aunt Liz, and that's why he bought it in the first place,' Kay cut in. 'For you. To make up for no more hopping. You know he did.'

'Yeah.' Liz patted her niece's hand, 'You're right there, Mog. He would 'ave died a little bit easier knowing he'd left me that hut on wheels.'

'Liz!' The bedroom door flew open and Laura stood in front of them grinning from ear to ear. 'That was the employment officer at Hammond's

on the phone! You've got the job! The crotchety old cow's turned out to be human after all.'

'Oh, Laura. I 'aven't worked for over five years.' A worried expression came to Liz's face.

'You'll fit into that canteen like a glove. The women are great, you'll love 'em.'

'What will I 'ave to do?'

'Serve the staff with tea and sandwiches. Couldn't be easier.'

'It will get you out of the house, aunt Liz,' Kay added.

Sighing, Liz rolled her eyes. 'When do I start?'

'Monday.' Laura grinned.

'What do I wear?'

'They'll give you a pink and white check overall and a little white hat.'

'But will they 'ave one in my size?'

'Will you care if it's a bit loose?'

'Do me a favour, Laura. Whose uniform will I be slipping into, two-ton Tessie's?'

Laura gave Liz a quick once-over. 'You've lost at least a stone Liz, I bet you're down to ten now.'

Liz liked that. She stood up and examined herself in the mirror. 'You could be right there, Mog. This frock's hanging off me. Reckon I'll 'ave to use a bit of the insurance money to buy some new clothes.'

An encouraging cheer went up from Kay and

Laura as Liz turned away, embarrassed. 'To please Bert, of course,' she added quickly. 'He wouldn't want me looking like a sack of potatoes.'

Making fun of her own position in the fashion department at Hammond's, Laura stood behind Liz and pulled at the spare fabric of her dress until it was skin-tight. 'This dress was simply *made* for modom! A little tuck here and a little tuck there.'

'Think I might 'ave a little rinse when I go to the hairdresser's. What d'yer reckon on a Deep Chestnut?' Liz was beginning to sound like her old self again.

'Only if you let me pay,' Laura said.

'You're on. Manicure?' she asked, pushing her luck.

'A bottle of nail varnish. If you behave yourself.' Laura turned to Kay and the smile drained from her face when she saw the holiday brochure in her hands.

Letting go of Liz's dress, Laura looked at the reflection in the mirror and raised an eyebrow. Then picking up one of the brochures she flicked through the brightly coloured pages and slowly shook her head.

'It's no good, Kay. Your dad won't budge on this one. No way he'll let you go abroad.'

'No?'

'No!'

'Pamela's parents can't seem to understand his attitude. She's ready and waiting to book. Waiting for me to make up my mind.' Kay was feigning indifference, determined to get her way in the end.

'She'll be going with a proper travel agent, Laura.'

'Talk to Jack, Liz, not me. She can go to Australia for all I care!' Laura stormed out of the spare room.

'She doesn't want you to go either, then?'

'No.' Kay was close to tears.

'It's only because they're worried about you. You're all they've got. You mean everything to 'em.'

How many times that thought had gone through Kay's mind she couldn't say. One thing was clear though. She was beginning to feel trapped by their devotion. Somehow she would have to make them realize that she was a person as well as their only child.

'I only wanna go for two weeks. And to Spain, not outer space.'

'Perhaps next year, eh? Give 'em time to get used to the idea that you're growing up.'

'Don't you mean *grown-up*?' Turning away Kay lowered her voice. 'And still a virgin, in case that's what's bothering them.' Before Liz had time to butt

in, she continued, 'And if they think I'm going all that way just to lose it to some Spaniard they need their brains looking at.'

'I don't think that's what's on their minds.' Liz couldn't help smiling.

'Oh, of course it is! Why else would they want to stop me?'

'You don't listen to a word I say, do you?'

'I heard what you said but I don't agree. It's not because I'm an only child!' She hid her face behind the pages and murmured, 'Anyway I'm going, no matter what they say.'

'You think I don't know that? You'll be forging his signature on your passport, knowing you.' With that risky remark, Liz quietly left the room.

Staring into space, Kay suddenly felt lighter inside as she remembered an article she had read in a woman's magazine. An astrologer had written that while some people felt trapped by invisible bindings others put on them, what they failed to realize was that all it took was an invisible knife to cut themselves free.

Turning back to the picture of white sand and turquoise sea, Kay knew that it was time for her to do just that. How that could be achieved and when was something else. But do it she would, before they suffocated her.

* * *

Reversing into the edge of the kerb outside Liz's house, Jack's face fell as he caught sight of the white blinds on the windows. A reminder of what they had left behind. 'You sure you'll be all right on your own, Liz?'

'You are gonna come in?' She tried to cover the concern in her voice.

''Course I am. I'm talking about once I've left.' He pulled the brake on and turned to face his sister. 'I would stop the night, but I've got the meeting—'

'I don't want you to stop the night,' Liz cut in. 'I've got to start fending for myself sometime.' She looked back into Jack's face. 'You can stay for a cup of tea though, can't yer?'

''Course I can. Don't 'ave to be there for another hour.'

Liz sat her handbag square on her lap and sighed. 'I hope you know what you're letting us all in for, Jack. If this strike spreads the way you want it to.'

'It will,' he cut in. 'We'll go for an all-out if the managers don't back down. Hundreds 'ave joined us already.'

'Yeah, and hundreds of wives will be wondering 'ow they're gonna feed their kids on strike pay.'

Jack leaned back in his seat and stared out of the window. 'I'm telling you, Liz, this is the beginning of the end. If we let the London Port Employers get

away with this one, they'll be replacing registered dockers with non-union and casual labourers in no time.' He looked her straight in the eye. 'I've got a horrible feeling that the Dock Labour Board might welsh on us. So far it's just their attitude, but it all starts with a look, don't it? I reckon they'll approve listed men to unload vessels. They'll be condoning this "unofficial strike" next; you see if I'm wrong.'

'You're spending a lot of time on this strike, Jack. Kay and Laura's not seen much of you, if anything.'

'I know that. But this is our livelihood, Lizzie. If we don't safeguard it, who knows what the future'll hold?' He gave her one of his cheeky winks. 'Our Kay might marry a docker for all we know. For all 'er grand ideas, she might just settle for living by the docks in the end.'

Liz didn't want to get into that conversation right then. She had argued enough with her brother that he should encourage Kay to see a bit more of the world.

'It's a changing world all right,' she said instead, shifting the subject. 'Remember I said it would be different in the sixties? There's a strong feeling in the air. It's as if someone's messing about with the electricity; new lights coming on and old ones going out.'

'Well, all the more reason then to make sure our light bulbs stay right where they are and linked to the power!' Jack reached out and pulled one of Liz's carrier bags from the back seat. 'Now get out and get in there! I'm gasping for a cup of tea.'

Once inside the small terraced back-to-back, Jack took the stairs two at a time, saying he needed to have a pee. Slowly pushing open Liz and Bert's bedroom door he took a deep breath and went inside, making for the double bed. With one swift movement he pulled both pillows together, centred them and laid the special sympathy card he had bought that day on the silky gold eiderdown. Jack knew that going to bed alone was going to be a crippling emotional experience for his sister. At least she would have his letter, which he had slipped inside the card to help her through that first night.

With his invisible blinkers firmly in place, Jack strode out of the room. The last thing he wanted was to see Bert's personal bits and pieces around. Had he looked down, he would have seen the brown socks beside the bed that his brother-in-law and best friend had peeled off the night before he died.

'You know, it wouldn't hurt you to get yourself a decent-sized telly out of the insurance money, Liz.' Jack had been racking his brains for what he

might suggest could fill his sister's lonely evenings. 'I know someone who'd snap up your old set.'

'We'll see, Jack, we'll see.' Liz didn't want to think about the insurance money. 'Don't rush me, eh?'

'I just don't like to think of you by yourself.'

'Are you kidding? By myself? I'll have to pretend I'm out once my bingo friends start coming round to see me.'

'Yeah, that's true.' Jack smiled. 'You've always drawn 'em like a magnet. I was forgetting.'

'You was getting downhearted, Jack, I know that. I'm not daft. You're sitting in your best mate's front room, drinking a cup of tea, and he's not here and never will be.' Liz seemed to be drawing strength from her brother's weakness.

'Lizzie! You're one in a million, you know that?' He shook his head at her. 'And you can read me like a book.'

'Yeah. Who d'yer wanna give my old television set to, then?' she asked with a knowing smile.

'No one! I was thinking about you!'

'So you wasn't trying to kill two birds with one stone?' She pulled her little blue tin out of her pocket and sprinkled some snuff on to the back of her hand.

''Course I wasn't.' Jack looked away and wondered if Liz could see into his mind. It was true, he

did have an ulterior motive, but the thought really had only just come to him.

'Anyway, if I do decide, I'll let you have first refusal,' Liz said, in a mock-posh voice.

'Don't do me any favours,' he grumbled and sipped his tea, wishing he hadn't mentioned it in the first place. Liz was a canny woman and probably had a hunch he was thinking of paying Patsy a visit.

As Kay gazed out of an upper window of the 253 bus into the city on her way to work, the idea of forging her father's name on a passport form became a real possibility. It seemed the only way, since Jack had repeated the night before that she would only be allowed to go abroad when she was twenty-one. Unable to contain herself, she flashed a smile at the plump West Indian lady sitting beside her. Kay blushed as she heard herself telling a complete stranger that she was going to Spain for a holiday. 'Any room in your suitcase for me?' The woman grinned, showing off gleaming white teeth. 'I could do with some sunshine in me bones.'

Standing up ready to get off at the next stop, Kay bent down and whispered into her travelling companion's ear, 'I'm gonna forge my passport form.'

The woman's eyes widened and before she could say anything, Kay shrugged. 'It's the only way. My

dad won't let me go.' Making her way along the aisle, she grabbed the handrail as the bus pulled to a halt. 'Don't look so worried,' she called back, 'it might never happen!'

'I hope for your sake that it don't!' The woman shook her head at another traveller. 'Kids,' she said, and suddenly burst out laughing. Her peals rang through the bus and caused a fever of excitement to light Kay up as she jumped down on to the pavement. The woman was wishing her luck.

Making her way towards the building where she worked as typist and Girl Friday in the company secretary's office of Thompson's Windows, Kay began to make a mental list of the clothes she would take on holiday and the things she would need to buy. Her fortnightly salary amounted to just under fifteen pounds after stoppages, and she had hardly any savings. She would have to take the part-time job she had been offered in the tobacconist's the previous week, which would mean a ten-minute walk after work. It would also mean that her Saturdays and Sunday mornings would be spent serving customers instead of seeing her mates in the coffee bar.

'Day-dreaming again?' Jane from the typing pool grinned as she leaned across Kay and caught the far-away look in her eyes.

'Yeah,' she smiled, 'well, you know.'

Laughing, Jane looked up at the big round clock which hung below the company sign. 'We're ten minutes early. Fancy a frothy coffee?'

'Yeah, but that would make us ten minutes late, and you know what Mr Grieves is like for punctuality.' Kay pushed open the heavy glass-panelled door.

'I'm sorry to hear about your uncle,' Jane said, pressing her finger on the small brass lift button.

'Thanks.' Kay didn't want to think about it.

The sudden arrival of the lift, and the crash as Alf threw back the metal concertina doors, ended the conversation. Alf was thick with establishment.

'Makes a change for you girls to be early,' he said in his high-handed way. 'After a rise, are you?'

'No, Alf,' Kay smirked as she stepped into the lift, 'we just can't wait to see your welcoming face.'

Looking at his watch, the stern-faced man put it to his ear to check it hadn't stopped. 'We'll wait a few minutes,' he said, raising his chin defiantly. 'No point in wasting energy. There'll be more staff arriving soon.'

'Don't worry about it, Alfred, we'll walk.' Kay stepped out of the lift followed by her friend, and together they quickly stepped up the wide granite stairway, their stiletto sling-back shoes creating a clicking echo as they raised their voices so that Alf

would hear them say how antiquated the lift was, and it was time the firm changed it for an automatic one. Then, slipping into one of the panelled boardrooms, they sat down on velvet-covered easy chairs and shared a filter-tip cigarette, keeping an eye on the frosted glass walls for anyone passing by.

Kay listened with keen interest as her friend related her crazy weekend adventure. She had met a gorgeous mod at the Tottenham Royal dance hall and was in love again. A feeling of envy flared briefly in Kay but soon died. She had had boyfriends and a fair share of dates, but none of them had made her feel the way she had about Zacchi, the gypsy she left behind on the hop fields in Kent, just over two years ago. One day he would appear on her doorstep – she felt sure of it.

'So what was you day-dreaming about earlier on?' her friend asked, hoping for a return love story.

'Nothing much.' Kay pushed back her chair ready to leave. 'Come on, we'd best get out of here before we're caught.' She had no intention of telling her about the plan, no matter how friendly they were. No one must know. They might just spill the beans and stop her doing something that now seemed the most important thing in her life – getting a passport.

Cautiously the girls crept out of the plush surroundings; if Kay had had any idea right then that

she would feel like ending her misery in that very same boardroom, after being falsely accused of a crime she did not commit, her smiles and hopes would have been shattered. She had had a glimpse of prison life as a young child, when her dad had taken her to see her uncle Bert's brother, Frank, on the Isle of Sheppey – before she was taken for a paddle in the sea.

'Hallo, Thompson's,' said Kay in her poshest accent, learned from Marge on the switchboard. 'Thank you – putting you through now.' She pulled a plug on a black lead and pushed it into the correct extension number; pushed another key forward and told another caller she was sorry to keep him waiting. Answered another outside line, pulled at another plug and put the customer through; pushed another key forward and told someone else that the extension they wanted was now free, that she was connecting her. Reflexes on the switchboard had to be fast and concentration at peak level. Kay loved it. It was the highlight of her day when she relieved one of the telephonists for an hour, and was always surprised at how the time had flown by once the woman returned to take up her position.

'Come on, Kay, up you get,' Marge smiled at her apprentice. 'You'll be putting me out of a job soon.'

'Did you remember to buy my fruit?' June, the second telephonist asked. 'I've lost four pounds already. Hallo Thompson's. Thank you, you're through – I forgot to ask you to get me some cottage cheese for my dinner tonight. Sorry to keep you – line's still engaged. I've got to lose a stone in three weeks.'

Laughing, Marge said that one day June would say the wrong thing to the wrong person and upset a caller. Turning to Kay, who was removing the headphones, she gave her a studious look. 'You're looking a bit serious, lovey. Nothing wrong is there?'

'No, I was just thinking about my second job. I should be starting next week. I've never served in a shop before.'

'Second job?' Marge was grave.

'Maynard's, up by the Angel station.'

There was a heavy silence as both Marge and June looked from her to each other and back again. 'They don't allow you to have a second job here, lovey.' Marge spoke as if it were written in blood.

'Well, I won't tell them then.'

June covered her ears and chuckled. 'I never heard a word of that.'

'If they find out, Kay, they could give you the sack.'

'Oh, Marge . . . they wouldn't do that!'

'It's happened before, sweetheart. They don't like

to think that your mind's not on the job they're paying you to do. And let's face it, Kay, you are a bit of a scatterbrain at times.'

'No I'm not! Well, not when it comes to my work.' The door suddenly flew open and Mr Grieves appeared, looking far from tranquil.

'Isn't it time you were back in the office, Kay?' He looked at his pocket watch. 'You should have been off the switchboard four minutes ago.' He let the door swing shut between them.

'See what I mean?' Marge said, half smiling.

'Yeah,' Kay was thoughtful. 'You two won't say anything, will yer?'

They shook their heads; they wouldn't dream of splitting on her, but they didn't think she should take the risk of losing her job.

'I need the money,' said Kay, walking towards the door, 'I'm saving up to go on holiday. To Spain.'

'I don't know,' Marge shook her head again. 'That kid seems to tempt providence at least once a month.'

Laura tried to keep the worry of Kay out of her mind while she was at work in the fashion department at Hammond's. She knew her daughter could be moody at times, but this business of going abroad seemed to have possessed her. She wasn't sure that, should

Kay get a taste of travelling, she would want to settle down again.

'I can't see anything wrong with it.' The customer looked sideways at herself in the long mirror.

'I'm not sure . . .' Laura was trying tactfully to persuade a fifty-year-old woman away from the trapeze-line dress which stopped just above the knee, and was beginning to lose interest. When Liz came bustling in she was more than pleased to see her.

'Laura – I don't think I can go through with it.' Liz looked flushed and out of breath. Perspiration was trickling from her forehead down the side of her face. 'This bloody watch Jack got me to replace the bangle I lost is losing time, I swear it.'

Laura lifted Liz's hand and checked the time. 'It's fast, Liz, by ten minutes.'

'I'm sweating like a pig.' Liz wiped her forehead with a hanky, and then her armpits, feeling acutely embarrassed when the customer threw her a disgusted look.

Laura knew this woman was capable of finding a few select words to make her sister-in-law feel like dirt, so she took Liz by the arm and guided her away.

'I shan't keep you a moment.' Turning from the smirking face she winked at Liz. Then looking back at the woman Laura paused, and pretended to admire

her from the short distance between them. 'You know I think you were right, that style and colour does suit you. I thought those pink roses were too much, but they bring out the colour of your eyes.'

'Oh really?' The woman lapped up the compliment like a cat with double cream.

'I'll leave you alone for a couple of minutes. Feel free to wheel the other mirror over so you can see how lovely you look from all sides.' Seeing the suppressed grin on Liz's face, Laura marched her away.

'She looks like a lampshade gone wrong,' Liz murmured, keeping a deadpan expression. 'How she couldn't tell you was giving her the old flannel, I'll never know.'

'It's what she wanted to hear,' Laura whispered.

'I didn't mean to be late, Laura. I didn't wanna let you down.'

'You're not late, Liz. Bang on time. Stop worrying – you're making *me* feel nervous.'

As they moved through the store and into the staff canteen, Laura felt Liz relax when she saw the other members of staff smiling and sharing a joke or two. Once they spotted Liz, they gathered round and made her welcome. Feeling comfortable about leaving her there, Laura went back to the ageing would-be Dior model in her own department.

*   *   *

After her first day at work, Liz was only too pleased to follow Laura through the green gate into Delamar Place to spend ten minutes with Kay's grandfather. Once inside that small haven with the old brick wall separating them from the busy Whitechapel Road, Liz sighed with relief and admired the tiny front gardens of the cottages which were full of daffodils, tulips and hyacinths. Laura's dad, known as Billy to Liz, looked up, smiled and stretched. He was proud of his front garden and even prouder of the lovely, weed-free old paved pathway.

'Well?' he grinned, showing off a new set of teeth. 'How'd you get on, Liz?'

'Piece of cake.'

He nodded and shrugged. 'And a nice cup of tea to go with it, I suppose?'

Laughing at his little joke, they waited while he finished the job in hand, easing a stubborn weed from between the stones.

'It's a wonder you don't do your back in, Billy, bending over like that,' said Liz with a touch of concern.

'My back's got more spring in it than a young chicken. And don't forget to wipe your feet.'

Following the old man into his small, cosy living

room, Laura couldn't help feeling a touch of regret at the passing of the old gas mantles which she had loved to hear burning as a child. The gentle hiss was a familiar, comforting sound. Only five months ago electric light bulbs had taken their place. The cottage had finally been converted and brought in line with the very modern world of the sixties.

'Three sugars, innit, Liz?'

'Yes, Billy, and strong.' Liz sank back into the comfortable old leather armchair and kicked her shoes off, while Laura bent down beside the small Victorian fireplace and poked at the orange glow before adding a bit more coke.

'He'll never change, will he?' Laura chuckled.

'Let's 'ope not.'

'I think it's where our Kay gets her stubbornness from.'

'You reckon?' Liz chuckled knowingly.

Laura ignored that. She knew her sister-in-law well enough to take the meaning. 'Look at this, Liz. He's still putting crumbs out for that mouse.'

'Better than having a dog to feed. Cheaper.'

'Yeah, but what happens when the mouse has babies?'

'It won't!' her dad yelled from the scullery. 'She's a boy!'

'And how do you know that?'

'Mice 'ave been trying to set up 'ome in this cottage for years and I've managed to keep them down. I should know the difference by now!'

'That's put you in your place.' Liz closed her eyes.

'We'll see,' Laura said, settling herself in the other armchair. 'Mr Know-all's not always right.'

'Thought I'd 'ave a bit of liver and bacon for me dinner,' Billy said as he arrived with the small tray. 'You found yourself a chap yet, Liz, or what?'

'Dad!' Feeling acutely embarrassed, Laura eyed Liz for her reaction.

'Thought I might move in with you, Billy,' Liz teased, hiding the hurt. 'You can get a good tune from an old fiddle.'

Setting the tray down on a small wooden table, the old man laughed. 'Not me, girl. Too set in me ways. And Billy's willy's had it. I haven't had a bone in me dick for years.'

Liz roared with laughter while Laura could do nothing but shake her head, mildly disapproving. Leaving them to talk over old times, Laura went into the part-modernized scullery to peel some potatoes ready for her father to boil, and to toss the thick slice of lamb's liver in flour. Gazing round the scullery she felt a mixture of pride and sadness at the way the old man kept it. He still used the fuel-fired copper boiler to do his washing, and her mum's old mangle

to squeeze the water from his clothes. She couldn't knock it though, his tea towels were sparkling white and the smell of washing powder, bleach and starch reminded her of the old days when she was a child and helped her mother with the Monday wash. She hoped he would never get rid of the old washboard propped in the corner.

'At least you can rest in peace, Mum. He takes good care of himself,' she murmured.

'I tell you, Liz!' her dad was shouting now, and laughing. 'When I woke up in that ditch the next morning . . .'

They were talking about Liz's favourite subject – hop-picking. At least they had their stories. Machines might have ripped away the future for hop-pickers but they couldn't snatch back the wonderful memories.

Folding a tea towel over a wooden rail, Laura's mind was filled again with Richard. She remembered having counted up the few weeks of each year they were together; it amounted to just five months. They had only ever seen each other during the hop-picking season, since both were married and committed to their families. The end of hop-picking had meant the end of their affair.

Richard often moved in and out of her thoughts. Apart from her husband, Jack, he had been her only

love. And they had loved each other. Possibly still did. But their relationship had to be left to fade away, for everyone's sake. Especially Kay's. Guilt swept through Laura as her daughter's face now filled her mind. The time when she cried to Laura that she knew about the affair and how she didn't want her mum and dad to get divorced.

'Laura!' Liz's voice broke into her thoughts. 'Your dad wants me to take a trip over to France with 'im! Can I trust 'im, or what?'

Laura tried to smile, but it was impossible when her mind was on other things. Not that she didn't want to be with Jack – she did. They were all right now. Both had worked at getting back what they had before the marriage went on the rocks. But it wasn't the same as Richard, and she knew in her heart that it never would be. It seemed to Laura that emotions had a will of their own, and no matter how hard the fight, she couldn't change what happened by itself, inside.

'What's up now?' Liz took Laura by surprise as she stood in the doorway. 'You look as if you've lost two bob and found a penny.'

'I'm all right. Miles away.' She forced a smile. 'I'd best be getting on home. Jack'll be wanting his tea before he goes out to his meeting.'

'All right, Mog, you do that. I'll stop a bit longer, keep your dad company.'

Kissing her father lightly on the forehead, Laura squeezed his arm. 'Phone if you want anything, Dad, won't yer?'

'If I want anything, I'll walk round and ask you. I'm not using that contraption unless I 'ave to. Don't know why your Jack went to the expense of having it put in here in the first place. Just another bloody bill to think about.'

Laura folded her arms and stared him out until he finally gave in.

'All right, all right. If I don't feel well enough to come round, I'll use the bloody thing.' He looked up at his daughter's insistent face. 'Especially if I take bad in the night.'

'Good. That's what it's there for. I'll pop in after work tomorrow. Have your laundry ready for me to iron, OK?'

'Yeah, yeah, yeah. Go on, get going. You should be there when your old man gets in from work.'

'From where?' Laura asked pointedly.

'Oh, right, I forgot. The strike. What's new?'

'Don't ask, Dad. I'm sick of hearing about it. One thing I do know, it's spreading fast. See you at work, Liz.' With that Laura left, closing the door quietly behind her.

As she walked along Cleveland Way, Laura mulled over Liz's words. *Lost two bob and found a penny.*

Little did her sister-in-law know how near to the mark she had been. Leaving Richard behind for Jack had felt a bit like that at the time. But the pennies were mounting up again, like the months that had passed. She half hoped that Richard would eventually fade from her mind altogether, leaving her free to love only those who were close to her.

Waves of guilt broke over her again. It wasn't fair on Jack that she should even be thinking about that time. He had done his utmost to make it up to her once they were back together. And he had turned out to be a good, caring husband. And loyal too.

Looking down from the makeshift platform at a meeting of dockers and speakers outside the gates of St Katharine's Dock, Jack was missing Bert's company and moral support. Some of the faces were familiar to him, but out of the hundreds of men there, he recognized only thirty or so from his own wharf. Blocking his emotions in order to deliver the rest of his speech, Jack tensed his body and clenched his fists.

'When they gave Bert's job to an outside man instead of a regular, they were doing no less than testing our strength! Over a dozen names were submitted and they chose one who just so happened

to be a casual worker! Coincidence? I don't think so! And as we all know, his wasn't the first job to go that way!

'That firm has over three hundred men on the permanent labour force! And this isn't the first time it's drawn on the casual labour pool for work!' He stopped for a breather while the men, aroused, yelled their own opinions on the subject.

'And now we hear rumours that the National Dock Labour Board has taken the decision that firms *may* use unregistered labour. Well, if that turns out to be the case, brothers, I vote the men in our wharf stay out until the decision is revoked!'

A loud cheer went up and the men raised their hands to show they would remain on strike. Bringing his speech to an end, Jack dropped his tone and spoke gravely.

'And for those few misguided anti-strikers who have been heard to say that I'm using Bert's death to attack the London Board, they are very much mistaken. When this dispute is over – and please God, may it be soon – and the London Port Employers have realized how wrong they were, then maybe we can say that something good did come out of something tragic, and Bert's death hasn't been a complete waste.'

A hush fell on the crowd as one by one they

removed their caps to show respect for a fellow docker.

Jack was pleased to see Kay as he strode along the Whitechapel Road on his way home from the meeting. She hadn't seen him, and he quickened his pace to catch her before she went into Lyon's coffee shop. He didn't dare call out for fear of embarrassing her, should there be a young man on the other side of the window she was peering into.

'All right, babe?' he playfully tapped her head with his folded newspaper.

'God, you scared the life out of me!'

Jack had been right; a quick glance into the shop and he could see young Pamela and a couple of boys inside. 'See you later,' he grinned, and walked on.

Checking her reflection, Kay pushed open the glass door and made her way towards the threesome.

'Coffee?' Tommy was quick off the mark.

'Please.' Kay remembered how she'd wished he was a bit taller when she first saw him.

'Cappuccino?'

'Prefer frothy coffee, if that's OK.'

Pamela started to giggle and tossed back her long, straight black hair. 'It's the same thing, Kay!'

Ray Charles's voice, on the juke box, broke through the embarrassing pause as he sang 'Hit the Road Jack'.

'Guess what I've got in my handbag?' Kay boasted.

'Can't be bothered.' Pamela pushed her fringe out of her eyes and made a point of not looking at Kay. She was irked about something, and Kay was in no doubt that she would let her know what it was once the boys had gone. She sat down and pushed her face up close to Pamela's.

'Think of a hot, sunny, sandy place – palm trees . . .'

'That's a lot to get in a little handbag!' Micky grinned.

'Two words: the first begins with "p" and the second with "f".'

Arriving with a steaming cup of coffee, Tommy started to laugh. 'A "p" and "f", eh?'

Before they started making crude guesses, Kay pulled a manila envelope out and waved it in Pamela's face. 'Passport form,' she grinned.

'It isn't!' she shrieked, shedding her sophistication. 'Honest?'

'Yep.'

'They said yes?'

'Not quite.'

'What d'yer mean, not quite? Either they did or they didn't!'

Kay shrugged. 'They didn't.'

Sitting back in her chair, Pamela pouted, sulking, and looked daggers at Kay. 'You're not funny.'

Leaning forward, Kay whispered to all three of them. 'I've got it down to a fine art now. I've been practising.' They waited. 'My dad's signature. I'm gonna forge it on to this very special visitor's passport form. And I went into the booth on Whitechapel station on my way here and got my snapshots done.'

'Let's 'ave a look then,' Tommy was making it clear just how keen he was on Kay.

Pulling them out of the pocket of her suede jacket, she passed them over without so much as a thought. Her mind was still on the passport form. 'So you can go ahead and book the tickets.' She sat back in her chair, sipped her coffee and winked at Pamela. 'Six weeks' time and we'll be sunning ourselves silly.'

'You can't do it, Kay,' Pamela shook her head.

'You watch me. This afternoon when Dad's at his strike meeting.'

'I mean it! You can't *do* it!'

'It doesn't matter what you say – it's as good as done.'

Looking at his watch, Tommy stood up. 'I'm gonna 'ave to go.' He passed the photographs back to Kay. 'Will you be in the Black Boy tonight?'

'No,' Pamela answered for her. 'The Beggar's. You get some good parties there.'

'Yeah. Good villains as well.' Tommy made it clear he wouldn't be going.

'How about the Prospect of Whitby?'

'Nar. Full of medical students.' He was having none of that.

'How about the Artichoke?'

'Sounds good to me,' Pamela chimed in.

'As long as we don't stay in there but go on to the Black Boy or the Two Puddings.'

'See you at eight,' Tommy said, smiling at Kay. The two boys strolled out as if they had all the time in the world.

'Thanks for flirting with Tommy.' Pamela was fuming.

'I never so much as showed a knee!' Pulling her mug shots out of the envelope, Kay was taken aback. 'Look at this! One's missing. Tommy must 'ave torn it off.'

There was a pause, and their eyes met, Pamela feeling jealous and Kay suddenly in the mood for love and romance.

'You're really gonna do it, then?'

'Yep. I've got my seven and six, my photographs and my form. I'm all set. Spain, here we come!'

Chapter Three

Liz was serving Bob, the fire officer, with a cup of tea and a cheese roll when Laura arrived looking flushed and unnerved.

'That'll be tenpence, love,' said Liz, giving Laura a quick once-over. 'What's up with you?' she asked, pressing a key on the till. 'Another snotty-nosed customer got under your skin?' She handed Bob the change and tut-tutted when he grabbed her hand playfully.

'Liz, ask one of the others to cover for you. I need to talk.'

'That bad?'

Laura couldn't answer; she was on the verge of tears. Dragging a chair out from under a table for two, she sat down and pulled a filter-tip cigarette from her packet and waited for Liz to join her.

'Try to hide your feelings a bit, Laura, for Christ's

sake. The world and all its children can see you're fuming about something.'

Laura sipped her tea and tried to compose herself. It wasn't going to be easy, confronting Liz, but it had to be done. She had to know right away whether her sister-in-law knew about the devastating secret that Jack had been keeping from her.

'Come on then,' Liz sniffed, 'spit it out. Who's upset yer?'

'Can't you guess?' Laura couldn't keep the spite out of her voice. 'Who's usually responsible for turning me inside out?'

Liz sighed. It had to be her brother Jack. Who else could bring out the worst in Laura? 'What's he done now?'

'*You* tell *me*.' She looked into Liz's eyes and waited.

'Tell you what?'

Laura drew a letter from the pocket of her red and navy blue dress and pushed it towards Liz. 'If you know about this, Liz, I would rather you said so. Please don't lie to me.'

While Liz slowly read through the letter, Laura talked quietly. 'I can't believe he's been keeping in touch with her all this time. I never made any demands. I just presumed he would put that part of his life out of his mind. Now I can't stop wondering

if he's been up there to see her; see their baby. Maybe he's waiting for the right time to tell me he wants to leave. Perhaps he's just been pretending he's happy with me, when all the time he's been making plans to leave once Kay's left the nest.'

'No, Laura! That's rubbish and you know it. He idolizes you. This was a serious mistake that he's still having to pay for.' Liz folded the letter and slipped it back into the envelope. 'How would you feel if he *had* wiped her and the boy out of his life?'

'How did you know it was a boy? It doesn't say so in that letter.'

'Jack told me.'

Covering her face with both hands, Laura took a deep breath and willed herself not to cry. She hoped Liz wouldn't try to get her to speak. She needn't have worried, they had known each other long enough to realize when silence was sacred.

Laura finally came out from behind her hands and managed a weak smile. 'It hurts,' she said with a touch of bitterness.

'If I talk,' Liz said, 'are you up to listening, or shall we wait till the day's done and we can be private?'

'Wait. I'll come round to you after work. I'll leave cold ham and salad for Kay and a note to say where I am.'

'And Jack?'

Laura turned away, swallowed hard. 'I'll leave enough for him as well.'

'Good girl.' Liz squeezed Laura's hand. 'It'll all come out right, you'll see.'

Laura raised her eyes and looked into Liz's face. 'Two years he's kept this from me. Sharing something as important as a child with someone else. There's a lot to be put right, Liz. I thought that like me, Jack had stopped living lies.'

'This is a lie left over from the past, Laura. That's different. Just remember that the little boy didn't ask to be part of this. He's innocent. Probably the only innocent one in this drama. You played your part in it as well. While Jack was happy somewhere else it gave you a clearer conscience to, well, you know . . . Richard Wright?'

'I might have known I'd be held responsible!'

Chuckling, Liz picked up the empty cups and saucers. 'That's more like it. Anger's better than sorrow any day. See you later.'

Once Laura was back in her own department, with no customers to attend to, she pulled out the letter and read it again.

Dear Jack,

Just a line to say that the chickenpox has finally gone and we are having peaceful nights

again. Thank you for the postal order, it's a weight off of my mind to know that I can pay a month's rent in advance. My mother is still asking me to move in with her but I know it would never work; not while I have little Jac with me. Only last week she dropped hints about my having him adopted. She means well.

I have managed to get some piece-work, machining zips into men's trousers. At least it means I can work and look after the sprat at the same time, and it puts bread on the table. No other news. I don't get out much, but my mother's making inquiries about a second-hand television she knows will be coming up for sale. Some lucky sod will be buying an eighteen-inch set, no doubt.

There seems to be more work up here, for the men that is. Especially skilled builders and decorators. Everyone seems to be having small extensions built. All right for some. Tom will be coming to sit with me tonight. He's been very kind and I'm growing fond of him.

Try to get up here soon. We don't want you to lose touch with your boy, do we?

Write soon,
Patsy.

*　　*　　*

Laura shivered, thinking back to the time she first discovered that Patsy was carrying Jack's child. She couldn't help wondering if she should have kicked him out then. She wondered what her present life might have been like now, had she done so. At the time her main concern had been Kay. She hadn't wanted to put her through the trauma of her parents splitting up, filing for divorce. Maybe she had been wrong. Maybe Jack had spent the past two years wishing he was with this other woman.

'Mum?' Kay's voice echoed around Laura's thoughts as she sat hunched over the letter, choked, with tears in her eyes. 'You OK?'

Snapping out of her melancholy, Laura looked up and blinked. 'Kay! It *is* you. I thought I heard your voice.'

'Of course it's me.' She eyed the letter in Laura's trembling hands. 'Bad news?'

'No, not really. A letter from an old friend. I was swept away with nostalgia for a minute.' She slipped the letter back into her pocket. 'What're you doing here? Shouldn't you be at work?'

'I pretended I didn't feel well this morning. Mr Grieves finally condescended to let me go after lunch-time.'

'You did what?' Laura felt herself tense, gazing at

her one and only child who seemed to be maturing by the day. She found herself wishing she could turn back the clock and relive those times when chubby little Kay with blue eyes and blonde hair would nuzzle up to her and fall asleep on her breast.

'I had somewhere to go, Mum. And I've got something to tell yer.'

Kay's voice hadn't really changed that much, she just said things differently now. Informed Laura of things instead of asking permission.

'Promise you won't shout at me?'

'I promise, babe,' Laura said, knowing she didn't have it in her at that moment to shout at anyone. She pulled another chair up close to hers and motioned for Kay to sit down, hoping a customer wouldn't suddenly appear. Cupping Kay's face, Laura leaned forward and kissed her soft, flushed cheek and gave her a reassuring smile. Her daughter looked as if she had all the troubles of the world on her shoulders.

'I've done something that's, well, criminal, I s'pose,' Kay chewed the inside of her cheek and studied her mother's face for a reaction.

'Criminal, eh?' Laura stopped herself laughing.

'I had to do it, Mum. It was the only way. I've got to get out of this country.'

Laura felt herself go cold. 'You've got to what?'

61

'Oh, no, I don't mean . . . I haven't done anything that means I've *got* to get out. I've done something so that I *can* get out.'

Laura sank back in her chair. 'Oh, I wish you wouldn't do that to me, you little cow,' she murmured feeling somewhat relieved. 'I know what you've done. You've gone and got yourself a passport.'

Kay nodded slowly and swallowed hard. 'I had to do it. I feel like I'm suffocating. I need to get away. I need to feel some space around me.'

Laura stood up and paced the floor, one hand on her forehead. 'Kay, am I getting this right?' She looked her daughter straight in the eye. 'Did you sign your father's name on a passport form?'

Kay looked back sheepishly. There was no need for her to say anything.

'Terrific! And what do you think he's going to say about that?'

'Oh, we mustn't tell him! Not until I'm on the way and it's too late for him to stop me. I'm trusting you not to tell him!'

'Thanks. That's very good of you.' Laura sat down again. 'I wonder what else is in my stars today?'

'I won't ever tell Dad that you knew.'

'Oh, right.' Laura could hardly believe her ears. Kay was becoming an independent young lady.

Laura's thoughts went back to Jack's two-year-old son and her heart sank. She felt suddenly alone.

'I wouldn't have done it if it didn't mean so much to me, honest.'

'No, love,' Laura sighed, 'I can see that. When do you go?'

'In five weeks' time.'

'And where's the money coming from? Or am I supposed to pay for you to give me all this aggravation?'

'No. I've got a part-time job. Working in a sweet shop after work and at weekends.'

'And when did that come about?' Laura wondered what else had been going on while she had been day-dreaming.

'I've been looking for a job for ages.'

'And where is this sweet shop?'

'Islington.'

'Islington. You couldn't have got one locally, of course. That would have been too straightforward.'

'What's wrong with it? I work in Clerkenwell – it's just up the road!' Kay was beginning to lose her cool.

'Which will mean you catching a train late at night and at weekends!'

'It won't be late at night. I finish at half past eight and will be home before nine.'

'And what time does it get dark in April?'

'Oh, Mum, this is ridiculous! I'll be eighteen this summer!'

'It's north London, Kay. The Angel Islington's not the sort of place to be hanging around stations.'

'I won't be hanging around anywhere. I'll go to work, catch a train, come home. Simple.'

Laura felt much older than her thirty-nine years. 'OK,' she shrugged, hoping Kay would pick up on the note of weariness in her voice and lift her from the depths she was reaching.

'And you won't say anything to Dad about the passport?'

'No, I won't say anything,' she said, realizing she was hoping for too much. Kay was on a different plane.

'Good.' Kissing her mother on the cheek, Kay gave her a hug. 'Love you,' she said and hurried off.

Laura watched her go and wondered why she felt so depressed. Nothing terrible had happened. Not really.

'Do you have any Mary Quant dresses?' A girl, Welsh, probably a student, appeared before Laura.

'No, love, this store is a bit more conservative than that.'

'Don't you mean boring?'

'Yeah, boring. That's right. It does need to move with the times.'

The student agreed and left, as if an emotional, watery-eyed saleslady were part of everyday life.

'We all need to move with the times,' Laura murmured to herself. 'Things are on a roll all right. It's enough just keeping up.' She pulled the letter out of her pocket again and quickly put it back as a bubbly blonde approached, grinning from ear to ear. Not really paying much attention to the customer, Laura took a comb from her handbag and checked her appearance in a tiny mirror.

'I didn't know you worked in 'ere, Laura.' It was Milly, a friend she hadn't seen in months, years in fact.

Laughing, Laura put her comb and mirror away. 'You're marvellous, Milly, you know that?'

'Am I?'

'Yes. I was feeling a bit low to tell you the truth, and seeing you dressed up to the nines and looking as lively as ever is a real tonic.'

'Yeah? That's good. I was a bit naughty down 'opping, wasn't I? Trying to tease your Jack away.' She looked pensive. 'Never did work though, did it?'

'How's Georgie?' Laura was feeling better by the second.

'Gets out next week. That's why I came in. Thought I'd buy a nice new coat to pick 'im up in.'

'Is that how long they gave him?'

'Yeah. Bleeders. And all for what? A few bangle watches and a coupl'a dozen bottles of whisky. Still. I think it's taught 'im a lesson. He thought he was too clever to get caught. He had a good run before they did nab 'im, mind. He swears blind he's gonna go straight from now on.'

'Well, perhaps it was blessing, eh?'

'Yeah. Now, then, I fancy a nice camel coat with a bit of fox on the collar. Something like the one in the window. What d'yer reckon?'

'I've got just the thing. Expensive though.'

'That's all right. George 'ad a bit put by, if you know what I mean.' She grinned and winked at Laura.

'Oh, Milly,' Laura let out a throaty laugh, 'I am pleased to see you. You're one in a million.'

'Funny you should say that! It's what I used to think about you. Always wished I could be as classy. Where d'yer get it from, eh? You're just a common old East Ender, after all's said and done.'

Laura dropped her mirror back into her handbag and shrugged. 'That's me, all right.'

'Come on, then. Bring me a coat I can be proud to

walk down the Whitechapel Road in. I'll show some of them women out there that I can afford to shop in 'ammond's!'

Walking away from the store after closing time, Laura did her utmost to persuade Liz that she felt much better about the letter, that she didn't need to talk about it any more. But Liz in her wisdom thought Laura was just shelving it. 'If you don't talk to me about it, Laura, you'll bottle it up and explode at Jack at the wrong time.'

'No, Liz. I won't. I know what I'm doing, believe me. I'm gonna handle this my way.'

'Oh yeah?' Liz looked worried. 'And what way's that when it's at home?'

'Never you mind. Now then, you coming in to have a cuppa with Dad, or not?'

''Course I am. I need old Billy-boy to keep up my sense of humour.'

'All he ever does when *I* go in is moan.'

'Ah, well, you've either got the gift or you 'aven't. I bring out the devil in 'im.'

Unlatching the green gate into the tiny cul-de-sac, Laura smiled to herself. It was the effect Milly had had on her. She couldn't think why, but what did that matter as long as it worked and she felt lighter.

'What are you gonna do about the letter, then?'

'I'll tell you – once I've done it. Fair enough?'

'No. But I can see it's all I'm gonna get.'

'Spot on, Liz, spot on.' Laura knocked loudly on the cottage door and then used her own key to let them in.

'I'm not deaf!' yelled her dad from his place by the fire.

'See what I mean?' Laura shrugged and closed the door behind them.

'You got that kettle on yet, Billy, or what?'

'I have. And what's more, I've been out specially to get a bit of angel cake. And it wasn't cheap!'

As Liz pulled her coat off, Laura collected Billy's ironing, kissed her dad hallo and goodbye.

'Save me a bit of that cake!' she called over her shoulder as she made to leave.

'I dunno why you can't sit down for five minutes,' Billy called back. 'Always on the bloody go!'

'When they invent irons that work by themselves I will!' Laura shut the door behind her, pleased that each of them was filling a tiny gap in the other's life.

'The London Port Employers can urge all they like. It's like whistling in the wind as far as I'm concerned.' Jack was on his high horse again. 'We're in a strong position all right – and they know it. You

wait and see the turnout on Sunday. This'll be a mass march to remember.'

'I'm pleased it's going well.' Laura sounded sincere as she dished up some shepherd's pie and handed a plate to Jack.

'Are yer? Makes a nice change. So far you've done nothing but tell me how we shouldn't be making all this trouble for the country. What's changed your mind?'

'If that many men are willing to come out it must be for a good reason.' She piled processed peas on to his plate. 'I hate to think of those oranges and bananas rotting in the ships, though.'

'You think we don't? There has to be some losses. Stands to reason. Better a bit of fruit than a whole bloody industry.'

'I suppose the march on Sunday'll take up most of the day?' Laura asked, trying to sound casual.

'Oh, yeah. Bound to. Why?'

'Oh, nothing really. I was just thinking I might go and visit Fran. I've been promising to go ever since she moved out.'

'Harlow?' Kay said, getting herself a glass of water. 'That's miles away.'

''Course it's not. Anyway there's an early train. We'd have most of the day together, then I could catch one back somewhere around seven.'

'Wouldn't catch me going all that way for just a day's visit.'

Laura was sorely tempted to ask Jack why not, since Leicester was much further, but she bit her tongue and bided her time. 'It was just an idea. If you'd rather I didn't go—'

'Tch. 'Course you can go. I'll treat you to the fare as well. I was only thinking of you tiring yourself out. You're bound to wanna cook me something hot when you get in.'

'Always thinking of your stomach, eh, Dad?' Kay teased.

'Have some carrots,' Laura grinned, approaching him with a large spoon.

'Careful! Don't wanna get gravy over me clean shirt. I'm seeing the lads tonight in the Grave Maurice.'

'You're what?'

Jack wiped some gravy from the corner of his mouth. 'The Grave Maurice. What's wrong with that?'

'You never use that pub.' Laura felt her heart sink.

'Bert's brothers do. And they suggested we meet some of the other union leaders there. It's not a problem.'

'Bert always said he wouldn't step inside that

place. It's where the villains meet up, you know it is.'

'Oh shut up, Laura, you're talking about men we know. Frank and Freddie? What d'yer think they're gonna do, pull a gun? Tch. Villains!' He eyed her carefully. 'It's only a pub.'

Letting out a worried sigh, Laura began to eat her dinner. 'Haven't seen Bert's brothers for a couple of years, other than at the funeral. Right couple of spivs they looked as well.'

'You haven't dished any up for Kay.' Jack looked questioningly at his daughter.

'Me and Pamela's having pie and mash.' She pinched a carrot from his plate as she left the kitchen.

'Good. More shepherd's pie for us.' He winked at Laura, waiting for her to reach out and pick up the dish from the top of the gas oven. But she ignored him, and felt a wave of satisfaction when he finally got up without saying a word and got it himself. There was hope yet for her changing his Victorian attitude towards a woman and her work in the kitchen.

Spooning more hot food on to his plate, Jack looked suddenly pensive, and Laura wondered if he was thinking about his small son. She could feel herself sinking again.

'They're gonna be debating this strike in the 'Ouse of Commons, you know.'

Relieved that she was wrong about his thoughts, Laura poured herself some water from the pink glass jug. 'You have to expect that, Jack. It's turning into a serious unofficial strike now. Everyone's talking about it. I heard a couple of blokes in the canteen saying that you'll never get the government behind you on this one.'

'We'll see. The longer we stay out, the deeper in trouble this government'll be. They know that. They're testing us, see how far we're prepared to go.'

'And?'

'How far? Until they give in. We're not just talking about a little dispute, Laura. We're talking about the future of dockers and the docks.' He sat down, picked up his fork, then pushed his plate away. 'I've lost me appetite thinkin' about it.'

Laura had never seen him like this before, and had a nagging feeling it was because he and the men were in a no-win situation. They might even have walked straight into a political plot to weaken the union. And if Laura's mind was working that way, she knew for sure that Jack's would be too.

'Bert's brothers aren't gonna get involved in this dispute, are they?'

Jack looked back at her, a reassuring smile on his face. 'They're probably already involved, Laura. People like me and the other union leaders are just spokesmen, if the truth be known. This country's run by villains and corrupt politicians.'

'You are joking?'

'Yeah. 'Course I'm bloody joking.' He winked at her. 'Don't suppose you fancy a cuddle on the sofa before I go out?'

'Too early in the day. You can wake me up when you get in tonight though.' She was surprised to find herself flirting with him. She thought they had been married too long for all that. There was no doubt in her mind that the letter she had found in his jacket pocket, before she sent it to the cleaners, had aroused a bit of jealousy.

Leaning forward in his chair, Jack reached out and caught her as she passed and landed a big kiss on her small round buttock. 'I fancy you rotten,' he grinned.

'Make sure you're home early then.' She tweaked his ear and made a sharp exit.

Standing in a short queue at the ticket office on Sunday morning, Laura began to have doubts about the trip she was embarking on. Up to now she had had her sights firmly fixed on seeing the woman and

73

Jack's illegitimate son; to find out for herself what she was like and just how deep the relationship was. Had she confronted Jack, she felt sure he would have lied to get himself off the hook.

She pushed her left foot further into the new shoe, trying to ease the blister that was developing on her heel. Pointed toes might look good but they were murder to get used to. Brushing a dust mark from her bottle green skirt, she wondered if the costume she had chosen was a bit too smart. Maybe she should have worn something a bit more casual. Slacks even.

She started to wonder about her dark auburn hair that tumbled down around her shoulders. Shouldn't she have swept it up into a topknot?

'A day return to Leicester please,' she heard herself say, as if part of her had decided to take the lead. Another part wanted to run back home and forget the whole business. In her heart, though, she knew that this was not something to be put off. She had found herself thinking about it every spare minute, and a night hadn't passed since she found the letter when it hadn't crept into her sleep, giving her nightmares.

Sitting on the platform waiting for the train, Laura glimpsed the headlines on someone's newspaper, *Docker's Strike Halts Exports!*

Even though it was a national issue, she felt sure it wouldn't be long before the newspapers would home in on the human interest stories. Bert's name would be spread across the front pages of the local rags, at least. She dreaded to think what it would do to Liz.

'Who'd 'ave thought it, eh?' The elderly woman sitting on the bench next to Laura grinned at her. 'Working classes holding the country to ransom. About bloody time as well. Good luck to them boys, that's what I say!'

Laura found herself smiling back at the stranger and wondering what she *would* say if she knew just how involved her family were. 'Is your husband a docker?' she asked instead.

'No, love. He's six foot under. Used to be a coalman. He was good an' all. A grafter. More's the pity. The pay was lousy and the work was hard. Humping coal on his back non-stop, and for what? To end up with 'is lungs full of black dust.' She folded her newspaper and placed it on her lap. 'I wouldn't mind if he got a bit of respect for the hard work and hours he put in. Still, there you are. That's a working man's lot, innit?'

Laura shrugged and sighed. What could she say? Pushing open the gold-coloured clasp of her handbag, she pulled out a bar of Fry's chocolate cream and an Aero. 'Which one d'yer fancy?'

75

The woman's face lit up. 'Wouldn't mind a small section of that Aero. It's my favourite.'

'Here, take it. I'm watching my weight.'

'Ta, love. I won't say no in that case. Mind you, lovely figure like yours.'

'Ah, but, it wouldn't be if I ate as much chocolate as I would like!'

'True.'

Feeling lighter inside, Laura watched as other trains pulled into other platforms, enjoying the hustle and bustle of King's Cross.

'Where you off to, then?' the woman carefully peeled back the wrapper and then the gold paper.

'Visiting an old school friend who's moved up to Leicester,' Laura lied. 'You?'

'Oh, I'm not going nowhere, love. Waiting for my daughter and grandchildren. They come every Sunday. We go over the park and 'ave a picnic. Her old man left 'er for someone else.'

Laura popped a piece of chocolate into her mouth and imagined herself being a grandmother. She tried to visualize Kay with a baby in her arms and maybe a little one pulling on her skirt. Then she remembered why she was there waiting for a train. There seemed to be no let-up to the constant reminder of her personal anxieties.

Stepping out of Leicester railway station, Laura

found herself face to face with two placards on either side of the newspaper seller. The scrawled headline on one was *Gunfire As East Germans Attempt Escape Over Berlin Wall*, and on the other, *More London Dockers Out!* There seemed to be no escape. Approaching the smiling face of a flower seller, Laura asked for directions to St David's Road.

'Taxi or walking?' The woman wrapped a bunch of daffodils and handed them to a customer.

'Walking,' Laura wondered why she had asked. If she had intended to go by taxi, surely the driver would know the way. 'If it is walking distance, that is,' she asked carefully.

'Along London Road, left into Evington Road, left into East Park, about half a mile on, past Spinney Park, left into St Saviour's, up the hill, past the Imperial Hotel and then,' she looked up at the sky thoughtfully. 'Then you'd best ask again. It's somewhere around that way. Big houses. Split into flats.'

'Thanks. I'll take a mixed bunch, please.'

'You can remember all that, can you?' The woman sounded surprised.

'Left, left and left; Evington, East Park and St Saviour's,' Laura confirmed.

'That's one way of looking at it. Two bob, love.'

Laura passed over the coin and thanked the woman again.

'Taxi won't cost you much, love. Otherwise it's gonna take you a good half an hour.'

'That's OK. I'm in no rush.' Turning away Laura found herself smiling. She suddenly realized what it was about the woman that had attracted her attention. 'You're a Londoner!' she called back.

'Too right. I was evacuated up here and never bothered to go back. Married a taxi driver!' She nodded towards the black cab parked a few yards away. Her husband was in the driving seat, sound asleep. A certain smile flickered between the two women.

'Business is quiet,' she shrugged.

Showing a hand, Laura walked away feeling more comfortable about being in a strange town. Leicester wasn't a bit like she had imagined. It reminded her very much of London south of the river. For some reason she had pictured it being a small grey town instead of the lively place it was.

Deep in thought, rehearsing over and over what she would say to Patsy when she opened the door, Laura almost missed her third left turning and was halfway across the road when she realized, stopping suddenly and causing a young man behind to bump into her. Feeling like an idiot, she quickly made her way towards St Saviour's Road and stepped up her pace as she walked uphill towards the beautiful

Victorian Imperial Hotel, but slowed down again when the three-faced clock on the bell tower struck the hour. Again she was reminded of London, and Big Ben.

On a wild impulse, she stepped into the hotel entrance, her heart beating nineteen to the dozen, and followed the sign to the lounge bar. Once inside she felt like turning away. It was mostly men, and the women there all had male partners. Bracing herself, she walked with her head held high to the bar, a confident, serene smile fixed on her face, and asked for two gin and tonics.

'My husband will be joining me in a minute,' she said, taking her purse from her handbag.

'That's quite all right, madam.' The barman took her by surprise as he made it clear that money need not pass between them. 'If you'd care to tell me your room number and name, I'll put it on your bill.'

'But we haven't registered yet,' Laura smiled, wondering how she would get out of this one. 'Just in from London. My husband's parking the car.'

'The name will be fine, madam.'

'Thank you. It's Mr and Mrs Smyth-Winter.' Where that fictitious name came from she had no idea, but she liked the sound of it, and surprised herself at how easily she slipped into the part.

'If madam would like to take a seat.'

'Thank you, yes.' Laura looked around her and spotted a small round table in a corner not far from the door. She could make a quick escape when he wasn't looking.

With a mixture of excitement and trepidation, Laura settled herself and idly turned the pages of the complimentary copy of *The Times* which had been left neatly folded on the table. Again a headline hit her: *Unofficial Dock Strike: Minister Against Intervention*.

Reading with interest, she hardly noticed the two gin and tonics being placed carefully before her. 'Would madam care for ice and lemon?'

'Thank you.' She stopped herself laughing as the waiter gracefully tonged ice cubes into each glass.

'I hope you enjoy your stay.' He smiled and walked away, balancing the small silver tray on fingers and thumb.

Gazing at the drinks, Laura wondered whether to finish one and leave, making it look as if she were on her way to the Ladies', or go for the kill and drink both. She took out a cigarette and decided to see how it went. If the lounge bar continued to fill up, she could easily go unnoticed and enjoy what would amount to a double. She certainly needed it. Not caring whether it was correct for women to smoke in that part of the country, she lit a cigarette, thankful

for the mock tortoiseshell lighter that Liz had given her. The usual box of matches would never do. Not in these smart surroundings.

'I say, is this seat taken?'

Laura looked up from her newspaper into the bleary eyes of a grey-haired man with a huge handle-bar moustache. 'Not at the moment, but it will be.' She tried to sound polite in case his intentions were honourable.

'I was about to join you.' He spoke as if he were doing her a favour.

Having finished one gin and tonic and not really in the mood for another, she was relieved that the intoxicated gentleman swaying before her had given her the best possible excuse to leave.

Dropping her cigarettes and lighter into her hand-bag, she threw the man a look and walked with dignity out of the bar. Once in the street she quickened her pace, terrified in case someone came after her.

Pushing one hand into the pocket of her costume jacket, she withdrew a crumpled piece of paper with Patsy's address scrawled on it. Having come from one embarrassing situation in the hotel she felt easier, somehow, at going into another. Not that her stomach wasn't churning, but at least the palpitations that kept coming and going on the train had eased off.

When she finally arrived at Patsy's door, Laura

felt her heart lurch. She stood for a moment, wondering whether she should turn back, when the sound of a child's cry weakened her. Before she knew it, her finger was on the bell-push clearly marked Flat 1.

Standing in the doorway with the young boy in her arms, Patsy's face was full of surprise as she gazed into Laura's. Neither of them said anything until the child grinned and pointed a chubby finger at Laura's black and gold brooch.

'Mummy's,' he said. There were still tears on his cheeks.

Unable to think of anything to say, Laura turned her attention to Jack's son. 'Why was he crying?' she said, feeling self-conscious.

'Fell over. Bump!' The child answered for Patsy.

'You'd best come in,' she said quietly, standing aside. 'In there.' She nodded towards a cream-coloured door.

Lifting the little boy into his play-pen, Patsy gave him a biscuit, which brought a smile to his face. Then she added a few toys which were spread around the floor. 'You can take your jacket off. I won't steal it,' Patsy joked.

'I'm not stopping.' Laura felt a pang of jealousy as the two-year-old looked up at her with Jack's blue eyes.

'No mistaking whose boy he is,' Laura smiled

weakly. Then turning away to hide the pain, she stared out of a large Victorian window. 'You knew who I was the moment you saw me.'

'Oh, Jack's very proud of his family. He's shown me photographs. A reminder, I suppose, that he's not free to come and go as he might like.'

'Jack is free to do what he wants, and don't kid yourself otherwise,' Laura hit back. Any compassion she felt when Patsy first opened the door was slipping away, and there was nothing she could do to stop her anger rising again, or unwelcome tears welling up in her eyes.

'So what brings you here, then, after all this time?'

'I don't know,' Laura said, turning to face her rival, not caring that the tears were now trickling down her cheeks. 'I wish I could say something sensible.' She wiped her face with the back of her hand. 'I hadn't bargained on the waterworks.'

'Here.' Patsy took a clean white handkerchief from a pile of ironing on the sideboard and pushed it into Laura's hand. 'You've got some pluck, I'll give you that. Many's the time I've wanted to knock on your door.'

'Why?' Laura composed herself, determined to maintain a level of dignity.

'Tell you about me and Jack.'

'You didn't have to. I already knew. I was waiting for it to blow over.'

Patsy gave a burst of mock laughter. 'And look what blew in before it "blew over".' She half turned so that Laura could have a full view of the small boy.

While Patsy was in the adjoining tiny kitchen, Laura looked around at her spotless, simply furnished room. It was obvious that she wasn't too strapped for cash. Little Jac was dressed in a clean, pale blue knitted suit and it was obvious from the pile of ironing on the sideboard that he had plenty of clothes and a grandmother, probably, who was very good at knitting.

'Does Jack often send you money?' Laura felt like biting her tongue. She hadn't meant it to come out quite like that.

Arriving with two cups of tea, Patsy shrugged. 'He does what he can. If I had my way I wouldn't take anything.'

'He should send you money. It's only right.'

'Are you going to sit down, then?' Patsy had a way of making an invitation sound like an order.

Laura peeled off her jacket, threw it on to the back of an armchair, and sat on the edge of the cushion. 'I found a letter in Jack's pocket. I was getting some clothes ready for the cleaner's. I wasn't looking for it. It came as quite a shock.'

'Why? You knew Jack had got me pregnant: at least he said he'd told you, when you were in Kent.'

'He did, I just didn't think.' Laura sighed and hung her head. 'I suppose I just buried my head in the sand. It stands to reason he wouldn't have just left you to . . .' Laura's voice trailed off.

'So what's your problem, then? I'm sure you didn't come all this way just to spend five minutes with Jack's little bastard.'

'I didn't come to make trouble.' She looked into Patsy's big brown eyes and felt a wave of guilt. 'I'm not angry any more, and I don't blame you.'

'Maybe you should. I knew what I was doing. I wanted his child.' She looked down at little Jac playing happily. 'Funny little bugger, isn't he?'

'And what about your feelings towards Jack?' Laura dreaded the answer, fearing the worst.

'I still admire him – got great shoulders.' She sipped her tea. 'I do have a boyfriend. My love for Jack soon faded. I would like my son to know his father. But that's asking too much, I suppose?' She eyed Laura carefully.

'Yes. I think it is.' There was a pause. 'It has to be all or nothing with me, none of this family sharing. It's not right.'

'Well, I don't want Jack any more, and he never did want me, not for a wife, that is.'

They sat there, quietly drinking their tea, eyes down. The only sounds came from Jac, content to sit and pick the chocolate chips out of his biscuit.

'My mother lives just around the corner,' said Patsy finally. 'I was about to get Jac ready to go round there for Sunday dinner. She always feeds us Sundays.'

'I'd best be going then. She'll be expecting you.'

'Yes, she will. I'm sorry you've had a wasted journey.' Patsy's tone was very cool. 'Waste of a train ticket.'

'No, I don't think it was.' Laura stood up and reached out for her jacket. 'I'll see that Jack sends you a regular amount of money.'

'That's very charitable. I must say I wouldn't be as soft. But then Jack's not the sort who needs his wife's permission to feed and clothe his own son, is he?'

'Of course it's a bit difficult at the moment, with the strike. But once it's over, he'll make up for the months.'

'That's a very nice costume. Looks classy. Expensive. And that brooch, by the way, is identical to one he gave me three years ago. Must have been a job lot.'

Laura felt the tears well up again. She pressed her lips together and composed herself. 'Look, I'm sorry if you've had a rough time.'

'Like I said, I've got a boyfriend. But he refuses to take on someone else's kid. Especially a southerner's. Can't blame him. So there we are. That's the fine mess your husband's got me into.'

'But you said it was your doing,' Laura whispered, realizing she had pushed Patsy too far when she saw her cheeks redden with anger.

'Oh, yeah,' she grinned, 'I forced him to have sex with me, if you can believe that.' She shook her head. 'Jack made love to me more times than you've given him a hot dinner! The fact that he was too drunk to care one night, when he didn't have something with him, is neither here nor there.'

'I've made things worse by coming.' Laura's stomach turned over.

'No. I don't think so. Hasn't affected *me* one way or the other, to be perfectly honest.'

'You seemed relieved to meet me when I first came.'

'I was.' She smiled serenely. 'I used to dread you coming after me, when I was in London having the affair with Jack. I was terrified of you. We can blame Jack for that.' She tossed her ginger curls off her face. 'And now I'm not. And you know why? Because I've got his son – and you haven't.' She was still smiling.

Laura could do nothing but look at Patsy's face,

waiting for some sign of remorse, regret, maybe a little shame?

'That's right,' Patsy grinned spitefully, 'I've got a son and you haven't.' She spoke the words slowly, deliberately.

'Please don't say that.' Laura could feel the old hurt moving back into her chest. 'You don't know what you're saying.'

'I do, actually. I heard nothing else for bloody years! That sacred child you lost. Well my boy is alive and kicking and needs clothes on his back. So it's useless coming at me with all that self-pity.'

'God, you are one strange woman.' Laura managed to regain her self-respect.

'I don't want to seem rude, but . . .' Patsy looked at her watch, 'especially after you've come all this way.'

Grabbing her handbag, Laura made for the door, and turned to Patsy. 'Your son is the image of my daughter. Except for the ginger hair. But still, maybe that will lighten as he gets older.'

'Maybe. I'll get Jack to keep you informed.'

Jack settled himself in a quiet corner of the Grave Maurice and wondered what he would be having for dinner that day. He had got it wrong about the strike meeting, it was a three o'clock start, so he had time

to spare. Maybe he and the boys would go off for something to eat once they'd had a couple of beers and a chat.

Not much had been said the night before, not by Bert's brothers in any case. They had been content to sit back and listen to Jack's opinions about the strike and his plans, throwing the occasional question his way. He undid a small knot of blue paper and shook salt into his bag of potato crisps.

'What you drinking, Jack?'

'Hallo, mate, I didn't see you come in. A pint'll do me.' Jack swallowed the remains of a beer in one go.

'Laura get off all right?' The immaculately dressed Frank sat down opposite Jack and motioned to his brother, who was standing at the bar, that both he and Jack would have a pint and a chaser.

'Yeah. Though why she wants to travel all that way to spend a few hours chin-wagging, beats me.'

'Nice part of the world, Suffolk.'

'Essex,' Jack corrected.

'What's the difference? Coupl'a miles?'

'Think so, yeah.'

'Well we won't argue about that, then.'

Jack had no intention of arguing about anything, not with either of Bert's younger brothers. They had changed quite a bit since the time when Jack taught

them to make paper aeroplanes, way back in 1938
when he was nineteen and they were seven and nine.
He suddenly found himself wondering what kind of a
mood Frank was in. He felt distinctly uncomfortable
and wasn't sure why.

'How's Liz coping?' Frank asked, trying to sound
interested.

'Seems OK, Frank. Likes her job in the canteen.'

'Good.' Slipping a hand inside his jacket, he
pulled out a thick white envelope. 'Give this to 'er
for me, will yer? Say it's from me and Freddie.'

'Oh, right.' Jack tucked the envelope into his
pocket.

'That should see her right for a while.' Frank
sat back in his chair with an air of pride and satisfaction.

Setting the drinks down on the table, the second
brother nodded at Jack. 'All right, mate?'

'Yeah. Not bad.' He swallowed some of the beer
and had a strange feeling he was going to need
the chaser.

Moving along the bench so that Freddie could sit
next to him, Frank began to stroke one of his thick
black eyebrows. 'So, Jack . . . another meeting this
afternoon, eh?'

'Yep. Should be quite a turnout.'

'Mmmm.' Frank sniffed and drank some of his beer, leaving a silence.

'There are some people, Jack,' Frank said, his face expressive, 'top-notch people, that is, who are not very happy about this strike. They seem to think it's all getting a bit out of hand.'

'Nothing wrong with that, is there? Should be good publicity.'

The brothers looked at each other, showing their mutual disapproval in the nicest way possible, with a half-smile.

'It's getting a little bit embarrassing – for us, that is. A couple of Members of Parliament are a bit put out as well.'

'Oh yeah?' Jack waited to hear what was on their minds.

'Letters and parcels bound for places like Argentina, East Africa, they're stuck in sorting offices. Not to mention other exports and imports, come to that. The Dock Labour Board ain't backing yer; and I hear that other unions think it's all a bit out of order.'

'Come to the meeting this afternoon and you'll see. Hear what the men 'ave got to say.'

'Yeah, but that's not really the point, is it, Jack?' Frank said, trying to keep a friendly tone. 'You've got the warehouse keepers up in arms. They've invested a lot of money increasing exports.'

'Ah, now we're getting there,' Jack said knowingly. 'Some of them warehouse keepers are friends of yours, I take it?'

'Colleagues. And not so much mates of ours, as Management.'

'I thought you boys were freelance?' Jack smiled, trying to lighten the atmosphere.

'Everyone has to answer to someone.' Freddie downed half his glass of beer. 'Can't have too many chiefs.'

'And us red indians don't do so bad,' Frank chimed in.

Suppressing his anger, Jack leaned his head to one side and looked the thirty-year-old in the eye. 'What's this about, Frank?'

'Don't ask,' he said, slowly shaking his head and smiling. 'It's far too complicated.'

'The thing is,' Freddie the fair-haired brother added, 'we definitely don't want our Bert's name spread across the newspapers. And we don't want him used any more for other people's ends.'

'That's never been the case!' Jack snarled. 'And you fucking well know it!'

'Come on, Jack boy, don't be like that,' Freddie said, lighting a cigar.

'I'll be any way I like! And not so much of the boy. I gave you a cuff round the ear sixteen years ago

when you was a small fry. Don't think I wouldn't do it again.'

The two brothers looked at each other and raised an eyebrow, hoping to undermine Jack.

'Do you two realize how important this dispute is? Have you any idea what could happen to the docks if we sit back and let them bastards do what they want?'

'Jack, Jack, Jack.' Freddie paused and blew smoke rings towards the ceiling. 'You can't stop progress. This is the sixties, not the thirties. New roads are planned. Containerization's on the cards. Bringing stuff in and out of the country through the docks'll be history. Another decade and they'll be flying it all in and out by aircraft as big as your smaller ships. And that'll only be the start.' He drew on his cigar again. 'You're bashing your 'ead against a brick wall, mate.'

'I can't believe I'm hearing this.' Jack felt choked and angry. Downing his whisky in one go, he stood up without saying a word. As he turned to leave, Freddie grabbed his arm. 'Keep Bert's name out of it, eh?'

'I think it might be a bit late for that.'

'It's never too late, Jack boy.' His smile was full of threat. 'Not if you've got a brain, that is.'

Jack scowled and pulled his arm away. He stormed

out of the pub, full of revulsion. As he marched along the Whitechapel Road he realized that Bert's brothers had changed quite a bit in the last seven or eight years since he used to drink with them regularly. He had often wondered why they had slipped out of the local social scene. Now he knew. The mohair suits, the thick gold bracelets, the new Jaguar, it added up. They moved in the world of hardened criminals now, and he had to admit that he might regret it if Bert's brothers became his enemies.

Passing the Blind Beggar, where some of his docker friends drank, Jack felt a strong desire to go in and let off steam. He walked straight past instead, and turned left into Cambridge Heath Road on his way to Liz's small terraced house in Bethnal Green. She would give him dinner and he could get rid of the envelope in his pocket. He felt like hurling it over a wall, but guessed that it might be more than his life was worth. And besides, why shouldn't Liz have some of their ill-gotten gains?

Nodding to a passing neighbour, Jack realized he was shivering, not from the crisp April day, but with the mild shock of knowing that he could be under threat from people more powerful than Bert's two flashy younger brothers.

Turning into Columbia Road he considered the

idea of emigrating. Maybe that would satisfy Kay's wanderlust! Arriving at Liz's door, he braced himself to face that living room with the brown fireside chair empty, where Bert should have been.

''Course I was expecting you!' Liz made her way along the narrow passage, Jack closing the door behind him. 'I heard the meeting wasn't till this afternoon and what with Laura goin' off to Harlow, I guessed you'd be round for a bit of Sunday dinner.'

Sitting down by the glowing gas fire, Jack warmed his hands and felt distinctly better now that he was in familiar surroundings, with the sound of the wireless in the background and the smell of roast beef drifting through from the kitchen.

'Where's the Sunday paper?'

'On my bed! I went back with it and a cup of tea this morning. It was bliss, I tell yer. A bit of luxury I should have allowed myself before now!'

'Why didn't yer? Bert wouldn't 'ave minded.'

'I know that. I just didn't, that's all. Wouldn't 'ave dreamed of it. Had to get the worker's breakfast, didn't I?'

'Leave off, Lizzie. Had to? You loved running round 'im and you know it.'

'I'm glad to see those two little sods didn't worry you too much.' Liz sat in the other armchair and

slowly shook her head. 'Bert used to love them boys. His baby brothers. Then they grew up into what they are now.'

'I'm not with you.' Jack couldn't see how she could possibly know about their little meeting.

'Wheels travel faster than legs, Jack.'

'Are you telling me those bastards came round here?'

'As soon as you left the pub.'

Jack sipped the tea Liz had put down in front of him. 'They're way out of order. Who do they think they're dealing with, eh? Don't they think I've got contacts? One phone call is all it'd take and they'd get a bloody good 'iding.'

'I think you're gonna 'ave to drop it, you know.'

'Oh yeah?'

'Take a back seat. Let someone else take the lead. You don't know the sort of people Bert's brothers mix with now.'

'The people they'd like to mix with, you mean! They're all mouth.'

Liz put her cup and saucer on the radiogram next to her and stood up. 'I'd best turn that meat over,' she murmured. She couldn't bring herself to tell her brother just how serious the situation was, and how important the message delivered by the two men.

'So they came to see you 'oping you'd talk me round?'

'Something like that, yeah.' Liz walked back into the kitchen.

Jack remembered the white envelope in his pocket and it made him feel confused. Maybe it wasn't out of the goodness of their hearts that they were treating Liz, nor out of respect for Bert. Looking down at the envelope he could see it hadn't been sealed and, as he pushed it open with his thumb, that it was crammed full with grubby five- and ten-pound notes. He reckoned there had to be three hundred quid in total. It was becoming very clear that while the boys held an invisible gun in one hand, aimed at Jack's head, the other was offering a financial settlement.

While Liz busied herself in the kitchen throwing vegetables into boiling water, Jack stared into the fire, working out the best way to handle the situation. He could, without too much loss of face, slip into the background and let the other union leaders rule the waves, or try to. He had a perfect excuse. He could say the constant reminder of losing Bert so suddenly, and his name being thrown about the way it had been, was proving too much for his family. Or that his sister was living in fear of the press knocking on her door. Or, better still, he could say she was

scared that her innocent Bert had become the cause of a widespread national strike.

A loud ring at the door startled Jack and for a second or two he felt genuinely scared. Shaking himself, he called to Liz that he would answer it.

'It'll be our Kay!' she called out.

'Will it?' Jack felt relieved and pleased. He hadn't seen much of his daughter since the strike had started and he was missing her. What he hadn't expected was to see Kay in tears and looking angry.

Settling her on the sofa, Jack took the small glass of brandy Liz offered and swallowed it in one go.

'That was meant for Kay!' Sometimes Liz couldn't believe her brother. 'That's typical, Jack, that really is.' She could see Kay found it amusing.

'It's all right, aunt Liz. I don't need a drink. I'm probably overreacting.'

'What d'yer mean, Kay, overreacting? About what?' It pained Jack to see his girl in tears, even if they were from frustration rather than grief.

'You'll only get annoyed if I tell yer.'

Sighing, Jack pushed his hand through his thick blond hair. 'I won't get annoyed, all right?'

Kay blew her nose and took a deep breath. 'Someone just shouted abuse at me.'

Liz and Jack waited patiently while she composed

herself. 'You didn't walk out in front of a car again, did yer?' Liz asked.

'No. 'Course not. I only did that once before, aunt Liz, and I was nine!'

'You frightened the life out of everyone around yer, including the poor driver,' Liz said, remembering.

'Yeah. And everyone screamed at me for being careless.'

'Never mind all that now,' Jack put his arm around Kay's shoulder, 'who's upset yer?'

'Promise you won't ask who she was?'

'I know 'er then, do I?' Jack spoke before he thought.

'See! You're interrogating me already!'

Liz caught his eye, her expression daring Jack to lose his rag. He shrugged and said he was sorry.

'That's all right,' Kay murmured. 'Just give me a minute.'

They sat waiting for the silence to end, having no idea what was coming next. Liz looked as if she were trying to suppress a giggle, and Jack noticed. He kept his eyes firmly fixed on the floor to avoid looking at his sister, knowing how easily they could both lose control at the amusing side of this scene.

'Someone just yelled and swore at me. Said it was my family's fault that she wouldn't be roasting a joint

today but making do with vegetables and Yorkshire. She said that Mum should try living on strike pay with six mouths to feed.' Kay lowered her voice, her head bent. 'She said you was happy to see the strike go on, so long as Mum and me kept you.'

'Did she now?' Jack spoke quietly, turning his head away so that neither she nor Liz could see his shame-filled face. He felt as if the mud was being hurled from all directions. He couldn't understand it. If he was doing something underhand, that would be different – but fighting for rights? He inhaled slowly as it dawned on him that when it came down to it, all he really wanted now was a quiet, uncomplicated life.

'Sorry, Dad. I should 'ave kept it to myself.'

'No,' Jack shook his head, 'you did the right thing. Next thing we know, they'll be cursing Bert's name.'

Taking Jack and Kay by surprise, Liz's sudden cry filled the room and she trembled from head to toe. Unable to control herself, she cried out, over and over, for Bert. Jack and Kay could do nothing but watch helplessly as she sobbed and rocked to and fro, grieving for the man they loved and missed, and the situation that had developed after his death. It seemed to be affecting all their lives.

After eating Sunday lunch in a less than happy mood, Liz, Jack and Kay curled up by the gas fire, watching television, and one by one fell asleep.

There had been a debate which almost turned into an argument over which programme they would have on. The FA Cup special, Burnley versus Tottenham, was on at ten minutes past two, and ran through Liz's favourite programme on the other side, *Interpol Calling*. Liz had argued that since the football was a repeat from the day before and she knew full well that Jack wouldn't have missed it, they should switch over for *Interpol Calling*, switch back to football once that was over, and then see her favourite actor in *The Big Steal*. There wasn't much Jack could say; she had laid down the law, arguing that since it was her house she would watch what she wanted. As it happened, it was exactly what Jack wanted too. He was astute when it came to his elder sister, who had been more like a mother to him since their parents died when he was a boy.

Stretched out on the sofa, Jack's low snoring drifted through the room, and it was a miracle that the vibrations hadn't woken either Kay or Liz who were fast asleep in the worn, feather-cushion armchairs. None of them had intended to sleep for so long, and when the doorbell pierced their slumber, they were

surprised to see that it was nearly seven o'clock and the sun was going down.

Easing herself out of her armchair, Liz steadied herself before walking along the narrow passageway. She knew that at her age it was unwise to rush about after a doze.

'Just woke up, Liz?' Laura could see she had.

'Bloody blimey,' Liz said, 'you're all here now. Shut the door behind yer.'

Laura followed Liz into the sitting room and could see at a glance that they had all been sleeping. 'Looks like I'm the only one awake enough to put the kettle on,' she joked.

Dropping back into her chair, Liz nodded. 'Couldn't agree more.'

'How did the meeting go then, Jack?' Laura called from the kitchen.

'Dunno. I missed it.' He pulled out his tobacco tin and pushed the lid off with his thumb.

'You did what?' She stood in the doorway, kettle in hand.

'I got it wrong. It wasn't this morning. It was this afternoon, and I fell asleep after my dinner.'

Liz knew why Jack hadn't gone to the meeting, but Kay looked puzzled. Her dad was lying and she knew it. He hadn't fallen asleep when he said he had.

'How's Fran settling down in Harlow, then?'

'She's OK, Jack. D'yer mind if I make myself a cold meat sandwich, Liz? I'm starving.'

''Course not. Help yourself. Do you want one, Kay?'

'No thanks, aunt Liz. Wouldn't mind another piece of that apple pie, though, with cream.'

'Well go and help yourself then. Don't leave it all to your mother.'

Once Kay was safely out of earshot, Liz leaned forward and spoke to Jack in a low voice. 'Why don't you sit down quietly tonight and tell Laura about Frank and Freddie? You won't be able to hide the fact that you're pulling out of the fight.'

'I'm not gonna pull out, Lizzie. I'll step down as spokesman, that's all.' He stood up and stretched. 'That sleep's done me good. I've got a clear head about it now.' He pulled his braces up over his shoulders. 'Anyway, I've said all I've got to say. Won't be a bad thing to let someone else have a go. Be all right if I 'ave a wash and shave?'

Liz looked up at her brother and shrugged. 'I suppose so,' she said thoughtfully. 'You'll 'ave to use Bert's razor.'

''Course I will. What's wrong with that?'

'I dunno.' Her face suddenly lit up. 'He might 'ave something to say about it though, if he can see down here.'

Jack looked up, cocked his head to one side and raised his voice. 'You don't care if I use your razor, do you, Bert?'

'Turn it in, Jack.' Liz tried not to laugh.

'Shhh . . . he's trying to tell me something.' Jack pretended to be listening. 'You know I wouldn't do a thing like that!' he said to the ceiling. 'Anyway, I don't like Imperial Leather, you know that!'

'You're bloody mad, Jack,' said Liz, wiping a tear from her eye.

Jack leaned forward and put his face close to Liz's. 'Yeah. And don't you forget it.'

'What's that supposed to mean?'

'It means, Lizzie, anyone who talks to the ceiling, or a chair, or the air, might be on course for losing some of their marbles.'

'You'll find some mustard made up in a little white eggcup, Laura! It's on the shelf above the green cupboard!' Liz called out, changing the subject and keeping her flushed face away from Jack.

'The next time that bubbly widower invites you to a seance, tell him to pick up the blower and talk to me. I'll give him a message or two!'

'I only went the once, Jack. Gawd knows how you got to know about it.'

Jack tapped the side of his nose. 'The East End's not all that big a place.' He gave her a wink.

'If he wants to date you, there's nothing wrong with that. But tell him you'd rather go to the pictures.'

'Leave off, Jack. Dates at my age?'

'You can bet on it. There's a lot of lonely men out there, Liz. Just make sure you don't pick the wrong one.'

'Honestly, Jack! Bert's not been gone five minutes—'

'I'm not talking about a bit of the other. I'm talking about companionship.'

'Oh right,' she said, embarrassed, 'I'll remember that when a bloke struggles to undo my Cross-Your-Heart brassiere.'

Jack left the room, laughing to himself. 'All right if I put one of Bert's shirts on?'

'Yeah, go on then.' Liz knew exactly what Jack was up to. He was bringing the memory of her Bert out into the open, and it made her feel good.

Walking arm in arm with Laura along Cambridge Heath Road, Jack was suddenly aware that Kay had dropped behind. Turning his head to call her, he realized that the last thing his teenage daughter wanted was to be seen out with her mum and dad. 'You all right, Kay?' he called, more out of habit than concern.

'Yeah. I'm gonna cut through Barmy park.'

'You'll 'ave to be quick then. The park keeper'll be locking them gates soon!'

With the experience of a townie, Kay zigzagged expertly between the traffic and disappeared into the wide gateway next to Bethnal Green tube station.

'Jack . . . there's something I want to tell you,' Laura pulled her arm away from his and pushed both hands into the pockets of her jacket.

'Fire away.'

'I didn't go to Harlow today.' She held her breath, ready to deliver the next crashing blow.

'I know that.' He sounded very matter-of-fact.

Laura stopped dead in her tracks and threw her shoulders back with an air of indignation. 'You what?'

He slipped his arm around her waist and walked her along the pavement, smiling into her mystified eyes.

'You found Patsy's letter, right?'

'Liz!' Laura couldn't believe her sister-in-law would go behind her back.

'Oh, charming. Liz knows about it as well. Why not tell the whole bloody world!'

'Well, if it wasn't Liz?'

'Oh, Laura! One day it was in my jacket pocket, the next day it was gone, then it was back again.'

'I don't know what to say.' Laura allowed him to

walk her under the railway arch instead of turning left for home.

'Wait till we get to the Carpenter's. I'll buy you a rum and black and we can talk about it.' He squeezed her arm. 'That sound all right?'

'I don't know. Do what you want. Let's not change the habit of a lifetime.' They walked on in silence, each wondering what the outcome of the evening would be.

Pushing open the door of the pub, Jack showed a hand to a few dockers who were drinking at the bar. He quickly looked round for a quiet table and pointed at one in the corner. Laura settled herself down while he had a word with his friends and ordered a round.

'Bit out of order, wasn't it, Jack? You not turning up this afternoon?' The man was a large docker and not someone to fall out with.

'Sometimes, Jim, problems at home are more important than anything.' He looked him straight in the eye and hoped for the best. 'We've just come from Liz's as well. Poor mare. Wouldn't stop crying over Bert.'

The man squeezed Jack's shoulder. 'Give Jack a whisky, will you, Dave.' The barman stopped what he was doing and pushed a glass under the optic.

Downing the whisky in one go, Jack shuddered.

'That's better,' he said, and forced a sigh. 'I think I'm gonna 'ave to take a back seat for a while.'

'Understandable, mate, understandable. We'll pass the word. Just show your face now and then though, eh? The men 'ave got a lot of respect for you, Jack.'

Feeling lighter, Jack paid for his round and carried the drinks to the table in the corner and sat down.

'I take it you saw Patsy?' Jack drew a deep breath and pulled his tobacco tin out of his pocket.

'And the little boy.'

'I'm sorry, Laura. It was the last thing I wanted, you seeing that letter.' He sighed. 'You had to find out sometime, I s'pose.'

'It's my own fault. I knew when she was pregnant. I should have worked it out for myself. But I wish you'd told me you were writing to her, Jack.' She sipped her rum and blackcurrant. 'I feel as if we've been living a lie.'

'Don't be daft, 'course we haven't. And look how you reacted once you did know! You was on the next train up there.'

'She's more attractive than I thought she'd be.' Laura felt the jealousy rise again. 'I'm surprised you're not living with her instead of me.' She tried to keep the anger out of her voice.

'Well that proves something, surely?'

'Does it?'

'Yes, it does. It proves I love you and not her.' He drank some of his beer and wiped the froth away from his mouth with the back of his hand. 'Always have done.'

'He looks so much like you and Kay . . .'

'Yeah?' Jack sounded pleased. 'I've only been the once. Just after he was born. Since then I've sent 'er a letter each month with a bit of cash in it for the rent.'

'Don't you think we should have done a bit more than that?' Laura could hardly believe she was saying it. 'He is Kay's brother, after all.'

'She didn't want any more than that. Only the rent. I wanted to see him, but . . .'

Laura pulled a packet of cigarettes out of her handbag. 'That's not the impression I got. I think she'd like some money for clothing. Not that Jac looked hard done by. I saw a pile of his things on the sideboard. I expect her parents and her boyfriend help out.'

'So.' Jack had had enough of this. 'Where does that leave us? Am I gonna be sent to Coventry or what?' He looked at her sheepishly.

'No. But you might find yourself on a train to Leicester if you're not careful.'

'Gimme a break, Laura.' Jack avoided her eyes

for fear he might see something he didn't care to. 'D'you want another drink, or what?'

'You should have told me you were writing to her, Jack. It opened up a very sore wound when I found that letter.'

'OK. I was in the wrong! I should 'ave told yer. What d'you want me to do, beg forgiveness?'

'I'll think of something.' Part of her wanted to say it was all right, but in her heart she knew she would be lying. 'Let it lie for now.'

Chapter Four

Standing behind the counter of Maynard's tobacconist's, Kay felt very nervous as she watched Gladys turn the *Open* sign around and unlock the front door. She was beginning to regret taking on the work and wondered if she would be able to cope. Arithmetic had never been her strongest subject at school, and she dreaded the thought of giving someone the wrong change.

'You'll be all right, luv,' Gladys winked at her. 'They won't bite your head off. Just watch me at first, you'll soon get the hang of it.'

Forcing a smile, Kay tried to ignore her rumbling stomach. 'My hands are sweating.'

Smiling, Gladys brushed her grey curls back off her face and peered into a small square mirror. 'That's why I took you on. I prefer to have sensitive people around me instead of some of the flashy women we've had in here from time to time.' She

squeezed Kay's arm. 'Why don't you put the kettle on? Only three sugars for me. I'm slimming.'

'Everyone seems to be on a diet in our firm,' Kay said, spooning sugar into both their mugs. 'They all wanna look like Jean Shrimpton.'

'You mean they all want to look like you! Seventeen . . . I wish I was your age again. Best time of your life. Or should be.' She looked sideways at Kay. 'Pity you 'ave to spend so much of your life working. Should be out there having fun. Money's not everything, you know.'

'It is when you need it. I'm saving to go abroad.'

'Ah . . . that's different. Money for fun – I'm all for that.'

'And my dad's on strike, otherwise my mum would have been able to help pay for the holiday.'

'Your *mum* would?'

'Dad doesn't want me to go.'

Gladys raised a hand, 'Say no more.'

Snapping two fingers off her Kit-Kat, she narrowed her eyes. 'What you wanna remember is this: don't go getting yourself locked into a courtship before you've turned twenty.' She dipped the chocolate biscuit into her coffee. 'I've seen more girls 'aving to get married before they've got the key to the front door than I've had baked beans. And I was one of the silly cows as well! It's the

eyes. They get you with their eyes. My Tom did. One look from him and the bit between my legs was throbbing.'

Kay liked her new boss, they got on like a house on fire, but as soon as it was time to get down to business, Gladys's personality changed. She was very efficient, and made it clear that she took pride in the shop; how it looked, how good the takings were and how long she had been manageress. Eight years sounded like a lifetime to Kay, but it made her feel comfortable knowing that Gladys knew exactly how to handle the awkward customers.

'You're a bit on the naïve side, Kay,' she said as they locked up at closing time, 'but there's no better way to learn about the human race than when they're parting with their money. They'll catch you if they can. You're gonna 'ave to learn how to read people's faces.'

When Kay walked into the kitchen later that evening, Laura and Jack were sitting waiting to see how she had got on. 'I've kept your dinner on steam. I don't think it will have spoiled,' Laura fussed around her.

'I don't care if it is. I'm starving!' Kay dropped on to a kitchen chair and smiled into Jack's grinning face. 'It was good, Dad! I liked it. And the extra cash'll come in handy.'

'For what?'

'New clothes, that sort of thing.' She hated lying to her dad but it was necessary.

'We're not on poor street, you know.'

'I know that. It's just that, you know, I wanna be independent.'

'Just like your mother, eh?'

Placing the hot plate in front of Kay, Laura tossed her hair back, proud. 'Nothing wrong with that.'

'True. So long as I don't end up being a spare part around here.'

They couldn't help smiling at the way he always put on the hangdog expression when he wanted a bit of attention and sympathy. Leaving the kitchen, he called back over his shoulder, 'Wouldn't mind a cup of tea by the telly!'

'Thanks for not telling Dad about my going to Spain, Mum.' Kay pushed a forkful of meat pudding into her mouth.

Laura looked at Kay, her eyes wide. 'God help me when you've gone and I do have to tell him. He'll hit the roof.'

There was a ring on the doorbell. 'That'll be Pamela,' Kay smiled, 'I knew she'd 'ave to come round to see how I got on. Anyone'd think this was my first job. Open the door for 'er, Mum.'

'What did your last slave die of?'

Kay laid down her cutlery. 'Sorry, I didn't mean to—'

'I'm only kidding. Don't be so sensitive!'

'Hallo!' Pamela's singsong voice reverberated along the passage and into the kitchen. 'Where is she?'

Looking up at her friend's sparkling face, Kay knew by her expression that she had something she couldn't wait to tell her.

'That looks nice.' She studied Kay's dinner.

'There's some left,' Laura said, following Pamela in. 'Have you eaten?'

'No, I'm on a diet.'

'You *are* joking?' Laura eyed the skinny form in front of her.

'I'm not. The girls at work say I've got enormous thighs. How can I wear a bikini with enormous thighs?'

'Keep your voice down!' Kay snapped. 'Dad's in the front room.'

'Sorry,' she mouthed. Turning to Laura, Pamela pulled her short skirt up above her knickers. 'See,' she said, looking as if she were about to cry. 'Look how thick they are.'

'But look how skinny the rest of your body is, love! You won't necessarily change your legs by

not eating. That's your natural shape. Family genes coming through.'

'You mean I'm always gonna have tree-trunks for legs?'

'That's right,' Kay said, 'just keep 'em covered up while you're out with me.'

Laura watched, bemused, as Pamela dropped on to a chair and wept.

'Take no notice, she's always doing that. It's not real crying. She only does it to get attention.'

'I do not!' Pamela sat up straight and the waterfall ceased instantly. 'I'll have some of that meat, Mrs Armstrong, but no pudding, thank you. I never eat stodge.'

'Help yourself.' Laura left them to it and joined Jack in the front room.

'You insult people all the time, Pamela.'

'Now what 'ave I said?'

Kay nodded towards the steak and kidney pudding in the steamer. '*I never eat stodge,*' she mimicked.

Pamela looked puzzled. 'What's insulting about that?'

'Just help yourself to what you want and shut up,' Kay grumbled, 'it's been a long day.'

Peering into the saucepan, Pamela turned up her nose. 'I don't think I'll bother. Can I make myself some toast instead?'

'Did you bring the holiday brochure?' Kay spoke quietly, coming straight to the point.

'Er . . . no.' There was a touch of worry in her voice.

'Why not?'

'Because there isn't one. Not for where we're going. Well there is, there's lots actually, but not for us.'

Kay narrowed her eyes and drew breath. 'What's that supposed to mean?'

'Well . . . the man who's arranging all this knows the hotel owner in the resort where we're going, on the Costa Brava and—'

'Which resort? You said you'd find out which one today!'

'I forgot. Anyway,' she grinned broadly, 'I've paid our deposits so we're definitely booked in. And we won't have to share a room with anyone else but each other. I saw a photograph of the hotel. It's very nice.'

'Where do we fly from?' Kay was losing her patience.

'We don't.' Pamela popped two slices of bread under the grill. 'How d'yer turn this thing on?'

'You're not telling me we go by boat and coach?'

'Oh no! Train, boat, then an overnight sleeper train, then a coach, then another train and then a

117

Spanish bus. That way we'll get to see more of France and Spain. And it keeps the price down.'

'You mean it's not gonna cost forty pounds, then?'

'Oh yeah. But the man who's arranging it said that was very cheap.'

'Only by three pounds! I checked in the other brochures. And that's flying!'

'Is it?'

Sighing, Kay pushed her plate away. 'I take it you *have* found out the date we go?'

'Yeah. In two weeks' time.'

'You said it would be four or five weeks, at least!'

Pamela looked thoughtful. 'Did I?'

Closing her eyes, Kay imagined herself strangling her best friend. 'It's all right for you,' she grumbled, 'you've already saved up for it.'

'No I haven't. I'm skint.'

Eyeing her carefully, Kay waited for a grin to appear on Pamela's face. She hoped it was a joke.

'I'm gonna have to borrow it.'

Pushing one hand through her hair, exasperated, Kay began to regret they had ever made plans to go away together.

'Who from?' she asked, not thinking for one second that she would get a sensible answer.

118

'My mum and dad of course.'

'How do you know they'll lend it to you?'

'Because they said they would.' Pamela eased the lid off the biscuit tin and helped herself to a chocolate finger. 'They'll lend you some as well if you want. They're loaded.'

'No.' Kay clenched her teeth. 'I'll manage,' she said, suddenly feeling low. There she was, working all hours to get the cash together, and Pamela could get it from her parents simply by asking. It didn't seem fair.

Kay scraped the remains of her dinner into the waste bin and washed her plate. 'I think I'll have a bath and an early night.'

'Right-ho. I only came to tell you that I've booked.' She helped herself to another biscuit. 'You could say thank you,' Pamela said, a hurt look on her face.

'Yeah. Thanks a bundle. You're a really good organizer.'

'At least I'm good at something, then,' she said, pleased with herself, taking Kay's sarcasm for real. 'I'll see if I can get the man who's arranging all this to let me borrow the photograph for you. The other girls think it's great.'

'Is it an all-girl party then?' Disillusionment was setting in with every passing second.

'Oh no. Four blokes, I think. And if they're all like the two I saw today,' she grimaced, 'they're about as exciting as boiled sausages.'

On the Friday morning before departure day, Laura smiled into Kay's worried face. 'You don't look very excited.'

'Scared more like. At what Dad'll say.'

'He won't find out.' Laura smiled. 'We've done a good job on him. He really believes you're off to the Isle of Sheppey to stay in aunt Liz's caravan. What the eye doesn't see.' Laura winked at Kay. 'We'll tell him once you're back. Won't have any choice then, will he? You'll be as brown as a berry.'

'Hope so.' Kay looked at the kitchen clock and quickly swallowed the remains of her tea. 'Thanks for the fiver. I'll bring you back a souvenir.'

'Don't be silly. You spend it on yourself. That's why I gave it to you. And if you run out—'

'I know, I know. Borrow it off of Moneybags.' She made for the door. 'Stop worrying, I'll have plenty. See you tonight.'

Arriving five minutes early at the bus stop, Kay let her mind wander, thinking of the next day. She tried to imagine herself lying on a long stretch of golden sand and swimming in a clear turquoise sea. She made a mental list of the few incidentals she would

have to buy during her lunch-break. Her aunt Liz had been round the day before and slipped five pounds in an envelope between her eiderdown and pillow. *A little treat* was scribbled on it in green biro.

When the bus arrived, Kay climbed aboard and looked for her West Indian friend.

'Over here, darlin'!' Juanita called out, her beautiful smile sending a surge of excitement through Kay. Sitting down next to her, Kay squeezed the woman's arm. 'I can't believe it's come round at last.'

'Have you told your father yet?'

'No.'

Juanita sucked her teeth and slowly shook her head. 'You're one hell of a brave girl, or somethin'.'

'What do you want me to bring you back?' Kay said, wanting to change the subject.

Juanita thought about it. 'A nice big Spanish señor!' She roared with laughter and her warm, sweet-smelling body shook.

Taking her arm, Kay moved closer and rested her head on Juanita's solid shoulder. 'I'm really looking forward to it, Juanita,' she sighed.

'I know, I know.' Juanita turned away and stared out of the window. 'Just be careful, eh? I want to see you back on this bus as happy as you are now.'

'I will be. The only difference'll be that I'll be blacker than you are.'

'You think so?' she tried not to laugh. 'With that skin?'

'Two weeks of non-stop sunshine.'

'And you'll look like a lobster.'

'I'm not stupid, you know. I have bought some protection cream. I'll wear that for the first few days, then I'll put oil on.'

Juanita looked at Kay with half-closed eyes. 'Oil?'

'Why not?'

'Listen. You don't put oil on, y'hear?' She raised her voice as if she were scolding a child. 'You put oil on that paper-thin white skin and you'll be covered in blisters!'

'All right, all right!' Kay felt her cheeks flush with embarrassment as other people on the bus looked at the two of them shouting at each other. 'No oil – OK?' Kay pulled away and folded her arms defiantly. 'Not until the end of the second week.'

'I don't know! As if I haven't got enough with three grown-up children to worry about, I have to get lumbered wit' you.'

'Perhaps I can meet these grown-up sons of yours when I get back, when I'm brown, when I won't stand out like a sore thumb.'

'Maybe. We'll see. You could do with some spice in your bones, that's for sure.'

For the rest of the short journey into the city, both Kay and Juanita were wrapped in their own thoughts as the bus crawled along through the rush-hour traffic.

'Show me the palm of your hand,' Juanita broke in.

Kay did as she was asked, making sure the bus conductor had seen that she wanted to get off at the next stop. With her eyes on him and her palm spread, Kay waited for Juanita to tell her fortune, assuming that was her intention. Instead of words of wisdom, Kay felt two coins being pressed into her palm, the size of half-crowns.

'I can't take that.'

'Why not? My money not good enough?' Juanita's big brown eyes widened.

Kay bent down and kissed her on the cheek. 'Thanks. I'll send you a postcard!' she said, as she ran along the aisle towards the exit.

'You don't have my address!'

'I'll send it to the bus!' Kay yelled and then jumped down on to the kerb. Waving through the window, she felt a lump in her own throat as she saw tears rolling down Juanita's brown cheeks. 'I'll be all right!' Kay called out, as the bus pulled away.

Using every bit of concentration she made a mental note of the bus's number-plate, and as she

crossed the road and walked along St John's Street, she repeated it over and over again.

'Six minutes early again?' Alf dragged the gates shut and pressed the button to ascend. 'You're getting a bit keen, ain't yer?' he accused.

Kay wouldn't answer him; she was still repeating the bus number-plate and didn't want to lose it.

'And no nipping into that boardroom! I've seen yer! Sneaking in like a cat burglar!' he called after her.

'Don't waste your breath on her, Alf,' the stocky canteen manageress called out. 'Lazy little cow's not worth it. None of 'em are. You should see them in the Ladies' at tea-break. Only supposed to take ten minutes. Ha! Fifteen, more like. Fill the place up with smoke and giggling and all.'

Alf crashed the gates closed. 'They should go in the army, the lot of 'em; boys and girls alike.'

Grabbing her notepad from her desktop, Kay jotted down the number-plate. When the door suddenly flew open and Mr Grieves marched in whistling a little tune Kay stiffened, knowing he would be embarrassed when he realized he had an audience, and a junior at that. She had never heard him whistling before.

'Morning Mr Grieves!' she said boldly, letting

him know she was there before he did anything else out of character.

'Eh? Oh, it's you, Kay. Yes, well, it's good to see you in early for a change.' He peered suspiciously at her. 'You're looking a bit flushed.' He instinctively looked around the office as if someone else might be there. Someone who shouldn't be.

'I arrive at the stop in good time every morning to catch my bus,' Kay was beginning to get annoyed, 'and I always catch it. If the traffic's bad, I'm a couple of minutes late; if it's good, I'm early.'

'Fetch me the P.R. Marshall file, would you please, Kay. We may as well make an early start.'

'I haven't taken my coat off yet.'

Mr Grieves looked at her over the top of his bifocals. 'So I see.'

Pulling her coat off, Kay threw it on to her typist's chair, dragged the file he wanted from a small grey cabinet and put it down on his desk.

'I'll take my coat to the cloakroom now, if that's all right.'

Mr Grieves said nothing. He gave her a look instead, which spoke for itself. She had better watch her manners.

Slipping her coat on to a hanger in the ladies' powder room, Kay turned to the other girls who

were busy studying their faces in the large wall mirrors, and applying make-up.

'What you looking so chuffed about?' said June from the switchboard, slipping a gold-cased lipstick into a white make-up bag.

'If you don't know now, you never will.' Kay grinned back at June's reflection.

'Oh, of course! It's tomorrow you're going away.'

'All right for some,' one of the girls from the typing pool said coldly. 'Must be nice to be an only child. Having your parents pay for you to go abroad.'

'That's where you're wrong!' Kay rejoined. 'It's coming out of my own purse, actually!'

'Yeah?' The girl flicked more mascara on to her upper lashes. 'Your purse must be like the magic porridge-pot then, the salary this tight-fisted firm pays.'

June threw Kay a look, warning her not to say too much. Kay was quick to pick up on it. 'I've been saving up for a year,' she said quietly. Wanting to end it before she was asked any more questions, Kay left the cloakroom without combing her hair.

'We've got a lot to get through today, Kay.' Mr Grieves spoke to her through the frosted glass partition that separated Kay's desk from his.

'You'll need to tie things up so that Doreen knows where everything is while you're away.'

Kay looked across at Doreen and they simultaneously rolled their eyes. Doreen was Kay's senior and had taught her everything she knew, efficiency being top of the list. Between them they had everything tied up, and each knew that Doreen could handle the responsibility for two weeks without too much difficulty.

'I want you to finish my letters before you start sorting the pay packets.' Mr Grieves sounded as if he begrudged her going away. In truth, he was probably feeling a bit peeved because he had never been abroad himself, and was Kay's senior by twenty years. He was in a rut.

'I'll start typing the registered envelopes as soon as you're ready.' She spoke quietly and with respect. Despite his sometimes austere manner, she knew he was an old softie at heart. It was the same every Friday fortnight on pay-day. The busiest day for the chief accounts clerk.

'I can always stop when you're ready to dictate,' she added, trying to ease the feeling of tension in the office.

'Good girl.' He went back to his figure work.

Pulling her typewriter forward, Kay caught Doreen's eye again and a smile passed between them. Doreen

often teased Kay that when she turned on the charm, Mr Grieves was like putty in her hands.

'Now then . . .' Kay started to talk to herself, a habit which could be irritating to others. Mr Grieves, James the junior and Doreen often complained about her mumbling.

'Where did I put the registered envelope list?' She pulled at each of the four drawers in her desk, and still couldn't find it. She tried them all again. No luck.

'Kay!' Grieves sighed loudly. 'If you open another drawer . . .' His voice was tinged with threat. 'I'm trying to concentrate!'

Kay apologized, and made an effort to make less noise. Searching through some papers in a wire tray on her desk, she finally found the list she needed.

'Seems I'm not the only one who chose this month to go away.' She was talking to herself again. 'One, two, three, four, five,' she quickly counted aloud, 'six, seven—'

'Shhh!' Grieves made his feelings known for the second time. Reprimanding herself, Kay settled down to work and tried not to be distracted. She was excited, and as much as she tried to act as if it were a normal busy pay-day, she couldn't stop the surge of excitement that swept over her from time to time.

Doing her utmost to concentrate on her work

and not think about the packed suitcase in her bedroom, Kay began to type addresses on the registered envelopes which were to be posted to members of staff who were away that week, either on holiday or off sick.

There were over six hundred people on the staff and it was Kay's responsibility to separate and put into bundles the departmental salaries, ready for collection.

Later that day, just as she was about to slip a pay packet into a registered envelope, the bell went for tea-break. Pushing her typewriter back, Kay had no idea that an empty registered envelope addressed to Mr Woods had also been forced to the back of her desk and had fallen behind it, hidden from view.

By late afternoon, several staff from various departments had been in to collect the salaries, and the filled registered envelopes had already gone to the post room.

'Afternoon.' The soft voice of Stephen Drake drifted into Kay's thoughts as she sat staring at nothing.

'Oh, sorry,' Kay said, 'I was miles away.' She looked up into the drawn face of the eighteen-year-old and grinned. 'Hope you haven't been standing there too long?'

'No, I've just arrived.'

Kay took the bundle of salaries from the tray, put them to one side and began to write in the receipt book. *Salaries – 8 M*, before realizing her mistake. 'You're not from the Mail Sales department, are you?'

'No. Bought Ledger,' said Drake quietly.

'I'm going mad.' She smiled, crossed out the M and wrote *Bought Ledger* instead.

The young man signed, flicked through the salaries, counting them under his breath, then turned to leave. As he reached the door he asked Kay what he should do about the head of department's salary, Mr Woods, who was away on holiday.

'Oh, his will be sent on by registered post,' she smiled, thinking that Woods wasn't the only one to be escaping Thompson's for a while.

'You're sure about that?' Drake asked.

'Oh yeah,' Kay wondered why he was blushing. She showed him the list on her desk and pointed out Mr Woods's name.

'Ah, right. Thanks.' A little awkward, the young man left the office. Something didn't feel right, but Kay couldn't decide what it was.

Once outside, Stephen Drake leaned by the door, looked through the salaries again, pulled out the one marked for Mr Woods and slipped it into his inside pocket.

As he walked along the corridor a broad grin swept across his red face. The stupid little tart had made a mistake and made his day. It was a fat pay packet, and Mr Woods being the head of department probably earned more in a week than he did in a month. And since he was on holiday leave, it meant that instead of a fortnight's salary in that packet, there would be four weeks' worth of cash.

It was true he had signed for eight salaries and would only be handing in seven, but the dizzy blonde had messed up the receipt book in any case, making another mistake over the name of his department. He was home and dry, and didn't give a toss as to how she would explain the missing salary. After all she was common as muck, from the worst part of London – probably came from a family of thieves. Whereas he, Stephen Drake, was the son of a Detective Superintendent at the Met.

Feeling pleased with himself, he pushed his finger on the lift bell for a few seconds longer than necessary.

'You're young enough to walk down!' Alf was far from pleased at being called up to the third floor by a junior.

'Sorry, I wasn't thinking.' Drake had taken on his innocent, shy look again, but there was no fooling Alf. He had seen dozens of people come and go at

Thompson's and prided himself on his perception of character.

Slamming the gates shut, Alf stared into Drake's face. 'Someone filed a complaint against me five weeks ago, he said I was a bit on the slow side. Said he had to wait five minutes for the lift.'

Drake shook his head. 'Some people have no respect for their elders. Whoever it was should have had a good dressing-down.'

Throwing the gates back on the ground floor, Alf felt a pang of concern. This young man was very smart, both in dress and thinking. The type to go far. The sort who could easily rise to a managerial position.

'I can assure you it wasn't me.' Drake looked straight into Alf's face, daring him to answer back.

'No. I just thought I would mention it, in case you knew.'

'If I hear anything.' Drake gave the worried lift man a friendly punch on the upper arm and walked with his head high out of the building to the annexe, where he worked as a junior office clerk.

Alf inhaled slowly, pursed his lips and wondered why that young man made him feel uncomfortable.

He wasn't the only one. There was no way Kay could have known that Drake was going to be the cause of a nightmare she would have to face after her holiday, but somehow she felt uneasy about him and couldn't think why. Looking up at the clock on the wall above Doreen's desk, she was relieved to see it was ten minutes past five.

After a hectic day, the office now had a calm air about it. 'You, er, you can knock off now, Kay.' Mr Grieves looked over the glass partition. 'I expect you've some packing to do?'

'I've been packed for a week,' she grinned.

'And don't get oil on my bikini!' Doreen placed the cover on her adding machine. 'Or my sundress!'

'Oil? You'll burn to a cinder.' Grieves pulled on his trilby. 'Now then.' He moved closer to Doreen and whispered something in her ear, causing her to turn around and smile at Kay. They both stood there, smiling at her.

'This is for you, love.' Doreen held out a white envelope. 'It's from me, the girls on the switchboard, and Mr Grieves.'

Moving slowly forward, Kay felt tears welling up in her eyes. They were giving her a card, wishing her *bon voyage*. Tearing it open, she kept her eyes down,

determined not to cry like a baby but to accept the gesture like an adult.

As she drew the card out and opened it her eyes nearly popped out of her head. Three crisp new ten-shilling notes were inside. Swallowing the lump in her throat, she pressed her lips together and nodded.

'It couldn't have been easy, love. What with your dad on strike.'

'Everyone's being so kind . . .'

'Compassion is only shown to those who deserve it, Kay.' Mr Grieves tipped his trilby and wished her a safe journey and Doreen a good weekend, and as the door swung shut behind him, Kay felt a certain sympathy for him.

'He's not a such bad bloke, is he?' she said.

'Not when you get to know him.' Doreen tied her silk Paisley scarf under her chin.

Standing by the door, Kay looked back at her tidy desk and felt a nagging worry, as if she had forgotten to do something important.

Turning the lights off, Doreen placed a hand on Kay's shoulder. 'It'll be there when you come back,' she smiled.

Tired at the end of a busy day, they left the silent office, the empty registered envelope addressed to Mr Woods still wedged between the back of Kay's desk and the partition.

On her return from Spain, she would have to face the consequences of that small accident, which would thrust her into the adult world more quickly than she could anticipate.

Chapter Five

Standing in the tiny sleeping compartment of the French train, heading for the Spanish border, Kay stared bleakly at the small top bunk. 'I can't sleep up there, Pamela, I just can't. I'll be sick again, I know I will.'

'No you won't. You've had your travel pills.' Pamela was beginning to lose her patience.

'They didn't work on the boat, did they!'

'Only because you didn't take them early enough. Now climb up there and try the bed out.'

'Call that a bed? If I'd 'ave known we'd be travelling for this long, I would never have come.'

'Stop moaning.'

'What if I need to be sick again?' She turned to one of the other women who was sharing the sleeping compartment with them. They had been doing their best to ignore her.

'Please let me sleep below.'

'I'm very sorry, but no!' One of the women cut in. 'I said all along that I wanted to be below. And we were here first!' She looked fiercely back at Kay. 'And please take something up there with you to be sick in. Should the occasion arise.'

'And if you are sick,' the woman's companion added, 'make sure you take the vessel away and wash it.'

'If you stop thinking about it, it probably won't happen,' her friend chimed in.

Kay gazed at the women and wished she had the energy to tell them what she thought, but she felt like death. And the prospect of sleeping on the train didn't help, with hours to go and still suffering from the after-effects of the rough crossing from Dover. She looked up at the bunk again and thought about her bedroom at home, where all would be so very still and quiet. Then she thought about her mum and dad, and two weeks suddenly seemed like a lifetime.

'Now, if you don't mind, my friend and I would like to eat our sandwiches without a running commentary on your stomach!' The women sat on the edge of their bunks and peeled greaseproof paper from their sandwiches. The smell of hard-boiled eggs filled the compartment.

After another visit to the lavatory, Kay opened a window and sucked in fresh air which tasted

wonderful. Feeling slightly better, she turned to Pamela. 'I'll be all right soon. Those bloody bitches don't help much.'

Pamela poured some lemonade into a paper cup. 'Here, get this down you.'

'When this train stops, I'm getting off.' Kay drank the lemonade down in one go.

'We'll all be getting off.'

'And I'm turning round and going back.' She let out a long, loud belch, and didn't care who heard her.

'Good. Can I borrow some of your clothes then?' Pamela knew how to handle Kay. They had, after all, been friends since nursery school.

'What 'appens after this train, anyway?'

'A nice long coach trip over the Pyrenees mountains which rise to . . .' Pamela closed her eyes, remembering what she had been told that day, 'over eleven thousand feet. That's high.'

'I hope you enjoy the view.'

''Course I will. We both will. No choice really. The roads are very narrow and winding.'

'At least you read up on it. I suppose that's something.'

'No I never. This woman at work told me all about it. She went last year. Never again, though.'

Kay stared into Pamela's face. 'Why not?'

'I don't know. I didn't ask. She just said never again.'

The biggest mistake of their arduous journey to Spain was that Kay allowed Pamela to talk her into sitting on the back seat of the coach. She said she would be better off away from the engine. Kay could see the sense in that, until she learned where the engine actually was. Then it was too late to change seats.

The Spanish coach driver was obviously used to the route across the mountains. It seemed as though he knew every hairpin bend. When the rear end of the coach tipped over the edge of a road, the madman would roar with laughter at the screams coming from Kay and Pamela. The higher the coach climbed, the faster the driver seemed to go. Kay wanted to be like the others and enjoy the view, but she couldn't bring herself to take her hands away from her eyes.

'You know what's worse than this?' Pamela murmured. 'We've got to go through it all again on the way back.'

When the nightmare ride finally came to an end and the mountains were behind them, Kay and Pamela fell asleep on each other's shoulders and didn't wake until the coach pulled up outside Hotel Ruiz, in the tiny resort of Costa Lana, four hours later.

Half asleep and exhausted, the girls struggled with their suitcases, following a porter who led them and a few others out of the small hotel and up a side-street. Neither of them could be bothered to ask where they were going. All they wanted were their beds. It was ten o'clock at night.

They were guided through the living room of a Spanish family, up a narrow staircase and into a small but clean twin-bedded room. Once the young Spanish porter left them, Kay dropped on to her bed and stayed there. She was almost asleep when she felt Pamela pulling at her arm.

'Kay, I'm starving. Let's go and get something to eat.'

Forcing her eyelids open Kay slowly shook her head. 'I'm too tired.'

'No you're not. It's all in the mind. Come on, we're in Spain now. It's early. People don't go out until now.' She poured the remains of the lemonade into a glass she found in the bathroom.

'Drink this and you'll feel better.'

Kay did as she was told but didn't feel better. The lemonade was warm. 'Can I go back to sleep now?'

'No. We're going out to explore the nightclubs.'

'You go. You're bound to see some of the people we travelled with. Talk to them.'

Leaning back on fat pillows, Pamela sipped her

lemonade. 'Did you clock that dishy bloke in Reception? He was gorgeous.'

'Go and talk to him, then.'

'He touched my hand deliberately when he handed me our key.'

Pulling herself up into a sitting position, Kay stared at her feet. 'I need a bath,' she yawned.

'No. A shower.'

'A nice long soak—' Kay stopped in her tracks. 'Why did you say no?'

'It's a lovely shower.'

'There isn't a bath, is there?'

'Spanish people must take showers,' she shrugged. 'I s'pose it's because there's a water shortage out here,' Pamela commented thoughtfully. 'Daft really, 'cos there's a lot of sea. What you wearing then?'

Kay peered at her through half-open eyes. 'What?'

'Tonight. When we go out to the nightclub. What you wearing?'

'You mean it. You really expect me to go dancing after all that travelling?'

'After your shower.' She grinned again. 'I'll unpack while you're in there. I'll hang everything up properly, in the ward—' she gazed around the room until her eyes settled on a painted cupboard. 'In the cupboard. You can have the best hangers.'

Kay felt a pang of guilt. Poor Pamela was trying

so hard, and all she had done was complain. 'Share the hangers out fair and square. But you don't have to unpack for me.'

'I want to.'

'You want to see what I've brought with me, you mean?'

''Course. I might wanna borrow something.'

Kay let herself be persuaded into the shower, and with warm water cascading down, she gently rubbed the spicy Spanish soap over her body until she was covered in suds. The water was much softer than at home, and she began to feel better than she had in a long time.

'Can I borrow your mini-dress? The black Mary Quant-style dress with the white thingumabobs down the front and back!' Pamela yelled from the other side of the door.

'Yeah, but not until I've worn it first. You can 'ave it tomorrow night.'

'But he'll 'ave seen you in it!'

'Exactly!' Kay laughed to herself. This felt more like it. This felt like being on holiday. She was beginning to relish the thought of nightclubs and fun.

'I heard someone say it's been really sunny!' Pamela couldn't keep the excitement out of her voice. 'We'll dance until the sun comes up and then sleep all day on the beach.'

143

Wrapping herself in a big white towel, Kay stepped out of the bathroom. 'I can't get over how warm the air is.'

'I can't get over those Spanish eyes,' Pamela said dreamily.

Dropping down on her bed, Kay drew her knees up and stretched her arms. 'I feel brilliant!'

'Thank God for that. I thought you was gonna die on that boat.'

'Don't! No more, Pamela. And I mean it. I want to forget that trip. OK?' She glared at her friend.

'I don't know whether to 'ave a shower or not.' Pamela turned away. 'And if you ever talk to me like that in front of anyone else,' she pulled a dress out of the cupboard, put it up to her and admired her reflection in the wall mirror, 'I'll talk about small cubes of pork fat on a piece of string.'

'Enough!' Kay screamed. 'It's not funny!'

'I know it's not bloody funny! The way you *talk* to me!' Pamela's face was white, her dark blue eyes alive with anger. 'You're always so bossy!' She turned her back on Kay and lowered her voice. 'Or putting me down, and sometimes in front of other people.'

Kay inhaled slowly and thought about it for a minute. 'It never occurred to me I was doing that.'

'Oh, it's not *you*! I don't even know why I said it.'

Seeing that Pamela was keeping her face turned away, Kay slowly circled her. 'Pamela? You OK? You're not crying are yer?'

'No, I'm not,' she sniffed, trying to control her face.

'Hey,' Kay put her arms around her best friend's shoulders. 'I'm sorry. I didn't realize I was being a cow.'

'It's not you.' Another pained expression suddenly spread across her face.

Guiding Pamela towards her bed, Kay sat down next to her and stroked her back. 'What is it, Pamela? You can tell me, surely?'

'It doesn't matter.'

'Of course it does.' Kay tried not to be upset. One of them had to be strong. They were, after all, in a strange country.

'It's my mum,' Pamela covered her face with her hands.

Kay was beginning to fear the worst. 'She's not ill, is she?'

'No.' There was a pause. 'I miss her.'

'You miss her?'

'And my dad.'

'You miss your dad as well?' Kay bit the inside of her cheek and didn't even smile.

'And my cat!' Pamela threw herself on to the

bed, buried her face in a pillow and howled. 'My cat'll be looking for me, I know he will! He'll be sitting outside my bedroom and he'll be crying and my mum'll start and so will my dad. They'll all be crying, and it's Sunday night!'

Kay wanted to ask what was significant about Sunday night but she didn't dare speak. She stuffed the corner of her pillow in her mouth and kept her back to Pamela as she lay on her own bed. Her body shook, and all she could hope was that should Pamela come out from under the pillow, she would think that Kay was crying, not laughing.

'My grandma and grandpa always pop in of a Sunday night,' Pamela sobbed, 'they'll be in a state as well. And that's bound to start Joey off!'

That was it. That was more than Kay could stand. She shrieked with laughter and couldn't stop. It was Joey that did it. Joey, the half-dead blackbird that the family were nursing back to life. The bird had been with them for four months. They had even bought it a cage, swing, small mirror and every other comfort available for the feathered pet.

Sitting bolt upright, Pamela stared disbelievingly at Kay. 'You're laughing!'

'And so would you be, if I was going on about a half-dead bird missing me!' Kay buried her head in

her pillow again. The next thing she knew, Pamela was thumping her with something soft, and she was happy to retaliate. The pair of them were enjoying a really good pillow fight.

Thirty minutes later they stood by the door of their room, admiring each other. Kay had given in over the Mary Quant-style dress and thought it looked better on Pamela in any case.

'Maybe I should have worn my denims . . .' Pamela stood awkwardly, checking her reflection in the mirror. 'I'm overdressed next to you.'

'I'll 'ave my frock back, in that case.'

'You think I look all right then?' Pamela was begging for a compliment.

'You look great. And the only reason I'm in jeans is because I . . . feel in that kind of a mood,' she shrugged. 'Come on! We've washed our hair, polished our shoes – now let's she what this place has to offer.'

Ten minutes later, they were handing in their key to Reception in order to let Pepe, the handsome receptionist, know that they were going out on the town.

'The Cellar!' he called after them as they waltzed out of the hotel. 'It's very best!'

'You have beautiful eyes!' Pepe shouted into Pamela's

ear as he held her close. 'They are like sky before night. Beautiful hair. It is like—'

'I love this song!' Pamela yelled back. She had to shout to make herself heard above the noise in the Cellar. Forgetting that she had always been singled out as a growler at school, she began to sing along to 'Rambling Rose' as she eased herself out of the tight grip that Pepe had on her.

'Why?' Pepe asked, gazing into her face, trying to win her over with his big brown cow-eyes.

'Why what?' she asked, irritated that he was interrupting the song.

'Why you no come close?' He tried his best to sound offended.

Even though Pamela had had quite a few Martinis she still had her wits about her. 'You're too hot, Pepe!' she laughed.

'Pamela!' Kay shouted, trying to be heard above the din. 'I'm going back to the hotel!'

'Why? This is great!'

'I'll see you later.' Weaving her way through the mass of bodies, Kay made for the exit, keeping her eyes down so she didn't have to acknowledge the smiles of local boys reaching out to stroke her long blonde hair.

Once outside Kay was grateful for the fresh air, which although warm was a lot cooler than the tiny

nightclub. Making her way back to the hotel she wondered how Pamela could be so full of energy after two days of travelling. She was ready for her bed. The bright white spotlights of the Cellar and the smoky atmosphere had made her eyes smart, and there was a dull ache spreading across her forehead.

Ignoring complimentary remarks from a group of Spanish boys, she walked quickly along the narrow pavement and turned left, believing that was the way back to the hotel. She couldn't stop the niggling feeling inside reminding her about Pamela's well-being. After all, it was only the first night. Remembering that her friend's dancing-partner worked at the hotel she felt easier, telling herself that Pamela was probably in less danger with a local than with one of the gorgeous French students they'd met at the Cellar. It was the delicious aroma of freshly baked bread that caused Kay to stop and take in her surroundings. At first she was interested to know where the smell was coming from, but when she realized that she had no idea where she was, a surge of panic shot through her. Had she taken the wrong turning? Or was it left out of the club and then the third on the right?

The narrow cobbled street was practically in darkness, only a glow coming from the windows of one

or two of the old terraced houses. Looking further along the street she could see that the bakery was lit up and the door was open. She quickly made her way towards it, praying that someone inside could speak English. Maybe he or she could direct her to her hotel.

Fear gripped Kay and she suddenly stopped in her tracks. She had forgotten the name of the hotel. Looking backwards, she wondered if she should retrace her steps to the nightclub. Knowing she would have to pass the local boys who were hanging around, she decided to go forward. Bracing herself and trying desperately to remember something about the hotel as a reference, she made for the bakery.

Standing in the doorway, Kay found herself face to face with a man, whom she imagined to be the baker's assistant, kneading dough on a large wooden table. She stood for a few seconds staring at him, wondering if her eyes were playing tricks. Was that Zacchi, her first love whom she'd met in Kent, on the hop fields?

'We're not open, but you are welcome to try some hot bread,' the young man smiled. 'Or a cake?' He pinched three strands of dough together at one end and began to plait with expertise.

It must have been the Martinis, thought Kay. Of

course it isn't Zacchi. He's taller, his eyes are a lighter brown, but his black hair and eyebrows and long lashes, they're nearly the same . . .

'You look as if you've lost your way.' He was laughing at her, and Kay could feel herself go weak at the knees. He had the most wonderful smile she had ever seen, and his golden skin showed off his pearly-white teeth.

'I have,' she said, unable to keep anxiety out of her voice. 'And I can't remember the name of my hotel.'

Smiling, he pulled some dough from a larger piece and threw it on to the floured surface. 'Can you remember your own name? Or do you wear a label around your neck?' He was flirting with her and she loved it.

'You've got flour on your hair and nose. And it's Kay.'

'You've got a very pretty face, and it's Chris.' He blew a loose strand of hair from his face and suddenly looked shy. 'I'm supposed to wear that hat.' He nodded to a sparkling white baseball cap.

'Well wear it, then!' Kay reached out and grabbed it, then placed it firmly on his head. 'Shall I tuck the loose curls in?'

He took a slow, deep breath. 'You want me to explode?' He shook his head. 'Those lovely slim

hands touching a man's neck would send sparks flying up and down his spine.'

'I'm sure.' Kay backed away from him, wondering if her mascara had run as her eyes had watered from the smoke at the nightclub.

'You arrived today, I take it?' He looked at her sideways.

Was he psychic too? 'How can you tell?'

'Lily-white skin,' he grinned, looking from her face to her hair and making it obvious he was impressed. 'It's very blonde. Do you bleach it?'

'No I don't!' How dare he suggest she used peroxide? 'I occasionally put lemon juice on it, but that's all.'

Carefully placing a second plaited loaf on a proving-tray, he nodded towards a wooden stool. 'If you want to sit down and wait for ten minutes, I'll help you find your hotel.'

Watching him work on another piece of dough, Kay studied his face to see what it was that made him so attractive.

Chris's eyes were almond-shaped; his nose straight; his jaw square, and his smooth skin had a deep golden tan. He had high cheek-bones and thick, dark eyebrows. He was very handsome and try as she might, Kay could not find any fault with his looks. And he had charisma.

He's probably the most conceited man on this earth, Kay told herself, turning her attention to the next best thing – hot crusty bread on the cooling-rack.

'If you look in that blue and white dish, you'll find some butter. Knife in the top drawer,' he nodded towards a small scrubbed pine table in the corner of the bakery. 'If you think we need plates, they're in the cupboard underneath.'

Was he a mind reader too? 'How come you speak such good English?' Kay said with a touch of suspicion in her voice. She couldn't help herself. This bloke was too good to be true.

'I lived in England from the ripe old age of two,' he said.

Kay smiled inwardly. That's what it was about him. 'You do look like a Londoner, as it 'appens.'

'Disappointed?'

'Why should I be?' She was noncommittal.

'I could be the first Spanish bloke you've spoken to, and I turn out to be regular old townie from back home.'

Pushing the last loaf of bread into shape, he slapped it down with the others and lifted the large metal tray with one hand, raising it level with his broad shoulders. 'Don't go away, I won't be a minute.'

Hearing him speak fluent Spanish to someone in the back room, she felt herself melt inside. Watch yourself, Kay . . .

Taking a small loaf of bread from the tray, she broke off two pieces and split them in half. Spreading unsalted butter thickly over each piece, she felt her mouth watering.

'This is delicious,' she told Chris as he strolled back in. He pulled off his white apron and proceeded to wash his hands under a tiny brass tap over a minute sink in a far corner of the room.

'I didn't realize how hungry I was.'

'Come on,' he said, pulling off his cap, 'we'll eat it going along, while you try and remember the name of your hotel.'

'I have remembered. It's Ruiz.'

'Oh, so you're only as thick as one plank, then?'

Ignoring the remark, Kay walked by his side, wishing Pamela could see her with this tall, handsome hunk of a bloke. She thought he must be twenty-two or twenty-three.

'So how long are you gonna be working over here for?' Kay asked as she tucked into the warm buttered bread.

Taking her hand and guiding her round a small group of Spanish boys, Chris smiled at her. 'For good. Or for bad; depends which way you look at it.'

Once they were safely past the noisy gang, instead of letting go of Kay's hand, Chris locked their fingers. 'I didn't want to go into my father's restaurant business, so we decided to leave home and set up here, in our family's village. Not that it's much like a fishing village any more,' he said, looking into her face.

'We?' Kay wondered if he was married.

'My brother bought a small bicycle shop – we'll pass it soon – and I took over the bakery. Neither of us are married. We've been here for just over a year.'

'Sounds perfect.'

'It could be,' he said, giving her a studious look. 'You know what I'm going to tell my brother tonight?'

'No.' She felt his eyes on her face and prayed she wasn't blushing.

'I'm going to tell him that tonight a star fell from the sky and landed in my bakery.'

Kay raised her eyebrows and gave a slow smile. 'Not a poet as well, are you?'

'No. I mean what I say.' He squeezed her hand.

'Yeah, I'm sure.' She wasn't going to fall for that one.

'Come on.' His face was full of fun. 'I'll introduce you to him. I know exactly which bar he'll be in. He's in love with the blonde German waitress.'

Before Kay could object, Chris was running and pulling her along with him. His laughter filled the air, and it was contagious. She was laughing too, and feeling very happy.

'Do you believe in love at first sight?' he yelled.

'Yes, I do, as a matter of fact!' She remembered Zacchi.

'So do I,' he said. Then without warning, he suddenly swept her up into the air and swung her round.

Shrieking and laughing, she begged him to stop. People were looking. He brought her gently back down to earth and cupped her face in his hands. 'I don't care who's staring at us,' he murmured.

'Neither do I.' Kay was surprised at her own words, and even more surprised when she stood on tiptoe and kissed him lightly on his full lips.

'Come on. I want my brother to meet you.' He tousled her hair and then put his arm around her shoulder, leading her into the small bar.

Chris introduced Kay to his brother Charles and a few friends who were there. 'She . . . is only sixteen, only sixteen . . .' Charles began to sing.

'Seventeen, actually,' said Kay, playfully indignant. She liked Charles instantly; the eighteen-year-old was full of himself, and she could imagine Pamela would go for him in a big way.

'Oh, well then.' He folded his arms and smiled at her and Chris. 'I expect you'll want me to stay out of the apartment tonight?' Before either of them could say anything he leaned forward, pushing his face up close to Kay's. 'But only if I get a turn tomorrow.'

Chris and the rest of them began to laugh as Kay became suddenly aware that she was a stranger, and fearful of what she had walked into. Stepping back, nearer the door, she looked at Chris and saw him in a different light. Maybe the instincts she'd had in his shop were right. He was too good to be true. Remembering how she had allowed herself to get into a dangerous situation with Zacchi, she felt herself go numb. Turning quickly, she ran out of the bar, angry as much with herself as with them.

She ran a short distance, then stopped and looked back. No one was following her. Composing herself she asked an English couple if they could direct her to the Hotel Ruiz.

'Turn around,' the man gave her a relaxed smile. 'It's behind you!' he said, in true pantomime style.

Kay was so relieved she felt like hugging the couple. She thanked them and went through Reception to the hotel bar, and was even more relieved to see Pamela.

'Where 'ave *you* been?' Pamela was beside herself. 'I was just about to get the manager to phone the police!'

Kay sat on a stool at the bar and slowly shook her head. 'I'll tell you later, when we're in bed. Where's Romeo?'

'Sitting at the hotel switchboard, can you believe? Talk about Jack of all trades and working all hours.' Pamela looked at her watch. 'He'll be finished in just over an hour. I'm waiting for him.'

'It's nearly three in the morning, for God's sake. Can't we go to bed?'

'You can. I'm not stopping yer.' Pamela looked as if she really had had one drink too many.

'Please come with me. I don't want to go to the annexe by myself. I'm scared.'

'What of?' Pamela studied Kay's pale, frightened face and nodded slowly. 'Tell Pepe I'll see him tomorrow, will yer, Juan?'

Juan, the barman, pushed his thumb forward. 'OK! Swinging!' Norman Vaughan's catch-phrase had obviously reached Spain.

Slipping down from the bar stool, Pamela looked sideways at her friend. 'You OK?'

'More or less.' Linking arms, the girls left the main hotel building and made their way to the annexe.

'Where did you get to, then?'

'I found a bakery.'

'You what?' Pamela cut in. 'I'm starving!'

Laughing quietly, Kay took an elastic band from her pocket and pulled her hair back into a pony-tail. 'I met the baker as well.'

'Did they have any cakes?' Pamela stopped in her tracks.

'Warm cakes, yeah, and hot bread.'

'What are we waiting for then?'

'You wouldn't catch me going back. Not in a million years.' Kay carried on walking.

'Where is it? I'll go.' Pamela stood her ground.

Turning back to look at her friend, Kay thought about it. 'OK,' she said, 'we'll go, but there's somewhere else I want to go first. A bar. I've got something to settle. Come on, I'll tell you about it on the way.'

Surprised but pleased with Kay's sudden change of heart, Pamela slipped her arm through Kay's. 'I had a great time in the Cellar after you left. A gorgeous Frenchie asked me to dance. We're meeting him on the beach in the morning.'

'Oh *are* we?'

'We don't have to stay with them. It's very casual. It's not a date or anything.'

'You said *them*?' Kay looked suspiciously at her.

'Yeah. A whole load of French students. Staying on a camp site. It's party night every night by the sound of it.' Pamela looked as if she had already been in the sun. She was positively glowing.

'Anyway, enough about me – your turn! What's so special about this old baker man?'

Kay shrugged nonchalantly, tucking her red blouse into her denims. 'He's just a kindly old man, that's all.' She smiled to herself and suddenly felt in the mood for a bit of fun.

'I said she would be back!' Charles looked happy to see Kay.

'Don't fall off your ego,' Kay snapped, a sulky expression on her face. 'I came to set the record straight.' She turned to Chris who was sitting by himself at a small table. 'You insulted me.'

'Kay!' Pamela spoke in a low whisper. 'You don't talk like that to a *god*.' She couldn't believe her own eyes.

'He never said a word!' Charles looked pleadingly at Kay, 'It was me. *I* owe you an apology.'

Kay looked from Charles back to Chris and waited. Chris said nothing, just looked back at her. With a cool expression on his face he slowly raised his legs and stretched them out on top of the table in front of him.

'What's going on, Kay?' Pamela whispered in her ear.

'This lot had a good laugh at my expense!' she deliberately raised her voice.

Charles made a display of innocent frustration. 'It was a joke!' He glared at Chris. 'Tell her then!'

Chris folded his arms defiantly and chewed on the wooden toothpick stuck in the corner of his mouth.

'Well, I dunno what's going on,' Pamela said, 'but I fancy a cappuccino.' She perched herself on a bar stool and smiled at the blonde barmaid, Sieglinde. 'Make that two,' she said. 'One for Kay.'

Sieglinde gave Pamela a thumbs-up sign and smiled. 'That's good,' she said, 'a good move.'

Leaving Sieglinde to it, Pamela swung around and looked from Kay to Chris. They were glaring at each other.

'It must be love,' Charles whispered in Pamela's ear. They both enjoyed the scene and within seconds were chatting away.

The other Spanish lads looked at each other and waited to see which of them would give in first and speak. They knew it would be a mistake for any one of *them* to start flirting with Kay.

Suddenly swinging his legs off the table, Chris sauntered over to the jukebox and studied the labels. Making his choice, he then turned away and took up

his earlier pose, keeping himself to himself. Charles and the other lads looked at each other, wondering which record Chris had chosen. It could make or break a possible romance.

Kay joined Pamela at the bar and sipped her coffee, keeping her back to the vain, loathsome man she had foolishly allowed herself to kiss. She hated him for the way he was behaving, and wondered how she was going to leave the bar with dignity. As the record started to play she felt Pamela's eyes on her face and resisted the urge to smile. They all listened with interest as the music drifted through the bar. Recognizing the record, Sieglinde reached up to the controls above the counter and turned up the sound, giving Kay a cheeky wink as the lyrics of 'Venus in Blue Jeans' filled the room.

> She's Venus in blue jeans,
> Mona Lisa with a pony-tail
> She's a walking, talking work of art
> She's the girl who's stole my heart . . .
> My Venus in blue jeans, is the Cinderella I adore . . .
> She's my very special angel too
> A fairy tale come true . . .

Resisting the urge to join in with the others, who had begun to pick up on the lyrics, Kay slowly swung

around and smiled back at Chris, who had his eyes fixed on her. His legs were no longer stretched out on the table.

They say there's seven wonders in the world,
But what they say is out of date.
There's more than seven wonders in this world . . .
I just met number eight . . .

Smiling, she walked towards Chris and took his outstretched hand. He pulled her down into the chair next to his.

'I suppose I'll have to walk you back to your hotel?' Charles grinned at Pamela.

'But no funny business!' She tossed back her long dark hair.

'Would that I dare?' he laughed. 'Don't want you setting Kay on me.'

'Never mind Kay,' Pamela stepped down from the bar stool. 'I can throw a good punch, you know.' She looked up into his cheeky face. 'Come on then, Goldilocks. I'm dead tired.'

'Tonight . . . they will make love on the beach.' A Spanish boy grinned.

'I think not,' said Sieglinde, drying glasses. 'Those girls are good.'

'You hope so, eh?'

'I am not worried. Two weeks, and the girl will be gone. I am here for a long time,' she shrugged.

It was almost four a.m. when Kay and Chris strolled hand in hand along the calm shore of the Mediterranean. 'You know what would be nice?' Gently he pulled Kay down on to the soft sand. 'If we could stay here and watch the sun come up.'

Kay curled herself into his strong, tanned arms. It was exactly what she had been thinking. 'Wake me up if I fall asleep,' she murmured.

'You won't fall asleep.' Chris kissed her gently on the mouth and she responded, her entire body beginning to throb with longing.

This was a new experience for Kay. Lying on a soft golden beach, waiting for dawn to break and listening to the sound of the sea lapping the shore. It was like a dream come true.

For Chris, it was just another holiday romance. Except that the girl lying next to him seemed different to all the others. She was natural and relaxing, comfortable to be with. It made him feel uneasy.

Chapter Six

Settling themselves in the living room by the gas fire, Laura and Jack tucked into their fish-and-chip supper and were enjoying an episode of *Coronation Street* on television. It had been a drizzling, grey day and Jack had stood for several hours outside the gates of the Royal Albert Dock. The mass meeting of dockers included men from Tilbury, Surrey and East India Docks.

Jack Dash, the union leader, had been there and spoken well. He had told the men that the situation in the Port of London was critical. He also confirmed that unregistered labour was being used at one of the wharves, while elsewhere, two thousand dockers could not obtain work.

'They're planning to fetch meat in by air, y'know?' Jack said, breaking off a small chunk of steaming hot crispy cod. 'Flying it in to Southend.'

'Oh yeah?' Laura tried to sound interested, but she

was involved in an argument going on between Ena Sharples and Annie Walker.

'Tilbury hasn't come out yet, but some of the Surrey men are with us. Bloody Joint Import Trades Committee sent a telegram to the Prime Minister requesting that importers get permission to unload their own cargoes! They want their bloody brains looked at.'

Making himself a chip sandwich, Jack tried to get interested in the weekly serial, but his mind was still full of the strike.

'Mead's going on about letting fleets of lorries into the docks to collect cargoes. I tell you, Laura, this country's gonna be in a sorry state if it goes on the way it is.'

'Try not to worry about it, Jack, eh?' Laura was bored with hearing about it.

A long ring on the doorbell broke into their thoughts. 'Who the hell's that?' Jack moaned.

'Might be Liz.' Laura hoped it was. Jack never went on about the strike when she was around. 'You get it, eh? I can't miss any of this. I think Annie Walker's gonna win.'

'It'd better be Liz,' Jack said, standing up. 'Anyone else can go for a quick walk. Especially if it's another Bible-basher.'

Pouring herself a glass of Tizer, expecting Liz to

walk in any minute, Laura focused on the row going on between her two favourite characters, ready to fill her sister-in-law in on the affairs of the Street.

Instead of coming back into the living room, Laura heard Jack go into the kitchen. She could hear men's voices and thought she recognized them. Opening the small serving-hatch between the rooms her heart sank when she saw Bert's two brothers, Frank and Freddie, sitting at the kitchen table.

'I'm just making a cup of tea, Laura. D'yer want one?' Jack looked far from happy.

'No, I'll wait till later. Don't forget your fish and chips,' she added, eyeing the brothers.

'All right, Laura?' Frank smiled.

'Fine thanks. You?'

'Could be better, but there you are. Heard from Kay yet?'

'Not yet, no, but I expect we will.' Laura managed a smile and nodded to Freddie before closing the hatch doors. Settling herself down again, she couldn't help wondering what the two villains wanted with Jack. She hoped he wasn't mixed up in anything that involved them.

'It's like old times, eh, Jack, us being 'ere in your flat.' Freddie said. 'I know we was here for the funeral, but that was different.'

'Last time before that was one Christmas a few

years ago. Bloody good party it was an' all. Bert sang 'is favourite song, naturally.'

All three men laughed at the memory. 'He didn't have a bad voice as it happens,' Jack said, pouring boiling water into the chrome teapot.

'No, you're right,' Frank lowered his head. 'I s'pose you're wondering why we're here?'

'If it's the envelope that's worrying yer?'

''Course not,' Frank cut in.

'I 'aven't given it to Liz yet, for a reason.'

'We didn't know you hadn't, Jack. That's not why we're 'ere.' Freddie rubbed his eyebrow. 'We 'aven't really felt right since we saw you in the Maurice. You looked a bit choked when you left.'

Jack felt like telling him that he wasn't upset, but angry. He thought better of it. 'I don't know if Liz'll take the cash, to tell you the truth. She can be a funny cow at times.' Jack poured milk into each cup.

'Beer money, Jack, that's all.'

Jack looked into Frank's suntanned face. 'Yeah?'

'Now that it's really sunk in about Bert,' Freddie began, quick to change the subject away from back-handers. 'He was a good bloke. We thought a lot of 'im.'

Frank covered his face with one hand. 'A fucking good brother as well.'

Freddie's eyes were filling with tears. 'We never saw much of 'im during the last couple of years. You know 'ow these things go. Families lose touch.'

Pouring the tea, Jack wondered what Frank and Freddie really wanted. They were upsetting him talking about Bert, and he wasn't sure how he would handle it if they had something else on their minds and were using his late best friend as a smokescreen.

'Bert was one of the best, Freddie. You only have to think back to the turnout at his funeral to see that. Anyway, what d'yer want with me?' He placed their tea in front of them and folded his arms, ready to stare them out if necessary.

'What you've just given us, Jack. A cup of tea and a chair.'

'If you two are winding me up, you can piss off now.' Jack could feel the blood pumping through his veins.

'We're not 'ere to wind you up,' Frank sighed. 'We miss Bert!'

'Fair enough . . . fair enough.' Jack sat down at the table and pulled his tobacco tin from his trouser pocket.

'You saw a lot of 'im, didn't yer?' Freddie said, wiping away a tear.

Jack sucked on his bottom lip and nodded, giving them the benefit of the doubt.

'He was happy enough, wasn't he? I mean, he didn't want for anything.'

'Drink your tea, Freddie. You're letting your emotions get the better of you.' Jack didn't need these two pouring their hearts out to him.

'How's Liz?' Frank blew his nose. 'She's all right, ain't she?'

'Doing 'er best. You know Lizzie.' He looked sideways at Frank. 'Well, you used to.'

'Don't be like that, Jack.' Freddie pulled a white envelope from his inside pocket. 'Don't you think we wished we'd 'ave visited them more often?' He dropped the envelope on the table. 'There's a bit more cash for Liz, and for you.' Freddie eyed Jack with caution.

Standing up, Freddie swallowed the remains of his tea. 'You ready, Frank?' He looked at his gold wrist-watch.

'Yep. We've got a little bit of business to see to, Jack. Otherwise we'd stay longer.'

With one hand on the kitchen door, Freddie turned and looked Jack in the eye. 'Sounds like the strike'll be over soon. You did the right thing.'

'Oh yeah?' Jack could feel his heart sink. 'What makes you say that?'

'Stands to reason. The attention's off of Bert. You've made things a lot more comfortable for us.' He held his hand out to shake Jack's.

'If you wanna use them notes to take Liz and Laura on a nice holiday abroad, that's fine by us.'

Before Jack could tell them to take their filthy money, the two brothers were out of the kitchen, heading for the front door.

'See yer, Jack!' Freddie called over his shoulder.

'Say hallo to Liz for us!' Frank added.

The street door slammed shut behind them. Jack shuddered. He stared at the white envelope in his hand. *Beer money*. That's what they had called it. Beer money.

Laura leaned in the kitchen doorway and folded her arms. 'Forget it, Jack. They're not worth losing sleep over.'

Jack looked up at her. His white face said it all. He was too bitter to speak. The only reason for Bert's brothers to call round was in the envelope. The second payment. The other half of the bribe.

'I feel like burning it, Laura.'

Snatching it up, Laura pushed it into her cardigan pocket. 'We'll tell Liz about it and let her decide. If we don't want this, Jack, there are a lot of people who will. People who won't know or care where it comes from so long as it puts clothing on their kids' backs.'

Jack laughed at her quietly. 'You gonna stand on the corner of Brick Lane Sunday morning and give it away, I s'pose?'

'All we 'ave to do is split it up and pop envelopes through doors. I know a lot of families on this estate who'd appreciate hard cash.'

Jack sighed heavily. 'It's filth money, Laura. From London scum.'

'Oh come on, Jack! *You're* so innocent?'

'No I'm not! I've nicked stuff from the docks and no doubt I'll do it again, but that's different! A box of Jersey spuds? A crate of oranges? Perks! They expect it!'

Laura knew it wasn't just the history of the money that was tormenting Jack, it was the reason it had been given that was tearing him apart. He believed in the strike, and wanted to be on his soapbox urging the men not to give in. And then there was his pride. Bert's two flash brothers had kicked it about as if it were an old tin can, and then crushed it flat.

'Come on. Come and cuddle up on the sofa.' She stroked his thick blond hair and pushed her slim fingers into his neck, gently massaging away his troubles.

Looking up at her with his light blue eyes, Jack reminded Laura of Kay and another worry swept

through her. She prayed she would be all right abroad, with all those foreigners.

Wrapped in each other's arms on the sofa, later that night, Jack and Laura were quiet. They had turned off the television, the lights were down low and they were listening to their favourite record, Nat King Cole singing 'Unforgettable'.

'I don't really understand why they gave you that money, Jack,' Laura said, after a while. 'Why don't they want the strike to go on? What's it to them?'

'It's probably all down to one warehouse keeper. Frank and Freddie are members of a certain firm, and that firm is probably involved in importing tea . . . sugar.'

'Yeah? So?'

'The tea and sugar doesn't come over in little bags.'

'I know that. Get to the point!'

'Well, hidden amongst all those billions of tea leaves and grains of sugar there'll be something else far more valuable.'

Laura sat up and stared, disbelievingly, into Jack's face. 'Drugs?'

'Now you know why it's scum money.' Jack reached for his tobacco tin.

'Blimey, Jack. It never occurred to me.' She shook her head slowly. 'Are you sure?'

'Why d'yer think some of them use casual labour when it suits 'em?'

'And you know this for a fact, do yer?'

'Common sense.'

'Are you saying that's the reason why this strike started up? That the wharf manager took a man on because they were running drugs and he was part of it?'

'No, of course not. That company's got nothing to do with it. It's the other one or two warehouses, here and there, who discourage the dockers from striking in their own sweet way. They wouldn't want anything to hold up the trafficking.'

'Bloody hell. I'm glad you've taken a back seat, Jack. You could 'ave ended up with your face slit.' Laura dropped her head back on to a cushion.

'Don't be silly. They don't do things like that. I would 'ave just disappeared, that's all. Man Missing Presumed to have Run Off with his Mistress.' Jack was trying to turn it into a joke.

'You could still 'ave 'ad your throat cut.' She felt a shiver run down her spine.

'Nar. A bullet through the 'ead, maybe,' he chuckled, lighting a roll-up.

'It's not funny, Jack.'

'You're telling me.' Jack didn't think any of it was funny. The East End had always had its thieves,

its gangs, but the past decade had seen America filtering through. Mafia-style firms were becoming more established.

'You know, I wouldn't mind getting out of this country. Emigrate to Australia.'

'Oh leave off, Jack,' Laura laughed, 'you? Emigrate? You nearly threw a fit when I suggested we all went to Spain for a holiday! If ever there was a home-bird, it's you.'

'Yeah well, I do love this country and I think it's worth working and fighting for.' He sighed and shook his head. 'It's corrupt, Laura. Corruption runs through every establishment you can think of. Even the law.'

'Maybe it's the same in other countries?'

'Maybe. Don't make it right though, does it?'

'I dunno, Jack. Right pair we are. How often do we sit here like this without having to worry about Kay crashing in any second?'

He grinned at her. 'Funny you should say that.'

'I thought you'd never ask.' Easing herself further down the sofa, Laura stretched out one leg, allowing her silky green skirt to rise above the top of her black suspender. 'Not bad for thirty-nine,' she teased.

Jack ran one finger from her knee upward and moved his hand across her flat stomach. 'You know what I'm gonna do tonight?'

'Tell me,' she kissed his neck and let her legs fall slightly apart.

'I'm gonna kiss every inch.' He began to unbutton her dress. 'Yep, every inch, if it takes all night.' He lowered his head and filled his mouth with her erect nipple, sucking and licking, sending a wave of delicious craving through her body.

Looking into her soft green eyes, Jack pushed his hand under her, cupping and squeezing, gently playing with the soft, dark curls between her legs. Then, easing her off the sofa and on to the rug in front of the gas fire, he began slowly to take off her clothes.

Chapter Seven

Liz had taken to Joe on her first day working in the canteen at Hammond's. He was the only one, it seemed, who could make her laugh and bring her out of a blue mood. Joe from maintenance, as he was known, was also on his own. His wife had died three years previously and to fill the gap he had joined a spiritualist group.

That evening the meeting was taking place in Rose Davenport's living room, and from the moment Liz entered the clean and polished two up two down, she wished she hadn't. Telling herself that this would be her last session, she sat at the round dining table feeling easier, knowing she would not have to put up with Rose's snobby ways after tonight. She was worse than some of the women who worked in Hammond's.

'We don't seem to understand who the message is for. Could you please spell out the name of the person

you wish to contact?' Rose's shrill voice broke the silence.

'I think someone else should be the contact,' Joe said quietly.

'Don't be silly, Joe. It just needs a bit more time, that's all. Come on.' Rose urged the spirit; 'Stop wasting our time!'

'You'll make it angry, Rosie. You've got to coax, not demand.' Joe took his finger off the glass.

'Oh, no that *won't* do, Joe! You've broken the link now.' Rose was beginning to lose her patience.

'I don't think it's going to work this evening,' Mary, the eighty-year-old, had had enough. 'I'm desperate for a pee and a cup of cocoa.' They always had hot chocolate after a chat with the spirits. 'Why don't we stop, eh?' She looked at Liz for support.

'Well, let's see if we can decipher what I've written first.' Rose was in before Liz had a chance. Pushing the paper towards Joe, she crossed her arms defiantly and eyed Liz. 'I think we have a non-believer in the room.'

Liz was only too pleased to make her escape into the kitchen. 'I'll make the cocoa if you like. Then you can get on with it.'

'Sit down, Lizzie. We're not finished yet. And anyway, it's Rosie's night to make the drinks.'

'You were going too bloody fast, Rose. There's

not one space in between these letters.' Joe tried to break and separate words from the continuous lines of scribble.

'If I'm not back in five minutes,' old Mary said, switching the lights on, 'start without me. I think that chocolate Ex-Lax is beginning to work, Liz.'

Liz smiled inwardly at Rose's loud sigh of disgust and wondered if she might come to just one more meeting after all. Lovely old Mary crossing swords with this woman was worth coming out in the rain for. She knew the old girl did it on purpose, slipping in what Rose would refer to as a *vulgarism* here and there.

'*YaK K hctaw*? It must mean something, it's repeated that three times.' Joe said.

'Let me see that!' Rose snatched the paper away. 'Well it's obvious what's happened! I sometimes do mirror writing when I'm in touch.'

'Well,' Joe looked thoughtful, 'if you have been writing backwards, Rosie, and nothing would surprise me, this message could be for you, Liz. *Watch K Kay*.'

Liz took the piece of paper from Joe. 'You could be right, you know. Let's give it another go.'

Enthusiasm was never far away with this group; within seconds they had their fingers poised over the glass.

'We'll wait for Mary,' Liz said. 'And I'll take down the message this time, as it's for me.'

No one could argue with that, not even Rose, who hid her feelings of rejection quite well. 'Someone should call up to that woman and ask if she's going to be there all night!'

Without wasting a moment, Liz was up and in the doorway. 'Is the chocolate working, Mary?'

'Yes! It's wonderful! I don't want to come down, start without me!'

Back in her place, eyes closed, head bowed, finger on the glass at the centre of the table, Liz took a deep breath and began. 'I'm sorry we broke away when you were trying—'

'Ask it if there's a message for anyone in the room!' Rose cut in.

Containing her impatience, Liz took another deep breath. 'If you do have a message for any one of us, please spell it out and I'll do my best to write it down.'

The glass moved quickly around the edge of the mirror, stopping at letters of the alphabet which had been marked on with Rose's black eyebrow pencil. Keeping her index finger in contact with the sherry glass, Liz carefully wrote down the message until the glass came to a pause.

'Lights!' ordered Rose.

'There's enough light.' Liz stared down at the notebook. 'Give me a minute,' she murmured.

'If this is a message from my Bert about our Kay, it's a bit muddled.' She slowly began to read. *Watch K K Watch her Trouble K Watch her.*

'I think I've had enough for one night.' Liz stood up and looked at her new friend. 'You don't have to leave yet, Joe, if you don't want to.'

Easing back into his chair, Joe looked at the others. 'As if I'd let you go through the backstreets by yourself.' Pulling his cap on and rising from the table, he turned to the others. 'See you in a fortnight. Keep smiling.'

Making their way along Vallance Road, stepping around small puddles, Liz and Joe enjoyed the warm evening air after rain. The smell of baking bread wafting along the narrow cobbled street made Liz feel hungry. 'I could eat a nice hot bagel, Joe. I'm—' Before she could finish the sentence, he was guiding her into the Blue and White all-night Jewish baker's.

Thankfully the little corner shop wasn't too busy. Just a couple of taxi-drivers enjoying a chat. 'This your new girlfriend, Joe?' one of them joked.

'I'm old enough to be your mother and you're young enough to go across my knee,' Liz returned, eyeing the cheesecake behind the glass counter.

'Well, let's hope you've got plenty of money.'

'Wouldn't mind a piece of that apple strudel, Becky,' Liz asked, wondering at the taxi-driver's last remark.

'I s'pose she's the reason we haven't seen you at the last two card games, eh, Joe?' The man wasn't going to leave it be.

'Nar,' Joe slowly shook his head. 'My prostate's been on the blink again.'

'Go on! Funny that. You've always seemed fit as a fiddle and twice as sharp. Still, I always did think you was a bit deep.'

Paying for her bagels and apple strudel, Liz bade them goodnight and she and Joe left the shop, a nagging doubt at the back of her mind. Was the taxi-driver trying to tell her something?

Turning on the fire in the small living room, Liz told Joe to pull the armchair up close to the heat while she put the kettle on. 'There's some rum in the sideboard if you fancy a drop.'

'I've been thinking,' he said, following her into the kitchen. 'I've got no money, Liz, and no sex to offer yer, but . . .' he took a deep breath, 'I'm yours if you want me.'

Smiling, Liz turned to face him. 'That's a lovely offer, Joe love, but it's a bit too soon.'

'Oh, I don't mean yet. Gawd, no. In time. If you

fancy a bit of company in the evenings. Someone there in the mornings.'

'Ask me again in a year, eh?' She kissed him lightly on the side of his face.

'So you don't mind, then? You know, about the . . .'

'Sex? 'Course I don't. I've got no interest in all that now. And as for the money, well, I've got none either and never have had. So what I haven't had I can't miss, can I?'

'That's true, Liz, that's true.'

'But to be honest, the pictures would suit me better than them bloody seances you keep taking me to.' She placed two mugs on a tray. 'Bert wouldn't really have approved and, well, it does upset me a bit, to tell you the truth.'

'Ah, you're just a bit upset over that message about Kay, that's all.'

'No,' she chuckled, 'I was pushing it with my finger the second time round. I'd had enough of that bloody Rose woman.'

Later that night, as Liz lay in her darkened bedroom, she couldn't help thinking about the taxi-driver. There was a look on his face, and she couldn't fathom what had been behind it. Sighing, she turned over and eased her shoulder under the soft feather pillow and tried not to worry about her Kay in a

foreign land. She had only told Joe a half-truth about pushing the glass. She had started to force it towards the letters but then it seemed to have a life of its own, moving by itself, regardless of Liz's fingers.

For the next two days, until her niece was home, safe and sound, Liz knew that the feeling of dread inside her would stay right where it was.

Chapter Eight

'It's me, Kay!' the voice screeched over the telephone. 'We're at Dover!'

'It's all right, Kay,' Laura laughed, 'you don't have to shout.' Laura was choked at hearing her daughter's voice again. 'What time will you be arriving at Victoria?'

'I dunno! There's trouble with the trains so I'm gonna be late whatever happens. You won't have to meet me. We've been offered a ride in a taxi.'

'What d'yer mean, offered a ride? Who with?'

'This man and woman we met on the boat. They live near Aunt Liz. They know her. Alf and Sarah. I'll have to go, Mum. Wait up for me, won't you?'

''Course we'll wait up for you,' Laura swallowed tears, 'I can't wait to see your silly freckled face.'

That Friday evening seemed the longest in Laura's life. Sitting beside Jack on the sofa, she tried to get absorbed in the television; *Take Your Pick*.

Lighting her second cigarette, she rehearsed to herself how she would deliver the news to Jack about Kay's holiday and where she had actually been. Time was running out and she would have to speak up soon. Kay might knock on the door any minute.

'What's with the chain-smoking?' Jack said casually, his eyes on the screen. 'What's on your mind?'

There was a moment's silence as Laura plucked up courage and searched for the right words. Jack was a placid man most of the time but experience had seen him flare up within seconds and take days to calm down.

'I'll tell you after this show,' she said, giving herself breathing space.

'That bad, eh?'

Loud banging on the front door startled them both. Jack peered across at Laura, his eyes narrowed. 'If that's not the copper's knock I don't know what is.' He pulled himself out of his armchair.

'Don't be daft,' Laura's face lit up, 'it's Kay!'

'No, that's not her.' Jack pulled his braces over his shoulders, sucking on his bottom lip. 'There's nothing I should know before I open that door, is there?' he asked, with more than a touch of worry in his voice. 'You've been on edge for a couple of days now.'

'No, of course not.' Jumping up quickly, Laura's hand flew to her face. 'Oh Christ! There's still a carton of cigarettes in the wardrobe!'

'No there's not. I got rid of 'em this afternoon.'

While Jack made for the street door, Laura stood in the darkened passageway, listening.

'Mr Armstrong?' she heard one of two uniformed officers ask.

'May we come in, sir?'

'I hope you're not the bringer of bad news? We've had more than our fair share lately.' Jack spoke in a low voice.

'There hasn't been an accident, sir. Nothing like that. We'd just like a few words with your daughter, Kay.'

'Oh yeah?'

Laura felt her heart sink as she recognized dread in Jack's voice. Something was wrong. Something bad had happened.

'If we could come in, sir? It shouldn't take long.'

Closing the door behind them, Jack led the way into the front room. Laura's brain worked nineteen to the dozen. She couldn't imagine Kay getting up to anything, not on holiday.

'I take it she has arrived back from her holiday, sir?'

'No, as a matter of fact she's late.'

Laura silently prayed that they hadn't found out about Kay forging Jack's signature on her passport form. Staring into their solemn faces, she heard herself telling them to sit down as she switched off the television.

'So what's my seventeen-year-old been up to, then?' Jack smiled. Trying to hide his concern, he dropped into his armchair and picked up his tobacco tin from the coffee table.

'We believe she's involved in something quite serious.'

Laura turned icy cold, unable to do anything but stare at the policeman who seemed at ease with the silence that hung heavy in the room.

'According to information given by her colleagues at work, your daughter was due home today?'

'That's right,' Jack lit a roll-up. 'Should be in any minute. We was getting a bit worried, as it happens. She is on the late side.' He drew on his cigarette. 'What's she been up to at work then?'

'What makes you ask that, sir?' asked the younger police officer.

'Stands to reason. You went there before you came 'ere.'

'She's under suspicion of theft,' the second officer added.

Jack roared with nervous laughter, then looked at

Laura and winked. Kay stealing? It was out of the question. 'What she s'posed to 'ave pinched then?'

'A pay packet's gone missing from the office where your daughter works. So far our inquiries lead us to believe that she might've taken it.' The officer shrugged and gave Jack a half-smile. 'Maybe she was a bit short of pesetas?'

Jack shook his head and grinned. 'You're barking up the wrong tree, mate. Kay's no thief. And she would hardly need pesetas on Sheppey.'

'You mean the Isle of Sheppey?' The officer looked across at his colleague. 'We were told she'd gone to Spain.'

'Do me a favour – Spain. She'd need a passport for that.'

Laura studied Jack's face, and when he smiled reassuringly back at her she was filled with remorse, knowing that at any second it would have to come out that she and Kay had gone behind his back. It would be devastating.

'You're confusing our Kay with someone else,' he said.

'I don't think we are.' The officer caught Laura's eye and waited. It was obvious from his expression that he knew she had something on her mind.

'She did go to Spain, Jack,' Laura murmured, keeping her eyes fixed on the floor.

Looking at his watch, the police officer sighed. 'Perhaps we'll call back tomorrow. I except her plane was late in.'

'What you talking about? How could she go abroad without a passport?' Then, as it dawned on him, Jack threw his head back as if he'd been struck by lightning, and swore. He shook his head slowly. 'Stone me. I never thought you'd go behind my back and sign that form.'

There was a tense silence and the officers looked from one to the other.

'What right did you 'ave to undermine me like that?' Full of anger, Jack couldn't see the warning looks Laura was giving him. She wanted to scream at him, tell him to keep quiet. Tell him to think before he spoke. But knowing that was one of Jack's weaker points, she began to get angry herself. He was playing his usual game of turning things around so that she was at fault. She had seen it before, many times. Now he was pushing it too far.

'You can be a silly bitch at times. D'yer think I didn't 'ave my reasons for not wanting her to go out there? She could 'ave got dragged off by some sodding—'

'I never undermined yer! She did! And all because you wouldn't let her go! She signed your name on

the form!' Laura screamed at him. 'It's *your* bloody fault! If you wasn't so stubborn.'

'She forged her father's signature? On a passport form?' The officer spoke slowly, emphasizing each word. 'And you don't think she's capable of taking a bit of spending money?' He turned to his colleague and a look passed between them.

'I think we'll wait for her to come in.' He sank back on the settee and folded his arms. 'Let's hope she's not too long.'

Clutching the handle of her suitcase, Kay waved goodbye to Alf and Sarah as the taxi pulled away from the grounds of the flats. It had just gone nine p.m. and as tired as she was, she couldn't wait to show off the presents she had brought back.

Pressing the lift button she felt excited at being back home in Stepney. The *No spitting* sign on the brick wall was like a welcome-home plaque, and the familiar smell of flowers from the cottage gardens opposite brought a smile to her face. The holiday had been wonderful. A dream come true. But it was good to be back, even if it did feel chilly. Almost as exciting as leaving in the first place. And Spain would always be there. Spain with its night life and eternal sun. Spain with its promise of a lifetime for her and Chris – running a small chain of bakeries.

Pulling the lift door open, she dragged her suitcase out and carried it to the front door. Finding the bell in the dark she held her finger on it for longer than she would normally, to announce her arrival.

It was a grim-faced Laura who opened the door. 'Hallo, Kay. I'm afraid we've . . .' unable to say any more, Laura reached out and drew her in. 'Oh, Kay. What have you done?'

'Mum?' Kay pulled back and looked into the haunted face. 'Dad's not that angry with me, is he?'

'No, love. He's not angry with yer.' She wiped her eyes with the back of her hand. 'Push your suitcase up against the passage wall.'

'But the presents. Can't I give 'em to you now?'

'Later, Kay. We've got visitors.'

When Kay saw the policemen, her heart sank. Had someone else died? Were they there to break the news?

'Kay, there's been some trouble at Thompson's. A wage packet's been stolen.'

A broad grin swept across Kay's face. 'At Thompson's? God. Trust me to miss all the drama.' She smiled at the two policemen. 'I don't know how I can help. I've been away. I've just got back from Spain.' Glancing at her dad, she lowered her eyes.

'So we gather. It came as a surprise to your father.'

The officer's tone and dour expression made it clear that they were not amused. 'We understand from your parents that your passport was obtained by a forged application form?'

Kay looked from Laura to Jack. Surely they hadn't betrayed her?

'They found out from your mates at work, Kay,' Laura murmured.

The senior officer looked from his watch to his assistant who seemed to read his mind. A brief nod passed between them. 'Kay Armstrong—'

'*No!*' Laura's green eyes were wide and full of fear. 'You can't do this!'

Grabbing Laura's arm, Jack swallowed hard. 'Leave it, Laura.' His instincts were to the fore. He had read the expression on the officers' faces and knew what was coming. Furious as he was, his only thoughts now were for Kay and how best to support her through the next few hours.

Pulling Kay in close, Jack felt a sudden surge of emotion, as though an electric current was passing through his body. They were going to arrest Kay. They were going to take his girl in for questioning.

'What's going on? Dad? What's happening?'

'Kay Armstrong, I am arresting you on suspicion of theft and forgery. You are not obliged to say anything unless you wish to do so. But what

193

you do say may be put in writing and given in evidence.'

'You can't do that,' Laura cut in, defying them to argue with her. 'You dare take my child away!'

'We'll be taking your daughter to King's Cross police station where she'll be questioned properly.'

Trembling, Jack nodded. 'I'll get my coat,' he managed to say, throwing a sheepish glance at Laura.

'I don't understand!' Kay's face became distorted and she burst into tears. 'I haven't done anything, I don't know what you're talking about.' She backed away and began to sob. 'You can't take me away! Dad, tell them! Tell them I'm not a thief!'

'It's all right, Kay, it's all right.' Jack moved towards Kay as her hand went for the veranda door. With one quick movement he reached out and grabbed her, pulling her in close. 'It's a mistake, babe. We'll get it sorted.'

'But they're arresting me! They're gonna put me in prison! You've got to stop it!' She was still gripping the handle of the glass doors. Dropping from the back balcony was one way of escape and Kay's mind was racing.

'No they're not, silly.' Jack stroked her hair. 'They just need to ask you a few questions, that's all.'

'Well let them ask me then.' She turned to the

police officers. 'Ask me anything you like. You don't need to take me with you.' She looked at each of the solemn faces. 'What am I supposed to have done?'

Jack knew it would be useless trying to soft-soap these two. They had their job to do and as far as he could tell, little scenarios like this left them cold. He silently prayed to God that Kay hadn't been silly enough to steal that money. He would rather die than see her cross-examined in a court of law.

A stream of words poured from Kay as they journeyed from Stepney to north London in the back of the squad car. As she sat between Laura and Jack, she turned from one to the other for reassurance.

'But you must know something, Dad? Whose salary went missing? What does Mr Grieves think? He knows I'm honest. I handle loads of money every fortnight. I've never taken a penny, they know that.' She had stopped crying but her voice was shaky and she was trembling from top to toe.

'They wouldn't trust me with all that cash if they thought I was a thief.'

'Never mind trust! They shouldn't 'ave given a seventeen-year-old that kind of responsibility. You

wait till this is over. I'll have something to say to that company!' Jack looked as if he might put his fist through a window.

The interview room at King's Cross was small, with just a few chairs and a small wooden table, a far cry from Laura and Jack's front room where they should have been at that moment.

Carrying a tray of hot tea, a uniformed officer arrived and his comforting smile eased the atmosphere. 'Would you like a biscuit? They're not very exciting.'

'No thank you,' Kay murmured, and started to cry again. The well-meant kindness was all it had taken to trigger her off.

Setting the tray down, the officer left the room and was instantly replaced by the arresting officer and the station sergeant.

While Laura looked as though she might pass out any minute, Jack's fists were clenched with anger. The officer was reporting to the sergeant his grounds for arresting Kay, and making it sound worse than it was. They were talking about her as if she were a criminal.

Once that was over, Laura and Jack were asked to leave the interview room and wait in the foyer while the female officer searched Kay and recorded her details.

'Your daughter will be interviewed by the detective constable and should he feel there is enough evidence against her, she will be charged and released on bail. If she's cooperative, it shouldn't take too long.' The constable threw Jack a look, advising him to leave him to it.

Taking Laura by the arm and avoiding his daughter's searching eyes, Jack led his wife out of the room.

The silence weighed heavily in the small room while the detective constable sat on the other side of the table and placed the red receipt book down, watching Kay for her reaction.

'How did that get here?' She stared down at the book. 'That's the salary receipt. I keep that in my top drawer, in my desk.'

Looking into Kay's face, DC McCormack sipped his tea. 'You do understand why you're here?'

'No, I don't, actually. I thought that you were only allowed to drag criminals into a place like this!' Knowing she was overstepping the mark, she added quickly, 'I s'pose for all you know I *am* a criminal.'

'You were brought in under suspicion of theft of a wage packet, and forging an official document.' Before she could interrupt, he quickly reminded her that she was still under caution. His stern voice

and strong presence caused Kay to cower in her chair.

Keeping his eyes lowered, the DC thumbed through the pages and then stopped. 'Can you tell me why you made this alteration, Kay?' He looked straight into her face.

Through watery eyes, she focused on the line written in the book and suddenly blushed as she remembered making the mistake. She leaned forward in her chair as she scene came flooding back. 'Mr Woods's salary?' Her voice was tinny. There was a pause while they waited for her to continue, but her mind was racing as she slipped back in time. There had been something about that moment. Something about the expression on the face of Stephen Drake when he asked her what she would do about Mr Woods's salary, since he was on holiday.

'It went by registered post.'

'That doesn't answer my question.'

'What question?' Kay had lost touch with the present; she was still back there in the office on that Friday afternoon.

'Why did you alter this entry?' He pointed to the line in question.

'It was a mistake.' She was remembering clearly now. 'I thought Mr Drake was from Mail Service but he wasn't. He was from Bought Ledger.' She smiled.

It had been a silly mistake after all. Soon she would be home and in her bed.

'Go on.'

'I wrote down eight salaries, then I was going to put Mail Service but I remembered where he was from, crossed out the M, and put Bought Ledger.' She was even beginning to enjoy the fact that she could throw light on the mystery.

'I see.' He sat back in his chair and rubbed his chin. 'So what happened to Mr Woods's salary, Kay?'

'He was on holiday. So it went by registered post.' She sipped her tea and began to enjoy the feeling of relief which was taking over from the turmoil inside.

'But Mr Woods never received it.'

Kay shrugged. 'Must 'ave got lost in the post, then.'

'Registered envelopes don't get lost. That's the point of having them registered in the first place.' He was taking on a more serious tone. 'And when your boss, Mr Grieves, checked with the post room, there was no sign of his name in the book. And the girl in the office couldn't remember seeing an envelope for him.'

'Well there was one. I remember typing it. And I remember pointing it out to Mr Drake when he asked about it.'

'You showed him the envelope?'

'No, I showed him my list of names of the staff whose salaries had to go by registered post.'

'Why didn't you show him the registered envelope?'

'I don't know!' He was beginning to irritate her. 'The list was there, right in front of me.'

'So you're saying that you definitely remember typing the envelope, putting the salary in and taking that, with the others, into the post room and giving all of them to Sylvia?'

'Yeah.' Kay smiled again. 'Ask Sylvia, she'll tell yer.'

'We did, and like I said, she doesn't remember it.'

There was another pause while Kay racked her brain. She didn't want to get her friend in trouble. Maybe Sylvia had taken the salary?

'Your father tells us you're not averse to a little forgery now and again?'

Kay bent her head, realizing that her foolish idea had turned out to be more serious than she had dreamed possible.

'Did you or did you not forge your father's name on an official document? An application form for a passport!' He was angry now. Angry, demanding and impatient.

Kay could feel the blood rushing to her face again. 'Yes,' she murmured.

'I'm sorry,' he said, cocking one ear, 'I didn't hear that.'

'I did!'

'You must have known that was a serious criminal act.' He leaned back in his chair and grinned. 'You've got some nerve, I'll say that. It takes a brazen face to pull off something like that.'

'It was the only way.'

'Mmmmm . . . and there's not much point being in a place like Spain if you've no pocket money.'

'I had pocket money. We're not exactly on poor street, you know.'

Giving her a warning look, the officer continued. 'Did you take Mr Woods's salary, Kay?'

'No. I'm not a thief.'

'But you are a forger? And some would say that's even more serious than stealing. What did you do with the empty registered envelope?'

'I took it to the post room with the salary in it.'

'But we've questioned three people in the post room. None of them can remember seeing it. Where did you get the money from to pay for this holiday abroad?'

'I worked for it.'

'But Thompson's only pay you seven pounds ten shillings a week.'

'I got another job. In the evenings. In the sweet shop.'

'Your boss doesn't seem to know anything about that. No one that we spoke to mentioned it. Seems a bit strange.'

'We're not meant to have a second job. Company policy.'

'So you're a liar too.'

'I am not!' Kay's voice was cracking, but she willed herself to stay calm. She wasn't going to let him beat her down.

'You told them you were breaking the rules, did you?'

'No. I didn't tell them anything. I would have got the sack if they'd found out.'

'You know what I think?' He leaned forward, pushed the red receipt book under her nose and slowly tapped the altered entry with his finger. 'I think you wrote *Salaries seven. Bought Ledger.* And that's what the young man signed for. Once he had left the office, you made the seven look like an M and wrote *eight* down next to it.'

Kay only took in half of that. She was more concerned with him saying that Stephen Drake had signed for eight. 'I remember now!' She sat up, a

smile on her face. 'I remember! He stood there and counted the salaries, they all do. They have to, before they sign. Then he asked me again what was gonna happen to Mr Woods's. He must have seen it there! I must have put it in the collection group instead of the registered envelope batch.'

'But you said you also remember typing the registered envelope. And putting the salary in. And taking it to the post room!'

'Well I got confused! You keep confusing me! I remember filling the envelopes. I can't be expected to remember every name! I don't know, I must have made a mistake!'

'So that leaves the empty registered envelope that you typed. Where do you think that is?'

'I don't know. Maybe I never typed one out for him! Maybe I forgot! Why don't you talk to Mr Drake?'

'We have. He flatly denies seeing a pay packet for Mr Woods. And I believe him. He also swears you didn't alter that entry while he was there.' The inspector raised one eyebrow and stared into Kay's flushed face. There was a long pause.

'Kay Armstrong, I am now going to have to charge you.'

'No!' Kay cried, 'No! I didn't do it! It's not fair!' As Kay stood up, moved behind her chair

and picked it up, McCormack's colleague was in like a flash, seizing her by the arms. The stream of words seemed to strike out and hit the centre of her stomach, sending flashes of white light and a million sparks up through her head.

Kay remembered little of the journey back to Stepney in the taxi. Sitting in the armchair in front of the gas fire at home, she didn't want to think about King's Cross police station. She would try to wipe it out for ever.

'D'yer want me to unpack for you, Kay? Or would you rather wait till the morning?'

'I'll wait.'

'You sure you don't want to show me your gifts?' Laura was doing her best to cheer Kay up.

'Give it a rest, Laura,' Jack said, 'it'll soon be bloody morning.'

'Yeah, don't feel like it though, does it? I don't know about you, but I can't see myself sleeping yet.'

'I'm gonna have to go through all that again.' Kay stared into the glow of the gas fire.

'Oh, no you're not!' snapped Jack. 'There'll be a solicitor present next time.'

'What good will that do? I'm a forger. I even admitted it.' She gazed up at him, almost trance-like. 'What does bail mean, Dad? I don't really understand.'

Jack rubbed his forehead and sighed. 'I dunno. They need time to investigate. Make more inquiries. It's all down to form-filling, I s'pose. Anyway, you're here and not locked up in a cell, that's something.'

The room fell quiet as the three of them gazed into the blue and yellow flames of the fire.

'How's aunt Liz?' Kay rubbed her swollen eyes, which were puffy from crying.

'She's all right. Been talking to your uncle Bert again,' he laughed. Catching Laura's eye and her scowl, he tried to keep a straight face. 'She's gonna drive us mad now, you wait and see.'

'Why?' Kay asked.

'Saw it all coming, didn't she? Reckons Bert sent her a message a couple of days ago. "Kay, watch Kay, trouble".'

'Dad!' Taking a sudden interest, Kay cupped her mug. 'You're kidding me?'

'Does seem strange, I must admit,' Jack conceded.

'Strange, nothing! She was worried about Kay being abroad, that's all. It was on her mind.'

'Yeah, I s'pose you're right.' Lying back in the armchair, Jack stared out. 'I might go with 'er one night. Wouldn't mind a word with Bert.' He ignored Laura's sigh. 'I wonder if Mum and Dad are with

him? Or our dog, even? Do dogs bark in heaven? That's the question.'

That was too much for Kay. She started to laugh. 'Be a noisy bloody place if they did.'

'Come on then. Let's see what you've dragged back from half way across the world.' Jack had achieved his goal, seeing the smile back on his daughter's pinched face.

'I haven't got the energy,' Kay said, hoping he would get the suitcase for her.

'We'll 'ave to wait till tomorrow then, won't we.' He sniffed and stretched his long legs.

'No you will not!' Kay jumped up from her armchair and marched out of the room. 'You'll look at everything now.'

'That was mean, Jack. You could have got it for her.'

'I know that, Laura.' He grinned and winked at her.

'Oh, right. Yeah. It worked too.' She chuckled then drew a deep breath. 'Talk about two peas in a pod.' She sipped her tea. 'What a life, eh?'

'It's only what you make it, Laura,' he said, looking up at the ceiling, wondering if she would remember her telling him that once.

She managed not to smile. 'It's not very nice when it crumbles before you though, is it?' She repeated

the answer he had made two years ago when they were going through a crisis in their marriage.

It amused Jack that she had remembered, and surprised him. Laura was just as deep as he was, then?

Chapter Nine

The following Monday morning before Kay left for Thompson's, she and Laura shared a gloomy breakfast, sitting in the kitchen.

'I don't want to go.' Kay broke off a piece of toast. 'They probably all think I did it.' Feeling sick inside, she sipped some water, hoping it would ease the nausea.

'You don't have any choice, Kay. If you don't go to work as normal it'll make you look guilty.' Laura tipped cold tea from the teapot into the sink. 'Try and eat a bit of that toast, love. You've hardly touched anything all weekend.'

'I can't. It'll get stuck in my throat again.' She dropped the toast on to her plate.

'My gut feeling is to go with you. Take a day off work. Mondays are always quiet. They'd give me the time off, I'm sure of it.'

'No. If I have to go, I'll go by myself.' Kay

dragged herself from the kitchen chair. 'I've got nothing to hide.'

'No. Someone has though, Kay, and wouldn't it be great if you found out who took that money?'

'Yeah. I s'pose it would.'

'You don't have to tell them you've been charged.'

'Oh yes I do!' A surge of defiance rose inside her. 'I'm gonna make sure everyone knows before they find out and whisper behind my back. Yeah, I'll go in. I'll show them. Don't you worry, Mum. They're not gonna get away with this, the bastards.'

'Kay! You're above that kind of language!'

'Am I? I don't feel it. Not any more.' Collecting her handbag and suede jacket, she swept her long blonde hair back off her face. 'I'm a hardened criminal now,' she half joked.

'Well, if you ain't a sight for sore eyes,' Juanita chuckled as Kay sat down beside her on the bus. 'I expected a little more colour in your cheeks. You look as if you've been dragged through hell.'

'I have,' Kay quietly said. 'Trouble is, I'm still there trying to crawl out.'

Juanita sucked her teeth and slowly shook her head. 'What happened to you out there, eh?' The smile had gone from her face.

'Out there was great. I fell in love. It's back here

210

that's the problem.' Kay turned away, willing herself to be strong. She mustn't cry. She would walk into Thompson's with her head held high.

'Are you ready for it?' Kay gave Juanita a wry smile.

'No, but you had better get it off your chest.'

Kay started at the very beginning when she made the crucial mistake and altered the receipt book. She gave a methodical account of the whole drama almost as if she were recounting it to herself. Remembering, conveying, in a detached voice, what had gone on since they had last spoke.

Before either of them realized, the bus was pulling up at Kay's stop. Taking a piece of paper from her pocket, Juanita quickly wrote down her telephone number. 'Phone me this evening or earlier if you want to talk. I'm usually home by four-thirty.'

Slipping the piece of paper into her pocket, Kay thanked her friend and jumped down from the bus feeling much better than when she got on. Her stomach was still in a turmoil, threatening to throw everything out one minute and striking her with pain the next. But not her mind. Her mind was clear. Her conscience was clear. And her determination strong.

From the minute she stepped into the lift, the

atmosphere could have been cut with a knife. Alf the lift man gave her a sympathetic smile while two of the women from the canteen threw her a knowing look. Their expression said it all. They thought she was guilty.

'I suppose the whole bloody building knows about it?' Kay said, firing the question at Alf.

'It's been the talk of the town,' he smiled. 'And a lot of people are very angry. We know you're a cheeky cow at times but we don't think you're a thief. So keep your chin up and don't let anyone put you down. If they do, come and see me for a pep talk.' Alf spoke in a fatherly fashion, which touched Kay.

'Thanks Alf.' She gave him a wink and walked away, pushing the swing doors with more vengeance then she meant to. Her plan was to remain cool. Cool and clever. Listening out for any remarks that were derogatory, any looks of suspicion. She needed to know who her friends were before she could attack the enemy. And she would attack. Verbal abuse or otherwise. Her bottled-up anger was bursting to escape.

Making a grand entrance into the Accounts office, Kay stood her ground, smiling defiantly at her colleagues. There was a deathly hush as each one turned to her. First it was Doreen, doing her best

to smile. Then James, the junior clerk who, though she couldn't swear to it, seemed to be sneering.

'Morning, Kay,' Mr Grieves finally said. 'I'd like a word in private.' He looked embarrassed.

'No need for that. Anything you've got to say can be said in public. My washing is already on the line.' She smiled back at him. 'And before you ask, no. I didn't do it. I've been charged, but I'm innocent. OK?'

There was a look of surprise from both Doreen and Mr Grieves. Even James looked as if he might fall off his chair.

'The question is,' Kay spoke as if she were in court, the prosecutor rather than the accused. 'Where *is* the missing registered envelope with its fat contents?'

They stared at her in disbelief. How could she joke at a time like this? 'Would you like me to arrange some coffee?' Doreen looked sick with worry.

'No thanks, Doreen. I'll wait for the break. I've got too much to do.' Charged with a new-found courage, Kay stepped towards her desk, pulled out the top drawer and tipped the contents into the middle of the office floor. She did the same with every drawer and container on her desk until there was nothing left. The others sat rooted to the spot,

staring down at the heap of office sundries, paper, notebooks and files.

'It's all right, I'm not gonna put a match to anything. Not yet.' Falling to her knees she began to search through the tip.

'Kay, we've already looked. Mr Grieves and I went through everything. That's why we came in early.'

'After this, it's your desk, James. And then Doreen's, and then yours, Mr Grieves. We must leave no stone unturned!'

Fearing for her state of mind, Mr Grieves stepped forward and offered his hand. 'Come on, Kay. There's no need for that.'

'No? Well you try being dragged off to a police station the minute you walk back from your holiday and see how it feels! You try being arrested! Being questioned and charged for a crime you didn't commit. Then come and tell me that!'

The opening of the office door broke the tension. 'Ah, Mr Grieves, the Chairman would like a word with both you and Kay.' Miss Jamieson, the Managing Director's secretary, stared down at the floor, at Kay and at the mess.

'Ah, Miss Jamieson!' Kay made no move to get up, but leaned back on her hands and tossed her silky blonde hair. 'That's a very smart outfit

you're wearing today. Straight from Harrods, no doubt?'

Ignoring the remark, Rebecca Jamieson turned to Mr Grieves. 'We have Mr Drake with us now.'

Quick to her feet, Kay stood in front of the haughty woman. 'Have we really? How splendid. Excuse me.' She pushed her aside and stormed out of the room, making her way to the Chairman's chambers.

Drake and the Chairman, Mr Thompson, stared blankly at Kay as she burst into the office. 'Everyone, it seems, has decided to get in early today. I wonder why?'

Paying no attention to the pleas from Doreen and Mr Grieves who were on her heels, Kay moved towards Drake. 'You're a liar. And I think you might be a thief as well.'

'Now then, Kay . . .' Mr Grieves's voice went over her head.

'And d'yer know what happens to a liar and a thief where I come from? You know, the other side of the tracks, where only the lowest of the low live?'

'I should think an old lag would have no trouble finding refuge in those Dickensian backstreets,' Drake flashed a knowing smile at the Chairman, 'code of silence and camaraderie.'

'You gormless overgrown *maggot*!' Kay slowly

shook her head and found herself laughing at him. 'Dickensian? It's time you woke up, cretin.' Not wanting to spend any more time in his company, she stepped forward, grabbed him by the lapels of his jacket and with strength borrowed from her anger, pushed him across the office, knocking an antique statue flying. '*We* get arrested! Even if we're innocent! Now get up! Get up and tell the truth, you spineless bastard!'

As Drake started to raise himself on to his elbows, Mr Grieves stepped forward, but Doreen grabbed his arm. 'Leave her,' she murmured. 'She knows more than we do.'

'You saw me alter that book and you know it!' Kay lunged towards Drake again, grabbing his tie and glaring into his eyes. 'Tell them the truth, you sodding coward! *Tell them!*'

'I have told them.' Curling his top lip, Drake pushed his face close to hers. 'You're no better than your scum family,' he sneered.

A flash of fury shot through Kay and before she could stop herself, she drew back her arm, clenched her fist and used all her power to land a punch square on his face. Overcome with anger and humiliation, Drake shot forward and grabbed Kay's hair, pulling until her head almost touched the floor. 'Apologize, you slut!'

'That's enough!' Grieves pushed Miss Jamieson out of his way. 'Let go of her, Drake, before I—'

'*Stephen*! Out here! Now!' The booming voice of Drake's father took them all by surprise. 'Move!'

Everyone's attention turned on the red-faced man standing in the doorway. 'I'll deal with this,' he said, assuming command. 'In *private*!'

The colour draining from his face, Stephen Drake pulled himself to his feet, pushed his shoulders back and tried to cover his fear. It was clear to everyone that his father reigned supreme. He instantly filled the room with his oppressive presence.

'And who are you, sir, to come barging into my office?' Mr Thompson was not the least pleased.

'Stephen's father,' he returned curtly, ending it.

'From the Met?' Kay smiled knowingly. 'Here to save your son's skin, no doubt.' She ignored the urgent look on Mr Grieves's face, warning her to take heed.

'I'll show the gentlemen into the boardroom,' Rebecca Jamieson smiled benignly as she led the way out of the Director's chambers. 'We hadn't realized you were dealing with this case—'

'I'm not!' he said definitively as he followed her out of the room.

Once Mr Thompson had ushered everyone except

Kay out of his office, he closed the door and sighed. 'It'll be much easier in the long run if you tell the truth, you know.'

With her back to him, Kay asked if she could have a glass of water. Filled with disappointment that he really believed she was guilty, the anger which had fuelled her actions earlier began to drain away and she made no effort to stop the tears.

'We shan't press charges, and *if* the police are prepared to drop the matter, we'll settle for your confession. Of course it will mean your finding employment elsewhere, and I can't promise to give you a clean reference.'

Taking the glass of water from him, Kay felt like giving in, saying that she had taken the money, and putting an end to the whole thing. It might be easier to confess than to fight. She could walk away from the building. Away from the accusing faces.

'Crime really doesn't pay, you know. I should have thought you would have learned that from your brother who spent time in prison.'

'I haven't got a brother,' she murmured.

'Oh, well, your uncle then.' He waved his hand impatiently.

Her uncle. So that had come out too. While she had been in Spain believing that her colleagues were struggling along without her, people had been

delving into her private family business, discussing her uncle. What right had they to do that? What right had they to accuse her of stealing when she had never once taken a penny that didn't belong to her? Who did these people think they were?

'Does your wife know you've been fornicating with your secretary?' She smiled into his shocked face. Fornicating. She liked that word. She remembered it from senior school. It had been the cause of a humorous debate between the teasing adolescent boys in her class and the naïve student teacher who thought they had been interested in her religious knowledge lesson.

'You could end up in court for that, you know,' Kay continued. 'If Jamieson's old man filed for a divorce you'd be—'

'That's enough!' His red angry face looked fit to burst. 'You insolent wench!'

'Not very nice, is it, Mr Thompson? To be accused of something you haven't done? How would you feel if your wife believed the lie and stopped trusting you?' By the expression on the Chairman's face, Kay had a feeling she might have touched a nerve.

A tapping on the door stopped her getting in too deep. She could hardly believe herself, speaking to the Chairman like that. She would have apologized

if Rebecca Jamieson's sickly smiling face had not appeared.

'Would you come to the boardroom please, Kay.' The polite request was delivered as if it were an order.

'No, I won't. I've had enough. You go and play detectives if it gives you a thrill. *I* am going home!'

'I don't think that would be wise.' Again the sickly smile.

'Oh, get out of here, both of you. I'm fed up to the back teeth with it.' Mr Thompson poured himself a whisky, keeping his back to them.

Kay pushed her way past Miss Jamieson and strode along the corridor towards the boardroom. Again she was filled with determination to prove her innocence, if only to put Jamieson in her place. Kay hadn't bargained for the scene that awaited her in the plush, oak-panelled room.

Stooping beside his thickset father, Stephen Drake was a different person. His cockiness had been replaced by a bent head and a twisted expression. 'I didn't mean to get you in trouble,' he said quietly.

'We can't tell *talk* from *mutter*!' His father barked into his ear, causing Drake to shudder. 'And *stand up straight*!'

As his ashen face lifted to Kay's, she was overwhelmed with pity, and felt like telling him not to

let himself be dictated to by his father, but the great bully of a man scared her too.

'I'm sorry for what I've put you through,' Drake inhaled slowly, doing his best to conduct himself with some self-respect. 'I'll set the record straight,' he said.

Kay's mind was racing. Why was she feeling guilty? Drake had deliberately lied, not giving a thought to the fact that she might have faced a prison sentence. Now he was offering to set the record straight, as if he were doing her a favour. As if *she* should be grateful. And the worst of it was, she did feel a sickening sense of gratitude. Looking from him to his father, Kay knew where to lay the blame: at the feet of this overbearing man who stood before her. The father, who was returning her scorn with a grimace, was at the root of the trouble. He was sending her a message. She was a loser.

'I always knew,' Rebecca Jamieson chimed in, startling Kay who had not heard her come in. 'Under the magnifying glass that M *was* clearly an M, not a seven. We felt sure you were innocent all along.'

'You lying cow! They told me at the station, *you* thought I did it. You *regretted* taking on someone from a housing estate. And this boy, as you called him, must be innocent, because he comes from a

good family. Because *his* father is a high-ranking officer in the Met!'

'Yes, well,' she smirked foolishly, 'you can hardly blame us for wondering.'

Without pausing for a second, Kay slapped the secretary's arrogant face and enjoyed the tingling it left in the palm of her hand. 'Now fuck off. All of you!'

As if suddenly struck dumb, the three of them stared at Kay as, turning her back on them, she let out a low whimper and hugged herself. Unable to cope with this display of emotion, they each scuttled faint-heartedly from the room, leaving her to it.

An excited buzz was spreading outside the board-room door, but Kay moved to the large window and stared out.

'He admitted it!' Doreen's voice rang through her brain. Why was everyone so overjoyed? Had they believed she'd done it? Didn't they realize that the truth would come out in the end? Now it was Marge from the switchboard who was shouting for joy. And Ivy the tea lady.

Turning from the window, she gazed at the frosted panelled glass wall, which separated the room from the corridor and Kay from her colleagues grouped together outside, enjoying the euphoria of a crisis

resolved. She felt as if she were acting in a film. A movie in which she was the star. Why were they reacting like this? Why weren't they angry? Or feeling like her, sad and let down? Why *did* she feel so hurt, so betrayed? It was a different pain inside now.

A large notepad and pen lying on the long, highly polished table caught Kay's eye. Sitting down on a padded chair, she picked up the biro and wrote in large letters THEY THOUGHT IT WAS ME. She looked up from the pad to the window, and feeling strangely drawn to it, she dragged herself from the chair.

Gazing down at the busy street, thoughts came flying at her. *Wouldn't it serve them right if I jumped? The crowd would soon gather round my broken body. Someone from Thompson's would hear the commotion and look out. Word would spread. I would be dead, and it would be their fault. No more having to face Drake or the police. No more threats of a prison sentence for forgery.*

Behind her, Kay heard the creaking of the heavy mahogany door as Mr Grieves pushed it open. 'Doreen said you'd be in here.'

Keeping her back to him, Kay kept her eyes on the street below. 'They thought I stole that money,' she repeated quietly.

'No, Kay.' He sounded choked. 'None of us believed it. That's why Doreen and I were in early. We searched the office from top to bottom.'

She could feel him moving towards her. 'Please don't come any closer.' Even to herself, Kay's voice sounded different, toneless.

'Doreen's fetching some sweet tea for you.'

'I don't want anything.' Kay opened the window and leaned out. The people below looked so small. The street noise was inviting.

'Why don't we sit down for a while?' Grieves was trying his best.

'Will you please tell Doreen I don't want any tea.' Kay spoke in a monotone. 'Would you please go.'

'No, Kay, I won't.' His voice was quiet but firm. 'You've been through a lot. I dare say you're still in a state of shock. I think we all are.'

'No. You don't know what it feels like. Otherwise you wouldn't be here. You'd want to be on your own.'

'Is that honestly what you want? A few minutes by yourself?'

She turned to him and smiled as she cried. 'Yeah. It's OK. I'm not gonna . . .' She looked at the open window. 'I'm not brave enough. If someone else came along and took the life from me, that would

224

be different.' She wiped her face with the back of her hand. 'Eternal sleep,' she grinned. 'I wouldn't say no.'

Ignoring Kay's request for solitude, Grieves moved closer and placed one arm around her shoulders. 'I wish you could feel as relieved as I do about that confession.'

Pleased that he hadn't left the room, Kay allowed her head to rest against his shoulder. 'Part of me feels good about it, but the rest of me?' She looked thoughtfully into his grey eyes, 'It's having to face everyone. They all know about it.'

'Oh, I'm sure they do. And you can bet that within the hour they'll also know about Drake's confession.' He smiled into her tear-stained face. 'It seems a shame to let them celebrate without you and, well, with your permission, I would like to demand that some of today is taken up with a meeting, in the canteen. I think the Chairman should make a public apology. On behalf of the firm, of course.'

'He wouldn't go for that.'

'Oh, I think he will. No choice really. I should think several of the staff have been toying with the idea of walking out. But if you were given a public apology . . .'

Kay screwed her face up and forced back tears.

'That would be—' she took a deep breath and exhaled slowly, 'that would be—' as much as she tried, she couldn't finish the sentence.

'You'd like that?' Grieves smiled broadly.

She nodded, her lips squeezed shut.

'Good. I'll see to it now.' He turned to leave and then stopped. 'Do you want to be present?' Her half-smiling, pained face said it all, and a slow nod of approval filled him with righteous indignation.

'We'll set the records straight, don't you worry.'

'There *is* something else.' Kay chewed on the inside of her cheek and wondered whether to continue.

'I know about your other extra employment, Kay. Doreen told me in confidence. It won't go any further.'

Kay sighed with relief. She was pleased he knew. 'What if Mr Thompson finds out?' She wiped a tear from her neck.

'I'll deal with that if and when it comes up. I don't think you have anything to worry about.' He winked at her and left the room.

Trying not to look too worried, Laura leaned on the balcony wall pretending she was taking the air and enjoying the last of the late afternoon sun.

She stubbed out a cigarette-end in the earth of the flower-filled window-boxes as she saw Jack striding through the playground, on his way back from a dockers' meeting. His unmistakable lean body and broad shoulders filled her with warmth. She gave him a wave and wondered how he had managed to get through the day.

'Kay back yet?' Jack tried to sound casual.

'No. Should be along any minute.' She followed him into the kitchen. 'How'd the meeting go?'

'OK.' He looked sheepishly at her. 'I s'pose Kay would 'ave phoned if that firm was giving her a hard time?'

'Of course she would.' She turned her back on him and covered her face with her hands.

'I wish I could say something to make you feel better, Laura, but I can't. I've been worried sick all day. And wild. Bloody wild, I'll tell yer.'

Sitting down opposite him at the Formica table, Laura lit another cigarette. 'They won't put her away, surely?'

'Who knows what they'll do. I'll tell you what, though—' Jack stopped dead in his tracks as he caught sight of Kay passing by the kitchen window. 'Here she is! Try to think of something else to talk about, for Christ's sake.'

'Why? Don't you think she'll want to talk about it?'

'I don't know what to think any more, tell the truth,' Jack said, staring down at the floor. He expected Kay to look depressed and drained, and tried to fix a smile on his face.

'Guess what?' Kay beamed as she stood in the doorway of the kitchen. 'He's confessed! I've had a public apology *and* the police are not gonna press charges over the passport form!' She paused for a breather. 'Kept my passport though. Said I've got to wait until next year till I apply for another one. Let me off with a stiff warning.' She spread her hands and hunched her shoulders, mimicking Pamela's Jewish father, to Jack and Laura's amusement. 'You could say *something*?'

'This isn't one of your silly jokes, is it?'

'No,' Kay dropped on to a chair, 'it's over.' She clicked her fingers. 'Just like that.' Then, realizing that her hand was still painful from punching Drake, she hid her discomfort. She would relate that scene later. 'What's for tea?'

'Dad's gonna get a Chinese take-away. And what d'yer mean, he confessed? Who confessed?'

'It's a long story. Can't I tell you tomorrow?'

'You're not having us on, are you?' Jack's eyes narrowed and he cocked his head to one side.

'Nope.' She stood up and kissed him on the forehead. 'It's over. I will tell you all about it. But not yet, eh?' Her eyes filled with tears again, but she managed to compose herself. 'I've really had it.' Reaching out for Laura, she gave her a big hug. 'I'm sorry I caused all that trouble. You know, signing the passport form. It was stupid. Immature.'

'Kay! Who confessed?' Jack's face was taking on an angry, determined look.

'The bloke who took it!'

'Yeah fine, but *who* took it?'

'I don't want to talk about it. It's over and done with!'

Laura looked at her daughter curiously. She seemed different, older. Her mind flashed to the holiday in Spain. 'Did you meet anyone nice on the Costa Brava?'

'What made you ask that?' Kay sounded both defensive and pleased that she had been asked.

'Just wondered.'

'I did as it happened. His name's Chris. He lives out there. Got his own bakery.'

'How old is he?' Jack's voice took on a different tone.

'Twenty-two,' she said, knowing he was in fact twenty-four.

Jack slowly nodded. 'Just as well you left him behind then. He's too old for you.' He looked her straight in the eye and made it clear that he meant what he said. 'Now then, sit down and fill me in on what happened today.'

'Oh please, Dad! I've had enough. Can't I just go round Pamela's and forget about it? Just for tonight? Pamela's mum'll feed me. You know what they're like for food.'

'Well if you'd rather 'ave herrings than sweet and sour pork.' Jack teased.

'Jewish people don't eat herrings *all* the time . . .'

'They smell like they do.'

'That's *so* insulting!'

'Your dad's tormenting you, Kay. You should know him by now.' She tried not to smile back at Jack.

'Go on, get going and ask Pamela's mother if she's made one of her nice poppy-seed cakes this week.'

'Now what was it you always told me? *Those who ask, don't get . . .*'

'I didn't ask you to ask, did I?' he grinned.

'*And those who don't ask, don't want.* I'm sure it went something like that.' Now Kay sounded as if she were talking to herself as she picked up her handbag and made for the door.

'I always gave you a tanner when you asked for a threepenny bit, though!' Jack called after her.

'Well,' Laura sighed, 'that's that then! We've been worrying ourselves sick all day, and she's been in seventh heaven.'

'Yeah. Puts years on you, don't it?' Jack looked genuinely concerned about himself. 'Why has Kay made me feel old all of a sudden?'

'Bernard! Bernard! Put up the closed sign will you? Supper is ready!' Pamela's mother shook her head at Kay. 'That man is so slow . . . It's a very sad thing. He reaches forty and settles for being old.'

'Why must you shout, Lillian?' Pamela's father stood in the doorway between the shop and the living quarters.

'Why? Because you are stone-deaf.' She shrugged at the girls. 'I would have thought that was obvious.'

'But if I am stone-deaf, why shout? Why not chalk messages on the blackboard?' Bernard winked at Pamela and Kay who were managing to keep a straight face. 'You don't look very brown, Kay.'

'Kay was arrested over the weekend.' Pamela couldn't contain it any longer. A silence fell as her parents gazed impassively at Kay.

'I was charged as well. They let me out on bail.'

Lillian and Bernard slowly and simultaneously lowered themselves into their chairs. 'Go on,' Lillian said, while scooping and serving fried fish. 'What happened?'

Kay told them the entire story from beginning to end, and the way they had treated her like royalty at Thompson's that day. She carefully skipped the bit about forging her passport form. She told them everything that Laura and Jack had wanted to know. Somehow it just seemed easier with this family. She knew they wouldn't continually throw questions at her, or butt in. They were listeners. At least to visitors. Not to each other. Not often.

'So what happened to the registered envelope?' Bernard asked after a respectful pause. Everyone waited while Kay searched for an answer.

'I don't know.'

'Would you like to know?'

'I would. I really would.' She became thoughtful. 'I think I typed the name and address on it. I remember the name.'

'What time of the day was it?' Bernard asked, in his usual calm manner.

'The afternoon. Before tea-break.'

'And this list? It was in alphabetical order?'

Kay thought about it. 'Yeah.'

'And his name?'

232

'Mr Woods.'

Bernard smiled quietly at her and ate a little more fish.

'I did type it. Just before tea-break,' Kay said, as it all came flooding back. 'It was the last one! I typed his *just* before the bell went!' She placed her knife and fork down. 'Do you think someone came in and stole the registered envelope?'

Bernard chuckled. 'Who wants an empty soiled envelope?' He took some potato salad.

'Well, what else could have happened to it?'

'What do you do the minute, or second, before you leave your desk to go to the canteen?' He looked at her with his brown, sleepy eyes.

Kay thought about it. 'I push my typewriter to the back of the desk. Don't ask me why.'

'Why?' Bernard looked from one to the other, hoping to get a reaction to his humour.

'It's a habit.' Kay shrugged in true Jewish style. Something she slipped into when in their company.

Disappointed that all three of them had missed his joke, he pressed on. 'Is there a gap?' He motioned with his fork.

Kay's face suddenly lit up as she remembered. 'Yes, there is! I sometimes push my biscuit crumbs down there to get rid of 'em.'

233

'Well, there we have it. Tomorrow you ask your boss to look. Let him find it. Tell him Mr Simmonds helped you remember, eh?'

'I will!' Kay grinned, 'I'll definitely tell him.'

'Pamela, why aren't you eating?' Lillian gazed at her daughter's full plate.

'I'm not hungry.'

'So?'

'If she's not hungry, Lillian, why must she eat?' Ignoring the scornful look from his wife, Bernard turned to Kay.

'When did you last visit your grandpa?'

'I don't know. Just before our holiday, I think. Why?'

'I saw him yesterday. In Petticoat Lane. The old man looked lonely. We had a chat.'

'He hasn't been in the shop lately as a matter of fact,' Lillian said. 'He always has the same thing: four rollmops and some cream cheese. Maybe he's gone off soused herrings. I don't think he came in for three weeks now; yes, it must be three weeks. Pamela, if you're not going to eat that, stop messing with it.'

'He asked me about the Brady Street Club.'

The three of them waited for him to finish what he was saying but he just shrugged.

Irritated by her father's measured nature, Pamela

sighed loudly. 'Well don't just leave it in the air. What was he asking?'

He gazed at all three of them in disbelief, 'It's not obvious?' There was an impatient pause. 'He asked me if he could be involved in some way.' He turned to Lillian. 'I think he misses the youth club.'

'But my grandfather's nearly seventy!'

'Once you've been involved with young people you get hooked.'

'Why can't he spend some time at the Brady Club then?' Pamela folded her napkin and looked sideways at him.

'Because he's not Jewish.' There was a touch of regret in his voice. 'I don't make the rules, Pamela.'

Preoccupied with her grandfather, Kay's mind wandered from the conversation. When she really thought about it she realized that she hadn't been in to see him for nearly a month, and he lived so close by. Suddenly filled with guilt, she pictured him in his tiny cottage going through his daily routine, which was centred around feeding himself and keeping himself and the house clean. His daily visit to the local was probably more for company than anything else.

'I think I'll go now, see if he's all right. You coming, Pam?'

'Hang on a minute. I have to speak with my parents.'

Bernard peered at her. 'She's after something, Lillian – hide the chequebook.'

Pamela raised an eyebrow and gave him one of her famous glares.

'So talk.' Lillian looked concerned.

'I'll wait until you've finished eating.'

'It's dirty talk?' She almost dropped her fork. 'I said something was wrong with this girl.' She narrowed her eyes, 'Did you get a period yesterday?'

'Oh, for heaven's sake!' She threw her fork down. 'Yes, I *did*!'

Lillian breathed a small sigh of relief. 'For small mercies.'

'I want to move out. Get myself a studio flat.'

Another silence filled the room and Kay almost choked on her lemonade as she watched the changing expressions on Lillian's face.

'You don't need a flat. You've got the best room.' She spoke in a determined, no-nonsense tone. 'A four-foot bed, an easy chair. A lovely carpet. Curtains that meet.'

'I want my independence.'

'At seventeen?' Bernard found it amusing.

'My grandfather's got a spare room,' Kay said, matter-of-factly.

'Has he? Right! What're we waiting for, then?' Pamela kissed her bemused father on the forehead and tried to catch her mother's left cheek, but Lillian pulled away. 'It'll kill two birds with one stone. Company for the old man and independence for me.'

'I was only saying—' Kay shrugged at Pamela's parents.

'It's a strange joke?' Lillian asked, once they had left.

'It's no more than a fancy,' Bernard reached across and patted her hand, 'it will pass. Stop worrying.'

Linking arms, Kay and Pamela strolled along the Whitechapel Road enjoying the early-evening buzz. There were only a few stalls left, clearing away, but still the 'waste' had a feeling of market day about it. People were rushing to and fro chasing buses, and an ambulance was racing along the main road with its emergency light and bell piercing through the air, making its way to the London Hospital.

'Everyone looks so pale and scrawny,' Kay said, looking around at the passers-by.

'I know. We've got to get back there before next year, Kay. I'm dying inside.'

'And where's the money coming from? You're in debt to your parents as it is. Now you want to get

a flat. That'll cost you. Even if you did move in with my grandfather, you'd still have to pay him something for your board and lodging.'

'I don't want a flat. I only said that. Give them something serious to worry about so that when I do ask if I can go back to Spain this year . . . when I "give in" over wanting my independence . . .'

'You conniving *cow*!' Kay began to laugh, but stopped the instant she remembered that her passport had been taken away. 'I won't be able to go,' she said miserably.

'I know. I can't help it, Kay. I've got to go back. I can't stop thinking about Charles.'

'Well you know what? I think we should be celebrating.' Kay was desperate to change the subject away from what now seemed like paradise. 'I'm a free woman! Come on.' She marched her friend forward. 'We're going to see an old friend of mine. You'll love him.'

Strolling along Vallance Road, they checked the numbers looking for Terry Button's house, and were surprised when a dark blue Jaguar pulled up beside them.

'I thought that was you, babe. Who you looking for?'

Peering into the car, Kay recognized Bert's brothers, Frank and Freddie, in the front seats. 'My friend lives

along here somewhere. Terry Button. Don't suppose you know him?'

'Terry Button?' Frank turned to his passenger in the back seat. 'Ring any bells, Reg?'

'Yeah, as it 'appens.' A knowing smile spread across the tanned face as he looked up at Kay. 'You'll find him in the Sun. He's got a lovely voice.' He looked away and smiled. 'Terri with an i.'

'Why?' Pamela looked puzzled.

'No . . . an *i*,' Reggie joked.

'The lead singer?' Freddie said with a wry smile.

'Give the girls a lift. Save 'em walking.' Reggie's quiet, serious voice caught Kay's attention. She couldn't help thinking how good-looking he was, with thick black hair and eyebrows to match. There was something about him. A mysterious, almost menacing quality.

She opened the back door and slid along the seat up close to Reggie, making room for Pamela. 'I love the smell of leather in cars.'

'Goes well with that perfume you're wearing.' Reggie winked at Kay.

'Thanks. It's Coty, *L'aimant*.' Kay liked the look of him even more close up. His mohair suit and gold cuff-links were quite impressive. She found herself wishing he were a bit younger.

'Bit like a getaway car really,' said Pamela, mock

innocent. The remark was a real killer. It suddenly went very quiet.

'How was Spain then?' Frank asked, looking at her in his mirror. 'Your friend's got more colour than you 'ave.'

'Don't tell her that or she'll sulk. I'm Pame*lia* by the way.' This slight variation on her name was a new one to Kay.

Reggie leaned forward and offered her his hand. 'Reggie. All right?'

'I think you'd better call us Uncle as well, Pame*lia*.' Freddie managed to keep a straight face.

'No, that's all right. You're Kay's uncles, not mine.' She could slip so easily into her sophisticated act.

'Spain was great!' Kay said. 'A bit too hot at times.'

'It was only ninety degrees.' Pamela combed her fingers through her long dark hair.

The men found that mildly amusing but kept it to themselves as they cruised along Roman Road. 'How long 'ave you known Terri?' Reggie asked Kay.

'Oh, years. We used to go down hoppin' on the same farm. Haven't seen him since the last time we went. I don't s'pose he's changed much.' She tried to imagine him two years older.

'I wouldn't bank on it,' Reggie said quietly, with a touch of concern in his voice.

'We were very close,' she looked into Reggie's deep brown eyes. 'We shared secrets.'

Reggie gave her a knowing smile, showing his admiration for her tact. 'The boys are gonna drop me off just along here, girls, so I shan't be having the pleasure of your lovely company.' He checked the time on his Rolex watch. 'It's a pity those two are your uncles.'

'As I said before,' Pamela cut in, leaning forward and smiling at him, 'they're not mine.'

'And that you're both so young,' he continued. 'This'll do, Frank.'

Screeching to a halt, Frankie put the car into neutral. 'See you later, Reg.'

'You're not coming to the Sun then?' Kay smiled, making it sound like an invitation. She knew her uncles would be disturbed by it but she couldn't help herself. She could feel herself drawn in by Reggie's presence.

'Bit of business to attend to.' Reggie gave the boys a show of his hand and Kay a flirtatious wink. 'If you're still footloose in five years, I'll take you to the best restaurant in town! That's a promise.'

'Why five years?' she called out of the window.

'You'll be five years older!'

Dropping back in the comfortable seat, Kay grinned at Pamela, who was sulking. 'Reggie, eh? Talk about chemistry.' She ignored the mocking laughter from her uncles. 'A thousand invisible silver darts flashed between us . . .' she recited melodramatically, trying to make light of the sudden crush she had on a total stranger.

Frank and Freddie found it amusing. 'Don't mention his name to your dad, babe, will yer.'

'Why?' Pamela quite fancied him too. 'He was really polite.'

'Don't they get on then?' Kay should have known her uncles wouldn't give much away.

'You could say that,' Freddie chuckled.

Walking into the pub, Kay felt as if she had entered another world. Terry was on the stage, belting out 'Kiss Me Honey Honey Kiss Me' and singing it beautifully. Even though he wore a long black evening dress and had dyed his hair auburn, still she recognized him. When her uncle Frank asked what she wanted to drink, she heard herself ask for a sweet Martini as if someone else were voicing her request.

She heard her uncles talking across her. 'I don't think she did know his deepest secret.' Frank was laughing.

'You'd better make hers a double,' Freddie added.

Settling herself into a chair, Kay fixed her eyes on her friend. He had changed, that was clear. Not his face – his figure. Or was it all padding? He looked taller, slimmer.

'What's wrong with you? Have you seen a ghost, or what?' Pamela looked from Kay to Terry. 'Surely you've seen a drag queen before?'

'Don't call him that.'

'Why not? What's wrong with drag queen?'

'His name is Terry, OK?'

Terry finished the number and gracefully drank in the applause, and then announced the arrival of a long-lost friend. Signalling to the stage-hand, he indicated to him to throw the spotlight on Kay. Before she could object, she was floodlit.

'My best friend of many years: Miss Kay Armstrong!' Terry proclaimed joyfully.

Deeply embarrassed, Kay could feel herself blushing. 'I'll kill you for this,' she mouthed to Terry as he approached, arms outstretched.

Hanging on to each other, gripping tight, they seemed locked together, Kay almost overpowered by his French perfume. People's eyes were on them, but neither cared.

'Kay . . .' Terry's voice, now quiet, was heavy with remorse. 'Stay with me. Don't go. Please don't walk out.'

Kay gently pulled back and looked into his brimming eyes. 'Why would I do that, you silly cow?' she grinned.

Laughing, he posed for her: 'What d'yer think then? Better than my old jeans and wellies, or what?' His eyes held secret doubt.

'Terry. Shut up.' Kay hugged him again, whispering into his ear. 'It's what's inside that counts.'

Terry let out a sigh and slowly shook his head. 'I dreaded you walking in 'ere one day. Seeing me.'

'What d'yer want to drink, Terri?' Frank called from the bar.

'No, it's all right, thanks!'

'Go on, have one, Tel. He's my uncle.'

Terry turned towards the bar. 'He's your *uncle*?' He looked impressed. 'OK, thanks, I will! G and T please, love!'

'He's not . . .' Kay suddenly felt embarrassed, 'you know. He's married.' She felt herself go hot around the neck.

'Leave off, Kay. I'm not after everything in pants you know. It's me, Terry. And I've got a friend, OK? I'm no different to you when it comes to relationships.' He wiped the lipstick from the corner of his mouth. 'I'm not a tart, and I only dress like this when I'm performing.'

Kay widened her eyes questioningly.

'Performing on the stage!'

Kay's lips parted in surprise.

'*Singing*!' he laughed. 'Mind you, I have been asked to do a bit of striptease. Not 'ere. In a night-club.'

'And?' Kay hoped for the right answer.

'Would you?' The humour stopped there.

'No I wouldn't.'

'And neither would I!'

'Our drinks are up, come on. Come and meet my other best friend.'

Seated round a corner table, Kay, Pamela, Terry and the two uncles got on famously. They talked about everything from hop-picking to the future of the London docks to unions and management. 'Don't talk to *me* about management,' Kay said after her second Martini. 'I'm up to here with it.'

'Listen,' Terry suddenly said, 'I'd love to sit and listen to your opinion on the subject, Kay, but I must get changed before Ray comes in. He 'ates seeing me in drag.'

'Ray? *The* Ray?' She was referring to an old friend of Terry's who threatened to punch him when he learned that Terry wasn't attracted to girls.

'Yeah,' Terry shrugged. 'I know. It was 'is way of not accepting what he was feeling. I should 'ave

known really. He was always going on about how
this one or that one was . . . you know. Once he
saw it wasn't the end of the world for me . . .' he
shrugged.

Kay remembered the naked midnight dip in the
Medway. Ray had been mouthing off about fancying
her. It obviously hadn't been her fierce warnings
which had kept him at bay. Suddenly his behaviour,
which used to exasperate her, made sense. Ray had
been trying to disprove something.

'Shame,' Kay murmured, 'we might have got on
a lot better if he'd admitted it.'

Leaving them to it, Terry swanned off to a back
room to change. Watching him, Kay couldn't help
thinking how he looked every bit a woman.

'Anyway, where was I?' Kay asked.

'Management, babe, and why you're celebrating
tonight.' Her curly-headed uncle chuckled.

Once again she related the story, pleased to offload
it and flattered that her uncles showed interest. She
knew Pamela was bored, wishing they could be
with younger company, but that was tough. Kay
had been through a lot and thought she deserved
some attention.

'So what d'yer wanna do about it?' Freddie spoke
in a matter-of-fact tone but there was a suggestion
of revenge in his voice.

'Nothing. Forget it, I suppose.' She shrugged and sipped her drink.

'It wasn't Friday the thirteenth was it?' Frank grinned.

'It was a Friday, yeah. But not the thirteenth.'

And that was enough. From her brief résumé, the brothers had worked out that the cash for the wages was collected from the local bank fortnightly and on a Friday.

'You're right, Kay babe. It's best to forget about it,' Freddie said, looking at his watch. 'Time we made a move, Frank.'

'You girls be all right walking back by yourselves? Or d'yer wanna lift?'

'We know these backstreets like the backs of our hands,' Kay said reassuringly, 'and besides, I want to see Terry before I go.'

'Mind how you *do* go,' Frank tousled Kay's hair. 'Goodbye, Pam*elia*. I expect we'll see you again,' he teased. 'That's if you can bear to stay in this cold, grey country.'

'Say hallo to your mum and dad for us, and your aunt Liz. Tell her we'll be round to see 'er soon.' Freddie winked at Kay and followed his brother out of the pub.

'You've got some dubious relations, Kay,' Pamela frowned. 'They look like criminals to me.'

'Silly cow. They're in import-export. I think they've got their own firm, or they've got top positions in one, according to my dad. I remember him and uncle Bert arguing about them once. They're not short of cash,' she added proudly.

'Anyone can see that. You should have asked them to lend you the money for Spain.'

'Kay, this is Ray. Ray, this silly cow is Kay from hop-picking – looking a lot more grown-up and sophisticated . . . and this is her friend Pamela.' Terry looked just like his old self in his jeans and white T-shirt, with most of his make-up wiped off.

'Hallo, Ray,' Kay reached out and shook his hand.

'Well. Where shall we go then?' Ray looked pleased to be in their company.

'You name it,' Pamela said, admiring Ray's good looks, feeling sorry that he preferred boys to girls.

'We can't afford the Kentucky but there's other little nightclubs. We could club-crawl.' Terry grinned.

'Kentucky Club,' Kay said thoughtfully. 'Where 'ave I heard that before?'

'From your uncles. That's where they'll be heading.'

'I said they were criminals. Only villains, film stars and politicians go to the Kentucky,' Pamela said in her high-handed way.

Making their way out of the Sun, Kay stopped in her tracks. 'Hang about you lot, we're broke. I've only got three pounds to last me the rest of the week.'

'The night's on us.' Terry turned to Ray, 'I haven't seen her for over two years.'

'Yeah, all right,' Ray nodded. 'But don't start asking for doubles.'

Chapter Ten

It was four weeks since the missing salary episode, and everyone at Thompson's appeared to have forgotten all about it. Everyone except Kay. Sitting at her desk, pulling and stretching a paper-clip until it became a single wire, she wondered what she would say when she handed in her notice. She shaped the wire into a spiral, pushed the two ends together and created a ring to slip on her finger. Her mind filled with Chris. She couldn't imagine getting through the year without seeing him.

Pushing herself around in her swivel chair, she turned her face towards the sun streaming in through the window, and tried to visualize herself on a white sandy beach, lying next to Chris's tanned body, holding his hand, waiting for him to turn over on to his stomach the way he did, and kiss her.

'I'm ready to sign today's letters, Kay.' Mr Grieves's voice drifted across the partition.

She could feel Chris's strong hand easing its way under the small of her back, and his muscular arm turning and lifting her on to his sweat-beaded chest.

'I've got one more memo to dictate, but that needn't be typed until tomorrow.'

He was kissing her neck now and pushing the palm of his hand across her sun-warmed stomach . . .

'Kay!' Grieves's face appeared above the glass partition. Kay looked from the grey-suited bulky body, distorted by frosted glass, up to his bespectacled face. 'My letters?'

'Mr Grieves . . .' Kay had left the beach but she wasn't quite back in the present. Somewhere in between. She gazed into his puzzled face. 'I'm leaving,' she said flatly. 'Who should I hand my notice to?'

A bemused smile crossing his face, Grieves raised an eyebrow. 'Why do you want to leave, Kay?'

She picked up the black folder containing the letters for signing and walked around to his side of the partition. 'Because I hate it here now.'

'You don't mean that.' Grieves leaned back in his chair and clicked the end of his biro several times.

'Do I have to give a week's notice, or is it a month?'

'If you are serious, I think we should have a private word.' He threw his pen down on the table, conveying his impatience.

'No, sorry. I'm not interested in company policy to persuade staff to stay on. I've made up my mind.' She offered him the black folder. 'We're all mad to work 'ere.'

'What's brought this on?' He opened the folder and began signing the letters with a flurry of speed.

Kay folded her arms and looked up thoughtfully at the ceiling. 'Well I suppose it could have started to dawn on me when I was accused of stealing that there might be better places to work.'

'Yes, I thought that might be at the bottom of this.' He sounded pleased, as if it were something he could talk to her about, make her see sense.

'I've been window-shopping, down the Brook Street Bureau. I can earn more money, get better conditions, good prospects.'

Grieves nudged his bifocals down his nose and looked up at her. 'You really mean to do it?'

'You make it sound like suicide.'

He pushed himself around in his chair and looked out at the modern office block opposite. 'It feels a bit like that. I wonder why?'

Taken aback by his tone, as if he were speaking to an equal instead of a junior, Kay felt warmness towards him. 'To leave here and go out there, you mean?'

He turned to her and gave a hint of a nod. 'Something like that.'

That line proved too near the mark. Grieves turned his attention again to his signing.

Kay couldn't be sure but she thought he sounded a bit choked. 'Would one week's notice be OK?'

Clearing his throat, Grieves said he would check with Rebecca Jamieson and let Kay know tomorrow, after she'd had a night to think it over.

'You don't want to rush into this,' he sighed, as if he were saying something he didn't really believe. 'We'll have another word in the morning.'

Kay nodded slowly and smiled. He was a funny man. Strict one minute and soft as anything the next. Yes, she would miss him too.

A slight feeling of doubt began nagging at Kay as she prepared for the next day. Friday. Pay-day. She looked up at the registered envelope that had been retrieved from behind the desk and was now stuck on the wall for everyone to see.

The small, dusty blue van had been parked in Clerkenwell Road for an hour by the time Kay strolled by the next morning on her way to work.

She was thinking about the way she might play games with Jamieson when she smiled patronizingly at her, saying that Kay would be hard-pressed to find another company as friendly as Thompson's. She had heard about the rehearsed company speech from one of her friends when she tried to leave. A rise of one pound a week and empty praise were all it had taken to persuade her to stay.

'I'm a bit pushed this morning, Kay,' Grieves said as she stood before him. 'I'll have a word with Management after lunch.'

'Fine.' Kay was in no hurry. Her mind was made up. As she turned away, he asked her not to let it distract her from her work.

'Don't worry. It won't happen twice.' She didn't try to keep the bitterness out of her voice as she walked away and out of the office.

And that's exactly why I'm leaving! She pushed open the door to the ladies' room and pulled a packet of five Weights from her cardigan pocket. *Bloody cheek.* It wasn't her fault. Anyone could have made that mistake. She lit a cigarette and stared out of the window at the street below. The dark blue van was still parked in the street, but meant nothing to her. *There he goes. James, upright in his three-piece suit, on his way to collect the wages.* Suddenly, without warning, Kay found herself crying, in anger, not

self-pity. She paced the floor. 'It's not fair,' she told the room. 'It shouldn't have happened! I hate them. I hate this place. I hope it burns down!' Dropping on to a chair, she stubbed out her cigarette with the heel of her shoe, not caring about the mess it made on the cold tiled floor.

'Mr Grieves is asking for you, Kay,' Doreen stood with her back against the door, keeping it open. 'We've all got a lot to do today.'

'I know. I wish I had the same enthusiasm I used to have. I can't help it, Doreen. That office. This building. It closes in on me. Sometimes I feel as if I'm suffocating.'

Laughing and shaking her head, Doreen waved her towards the door. 'I think you've missed your cue in life, Kay. You should have been an actress.'

'There's still time,' Kay forced a smile, 'I'm not exactly old.'

'Come on, be a good girl. You always said Friday was your best day. Think of the party tomorrow night. That should put some life into you.'

Walking back along the corridor to their office, Kay told Doreen that she was going to hand in her notice. She was a bit disappointed when the only reaction was slight annoyance that she would have to train someone all over again.

'I wish I had known a year ago you had no

intention of staying,' Doreen said as she sat down at her own desk. 'There were two others after that position.' She began typing. 'Now they're established in Bought Ledger and Cost Office.'

Kay felt a flush of anger when Doreen mentioned Bought Ledger. 'That's where Drake worked, till he was transferred to one of the subsidiary companies, after that embarrassing little episode! It would have been a different story if I'd been the guilty one. But then, *I'm* only a docker's daughter!'

She pulled the cover off her typewriter and shoved it in the small cupboard next to her. 'I suppose they've given Drake promotion at the same time for his troubles brought on by the silly mistake of a fellow employee!'

'If you could pop round, Kay? I would like to dictate a couple of memos.' Grieves was obviously in a mood and didn't want to hear her grievances. There was no smile in his voice today.

Collecting her notepad, Kay accidentally knocked against James's chair which fell forward, knocking his filing tray on to the floor.

'Leave it, Kay!' The impatient voice warned her to do as she was told and not argue.

'I'm sorry,' she said, leaning on the partition, looking down at Mr Grieves. 'I couldn't help it.'

Scratching his neck, he frowned. 'I realize that. We'll get on then, shall we?'

Kay felt an overwhelming desire to run out of the office, away from the building. It was stifling her again. She looked out of the window, trying to remind herself that fresh air and sunshine were still out there and always would be, even though the sun didn't shine as much here as it did in Spain.

Glancing down she saw something which caused her to freeze to the spot and then break into a sweat as she saw two men with stockings pulled over their heads jump out of the dark blue van. One of them had a cosh.

'Mr Grieves! *Quick!* They're going for James!'

Grieves was at the window in a flash. The men weren't using the cosh, just threatening James who was handing over the holdall containing the money for the salaries which had just been drawn from the bank.

Kay felt as if she were watching a film that was over in seconds. The robbers were back in the van and roaring along Clerkenwell Road before any passers-by had a chance to realize what was going on. As she stood between Doreen and Mr Grieves, it seemed as if all three of them had suddenly turned to stone.

Snatches of conversation flashed across Kay's

mind as she remembered the evening in the pub with her uncles. *So what d'yer wanna do about it, Kay . . . You've got some dubious relations. Kay. They look like criminals to me . . . Only villains, film stars and politicians go to the Kentucky . . . Wasn't Friday the thirteenth, was it? No. But it was a Friday. We get paid fortnightly.*

Kay remembered the look that had passed between the two men. It had crossed her mind that they had been talking to her with something else on their minds. But never, not in a thousand years, had she thought that they were already planning to square the accounts. It all suddenly fell into place. Some of the things her dad had said about her uncles and the way they had always seemed to have money to throw around. They *were* villains. They really were.

Leaning against the window-sill, Kay left every-one else to the drama, finding it difficult to stop herself smiling. Would they dare to interrogate her again? Would they dare to accuse her of being an insider? She looked out of the window again at the crowd who had gathered around James. The hero. It would probably add colour to his grey image. No, they would never dream that it was her people who had performed that swift, professional snatch. And if they did? Kay was no longer smiling but quietly laughing. If they did have any reason to suspect her,

she felt confident Frank and Freddie would have left no trace of a clue.

When Kay officially handed in her notice that day, she thought Rebecca Jamieson might have detected the smugness in her voice. She had given her a long, puzzled look, but had said nothing.

Chapter Eleven

Wearing her favourite light blue button-through shift dress and matching sling-back shoes, Kay made her way along Lombard Street on a sweltering June afternoon. Weaving her way between pedestrians she arrived at the address on the slip of paper given to her by the employment bureau, and felt her heart sink. She peered in through one of the windows and saw that the ugly Victorian building was even worse inside.

Telling herself she had nothing to lose, Kay entered the dim reception area and made her way towards a long dark desk, deciding that she would go through with the interview now that she was here, but would not accept the position for which she was applying. This was another world. An alien world, where the staff walked around like sad robots with half-smiles fixed on their pale faces. It was as if all colour had been left at

the door. Black, white and grey surrounded her. Not the starkly contrasting black and white décor that Kay loved, but a heavy, old-fashioned drab interior.

'Mr Trillington will be down shortly.' The middle-aged woman spoke without looking up. 'If you would like to take a seat.' She swept a long red fingernail across the nape of her thin neck, capturing a few loose strands and slipping them under a tight French pleat of silver-grey hair.

'What's it like working here?' Kay wasn't really interested, she just wanted to see what was under the layers that seemed to prevent this woman from communicating.

Glancing briefly at Kay, she wound a sheet of paper into her grey typewriter. 'I shouldn't worry too much about that.' There was enough smugness in her voice to last a working lifetime.

'I wasn't.' Kay carefully leaned forward and lifted a hair from the grey padded shoulder. 'It's just that you don't seem full of the joys of spring.'

'Really?' Shooting her a ferocious look, the woman answered the internal telephone system.

'This carpet needs fumigating.' Kay slowly shook her head. 'It smells of stale cigarette smoke and yet still the moths lay their eggs.' She leaned on the edge of the archaic desktop and looked into the woman's

face. 'Doesn't it bother anyone? This building smells like an old metal ashtray.'

'Mr Trillington will see you now. Third floor, second door on the left.'

'Thank you.' Kay stood for a moment, wondering whether to bother. 'This is only the second interview I've ever been to. I really wasn't asking you for much. Just a few words. Anything that just might have made me feel a bit more at ease.' Kay was surprised at her own audacity.

Studiously examining her notebook, the receptionist looked as if she might be a touch embarrassed. 'Knock before you enter.'

During the lightning tour of the offices, seen through windows from the long dark corridor, Kay did her best to be polite and hide her boredom.

'Why do all the girls and women wear black and white? Is it a rule?' she asked, as they stood outside the typing pool, staring in.

'It's not exactly compulsory.' Trillington nervously scratched his nose and smiled down at her. 'We're a very conservative firm and a very busy one. It wouldn't do to have valuable time wasted.' He folded his arms and curled his bottom lip over. 'I'm talking about the male members of staff, of course. Can't expect them not to be interested in women. Bit of an old dog myself. I'm afraid your sort of colours

wouldn't do at all. They'd spend most of their time ogling. Then of course there's your hair.'

Kay checked her reflection in a darker part of the window. Her new short-bob turned perfectly under her chin and the thick fringe was dead straight and sat level with her eyebrows. So what was wrong?

'I'm afraid you simply wouldn't fit in. But you seem a bright girl; I expect you've worked that out for yourself. Nothing to do with you, of course. Just your appearance. The blonde "sex kitten",' he smiled. 'The directors would throw a fit if I took you on.'

Sex kitten? He couldn't, as far as Kay was concerned, have insulted her more. She hated the label blondes were given, especially if, like her, they happened to be five foot eight. 'My hair's natural.' She found herself making excuses and feeling ashamed. 'And I'm too thin to be classed as a sex kitten.' She could feel the blood rushing to her face again and hated herself for being embarrassed when she should be giving this pompous git a piece of her mind.

'Those girls,' she could hear the tremor in her voice and cleared her throat, 'they may be wearing traditional black and white but they look like tarts. Their skirts are too tight and too short and the fact that they wear their blouse collars up makes them

look as if they're Teddy girls. And they're wearing too much make-up.'

Trillington placed one arm around her waist and steered her away from the window back along the corridor towards his office. 'Come and take the weight off your feet. I'll explain about personal appearance. The difference between what you might wear when you go out with a boyfriend and what you ought to wear when—'

'No thanks.' Kay pulled away from his clammy hand. 'I think I can work that out for myself.'

Looking at his watch, he raised an eyebrow. 'Almost noon. I think I could get away with an early lunch.' He winked at Kay. 'A drink and a quick sandwich sound OK?'

She could hardly believe her ears. A man who must be old enough to be her father and from a different class was asking her out to lunch?

'Unless you want to come back after business hours.' He lifted her chin with his forefinger so she had to look into his leering eyes.

Pushing his hand away she shot him a look of disgust and turned away, her low stiletto heels thudding on the dust-filled carpet. And as she walked quickly down the stairs she willed herself not to break down. 'I won't cry,' she said aloud, 'I won't.'

For most of her life Kay had been told she was too

sensitive, bursting into tears at the least thing. But not this time. And, she was determined, not ever again. At least she had Thompson's to thank for that. She had made a resolution when she walked out of the building for the last time that she would never cry again, unless someone she loved were to die. She would allow herself tears then, but not for anything or anyone else would she ever weaken. Her crying days were over.

Sitting outside a small Italian café Kay enjoyed the sun on her face while she waited to be served. She was reminded of Spain and began to fantasize about her future, living with Chris in that small fishing village. For five weeks, since returning to England to face the music, she had quietly begged God to let there be a letter from Chris when she returned from work. So far there had been nothing. Not a word. She had written and posted the first letter.

Maybe they were all the same? Out of sight, out of mind. She had given up on Zacchi a long time ago.

She sipped her coffee and wondered if it was time yet to make a secret appointment with Doctor Brynberg. She was now three weeks late and seriously worried. Would her family ever believe that she had gone out there a virgin and had only made love with Chris twice?

Ignoring the butterflies in her stomach, Kay pushed

open the glass swing doors leading into the reception of Waterman's Publishing. Her second interview that day. The first had managed to crush her self-esteem and she wondered how she would react if she were put down a second time.

This time she decided to try harder with her accent. She recalled her teacher drilling into her and the other girls on the commerce course that a 't' was on the end of a word for a reason, and that they must sound it. She had been just as pedantic too about not dropping aitches.

'My name is Kay Armstrong.' She assumed the voice she used when working on the switchboard at Thompson's. 'I have an appointment at two o'clock.' She quickly checked the piece of paper for the personnel officer's name.

'Oh right, yeah,' the young girl checked her diary. 'Mrs Jarold's expecting yer. She's gonna be tied up for ten minutes though. D'yer wanna cuppa coffee while yer wait?' Pushing back her chair the curly-headed receptionist stood up. 'It tastes like camel's piss smells, but if you eat a square of chocolate with it,' she shrugged and grimaced.

'It's OK,' Kay laughed, 'I've just had a cappuccino. Is it all right if I have a cigarette while I'm waiting?' She had dropped her telephonist's voice and

compromised, not slipping back completely into her everyday East End tones.

'Not s'posed to smoke in Reception, but I'll keep my eye out for Mr Branson. He's 'ead of staff. Struts about like a peacock with a slipped disc. We've got a smoking room but it's on the second floor.'

'I'll wait till later. Thanks anyway.'

'No. Go on. It's bloody nerve-rackin' goin' for interviews. You wanna fag – have one!'

'No, honestly, I'm not a proper smoker. Just like one now and again.' She sat down on the edge of the red and white sofa and placed her handbag on the glass-topped table. 'What's it like working here?'

'Fucking brilliant, I tell yer. Some of the journalists.' She rolled her eyes and puckered her full pink lips. 'Keep arm's length with the married ones though. They'd 'ave you in the corridor if they could.' She picked up her emery board and filed a broken fingernail.

'I'm being transferred to the subscriptions department. They need a fast typist, or so they said.' She leaned forward and lowered her voice. 'I think Mr Branson told Mrs Jarold that I'm a bit too common for Reception. Fucking cheek. I got caught right out last week though. Couldn't be bothered to go into the cloakroom to do me hair, so I used that big pink mirror.

'There I was, backcombing away like mad, trying to straighten this lot. Me hair was sticking out all over the place and in walks two really important clients. And guess who was with 'em?'

'Mr Branson?'

'Bang on. I tell yer, it was really embarrassing. For the men I mean. Didn't know where to put their faces.' She unscrewed the lid of her nail varnish and carefully painted over the repaired nail. 'It didn't bovver me. I 'ad me make-up on so I knew me face was all right when I took their coats. Cashmere they was. Think they were quite important as it 'appens. Still, there you go. I'd rather be in Subs anyway. The blokes are a right laugh and I quite fancy the driver, Roger. You wait till you see 'im.'

The interview went well. Kay liked Mrs Jarold and from what she could tell the feeling was mutual, and she passed her typing test with flying colours. She was then offered the position either of Receptionist or Production Assistant on the fortnightly magazine *Stock Market*, where she would be working closely with the journalists. Her role would be to ensure that copy was properly typed up and in on time. She opted for Receptionist but asked if she could type copy as well. The one thing Kay hated most was to be bored.

As she stepped on to the train at Moorgate underground a sudden wave of pleasure flowed through

her. Her salary had shot up overnight from seven pounds ten shillings to twelve pounds ten a week, and she would get luncheon vouchers on top. But more importantly, she had been treated with respect at the interview.

The train pulled away; just one stop to go, Bethnal Green. Kay felt as if she had been given another start in life; a career she felt sure would hold excellent prospects. Working for a publisher alongside writers was a dream she hadn't imagined could ever happen. Catching sight of her reflection in the train window she decided that her new hairstyle was a success. She liked it, now that she was getting used to it. It had been rather a shock when the scissors were first taken to her long hair.

Suddenly aware of her silly smile, she felt embarrassed at admiring her reflection. She cast her eyes along the car to check if anyone had been watching and noticed the smartly dressed drunk who was hanging on to a rail for dear life. She wondered where in the world he came from. Not the East End, that was for sure. But then, had it not been for his three-piece suit and silver-topped walking stick, the thought would not have crossed her mind.

'Clothes maketh the man' was something her art teacher always used to say. If clothes made this man, then alcohol had certainly done the opposite. His

red face and glassy eyes reminded her of the meths drinkers who sometimes lay in the gutter, blood seeping from bandaged heads, outside the Salvation Army hostel in Whitechapel.

Instead of going home after her interview Kay found herself unlatching the gate leading into Delamar Place. Since Pamela's parents had pointed out, and probably deliberately, that her grandfather was a lonely old man, she had made a point of seeing more of him and had gained much by it. Laura had always said he was a rough diamond, and up until recently Kay had not really understood what her mother meant. Now she knew. She had got to know Billy more during the past couple of weeks than in all her seventeen years.

'I'm pleased about your job, Kay,' Billy said, handing his granddaughter a cup of tea, 'but I can't say it eases my mind.'

'Tell me what's *on* your mind and perhaps I can ease it for yer.' She dipped a chocolate Bourbon into her tea.

'I think you know.' He sank into his cushioned armchair and waited.

'Know what?' Kay could feel her heart begin to beat faster. Surely he hadn't picked up on her worst fears?

Billy said nothing; he was wise enough to know

that a short silence could say more than a stream of words. He sipped his tea and stared down at the floor.

'You tell me what you think it is and I'll tell you if you're hot, warm or cold. A new version of I Spy.'

Still he said nothing, pretending to be interested in a worn patch on the arm of his chair.

'You're not clever, Billy. I can see right through you.'

'Oh, yeah?'

'Yes.' She leaned back in her chair and kicked her shoes off. 'I'm quite happy to sit and enjoy this silence.'

'Good.'

Listening to the loud tick of the large wooden clock on Billy's shelf, Kay began to count the seconds to see how long he could sit it out. She knew he loved to chat, and it hadn't slipped her notice that he had brought out his oldest photograph album. The one he had promised to show her when he found it. The one that was full of pictures of his daughter, Laura, who, apart from her dark hair, looked so much like Kay.

She counted two hundred and fifty seconds and was beginning to get cross with him for the casual way he sat there, unperturbed.

'OK, so I'm worried about something, am I?'

she said finally. 'So what? Everyone has some-thing to beef about.' She was slipping into his language again.

Billy swallowed the remains of his tea, carefully placed the bone-china cup on the saucer, sat back again and folded his arms. This time he looked tenderly into her face and shook his head. His expression said it all. He knew she had been a silly girl.

'You haven't said anything to Mum, 'ave yer?' she murmured, ashamed.

Pursing his lips, Billy shook his head defiantly. 'That's something you're gonna have to do, Kay, and soon.' He raised his eyebrows. 'I suppose it did happen in that bloody foreign country?' There was hope in his voice that he might be wrong.

Kay nodded and covered her face with her hands. 'He *was* English though – well, practically – and he *was* the first.'

'You don't have to tell me that, Kay. I saw the difference in your face when you got back. I can't tell you what the look is, but I saw it in your mother's face when your dad had first carried her through the bluebells.'

'Dad'll go mad.' Kay's mind was suddenly filled with Jack; the way he still treated her like his baby girl.

'Your dad knows already. Well, not about . . .' he nodded towards her stomach. 'He's kept the letters back. Didn't read any of 'em. But he's not daft. He knows they're love letters.'

'He did *what*?' Kay could hardly believe her ears. 'Are you telling me that Chris has written to me?'

'Don't be too hard on him, Kay. He was hoping it would blow over and you'd forget him if you thought he'd forgotten you.'

'That's horrible! How could he do that to me?' She was about to cry and remembered her resolve not to. Taking a deep breath she stood up, keeping her back to Billy. 'He'll think I don't care. He'll think I was just using him.'

A loud banging on the door stopped her dead. They both knew it would be Laura come to check up on him on her way home from Hammond's.

'Don't say anything. Not a word.' Kay stormed out of the room.

Opening the door to her mother, Kay forced herself to smile. 'I got the second interview I went for!'

'What did you do wrong on the first one?' Laura teased, and opened her arms to Kay who sprang into them.

'I've just had a phone call from your dad.' Laura walked arm in arm with Kay along the passage. 'You've got a visitor.'

'Where's today's paper, then?' Billy asked as Laura bent down to kiss his head. 'And where's Liz got to? This is the second time I cut up some fruit bread for the pair of you.'

'She's tired, Dad. Had a busy day. It was our floor manager's birthday and they made a bit of a fuss in the canteen. She's been with the firm for fifteen years.'

'Mum! You said I had a visitor.'

'And you've still got one.' Laura's broad smile was catching. Kay and her grandfather looked at each other and grinned.

'Male or female?' Kay asked, knowing somehow it was male and yet not understanding why her parents weren't hitting the roof. Chris might speak perfect English, but he had Spanish eyes all right.

'Male. Dark hair. Very attractive.'

'Chris?' Kay couldn't believe it.

'No, love. I think his name is Zacchi.' Laura couldn't contain herself. She was as excited as Kay should have been.

'Zacchi?' She could hardly believe it. 'But how do you know it's him?'

'Because your dad said so.'

'And he doesn't mind him turning up?'

'No. He sounded quite chuffed.'

Grabbing her handbag, Kay ran from the cottage

out of the courtyard and through the backstreets, almost knocking over a woman as she stepped out of Higgins's, the corner shop. 'Sorry!' she yelled back, not stopping until she finally arrived at the stairs leading up to the second-floor flat where Zacchi would be waiting. She leaned on the white-tiled wall and caught her breath.

'Where've you been, Kay? He's been 'ere for about two hours.' Jack seemed far from pleased.

'Looking for a job, Dad. It does take time, you know.'

'I've run out of things to talk about,' he whispered.

'What does he look like?'

'What d'yer think he looks like? An old man? It's only been just over two years.'

'Nearly three, actually.'

'Anyway, go and see for yourself. I'll put the kettle on. He's in the front room.'

'Dad!' Kay whispered.

He turned and looked at her. 'What?'

'Do I look all right?'

''Course you do.'

'Not too – you know, smart?'

Smiling, he stroked her hair and admired her face. 'You look lovely. Now go in and see 'im.'

Slowly pushing open the door to the living room, Kay tried to stop herself grinning like an idiot.

'Hallo, Zac.'

Spinning round on the heels of his black cowboy boots, Zacchi faced her, looking shy and awkward in his Italian suit. 'You've had your hair cut,' was all he managed to say.

'Yeah. On Saturday.'

'I like it,' he smiled. 'It suits you.'

'Thanks.'

There was a pause while each wondered what to say next. Kay was completely lost for words. There was so much to talk about, but she couldn't think of anything to say. He did look different. Especially in a suit. She hadn't expected that.

'We've left the road,' Zacchi suddenly said. 'Joined the settled travellers.'

'You're kidding?'

'No. It's getting more difficult now, finding places to stop, seasonal work. Gypsies are out of fashion.' He flashed her a smile.

'That's terrible, Zacchi. Your family must hate it.'

Shrugging, he looked out of the window. 'It's not all bad. It means the young ones can go to school.' He turned to face her. 'We're not in a council house, not yet. We're on a site with other travellers. It's a bit like living on the common. Hop-picking.'

'Can't knock that.' Kay was wandering from the

conversation again, looking into that familiar handsome face and those dark blue eyes. His wavy hair was just as thick and shiny, maybe a bit shorter.

Zacchi played with a cuff-link on his shirtsleeve. 'I don't suppose you feel like going for a walk?'

'I thought you'd never ask.'

Popping his head round the door, Jack asked Kay if she wanted tea or coffee. He didn't look too perturbed when she told him they were going out.

'Thanks for your hospitality, Mr Armstrong,' Zacchi said, shaking Jack's hand.

'That's all right, son. And good luck with your new job.' He winked at him and squeezed Zacchi's hand in a fatherly fashion. 'You'll soon get used to the nine-to-five routine.'

Strolling hand in hand they walked under the railway arch, heading for Bethnal Green park. It amused Zacchi the way Kay's voice suddenly had an echo, and before long they were making whooping war cries between bursts of laughter.

'This isn't the way I imagined it would be.' Zacchi put his arm around Kay's shoulder and kissed her lightly on the cheek. 'I didn't really know what to expect, but I never dreamed we'd be standing under an arch making silly echoes.'

'I never imagined you in a suit.'

'No. Neither did I. It goes with the job.'

'What's that?'

He took her hand again and for the first time looked relaxed and happy. 'It's all your fault! I've spent the past two years studying to take an O-level in English – while we were still on the road. It started with my buying a dictionary so I could look up some impressive words when I wrote to you.'

'But you never did write, Zacchi.'

'No. I decided to wait.' He pulled her close to him. 'And here I am.'

'You still haven't told me what your job is.'

'Well, because of my years spent travelling and because I seem to have a way with words, and . . .'

'The poetry! Of course, I'd forgotten you wrote all those lovely poems.'

'The pay's not brilliant but it's really good, having my own weekly column . . .' He waited for her reaction.

'I don't suppose you've got any of your poems with you? The ones you wrote specially for me, for instance?'

'. . . "Travelling the Dusty Road – Around Britain". The circulation figures have gone up since they took me on.'

'What are you talking about, Zacchi?'

279

'I'm a feature writer on the local rag, the Walthamstow *Guardian*.'

Kay stared at him, hardly able to take it in. Zacchi, a professional journalist? Her gypsy boyfriend doing something she had always secretly wanted to do? 'Honestly, Zac? You're not pulling my leg?'

'No I'm not,' he laughed, 'but if you're offering . . .'

Feeling herself blush, she looked away, her mind suddenly full of the time when she almost lost her virginity to him. Then, remembering her own sorry state of affairs, she went quiet.

'I was joking, Kay.'

'I know.' She didn't want to think about that side of their relationship which, as far as she could see, had been ruined by her holiday romance.

Turning into the gateway leading to the park, Kay suggested they sit on the low wall that surrounded the large paddling pond. 'That's old Sid,' she smiled, nodding towards an elderly man handing out tracts to passers-by. 'Bible Sid. He'll start singing a hymn soon and if we're lucky, dancing too.'

Zacchi took Kay's hand and stroked her fingers with the tip of his thumb. 'I said I would come for you, one day—'

'I told you, didn't I?' she interrupted. 'There he goes. The kids love him.' They looked across at the smiling old man.

'Don't the parents worry?'

'No, never. Sid's been around since I can remember. He's harmless. Never begs. Never asks for anything. Some people reckon he's really a millionaire, an eccentric. It wouldn't surprise me.'

'I still feel the same about you, Kay.' He gazed at her face. 'Why won't you look at me?'

'Zacchi—' She felt herself blushing again and wondered if she would ever grow out of it. 'There's something—'

'Don't you mean some*one*? Someone else?'

Kay dropped her head back and sighed. 'It's hopeless, Zac.'

'Why?' His voice, as ever, was sincere.

'I went to Spain earlier this year. For a holiday. I met someone. Chris. He looked so much like you.' She bit her bottom lip and wondered if she should stop there.

'He's the first real boyfriend since you.' She said it quickly. 'And I'm afraid this time I didn't stop when I should have.' There. It was out. The ball was in his court.

He slowly withdrew his hand from hers, and she could feel his body tense even though they weren't touching. She wanted to say how sorry she was and yet somehow that would have been disloyal to Chris, whom she did, or at least she thought she

did, love. Now that Zacchi was close to her again, she wasn't sure.

'I've been tempted enough times,' he said, 'but it would have been for sex and nothing else. I chose to bury myself in my study and writing instead. I was daft enough to believe you might wait for me.'

'Well that's a bit much, isn't it? Nearly three years and not a word from you! As far as I was concerned you'd wiped me out!'

'It wasn't that easy for me.' His voice was shot through with disappointment.

'Well why *didn't* you write?' she cried, not caring about two women who were sitting close by, listening intently.

'I did write!' He lowered his voice. 'I just couldn't bring myself to send the letters. I don't know why. I don't know.'

Narrowing her eyes, Kay studied his face. 'I don't think I believe you.'

'Thanks.'

They sat there while Sid drew people towards him on the opposite side of the pond. Kay began to feel as if she were sitting next to a stranger. Part of her wanted to suggest they make their way back, and another part wanted to stay with him and rekindle the special feelings they had shared.

'I had a lot of girlfriends before you, Kay. Some I

liked a lot more than others. I even thought I loved a couple of them. Then I met you. And I realized what love meant.' He slowly shook his head. 'I loved you so much, a day didn't go by when I wasn't making plans. Thinking about the future, reliving the past, helped me live the present. And if you think that sounds too corny, then you'll know why I couldn't bring myself to post the love letters I wrote you.'

'I felt the same,' Kay kept her head lowered. 'The difference was that I didn't have an address to write to. I had to wait until you contacted me. I had to get through every day trying to hold the smell of your spicy soap in my mind.'

Zacchi chuckled and shook his head. 'That soap meant more to you than I did.'

'At least you took the trouble to use it today,' she murmured, trying not to smile.

'I had to twist my uncle's arm to get it. You can't buy it in the shops. My grandmother made it to an old family recipe.'

'And she doesn't any more?'

'No. She died last year. That's when my family decided to settle down. We burned her wagon. It's an old gypsy custom.'

'I'm sorry, Zacchi. It must have been traumatic giving up your way of life.'

'It was. But we're adjusting. So long as we stick

together, we'll be OK.' He was bending over now, resting his elbows on his knees, his head lowered.

'My uncle Bert died, too. Earlier this year.' Kay could feel the old familiar sadness sweep over her.

'That must have been hard for your aunt Liz.'

Kay was touched that he still remembered her family. 'She's still getting over it. We all are.'

'I'm still in love with you, Kay.'

Covering her face with her hands, Kay willed herself not to cry. 'The trouble is—' she stopped. The words stuck in her throat. How could she tell him she might be having Chris's baby?

'Go on.' His voice was serious, almost as if he had picked up on the gravity of the situation.

'You'll hate me,' she warned.

'Maybe.'

'I think I might be pregnant.'

Zacchi wanted to hear no more. He stood up, and keeping his back to her, composed himself and walked away. Kay made no move to leave. She sat staring into the pond, at the ripples made by a few children who were still paddling.

When she finally checked the clock hanging on the wall of the umbrella factory just outside the park, it was five minutes to seven. The park keeper would be locking the gates in five minutes. She had been

sitting there for over an hour and it had seemed like seconds.

Sid had moved to her side of the pond and sat near by, his Bible and hymn-book on his lap. They were the only two there. As she gazed blankly at him, he turned his head sideways and smiled back at her. Then, without thinking, she walked up to him and sat down.

'Hallo, Sid,' she said quietly.

'There's no point worrying. If it's going to happen, it will,' he said, not looking at her.

'It already has.'

'I don't see a happening.' He studied the air around them.

'How could you see what's inside me?' she said, hoping he wouldn't realize what it was she had allowed to slip out.

'If it's inside – it hasn't happened. When it's outside, and you can see it, touch it—'

'Do you know what I'm talking about?'

'It's more important that *you* do.' He stood up, doffing his battered trilby. Then, with one hand flat on his Bible he smiled. 'Thou shalt not kill.'

Kay sat by herself for the last couple of minutes. Sid always left her with a feeling of comfort inside, a safe feeling. Even when she was a child and listened to him with the rest of the crowd, he was

special, and somehow managed to find his way into people's hearts.

Thou shalt not kill. His voice hung in her mind. He needn't have worried. That was the last thing she intended to do. If there was a baby growing inside, she would feed it until it was ready to come out into the big wide world. Then she would love it and protect it.

With her hand on her stomach, she wondered if it might be a girl or a boy. She was no longer filled with worry, but with a warmth which she would share with no one until she was sure. She would make an appointment with the doctor before going home.

'He seemed decent enough,' Jack said from behind his newspaper. 'Get rid of that earring, and you'd never guess he was a gyppo.'

'That'd be a shame. It's what I find most attractive about him,' Kay retorted, knowing that was the best way to deal with her dad when he pretended he was racist.

'You'll be buying a wagon next and going on the road.'

'Chance would be a fine thing.'

Jack bent back his newspaper and looked quizzically at her. 'You think you'd enjoy not being able to take a bath when you wanted, do you?'

Not wishing to get into a no-win argument, Kay changed the subject. 'Do you think I could have my letters now? You know, the ones from Spain?'

'Don't know what you're talking about.' He shook his paper and hid his face.

'I've got a friend in the sorting office, so I know there's been letters for me. And I want them!'

'Top drawer in the sideboard. You should 'ave asked before now, I'd forgotten about them.'

'Liar!' She stormed out of the kitchen.

'If you think you're going out there to see a Spaniard, you've got another think coming! Why can't you go out with a local boy? Make life a bit easier, wouldn't it?' he called after her.

In the privacy of her room, Kay sat on the edge of the bed and began to open her letters. She had put them in date order, and opened the first one. It was full of love and promise. Chris wanted her to go back out there for a holiday in the autumn. He even offered to pay half her expenses. The second letter was full of questions. Why hadn't she answered? Had she met someone else? Maybe she had written and the letter had gone astray? The third was all disappointment; the fourth and fifth angry, hurt and desperate.

'How could you have done this?' The tears were pouring down her cheeks. 'He's practically suicidal!'

'I couldn't see the point!' Jack spat back, aloof.

'We loved each other! Isn't that enough? Does there have to be a point?' Kay knew she was hysterical, but the tone of Chris's last letter had been so awful all she wanted was to be with him, to tell him what had happened; to tell him she did love him.

'If you'd met him, you'd never treat him like this!' She gripped the letters angrily in one hand, waving them in Jack's sorry face. 'Read them! Read what you've put him through, and then tell me you were right!'

Jack covered his face with his hands. 'All right, babe. I was wrong. I'm sorry, I shouldn't 'ave done it.' He sighed loudly. 'I can be a silly bastard at times.' He reached out and pulled Kay close, patting her back the way he used to when she was a baby.

'I didn't wanna lose you. I don't want you living a million miles away.'

'It's not even three *hours* away.'

'Yeah, I s'pose that's one way of looking at it.' He gazed into her face. 'You're not scheming up any more wild ideas, are yer? Forging a passport once was bloody risky, a second time would mean prison.'

'I wouldn't do that. I can wait till next year. But at least he should know why I can't go till then.'

288

'Who is he, anyway? I don't know a thing about 'im.' Jack found it difficult not to show his frustration.

'He was born and bred in this country. He doesn't even have a Spanish accent. And he went to a good school. Better than the one I went to!'

'So what's he doing out there then?' Jack looked relieved.

'It's his family's village. His grandparents are there and some of his other relatives. He's got a small bakery. It's what he's always wanted.'

'He's what?' Jack's eyes narrowed.

'Bought his own bakery.' Kay read his mind. 'He's only twenty-two, Dad, and he bought it from an uncle, so it didn't cost the earth.' She gave him a wink to lighten things. 'You should taste his hot bread, Dad. It's out of this world. And the cakes.'

'I suppose you'd better phone 'im,' Jack said indifferently.

'Phone?' Kay could hardly believe it. It would cost a fortune.

'Well it's cheaper than going out there, innit? Go on.' He tapped one of the letters she held in her hand. 'Look. He's put the number in the corner.'

'You really mean it?' She felt like screaming for joy.

'Yeah, go on. But keep it short!'

* * *

'Well, where is he?' Laura unpacked some shopping from her bag on to the kitchen table.

'Who?' Jack knew very well who, but he was in one of his mischievous moods.

'Zacchi of course.'

'Dunno. They went out for a walk; she came back by herself.' He shrugged. 'Then she spent over an hour on the phone to Spain.'

'She did *what*?'

'Well, five minutes anyway. It felt like an hour. Christ knows what it cost.'

'Jack. What's going on. What has Zacchi coming here got to do with her phoning Spain?'

'Search me. She's in her room. Go and ask 'er.'

'I think I will.' Laura marched out of the kitchen and rapped on her door.

'Not now!' came the sorry reply.

'Kay? What's wrong?'

'I'll tell you later, Mum! I need to be by myself.'

'She's not crying, is she?' Jack joined Laura at Kay's door. They both stood there wondering what to do next.

'He doesn't want to know me any more. I couldn't tell him that Dad hid the letters, so I lied and said I'd been too ill to write. He didn't believe me!'

'I warned you.' Laura pointed a finger into Jack's

face. 'I said something like this would happen!' She stormed into the kitchen.

'Hiding your daughter's letters! You and your stupid Victorian attitudes! Don't blame me if she ups and leaves!'

Jack turned his back on her and stared out of the window at nothing. 'Of all the nerve. Who does he think he is, doesn't wanna know? Doesn't wanna know our Kay? I'll strangle the little bastard.'

'Yeah, that's it, Jack. Turn it around. Put the blame somewhere else. Like you always do!'

He turned to face her, his eyes fiery with anger. She'd never seen him look so menacing. 'Good job he's miles away,' she murmured, half smiling.

'I'll phone 'im. Yeah. That's it. Go and get one of them letters. The number'll be on it.' Jack tapped a roll-up on the lid of his tin. 'I'll soon knock the little drip off his pedestal.'

'No!' Laura was unhesitating. 'Definitely no!'

Jack spread his hands in the air and shrugged. 'I can't just leave it, Laura. Either I phone, or I push my fist through a window.'

'You'll do neither. Because both would be costly, and I'm not gonna add to the expense that boy's cost us already!' She hoped that would bring Jack's temper down enough to make him see reason.

'So what then?' he demanded pathetically.

'So we leave it. I'm afraid she's gonna have to learn to deal with her own heartaches. Everyone has to in the end. You've got to learn to let her go, Jack.'

Drawing hard on his cigarette, he nodded. 'You're a lot of help.'

'How d'yer think I feel? I wasn't cast in iron, you know.'

'I know.' He stretched out one arm and pulled her to him. 'When does it end, eh? The pain we go through with kids?'

'Never, according to Liz. She still worries about her David and his snooty wife.'

'Yeah, but it's different with us and our Kay.'

'Everyone thinks that about their own. We all love the little sods too much for our own good.'

'Yeah. You can say that again.'

Sitting on Pamela's bed with the pillows propped behind her, Kay waited for her friend to put the finishing touches to her make-up. She hadn't told her about the visit from Zacchi that day, or the call to Spain. She would wait until she had her full attention.

'So when do you start this new and exciting job?' Mouth gaping, Pamela brushed on more mascara.

'Tomorrow.'

'Blimey. Don't give you much time to dwell on it, do they?'

'I didn't ask for time, I wanted to start straight away. No point sitting around being bored.'

'I dunno,' Pamela admired her reflection. 'Some people have all the luck.' She turned to face Kay. 'You don't seem very excited. I'll go in your place if you like and you can take my boring old job. If I 'ave to fill in another claims form I'll go mad.'

'Are you ready yet?' Kay was beginning to lose patience. She had been there for over an hour while Pamela titivated herself. They were, after all, only going for a drink in the Black Boy and it being a Monday, it was unlikely that any of the usual crowd would be there.

'Does this new lipstick suit?' Pamela puckered her pale apricot lips.

'I prefer the pink you usually wear.'

'You don't like it.' She picked up a tissue ready to wipe it off.

'I do! I just prefer you in pink. I'll get used to it. Now leave it alone!'

'Sorry for breathing.'

'Well, what d'yer expect? I want to go *out*,' she snapped. Lowering her voice, she trailed her finger round a flowing leaf on Pamela's bedspread. 'I've got loads to tell yer.'

'Like what?' Pamela pulled on a baggy mohair cardigan. The deep purple made her big brown eyes stand out more than ever.

'Like who my visitor was today. And who I spoke to on the phone – long distance.' Kay suddenly felt lighter. As pleased as punch.

Unable to stop a cocky smile spreading across her face, she began to chuckle. Pamela stared at her forlornly. 'I've got their number,' Kay sang tauntingly.

'You liar!'

'Suit yourself.' Kay slipped down from the pillows and stretched herself out on the bed. 'It was as if he were standing in the same room,' she said, full of swank.

'Where'd you get his number from then, Miss Clever-drawers?'

'From one of the letters he sent me.'

Pamela turned back to the mirror and carefully wiped off the apricot lipstick. 'I'm sure,' she murmured.

'He sent four in all.' Kay's mind clouded over as she remembered how her dad had ruined their relationship. 'My dad kept the letters back,' she said. 'He thought he was doing it in my best interests.'

'Kay!' Pamela sounded angry. 'Stop messing

about. You know how depressed I've been not hearing from Charles!'

'He lost your address. Chris wrote that Charles asked if I would get you to write.' Kay pulled a piece of paper from her pocket. 'Here. I've written it down for yer.'

Snatching it from her friend, Pamela screeched with joy until her mother appeared in the doorway. 'What's happened?' She turned to Kay. 'You told her she looked like a model with that new lipstick?'

'Charles lost my address!' She brought her face close to her mother's. 'He lost it. That's why he hasn't been in touch.' She kissed the piece of paper. 'I knew he loved me.'

Lillian raised her eyebrows and shrugged. 'I suppose he's a goy?'

'He's Spanish! And if I have to, I'll convert to Catholicism!'

'Sure you will.' With a smug half-smile on her face, Lillian closed the door behind her, leaving the girls to themselves.

'If I said that to my mum or dad, they'd hit the roof.'

'Why? This faith, that faith, what's the difference? We're all flesh and blood underneath.' She kissed the piece of paper again. 'Give me his phone number! I must talk to him.'

'I don't have it. Only Chris's. And I'm certainly not giving that to you. Not after what he said to me.' Kay turned her back on Pamela and wondered why she didn't actually feel sad any more. She wondered why it was Zacchi's face that filled her mind instead.

'What d'yer mean?' Pamela circled the bed. 'Kay, what did he say?'

'He's gone back with his fiancé. A local girl. I was on the rebound.' Kay sat up and hugged her knees. 'He blamed it on the fact that he wrote four letters for my one. Said he had suffered so much pain, and when she appeared in the doorway one day he realized how much he had loved her.'

'I can't believe it,' Pamela shook her head. 'You're not messing about, either, are you.'

'It's OK. I've done my crying. And that's what gets me really mad. I vowed I wasn't gonna let anyone make me cry again and I did. I hate him for that.' She turned the signet ring on her right hand. 'Zacchi was so warm and oh, I dunno, kind of loving, in a way.'

'Zacchi?' Pamela looked totally confused. 'Today is Monday, isn't it. And I did see you yesterday? And none of this had happened then?'

'All in a day!' Kay forced a smile. 'I gained a new career and lost two boyfriends. Not bad, eh?'

'Lost?'

'Yeah. Come on, let's go for a drink. I'll tell you on the way.'

Walking along the Mile End Road, Kay filled Pamela in, except on the one worry that she was keeping to herself. She couldn't bring herself to tell her best friend her worst fears, or about her visit to the doctor. The two pills he had given her were in an envelope in her handbag. She was to take them that evening and if she wasn't pregnant, her period would come the next day or so. She was almost too scared to take them in case nothing happened.

It was the best thing that could have happened, Tommy and Micky being in the Black Boy. They looked handsome leaning against the bar, each enjoying a pint. Kay looked from them to Pamela. 'Look who's here.'

She felt sure they would take her mind off Zacchi, even though she found herself wishing he would walk in.

'Oh, you made it then,' Pamela said in her haughty way.

'Wouldn't miss it for the world,' said Tommy, looking at Kay.

'You might 'ave told me!' Kay was caught off

guard, and was embarrassed that he wouldn't take his eyes off her.

'Haven't seen you around lately,' Tommy slipped between Kay and Pamela, trying to separate her from the group.

'Life's been a bit hectic since Spain,' Kay smiled shyly back at him.

'What she means is that we've been spending time seeing how the other half live.' Pamela showed a limp wrist. 'Her friend Terry's been showing us the town.'

'Oh yeah? Gay, was it?' Micky threw his head back and laughed. 'Hope we're not too butch for yer!'

'No.' Kay looked them up and down, an impertinent smirk on her face.

Enjoying her sense of humour, Tommy walked over to the jukebox while his friend ordered the drinks. Kay watched him as he studied the labels and thought what a coincidence it would be if he chose the same song as Chris had done in Spain.

'This is just for you.' He winked at Kay as Bobby Vee's voice filled the room with 'Rubber Ball'.

Lying in bed that night, Kay lined up in her imagination the three young men she had spoken to that day and measured each against the other. Zacchi

definitely came out on top but he was the only one
who knew her secret, so she didn't want to face him
again. Tommy came second for his good looks and
the modern way he dressed. And Chris came last.
Had he not told her rather belatedly that he had been
engaged before they met, he would have come out
on top and she would be making plans to fly out
there the following year, 1963, quite possibly with
his baby in her arms.

Deciding not to take the pills that night for fear
of anything spoiling her first day at her new job she
turned over, buried her head in her pillow and quietly
prayed that everything would turn out all right. It
had been a long, eventful day and within a minute
of closing her eyes, Kay fell into a deep sleep.

*'The Managing Director wishes to meet you,
Kay. Please follow me.' Rebecca Jamieson was
wearing a smart, tight-fitting black dress and a
beautiful diamond necklace. 'Let's not keep him
waiting.'*

*Jamieson had left Thompson's and was now work-
ing for Waterman's. Kay pushed her chair back
ready to stand, but on looking down was shocked
to see that she had forgotten to put on the skirt
she had laid out the night before and was wearing
only one stocking. The suspenders from the horrid
old-fashioned pink roll-on were dangling down one*

leg, the elastic so old and loose that the button and clip almost touched her knee.

Leaning on the reception desk, Jamieson pushed her head closer to Kay. 'You're going to have to stand up, you know. You can't hide behind that desk all day. Get up! Now!'

Hot and panicky, Kay pleaded with her, but the words in her mind were not the ones that left her mouth. She was saying the wrong things and her head felt as if it were on fire and would burst into flames. Dripping with perspiration she wiped her legs with her damp dress and was horrified to see the dark red liquid oozing from her and dripping onto the light carpet.

'Get up! The Chairman is coming.' There was an evil sickly smile on Jamieson's face.

'No! Please, no! It hurts! I'm in pain! I want my mother! Please phone for my mother!'

'Your mother is in the next office. She doesn't want to see you.'

Kay looked through a window, and could see Laura. She called out to her, but she just threw her a look of disgust and carried on with her work. 'MUMMY! MUMMY, PLEASE! HELP ME!'

'Kay . . . ? Oh Kay, baby, it's all right.' Laura was at Kay's bedside in a flash, cradling and rocking her daughter. 'Just a nightmare, love. Just a silly dream.'

'Mum! I've got cramp! It's worse than I've *ever* had before.' Kay gripped Laura's arm as a searing pain shot through her womb.

Shocked by Kay's harrowing scream, Laura whipped back the bedcovers to see that her daughter was lying in a pool of sticky blood. Grabbing her mother by the arms again, Kay caught her breath as her stomach contracted and another pain pierced her.

'All right, baby, all right. Just lie still. Don't move.' Realising the gravity of the situation, Laura felt herself shiver.

'It's just a heavy period, isn't it?' Kay dragged the covers back over herself and dropped back on to her pillow, looking deathly white.

'I expect so.' Laura spun around as Jack arrived. 'Don't ask questions,' Laura warned, 'just sit there and hold her hand.'

'Where are you going?' Jack's eyes were heavy with sleep.

'To phone the doctor!'

Another cry from Kay snapped Jack into action. He was by her side and holding her before he could think.

'It's a late period, Dad, that's all.' Kay went limp in his arms.

Smiling bravely into her face, he stroked Kay's

perspiration-damp hair. 'Try to relax, eh?' He closed his hand around hers and prayed that the worst hadn't happened. 'I'll run you a nice warm bath in a minute.'

While they waited for the emergency doctor to arrive, Laura busied herself, making Kay as comfortable as she could, after changing the sheets. Jack had been sent into the kitchen where he could let go of his bottled-up emotion in private and make them all some hot, sweet tea.

'It's more than just blood, isn't it, Mum?' Kay turned her head away as Laura carefully slid the heavily soiled sheet into a plastic bag.

'Try not to think about it.'

'I've never known pain like that before. You *will* tell the doctor how bad it was!' She arched her back again and struggled with another minor contraction. 'In case it gets bad again,' she managed to say.

Laura looked into Kay's drawn face. 'How bad is it now?'

'Worse than a normal period.' She laid back and sighed with relief as the pain subsided. 'It was as if a knife was—'

'Yeah all right.' Laura didn't want to hear the rest. She glanced at the small alarm clock on Kay's bedside table and was just about to say that the doctor should be here by now when the doorbell rang.

* * *

'It's barely termed as a miscarriage, Mrs Armstrong but your daughter was five or six weeks pregnant. It looks as if she's passed as many clots as she's likely to and the flow seems to be easing. A few days bed-rest and she'll be fine. Just keep her warm and comfortable.'

Laura nodded, avoiding the doctor's eyes. 'We didn't . . . Kay didn't . . .' She took a deep breath. 'It's not an abortion.' She blurted out the words quickly, wanting to get that bit over with.

The doctor smiled. 'I realise that. We *can* tell you know. I doubt if she has had intercourse more than two or three times in her life.'

'Well, that's something to be thankful for, I suppose.'

'At seventeen? I would have thought so. These days.'

Once the doctor had gone and Kay had been given pain killers, Laura braced herself to face Jack. Now he really would have to accept the fact that his baby-girl had experienced full woman-hood. Like it or not.

Wrapped in her towelling dressing gown, curled up in an armchair, Kay thanked her lucky stars. One way or another, Mother Nature had seen fit to map out the following year or so of her life.

'I'll have to go to work, Kay, but Dad'll get you anything you want. He'll only be gone a couple of hours.' Laura handed her a milky drink.

'Did Mrs Jarold really sound OK about my not turning up?'

'Yes, for the third time. I told her you had a stomach bug as well as a period and that you wouldn't be taking a day off every month. She was fine about it. OK?' She kissed Kay on the forehead. 'Stop worrying.'

'Thanks, Mum.'

'You'll be all right, then?'

'Yeah.' She waved a library book. 'It'll be nice to get in some reading.'

'Charles Dickens again?' Laura sounded pleased. 'You'll be so well read, we soon won't be able to talk to you.'

'Did I tell you that Zacchi's a feature writer?'

Standing by the door, Laura smiled back at Kay. 'Yes, love, you did. And I'm just as proud of him as you are.'

Once alone, Kay laid her book down on the arm of her chair and closed her eyes, thinking about Zacchi. She tried to put herself in his place and imagine how she would have felt if he had told her he had met someone else and that she was having his baby. She would have hated it.

Full of remorse at having broken her promise to wait for him, she decided to write a letter saying she was sorry. With pen poised, she tried to think of the right words to say. For ten minutes she sat staring at the blank page until it dawned on her why she wasn't scribbling away like mad. She was sorry she hadn't waited . . . but she didn't think she should apologize. Zacchi should have written to her. How was she to know if he was ever going to contact her after two and a half years? No: he was to blame, not her. She would not write.

Tossing the pen and notepad to the floor, she continued to read *The Old Curiosity Shop*. If Zacchi was half as interested in her as she was in him, he would get in touch. If not, at least she knew where she stood.

Ten minutes later, Kay was asking Directory Enquiries for the number of the Walthamstow *Guardian*.

Not knowing quite what to say to him once she was put through, Kay found herself asking why he had walked away from her the day before.

'If you don't know, there's no point in my trying to explain,' he said flatly.

'I'm not pregnant, by the way,' she blurted, 'if that's what bothered you!'

There was a pause. 'Why did you say you were then?'

'I thought I was. Today proved different. I'm at home. I couldn't go to work and it was my first day as well.'

'Did you love him?' Zacchi was never one for mincing his words.

'I thought I did till you turned up.'

'I'll come and see you at the weekend.' Still there was no enthusiasm in his voice. 'Saturday morning, around eleven. I hope you feel better soon.' With that he replaced the receiver.

Feeling frustrated, Kay slammed the phone down. She had hardly said anything to him. She hadn't said how sorry she was, or how she couldn't stop thinking about him. Saturday seemed a lifetime away.

Chapter Twelve

At the end of her first week as receptionist/copy typist at Waterman's, Kay was feeling pleased with herself. Standing in front of the large pink-tinted mirror in Reception, she admired the new Italian suit she had bought in Petticoat Lane that lunchtime.

'Prince of Wales check. It suits you.' Mrs Jarold's sunny face smiled in the mirror as she stood behind Kay. The Staff Liaison Officer had taken a liking to Kay and Kay to her.

'You've made a good impression, you know. The editor of *Stock Market* wants to know if you can be transferred to his department.'

'Really?' Kay beamed, but then remembered that her shorthand wasn't as good as it could be. 'I don't suppose he uses a dictaphone?'

A look of concern came to Mrs Jarold's face. 'I thought you could work with one?'

'I can. I was worried in case he might want a shorthand typist.'

'Ah,' the smile returned to her face. 'No, my boss is the only old-fashioned one here. So? What do you think?'

Kay wasn't sure. She really enjoyed dealing with clients and having a bit of fun with the journalists when they dropped by for a chat. She would miss that. And the *Stock Market* wasn't exactly the most exciting journal.

'Can I let you know on Monday?'

'Of course you can.' She pushed open the smoked glass main door. 'I suppose I had better tell you that the *Mirror* has asked for you as well.' She winked at Kay. 'But don't let it go to your head.'

Staring after her as she walked out of the building, Kay couldn't help feeling thrilled.

'Have a good weekend!' A tall, dark-haired attractive woman in her early thirties passed Kay on her way out of the building.

'Excuse me!' Kay called after her.

Stopping in her tracks, she turned to face Kay. 'Yes?'

'Don't you work for *Female Weekly*?'

'Excellent memory! You've only been to our department once. We must have made an impression,' she smiled.

'Yeah, you did. There's kind of a buzz.'

'Glad you picked up on it. We're not always buzzing, though. It's a nightmare the day before we go to print. Tempers get a bit frayed to say the least.' She pushed the door open with her shoulder and gave Kay a show of her hand. 'See you Monday.'

That was it: that was her goal. Kay would ask if there were any chance of her working her way towards being part of *Female Weekly*'s team. She would turn down *Stock Market* and continue in Reception until a vacancy came up. It was a strange feeling, but she just knew by instinct that she would find her niche on that busy weekly, should the opportunity arise.

Squeezing into the stuffy carriage on the underground, this time Kay didn't mind being squashed like a sardine. She couldn't wait to tell her parents about the new job offers. Her mind went back to Thompson's and found herself believing in fate. If it hadn't been for that terrible incident she would never have left. She would still be working in that backwater instead of experiencing a thriving, lively company.

Her thoughts began to race. Maybe she would go to evening classes and learn about journalism. Maybe she could be trained as an editor. She had already

done a bit of proofreading for one of the journalists and she had only been working there four days. If she could achieve that much in such a short time, what could she achieve in a lifetime? Or at least before she settled into marriage and having children. She couldn't remember a time when she felt as happy and optimistic.

Walking home through Bethnal Green park, passing a couple of heavy drinkers who were sleeping it off, she wondered what it would be like to have her own flat in another part of town. Not that she didn't like living in the East End, but London was a big place and Kay had often felt the desire to live in other areas. A whole new life was out there, and in her mind's eye she likened it to a large cut-crystal globe, each facet showing a different Technicolor film, a hundred worlds existing at the same time.

'Hallo, babe. Your mum said you would be along any minute.' Frank and Freddie were walking down the stairs as Kay was on her way up. 'Like your new haircut. Suits yer,' her curly-headed uncle grinned.

'We was hoping to see you, Kay,' Frank said, slipping his hand into an inside pocket. 'This is for you.' He handed her a thick white envelope.

'What is it?' She had a horrible feeling she knew.

'It fell off the back of a van. Enjoy spending

it but don't let Mum or Dad know. They'd do their nuts.'

Laughing quietly, Frank carried on down the stairs. 'I take it there was no comeback for you?' he asked, a hopeful look on his face.

Trying to stop herself grinning, Kay slowly shook her head. 'I can't take this.'

'Now don't be a silly girl! That place deserved what it got and you deserve that. You don't have to spend it straight away, all at once, like. Wait till you see something you want.'

Leaving her speechless, they disappeared down the next flight of stairs. 'If you wanna bring your friends to the Kentucky, make it a Monday when it's quiet.' Frank's voice echoed in the stairwell.

Leaning over the green-painted metal banisters, Kay called down to them. 'Will Reg be there?'

'Probably . . . with his fiancée!'

Going directly to her room, Kay sat on the edge of the bed and drew a wad of banknotes out of the envelope. She felt a deep thrill as she began counting. Two hundred and fifty pounds. She swept her fingers across the fanned notes and wondered if she dared use it.

Hearing footsteps in the passage, she pushed the money back into the envelope and tossed it on top of the wardrobe.

'I thought I heard you come in,' Laura stood in the doorway. 'Zacchi phoned. Said he won't be able to make it tomorrow after all. He's got to cover a story.'

'You reckon?' Kay could feel herself sink. 'I'm not the same fifteen-year-old he fell in love with.'

Laura let out a throaty chuckle. 'Anyone'd think you were an old woman.' Stroking Kay's hair, she tried to stop herself smiling. 'So he's coming tonight instead.'

'Mum, that's not funny! You could have said.'

'I just did.'

'Yeah. Bit late though.'

''Cos you let your mum see how much you like him?' Laura teased. 'You won't need any tea.' Cocking her head to one side, she affected a cut-glass accent. 'He's taking you out to dinner. Do you want me to run you a bath? While I press whatever madam decides to wear?'

'My herring-bone suit and white short sleeves'll be all right, won't it? Or the pink and navy?'

Leaving the room, Laura told her not to worry – whatever she wore, she would knock Zacchi for six, if she hadn't already.

Knock him for six. The words rang around her head. Maybe that was the order of the day? She looked at herself in the full-length mirror and doubt

clouded her mind. *I'm not the same though, am I.*
I'm not a virgin any more. He's probably taking
me out to dinner to tell me it's over before it all
starts up again. He's probably guessed that I was
pregnant.

Opening the drawer of her dressing table, she took
out the false eyelashes she had bought but never
worn. Tonight they would get an airing. If Pamela
could wear them, so could she.

Pamela! She suddenly remembered. 'Mum!' She
stepped into the passage. 'I'm supposed to be going
to the Black Boy with Pam!'

'Phone her! She'll understand!' Showing her face
in the kitchen doorway, Laura shrugged. 'It had to
happen sometime, Kay. You're both gonna get dates,
and not always in a foursome.

'Did you pass Frank and Freddie by the way? They
left just before you came in.'

Kay slipped back into her bedroom. 'They just
said hallo and goodbye.'

'I'm not sure why they came, really,' Laura called
back. 'Probably wanted to see your dad about something.'

'Dunno!'

Pleased that she had managed to get the false
eyelashes on without making her eyes water, Kay
applied a touch of mascara, remembering that Zacchi

313

didn't think much of painted faces. She slicked on just a touch of ice-pink lipstick.

'He's here, Kay!' yelled Laura from the kitchen. Seconds later there was a knock at the door.

Zacchi stood on the doorstep looking as handsome as ever. 'I'm ready, but you can come in if you like.'

'I've waited too long to share you with anyone else.' He held out his hand and smiled.

Arm in arm, their stormy parting forgotten, they walked slowly through the backstreets. It was as if the three-year gap had never been. 'Where do you want to go?' Zacchi asked.

'Don't mind.'

Then without warning, he grabbed her by both arms and pulled her to him, not caring about the passers-by. They melted into a long kiss. 'I was mad to think there wouldn't be anyone else, Kay.'

'I did wait, Zac, I really did. But being in Spain and him looking so much like you—'

'That's history. Now it's just you and me.'

'Do you know what I would really like to do? Show you around the East End. Show you that it's not quite as Dickensian as people think.'

'If you must,' he groaned.

Carrying two cups of tea to a table in the canteen at

Hammond's, Laura waited for Liz to join her. She always took her tea-break when her sister-in-law was not so busy. That way they could sit and natter.

'You seemed a bit quiet at lunch-time.' Laura bit off the corner of her biscuit and waited.

'Did I?' Liz kept her eyes down. 'Bit tired, that's all.'

'Sure?'

'Yes, Laura. I'm sure. Stop digging.'

'There is something to dig for, then?'

Shaking her head and smiling, Liz sipped her tea. 'You're getting as bad as me.'

'Good. Well then?' Laura smiled, but she couldn't stop the nagging feeling. Liz had looked downcast for a couple of days now.

'You know Joe's retiring at the end of this month, don't you?'

'You already told me that. You're not fretting over it, surely?'

'No. Not over that. It's just that . . .' Liz sat back in her chair and pursed her lips. 'He's not all he's made out to be.'

That came as no surprise. Laura had always known that Joe liked the women, and if Liz hadn't been mourning for Bert when she met him, she would have given her a word of warning. As it was, it seemed best to leave it and hope for the best.

'He's a gold-digger,' Liz said at last. 'Thought I had a packet to come from the insurance policies. Ever since I told him that wasn't the case, he's been a bit standoffish.'

'Just as well you found out when you did.' Laura tried not to let her anger get the better of her for the sake of Liz's pride.

'I thought I'd found a friend. Someone I could talk to, a soul mate. Another person to watch television with. Maybe go to the pictures with, now and then.'

'You can always come round to us, Liz, you know that.'

'You know what's worse? The feeling of being used. I should 'ave known better. I'm no spring chicken.' She pulled her little blue tin out, checked that no one was watching and sprinkled some snuff on the back of her hand.

'I passed him on the stairs this morning; he was charming the woman who comes in to clean the telephones. I wouldn't mind betting she's a widow as well.'

'His type ain't worth upsetting yourself for, Liz.' Laura tried to think of something to lift her. 'I'll tell you what,' she smiled. 'My dad's missed you popping in to see him.'

'Poor old Billy,' Liz laughed. 'Missing someone like me? Must be desperate.'

'Come on, Liz. You don't mean that. You know the pair of you can make each other laugh about nothing.'

'Yeah, that's true. I'll drop in after work. Take him a couple of buns.'

'Good. And try not to think about Joe,' Laura stood up. 'He's a loser, Liz – if only he knew it.'

Walking out of the canteen, Laura stopped in the doorway and looked back at Liz. Telepathy or not, she knew that there was a question on Liz's mind, so she walked slowly back and stood next to her.

'You don't think your dad would wanna move in with me, do you?'

'No chance, Liz. But I know he'd love it if you took his spare room. My old bedroom.'

There was a pause as Liz thought about it. 'It's a smashing little cottage,' she said softly.

'Shut away from the rest of the world behind that old green door in the wall,' Laura persuaded.

'I suppose he does get on with the neighbours?'

'They're all pensioners, Liz. All worked for the brewery. They all know each other. It'd be like hop-picking without the hardships.'

'And you think Billy'd go for that? Me moving around in his little house?'

'Ask him.'

*   *   *

317

Laura hadn't seen Jack look so happy in a very long time. Now, in the middle of July, the London dock strike was over and the men were going back to work the next day. While he wasn't that pleased with the outcome it was obvious that he, like hundreds of other men, was sick of just passing the time of day.

Pressing the collar of his shirt, Laura felt a rush of admiration for him. He was giving the blade of his docker's hook a good polish.

'You did well. All of yer. You let this country know the strength of the dockers.'

'Maybe,' Jack said, trying to hide his true feelings. He couldn't wait to get back to the dockside, and she knew it. 'There's gonna be an investigation by a government-sponsored committee next week. At least it's woken 'em up a bit. If we hadn't have agreed to go back, they would have had to move troops in, you know, to move the perishables.' There was a touch of pride in his voice.

'Well, maybe they'll think twice now before they take on outside labour.'

'You can bet your life on it.' Changing the subject, he brought the conversation around to Liz.

'I saw your dad down the waste today. At the fruit and veg stall. Looked happy as a sandboy,

318

picking out a fresh cauliflower.' Jack chuckled. 'D'yer reckon they'll get married, or what?'

''Course they won't. She's gonna be his lodger and that's all they want.' She hung his shirt on a hanger and checked the cuffs. 'That's all that matters at the end of the day, a bit of company. Someone to say goodnight to.'

'I never did trust that bloke of hers. Taking her to seance meetings. She wouldn't listen, though.'

'No, and neither would you if the boot was on the other foot.'

'Kay's late in,' he said, looking at his watch.

'She's nearly eighteen, Jack, and it's only just gone half past eleven.'

'Half past eleven,' he said, staring out. 'I always had to get you back home by ten.'

'Yeah well, times have changed, thank God. You can do the same thing at midnight as you can before ten. As you well know,' she half smiled.

'I never laid a hand on you till you begged me.'

'Bloody cheek! Me, beg? That'll be the day.'

'Yes you did. With your eyes.' He laid down his sharpening stone. 'Coming to bed?'

Laura pulled the plug out of the socket and stood the iron on the tiled fireplace to cool down. 'I thought you'd never ask.'

'What d'yer think about this gypsy, then?' Jack said.

'Oh, don't keep calling him that, Jack, it's not funny. He's a good kid and she likes him a lot.'

'That's what worries me.'

'He doesn't live in Spain . . .' She had been saving that one.

'That's true,' he said, rubbing his eyes. 'What am I gonna do about this money, Laura?'

'I can't keep up with you. Your mind flashes from one thing to another. What money?'

'The envelopes, for Liz.'

'You should have given them to her by now.'

'I know. I can't bring myself to, though. I suppose I don't want her to have it.' He stood up and stretched. 'Scum money.'

'Oh, shut up. You don't know it's from drugs. You're just guessing. Anyway, you should leave it to Liz to decide. You're not her keeper.'

'Yeah. I s'pose you're right. I'll pop round there after work tomorrow.'

Laura folded the ironing-board and leaned it against the wall. 'I know what I'd do with it.'

He looked at her and waited.

'I'd book a cruise for her and Billy. Tell her you had a good win on the dogs. She won't ask any questions. Neither will Dad.'

'You serious?'

'Yes, Jack, I am. Sod it! Why shouldn't the pair of them see a bit of the world? If that money goes back to the boys it'll just get pissed away.'

'Oy, oy, oy! Language,' Jack scolded.

Laura knew he hated to hear her being coarse, but she knew how to distract him. 'It's true though. You know it is.' She moved close to him and rested her hands on his broad shoulders. 'Where's the harm in it, eh? Try to think of it as unearned income that the taxman won't get his hands on.'

'You mean it, don't yer?'

'Both of them have worked hard all their lives. As hard as any self-made millionaire. So why shouldn't they have a thin slice of what the rich enjoy most of the time?'

'Well,' Jack grinned, 'put like that, what can I say?' He put his strong hands on her small waist, pulled her to him and kissed her with passion.

They would have made love on the rug if the doorbell hadn't brought them down from the heady heights.

'She's forgotten her key again,' Laura couldn't help laughing. 'I'll see her in. You go and warm up the bed.'

Sitting on the edge of the sofa, Laura waited patiently for Kay to stop crying. She knew it was

no use trying to comfort her. She had seen her like this before. She'd stop soon enough.

'What will I *do*?' Kay could hardly speak. 'A whole month! Four weeks.' She buried her head in Laura's shoulder and wailed louder.

Suppressing a smile, Laura tried to see the sad side of it, but it seemed impossible. Zacchi had been commissioned to travel through France and Spain, finding and following Romany travellers, and collecting material for a book about them.

'It'll soon pass, Kay.' Laura could have bitten her tongue. She knew that was the last thing her daughter needed to hear.

'How am I gonna live without him?' Kay looked pleadingly at her out of red, swollen eyes.

Her fingers pressed against her mouth, Laura managed to ask if Kay would like a hot milky drink. Thankfully she did, which gave her a chance to get into the kitchen where she could be alone to let out the pent-up laughter. *My God!* She slowly shook her head. *Did I ever feel like that about anyone?* Then she remembered the feeling of emptiness each year that came when she left Richard in Kent.

Knowing Jack was waiting for her in bed, she suddenly felt guilty for thinking about another man. She wondered if Richard would ever fade from her memory.

'You coming to bed, Laura, or what?' Half asleep, Jack stood in the kitchen doorway.

'Kay's upset. Zacchi's got to go away for a month; they want him to write a book. She's sobbing her heart out in there.'

Jack looked at her blankly. 'A month's not that long, is it?'

'She reckons she won't be able to live without him.' Laura managed to sound serious in case he got annoyed with her for treating it lightly.

'Four weeks?' Jack raised an eyebrow and grinned.

'Jack, don't. If she hears you . . .'

With his hand on his mouth, he practically ran along the passage and into the bedroom where Laura could be sure he would bury his face in his pillow to muffle his laughter.

Pouring the hot milk on to Horlicks in Kay's mug, Laura wondered what she could say to her baby to cheer her up. She remembered the blue box in the sideboard.

Curled up on the sofa, Kay sipped her drink between small, spasmodic sobs. 'Thanks, Mum. This is lovely.'

Sitting next to her, Laura held out a hand and offered Kay the ring box. 'This was your grand-father's, your dad's dad. Aunt Liz won't mind if you have it. It's not that valuable, but it is gold.'

Kay took it and pushed the lid up with her thumb. 'This is a man's ring, Mum.'

'Of course it is. I told yer. It was your grandad's. That stone's an onyx.'

'Why are you giving it to me?'

'So that you can give it to Zacchi.'

A smile lit up her face. 'Are you sure?'

'I've never been surer. While he's wearing that, part of you will be with him.'

As she lay next to Jack in bed, Laura hoped he wouldn't hit the roof when she told him about his dad's ring.

'You asleep?' she whispered in his ear, and then kissed his cheek.

'Give my leg a massage, will yer. It's gone dead.'

Slipping her hand down his thigh, Laura began to giggle. 'You lying sod! You've been lying there thinking about me.'

'No I haven't. I've been dreaming about Sophia Loren.'

Turning over, she switched off the bedside lamp and then climbed out of bed.

'Where are you going?' Jack was suddenly awake.

'Just opening the curtains a bit. I want to see you in the lamplight.'

A deep sigh escaped him as he reached out for her.

'Everything seems to be turning out all right then,' Laura said. 'With our Kay, I mean. Happy in love and happy at work.'

'Yeah, but that don't mean she won't do an about-turn all of a sudden. Little cow. I've never known anyone so unpredictable.'

'No?' Laura slipped in beside him. 'I think she's a chip off the old block.' She kissed him lightly on the mouth.

'Your block – not mine,' he joked, and pulled her on top of him.

At Waterman's, Kay got what she had asked for. Once word was out that she could not only type fast but accurately, the journalists threw handwritten copy at her, and she was forever being asked to help someone out with the dictaphone. She was also bombarded with offers to go to the pub after work.

'So who's the lucky fellow?' John from *Stock Market* handed Kay a vodka and tonic.

'What makes you think there is one?' Kay was flirting with him, but it was expected with this lot.

'You're not interested in any of *us*,' he said with a touch of hope in his smile.

'His name's Zacchi. He's a travel writer.'

'What kind of a name's that?'

'He's a Romany.' Her back stiffened as she shot

him a warning glance, before he started being offensive.

'Tall, dark and handsome?'

'Not quite as tall as you. Probably not as handsome.'

'But?'

'But . . . he's got it.' Kay sipped her drink. 'Whatever *it* is.'

'You mean you don't know?'

'Does any of us?'

John thought about that, then shrugged. 'So where is he tonight, while you're out with all the journos?'

Fed up with being jostled by the pub crowd, Kay looked around for somewhere to sit. 'He's travelling in France.'

'Over there,' John cut in, 'in the corner. Push your way through. I'll follow.'

Once they were settled, John's manner seemed to change. He was more at ease. 'My fiancée's taking our bridesmaids for a fitting,' he said, unable to keep the pride out of his voice.

'You're getting married!' Why Kay should feel so pleased for him she had no idea. They had hardly spoken at work. Polite greetings as he passed on his way in and out of Reception was all that had passed between them, except when he gave her copy to type up.

'You look relieved,' he smiled and drank his beer.

'I suppose I am really. Don't know why, though.'

'You feel safe,' he teased. 'I'm not the lecher you thought I was.'

She had to admit to herself that he was right. They could talk easily now. The guard was down. No need to read into every line. 'How long have you been engaged?'

'Three years. On and off. Five times off.'

'And now you're sure?'

'As much as I'll ever be. What about you, yours serious?'

Kay was impressed that he seemed genuinely interested. 'Very. But it's early days.' She looked into his face. 'Can you tell me something?'

John raised an eyebrow. 'Depends.'

'Why do blokes usually talk to us girls as if you're chatting us up? I don't mean now. Now we're talking normally.'

'We have proof of nothing but our own existence,' he cut in.

'Come again?'

'Ego. Over-concerned about our image,' he said thoughtfully. 'Or . . . scared of coming across as boring?'

'But the chat-up lines and the tone you use, all

the eye contact, that *is* boring. All you can see is the method. The man's hidden.'

'There's your answer. Think about it.' He finished his beer, placed the glass on the table and looked into her bemused face. 'Now then, how about you getting a round?'

Taken aback, she found herself laughing. 'That's the first time a bloke has ever asked me!'

'You're one of us now.'

'Good.' She took that as the best compliment ever paid. 'What's yours?'

'Gin and tonic, please.'

'OK.' Kay looked at the crowded bar. There were a few women, but it was mostly men she'd have to find her way through. 'I don't suppose—'

'You want me to get them in?'

'Would you?' She handed him a ten-shilling note and felt herself blush. 'I'm not used to this.'

Taking the money, he suddenly stroked her face, and withdrew his hand like lightning. 'Sorry.' He jokingly put up both hands as if in surrender.

'It's OK. Don't push it though,' she joked.

While she waited for him to bring the drinks, gazing at the red and gold wallpaper, Kay tried to clarify her feelings. She thought about Zacchi and how much she loved him. She thought about Chris and remembered how she had felt. Now there was

John. She was beginning to like him a lot and felt guilty that she was enjoying his company.

'A penny for them?' He placed their drinks down and handed her the change.

'You really want to know?'

'Can't wait,' he leaned back in his chair.

'Well . . . I was wondering about love.'

'Oh *that*,' he let out a small embarrassed chuckle. 'Not to be confused with sexual attraction.'

'Right. So how do we know when it's the real thing?'

'You shouldn't have to ask. You just know.'

Kay became pensive. Somehow, deep down, she felt he must be right. 'Can two people of the opposite sex have a strong liking for each other without . . .' she shrugged, 'you know.'

'Of course. And so can two people of the same sex.' He offered her a cigarette. 'It's affection.'

'And affection's not love?' She waved away the packet.

'No. It's when all the emotions are going that love ends up on the table.' He leaned forward. 'And we blocked sexual attraction when we spoke about our *betrothed*.' He lit his cigarette. 'Got it?'

'I think so. What you're saying is . . . we can love more than one person, but we only really love the one.'

'At the time,' he broke in. 'I love Pauline – that's her name – and I love my sisters, sometimes. I also love my parents. Some of my colleagues. My friends. And now you.'

Kay looked at him worriedly. If he was so clever, so philosophical about it, why had he singled her out instead of grouping her together with his friends?

'You, my new friend and colleague,' he reassured, reading her thoughts.

'You're such a clever dick,' she laughed.

'No. I had to read up on it. Sort myself out. I'm the one who's getting married, don't forget. I had to be sure. And you know what the bottom line was? The questions I asked myself? Would I want this person to bear my children? Did I want part of me and her to make a whole?' He sipped his drink and sighed. 'That was when I knew. This was for real and for good.'

Wondering why she felt a sudden pang of jealousy, Kay decided it was time for her to leave. She looked at her watch and faked her surprise at the time. 'My mum'll go mad! I said I would be going straight home tonight.'

'Phone her.' John sounded very casual about it. 'Your parents'll have to get used to it. We spend most of our time in the pub. It's part of the job. Where we pick up our little tips.'

Before she had time to decide, Jeannie arrived. 'Hi! What're you two up to?'

'Hallo, how's tricks?' John eyed her slim, shapely body.

'I wouldn't know. I never play them.' She turned to Kay and winked. 'I hope he hasn't been trying to turn your head?'

'If discussing bridesmaids is turning a head, the answer's yes,' he grinned sardonically.

'Oh, well done you,' she said to Kay. 'When they begin to tell you about the domestic, it means you've been initiated. Welcome to the club.' Jeannie pulled up a chair and squeezed it into a tiny gap around the table.

'Of course you'll be treated quite differently now. One of the chaps. Expect lots of jokes and no more real lustful looks.'

'You make us sound undesirable! Mine's a gin and tonic.'

'You know where the bar is.' She pulled a pound note out of her pocket. 'Get one for Kay. Whisky mac for yours truly.'

'You've done well for yourself.' She eased herself forward, allowing just enough room for John to pass. 'It usually takes longer for them to accept you as one of *them*.'

'What kind of jokes should I expect?' Kay was

beginning to like the idea of being part of this new life.

'Oh, all sorts. They'll hide your handbag in the Gents'. Glue your coffee mug to the blotting pad, that sort of thing. Until the next new girl comes along.' She lit a cigarette and kept it dangling from the corner of her mouth while she pulled a tiny face mirror from her handbag.

'Do you enjoy working in Reception, Kay?' she said, checking her reflection.

'They keep me busy. I like that.'

'Well let me know when you've had enough. We need someone to sort us out.'

'I enjoyed the article I typed up for you last week. I didn't realize you were allowed to write about something as serious as that and show the humorous side of it as well.'

'Life and death, love. Get too heavy and you're pulled. And I'm not talking bed.' She took a long draw on her cigarette. 'If you read our mag, you'll see what I mean.'

'I keep meaning to. Don't seem to get the time.'

'Ever thought about scribbling?' Jeannie peered into Kay's face. 'You never know, you might be good.'

'I suppose everyone's had that dream,' Kay shrugged, 'but I'm just a girl from the East End. In

my school the teachers were there more to keep order than to teach. My holes have got a little grammar in them, you might say.'

'Grammar! That's the least of your problems. That, my love, can be taught. Talent cannot.'

'Talking about me again?' John set down a tray of drinks.

'Kay's going to write a feature for *Female Weekly*. What It's Like Living in the East End.'

'Am I?'

'Deadline Wednesday, five o'clock. That gives you the weekend plus three days. No more than a thousand words, double-spaced. Tell us about the wheeling and dealing; the pub life; poverty, and—' she closed her eyes '—Oh, yes,' she smiled, 'the lack of education and rule in schools.'

'OK,' Kay swallowed half her drink, 'you're on. One condition though. You check my spelling on the first draft.'

John roared with laughter. 'She's the worst speller in the whole building. Give it to me, I'll sort it.'

Looking questioningly at Jeannie, Kay was a little surprised to see that she was nodding.

'He's right, the cheeky bastard. And he's probably the best guide you could get. Even though it pains me to say so.'

Within minutes of Jeannie joining them, others

arrived and were duly introduced to Kay. Some she had already seen to say hallo to at work, and others who wrote for other publications. Drinks were offered one after the other, and more than one conversation went on at a time. Most of which went over Kay's head. But she enjoyed it all the same; the buzz was fantastic, and she made up her mind there and then that this was the world for her. She would catch up. She would read up. Soon she would know what they were talking about and understand all the in-house jokes.

Feeling more than light-headed, she made her way to the tube and wondered if her parents would smell the drink on her breath. It was nine-thirty. She thanked her lucky stars that a night in had been the intention, otherwise a very angry Pam*elia* would be waiting for her.

'Hallo, Liz. Did you fetch the haddock?' Billy asked as he closed his front door behind her.

'Yeah. Richard Wood was up the market so I bought it from 'im. Cheaper and a bit fresher. I could do with a cup of tea.'

'I'll put the kettle on. Take the weight off your feet.' He pulled a kitchen chair out from under his green-painted table.

'I don't know,' Liz kicked off her shoes and

relaxed. 'I used to love the sunshine, but give me a light cloudy day any time.'

'Laura's old room don't get a lot of sunshine, you know. Time it gets round to the back of the house it's gone down too far.' He shovelled tea into the aluminium teapot. 'I thought I'd give the walls a coat of primrose to brighten it up a bit. I don't know what you think about this brilliant white that's in. For the paintwork, I mean.'

'Jack said he'd do any decorating for yer, Billy. You don't 'ave to push yourself,' Liz said, yawning and rubbing her eyes.

'It keeps me busy. And how come you're so tired? You 'ad a lie-in today, surely? Your day off?'

'Yeah, I know. But I was up at six all the same. Sorting out my things. Where does it all come from, eh?'

'You were married a long time, Lizzie.' He handed her a cup of tea. 'When's the second-hand dealer meant to be giving you a price?'

'Charlie's coming round at seven.' Sipping her tea, Liz looked over her cup at him. 'You sure we're doing the right thing?'

''Course we are. Makes sense. One set of bills instead of two.'

'Yeah, but, oh, I don't know.' She shook her

head. 'I just 'ope you won't regret it, that's all. You must 'ave got used to having the place to yerself.'

'You can always get used to loneliness, gal. That doesn't mean to say you like it. What time shall I cook the haddock?'

'About one'll do.' Liz looked at the small orange clock on the kitchen dresser. Five past ten. 'That's fast, innit?'

'Yeah. Ten minutes. Don't ask me why I like to keep it that way, I still haven't worked it out. Need anything down the waste?'

Liz thought about it. 'I wouldn't mind treating myself to a new dressing gown. I wonder if that knock-down stall's out this week?'

'Bound to be. We'll go once we've drunk this. Wanna biscuit?'

'No. I had a big bowl of porridge this morning. I'm still in the habit of making enough for two.' She lowered her eyes, appreciating the silence. That was the good thing about her and Billy. They had known each other long enough to realize when to keep quiet.

'How about a nice lemon housecoat? To go with your new bedroom,' Billy grinned as he pulled on his cap.

'No. I fancy a pale blue candlewick,' said Liz with

conviction as she pulled the old gate shut behind them. 'If not pale blue, then rose pink.'

'It's your money,' he said, striding along Cleveland Way, swinging his arms.

'Slow down, Billy, for Gawd's sake.' Liz had been trying to keep up with him. 'I'm nearly out of breath already. And my throat's dry.'

'I'll treat you to a nice cold sarsaparilla from Becky's sweet shop.'

Liz stopped in her tracks. 'If you don't slow down, I'm going back! I mean it, Billy,' she said, shaking her head at him. 'You're gonna have to get out of that habit of walking fast when you're out with me.'

'All right, gal,' he said, waiting for her. 'Don't get your knickers in a twist. I was rushing to get this bet on, that's all.'

'Oh, right. Go on then, I'll catch you up. I don't want you to miss it. Expect you've been studying form since five this morning.'

'Paper didn't come till half past six. Shall I put one on for you?' he called back over his shoulder.

'Yeah, go on then. A dollar to win on whatever you've picked!'

'A dollar? Bit steep, innit?' He stood on the pavement, pushed his cap back and rubbed his chin. 'If you're gonna spend that much, why not go for a treble?'

'All right. You sort 'em out. But a treble win! I don't wanna place-bet. Not worth it.'

Laughing quietly to himself, Billy walked on, a bit slower. Liz knew he was giving himself time to think about this morning's study, remembering which horses were in good form.

Arriving outside the betting shop, she perched herself on the low window-sill and was content to watch the Saturday shoppers go by. Facing Hammond's side entrance, she was pleased not to be in there working. Monday would come around soon enough.

'Hallo, Liz.' Milly's cheery voice broke into her thoughts. 'I'm just going in to see Laura. I know she finishes at twelve, so I mustn't stop.'

Liz blinked twice as she turned to face her friend whom she hadn't seen in ages. 'Talk about a face from the past,' she chuckled.

'I always go down the waste on a Saturday, Liz. It's you who's out of your territory. Bethnal Green market going downhill, is it?'

'No, I'm just waiting for Billy. Laura's dad. He's in there,' she tilted her head towards the door. 'How's tricks then? Georgie's leg still playing him up?'

'No. Did him the world of good, that little stretch inside. He's a changed man. They knocked the loafer out of him, I'll tell yer.' She looked and sounded

happier than Liz had ever seen her. 'I miss 'oppin', though, don't you?'

Realizing that Milly couldn't have heard her bad news, Liz braced herself. 'My Bert passed away you know,' she said quietly.

'Oh, Liz. Surely not? Not Bert?' Her eyes filled up in seconds.

'Yeah,' Liz sighed. 'It was a bit of a shock. Heart. Died in his sleep, more or less . . . you know.' Liz swallowed hard.

'I'm sorry, love.' Milly shook her head. 'When I think of the bastards who are walking about and shouldn't be.'

'Do you ever see Mrs Brown?' Liz was quick to change the subject. She hardly needed reminding that Bert should still be by her side.

'Yeah, poor cow. Walks about as if she's in another world. He left her in the end you know. Gawd knows where to. Still, she's better off I suppose. At least she's not covered in bruises any more. Can't be easy though, bringing up four kids on her own.'

'So why you going in to see my Laura, then? Gonna treat yourself to a nice new frock?'

'As it 'appens. My Brianny's getting married, can you believe? We've booked the room above the Artichoke. Got a band and everything. Her family's

from Tonbridge. Little bit on the posh side, so I wanna make a good impression, see?'

''Course you do, Milly, and why not?'

Checking the narrow road for traffic, Milly looked back. 'Why don't you and Laura come for half hour? It'll be like old times.'

'What about Jack? He's still around, you know,' Liz smiled.

'Yeah, 'course, I just thought you might feel . . . oh, I dunno.'

'I'll bring Billy with me if that makes you feel better.'

'Do that.' She stepped out into the road. 'Billy, eh? Didn't take you long, did it,' she teased.

Liz smiled but inside she hurt. The remark cut deep. But then she would have to contend with more of that in the future, especially once she had moved into his cottage. But she could cope with it. She knew why she and Billy needed to share the same roof. Loneliness could turn a good day into a nightmare, and there were lots of days ahead of them both. God willing.

'Our Kay seems to be all right now,' Billy said as he and Liz strolled along the waste.

'What's that supposed to mean?' Liz was sharp enough to realize he might be trying to tell her something.

'I was a bit concerned. When she came back from that Spanish holiday of hers, she looked drawn in the face, as if she had something on her mind.'

'She fell in love, Billy. What d'yer expect?'

'That's what worried me.'

'In case her lover-boy had been dipping his lolly in the sherbet, you mean?'

'Something like that, yeah,' he laughed. 'You can be crude at times, Liz, you know that?'

'It's honesty in my book. Anyway, she's all right. Not in the club, if that's what's worrying yer.'

'You know that, do you?'

'Yes, Billy. I do.'

'That's all right then. All we have to hope is that she behaves herself with that gypsy.' He nodded towards the delicatessen. 'I just wanna pop in and get a couple of Barron's New Green cucumbers to go with our fried fish.'

Waiting outside for him, enjoying the sun on her face, Liz spotted Kay's best friend Pamela walking towards her. She was grinning like a Cheshire cat.

'What you looking so pleased about?' Liz said.

'My boyfriend's coming over from Spain, for a holiday. Next week. Don't tell Kay though, I want it to be a surprise. I want to watch her face when we all turn up on her doorstep.'

'All?'

341

'Charles, that's my young man's name, and Chris . . . Kay's friend.'

'Let's hope Zacchi doesn't get jealous.'

'Zacchi won't be here though, will he? He'll be out of the country while Chris's in it. Perfect timing.'

'So long as it's not two-timing.' Liz was feeling rattled at Pamela's attitude.

Shrugging, Pamela made to step into her parents' delicatessen. 'Why are you standing out here anyway?'

Liz nodded towards Billy who was paying for his pickled cucumbers. 'Kay's grandfather's doing a bit of shopping.'

Pamela looked thoughtful. 'You're gonna move into his spare room, aren't you? Never too old, eh?' she smiled, leaving Liz open-mouthed.

Feeling her anger rising, Liz inhaled slowly. Had Pamela not slipped out of her hands so quickly, she would have given her a piece of her mind about showing respect to her elders. One thing was becoming very clear: Liz was going to have to accept the fact that people jumped to the obvious conclusions about her and Billy.

'Come on,' Liz walked ahead as her friend joined her. 'I fancy a walk around the art gallery.'

'You what?' Billy shoved the well-wrapped pickles into his jacket pocket.

'The Whitechapel art gallery. It's cool, peaceful and there are nice pictures to look at.'

'Fair enough,' he took her by the hand and led her through the doors. 'This feels a bit like courting to me,' he smiled.

'Don't start that, Billy. We're friends. Don't spoil it.'

'It was a joke, Liz. I'm too old for all that.'

'You reckon?' Liz threw him a mischievous look. 'I wouldn't bank on it.'

Instead of making her way towards her and Pamela's favourite coffee bar, Kay found herself walking along Bethnal Green, heading for the second-hand office equipment shop. She had decided to borrow ten pounds from the envelope to buy herself a typewriter.

Sitting down at the desk, she tried out the used Underwood machine. It took her back to her school days and the commerce course. It was identical to the one on which she had learned to type. She remembered her teacher fighting to have proper desks and typewriters brought in.

'You won't find anything cheaper in that condition.' The owner of the small office equipment shop ran his hand through a thick mop of frizzy, light brown hair. 'And since you're such a pretty

face, I'll throw in a spare ribbon.' He crossed his thick, heavily freckled arms and cupped his reddish beard, giving her a fatherly wink.

'Done,' Kay smiled shyly. She felt like yelling for joy. Her own typewriter! Now she could tuck herself away in her room and write whenever she felt like it.

'Gonna write a book, are yer?' he smiled.

'Who knows?' She swept her hand across the keys. 'I always wanted to, when I was little. I begged my dad to buy me a John Bull printing set. He got me a little printing gadget instead. He thought it would be better because it was more up to date.' She looked back at the shop owner, 'I needed a hand-held printing set.'

'The ones with rubber letters all in a row?'

'And you cut them up and used tweezers to space them into the words you wanted to make up and print.'

'Be a lot quicker with this.' He tapped out *I am a writer!* 'Never forget that, and you'll soon 'ave other people believing it.'

Kay felt a tingling in her fingertips. 'I wish it was true.'

'It is true. It's written all over you.' He pointed a friendly finger in her face. 'It's up to you. There's no law to stop you. And every day has twenty-four hours.'

'You sound as if you know something about it.' Kay was warming to him by the second.

'There are three novels gathering dust on my shelf. A collection of my poems and a few short stories. One day I'll send something off to a publisher,' he said, obviously embarrassed.

'Can I read one of the novels?' Kay asked.

'No one ever gets to see the rubbish I write.' There was an underlying tone of disappointment in his blunt voice.

'OK, but what if I do manage to type a book?'

'*Write* a book,' he corrected.

'OK, write a book. We could swap and read each other's. I'll promise to tell you honestly if I think it's good or not – if you'll do the same for mine.'

'How to lose a friend!' he laughed.

'I've never met anyone who's actually written a novel. I work with journalists, but three novels, poetry, short stories! You must be good.'

'Well, I think I am, but . . .' he shrugged and spread his hands. 'Tell you what, come back next Saturday and I'll have sorted out a short story for you to take away and read. So long as you don't nick my ideas.'

'That'd be great. A good excuse to come back in here as well.' She spun herself around on the typist's chair. 'I love the smell of oil and ink and

metal, and all these different typewriters. Some look as if they've come out of the ark.'

'They'll be worth a lot of money in the future. Collector's pieces.'

'You reckon?' Kay shook her head and laughed at him. 'I doubt it.'

Proudly carrying her typewriter in its case, Kay walked into the living room to find Laura and Jack sitting quietly with their heads lowered. There was a heavy atmosphere in the room.

'You'd best sit down, Kay,' Laura murmured. 'There's something your dad wants to talk to you about.' She gave Jack a nudge with her foot to urge him.

Folding the letter which had brought the news, Jack leaned back in his armchair and sighed. 'Take the weight off your feet then,' he smiled sheepishly at her, wondering how she would react to his thunderbolt.

Sitting on the edge of the sofa, Kay looked from her dad to her mum and back to her dad again. 'What's happened now?'

'It's more a case of what happened nearly three years ago.'

Jack took his tobacco tin from his cardigan pocket. 'I know it didn't escape your notice that Mum and me went through a bad patch.'

'It could hardly escape my notice, Dad. It went on for years before it all came to a head.' She didn't want those memories to come flooding back. 'I thought that was all in the past. Dead and buried?'

'It is, babe. As far as your mum and me are concerned. We've never been as happy together as we are now.' His voice trailed off.

'So what, then?' She knew it was serious from his face.

'Well . . .' Jack was finding it difficult to choose the right words. 'I was—' he shook his head, 'I've been a silly boy.'

'You're not a boy, Dad!'

'No. OK. Fair enough. When your mum and me were sleeping in separate rooms there was a reason for it. I was full of guilt, OK? I was having an affair with someone called—'

'I don't want to know her name!' Kay clenched her fists, forcing herself not to get emotional. 'I knew about her at the time, so it's not news now! And you know that, so what's different?'

'You've got a half-brother.'

It didn't go in, not at first. Kay deliberately blocked it. She felt a sudden surge of hate for her father. Hate and disgust. 'I'm going to my room,' she stood up, not looking at either of them.

'Sit down!' Jack ordered. 'Sit down and listen!

And stop acting the madam!' His face was red and the veins on his neck stood out as if ready to burst.

'I'm not acting! I hate you!' she screamed. 'You make me feel sick. Dirty! I wish I had nothing to do with you!'

'That's enough, Kay!' Laura yelled. 'You high-and-mighty little cow. Do as your dad says and sit back down *now*!'

Reluctantly, Kay threw herself on to the sofa, crossed her arms and legs and glared at Jack. 'I'm listening!'

'Your brother's—'

'I haven't got a brother!'

'Your brother is two and a half years old.' Jack spoke slowly, emphasizing each word, daring her not to deny him. 'And he's a dead ringer for you.'

'And that's supposed to make me feel better, is it?'

'I'm not asking you to feel anything, Kay. I know this has come as a shock.'

'You should have told me before now.' She stood up and paced the floor. 'How dare you not tell me I've got a brother? What right have you to keep that from me?' Kay felt as if she were going to explode. She couldn't believe how insensitive they could be.

'Sit *down*, Kay,' Laura pleaded. She was finding

it difficult too. 'Your dad's really upset about this letter he got today.'

'I'm not gonna sit down.' She breathed hard. 'What letter?'

'It's from the child's mother.' Jack carefully avoided calling Patsy by her name. He knew exactly why Kay didn't want to hear it.

'She's getting married, and her boyfriend refuses to take on someone else's—' Jack swallowed hard, looking at the letter in his hand, 'bastard,' he murmured, heavy with guilt.

'Bloody cheek. How dare any one say that about an innocent two-year-old?'

'The thing is, little Jac—'

'Little *who*? You named him after you?' Now she did feel the effect of the shock. It struck instantly. As if someone had tapped the top of her head with a wand and said *Freeze!*

'There's a little boy,' she spoke in a monotone, not moving, not looking, staring ahead, 'who looks like me. My brother. I have a brother. And his name is the same as my dad's. You've been loving him all this time.' The tears were warm as they rolled down her cheeks, cold by the time they reached her neck.

'But I had to be kept out of it. You didn't want me to see my brother?' She looked at Jack, appealing. 'Why did you do that? Why have you kept us apart?

You must love him a lot. You called him Jack. You named him after you. You didn't name me after Mum.' She could hardly focus through her tears.

'*She* called him that, not me!' Jack clenched his teeth. 'And now she's dumped him in a *home*.' Covering his face, Jack began to cry.

Kay had never seen her dad like this before. Loud wailing sounds were coming from him. His body was shaking, almost going into convulsions. Then she remembered coming round after the drowning accident in Kent. She had heard him crying then. It was the same desperate sobbing.

'They've put the poor little sod out, Kay,' he looked up at her, 'dumped him. She's got 'er way in the end. She wanted to get rid of him from the start.' He felt a sharp kick from Laura, and could have bit his tongue.

'No!'

Laura found her voice again. 'A small children's home in Leicester.'

'How could she do a thing like that?'

'She's not all bad. Poor cow probably had no choice. He must have given her an ultimatum. And when you love someone . . .'

'So you want to know how I feel about you taking him?' Kay said.

'No.' Jack shook his head. 'She's made it very

clear that she wants him kept in the neighbourhood so that she and the grandparents can visit him at weekends.' He mopped his face with his handkerchief and made an effort to compose himself.

'She wants to have her cake and eat it. Well, we're not just gonna leave it like that, are we?' Kay looked from one parent to the other.

'We'll try applying to the authorities to foster him but it'll take ages, and there's not much of a chance that we'll get him. Mostly because of us living out of the area.'

'So while we've got a home to offer, a loving family, a room of his own, he has to stay in a home?' Kay raised her eyebrows. 'They need their brains tested if they think we're gonna put up with that.'

'It'll take months, years of fighting and meanwhile, that little kid finds himself in a strange place full of people he doesn't know.' Jack's eyes were blazing. 'It beats me how anyone can do that!'

'Especially to a little darling like Jac,' Laura hung her head.

'You've been seeing him too?' Another blow for Kay.

'Only the once. I found a letter in your dad's jacket pocket. I went to Leicester to punch her in the face, but when I got there . . . saw that little tot in his play-pen . . .' Laura found she could barely speak.

'And he is the image of you, Kay. I could hardly believe it.'

'Right,' Kay said, her voice full of determination. 'You two are obviously too upset to do anything, so I suppose it's up to me. I'll get him out.'

'You can't do that,' Jack smiled at her through his tears. 'The law's an ass and all that, but try fighting it.'

'I don't give a *fuck* about the law any more! I've had it up to here with the law and its double standards!'

'Oh, Kay, please don't swear. Don't get bitter,' Laura pleaded.

But Kay could not be stopped. 'Sometimes we have to ignore what's written as wrong – when we know it's right. And that's just what I intend to do.'

Jack frowned at her. 'What's on your mind, babe?'

'You'll see.' She left the room, slamming the door behind her.

'D'yer think Kay took it to heart, you know, when I talked about Patsy wanting to get rid of—'

'Oh, shut up, Jack. She's put it out of her mind – why can't you do the same?'

Jack leaned back in his chair and closed his eyes. 'Because I'm still gutted over it, that's why. I know what I'd like to do to that Spaniard.'

'And I thought you were ready to forgive and forget. Silly me!'

'I'll never forget. Never. Just let him show his face, that's all!'

Chapter Thirteen

Standing in the doorway of *Female Weekly*, Kay saw before her yet another new and exciting world. The sound of electric typewriters clacking busily, the whirr of the photocopying machine and the conversation of people in the office and on the telephone conducting interviews sent a thrill of possibility to Kay's core. She caught sight of Jeannie across the room and cautiously wove her way around workers and desks to join her.

'I suppose you're too busy to talk to me?' Kay said, worried she might be disturbing her train of thought.

Switching off her machine, Jeannie leaned back in her chair and smiled. 'Don't tell me you've finished the article already?'

'No. I haven't even started it.'

Her superior's expression changed instantly. Without uttering a word, she was asking Kay what, in that case, was she doing there.

'Can I sit down?'

Looking at her watch, she narrowed her eyes. 'Five minutes. I'm running late.'

Pulling the chair close so no one would hear, Kay leaned forward. 'I've given it a lot of thought over the weekend, and I honestly don't think that writing about life in the East End will make good copy. We're not that much different from anyone else.'

'Have you spent time in other parts of London, seeing the way other people go through their days?'

'No. And that's another thing. I've got nothing to compare our way of life with.'

'That's the point.' Jeannie examined her fingernails and shrugged. 'Oh well, it was just an idea.'

'I do have another one,' said Kay quickly, before Jeannie's forefinger hit the on switch of the typewriter.

'Go on. But be brief,' she warned.

'I've read a couple of the magazines now, so I've got more of an idea of the house style. The kind of stories you—'

'You're waffling,' she said, in a singsong voice.

'OK. I want to write an article about a seventeen-year-old who suddenly discovers she's got a brother, and what it feels like to know that he's in a children's home.'

Jeannie reached for a packet of cigarettes, a look of interest on her face. 'You?'

'Yeah. I only just found out.'

'And you're prepared to give us the story?'

'I don't see why not. My name won't go in, will it?'

'Not if you don't want it to. We can change all the names. But it's the only way to get yourself known as a feature writer.'

'That's not why I'm doing it. Maybe the next article, but not this one.' Kay could hardly believe herself. She sounded positive: any self-consciousness had gone.

'Why do you want to do it?'

Kay took a deep breath. She was beginning to feel slightly emotional. 'If I can let other parents know the harm they're doing when they make such decisions—'

'Your parents put him in there?'

'No, I mean – *his* parents. His mother.' Kay rolled her eyes. 'He's my father's illegitimate son.'

'Ah.'

'The other woman's getting married and her bloke won't take on someone else's son. Mum and Dad want to adopt him, but she wants him in a home in Leicester near her, so she can visit him.' Kay eyed Jeannie's packet of cigarettes.

'Help yourself.'

'Thanks. I'm going to do something about it. But that'll be the next instalment.'

'Fine.' Jeannie pushed against the desk with her foot and spun around slowly in her swivel chair. 'And what exactly had you in mind?'

'I'm going to Leicester. Get him out of that home and bring him back.'

Slowly shaking her head, Jeannie made it very clear that it was a bad idea. 'The law takes a dim view of kidnapping.'

Determined not to be swayed, Kay avoided making eye contact. 'I've got a couple of uncles who I think will help. They can drive me there, wait while I go in, then drive us both back to Stepney.'

'You've been reading too many bad paperbacks,' she said, not mincing her words.

Angrily Kay stubbed out her cigarette in the ashtray. She hadn't meant to disclose her plan, and was annoyed with herself.

Too late to retract it, she could only hope that the editor would dismiss it. 'I'll just write up the bit about my finding out about him, then.'

'I'm not interested.' She switched on her machine and began to type.

'Why not? You were at first.'

'Yep. It sounded good. Our readers would have loved it.'

'So?'

'I don't want one of our writers getting mixed up

in what you have in mind. We can do without that kind of publicity, thank you.' She looked up at Kay. 'A member of *Female Weekly* going to prison?'

'Don't be daft. Prison?' Kay smiled nervously. That word had been bandied about too much of late.

'Listen. Don't even think about it. Drive it out of that silly head of yours. Go for plans B or C.'

Kay looked at her, puzzled. She hadn't mentioned any other plans – she didn't *have* any other plans. Jeannie was half smiling, waiting for the penny to drop.

'You mean I should have thought of other ways?'

An impatient sigh escaped her. 'Something like that, yes.'

Kay shrugged forlornly. 'I couldn't think of any other way. I've gone over it so many times.'

'Look. Write your article and meanwhile, I'll give it some thought. Legal thought.'

'Fighting for an adoption could take *years*!' Kay knew she was out of order talking to her senior like that, but something inside was beginning to snap. 'And meanwhile that poor little two-year-old is with strangers! It's my baby brother we're talking about—' Her voice cracked and she had to turn away.

A comforting, feeling arm went around her shoulder.

'We'll think of something, Kay, don't upset yourself. She can't be made of stone, his mother. And if she is, we could always wield the threat of the power of the pen.'

'You mean you'd write to her?'

'No, silly! I'll see if I can set up a meeting. Don't worry, I'll be gentle. I'm a good journo. I know how to handle people. Especially women. She'll see us, I promise you.'

'I'd got it all planned out, as well. I was gonna rush in and carry him off.'

'And scare the bloody life out of the poor kid?'

Kay suddenly felt foolish. 'Doesn't know me from Adam, does he? It was a pretty dumb idea.'

'No it wasn't. It was a lovely, thoughtful gesture. And when I tell my fiancé about it, he'll want to marry you instead of me.'

'Oh no, please don't tell anyone!' Kay felt her world changing again, slipping out of her control.

'We'll need him,' Jeannie said, lowering her voice. 'He'll find all the ins and outs for us. He's an investigative journalist and a bloody good one.'

Turning back to her work, she added brightly, 'Welcome to our inner circle. The one outside work and pub sessions. Join us for dinner tomorrow night, OK?'

Kay nodded and retreated, believing she had found another friend.

'And get the article in on time!' she called out as Kay was leaving the office.

'What was all that about?' asked a tall, thin woman draped in layers of mauve and black. 'You're not getting her to write about life as a docker's daughter, are you?' she smiled sarcastically.

'The kid's just discovering she's a writer. I don't suppose you can remember what that felt like?' Jeannie said, putting the seasoned journalist in her place. 'Too long ago, I would have thought.'

Drawing on a long ebony cigarette-holder, the woman blew a smoke ring into the air. 'She can hardly string a sentence together, let alone write a decent feature.'

'You think so? We'll see.' She began to type again. 'She might end up Chief Editor – before she goes on to other things.'

Surprised and pleased with Kay's first feature article, Jeannie decided to hold it back until a sound plan had been worked out regarding the meeting with Patsy.

'I won't alter your story, Kay. Just turn a few sentences around for the sake of grammar. Once you've seen what I've done, you'll know for the next time. I have a feeling you're a quick learner.'

'What about my spelling?' Kay whispered. She didn't want any staff passing through Reception to overhear.

'John went through it for me. I'm afraid even your spelling mistakes had spelling mistakes.'

'Oh God, how *embarrassing*.' Kay suddenly wished she had never had ideas above her station.

'Don't be silly! You're a good writer. Spelling comes once you've learned a few of the rules. Take a dictionary to bed instead of a paperback. I did. It worked wonders.' She winked at Kay and left her to go back to the *Female Weekly* office.

You're a good writer . . . The words drifted through Kay's mind, once, twice, three times. She couldn't stop smiling as the bearded face of the man in the office equipment shop came into her thoughts. Remembering the line he'd typed on her machine she clenched her fists and yelled, *'Yes!'*

Now that she had handed in her article she felt a sense of loss. Nothing else for it, she told herself, I'll just have to make a start on that novel. She leaned back in her chair and began planning. It would be a psychological thriller about a woman betrayed. She would wander the streets at night tracking down men who were out looking for women instead of at home with their wives and children.

Her heroine wouldn't kill the men, she would just terrorize them; maybe cut off a lock of their hair as a warning. A warning that should she catch them out again, she would hack off all their hair. *The Woman in Black* is what she would call her first novel. Or better still, *The Woman Who Terrifies* . . .

'Couldn't type up this copy for me, could you, Kay?' John's voice brought her back to earth. 'Dreaming about that gypsy of yours again?' he teased.

Feeling herself blush, she told him how clever he was, reading her thoughts like that.

'Pop it on my desk when you've done. You up for a drink after work?'

'No, not tonight. Apparently Pamela's arranged some kind of a surprise date.' She lifted her nose.

'Two-timing, eh?'

'What if I was?'

'Enjoy it while you may,' he grinned. 'If you fancy 'em, bed 'em, that's what I say.'

Kay tried not to look shocked. 'You don't mean that?'

'Of course I do.' He was very matter-of-fact.

'You mean, if you met a girl, say, in the pub tonight, and she and you – well, you know – sparks flying and all that.'

'Yes,' he grinned, cutting in.

'But you're already getting married?'

'So?'

'You *can't* love two people at once.'

'Who said anything about that? I don't have to fall for every girl I fancy.' He perched himself on the corner of her desk. 'I'm not in love with you, am I?'

'Don't be stupid.'

'Well, there you are then. I fancied you rotten at first. Then I found I really liked you. But that's all. It stops there.' He pushed his face up close to hers. 'You don't have to love those you like a lot. You can have friends of the opposite sex. It's not against the law.' He stood up, shook his head and walked away chuckling.

Hating him for being so cocksure, she secretly stuck two fingers up to him. He certainly had a way of making her think. She had always believed that if you began to like a boy you stayed with him until you fell in love. If you didn't fall in love, you said goodbye. But now she was seeing things in another light. Each friend, male or female, was just part of her world. Different mates for different reasons. Love was something else.

She looked down at the copy John had left her. He had scribbled across the top in red pen *To*

be typed by the sexiest girl in the whole bloody building. And for some reason she felt flattered instead of affronted. He hadn't meant anything by it other than a bit of fun. It dawned on her that she had been taking life, and people, far too seriously.

Feeding a sheet of paper into her typewriter, she tried to guess what the surprise date was that Pamela had lined up. Probably Tommy and Micky were going to take them to the Prospect of Whitby at last. She had begged them enough times in the past to change their regular pub-crawl and enjoy a drink overlooking the Thames.

'But my twin-tub does boil up the whites, Billy! And it's a lot less trouble than that old boiler.' Having lost over the refrigerator, Liz was determined to have her way and install her washing-machine into his old-fashioned kitchen.

'That's as may be, Liz. But I'm used to that copper. And anyway we can hardly get it carted away. It'd cost a bomb to move it.'

'We won't need to. We can plant some lovely indoor bulbs. My machine'll go over there, in that corner, near the butler sink.'

'Indoor bulbs?' His blue eyes twinkled at the thought of it.

'Yeah. One of my friends did it when she modernized. It looks lovely. Brightens up her old scullery, I can tell yer.' She was winning him over and knew it.

'Now then, what about getting rid of this old gas stove?'

'But there's nothing wrong with it. Clean as a whistle, and does my Sunday joint a treat.'

'Yeah, but mine's electric,' Liz said proudly.

'I'm not having electric and that's definite!' Billy marched out of the scullery. 'You can fetch your washing-machine in, but that's all!'

Looking out of the window on to his tiny back garden, Liz suddenly felt very happy. It was full of lupins, Canterbury bells and roses. Her eyes went from the rich black earth to the old brick wall that was covered in purple clematis.

'If you wanna make yourself at home, you could put the kettle on the gas stove,' Billy called from the living room. 'Matches are on the shelf above it. Cups are in the dresser!'

Liz couldn't help smiling. This was a break-through. So far he had always insisted that he made the tea. She couldn't think why. 'Two sugars?'

'Two and half!' he corrected, yelling above the sound of the television he had just switched on. 'The six o'clock news'll be on in a minute, if you wanna see it!'

'I do, Billy, yeah. You gonna 'ave a piece of this angel cake?'

'No, ta, I'm not keen. A couple of digestives'll do me!'

Pouring boiling water into the teapot, Liz began to feel more and more at home. Waiting for the tea to brew, she became pensive. Moving in with Billy felt right. And she knew that Bert would be chuffed to bits if he could see her. She felt sad that that night would be the last she would spend in her own two-up, two-down. Tomorrow was the official moving-in day. Jack had borrowed a van from a friend and was going to bring her bits and pieces over during Saturday. Most of the larger pieces had been sold off to the second-hand dealer.

'Do you play cards, Billy?' Liz asked, handing him his tea.

'Haven't done for years.' He sat back and thought about it. 'Three card brag. Pontoon. Rummy. Three of One and Four of the Other, as young Kay used to call it.' He dipped his biscuit into his tea. 'I dunno, Liz, you keep bringing memories back,' he chuckled.

'Only there's a couple of friends of mine who like to play. Perhaps we could invite them over one night in the week, for a game?' Liz knew it was rather early on to suggest changing his routine, but she felt it best

to start as she meant to go on. Billy was set in his ways and he could be a bit on the stubborn side.

'Could do, yeah. Leave it a for a couple of weeks though, eh? Till I get used to having you around the place.'

'Yeah, all right.' Liz smiled inwardly. At least he was willing to try.

'We'll 'ave to sort out the finances, Liz. I don't want anything for the rent but perhaps you could chuck a little bit in for groceries. What d'yer reckon?'

'I'll pay half the rent, half the electric, half the gas. And half for the shopping. You can buy your own tobacco and I'll pay for my own sweets. I always keep a tin of Quality Street in the cupboard and I buy a half-pound of chocolate off the stall on Saturdays. Other than that, I don't need much else.'

'You're not paying my rent,' he said, insistent.

'Yes I am.'

'Oh, no.'

'Oh, yes.'

'I said no, Liz!'

'And I said yes, Billy!'

Shifting about in his chair, Billy shook his head. 'Jack warned me you were obstinate,' he murmured.

'Good. That's settled then.' She sat back in the armchair and focused on the television. 'That's a

good picture, Billy, much better than mine.' She knew how to get round him.

'I get it serviced regularly so it'll always go. Bit like my bowels. A dose of Epsom salts every night to keep myself open,' he grinned.

Liz found that amusing. She had never heard anyone compare themselves to a television set before.

Feeling relaxed, she lay back and let the six o'clock news go over her head, while her mind filled with her son, his wife and their lack of interest in having children. Liz longed for a grandchild and at sixty, she reckoned she was entitled to one. If David didn't get a move on, his wife would soon be past safe child-bearing age.

'What d'yer reckon about Kay and this Zacchi, then, Billy? Fancy gypsies for in-laws, do you?'

'Don't bother me, so long as she's happy. He seems nice enough. Clean. Very clean. Gets a good shine on his shoes as well. That says a lot. Why, you're not prejudiced, are yer?'

'Hardly. If the truth be known, there's gypsy in our family line, and not all that far back neither. No. It'll be strange seeing Gypsy Rose again. I expect we'll meet up now. She always said we would.' Liz smiled and drifted off into a light sleep as sunny hop-picking days came flooding back. Anyone looking into that small living room could be forgiven for thinking that

seventy-year-old Billy and his new lodger, Liz, had been living there together for decades. All that was missing was a cat curled up at their feet. Liz would soon see to that though. Her fifteen-year-old mog, Blackie, would be moving in with her the next day.

'Kay'll give you a hand with your packing if you ask her,' Billy said.

'I wouldn't dream of it. My niece 'as got 'er own life to get on with. She's gonna be a writer, you know.'

'Oh yeah?' It made Billy feel uncomfortable, Liz talking about his granddaughter as if she were as close to Kay as he was. 'What makes you say that?'

'Don't know. Just feel it in my bones, that's all.'

'Let's 'ope you're right. She can look after us in our old age.'

Liz liked that. At last Billy had stopped thinking of himself as slipping into the grave. There was life in the old boy yet.

While Liz and Billy were fantasizing about Kay, she was on her way to the date Pamela had set up for them. Strolling along with all the time in the world, she enjoyed the warmth of the late sun as it began to go down. It had been a flaming hot day and the tar on the narrow road felt soft underfoot as she crossed

from one side of Brady Street to the other. Pamela had insisted she meet her outside the Whitechapel art gallery on the dot of eight.

Kay passed a young woman who was studying a tricycle in a toy shop window, while wiping some ice-cream from the chin of her small child in a pushchair, and it made her wonder what her brother looked like. She had been thinking about him on and off since she discovered that she wasn't an only child. She had begun to miss him. Miss the little boy she had never met! It seemed silly to her but she just couldn't help what she was feeling inside; a feeling of loss. She had a brother, and she wanted to hold him. She wanted that more than anything else in the world.

As much as Kay realized that her original idea of walking into the children's home and carrying Jac off had been a reckless one, she couldn't quite get it out of her mind. Jeannie had been right to suggest they handle it her way. Kay felt sure of that but even so, she was anxious to do something, and soon. She couldn't help worrying that little Jac might be very unhappy at being dumped in a strange place with strange people.

In no real mood for fun, Kay approached the art gallery wishing she had never agreed on the rendezvous. She missed Zacchi and would rather

have been at home in her room, typing the short story she had begun to write. At the moment she much preferred to be in a world of her own creation than the real one.

'Fifteen minutes late!' Pamela looked angry and nervous.

'So?' Kay was beginning to wonder about the surprise her friend had in store. 'Where's the fire?'

'In here,' a familiar voice spoke from behind her.

Spinning around, Kay came face to face with Chris's smile. He had his hand on his heart. 'I just couldn't put out the flame.'

Arm in arm with Charles, who had also stepped out from the shadows, Pamela was laughing. 'Look at her face! Anyone'd think she'd seen a ghost! A very tanned ghost.'

'You should have told me,' Kay snapped at her friend. 'You're not clever!'

'Someone doesn't seem very pleased to see me,' Chris dropped his head to one side and looked into her face. 'Maybe I shouldn't have flown all this way? Maybe you should have written Return to Sender on my letters?' There was a touch of anger in his voice. 'Instead of making up stories about your dad holding them back!'

'It was true! And where's your fiancée? Being fitted up for her wedding dress?'

'You really did fall for that one?' He took Kay by the arm and led her away. 'We'll meet you in the Beggar's in half an hour,' he called back to Pamela and Charles.

'If you were lying then you could be lying now!' Kay caught a whiff of the familiar aftershave he wore and felt her heart beat more rapidly.

'Maybe you haven't experienced hurt pride? You do anything to hide it. Anything. Until time helps to dull the pain.' He looked away, pretending to be interested in dogs fighting across the busy Whitechapel Road.

'I wasn't lying, Chris. My dad really did keep the letters from me. He thought I might go rushing off to Spain to live.'

'What's so terrible about that?'

'I'm an only child.' She felt her heart sink as she said the words but it wasn't the right time to go into all of that. Nevertheless, the two-year-old flooded back into her thoughts no matter how hard she tried not to think about him. Then the other loss filled her mind. Chris's baby.

'You're really upset.' He squeezed her hand. 'I'm sorry. I shouldn't have lied about loving someone else.' He flashed a smile. 'To tell the truth, I've never had to do the chasing before.'

'No, I can understand that.' She gave in and

smiled at him. 'You're too bloody attractive for your own good.'

'And you're not?'

'I don't know what I am. I've never really thought about it. I think more about what I feel than what I look like. And if beauty's judged on that, I'm very dull.'

'You don't mean that, so why say it?' A frown replaced his smile.

'No, I don't mean that, you're right. But I did up until recently.'

'What happened to change it?' He pushed open the door of the Blind Beggar.

'Quite a lot actually. I was kind of pushed into leaving one job and starting another. It was the best thing that's ever happened to me, as it turned out.' Her mind was still full of the miscarriage. Her secret.

'What about us? Doesn't that compare?' Chris leaned on the bar and tried to catch the barmaid's attention.

'No. That was much more special. More special than anything.' Determined to start as she meant to go on, Kay took a breath and said, '*Was.*'

He cupped his face with one hand, pushing his elbow on to the bar, and looked straight ahead, studying the bottles of spirits above the optics. It was obvious to Kay he knew exactly what she was saying.

'It's not that I feel any different. You affect me exactly the same way, if not more. But I mistook it for love when it was, I don't know, chemistry.'

'Thanks a bundle.' Still he wouldn't look at her.

'I didn't mean it was only that. I did fall in love, but wasn't it just a holiday romance?'

'You'd best get out while you're ahead.' There was humour in his voice. 'What do you want to drink?'

'I can't be in love with two of you, surely?'

He faced her and raised an eyebrow. 'I never realized you were boss-eyed – two of me? That's original.'

'You remember I told you about Zacchi? Well he came back.'

'Hoo-bloody-ray. Three cheers for the gypsy!' He turned his back to the bar and leaned on it. 'So it's one door closes, another one opens?' He looked angry. 'And I'm out in the cold.'

'It's not like that,' Kay was feeling more wretched by the minute.

'No? Well what is it then? What am I supposed to think, or feel?'

She looked into his warm brown eyes and all the old feelings came flooding back. 'I don't know.'

'I'm here for a week. Then it's back to work. Back to the bakery. Either we carry on where we left off

or end it. It's up to you. You've got six days to think about it.'

In bed that night, Kay tried to weigh everything up. She tried to analyse the two weeks with Chris in Spain, and then how she and Zacchi were together again, after nearly three years.

Closing her eyes, Kay tried to clear her mind of all that was worrying and upsetting her. As she began to doze off, the noise of trains and traffic moved further into the distance and the imagined face of Zacchi filled her with a comforting feeling. Soon he would be back. She hadn't realized just how much she was missing him.

She wondered whether she would have felt comfortable taking him with her to the dinner party at Jeannie's if he had been around. What should she wear, and who else would be there? More importantly, she feared she might feel right out of her depth.

'Jeannie – you've done it again! This goulash is even better than Tibor serves in the Budapest, and that's saying something.' Bill, a commercial artist, lifted his glass of Bull's Blood and winked at the proud hostess.

'I do my best,' Jeannie was in her element.

'It's really nice,' Kay smiled shyly. 'I've never tasted it before.'

There was a brief hush as all attention was turned to her. 'You mean you haven't been to the Budapest or the Gay Hussar?' Bill's Hungarian wife raised an eyebrow and smiled.

'Oh, oh!' Bill laughed. 'Susie looks as if she's just found a new disciple.'

'The next time we go, you must come. And in return, you could take us to a pie and mash shop in the East End. I love the East End.' Susie turned to the others. 'Cockneys are truly wonderful people.'

With trepidation Kay told Susie she would be pleased to take them on a pub-crawl if they wanted. All eight guests thought that a wonderful idea, and raised their glasses to Kay who was already feeling tipsy from the wine. Jeannie's fiancé, Rob, turned out to be a lot of fun as well as a really nice person. Sitting next to Kay on the green velvet Victorian *chaise longue*, he explained a few things about writing fiction as well as good copy. His friend Harold, a playwright, threw in a couple of tips about characterization and dialogue. They had obviously been filled in by Jeannie about Kay wanting to write, and having some talent in that direction.

'*Monsieur Hulot's Holiday* is a fine example of good use of the camera. Hardly any dialogue, but

full of innuendo and subtext. Have you seen it, Kay?'
Rob asked.

'No, I haven't. I haven't seen that many films
since I was a child. My aunt Liz used to sell
ice-cream at the local cinema, so I could always
get in free. I loved it.'

'Paris Pullman. That's the place.' Bill turned to
the others. 'We could go now!'

A chorus of *No!* resounded through the room.
Everyone was enjoying themselves enough not to
want to go out.

'I've never heard of the Paris Pullman. Is it a
theatre?'

'No, love. It's one of the best little cinemas
in town.'

'We'll take you there too. After we've eaten
at—'

'The Budapest!' they all yelled, poking fun at
Susie.

'Well I don't know about you lot, but I'm making a
move,' said a petite redhead called Christine. 'I want
to be down Portobello good and early. I'm very low
on stock.'

'Ah, speaking of which, Chris darling,' Rob placed
his arm around her slim waist. 'I've seen a lovely
little stripped pine table in your window which would
double up as a writing-desk for yours truly . . .'

'Thirty pounds to you,' she kissed him lightly on the cheek.

'Make it twenty-four and you've got a sale.'

'When can you collect?'

'And I saw a pair of Vicky serving spoons.' Jeannie gently pulled Rob away from Christine. 'If you're to have the table, my love . . .' she said, seducing him with her green almond-shaped eyes.

'I know the ones you mean. Silver plate, I'm afraid. Bit pricey.'

'How pricey?'

'Eighteen.'

Conversation bubbled and rose between the eight guests as Kay sat with her feet tucked under her, on an enormous old worn African pouffe. She was out of the action now. They were discussing antiques and the best auction rooms where you could still pick up a bargain. She was more than happy to sit and watch in the lovely Georgian sitting room of Jeannie's flat, which was crammed full of interesting furniture, rugs and pictures, a mix of attractive old furniture and genuine antiques.

Picking up her hand-painted pottery cup, she remembered the Whitechapel art gallery where she used to go on Saturday mornings. She had never quite got the hang of the potter's wheel. Running

her finger round the rim of the chunky cup, she thought how nice it would be to own a set like this one. Greyish-mauve with delicately painted leaves.

'Carnaby Street, love. And not as expensive as it looks. Tiny shop where they throw the pots themselves. First on the left after Liberty's on the right.' Rob winked at her, and she couldn't help laughing at him. He was as drunk as her dad and uncles got when they had a beer party.

'What are we gonna do about this brother of yours, eh? That is the question!'

'I'm not allowed to kidnap him.' Kay wondered why she had said that; she wasn't thinking it. Maybe it was the wine, not to mention the liqueurs.

'Oh no. Mustn't do that.' He tapped his nose. 'I'll think of something, worry not!'

'I've got the address now, of his mother. I know where she lives. I got it out of my mum, eventually.'

'Did you now? Clever girl. The art of good journalism is—'

'Stop boring her, Rob.' Jeannie smiled down at Kay. 'You look all in, love.'

'I think I'm drunk. I could fall asleep on the spot.'

'Well, no need for that. Come on. I'll see you safely to the boxroom.'

Having said her goodbyes, and accepted all kinds of invites to dinner, Kay was pleased to be alone in the tiny guest room. The single, old brass bed felt very welcoming as she slipped between crisp white sheets. Two minutes later, she was fast asleep.

Kay could not be sure whether it was the chime from the grandfather clock in the hall or the loud laughter coming from below that had woken her, and she peered at her watch. It was almost two-thirty in the morning.

Creeping out of her room and heading for the bathroom, she picked up a strange but somehow familiar smell drifting up the stairs. It reminded her of the bonfires her grandfather made in the back garden when he was burning dead leaves.

From the lower half of the staircase she could see the group through an open door. They certainly knew how to enjoy themselves, talking and laughing, some more hysterical than others. Jeannie and Rob were sitting cross-legged on the floor, listening with amusement to Bill relating a story from his travels in India the previous year.

There were more empty wine bottles on the coffee table and a bottle of whisky, two-thirds empty. Kay guessed they were all a bit tiddly, hence the excellent

party mood. Sitting herself down on the stairs, she sniffed the air. It was a good smell. She liked it. Looking back at the group, she saw Jeannie draw long and hard on a cigarette and then pass it to Bill. The penny dropped. This was no ordinary smoke. It was a reefer.

Feeling like a spy, she quickly made her way back to her room and threw herself on the bed. So this is what they got up to. Drugs! She wondered why it didn't shock her the way she expected it to. Maybe it was because they all looked and sounded so happy.

If her dad could see what they were up to he would throw a fit and drag her away. Just as well he would never know.

As her head sank back into the feather pillow she felt strangely flattered to be there. It was a pity they didn't trust her enough to smoke while she was in the sitting room. Maybe another time they might invite her to join them?

Turning over and settling down again, she was more than pleased to be a guest in this other world which was so different from her own. She had no doubt that Zacchi would fit in perfectly. Susie the Hungarian had gone on quite a bit about gypsies and how much she admired their way of life and their ancestry.

Yes, Kay found herself thinking: it was Zacchi

who would fit in, and not Chris. It was becoming clearer by the day which one of them she was really in love with.

The Friday evening before Zacchi was due home, Kay and Pamela went to the Black Boy with their friends. Tommy and Micky were there, as usual, chatting up the girls.

'So whose house are we gonna go back to then?' Micky was ready for a party.

'Not mine. The old man's decided to return to the nest – unfortunately.' A tall, broad-shouldered mod piped up.

'Your old lady still on 'oliday, Tommy?'

'Yep.'

'Well then?'

'Nope,' he looked across at Kay and winked. 'I've got other plans.'

The small crowd let out a chorus of catcalls and whistles which angered Kay. 'I hope you're not referring to me. I'm not in the habit of visiting strange men's homes.'

'No? Oh well,' he shrugged, 'I just had this feeling.'

'Well get rid of it then,' Kay smiled, 'my boy-friend's due back tomorrow.' She tried her best not to put Tommy down.

It didn't take long before the incident was forgotten, at least by most of the crowd. The chatting up continued to the sound of the jukebox and Bobby Vee, singing 'Run to Him', filled the bar.

Amused by Tommy's sense of humour at choosing the record, Kay gave him a broad smile.

'Can't win 'em all!' Tommy shrugged, making his way towards her.

'I'm just an old-fashioned girl who doesn't two-time,' Kay said.

'That's what I like about you. You're decent.'

Kay looked around to see where Pamela had got to. She was across the room having what looked like an intimate conversation with one of the other boys. So much for her undying love for Charles.

As Tommy drank his pint, Kay noticed his attention drawn to the bar door as it opened. Within seconds a hush had settled on the group. Turning to see who had walked in, Kay was delighted to see Terry and Ray. She was just about to wave them over when a tall eighteen-year-old blocked her view. He was standing close to Terry and indicating with his thumb that he and his friend should leave. Terry and Ray stood their ground and an argument began to break out. Unable to get through the mob that had moved forward, Kay felt her pulse quicken.

Pulling on Tommy's sleeve she shouted at him,

but he wasn't listening. 'They're my friends!' she yelled at one of the men behind the bar.

'It only takes one to set the rest of them off,' he shrugged.

Trapped on the wrong side of the small crowd which was gathering around Terry and Ray, Kay used all her strength to push her way through until she almost fell through the door and on to the ground outside.

Still cursing and screaming at the mob to leave them be, she grabbed at one of their jackets. A strong arm swung backwards at her, hitting the side of her face. Defiantly, she went back again and yelled for Tommy who turned and glared at her.

'Get inside!' He looked fit to kill. No longer the handsome smiling face she had warmed to, but a very different, ugly person.

Through the crowd she could see that Terry was on the floor, that they were kicking him. Ray was being held back by two others, having to watch his mate take a hiding. She could see Terry's face as it screwed up in agony as one kick after the other went in. When she saw a black shoe ramming into his head she let out a shrill scream, which was lost in the roar of wild abuse.

Blood was oozing thickly from Terry's ear and his eyes were closed. Still they continued to kick

until the sound of a police car could be heard in the distance.

Sobbing, Kay grabbed Tommy's arm as, with the others, he turned to run. 'Why did you do that? I don't understand!'

Pulling away from her, he spat on the ground in disgust and ran from the scene, disappearing down an alley.

'His head, Kay! His head!' Ray was kneeling beside Terry and crying. 'Look at his head.'

Wiping her tears with the back of her hand, Kay nodded. 'He'll be all right, he'll be all right,' she mumbled over and over, wanting desperately to believe it.

The blood trickling from Terry's ear began to flow more heavily, and then came in short, dark red bursts. She looked from Terry to Ray, unable to move, while Ray's face was turning white before her eyes. When he passed out and dropped to the floor she could do nothing but stare at their limp bodies on the pavement, the sound of bells ringing loud as the police arrived.

'You can't lie in bed crying all day, Kay,' Jack quietly scolded. He didn't know how to comfort her when he was so full of anger himself. Laura had taken the news badly and had gone to see

Terry's mother, hoping to hear that he had survived the savage attack.

'You should have been there . . . you can't imagine how quickly they changed. My friends changed from really nice blokes to a vicious mob. It was like they became animals.'

Jack sat on the edge of her bed and stroked her hair. 'I know, babe. I've seen it before, worse luck. I can't explain it to you. No one can. Animal instincts, I suppose.' He sighed heavily. 'But I do know this much. If me and a few others had been passing by, we would have given them flash boys an 'idin'. The difference is we'd 'ave used our fists and not our feet.'

'I begged Tommy, but it was as if he couldn't hear or didn't want to. I can't believe how he changed in seconds.'

'How about a nice hot cup of sweet tea?' Jack was finding the conversation too much.

'I think Terry's gonna die, Dad.'

'Now don't say that! Of course he's not!'

'You didn't see what a mess they made of his head. Never mind the rest of his body.'

'Your mother'll be back soon with the news. If you get yourself up, have a nice bath, then I'll take you to the hospital to see him. How's that sound?'

'If he doesn't die, he'll have brain damage.' Kay stared up at the ceiling.

'Now stop it!' Jack shouted. 'Get up and get dressed. Do something positive, instead of lying there feeling sorry for yourself!'

Once outside her room, Jack drew his hand across his face and gritted his teeth. It wouldn't do for him to shed tears. Not right then.

'I'll make some toast as well! Your mother'll kill me if I let you starve—' He just stopped himself from saying *to death*.

When Kay opened the door to Zacchi later that day, she fell into his arms and wept on his shoulder. He had telephoned from Dover earlier on, and all she had managed to say in between sobs was that something terrible had happened to Terry.

'I could do with a cup of tea.' He was too moved at seeing her grief to give her words of comfort. Her lovely face was swollen and her silky blonde hair was all over the place and damp with tears.

'They kicked Terry's head,' her voice was a whisper in his ear. 'My friends almost kicked the life out of him.'

Gently withdrawing himself from her arms, he looked into her face. 'Kay?' Again he could not find the words.

'They didn't kill him.' She pulled a handkerchief

from her sleeve and blew her red nose. 'He's in hospital though. Intensive care.'

'Are we allowed to visit?' he said quietly.

'I think so. I'm not sure. Let's go anyway, Zac, please?'

''Course we'll go.' He walked her into the kitchen. 'I bought this bottle of duty-free for your parents.' He held the bottle hopefully.

Kay smiled. 'Brandy. Yeah, they won't mind if we open it. You've only just missed 'em. They've popped round the Eagle for a quick drink. This 'as really gutted them.'

'I'm sure.' Zacchi turned away and filled the kettle. 'It's not easy to take in, is it?'

Sitting down, Kay felt a wave of comfort. It was good to have him back. She wanted to tell him how much she had missed him. But it didn't seem the right time.

'We'll go after we've had coffee, then?'

'Yep. After coffee.' Zacchi knew she couldn't wait to see how her friend was but he also knew she needed to relax a little before they left. 'They might not let us in. You should be prepared for that.'

''Course they will,' she snapped at him, as if by saying it he was siding with authority.

'I have to obey orders,' the slim, dark-haired nurse

was sorry. 'I daren't let you go in. Only his next of kin. Leave it a couple of days.'

'But I'm like his sister! Just ask him if he wants to see me. Please! Just go and ask him.'

Looking from Kay to Zacchi, she shrugged. 'Wouldn't be much point. He hasn't regained consciousness.' She backed away and gave a reassuring smile. 'Phone tomorrow evening, around this time. Ask for Nurse Derrick. I'll tell you how he is then. OK?'

'Will he live?' Kay could not contain herself. 'He's not gonna die, is he?' She was daring the nurse to say yes.

'Try not to think the worst. There's a chapel on the second floor. Why not pray for him?'

The sound of the nurse's heels on the marble floor echoed as she walked quickly away down the corridor. *Pray for him . . . Pray for him . . . Pray for him . . .* The words ran through Kay's brain. She looked pleadingly into Zacchi's eyes.

'Come on,' he managed, 'we'll go for a walk.'

Arriving at Bethnal Green Park an hour before the gates were due to close, Kay was secretly pleased to see that old Sid was there, enjoying an ice-cream.

'OK if we join you?' Kay knew it would be and sat close beside him on the sun-heated wall, with just his big black Bible between them.

'That's some accordion you're got there,' said Zacchi, and he swept his fingers over the ornate polished brass edging that glinted in the evening sun.

Sid studied Zacchi's face and then smiled. A twinkle returned to his blue eyes and the guarded look dissolved. 'Romany?' he said.

'That obvious?' Zacchi took an instant liking to the old man.

Turning his attention to Kay, Sid pursed his lips and waited, as she twisted a handkerchief in her hands.

'My friend's in hospital,' she said. 'On the danger list.'

'Does he know anything about it?'

'He's unconscious, if that's what you mean.'

'Then he probably doesn't.' Sid wiped ice-cream from his fingers on one of the rolled-up newspapers that were stuffed inside his old gabardine mackintosh.

'He might not survive.'

Sid's mischievous, knowing laughter stopped Kay in her tracks. Sometimes he could be irritating. She bit her lip while he picked up his accordion and began to play softly.

'How can you laugh, Sid?' She was begging him to say something that would make her feel better.

'Would he want us to cry?'

'Maybe!'

'No. If he is hovering between this world and the next, he'll be able to see you. And it's my humble opinion that if he had a voice, he would tell you the real meaning of death and birth and life, body and soul.' Before Kay could ask any more questions, Sid began to play and sing.

> Lead us, heavenly Father, lead us
> O'er the world's tempestuous sea;
> Guard us, guide us, keep us, feed us,
> For we have no help but thee;
> Yet possessing every blessing,
> If our God our Father be . . .

Without any prompting from Sid, Kay joined in on the second verse. Zacchi was too moved to sing, and the hair on his neck stood up. Once that verse was finished, Sid began to walk away, his voice filling the empty park grounds.

> Spirit of our God, descending,
> Fill our hearts with heavenly joy,
> Love with every passion blending,
> Pleasure that can never cloy;
> Thus provided, pardoned, guided,
> Nothing can our peace destroy

*   *   *

'He's special all right. You're lucky to have him in your part of the world,' said Zacchi.

'He's always been here.'

'No, not always. Since as far back as you can remember. He must be in his seventies, and you're only seventeen.'

'That's true. I hadn't thought about that. He doesn't have a cockney accent, as it 'appens,' she remarked.

'Doesn't have any accent. The man from nowhere.' Zacchi grabbed Kay's hand. 'Come on, before we get locked in for the night.'

Taking his hand in hers she pulled him towards her, and as they clung together, drawing comfort, Kay realized that Zacchi had become the mainstay of her existence. She couldn't imagine herself without him. He was part of her, and of her world.

Nuzzling into his neck she kissed him lightly. 'I love you,' she murmured.

Cupping her face, Zacchi looked more serious than she had ever seen him. He sighed and nodded briefly. It was his way of saying he loved her too. 'Where to now?'

'Hackney?'

'Kay, this is my first day back. Can't we just sit in the nearest pub garden?'

'If I sit still, I'll start thinking about last night and Terry, I know I will.'

'OK. So who lives in Hackney?' He sounded bored and tired.

'It's only a fifteen-minute walk. And I've got loads to tell you.' She took his hand and led him along towards the library. 'You'll never guess what I've got.'

'Go on then. Shock me.'

'A little brother,' she grinned.

Looking puzzled at her, he frowned until his dark eyebrows met. 'You're sure about that, are you? I've only been away two weeks and the last time I saw your mother she looked very slim.'

'Half-brother. Dad's been a naughty boy.'

He let out a low whistle. 'Yes, well, that's fairly shocking. How did you find out?'

By the time they had reached the Bethnal Green museum she had filled him in on everything; her first plan to snatch Jac, and the second more sensible one of Jeannie's, to use the power of the pen.

'We thought that if I went to see her and explained why he should be with us and not in a home she might see sense, and if she doesn't, tell her how bad it would look in a national newspaper—'

'National newspaper?' Zacchi cut in.

'So, I'd be telling a white lie. Jeannie said it would

394

go in *Female Weekly* so it's not that much of a fib, is it? We just thought it would sound more threatening if it was a daily.'

'You're evil.'

'And she's not? Putting a two-and-a-half-year-old in a home, with strangers? When he could be with his blood-father?'

Zacchi eyed her suspiciously. 'So who is it lives in Hackney?'

'Don't worry, not her. She's up in Leicester. We're going to see a very good friend of mine who I used to see on the bus when I worked at Thompson's. I miss her.'

As they turned into Tanner Street, Kay began to tell Zacchi about the dinner party she'd been to in the week. Her new arty friends in Hampstead. How they were both invited the following Friday to one of the guests' flats for dinner somewhere in Chelsea. He was an abstract painter and she a sculptor.

'Count me out thanks.' Zacchi sounded resolute.

'What do you mean, count you out? Don't be so bloody pompous!'

'I've met their kind, they bore the life out of me. So you go and have nice long debates about life, the universe and art. See how long you last.' He winked cheekily at her.

'I like them, Zacchi. I really enjoy being in their

company. It's got to be better than just standing in a pub listening to the jukebox.'

'What did they give you to eat, then?' he smirked.

'Hungarian goulash. With small dumplings and cucumber salad. God, you can be annoying.' She pulled her hand out of his. 'You think you're above it all. I don't suppose you'll like Juanita either!' She pressed her finger on the black and white porcelain bell.

The door slowly opened and a very tall, very good-looking, broad-shouldered young man stood smiling at them, as if quite aware of his beautiful row of even, sparkling white teeth.

'Hey, you brought a chaperone!'

'Sorry?' Kay thought he must be mixing her with someone else.

'We don't eat white girls, you know. Come in.' Malcolm stood aside, bowed and waved them in.

'Mum and Dad should be back in an hour. Tea or cold drink?'

'Nothing, thanks.' She cleared her throat. 'Do you know who I am?'

'The lovely Kay. The daughter she should have had – you see what I'm saying? Never mind the white skin.' He turned to Zacchi. 'We've all been waiting to meet her. All three sons. Shame about you – know what I mean?' he grinned.

'Who plays the guitar?' Zacchi asked, ignoring the flirting going on between Malcolm and Kay.

Eyeing a soft armchair, Kay was tempted to push her shoes off and drop into it. 'Do you mind if I sit down? I feel as if I've walked miles.'

'My pleasure.' Picking up his guitar, he lovingly drew his fingers across the strings. 'It's mine. You see what I'm saying? My woman. The only woman I've had the pleasure of . . .' he lightly strummed a few chords.

'If you can believe that,' Kay rolled her eyes. 'Give us a song, then.' She looked across at Zacchi. 'Don't suppose you still keep the old mouth-organ in your pocket?'

'New mouth-organ.'

'Hey! Fab. Let's make some music.' Malcolm threw the guitar strap over his shoulder.

Curling her legs under her, Kay felt very much at home. She liked the way the room was furnished, it reminded her of Juanita. The well-polished second-hand oak furniture was simple, and the embroidered chair-back covers on the three-piece suite brightened up the dark green upholstery.

'What can you play?' she asked.

'You name it.' Malcolm hugged his guitar.

'You want me to choose?' She was enjoying being made to feel special. It was just what she needed.

'Be my guest.' He took a bow.

'That'll do for a starter.'

'"Be My Guest?" OK.' He turned to Zacchi. 'Know it?'

'You play – I'll come in.'

Within minutes, the room was filled with lively music and song. It was one of Kay's favourites. Turning her attention to the door which was slowly opening, she was amused to see Malcolm's brother dance his way in. It didn't take him long to pick up the tune on the piano and belt out the words.

A bit later, while they were performing 'Teddy Bear', Kay remembered Terry. This was one of his favourite Elvis Presley numbers which he used to sing accompanying himself on his guitar.

While the two brothers and Zacchi were hamming it up for fun, Kay felt a pang of guilt. Her best friend was lying in hospital, his life in the balance, and she was enjoying herself.

'I want to go now, Zac.' She stood up and tried to get his attention. 'Zacchi, I want to go.'

Involved now and enjoying themselves, they circled her, singing and playing louder and louder.

'I'll wait outside, OK?' she tried to smile. 'I've got a headache,' she said, searching for an excuse.

Once outside, Kay leaned on the brick wall and waited, while they finished the song and started on

another – which was obviously meant for her. The chorus drifted out through the open door.

Qué sera, sera . . . They could never know just how much their mock crooning was causing her pain. Not wishing to dampen their spirits, she walked slowly away.

'I was getting a kick out of that,' Zacchi said, arriving by her side out of breath. 'Why did you leave?'

'I'm sorry, Zac. I needed some air.'

'Now that's what I call good company.'

'I know. I had a feeling it would be OK. I took to Juanita when we first met, as well. It was as if we'd known each other for years.'

'Bit like when we first spoke,' Zacchi lifted her hand and gently kissed it. 'Terry'll be all right, you'll see.'

Pressing her lips together she nodded. There was no need for explanations. He knew what she was going through.

The following day, unable to lie in as she normally did on Sundays, Kay was up at the crack of dawn drafting out a letter to Patsy. She was taking Zacchi's advice and writing to ask if she would please think about letting her family adopt Jac. She promised they would send the fare so that Patsy could visit every

week for a year. She would send it all, one sum of money, which she had been left by an uncle.

Glancing up at the top of her wardrobe, she felt relieved to have found what she believed was an acceptable way of disposing of Frank and Freddie's envelope. Finishing the letter, she urged:

> I feel as if we are related in a kind of way, you being the mother of my brother. I hope we can meet. I would be on the next train if I thought you wouldn't mind. A day doesn't go by when I'm not thinking about my brother. I wish my dad had told me before now. Before good news became bad news. I'm referring to Jac being in a home amongst strangers.
>
> My very best wishes,
> Kay Armstrong

She looked across at her typewriter on her dressing table and wondered whether to type it out or rewrite it in her best handwriting. She decided on the latter.

By nine o'clock both Laura and Jack were up and Kay was on her way out to post the letter which was hidden in her jeans pocket. 'I'm going round Terry's. See if there's any news.'

Laura frowned, throwing some strips of bacon into the frying pan. 'I'm not sure that's a good

idea, Kay. His mum wasn't the least bit pleased to see me yesterday. Well, that was the impression I got, anyway.'

'She always was a bit moody.' Kay grabbed an apple from the fruit dish. 'Probably be all right today. I'll buy her a box of Dairy Milk on the way.'

Stepping out into the quiet, sunny morning lifted Kay. As she pushed the doorbell and waited for Terry's mother to answer, she felt good having posted her letter, and looked forward to the response, if any. One way or another it would get things moving. If Patsy's reply was negative, she would put plan B into action. She would take a train to Leicester and see her in person. If that didn't work, she would carry out Jeannie's plan of threatening to write the article.

'You've got a nerve showing up here.' Terry's mum caught her off guard. 'It's because of you that my son's where he is now.' She stepped back and looked ready to slam the door shut.

Kay could hardly believe her ears. 'But I had nothing to do with it!' She pushed her hand against the closing door. 'Please don't—'

'You and your flash friends. He would never 'ave gone to that pub if it wasn't for you. Why couldn't you have stayed away, left him be? If the truth were known, you're partly to blame for the way he's

turned out anyway. Picking blackberries with you when he should have been kicking a ball about!'

'Terry's the way he is because that's the way he was born. He knows that, and so should you by now!' Knowing she had overstepped the mark she tried to apologize, but the door slammed shut between them.

Determined to have her way, she grabbed the iron knocker and banged it three times. When the door abruptly opened again she pushed her shoulder against it and forced a foot forward. 'If you shut the door on me again, you'll crush my leg.'

'Just go away and leave me to mourn my son!'

Kay swallowed hard. Mourn her son? 'What are you saying?' She just managed to get the words out.

'You surely don't expect him to pull through this, do you? A cat tied to a tree and stoned would stand more chance!'

'You mustn't say that. Terry will live, I know he will.'

'And when it's time to bury him? Where's the money gonna come from, eh? I don't even have enough to buy a cheap coffin!' Mrs Button grabbed the edge of the door for support as her legs buckled under her.

In a flash Kay was there, catching her before she

fell to the floor, pulling her inside and closing the door behind them. She ran into the front room and grabbed a couple of cushions from the sofa, placing one under her head and one under her knees.

'It's OK, Mrs Button. I'll get you a glass of water. You'll be fine. You fainted, that's all.'

Mrs Button moaned and rolled her eyes as Kay backed into the kitchen. Filling a glass, she forced back the tears. It wouldn't help to get emotional.

Supporting her head, Kay brought the glass to her lips. 'Sip this. You'll soon feel better.'

'Can you help me into the front room? I'd rather be sitting up, in an armchair.'

Once she had settled Mrs Button and made her comfortable, Kay went into the kitchen to make them both a cup of sweet weak tea. Waiting for the kettle to boil, she scanned the small back room. Apart from all the crockery on the blue-and-yellow-painted units, in one corner on the Formica surface was a tray with two of everything. Two dinner plates, two cups, two saucers, two tea plates, two soup bowls.

'Oh, Terry . . .' Kay murmured. 'You mustn't die. You mustn't.' A shrill whistle made her jump as steam forced its way out of the spout.

'I didn't mean what I said earlier, love. I'm all at sixes and sevens.' As Mrs Button looked at her,

Kay couldn't help noticing her eyelids which were rapidly twitching above her tired eyes.

'Do you think they'd let me see him today? If I went in with you?' Kay hugged her cup of tea and hoped she might say yes.

'No. They're very strict about that sort of thing. Daft really. I could do with someone by my side.' Her voice trailed off and her eyes filled with tears. 'There's only my sister, and she's emigrated to Canada. God knows where Terry's dad is.'

'Why don't you ask the police if they can trace him?' Kay couldn't imagine herself lying critically ill and her dad not being there.

'We'll see.' Terry's mum let her head drop back in the cushioned armchair. Staring up at the ceiling, she slipped deep into her own thoughts.

'Is there anything I can do?' Kay asked.

No reply came. It was as if she hadn't spoken. As if she wasn't there. 'I could stay overnight if you wanted?'

Still the tired face showed no sign of response. The woman looked drained and beaten. Kay tried to stop herself thinking the worst. If Terry didn't survive the beating, his mother would have nothing to live for, and it showed.

Looking around the room, it was evident that they had not had an easy time of it. The floor was covered

in a cheap brown lino which, though highly polished, showed signs of age. There were cracks and worn patches and a threadbare rug did nothing to make the room look cosy. The skimpy, faded gold and white curtains on each side of the bay window were unlined and Kay doubted that once drawn together they would meet.

Her mind went to the envelope and the money she had promised to Patsy. She felt suddenly guilty at having had such a comfortable upbringing. Her family had never really wanted for anything, in comparison to the existence she had seen in Terry's home.

Kay didn't want to leave the woman by herself, but she could see that staying would not only be a waste of time but an intrusion. Mrs Button wanted no one but her son and Kay could do nothing for her there. Nothing could be said or done to make either of them feel any better.

Walking home through the backstreets, Kay decided that until she was allowed to visit, any information about Terry would have to be drawn from the nurse she had spoken to the previous day. She would phone her for updates on his condition.

Life seemed so unfair. Her friend Terry was the very person she had chosen to tell about the way she felt inside about losing her baby. It would have

been easier somehow, talking to him. Pamela would not have let her forget it as easily as he would. Now she would have to keep it bottled up inside for a while longer – until he was up and smiling again.

Chapter Fourteen

Three weeks had passed since Kay first wrote to Patsy, and they had exchanged several letters. Bernard and Lillian found it strange that mail care of them had been arriving for Kay, but said nothing, after their first interrogation with Pamela. She had told them it was very personal and private – a confidential family matter.

'There's nothing else for it but to go up there,' Kay said, as they sat in Pamela's bedroom.

'Rather you than me.' Pamela was more interested in the *Melody Maker* she was reading.

'I don't suppose you fancy coming with me?'

'No.'

'Thanks. I always knew I could count on you.' Kay was beginning to wonder if she and her childhood friend were drifting away from each other. They seemed to have different attitudes about everything lately. Pamela hadn't even been with her to see Terry in hospital.

'I don't know why you don't drop it. She doesn't want the kid to move in with your family, surely that's obvious by now.' She didn't look up from her paper.

'Think I'll go tomorrow, get the early train. Go straight to the children's home. Say I'm a cousin or something.'

Looking defiantly at Kay, Pamela pushed her hair away from her face. 'You said you would come up west with me!'

'I think this is a little more important than you buying a new dress.'

'Well I don't! I want it for the party tomorrow night. We haven't been out since Terry's . . . you know.' She pretended to be absorbed in something she saw in the paper. 'If you're not seeing your precious Zacchi, you're brooding over him.'

'I do not brood over Terry. I happen to think he's better off where he is at the moment, than out here.'

'You're only saying that so you don't have to face the truth. He's on his deathbed and you know it.'

Lighting herself a cigarette, Kay leaned back on Pamela's bed. 'I'm longing to see my little brother.' She tried to blow a smoke ring towards the ceiling. 'They say he looks just like me.'

'Oh, bloody well go then! Get it over with.' Pamela was sick of hearing it.

'I intend to. Might even bring him back with me.'

'Don't talk rubbish.' She licked her finger and flicked a page over. 'When are we supposed to appear in court then?'

'I don't know.' It was the last thing Kay wanted to think about.

'I suppose we'll get a letter?'

'Yes.'

'Put the bastards away once and for all.' She gazed up at Kay, a different expression on her face. 'What made them do it?'

'I don't want to talk about it, Pam. I don't want to think about it, OK?' Her voice was remote with tension. 'Anyway, we might not have to go. There were other witnesses. My dad's trying to get us out of it.'

'Why? I'll go! I don't care. I'll bloody well tell them what happened. Wicked gits. I'll never forget what they did—'

'Shut up!' Kay clenched her fists. 'Mention it again and I'll put my hand through a window!' She glared at her friend, daring her to answer back.

'OK, OK! Fair enough. Calm down.'

'Terry's all right. He's not in as much pain now. Right?'

'Yeah, yeah, you're right, of course you are,' Pamela smiled and held out her hand, but Kay edged away.

'I'll be round on Sunday.'

'What about the party tomorrow night?' Pamela was losing her patience.

'Count me out. I'm not in the mood for dancing. Anyway, you never know what kind of people you're mixing with. Not any more, anyway.'

Kay and Laura were in the kitchen idly looking through a mail-order catalogue when Jack's piercing cry shot through the flat. Looking up, they waited to hear what might follow. Nothing came. A haunting silence filled the place.

Shrugging at Kay, Laura cautiously left the kitchen and went into the living room. 'What now?' she asked, dreading the answer.

As Jack sat there, head turned away, she caught sight of the headlines on the newspaper in his hands. *VICIOUS ATTACK LEADS TO SUICIDE.*

Jack jumped up from his armchair and stormed out of the living room, throwing Laura into shock. She stood paralysed.

Once on the back balcony, the newspaper still in his clenched fist, Jack punched the brick wall over and over, crying and cursing until his knuckles bled.

Staring at his fist he shouted out loud. 'Bastards! Bastards! Bastards!'

Kay rushed past Laura and stood in the veranda doorway.

'What is it, Dad? What's happened?'

Slowly raising his head, Jack's face twisted as he began to cry. 'Kay . . . I'm sorry, babe,' he shook his head. 'I don't know what else to say.' He handed them the newspaper and walked into the living room crouching down on the edge of an armchair.

Reading the lead story, Kay's face was slack with disbelief. 'He was terrified of coming out of hospital,' she murmured. 'He slashed his wrists.' She dropped the paper on the floor and walked out of the room and out of the flat.

Heading for nowhere in particular, Kay just kept walking. Thoughts seemed to be flying over her head instead of through it.

Nothing to think about. Not the past, not the present, not the future. No one. No one must be in her mind. They must all be cleared out. Friends, family, colleagues. An empty space. Empty room. Her head must be like an empty room. Only she would be there, standing alone. On a platform ordering everyone out. One by one they go. Out of the door, everyone. Only herself in the big, empty silent room. None to be allowed back in. Not then. Not ever. She would

*stay there for ever. By herself . . . by herself . . .
by herself. Until she was ready to let new friends
in. Jeannie and other people. Other people who
led uncomplicated lives. Her legs would be strong.
They would support her. She would walk around the
empty room. Around the room. Around and around
the room . . . By herself. Up and down. By herself.*

'I couldn't believe it. I wasn't going fast, just
biking along. And she walked out. I don't know
how I missed her. She just seemed to drop down in
front of me.' The man stood on the doorstep, his pale
face pleading with Laura to believe him. 'I promise
yer, I didn't knock her down. I think she's coming
round now. Nearly gave me heart attack an' all!'

'Bring her in,' Laura waved the small group of
curious children away from the door. Having seen
Kay being carried by the stranger, they wanted to be
part of the drama.

Laying her gently down on the sofa, the man shook
his head. 'Scared the life out of me, I tell yer.'

'What happened?' Kay moaned.

'She didn't look right you know. It was like she
was sleepwalking or something.' He was becoming
less defensive by the second. 'I mean, if she's ill
I don't think . . . I mean I could have bloody
killed her!'

'Look, I would offer you a cup of tea but we've

412

had a bit of a shock. A tragedy.' Laura hoped he would just go.

'That ginger-headed kid'll tell you. She saw what happened. I don't know how I managed to swerve in time! My bike's bound to have some scratches.' Remembering his bike gave him something else to think about. 'That balcony looks out on the road, don't it?' He rushed out to check what was happening below.

'Mum . . .' Kay was trying to focus, get her bearings.

'It's all right. Lie back and rest.' Laura's attention was half on her, half on the hyperactive cyclist, with his mac flapping around him.

Rushing through the room, the man almost tripped over his own feet. 'Bloody kids all round it now. Little sods. Bound to nick me pump!' His voice disappeared with him as he rushed through the flat.

'Who was that?'

'I have no idea, Kay.' Laura tried to keep a straight face. 'You OK?'

'Is Terry really dead?' her glazed eyes questioning.

'Yeah.' Laura parted her lips and took in a deep breath. She was lost for words. What could she say?

'It's all right, I'm not gonna cry. I'm really not.'

Kay raised herself on one elbow. 'I tried to. For the first time in my life I actually tried to cry instead of trying to stop. I'm all dried up. Terry's dead. So? He's better out of it anyway. No one in their right mind would choose to be born, would they? Not if they knew what you have to put up with. And yet we kick and fight against leaving. Mad. We're all mad.'

She sat up and stared at nothing. 'I would swap places with Terry like a shot.' Feeling weak, she flopped back on to a cushion.

'You don't mean that.' Laura was unsure how to deal with Kay's mood.

'Oh, I do. Yeah. Sorry, Mum. But I do.' She smiled, closed her eyes and left Laura to do the crying.

After what seemed the longest night in her life, Kay sat in the kitchen with Laura. Neither of them had slept much, and when one did manage to doze off she was disturbed by the other moving around the flat. It wasn't until five o'clock that they were up at the same time.

'I had no idea, Mum. If you'd have seen their living room. Just a few sticks of furniture.' Kay remembered what Terry's mother had said about the funeral. 'She won't even be able to afford a decent coffin.'

'Yes she will. I've seen to it. Yesterday afternoon.'

'How d'yer mean?'

Laura rubbed her eyes and decided it was time to tell Kay a few home truths about some of her relations. 'Freddie and Frank gave your dad some money for aunt Liz. Well, that's who they said it was for.' She sipped her tea and studied Kay's face for a reaction. There was none.

'The money they come by . . . well, it's not exactly kosher.' Again she looked for a response.

'What are you trying to say?' Kay sounded more impatient than surprised.

'Well they're, you know, small-time thieves.'

'Yeah? So?'

'Well we didn't think your aunt Liz'd want to take it—'

''Course she would!' Kay was on the edge of swearing at her mother for being soft.

'I popped an envelope – two hundred pounds – into Mrs Button's letter-box. Just wrote that it was from a well-wisher.' She expected a raised eyebrow from Kay.

'I'm glad you did that, but I'm not sure it's fair on aunt Liz. You should have asked her first.'

Laura found it strange taking advice from her daughter. The tables had certainly turned in the

past few months. 'There were two envelopes handed over. The other one's got three hundred pounds in it.'

'Oh, that's all right then.' Kay swallowed the rest of her tea.

'It doesn't bother you? Your uncles being crooks?'

'No, why should it? At least they don't go round kicking people's heads in.' She poured herself another cup of tea. 'I really like Freddie and Frank. They're good-hearted and generous. I'm not bothered where they get their money from.'

Laura's heart sank as she listened to her daughter who seemed to be getting more hardened by the minute. She felt sure it was the shock of Terry's death, besides everything else that had happened so far that year.

'They invited me and Pamela to the Kentucky Club. I might go.' Kay was being deliberately rebellious. She knew it would upset and worry Laura.

'I can't stop you from doing what you want, Kay, but I will say this. If you do start going down the wrong pathways, it won't be so easy to find your way back to your normal way of living.'

Kay half smiled. 'What's wrong with that?' She had no intention of turning against her uncles. The reverse, in fact. She had been invited to the Kentucky

and that was where she would go. If her uncles could so easily repay one debt, they could repay another. Those flash bastards whom she had thought to be her mates were not going to get away with causing the death of her best and closest friend.

Sitting on the edge of her bed, Kay waited for eight-thirty to come round on her small alarm clock. She thought that was probably the time they would be drinking at the club. A drink before they went for a Chinese meal, is what she imagined.

Approaching the unassuming building she could feel her heart pumping faster, and as she got closer she was puzzled by the exterior of the Kentucky Club. Surely this wasn't it? She had expected bright lights and glitter. Film stars and politicians is what Pamela had said. Famous and important people in a place like this?

Beside a small door, she could not miss the sign in black-painted letters, *No. 106A Kentucky Club. Strictly members only.* Smiling to herself but with her heart still thumping, she knocked on the door and was surprised by a sudden movement from the wide letter-box as a make-shift shutter was pulled to one side. Bending down, she tried to sound positive. 'I want to see my uncles. Frank and Freddie.' In a flash the door opened and there stood three men, bouncers. They showed no trace of a smile as they stared her

out. Behind them she saw the sign *All guests must be signed in*.

'My name's Kay Armstrong and I want to see my uncles.'

'They're not here, love. But you can come in and wait.' No trace of compassion in their voices, never mind the endearment.

Stepping inside the bar, she looked around at the seedy club. The smell reminded her of the horrid building in the City where she had gone for an interview. Old metal ashtrays, she thought. Old metal ashtrays and bad lighting. The dark red-embossed flock wallpaper reminded her of the small corner pub where she had once gone to pay her dad's union dues when he had the flu.

In the smoky room, amidst the many smartly dressed bodies, she thought she recognized some of the guests. Famous faces were laughing and talking. Is this it, she thought, is this really how the rich and famous like to spend an evening?

'Give Kay a drink.' One of the bouncers had followed her through. 'She's waiting for Freddie and Frank.'

'No, it's OK. I'm not staying.' She backed towards the open door.

'Any message?'

'No. You don't even have to say I came. It's OK

418

now. I've just remembered I don't need to ask them what I thought I needed to . . .' She had to get out of there. There was a feeling in the air. A strange feeling of importance, fear and something else she couldn't identify.

Once outside, she leaned on a wall and breathed deep lungfuls of fresh air. 'Sorry, Terry,' she murmured, 'I can't do it.'

With tears streaming down her face she made her way through the backstreets, past the brewery and towards the safety of her home. Still she found herself thinking that Terry was better off out of it. If he went to clubs anything like the one she had just been to, his life could not have been that rich. Law and justice, she decided, would have to seal the fate of the boys who almost kicked the life out of him.

There was no doubt in her mind now. She would have to get away from this sordid part of the world. There had to be better places. Had to be.

When she arrived at the block of flats she sat down on a stone step and cried for the friend she would never see again. She wished over and over that she could turn back the clock. Maybe give him different advice, when they were hop-picking. Safer advice, like don't let anyone know. Hide behind a grey suit. Do anything to stay safe, to stay *alive*.

One thing she did know. Life really was what you made it. And tomorrow she would do her best to make her brother's life happier, come what may.

Standing on the doorstep, the morning sun warming her, Kay felt her anxiety begin to lessen. She could hear the sound of children playing in the garden behind the large Victorian house and wondered if little Jac was one of those laughing. Full of apprehension, she pressed her finger on the doorbell and prayed that she was doing the right thing.

The matron, a woman in her early thirties, looked her up and down as she stood in the doorway of the entrance hall. 'Can I help you?' Her face broke into a warm smile.

A surge of embarrassment rushed through Kay as she struggled to find the right words. 'I wonder if I could come in and talk to someone?'

'To do with—?' The matron's smile was instantly replaced with a look of concern.

'My cousin,' she lied without thinking. 'He lives here.'

'Name?'

'Kay Armstrong.' She felt as if she were being interviewed.

'I'm sorry. We have no one here by that name.' Her bright but firm tone conveyed the message

that she wanted to end the conversation then and there.

Smiling nervously, Kay shook her head. 'No. That's my name. The little boy's called Jac. I was in the area and thought I might pay him a visit.'

'You'd best come in. Though I warn you, we don't allow visitors without parental consent.' She led Kay into a large, old-fashioned room. It wasn't how she had imagined it would be. The curtains with sunflowers printed on them were faded and reminded her of those which used to hang in her grandparents' cottage when she was small, and the green carpet, although spotlessly clean, had several worn patches.

'Would you like a cup of tea while you're waiting?' The matron smiled.

'Yes I would, thanks.'

'Don't hold out too much hope, will you. We'll have to speak to his mother on the phone before we can go forward.' She closed the door behind her and left Kay wondering if she had made a mistake in coming. Trying to imagine what Jac looked like, she warmed again to the thought of having a brother. She felt strongly that she had every right to see him.

Sitting down in one of the armchairs, Kay gazed out of the glass french doors and watched the gardener as he dug over a flower-bed. He reminded her of her grandfather, Billy.

'Good news and bad news,' Matron said as she handed her a cup of tea. 'Mrs Hemmingway doesn't want you to see the boy, but she is on her way here. She wants to meet you.' She sat down opposite Kay. 'Mr Watson, our resident house-uncle, will bring the boy's mother in once she arrives.'

'I suppose she told you who I really am – Jac's sister?'

'Half-sister,' she corrected.

'I'm sorry, but I don't see it like that. He's my dad's son and that makes me his sister as far as I'm concerned. Neither of us are half a person.'

'True,' she smiled again. 'It's always a difficult one—'

'You mean this isn't the first time you've had someone like me knocking on the door?'

'Similar cases. We usually manage to work something out, but it takes time. Be prepared for that.'

'We'll see,' Kay murmured.

'How long have you known about Jac?'

'Not long, a few weeks. I've been writing to his mother. I've asked her if my mum and dad could adopt him. We've got a spare room and even though we live in flats, there's plenty of playing area. Grass as well as tarmac.'

The matron looked back at Kay with sympathy in her eyes, as if she were trying for the impossible.

'I can't wait to see him.' Kay sighed and leaned back in the armchair. 'It's strange. I can't explain it, but ever since I was told, it's as if I've always known, deep down. It might have something to do with my baby brother who died at three months old. I was five or six at the time. I don't really remember, but sometimes I think I do. If that makes sense.'

Both Kay and the matron looked up as the door opened and the house-uncle appeared, followed by Patsy, who looked less than pleased. 'I told you in my letter not to come here,' she said at once.

'Please,' Kay felt a familiar, unwanted mood rising. 'I just want to say hallo to him.' Her tears streamed down despite herself. 'You don't know what it's like.' She wiped her eyes with both hands. 'I think about him all the time; dream about him, have nightmares that he's locked up in a cupboard.' She tried to stop but the words tumbled from her as if she had no control, and her body began to shake.

'I—' she tried to speak but then couldn't get the words out.

'My God. I didn't think she would be *this* concerned,' Patsy said.

'Miss Armstrong is more than upset,' the Matron placed one arm around Kay's shoulder and did her best to comfort her.

'My friend—' Kay tried again, but it was no use.

She looked into the Matron's face, desperate to tell her about Terry. 'My friend—'

'It's OK. Just try to relax. I'm sure Doctor will give you something to calm you.' She glanced up at the house-uncle hoping to get his attention, but he was gazing trancelike at Kay, moved by her sorrow.

'Has something else happened,' the Matron asked, 'apart from finding out about your brother?'

Kay could only nod and make whimpering sounds.

'Wait until you feel better. Then tell me.' She gently held her trembling hands. 'It will pass, I promise you. Just let go for now. Don't try to stop. It's your body reacting. I expect you've been bottling things up.'

'I don't want you to fetch Jac, not now – not with me like this,' Kay managed to stammer.

'You've got yourself in a real state over this, haven't you?' Patsy smiled.

Kay tried to return her smile, but her face felt numb. She sipped her tea, thankful for the warm liquid on her dry throat. After a few silent minutes, she began to feel slightly better. 'I'm sorry about this.'

'No more than I am,' Patsy looked ashamed. 'I've been a bit selfish. Just thinking of number one.' She turned to the house-uncle. 'I had no idea they felt this strongly about Jac.'

'Dad's really cut up about it.'

'Poor Jack. He's not a bad bloke. I just tried to make myself think that way to ease the hurt. I did love him, you know.'

It wasn't what Kay wanted to hear, but it was better than being yelled at, which is what she had half expected.

'Once you've pulled yourself together, we'll bring our Jac in. I think you're gonna be in for a surprise,' she chuckled.

'Mum said he looks like me.' Kay's puffy eyelids and flushed cheeks made her look younger than her seventeen years.

'He does.'

'Are you sure this is what you want, Patsy?' The house-uncle asked, hoping it was.

'It is, actually. Now that I've seen this young lady. She is my Jac's big sister, after all's said and done.'

'Who's that?' Jac pushed a chubby finger in Kay's face, making her laugh.

'*That* is your big sister,' Patsy said with a touch of pride in her voice.

'Isn't,' Jac said quietly, a strange look on his face.

'Oh, yes it is. You gonna give your sister Kay a kiss then?'

Without any prompting, Jac leaned forward and landed a big wet kiss on Kay's mouth.

'Coming?' Kay held out her arms.

'No!'

'I'll go away again.'

'No!'

'I will . . .'

Throwing himself into Kay's arms, he almost knocked Patsy off balance and thought it was hilarious when she pretended it was worse and landed on her bottom.

The three of them spent an hour together, walking around the grounds, playing chase with Jac and swinging him by his arms. An earlier rainstorm had passed, and the sun was warming the wet grass again.

'You can see why I don't want him to be miles away from me. This way I get to see him when I like.'

'Does he mind being here? I would have thought he'd miss his own home.'

Patsy sighed. 'Not at first. It was a novelty, like full-time nursery school. He's been a bit quiet the last couple of visits, mind. He probably thinks this is just a little holiday and that he'll be coming home soon.'

'What will you do if he starts crying when you leave? I couldn't bear that.'

'I don't know, to be perfectly honest. I'll just have to wait and see. It's no worse than boarding school, and plenty of children go there. And look at this place. It's much better than the place we live in, I can tell you.'

'And you wouldn't consider him living with—'

'No.' Patsy wasn't prepared to discuss it. 'But you can visit him, providing you let me know you're coming.'

'Sounds fair.' Kay scooped Jac up again and kissed him on the cheek. 'I'm going home now. But I'll be back to see you, Master Jac.'

'Master Jac,' he giggled, and playfully slapped Kay's face.

'What do you want me to do with the money? Keep it until you come back, or send it by registered post?'

'Keep it for now.' Kay looked at her watch. 'I'm gonna have to run, or I'll miss my train.'

After hugs all round, Kay left the house, smiling and waving and promising she'd see them again soon.

'Kay! What's the flat like, anyway?' Patsy suddenly called after her.

'Nice. And plenty of room to play. See you!'

Waiting on the platform for her train, Kay wondered why Patsy had asked about the flat. Maybe she

was having second thoughts about Jac going down
for a weekend visit.

Zacchi had turned up unexpectedly at Jack and
Laura's flat, and was slightly miffed that neither
of Kay's parents seemed to know where she was.
He waited two hours before deciding to leave.

'I'll phone later this evening, see if she's back.'

'OK, son. I'm sorry about this. Seems daft us not
knowing where she's got to. We assumed she was
round Pamela's. I'll tell her to stay in and wait for
your call once she does come in. OK?' Jack gave
Zacchi a friendly punch on the shoulder.

After seeing Zacchi out, Jack returned to the
kitchen in a black mood. 'What does she think she's
playing at?'

'Don't start, Jack. I've had enough. She's got
other friends, you know. Zacchi said something
about Juanita, someone she used to meet on the
bus. Maybe that's where she is.'

'I've no doubt. What *I'm* saying is she should tell
us if she's gonna be gone all day!'

Laura bit the end of a thumbnail, something she
had never done in her life. 'I've got a horrible
feeling we're gonna be saying goodbye to Kay
soon.'

Jack got himself a glass of water. 'What makes

you say that?' The tone of his voice said it all. He felt exactly the same.

'She's gonna go. Move out. Away from here.' She pulled her thumb away from her mouth and tucked her hands under her arms. 'She's crossed that line between depending on us and needing to live her own life.'

'Yeah, I know. She's young though, Laura. Eighteen next week. What age is that?'

'I think Zacchi knows it too. She's gonna slip through his net as well, you see if I'm wrong.'

Listening to the dripping of the cold tap that Jack hadn't turned off properly, they sat in the otherwise quiet kitchen. It had been a heavy, stormy day and now, in the late afternoon, black clouds filled the sky darkening the kitchen, but neither Jack nor Laura could be bothered to switch on the light.

When Kay finally came into the kitchen as if it had been just another day, Jack shocked her by slamming his fist down on the kitchen table, his pale face pinched with fury.

'You 'ad no right to go behind my back! First your mother and then you! What am I around 'ere? A fucking ghost or what?' he yelled.

'I was only trying to put right what you've messed up!' Kay shouted back at him. 'I should have been

told about Jac! Keeping my letters from me is one thing,' she clenched her fists and screamed, 'it's not fair!'

Drying her hands on a tea towel, Laura stood between them. 'Have either of you given a thought to what I might be going through?' She threw the tea towel on to the table and turned on Kay.

'Your father's right. You shouldn't have gone without talking to us about it. It wasn't clever!' She took a deep breath, spun around and turned on Jack. 'And as for you, playing silly games, knowing full well I was planning to go to Leicester and not letting on.' She walked out of the kitchen. 'I'm packing my bags and leaving you to it, both of you! Because *I* have had enough!'

The remark took the wind out of both Jack and Kay's sails. They knew Laura well enough to know this might not be an empty threat. Once she made up her mind to do something, she carried it through.

'Now see what you've done?' Jack balled an empty tobacco packet in his fist. 'You'd better go and talk her round before she does something silly.'

'Look me in the eye and say that, you sod!' Kay snapped back.

Jack made a sudden jerking movement towards her but thought better of it. 'Get out of 'ere before

I give you a right-hander!' He hurled the green and gold wrapping across the room.

'No! *You* get out of here and do something positive for a change.'

Inhaling deeply, Jack looked fit to burst. 'Like what?'

'Apologizing to Mum for giving another woman the son that she would have liked, for a start!'

Pushing both hands through his hair, Jack leaned forward, resting his elbows on his knees. 'Leave me alone,' he murmured and then shouted louder than she had ever heard him. 'Leave me fucking alone!'

'We did. And look where that got us!' With that insolent remark, Kay moved like lightning across the kitchen, heading for the door. She knew it was time to lock herself in her bedroom.

With her weekend bag firmly in one hand, Laura stormed out of the flat. She had no idea where she was heading. Maybe Harlow. Not Billy's cottage, that was for sure. The last thing she needed was to be told by her dad that her place was in the home.

Making her way through the backstreets, Jack's misdeeds flew through her mind. He had played the field back in the old days and had got away with it scot-free. She remembered Patsy's words; *Jack made love to me more times than you've given him a hot dinner.*

Seething, she walked briskly across the Mile End Road, daring the traffic to come anywhere near her. Having reached the other side in one piece, she reacted to an angry motorist by showing him two fingers.

'Hallo, Laura, mate.' Milly stood in her door full of smiles, wearing a flimsy pink housecoat and holding a green chiffon scarf. 'I've bin trying out my vacuum cleaner. Come and watch this,' she giggled. Following her friend through the brightly decorated passage, Laura couldn't help smiling. Nothing seemed to surprise Milly. Hadn't she seen her overnight suitcase?

'I only got it yesterday. Can't bring myself to suck any dirt into it.' Holding the delicate scarf in front of the brush, she pressed the switch on the vacuum cleaner and was overjoyed when the scarf disappeared into the machine.

'A kid with a new toy,' Laura smiled.

'I know.' She unzipped the cloth bag and pulled out the scarf with a flourish. 'Hey Presto!'

'You're mad.'

'Stopping long, are yer?' Milly asked, eyeing the small suitcase.

'I wouldn't mind hiding for a couple of days. Pigeons have come home to roost.' She shrugged and smiled.

432

''Course you can stop. Do Jack good to wonder where you've got to. I take it you didn't tell 'im?'

'I didn't know where I was going myself till I got here.'

'Oh, I'd love to do something like that.' She switched on the electric kettle. 'Especially when George and Brianny get going. He's not been out five minutes and they've clashed already.'

Pushing her shoes off, Laura lay back in an armchair. 'And you really don't mind my staying?'

''Course I don't. Be company for me. 'Ow many sugars?'

'Two. How's the wedding arrangements going?'

'Lovely. I've got myself a nice turquoise number – hat to match. I can't wait to get all dressed up, to tell the truth.'

'What about Georgie?'

'Dunno really. He shows a bit of interest sometimes, when I remind 'im that he's getting rid of his son.' She placed a cup of tea in front of Laura and sat down. 'He's changed a bit. It's all the sex he's getting now. Won't leave me alone. Thinks he's a young man again.'

'Not jumping off the wardrobe, is he?' Laura was beginning to enjoy herself. This was what she needed. A little break from all her worries.

'No, but—'

'Mum!' Brianny burst into the kitchen. 'Dad's only gone and nicked my best Ben Sherman shirt! That's twice this week!'

Laura laughed so much she had to cross her legs. Georgie Smith in a Ben Sherman – she couldn't imagine it. 'He's not wearing winkle-pickers as well, is he?' she managed to say.

'Yeah, as it 'appens,' Milly sipped her tea. 'Bought 'em off a stall down Chris Street market last week.'

'I warned 'im,' Brianny barked, 'I said I'd 'ave his suede tie if he did it again!'

'I hear you're getting married, Brianny?' Laura was longing to find out a bit more about his fiancée.

'Yeah, worse luck. Bloody country bumpkin, ain't she.' He narrowed his eyes and grinned. 'You remember – Richard Wright's little maid, Janet.' He left the room whistling.

'They been together all this time?' Laura tried not to let Richard creep into her mind.

'Yeah. Love, eh? Still, she's a good kid. She'll keep a nice front door and step. Helped me polish my windows last week as well.' Milly snatched a Rich Tea out of the biscuit barrel. 'You'll never guess who she's invited to the wedding?'

'You are joking?' Laura knew exactly who Milly was referring to. Her face said it all.

'They're coming as well.' She looked serious for a second. 'That's why I wanna look my best. Lord and lady of the manor coming to my son's wedding! Turn-up for the books, eh?'

'So Richard Wright did employ Brianny after all?' she said casually.

'Up until a few months ago when Brianny's uncle offered him work in London. He'd had enough of country life – thank Gawd.' She pulled a tiny patterned handkerchief from her pocket and wiped crumbs from the corners of her mouth. 'Getting in practise for the big day,' she giggled.

'You knew the Wrights were coming when you invited me and Liz, I suppose?'

''Course. That's why I didn't ask Jack.'

Once Milly had let Laura know that she had learned about her romance from Brianny, the floodgates opened. Laura told Milly everything and she was all ears.

'You don't still love 'im, surely?' Milly wanted more.

'No, I don't. And to tell the truth, I don't think I ever did.' She became pensive. 'I've been weighing things up this last couple of weeks, once I knew about little Jac.' She pulled her cigarettes out of her handbag and offered one to Milly.

'We weren't in love. It was unreal. We needed

435

each other just then, that's all. We'd both arrived at a difficult patch in our lives—'

'Give over, Laura,' Milly managed to grin even though a cigarette was dangling from the side of her mouth. 'You were madly in love, the pair of you. And just about everyone on the hop fields knew it.'

'You reckon?' Laura felt herself sink again. 'I don't know. I don't know anything any more.'

'What's gonna 'appen about Jack's kid then?' Milly had a way with words no one could match. Every line was spoken as if the words were from a song. 'Gonna dump 'im on yer, is she?'

'Chance would be a fine thing, no. And that's what all the upset's about really . . . well, that and other things that have been happening lately. Horrible things.'

Milly bent her head and her eyes filled with tears. 'Yeah, I know. Poor Terry, eh? Your Kay must 'ave taken that badly.'

'Fucking 'ell, Mum!' The freckled face appeared in the doorway again. 'Dad's took me suede jacket an' all!'

'See?' Milly shrugged at Laura, 'I told yer.' She tapped one side of her head. 'Gone mad. Thinks he's nineteen instead of turned forty. You're in for a treat. He'll be back from the pub soon.'

'I'm going down there. Pull it off 'is bloody back.' Brianny grabbed some biscuits and disappeared, banging the front door behind him.

It was Milly who started to laugh first, and Laura couldn't wait for Georgie to walk through the door wearing his new look.

Her fingers flying over the keys of her typewriter, Kay was in another world. The article she had begun writing the week before had somehow turned into a short story and was now developing into a novel. More and more ideas had come to her as the main plot developed. She had started to type to take her mind off the way she had upset her mum enough to make her walk out. She was also trying to block out the picture that kept flashing through her mind of the little boy she had left behind. Last but not least, she wanted to be free from her feelings about Terry.

The room where the orphans played was light and cheerful and looked out on to a small garden. Sarah pulled the sunflower-patterned curtains slightly to one side and was reminded once again of her childhood. The young man digging the garden looked just like her brother John, who had joined the merchant navy.

'Her Ladyship will see you now.' The austere

face of Mrs Johnson showed no signs of a smile.

'How many children are there?' Sarah regretted the words as soon as they were said. She knew by the woman's reaction that it was not her place to ask and the atmosphere at Wynchling Manor was enough for anyone to realize that not only children but staff must speak only when spoken to.

Pausing to read what she had written, Kay wound back the sheet of paper in the typewriter, moved along to the word *slightly* and typed a row of x's through it.

'Kay? You coming out of there now, or what?' Jack tried to sound indifferent.

She was up and unlocking her door in no time. 'It's going really well. I don't want to stop.' Her face was glowing. She splayed her fingers and wiggled them. 'I couldn't stop,' she grinned. 'I feel as if I could go on and on writing, in my other world.'

'Yeah, well, maybe we'd best sit down and look at what's 'appening in this one.' Jack went back into the kitchen.

'I can't believe it's nine o'clock already!' Kay rummaged around in the cupboard. 'I s'pose you're worried about Mum?'

'No. I couldn't care less. She won't have gone far. Probably having a chin-wag with Liz.'

'So what did you want then?' Finding a jar of peanut butter, she opened a drawer and took out the bread knife.

'Just wondered if you was all right in there, that's all,' Jack didn't sound too convincing.

'Do you want a slice of bread and butter? There's some cheese in the fridge.'

'No thanks. I'm not hungry.' He poured himself a glass of milk. 'So what's all these hints you've been giving out lately, about moving out?'

'Jeannie at work's got a friend who's got a studio flat for rent. In Highgate. Three pounds fifty a week.' Kay reeled it off quickly while she had him listening.

'And who's gonna do your washing? Cook your dinners?'

'Me, of course.'

'And what about Zac? Where does he fit in with all this?' Jack seemed almost to be coming round to the idea.

'Things won't be any different to what they are now. He'll get a train over there instead of here, that's all.'

'Your mum won't like it, Kay. I'll tell you that now.'

'What about you? You gonna stick up for me?' She studied his face and waited.

'I s'pose I'll have to. Little cow. You're gonna go one of these days, in any case. No matter what I say.'

'I don't do it on purpose, you know. I mean I'm not deliberately setting out to cause trouble or anything.'

'No?' Jack flashed her a smile.

'I'm *not*!'

'You're a natural rebel, babe. You don't even know you're doing it. Promise me one thing, though.' He looked her straight in the eye.

'What?'

'If you ever decide you wanna get married before you're twenty-one, you won't forge my signature on the marriage certificate form.'

'You've put the idea in my head now,' she grinned.

'No, I mean it, Kay. That would really cut me up. I don't think I could forgive you if you did that.'

'Well I won't then. See, Dad, all you have to do is talk these things over with me—'

'But you're only a kid!' He was getting angry again. 'I shouldn't have to—'

'Dad!' Kay cut in. 'It doesn't matter how old or young I am. You mustn't – oh, I don't know! I can't

stand to feel as if I'm not free to come and go as I please. I've got to feel free! Otherwise it's like I'm suffocating.'

'You're overdoing it, but all right! All right. I'll try to let you fly if you must. But I tell you what, Kay. You're not gonna be able to make these demands when you get married. You can kiss your freedom goodbye then.'

'It doesn't have to be that way! Two people can . . .' Kay's voice trailed off as the sound of a woman talking to a child drifted through the open kitchen window. Both of them recognized the accent but could hardly believe their ears. Dumbstruck, they waited for the sound of the doorbell. Instead they heard three short, sharp raps on the knocker.

'You gonna answer that?' Jack had suddenly lost his nerve.

'Is that who I think it is?'

'We won't know till you answer it, Kay – will we?'

'There she is, then,' Patsy said to Jac as Kay stood in the street doorway. 'Your big sister.' She looked at Kay and managed a smile. 'He cried once you'd gone. Cried for you, I mean.'

'I can't believe you're here!' Kay laughed as Jac put his chubby arms out to her and almost leapt from Patsy's arms. She was suddenly caught between the

devil and the deep blue sea. Her mum could arrive back any minute.

'Dad's in. I don't suppose . . . ?'

'Why not,' Patsy sighed and braced herself.

'Yeah,' Kay grinned broadly, 'why not?'

Leading the way, she hugged Jac and smothered his face with kisses. 'Look who the wind's blown in, Dad.'

So wrapped up in the moment, it had escaped Kay that Jack was looking at the son he hadn't seen for nearly two and a half years.

'What's going on, Patsy?' He spoke as if little Jac were still a well-kept secret.

'Is that all you can say?' Kay kissed Jac's smiling face again. 'This funny man is your daddy. And mine. You gonna say hallo?'

'No.' Jac placed his hands either side of Kay's face and pushed her cheeks together.

'You gonna give him a kiss?'

'No.'

Jack couldn't take it in. He looked drained and ready for his bed.

Turning to Patsy, Kay pulled her into the kitchen.

'Hallo, Jack,' she said, shyly.

Swallowing hard, Jack sucked on his bottom lip and kept his eyes down. 'You OK?'

The little boy answered for her. 'Hallo – Jack!'

he giggled, which started Kay and Patsy off. 'Hallo, Jack!' Jac loved having an audience. Pointing one chubby finger at himself he said, 'Me Jac!'

Smiling through tears, Jack looked up at his small son. 'So am I.' He leaned forward and offered his hand. 'How d'yer do?'

Jac took his hand and shook it in a very grown-up fashion.

'Pleased to meet you.' He glanced sheepishly at Patsy. 'You didn't come all this way by train, did yer?'

'No. Tom drove me. He's waiting downstairs. I just thought maybe . . . try it for a week. Think of it as a little holiday.' She stroked her son's hair.

'Why don't you fetch What's-his-name up? Tom?'

'You must be joking. He's scared of what you might do to him.'

'What am I gonna do, Patsy? I've got no grudge against the man. Why should I?'

'Because he won't bring up your son?'

'Can't blame 'im for that. I'd be the same in 'is shoes.'

'You would not, Jack, and you know it.' Patsy caught his eye and a smile passed between them.

'So I'm allowed him for a week then?'

'If Jac likes it, he can stay a bit longer.' She wiped

the dribble from her son's chin. 'Do you think you'll like it, then?'

'No garden!' Jac exclaimed splaying his hands.

'Five minutes walk away. A very big garden. It's called Barmy Park and it's got swings as well.' Jack put his arms out to Jac. 'Come on. Come to your dad while your sister makes us all a cup of tea. We'll go and tell Tom to come up, shall we?'

'Yes.' Jac thought that was a good idea. 'Yes!' He looked into his father's face and repeated what he had heard so many times from Patsy. 'Got Jac's eyes!'

'No,' Patsy laughed, 'you have got your daddy's eyes.'

'No!' He pressed a finger on to each of his lids and almost whispered, 'My eyes.'

'Go on then, go to your sister. I won't be a minute.' Placing Jac in Kay's arms, Jack grinned at her. 'Still gonna move out, are yer?'

'I didn't say straight away! Maybe in six months or so.' Kay put a tissue up to Jac's nose and told him to blow.

Once Jack had left the flat to fetch Tom, Patsy sighed with relief and sat down. 'Where's your mother?' She sat erect, preparing herself for a confrontation.

'Don't ask.' Kay smiled.

'Fair enough,' Patsy shoved her hand into her pale

lilac summer coat. 'I've brought the envelope back.'

'No. I mean it, Patsy. Use it for the fare money so you can come down regularly. It's only fair on Jac. And anyway, Mum and Dad don't know about it. A couple of my relations treated me. Let's leave it at that.'

'Well, I'm not going to argue with you. Thanks.' She slipped it back in her pocket. 'I only hope I'm doing the right thing, that's all.'

'It's not carved in stone.' Kay shrugged. 'If it doesn't work out . . . Come on. Let's show Jac where he'll be sleeping. Bring his bags.'

'These are full of toys and teddy bears. The back seat of the car's full of boxes and bags of his clothes. I didn't want to bring them up in case—'

'You didn't like the look of the flat?'

'Something like that, yeah. Your mum's in for a shock when she gets back.'

'You're not kidding.' Kay let out a sigh of relief. 'She'll be pleased, Patsy. It'll be good for her.'

No sooner had Jack left than he was back. 'Tom's a funny sort of bloke, ain't he, Patsy? Kept shaking my 'and but wouldn't come up!' Jack sounded pleased about it.

'He's all right. You leave him be.' Patsy gave Jack a look of scorn. 'I'm going now. I'll phone tomorrow, see if he's settled.'

Bending down to kiss Jac goodbye, she was taken aback when he turned away and snuggled up against his new sister.

'Kiss Mummy, Jac. Don't be silly!' Kay's mildly scolding voice worked. He gave Patsy a hug and kiss.

'Be a good boy and I'll see you very soon. OK?' Swallowing hard and rolling her eyes at Kay, Patsy forced back her tears.

Jac put his thumb up. 'OK!'

'Right. I'll be on my way.' She turned to Jack and gave him a teasing smile. 'You've still got great shoulders.'

'I'm not sure I can go along with this,' Georgie Smith said, tucking into his supper of cold meat, bread and pickle. 'You should be at home with your old man, Laura.'

'She's stopping and that's final.' Milly clinked her glass of port and lemon against Laura's. 'And you can do the same for me one day,' she gave Georgie a mock warning look.

'I'll tell you what, George. I'll phone and let Jack know where I am. How's that?'

'That's more like it,' he said. 'Now then, what's on the telly?'

Leaning back in her chair, Laura decided there and then that she would only stop overnight. That

446

would be enough time for Jack and Kay to have a chat and sort themselves out.

'What's your birth sign, Laura?' Milly was studying the horoscopes in the Sunday paper.

'Virgo.'

Milly began to read. *'You are seldom at your best this time of the year. However, you will soon realize that nothing you have gone through has been wasted or in vain. Yesterday's lessons are tomorrow's guidelines.'*

'Thanks, Milly. That makes me feel a lot better.'

'Load of bloody rubbish,' Georgie switched on the television set. 'Life's what you make it.'

Laura smiled to herself. He was dead right there. Her mind was full of Kay and what she would make of her life. It was plain enough that she was on course for a change.

'I don't suppose you fancy giving me a lift home do you, George?'

He stared at his watch. 'It's gone eleven!'

'I know but, you know . . .'

Milly yawned. 'I knew she wouldn't make it through the night. Go on, get going. But come and see me again. I've enjoyed tonight. Had a good laugh. Done my stomach good, that 'as.'

After thanking Georgie and waving him off, Laura walked slowly up the concrete stairs and could

almost hear the echo of her own breath, as well as her footsteps. She couldn't wait to see Jack's face. He would be worried and upset. His self-esteem had been a bit on the low side.

Not surprised to see the lights were still on at that late hour, she turned the key and closed the door quietly behind her in case Kay was in bed, and made for the living room.

'Oh, you're back then?'

Laura looked from Jack to Kay. They didn't look too worried. The reverse, in fact.

'I thought, you know, you just might have been a bit concerned!' Laura cursed herself for coming back too soon. She should have stayed the night and given them both something to think about.

Getting up, Jack took Laura by the arm. 'I've got something to show you.'

With one finger on his lips, he carefully opened the spare-bedroom door. A small night-light was on and the soft glow just allowed them to see Jac with his thumb in his mouth and an old brown toy dog under one arm. He was sound asleep.

Laura crept forward and gazed down at him. With her hand firmly over her mouth she looked to Jack for an answer. He just shrugged, pressed his lips together and did his utmost not to cry, but a tear was in each eye and beginning to trickle down.

Kissing Laura and Jack goodnight, Kay went to her room without saying a word. She knew that this was probably one of the greatest experiences they would ever have; the best thing in the world for them was to share it together, without her. Besides which, she couldn't wait to get back to her story which was almost certainly going to include Jac. She could write down her innermost feelings and maybe one day her mum and dad would read what had really been going on.

'Can't you advise us where to go? This is all foreign to us. We haven't been further than the Isle of Sheppey.'

'Isle of Wight,' Billy corrected. 'I always took Laura and her mother to the Isle of Wight when she was small. I've never much fancied Sheppey.'

The travel agent leaned back in the chair, narrowed his eyes and suggested a tour. 'I'm thinking of Austria. Mountains and lakes. Holland and the tulip fields. Clean air, not too hot. Flowers everywhere. Springtime.'

'Tulips from Amsterdam . . .' Billy was warming to the idea.

'How far is it?' Liz was beginning to wish she hadn't accepted Jack and Laura's offer. The Isle of Sheppey would have suited her.

'I take it you do have passports?' The travel agent seemed to be in a world of his own.

'No. But our Kay can fill us in on what to do. She's been abroad. Went to Spain, if you don't mind! Cheeky cow forged her passport form.'

'That's it, tell the whole bloody world!' Liz shot Billy a look to kill.

'Why not take a brochure and have a browse at your leisure?' The man smiled benignly at them.

'What about foreign money? How do we go about that?' Liz asked.

'We can arrange currency for you.' He pushed a colourful brochure in front of them. 'Please come back when you've found something you like.' He looked at his watch and raised his eyebrows.

'Dutch people, innit? Over there?'

'Ye – es. In the main, in Holland.'

Liz flicked through the shiny pages. 'So we'd get from one place to another by coach?'

'Mmmm. That's usually the way.'

'And stop in different hotels?'

'Yes. You'll be moving on from place to place.'

'And how much is this gonna cost?' Billy had no intention of leaving until the man had answered all his questions.

Having little faith that his time spent with this couple would achieve a sale, the travel agent pulled

the brochure towards him and turned to a page near the back. 'All the prices, for the different tours, are listed here.' He showed them a pink insert.

'Mmmm. The small print,' Liz said suspiciously. She sniffed and looked at Billy. 'I don't know what you've got against Sheppey.'

'OK,' Billy suddenly said to the man. 'You're on. We'll take it. Two to Austria. We'll leave it to you to sort the coaches and that. Send us a bill with all the charges on.' He reeled off his address and slapped his cap back on. 'We'll get the passports sorted out.'

Pushing his hand into the travel agent's palm, he gripped it tight and shook heartily. 'Thanks for all your 'elp.'

'It doesn't quite work that way.' The bemused man tried to keep a straight face. 'You choose, and we—'

'Stone me. D'yer want our business or not? Just pick what you think'd suit us. Come on, Liz, let's get going. My belly's rumbling.' He gave the man a show of his hand. 'You've got an honest face. We trust you to sort something out. All the best.'

Surprised by this sudden sweeping conclusion, Liz could only shrug at the man behind the desk. 'I s'pose that's it, then?'

'It would appear so.' He looked far from pleased.

'Make sure we're in separate rooms, only we're not married,' she smiled, and followed Billy out.

Tucking into their dinner in the pie shop, Billy grimaced at a family with five children who were making a racket. 'I'd show 'em my belt if they were mine.'

'You never used it on Laura, surely?'

'Never 'ad to. Any cheek and my hand went to the buckle. She soon came round. Never 'ad to lay a finger on 'er. A look was enough.'

'I bet it was.' Liz dipped a forkful of pie into the liquor.

'So where d'yer reckon this money did come from then? If it wasn't a win on the dogs?'

'I know where it came from, Billy. I know full well. Bert's brothers. The Brothers Bung, as I used to call 'em. It's not the first time they've bunged me a little treat on the quiet. Bert would 'ave blown 'is top if he'd 'ave known. Pride, eh?'

'Jack's just as bad. Let 'im try eating pride. Soon lose weight.'

'What sort of foreign food d'yer reckon they eat out there in Austria?'

'Dunno. Kangaroos, perhaps?'

'Silly bleeder. That's Australia.'

'Is it? Oh well . . . you never know.'

Liz waited for him to finish his sentence but it

became apparent that he had. 'You never know what?'

'We might go out there an' all, one day. Australia. I expect that's where our Kay'll end up.'

Willing herself not to laugh at him, she asked why Australia.

''Cos that's the furthest bloody corner of the world, innit?'

Sitting cross-legged by Terry's freshly dug grave, Kay ran her fingers over the flowers and dried wild hops she had brought with her, and wondered why she felt so light inside.

'You don't know how pleased I am to see you here.' It was Ray. He looked tired and drawn. 'Of all people you're the only one he really cared about, apart from his mum.'

Kay reached out and took Ray's hand. 'Come and sit down. It feels OK. And it's as close as we're gonna get.'

'So what now?' Ray said, settling himself down beside her.

'I don't know. One day at a time, I suppose?'

'Yeah. That's it. One day at a time.' He smiled at her and nodded. 'Thanks for being here.'

'And you,' she took his slim hand in hers and squeezed it. 'We'll be OK. We'll be fine.'

'So long as this weather holds out,' he said, admiring the blue sky dotted with cotton wool clouds.

'Yep. So long as that sun keeps on keeping on, eh?' She leaned her head on his shoulder and he responded by rubbing his cheek on her blonde silky hair.

'How's Zacchi?'

'Oh, he's OK. Wrote a nice poem for Terry. I'll let you have a copy.'

'Will you talk to me about him, Kay? All those years when you played together down hoppin' – all of it?'

''Course I will. But not now though, eh? In time. Bit by bit. Until we can laugh at him again. That's when we'll know we're over it. It will happen. It's beginning to already with my uncle Bert. I can think about him now, the way he really was. And it's OK.'

'That's good.'

'Did I tell you I've got a little brother now?'

'No. I didn't know that.'

'Yeah, he's lovely. And he looks like me.'

'I've got a little sister. She can be a cow sometimes . . . nearly three and bossy already.'

'But you wouldn't be without her.'

'No. I wouldn't be without her.'

Kay trailed one finger across the dark mound of rich earth and remembered Sid in the park and what he had said about Terry when he was in hospital. *If he is hovering between this world and the next he'll be able to see you* . . .

Kay had a strong feeling that Terry was hovering close to them now, and smiling. She couldn't describe it, but she felt his warm happy presence and from the way Ray was relaxed with his face to the sun, she imagined he too could feel that Terry had not quite made that final departure.

Her mind was full of that black tin hoppers' hut on the common, the white sheets smelling of washing powder and starch. His mum's faded curtain. The small Primus stove and the oil-lamp nailed to a wooden stretcher on the wall. It was as if it still existed. But of course it didn't. The hut, like all the others on the common, had been smashed to the ground and grass was growing where Terry's mum's polished lino used to lie.

But still in Kay's mind the hut was as real now as it was then. And so was Terry. Nothing could destroy what was in her mind. The memory of him would be with her forever. And one day she would be able to think back and enjoy their times together all over again, no matter which part of the world she chose to live in.

Looking around and admiring the small, well-kept patches of garden dotted between the white marble tombstones, Ray slowly nodded. 'It's funny; I never imagined a graveyard to be like this. It's really peaceful and, I dunno . . . alive. All these flowers.'

'Yeah. I know what you mean.'

Enjoying the tranquillity, the two of them sat there in the warmth of the sun, allowing time and space to move in and begin to soothe the knots of pain inside.

They were by no means alone. Others were there. Some removing fading flowers and replacing them with fresh ones. The bereaved, quietly getting on and dealing with their loss in their own way. One or two were tearful, but on the whole most of the relatives and friends looked happy – some were even smiling as they chatted to each other between the graves.

'We'll be all right,' Kay murmured, and locked her fingers in Ray's. 'We'll be fine. You'll see.'

CHRISTMAS IN HIS ROYAL BED

HEIDI BETTS

In loving memory of Helen Brown. When she passed away this time last year after a long and valiant battle with breast cancer, I lost a friend, and the romance world lost a dedicated fan. We miss you, Helen. And if Heaven is any kind of Heaven at all, it will be filled with romance novels for you to enjoy.

And with much appreciation to loyal reader Jennifer Yates, who, when I challenged readers to help me out, came up with many of the names used in this story. Thanks, Jennifer!

One

Only she would do.

Prince Stephan Nicolas Braedon of Glendovia watched the ebony-haired beauty from afar. Tall and lithe, with an hourglass figure, she had silky black hair that fell in a straight curtain to her hips. He was too far away to know the color of her eyes or see the full pout of her lips, but he trusted the feeling in his gut that told him both would be just as alluring as the rest of her.

Cocking his head toward the tall, suited man

at his side, he said in a low voice, "Find out her name."

His bodyguard followed the direction of his gaze, then gave a stiff nod before moving away. Nicolas didn't need to ask how Osric intended to get the information, nor did he care.

A few minutes later, his bodyguard returned, standing at attention at Nicolas's side.

"Her name is Alandra Sanchez, Your Highness. She is in charge of the organization of this evening's event."

Alandra. A beautiful name for a beautiful woman.

She floated around the large, crowded ballroom, smiling, chatting with guests, making sure everything was running smoothly. The full-length lavender gown she wore shimmered in the muted lighting every time she moved, and fit her perfect feminine curves like a glove.

Nicolas hadn't attended this fund-raising dinner in hopes of finding a lover, but now that he'd seen her, he knew he wouldn't be leaving the United States without making arrangements for her to become his next mistress.

It was true that he was the member of the royal

family in charge of overseeing Glendovia's charitable organizations, but his duties did not extend to attending charitable events outside of his own country. That, he usually left to his sister or one of his two brothers.

But though his sister, Mia, had been scheduled to make the trip to the States and attend this dinner to raise funds for a new children's wing at a central Texas hospital, she'd had to cancel at the last minute. Since Nicolas was to meet with very wealthy oilmen to discuss fuel for his country, he decided to attend.

Until a few minutes ago, he had been resenting the interruption of his own life and plans, and all but cursing his sister for being the cause. Now, however, he was considering sending Mia a bouquet of flowers or a box of her favorite truffles. He wanted to thank her for putting him on a path to what could turn out to be an extremely pleasurable experience.

Smiling so brightly the muscles in her cheeks ached, Alandra Sanchez moved around the room, making sure everything was running smoothly. She'd been working to set up this gala for months now, in hopes of raising both awareness and money for the new children's hospital wing.

Unfortunately, things weren't going quite as well as she'd hoped, and Alandra knew she had only herself to blame.

Everyone in the room seemed to be watching her. She could see their curiosity. Sense their condemnation.

All because she'd had the dreadful misfortune to get mixed up with the wrong man.

Of all the things that could have happened to put a damper on this evening's event, this was the worst. A hurricane, a flash flood, even the hotel catching on fire…

Those were all disasters she could have handled. They barely would have caused a blip on her radar. But instead, she was being personally attacked, her reputation besmirched.

It served her right for ever getting involved with Blake Winters in the first place. She should have known the minute she met him that he would end up causing her nothing but trouble.

And now everyone in this room—everyone in Gabriel's Crossing, the great state of Texas and possibly the entire United States of America—thought she was a home-wrecking adulteress.

That's what the newspaper gossip columns were saying about her. Her picture, along with Blake's and that of his wife and two children, had been plastered everywhere, with glaring, slanderous headlines.

Ignoring the stares and whispers she knew were aimed in her direction, Alandra held her head high and continued wending her way through the ballroom, acting as though nothing was wrong. As though her heart wasn't racing, her face wasn't flushed with humiliation and her palms weren't damp with anxiety.

Nothing that had happened in the week since the story of her affair with Blake Winters broke had led her to believe the fund-raising dinner wouldn't still be a complete success. None of the invited guests had cancelled, making excuses for why they couldn't attend. No one from the hospital benevolence society had called to complain about the scandal she found herself suddenly embroiled in, or to voice concerns about her name being linked to the organization.

All of which led her to believe everything would be fine. That even though reporters were camped out on her front lawn, the rest of her life continued to run smoothly.

Now, though, she wasn't so sure. Now, she thought perhaps every seat in the room was filled because the cream of central Texas high society wanted an up-close-and-personal glimpse of one of their own who had so recently fallen from grace.

She might as well have a scarlet letter pinned to her chest or a piece of spinach stuck in her teeth, for all the attention being focused on her every move.

The attention—even negative attention—she could handle. What concerned her more than the stares and whispers was the impact her newly sullied reputation might have on the amount of money collected this evening.

She'd worked so hard to put this event together, was so passionate about her philanthropy, giving of both her time and money to support the causes she felt most strongly about. And she had always been quite successful in convincing others to give to those causes, too.

Usually, by this point in the evening, she would

already have collected a dozen extremely generous checks slipped to her by those in attendance, with more to follow at the end of the night. Tonight, however, her hands—and the hospital's coffers—were still empty.

Because she'd had the misfortune of meeting Blake Winters at another fund-raiser last year, and hadn't been wise enough to turn him away when he'd started asking her out, those who were most in need could very well end up going without.

The prospect broke her heart, and she pressed a hand to the snug satin stays sewn into the lining of her gown in an attempt to settle the nervous caterpillars squirming and wiggling in her belly.

She would act as though nothing was wrong, nothing was out of the ordinary—and pray like the dickens that the crowd got over their curiosity and remembered their true purpose for being here before the evening was over. Otherwise, she had a sneaking suspicion her personal bank account would be taking a hard hit when she attempted to single-handedly make up for what the children's wing fund should have earned tonight. And probably would have, if not for her bad luck and some of the poor decisions she'd made recently.

Once she'd made her loop through the crowd to be sure every seat was filled, every guest served and everything was running as smoothly as possible, she returned to her own place at the front of the room, where a raised dais had been set up for the event's organizers. She made small talk with the women on either side of her and choked down her meal, barely tasting a bite.

Next came a speech from the organization's president, and a short ceremony where plaques were given to several members who had gone above and beyond in the past year. Even Alandra received one, for her continued dedication to raising money for the hospital.

Finally, the evening drew to an end, and she breathed a sigh of relief. She was now holding a few generous checks, and had received promises for more. Not as many as she'd collected in the past, and she had definitely noticed a distinct difference in the way people had treated her throughout the evening. But at least things were looking a bit brighter than they had when the night began.

She made a final round of the room, nodding farewells to guests as they exited the ballroom, and making sure no one left anything behind before the hotel staff started cleaning up.

Gathering her own small, beaded clutch and shawl from her seat, she found her mind racing ahead to what she needed to do the next day—thoughts that were interrupted when she heard a low, masculine voice call her name.

"Miss Sanchez?"

Turning, she found herself dwarfed by a wide-shouldered, dark-haired mountain of a man.

She swallowed once before pasting a smile on her face and tipping her head up, up, up to meet his gaze.

"Yes?"

"If you have a minute, my employer would like to speak with you."

He inclined his head, drawing her attention to the back of the room, where a lone gentleman sat at one of the now-cleared round tables.

From what she could see at this distance, he was quite handsome.

He was also staring at her.

"Your employer?" she asked.

"Yes, miss."

So much for gaining more information about who, exactly, the mountain's employer was.

But if he had attended tonight's dinner, then he was likely a current or potential donor, and she always had time to speak with a contributor. Especially one who could afford his own bodyguard, or CIA agent, or professional wrestler....

"Of course," she said, maintaining her bright, upbeat demeanor.

Turning sideways, the giant gestured for her to move ahead of him, and then escorted her across the nearly empty room. Around them, dishes clinked and stacked chairs clattered as the kitchen and cleaning staff worked to disassemble what had taken all day to set up.

As she approached the man who wished to speak with her, he lifted a flute of champagne and took a long sip.

He wore a smartly tailored jacket of navy blue, cut quite differently than most of those she'd seen throughout the night. He definitely was not a local.

She also noticed that her earlier perception of

him being "quite handsome" was a gross inaccuracy. He was movie-star gorgeous, with dark hair and startling blue eyes that seemed to bore into her like laser beams.

Holding out her hand, she introduced herself. "Hello, I'm Alandra Sanchez."

"I know," he replied, taking her hand and refusing to let it go as he tugged her gently forward. "Have a seat, won't you, please."

Letting her shawl fall lower on her bare back, she slid onto the chair beside him. "Your…employee said you wanted to speak to me."

"Yes," he replied slowly. "May I offer you a glass of champagne?"

She opened her mouth to refuse, but the hulk was already pouring and setting a glass in front of her.

"Thank you."

Though they both had drinks now, and the evening's event was clearly over, the man seated beside her still didn't speak. The silence made Alandra shift uncomfortably, and caused gooseflesh to break out along her arms.

"What did you need to speak with me about,

Mr...." she finally pressed, careful to remain as polite as possible.

"You may call me Nicolas," he replied.

His voice carried a slight accent. Perhaps the hint of a British lilt, but Alandra couldn't place it.

"Nicolas," she repeated, because he seemed to expect it. Then she continued in her attempts to get to his reason for wanting to speak with her.

"Were you interested in making a donation to the fund for the new children's cancer wing of the hospital?" she asked. "If so, I would be happy to accept a check tonight. Or if you'd prefer, I can put you in touch with someone from the organization you can speak with, to make your contribution personally."

For a moment after she finished, he simply continued to study her, his lapis-blue eyes sharp and commandingly intense.

After taking another sip of the expensive champagne, he slowly said, "I would be happy to give to your little...cause. However, that is not why I invited you over here."

Alandra's eyes widened fractionally at that, but she did her best to hide her consternation.

"I am staying in a suite of rooms here in this hotel," he informed her. "I'd like for you to return there with me. Spend the rest of the evening in my bed. If things go well and we are…compatible, perhaps we can discuss further arrangements."

Alandra blinked, but otherwise remained frozen in place, her entire body mannequin-stiff and unmoving. She couldn't have been more stunned if he'd lifted a hand and slapped her across the face.

She didn't know what to say. Didn't know what she *should* say.

This certainly wasn't the first time she'd been propositioned. Young or old, rich or poor, men had always been attracted to her, and she'd had more than her share of invitations to dinner, the theater, even romantic jaunts to private island hideaways.

And, yes, she was well aware that every single one of those men had hopes that dinner, the theater and tropical getaways would help him to seduce her into his bed.

But never—*never*—had any of them been so bold, so brash, as to flat-out ask her to sleep with him.

This was all because of the scandal, she realized

suddenly, her spine snapping straight with offense. Those bloody articles had labeled her an immoral home wrecker. And this man had obviously gotten wind of that and decided she wouldn't be averse to an indecent proposal.

Well, she was averse. She was disgusted and thoroughly insulted.

Pushing her chair back, she rose to her feet, re-arranged her shawl across her back and arms, and tightened her fingers on her small clutch purse. Concentrating on her breathing, she stood per-fectly rigid, looking down at him.

"I don't know what kind of woman you think I am. But I can assure you I'm *not* the kind to go to bed with a man I've just met."

She cut a quick glance at the bear standing at attention a yard or two away. "Maybe your body-guard can find someone a little more willing and a lot less discriminating to go back to your room with you tonight. That is, if you're utterly inca-pable of finding her on your own."

With that, Alandra turned on her heel and marched out of the ballroom to the elevator.

Just who the hell did the man think he was?

Two

Who did she think she was to speak to him in such a manner?

Nicolas had never been turned down like that before.

He blinked once, slowly, searching his memory for a similar incident that might have taken place during his lifetime.

No, he didn't think he'd been turned down *ever*.

Had she actually implied that he was incapable of finding his own female companionship? Or that he had to order Osric to *pay* a woman to spend time with him?

He shook his head, still not quite believing what had just taken place. Behind him, Osric shuffled closer, looming over his right shoulder.

"Your Highness, shall I go after her and bring her back so that you may finish your conversation?"

Nicolas could picture his oversize bodyguard, who closely resembled a brick wall, tackling Miss Sanchez to the ground and carting her back to him…and the fuss the lady would kick up if he so much as tried.

"No, thank you, Osric," he replied. "I believe I'll be returning to the suite alone this evening."

Placing his hands on the tabletop in front of him, he stood and straightened the front of his jacket, then started out of the ballroom, with his trusty security guard close on his heels.

He should be upset, Nicolas thought, as they made their way through the hotel to his private, luxurious suite on the thirty-third floor.

Ironically, he was more intrigued than ever by the ebony-haired beauty. It was her face and figure that had first caught his attention, and seeing her up close hadn't changed his mind about having her in his bed.

He would have expected a dressing-down such as she'd given him to turn him off, to make him realize he didn't want to sleep with a woman who possessed such a sharp tongue. Instead, her spirit fired his blood.

If anything, he found himself wanting her more. She was lovely and fierce, and he could only imagine how passionately those qualities would translate between the sheets.

Alandra Sanchez might think she'd gotten in the last word downstairs, when she'd all but told him to take his offer and go straight to the devil. But Prince Stephan Nicolas Braedon was used to getting his way, getting what he wanted.

And he wanted *her*.

So he would have her. He only had to figure out how.

One week later...

"Pop? Alandra? Is anybody here?"

Alandra heard her sister calling from downstairs,

and was more than happy to take a break from the event plans she'd been working on all afternoon.

Since Elena had moved out of their father's house and into her own with her new husband, Chase, Alandra didn't get to see her as often as she used to.

Abandoning her desk, she found her sister looking slightly frazzled as she flipped through a pile of mail stacked beside a large arrangement of fresh flowers on the round table in the center of the foyer. When she heard Alandra's approach, Elena raised her head and rolled her eyes.

"A reporter tried to follow my car through the security gate," she snapped, waving a hand over her shoulder in the direction of the front door. "He was camped out front, waiting."

Alandra frowned, moving closer to give her sister a gentle squeeze. "I'm so sorry. I really thought they'd have lost interest by now and moved on to something else."

"It's not your fault," Elena said with a sigh, returning Alandra's hug. "And eventually they *will* lose interest and move on."

"So what are you doing here?" she asked distractedly, her mind still on the reporter. It was one thing for *her* to be harassed and annoyed because of her own foolish actions, but it was another for her family to be dragged into this mess.

"Since Chase won't be home for dinner because of a late meeting, I thought I'd stop by to say hello, see how you and Pop are doing, and grab a bite to eat. Not to mention picking up any stray mail," she added, stuffing a few letters into the side pocket of her handbag.

Her sister had married and moved out last year, but the change-of-address process took time, and the odd letter or piece of mail showed up for her occasionally.

"Well, dinner will be served at seven, as usual, and as far as I know, everything is fine around here. Pop is still at the office, and I've just been working on the plans for that fund-raiser for the animal shelters."

"Will Chase and I be invited?" Elena asked.

"Of course."

"Looks like you got something important," her sister said, nodding toward the letter left on top of the stack.

Alandra picked up the thick envelope and read the return address, which was embossed in dark blue, fancy raised script on parchment-quality stationery. "H.R.H. Prince Stephan Nicolas Braedon, Kingdom of Glendovia."

"His Royal Highness?" Elena asked. "Really? You got a letter from a prince?"

"It appears so." She opened the envelope and skimmed the official-looking letterhead and neatly typed text of the top page. Then, heart stuttering, she read it again. "Oh, my God," she breathed.

"What?"

"This Prince Stephan wants me to come to his kingdom and oversee all of their fund-raising organizations."

Both sisters scanned the letter. It touched on Alandra's past fund-raising accomplishments, which the prince claimed were very impressive, and stressed how much Glendovia could use her assistance. He even went so far as to enclose copies of a contract for her employment that he hoped she would peruse and strongly consider signing.

Lifting the cover sheet, Alandra read the one-page agreement. It briefly outlined her duties and obligations, if she chose to accept the royal family's offer, as well as their obligations to her.

"Do you think this is legitimate?" Elena demanded.

The Braedon name did ring some bells. "I guess it would be easy enough to check out," she replied.

The two of them went into Alandra's office, where she started going through her guest lists, and her sister did a quick search on the Internet.

"Huh," Elena said when they discovered at almost the same moment that Stephan Nicolas Braedon was, indeed, a bona fide prince, and the island of Glendovia really did exist. According to Alandra's records, another member of the Braedon royal family—a Princess Mia—had attended one of her recent fund-raisers.

"What are you going to do?" Elena asked.

"Well, I'll reply, of course, and thank him for the generous offer, but I can't possibly accept. I'm already knee-deep in organizing my next event, and Christmas is a month off. I don't want to be away from my family over the holidays."

"I don't blame you, but you have to admit it's a flattering offer."

Extremely flattering, Alandra thought, glancing once again at the raised script of the letterhead. She almost wanted to reach out and run her fingertips over the prince's name. Her letter of refusal definitely wouldn't be an easy one to write.

"But maybe…"

Alandra glanced at her sister. "What?"

"I was just thinking that maybe this position in Glendovia is exactly what you need."

Alandra frowned. "What?"

"Well, things are anything but simple around here for you right now. You've got a reporter camped outside the house, that jerk Winters still calling you, and…well…" Her gaze skittered away and her voice softened slightly. "I heard that last week's fund-raiser didn't go as well as your events usually do."

Alandra took a breath, trying not to let the pain of having her shortcomings pointed out by her own flesh and blood overwhelm her.

Running a supportive hand down her arm, Elena continued. "I was just thinking that if you got away for a while, where no one could find you, this would all blow over. And when you came back, you could get on with your life as though none of it had ever happened."

"But I would be away from you guys," Alandra murmured. "Over Christmas."

"You could come back before then. But even if you didn't, it's only one holiday. There's always next year." Wrapping an arm around her shoulders, her sister added, "I don't necessarily *want* you to go, I'm just saying that maybe you should think it over and do what's best for you. I think Pop would agree."

"I'll consider it," Alandra said, realizing her sister was making a good point. Perhaps the best way to leave all this scandal behind *was* to fly off to a foreign country.

Three

Less than a week later, the Saturday after Thanksgiving, Alandra arrived on the island of Glendovia, hoping against hope that she'd made the right decision.

Her flight had been uneventful. And a limousine had been waiting at the airport for her, as promised in the itinerary that had been faxed to her as soon as she'd accepted Prince Stephan's offer.

Staring out the window as the car sped through the countryside, Alandra was swept away by the beauty of the tiny island country. Located in a northern area of the Mediterranean, it was postcard perfect, with a clear azure sky, rolling emerald hills, and the sprawling blue-green of the sea visible in the distance.

Even what she assumed to be the center of the capital seemed more quaint and clean than anywhere she'd traveled in America or Europe. The buildings were tall, but not mammoth. The streets were busy, but not crowded and harried.

Things seemed more tranquil here, and for the first time since scrawling her name across the bottom of that employment contract, she thought she might actually be glad she'd agreed to come.

Her family had supported the decision wholeheartedly, wanting her to be happy and get away from the scandal they knew was causing her such pain. She had accepted the position in order to protect them from a part of her life that had gotten ugly, in hope it would not spill over onto them.

The limousine slowed and waited for a tall, antique iron gate to slide open. They drove up a long, winding lane that ran among pristine, well-manicured lawns and gardens.

The house—*palace* was a better word—was somewhat historical in design, but looked updated and modern. Eggshell-white, with pillars and balconies and a myriad of floor-to-ceiling windows, it stood atop a small rise overlooking the splashing waves of the Mediterranean.

As the driver opened the door and helped her out of the vehicle, she couldn't tear her eyes away from the breathtaking view. Alandra continued to gawk while the driver removed her bags from the trunk and escorted her to the front door.

A butler opened it and invited her inside, where a handful of maids dressed in matching gray uniforms collected her luggage and trotted off with it.

The butler said, "The prince has requested you be brought to him immediately upon your arrival, Miss Sanchez. If you'll follow me."

Feeling as though she'd just stepped into a fairy tale, Alandra did just that, taking in every detail of the foyer as they passed.

The floor was of highly polished marble in squares of black and a mottled gray-white. A chandelier the size of a small bus hung overhead, with thousands of dangling crystals twinkling in the natural light. Directly across from the front entrance stood a wide staircase leading halfway to the second level before branching off to either side.

The butler led her to the right of the foyer and down a carpeted corridor lined with priceless artwork. He paused at one of the closed doors and knocked. When a low, muffled voice bade him enter, he stepped inside, announced Alandra's presence and then moved aside for her to pass.

The personal office was decidedly masculine, with a dark area rug, built-in bookshelves lining three of the four walls, and a large cherrywood desk taking up a good portion of the room.

Dragging her gaze from the impressive surroundings, Alandra turned her attention to the man sitting behind that desk…only to feel her eyes go wide and her mouth fall open.

"You."

"Miss Sanchez." He rose and regally rounded the desk until he stood directly in front of her. "How good of you to accept my offer and come to work for our family."

"You're Prince Stephan—"

"Nicolas Braedon of Glendovia, yes. You may call me Nicolas."

Nicolas. The same Nicolas who had asked her over for a glass of champagne and then invited her to sleep with him.

Her mouth went dry with shock, her stomach clenching and her pulse kicking as though she'd just run a marathon.

How could this be happening?

"I don't understand," she said, her voice faint as she struggled to put her thoughts into words. "Why would you invite me to work for you after the way we parted? All you wanted from me then was…"

Realization dawned.

"You did this on purpose. You lured me here under false pretenses so that I would sleep with you."

"My dear Miss Sanchez," he replied, standing straight as a sword, with his hands clasped behind his back, "Glendovia is very much in need of someone to organize its charitable foundations. And, after seeing you in action, I decided you would be the perfect person for the job."

"And you've changed your mind about wanting me in your bed?" she challenged.

Nicolas studied the woman in front of him, struggling not to smile at her forthright manner and the fury snapping in her brown, almond-shaped eyes. It was a sight to behold, and only made him more certain of the wisdom of the campaign he'd put in motion.

Her rejection of him during his stay in America hadn't dulled his desire for her at all. He had decided, not long after, that since the direct approach hadn't worked, perhaps he needed to go about attaining his goal in a more subtle way.

When it came to Alandra Sanchez, it seemed a bit of seduction was in order.

It had taken him a few days after returning home to land on the idea of asking her to his country for an extended stay. He knew she wouldn't accept if he merely invited her...or if she knew he was extending the invitation, for that matter.

But because they had philanthropy in common, he knew that was the one motive that had a chance of catching her attention. There was also the rather generous bonus he'd included in the employment contract as an added incentive—two hundred and fifty thousand dollars to be donated by him to a charity of her choosing once she'd fulfilled her part of the bargain.

And now she was here, exactly where he wanted her.

Not that she looked even remotely willing to jump into bed with him at the moment. But as with everything else, that would come.

He would see to it.

"I wouldn't say that," he murmured, replying to her question about whether or not he'd changed his mind about wanting her in his bed. "But I am certainly capable of separating business from pleasure."

Without giving her a chance to argue, he continued. "Come. I'll show you to your room, where you can unpack and perhaps rest before supper."

Dropping his arms to his sides, he stepped around her and crossed the room to open the door.

"Don't bother," she replied curtly behind his back. "I'm not staying."

Half turning to face her once again, he maintained a neutral expression. "Don't be ridiculous. Of course you are. You signed a contract."

"Contract be damned." She started for the door, her demeanor icy.

He waited for her to pass, then caught her arm as she marched down the empty hallway. "Are you really willing to deprive one of your favorite charities of a quarter of a million dollars?"

The reminder stopped her in her tracks, and he pressed his advantage. "If you leave, reneging on the agreement, you forfeit the bonus. Stay through the month of December and you will not only be paid the agreed-upon wage, but will also earn a hefty sum to bestow as you see fit."

He could almost hear the gears turning in her head as she weighed her options. Leave, and she would be safe from him; he would have no opportunity to try to lure her into his bed. Stay, and she would be all but walking into the lion's den, but would also end up earning a quarter of a million dollars to fund one of her pet projects. It was a compelling enticement.

The seconds ticked by while she stood in the middle of the hall, wracked with indecision. Once again, he chose to give her a small nudge in the direction he wished her to go.

Moving closer, he placed a hand at the small of her back. She stiffened and pulled away just enough to break the contact.

"Please," he said diplomatically, "allow me to show you where you'll be staying if you elect to remain and fulfill your contract. The family will gather in the dining room for dinner at eight o'clock. I'd like you to be there, if you would, to meet everyone. After that, if you still wish to return to the United States…"

He paused, choosing his words carefully. "I won't say I'll let you go without penalty, but I will be willing to discuss the situation further."

For a moment, he thought she would continue her retreat. And then the rigid line of her spine relaxed slightly and her shoulders lifted as she inhaled a deep breath.

Without turning around, she said, "Fine. I'll stay through dinner."

"Excellent. Come along, then," he replied, careful not to let his satisfaction show as he stepped around her and walked the rest of the way down the hall.

He led her through the foyer and up the curved staircase, toward the west wing. There were more hallways and a second set of stairs before they reached the suites of rooms reserved for guests.

The royal family's quarters were located in the east wing, on the opposite end of the palace. But that was for the best. If his plan to seduce Alandra succeeded, their relationship could be kept almost completely secret, thanks to the relative privacy of the west wing and the fact that she would be the only person in residence there for the next month.

Reaching her suite, he opened the heavy, carved mahogany door, standing just inside to allow her to enter ahead of him. Briefly, he showed her the sprawling sitting room, with its large-screen plasma television and DVD library. Nicolas hadn't known her personal tastes, so he'd ordered the room to be stocked with a variety of choices, any of which she could exchange in the family's entertainment room whenever she liked.

Glancing through the bedroom door, Nicolas was happy to note that Alandra's things had already been unpacked and put away. She was carefully observing her surroundings, and if she was offended that the palace staff had handled her belongings, she didn't say so. She looked pleased with the accommodations, her expressive eyes taking in every detail of the beautifully decorated rooms.

"I'll leave you alone now, to rest or take a tour of the grounds, whatever you like. One of the staff can show you to the dining room when you're ready."

Turning on his heel, he left her standing in the middle of the bedroom.

Alandra watched him go, still seething at his manipulation, and yet not so angry that she failed to notice the handsome, regal picture he made as he exited.

She supposed she should be flattered that a prince wanted her in his bed. Most women would be, she imagined.

The problem was that he hadn't seemed interested in *her*, in getting to know her or starting a relationship with her. His request when they'd met in Texas was to take her to bed for a night—or perhaps a handful of nights. And because of who he was, he expected her to simply acquiesce.

Even if she might have been attracted to him otherwise, that fact turned her off entirely. She didn't want to be some playboy prince's temporary intimate diversion.

With a sigh, she began to explore her rooms,

checking to see where all her things had been stored. Dresses, blouses and slacks hung in the wardrobe. More casual tops and pants had been folded and stacked in the dresser, along with her underthings. And her toiletries had been lined up on the bathroom counter or tucked into the available drawers. Even the books and folders she'd brought, for work and for leisure, had been neatly stacked on a small desk set before one of the windows overlooking the balcony.

She hadn't made up her mind yet about whether she planned to stay, but had to admit that if she *did* decide to fulfill her bargain with the Prince of Lies, the view alone would make her visit feel less like manipulation and more like a paid vacation.

Stepping onto the wide stone balcony, she moved to the railing and gazed out at the ocean beyond. Waves rolled to the shore, bringing with them a gentle lulling sound that could soothe even the most restless soul.

Glancing at her watch, Alandra saw that she still had a couple of hours before she needed to start getting ready for dinner with the royal family. The thought of meeting them caused her stomach to dip dizzily.

But she would deal with that when she had to. For now, she would call home to let her father and sister know she'd arrived safely, and to maybe get Elena's advice about her current situation.

Should she stay or should she go? Should she tell the prince just what he could do with his devious, conniving contract, and walk away from the chance to gift a quarter of a million dollars to a charity that could dearly use the money? Or should she swallow her pride and do what she had to to get through the month?

Four

At five minutes to eight that evening, Alandra followed the maze of hallways on the palace's second floor and found her way to the main staircase. The maid who had come to check up on her earlier had given her general directions to the dining room, and Alandra thought she could find it on her own.

But she needn't have worried. As soon as she reached the stairs, she found Nicolas standing at the bottom, waiting for her.

He was dressed in a dark suit, which made her feel better about her own outfit. She hadn't known quite what to wear to her first dinner with a royal family, so had opted for a simple blue silk dress.

"Good evening," Nicolas said in greeting, watching her intently as she descended the stairs.

Alandra felt a skittering of awareness as his gaze swept her from head to toe. No doubt about it, this man was dangerous. If she decided to stay, she would have to be very careful not to let those blue eyes and his handsome face lure her in and make her do something she wouldn't normally do.

"Good evening," she replied, pausing at the bottom of the stairs.

"May I?" he asked, offering his arm.

She hesitated only a second before accepting, lightly slipping her hand around his elbow.

"You look lovely," he told her as they crossed the marble floor. The chandelier had been turned on, sending bright, twinkling light throughout the foyer and beyond.

"Thank you."

She was saved from having to make further conversation as they reached the dining room. Nicolas opened one of the tall double doors, ushering her inside.

The room was as opulent as the rest of the palace. A long, narrow trestle table ran the length of it, surrounded by heavy, high-backed chairs with seats embroidered with what must be the Braedon family crest. Light trickled down from another chandelier hanging over the table, and glowed from many wall sconces.

The queen and king were already seated at the table, which held intricate place settings laid out for six guests. Nicolas guided her forward, stopping near what she assumed would be her seat.

"Mother, Father, I'd like you to meet Alandra Sanchez. She's from the United States and will be our guest for the next month while she works to help us better organize Glendovia's charitable foundations. And hopefully increase their profit margin. Alandra, this is my father, King Halden, and my mother, Queen Eleanor."

The older man rose and came halfway around the table, taking her hand and pressing a soft kiss to her knuckles. "Welcome to Glendovia, my dear.

We appreciate the work you'll be doing on behalf of our country."

"Thank you, Your Highness," she replied, only slightly intimidated by meeting and speaking with a real live king. "It's a pleasure to meet you."

Turning toward the queen, Alandra noticed that she'd remained seated. And when Alandra approached, she didn't offer to shake her hand.

"Your Highness," Alandra murmured politely and respectfully, pausing before the older woman.

She was greeted with a rather stiff nod, giving her the uncomfortable feeling that she wasn't as welcome as Nicolas and his father would have her believe.

"Please be seated," the queen told her. "Dinner will be served soon."

Returning to Nicolas's side, Alandra allowed him to hold her chair for her before he made his way around the table to the place directly across from her.

A second later, the dining room doors opened again and another couple swept in. It was obvious to Alandra that the gentleman, at least, was related to Nicolas. He had the same build, coloring and facial structure as Nicolas and the king.

The woman had similar physical traits, but Alandra didn't want to assume anything for fear she was a wife or girlfriend rather than a sister.

"Good evening, everyone," the man boomed, smiling easily.

"Mother, Father," the young woman intoned, removing any doubt of her relation to the others. "Nicolas," she added, laying her hands on his shoulders and leaning in to press a kiss to his cheek.

"Menace," he replied, one corner of his mouth quirking up in a grin before he shifted his attention back to Alandra. "I'd like you to meet my younger brother, Sebastian, and my sister, Mia, the baby of the family."

Princess Mia gave a short, harried sigh. "I hate it when you introduce me that way," she told him.

"I know. That's why I do it," he countered. Alandra didn't miss the affectionate sparkle in his eyes or the amusement that lingered on his sister's face as she strolled around the table to take the seat to Alandra's left.

"Our eldest brother, Dominick, is out of the country right now, but hopefully you'll meet him before you leave."

Shaking out the napkin on her plate and placing it neatly in her lap, Mia said, "It's nice to meet you, Alandra. Nicolas mentioned that you would be coming. He says you have brilliant ideas about increasing the amount of funds taken in by non-profit organizations."

Alandra's gaze flashed to Nicolas, flattered by his indirect praise, but he was looking at his sister.

"She's done terrific work with several charities back in the States," he announced.

From his seat across the table, Sebastian said, "That's good. We certainly have our share of worthy causes here on the island that could use a bit of a boost. And it helps that she's quite the beauty." Glancing in her direction, Sebastian winked.

For a moment, Alandra was startled by his brash behavior—in front of his family, no less. Then she realized this must simply be his personality. He was the youngest son, the one furthest in line from taking over the throne, and from the looks of it, a bit of a playboy, to boot.

She returned his good-natured smile before noticing the scowl on Nicolas's face. Her enjoyment fled immediately, replaced by a strange sensation in the pit of her belly. She didn't know whether to be concerned or intimidated, or even amused.

He had brought her here to be his mistress; she knew that. Under the pretense of working for his family, perhaps, but that didn't change the fact that he wanted her in his bed.

However, that didn't explain why he would look so cross at his brother's harmless comment and teasing.

Unless Nicolas and Sebastian had fought over— or perhaps shared—women before. Was Nicolas concerned that his brother would catch her eye before he'd had a chance to seduce her himself?

Oh, that was an interesting twist. And it would serve him right for spinning such a web of deceit to bring her here in the first place.

Servants arrived then to pour glasses of water and rich red wine. When the salad course was served, conversation turned to family and Glendovian affairs. Alandra ate in relative silence, finding the topics interesting, but having few comments of her own to add.

During dessert, Mia and Sebastian asked her about her own family and life back in Texas. She was only too happy to answer, but avoided any mention of the scandal that had driven her away.

"And what are your plans now that you're here?" Mia inquired. "Where do you think you'll begin with the charities?"

Before Alandra could answer, Nicolas interrupted. "That's something I intend to discuss with her at great length, but she's just arrived and I haven't had the chance to fill her in yet on everything she'll need to know." Pushing back his chair, he rose to his feet. "In fact, if you'll excuse us, I'd like to get started on that now."

He came around to her side of the table, taking her arm and giving her little choice but to leave with him. She said her good-nights and followed him across the room.

"Nicolas," the queen called out as he reached the door. "I'd like a word with you."

"Certainly, Mother," he replied in a respectful tone. "As soon as I see Alandra to her rooms, I'll return to the library. We can speak there."

His mother offered an almost imperceptible nod and they left.

With his hand once again at the small of her

back, he guided Alandra to the main stairwell, and they started slowly up the steps. She didn't miss his continued attempts at familiarity. And while his fingertips warmed her through the material of her dress, sending tiny shocks of desire through her system, she had to wonder if it was merely the first phase of his orchestrated attempts at seduction.

Even if it was, it wouldn't work.

She was stronger than that. Nicolas might be charming and gorgeous, his status as a prince alluring, but he had brought her here under false pretenses, and she was not going to be won over.

"So," he began, his voice low and persuasive, "have you had a chance to look over the files I left in your room?"

He had, indeed. A pile of colored folders had been left on the desk, each summarizing a different Glendovian charity she assumed she would be working with if she decided to stay.

"I glanced at them," she said.

"And…"

"You have some interesting organizations set up."

"They're not running as well as they should," he said.

"I noticed."

"Do you think you can fix them?"

That was the problem—she did. Even looking over the files for a few minutes before she'd started getting ready for dinner, she'd had a dozen ideas for improvements. Not to mention raising awareness and drawing in larger amounts of funding.

They were concepts she was excited about and eager to put into effect. But in order to do that, she would have to remain in Glendovia and fulfill the terms of her contract.

"I have some ideas," she replied guardedly, as they turned down the hall that led to her suite.

"Excellent." He waited a beat before continuing. "Does this mean you've decided to stay and work here?"

"I'll stay," she told him. "I'll stay through the month, as agreed in the contract, and at the end of the month you'll give me the bonus you promised."

"Of course."

He might have said more at that point, but she cut him off. "And no matter what your reason for bringing me here, no matter what you expected to happen, I will *not* be sleeping with you. You can cross that little item right off your Christmas wish list."

At that, she turned the knob, spun on her heel and disappeared into the suite.

Five

The door to the library was open when Nicolas arrived. His mother was sitting in one of the armchairs before the fireplace, sipping a glass of sherry and staring at the flames leaping in the hearth. Closing the door behind him, he moved to the sideboard and poured himself a drink before joining her.

"You wanted to speak with me?" he asked, leaning back.

Typical of his mother, she got right to the point. "What is she doing here, Nicolas?"

He didn't pretend to misunderstand the question. "As I told you at dinner, I hired her to help with our charities. She's very good at what she does. I think she'll be a boon to the organizations."

"And that's the only reason," his mother said shortly, eyeing him over the rim of her glass. "Nothing else?"

He took a sip of his brandy. "What other reason would there be?"

"Come now, Nicolas. I may be your mother, and therefore not your first choice of confidante about your love life, but I'm well aware of your… leisure pursuits. Are you sure you didn't bring her here to be your next conquest?"

While his personal relationships were no one's concern but his own, it was hard—not to mention foolish—to tell the queen to mind her own business. Even if she was his mother.

So he did what he and his siblings had done many times while growing up. He looked her straight in the eye and lied.

"Of course not. I take my responsibilities to our country very seriously. As soon as I saw what Alandra had done with the event I attended in

America, I knew she would be a great benefit to our own charitable causes."

His mother narrowed her gaze momentarily, as though gauging the truthfulness of his statement. "I'm glad to hear that. You understand, I'm sure, that it wouldn't do for your little associations to become public this close to announcing your engagement. We both know that you haven't been celibate since you agreed to wed Princess Lisette, but it's important that you keep up pretenses and do nothing to upset her or her family. This marriage will create a very important bond between her country and ours."

A brief second passed, and when she spoke again, both her tone and expression were sharper. "We can't jeopardize that association simply because you can't keep your hands off some American commoner."

Letting another swallow of brandy warm its way through his system, Nicolas consciously unclenched his jaw and forced himself to remain respectful.

"I know my duties, Mother. You needn't worry about me causing any problems with Lisette.

Alandra is a lovely woman, but she's no threat to my engagement, believe me."

"That's good to hear. But just in case you change your mind, or Miss Sanchez suddenly begins to look like an amusing diversion while she's visiting, I have something I think you should see."

With that, she reached between the side of her chair and the cushion and removed a folded piece of paper. She handed it to Nicolas and then sat back, every inch the queen as she awaited his reaction.

Unfolding the page, he found himself staring at a printout of a newspaper article with Alandra's picture. On either side of her photo were two others with jagged edges.

The headline accused Alandra of coming between the man and woman depicted, of being the ruin of a happy home and marriage. He scanned the write-up, which made Alandra sound like a selfish, devious trollop with no compunction about carrying on a torrid affair with a married father of two.

"She isn't one of us, Nicolas," his mother intoned. "She created a scandal in the States and brought shame upon her own family with her promiscuousness. We don't need her here, doing the same to us."

Nicolas tensed in response to both the content of the article and his mother's high-handed warning, then relaxed. This revelation about Alandra surprised him, but didn't concern him. And it certainly didn't change his mind about wanting her in his bed, despite his mother's cautionary warning.

"I appreciate your trepidation, Mother, but I think you're making too much of Alandra's visit. She's only here for a month, and only to help with the charities. Nothing more."

The queen arched a brow, but remained silent, making it clear she doubted his claims. But his life was still his own, and until he had actually taken his wedding vows with Princess Lisette, he owed no explanation to anyone.

Refolding the printout and slipping it into the front pocket of his jacket, he pushed himself to his feet and returned his empty glass to the sideboard before crossing to his mother's chair and leaning down to press a kiss to her cheek. "Good night, Mother. I'll see you in the morning."

* * *

Alandra was up early the next day, ready to get to work and start putting some of her strategies into action.

She also hoped to see more of the island and get *away* from Nicolas. He was dangerous to her peace of mind, and the less time they spent together during her stay, the better.

Carrying a briefcase stuffed with papers, she arrived in the dining room. The family was already gathered and eating. A plate was quickly set before her, and Alandra enjoyed her breakfast until the queen inquired about her plans for the day. Alandra still had the distinct feeling Nicolas's mother didn't like her.

"After studying the notes Nicolas gave me, I thought the local orphanage would be the best place to start," she answered. "I've got an idea directly connected to the holidays that I think will be quite successful, but since Christmas is right around the corner, it's important to get things moving as soon as possible."

If the queen was pleased with Alandra's response, she didn't show it. Instead, Nicolas replied. "I'll have a car brought around to take us to the children's home," he said, pushing back his chair and moving toward the dining room's double doors.

"You're...coming along?" Alandra asked, her words stumbling over themselves as her heart thudded. She really, *really* didn't want to spend the day with him.

He stopped at the door and turned back to face her. "Of course."

Swallowing past the lump in her throat, she tried to ignore the heat suddenly licking its way through her insides. "That isn't necessary."

"But it is," he replied softly. "Glendovia's national charities are my responsibility. I take that duty seriously and intend to work quite closely with you over the next month. I hope you don't mind."

He added the last, she was sure, for the benefit of his family, all of whom were watching and listening attentively. Because it was clear that even if she did mind—which she did—it would make absolutely no difference.

If they had been alone, she might have argued,

but she certainly wasn't going to put up a fuss in front of the royal family.

Forcing the words past her tight throat, she said, "No, I don't mind at all."

His lips curved in a smile that told her he knew exactly how much it had pained her to acquiesce. "I'll meet you at the car, then," he murmured, before walking out of the room.

Ten minutes later, they were seated in the back of a luxurious black sedan, driving away from the palace. According to the map of the island she'd studied the night before, the orphanage was nearby.

She was happy to simply gaze out the window at the passing scenery and mentally review what she hoped to accomplish at the children's home. But she should have known Nicolas would never allow her to keep to herself for long.

"So tell me about this holiday idea you have for the orphanage. I'm surprised you've begun to devise a plan already, without even having visited."

Keeping her fingers tightly wrapped around the folders on her lap, she tore her gaze away from the view and turned to face him.

"The files you supplied gave me a general impression of the home, and the type of event I have in mind is something I've been a part of before. It seems to go over well and is usually successful in getting the community involved."

"Sounds promising," he intoned. "What is it?"

"Basically, we throw a small party where Santa Claus visits the children and hands out gifts, and we invite the press and locals to attend. The goal is to draw attention to the orphanage, reminding people that the children are alone and in need not only over the holidays, but year-round."

Nicolas nodded, his mouth pursed in thought. "Interesting. And who provides the presents for the children, given that your fund-raising efforts haven't yet been put into effect?"

She smiled. "You do."

He raised a brow, and she hurried to elaborate. "Or rather, the royal family does. We'll be sure to mention that to the press, throwing your family into a very positive light. In fact, if this goes over as well as I think it will, you may want to consider sponsoring the event every year. Back home, we've made the visit from Santa an annual event, and it goes over extremely well."

Inclining his head, he said, "I'm sure that's something my family would be willing to consider."

The car eased to a stop in front of the children's home. A second later the driver came around to open Nicolas's door. He stepped out, and a bevy of flashbulbs immediately began going off in his face.

Alandra had slid across the seat to exit behind him, but rather than reaching for his hand, which he held out to her, she lifted an arm to shield her eyes from the blinding onslaught.

"Who are all these people?" she called to him.

He leaned in a bit closer to keep from having to raise his voice. "Just members of the press you were speaking of. They tend to follow members of the royal family wherever we go."

Reaching for her hand again, he said, "Come along. It's time to go in, and you'll get used to the attention."

She wasn't so sure of that. Where she had been happy a moment ago, and eager to get to work, she now dreaded having to step outside the vehicle into the crowd of photographers circling like vultures. She'd had quite enough of that back in Texas.

She'd come to Glendovia to get away from the

media. Now here she was, smack in the middle of the frenzy once again.

Of course, she wasn't the center of their attention this time, which she considered a blessing. But that didn't mean she appreciated having her picture taken without her permission here any more than she had back home.

Drawing a breath, she pushed aside the anxieties swirling in her chest as best she could, then placed her hand in Nicolas's and let him help her from the car.

She stared straight ahead, at the redbrick building they were about to enter. The fingers of her left hand tightened almost desperately on the handle of her briefcase, while she concentrated on keeping those of her right loose and relaxed. She didn't want to give Nicolas a single sign of just how disturbed she was by the reporters crowding around, still snapping pictures and calling out to the prince.

Nicolas smiled and gave a polite wave, but otherwise ignored them as he led her forward. The sea of photographers parted at his approach, and finally they were inside.

Releasing her pent-up breath, she let go of his

hand and stepped away, leaving a safer distance between them. When she lifted her gaze to his, she found him watching her, an amused glint in his eyes.

The move had been an act of self-preservation, and he knew it.

Dammit, he must sense that she was attracted to him, and he probably took it as a sign that he was that much closer to his objective: seducing her into his bed.

"Your Highness," a voice called, and footsteps clacked as an older woman came forward to greet them.

She offered him a small curtsy and smiled at Alandra. "I'm Mrs. Vincenza, administrator of the children's home. We're delighted to have you visit us. I hope you'll find everything to your liking, and we'll happily do everything we can to help you with your efforts."

"Thank you, Mrs. Vincenza," Nicolas replied with a small bow. "This is Alandra Sanchez. She'll be handling the fund-raising plans."

"Where *are* the children?" Alandra asked, scanning the open space, with its center stairwell leading to the upper floor.

"The older ones are in school, of course, and the younger ones are upstairs in the nursery. Would you like to meet them?"

"I'd love to," she answered.

She followed Mrs. Vincenza up to the second floor, with Nicolas behind them.

They toured the nursery, where Alandra played with the babies and toddlers for a bit, then met a few other members of the staff. From there, Mrs. Vincenza showed them the children's bedrooms, dining hall, playroom and reception area.

The reception area, Alandra realized as soon as she saw it, would be the perfect place to set up the Santa Claus event. It was large enough for all the children, the media and any number of guests they might invite. There was even a lovely tree already set up and decorated in the far cor-ner.

She jotted down notes as fast as she could, her mind racing ahead to everything that would need to be done. At the same time, she shared her plans with Mrs. Vincenza, whose eyes lit up at the prospect.

Behind them, standing tall and straight in the doorway, Nicolas listened silently. Alandra assumed that meant he approved of the project so far. She was certain he'd let her know if he objected to anything.

An hour later, she'd finalized the initial plans with the administrator and had a list of tasks to deal with herself. After thanking the woman for her time and enthusiasm, she and Nicolas made their way back outside, through the throng of reporters still hovering on the sidewalk, and into the back-seat of the waiting car.

The vehicle had barely started rolling away from the curb before Nicolas faced her and asked, "How do you feel it went?"

"Very well," she answered, flipping through the pages of her spiral pad and reviewing some of the notations she'd made. "Mrs. Vincenza is eager to help us because she knows it will ultimately help *her*, and even though there's a lot of work to do, I think we've got enough time to set everything up so it goes smoothly."

A small smile touched his lips. "I have to admit, I was quite impressed with what you said to her. You're very good at describing your visions so that others can see them clearly."

Her cheeks flushed with pleasure at his compliment and she nodded a silent thank-you.

"Allow me to buy you lunch at one of our local eateries to show my appreciation for all your hard work. We can discuss what else needs to be done to have everything ready by the week before Christmas."

Although she was starting to feel hungry and certainly could have used a bite to eat, she didn't think it was a good idea to spend any more time with him than absolutely necessary. It would be better to go back to the palace and ask for something to be sent to her rooms, where she could hide out and get some work done *away* from Nicolas.

Without meeting his gaze, she said, "Thank you, but no. I'd prefer to go back and get straight to work."

His eyes narrowed slightly at her refusal, and she almost expected him to argue. But then he turned to look forward and said, "Very well. You should remember one thing, however."

"What's that?"

His eyes returned to hers, bright blue and blazing. "You can't avoid me forever."

Six

For the third time in ten minutes, Nicolas checked his watch. He was standing at the bottom of the main stairwell, awaiting Alandra's arrival, while everyone else was gathered in the dining room, ready for dinner.

But the minutes continued to tick by, and still there was no sign of her.

Spotting a maid leaving the dining room, he motioned her over. "Would you please run up to

Miss Sanchez's room and find out why she's running late for dinner?"

"I'm sorry, sir, but she called down earlier to make her excuses and ask for a tray to be brought to her room."

"Is she ill?" he asked, his brows knitting with genuine concern.

"I'm not sure, sir. She didn't say so."

"Thank you," he said, nodding to dismiss the maid.

As soon as the maid disappeared around the corner, he turned and started up the stairs. Minutes later, he was knocking on Alandra's door.

He heard her call that she was coming, and then the door swung open. She was standing there in a short, turquoise-blue nightgown and a matching robe in some slinky material that made his mouth go instantly dry. Her hair was pulled up and twisted into a loose knot at the crown of her head.

Her lovely chocolate-brown eyes went wide with surprise for a second before narrowing with annoyance.

Noticing that his gaze was inexorably drawn to

the shadowed valley between her breasts, she raised a hand to close the edges of her robe.

"May I help you?" she asked in a tone that surely wasn't often directed toward someone of royal lineage.

Biting back his amusement, he kept a straight face and linked his hands behind him. "I heard you weren't coming down to dinner and wanted to make sure you were feeling well. Is everything all right?"

Her expression softened at his inquiry. "I'm fine, thank you. I just decided to have my meal in my room so I could continue to work."

"You've been working since we returned from the children's home," he said, more of a statement than a question.

"That *is* why you hired me," she replied with a tiny smile.

Her grip on the front of her robe loosened and he caught another quick glimpse of cleavage. His body immediately went tight and hot.

Clearing his throat, he struggled to make his brain work past the thought of stripping her bare and having her writhing beneath him. When he couldn't seem to manage that, he gave a curt nod and headed back the way he'd come.

It took him the full length of both hallways and the staircase to regain his reason and decide on a course of action.

First, he strode into the dining room, where the rest of the family had already been served, and told them he wouldn't be sharing dinner with them. Then he went to the rear of the palace and entered the kitchens, asking that two trays be made up and taken to Alandra's suite rather than only one.

He waited while that was done, and then accompanied the servant as the young man delivered the cart. Alandra answered the door when he knocked, a frown marring her brow when she noticed Nicolas trailing behind. To her credit, she held her tongue as the cart was wheeled into the center of the sitting room.

Glancing toward Nicolas, the servant waited to be told where they wished their meals to be served.

"That's fine, Franc. I'll take it from here. Thank you."

The young man inclined his head and quickly

made his way from the room, closing the door behind him and leaving Nicolas and Alandra alone.

Her gaze skated from the cart, with its silver-domed platters and bottle of wine, to him. "You're not planning on eating with me?" she asked, not bothering with even a modicum of civility as she crossed her arms beneath her breasts and tapped the red-tipped toes of one bare foot impatiently.

"We have a lot to do, as you've said, and I agree that taking dinner in your rooms is a good way to make rapid progress. We'll eat on the balcony," he added, pulling the cart out onto the terrace. "You'll like it out there. Bring some of your files, if you like, and we can discuss them while we eat."

She didn't say anything, but he wouldn't have stopped if she had. Giving her the chance to respond was only inviting a refusal, and he had no intention of being put off.

She followed him to the French doors, still without uttering a word, but stopped before actually stepping onto the balcony.

It was still light outside, edging into dusk, and the bright shades of sunset could be seen on the far horizon. The temperature, normally quite comfortable at this time of year, was even warmer than usual, giving him no qualms about inviting her out in little more than a thin slip of satiny material.

And if she got cold…well, he could think of several ways to heat things up quickly enough.

He moved to the round, glass-topped table outside, and pretended not to be watching her as he transferred their dinner from the cart. In reality, however, he kept track of her in his peripheral view. He saw her fingers twisting nervously on the frame of the open double doors, and her bare toes curling on the threshold rather than taking the step that would bring her out onto the balcony.

"Maybe I should change," she said in a soft voice.

Though he was careful not to let it show, he felt a flash of triumph. She had apparently accepted that arguing or asking him to leave was futile. He was here for dinner, and he meant to stay.

Raising his head, he once again looked directly at her. He wanted her sitting across from him just like that, with her legs bare and the turquoise fabric bringing out the sparkle in her dark eyes.

"What you're wearing is fine," he replied. "This is a casual meal, and we'll be talking about the charities most of the time. In fact, I'll join you in getting more comfortable."

Shrugging out of his suit jacket, he hung it neatly over the back of his chair, removed his tie and rolled up his shirtsleeves. "How's that?" he asked, giving her a moment to study his appearance. "I can remove more of my clothing if you like, but I have a feeling you would consider that a bit *too* casual. Am I right?"

He cocked a brow, silently challenging her to deny it. If he had his way, they would both be naked before the night was over.

For a second, she returned his look with a steady, rebellious one of her own, then spun around and disappeared into the bedroom.

At first, he thought she'd gone to cover herself in battle armor. But she reappeared a moment later, still wearing the same nightgown and robe, and not a stitch more. She was also carrying a legal pad and small stack of folders.

She took a seat and pulled her chair closer to the table, acting as though she was sitting down to a business lunch in a full business suit. But he certainly wasn't going to complain now that he had her exactly where he wanted her.

Following her lead, he lifted the silver covers from both plates and set them aside, then took his own seat across from her. He uncorked the bottle of wine, from one of Glendovia's own vineyards, and poured a healthy portion for each of them.

Nicolas made small talk while they ate. And though Alandra's side of the conversation was stilted at first, eventually she relaxed and spoke to him as easily as she would anyone else.

They'd just begun discussing the plans for the children's home when a knock sounded at the sitting room door.

"That will be dessert," Nicolas announced. Rising to his feet, he slung his jacket over his arm. "Let's move things into the other room, shall we?"

He strolled in that direction, leaving her to follow with her stack of files.

Before the waiting servant had a chance to knock a second time, Nicolas pulled the door open, gestured for him to enter and instructed him to serve the coffee and dessert at the low, square table in front of the fireplace.

While that was being taken care of, Nicolas

lowered the lights, then proceeded to build a small fire in the hearth.

Alandra watched from the bedroom doorway, chagrined to find herself admiring the broad expanse of the prince's back. The narrow span of his waist. The ripple of muscles beneath his crisp white shirt and dark trousers as he moved.

She swallowed hard, feeling a flush of heat flow over her chest, up her neck and into her cheeks.

Noticing Nicolas's considerable physical attributes was the last thing she should be doing. Finding him attractive at all, in any way, would be the kiss of death. A risk she could not afford.

And yet she couldn't seem to tear her eyes away from him.

"Isn't it a little warm for a fire?" she asked as the servant finished his task and slipped silently from the room.

"I thought you might be chilly," the prince replied, turning from the flickering flames and glancing in her direction.

His attention lingered on her bare legs, she noticed, and it took all her willpower not to shift uncomfortably or attempt to cover herself. The only thing that kept her from doing either was the knowledge that he'd noticed the tiny goose bumps beginning to break out on her arms and legs earlier. She was unaccountably touched by his consideration, which was *not* what she wanted to be feeling.

"We won't get too close," he said, dragging the table back from the hearth a few more inches before taking two cushions from the sofa. "Come, have a seat."

He lowered himself onto one of the cushions on the floor and sat cross-legged, leaving the other for her. Instead of sitting across from each other, they would now be much closer, with only one small corner of a rather small table between them.

It wasn't the typical setup for a business meeting. But then, her attire wasn't exactly typical, either. None of this was.

Striding across the room in her bare feet, she set her files aside and curled her legs beneath her as she sat down.

Nicolas poured coffee from a brightly polished silver carafe while Alandra studied the dessert. A fluffy, golden pastry was sliced into layers and

filled with large, juicy strawberries and a decadent amount of rich cream. Her mouth watered
just looking at it.

Because this situation could easily begin to take
on a romantic feel, Alandra immediately started
back on the topic of Christmas at the orphanage,
and didn't stop until they'd made it through the
pastries and a cup of coffee each. To his credit,
Nicolas stuck with the conversation, never trying
to change the subject or insert a level of intimacy
that didn't belong.

His enthusiasm and participation delighted her.
She'd expected him to put in only a minimum
amount of effort, to convince her he'd brought her
to his country for legitimate reasons rather than
simply to become the latest in what she was sure
was a string of lovers.

But he was taking their conversations and the
business of organizing these fund-raisers seriously.
Taking *her* seriously.

It was a welcome change after being made the
butt of any number of jokes and cruel jibes back
home once the rumors had spread that she'd been
sleeping with a married man.

Despite the cup of coffee she'd just consumed, Alandra found herself blinking tired eyes and covering her mouth to stifle a yawn. And maybe she was off her game, maybe her defenses were down, because it seemed sensible, almost natural, to join Nicolas when he moved closer to the fire.

She reclined beside him, letting the flickering flames and the opulence of her surroundings lull her. Keeping company with a gorgeous prince didn't hurt, either, even if she had to steel herself against his charms, his looks, the spicy scent of his cologne.

And he was about as handsome as a man could be. If he weren't already a prince, she would think he should be. A prince or perhaps a movie star.

"What are you thinking?" he asked softly from only inches away.

He had a nice voice, too. Low and slightly husky, it rumbled up from his chest and straight down her spine, causing her bare toes to curl.

If he wasn't a royal, constantly being followed by paparazzi, and if she hadn't recently been slandered and torn apart by vicious rumor and innuendo, she might just be willing to throw caution to the wind and sleep with him, after all. Not become his mistress—that was a bit beyond even her—but spend one passionate, sure-to-be-glorious evening making love with a man who had the power to turn her knees to jelly.

Thank goodness he didn't know that. Thank goodness he couldn't tell exactly what she *was* thinking. Otherwise all her good intentions, her insistence that her presence here was purely business, with no possibility of pleasure being thrown into the mix, would drift away like a wisp of fog on the ocean breeze.

Thank goodness.

"Only that this is nice," she replied. "Relaxing. I should still be working, but I think I'm too tired."

He turned, and she found her own shimmery image reflected in his pupils.

"Would you like to go to bed?"

It was on the tip of her tongue to say, "Yes, very much," before her hazy brain identified the danger his question posed.

"Clever," she said with a chuckle, feeling just tranquil enough to find his attempt to trap her amusing. "But while I would like to go to bed… eventually…I won't be doing it with you."

"What a shame. Although there's always to-morrow."

There it was again, that calm, cajoling tone. The voice that thickened her blood and sent warm, tingling sensations to areas she'd rather not have tingling in his presence.

"I didn't come here for that," she replied quietly.

He was only an inch away now, his heated breath dancing over her cheeks and eyelashes. His mouth looked incredibly inviting, sexy and about seven kinds of sinful.

Surely one little kiss wouldn't hurt anything. One tiny peck to satisfy an overwhelming curiosity.

It wasn't smart. Was, in fact, ludicrous.

Before she had a chance to decide if she could afford a momentary lapse of sanity, Nicolas made the decision for her.

Seven

Oh, my.

He tasted of wine and the strawberries and cream that had been part of their dessert, with a hint of the coffee he'd sipped afterward. Sweet and tart and smoky all at the same time.

It was a heady mixture, but nothing compared to the feel of his tongue sweeping into her mouth, tasting, stroking, claiming.

His hands gripped her shoulder and the side of her face, gently pulling her up. She wasn't sure how it happened, had no conscious memory of moving, but suddenly she was on her knees, pressed chest to chest with Nicolas and kissing him back with equal vigor.

While his hands kneaded and caressed her upper arms, hers clutched at his shirt, desperately holding on and pulling him closer. Her breasts were squashed between them, but she could still feel her nipples beading. Heat gathered and pooled low in her belly, and her heartbeat was a thunderbolt blasting in her ears.

She'd been wrong about keeping her distance, wrong about trying to convince herself she wasn't interested in this man. He was hard and strong and self-assured, and brought to life emotions she'd never felt before, at least not to this degree.

Her fingers trailed upward to tangle in the short strands of his silky hair. The two of them were already mouth to mouth, body to body, as close as they could be while still clothed, but that didn't keep her from exerting a small amount of pressure at the back of his skull and—if it was possible—taking the kiss even deeper.

With a groan, Nicolas moved his hands to skim

the undersides of her breasts. He cupped them in his palms, measuring their fullness and weight before letting his thumbs slide up and over the tight peaks of her nipples.

The caress, made even more erotic by the thin layer of cool, slick material between her flesh and his fingers, gave her shivers.

As she wriggled in his grasp, her knee bumped into the coffee cup she'd set aside earlier. The rattle of the porcelain on the saucer startled her out of the haze of passion and arousal she'd been lost in.

She pulled back slightly, breaking the kiss even though her body cried out for more. Her lungs heaved, straining for breath. Her arms and legs quivered, overcome with a lassitude she couldn't remember ever feeling before.

Good Lord, what had she almost done? How could she have gotten so wrapped up, so swept away by a single kiss?

His hands remained at her breasts, his fingers lightly brushing the rigid peaks. His eyes blazed a deep, dark sapphire in the firelight, no less heated than a moment ago.

Did he not realize she'd pulled away, or was he as blinded by desire as she'd been?

Regardless, she had to stop this, had to make it clear to him that what had just taken place between them was a mistake. A mistake of monumental proportions that could not, *would* not happen again.

"Stop," she gasped.

"What's wrong?" he asked in a ragged voice. Though he dropped his arms to his sides, he clenched his hands, betraying the tension vibrating through him.

"This is not going to happen," she said, though her tone was less firm than she'd have liked. Still on her knees, she inched away, afraid that he might reach for her again and she wouldn't have the conviction to fend him off.

One dark eyebrow hitched upward. "I thought we were off to a fairly adequate start," he replied.

Without looking at Nicolas, she rose to her feet. "I told you before that I didn't come to Glendovia to become your latest conquest. I'm here strictly for business purposes. That kiss was a mistake. It never should have happened, and it won't happen again. Things only got as far as they did because I'm tired and let my guard down."

But Nicolas wasn't ready to walk away, not quite yet.

He also got to his feet, then touched her elbow, stroking the satin fabric of her sleeve. "I could stay," he whispered smoothly, seductively. "Make sure the rest of your evening is both restful and enjoyable. Infinitely enjoyable."

The spark in her eyes let him know he'd over-stepped his bounds. She shrugged out of his hold and moved passed him. Wrenching open the door, she stood back, body rigid, and glared.

"Good night, Your Highness," she said, her tone only a shade shy of disrespectful.

If he weren't such a patient man, intent on his goal, he might have taken exception.

But he *was* a patient man, and he knew that pushing Alandra was not the way to win her over, not the way to lure her into his bed. Better to take things slowly, to woo and seduce her properly.

"I'll see you in the morning, then," he said politely, moving to stand before her, giving no indication that her attitude or demands disturbed him in the least.

Though she remained stiff, he took her hand and lifted it to his mouth, pressing a soft kiss to the back of it.

"Thank you for being such a lovely dinner companion, and for all of your hard work on behalf of the children's home. I knew bringing you here was the right thing to do."

With a swift grin, he left the room and strode casually down the hall. A few seconds later, he heard her door close with a slam, and his smile widened.

Alandra Sanchez was a fiery, passionate woman with a temper to match. She thought she was brushing him off, holding him at bay, but her reluctance merely intrigued him all the more.

For the next two weeks, Alandra did her best to avoid Nicolas whenever she could, and treat him with cool professionalism whenever she couldn't.

Nicolas, meanwhile, did *his* best to get her alone as often as possible, to touch her hand, her arm, her cheek on a regular basis, and to romance her into letting down her guard and inviting him into her bed.

So far, she'd remained firm in her commitment

not to be seduced. But she had to admit, at least to herself, that it had been no simple feat.

Nicolas was nearly irresistible. He was attractive and charming, and if he hadn't approached her to sleep with him before getting to know her—which she found gallingly arrogant—she very well might have fallen into bed with him by now.

Sad but true, and rather ironic. If he'd gone about courting her in a more traditional manner, he'd have likely gotten lucky.

Alandra might be considered beautiful by many—a fact of life that was sometimes a blessing and sometimes a curse for her—but she was anything but compliant.

And then there was the continued guilt and humiliation over the scandal that still clung to her name back in Texas.

She'd phoned home numerous times since arriving in Glendovia, and each time she'd asked her sister about the scandal she'd been running away from. Elena had admitted that people were still talking, but the reporters had finally stopped camping out at the house.

But even though the attention had died down,

Alandra knew she'd been right to leave town when she had. She was also even more determined never to leave herself open to disgrace again.

She reminded herself of this, firmly and repeatedly, as she made her way down to the foyer.

In the time she'd been a guest of the royal family, the palace's decor had gone from tidily opulent to brimming with holiday cheer.

The banister had been strung with long, twisting garlands of holly and ivy. Giant wreaths hung on both the outside and inside of all the main doors. And in the center of the foyer was a towering evergreen tree, covered with gold ornaments. A golden angel perched gloriously at the very top.

The holiday decorations were helping Alandra feel more at home. She missed her family terribly, and it broke her heart to think that she wouldn't be spending Christmas with them. But she found it soothing to be surrounded by all this cheer.

She was smiling when she reached the front door, where Nicolas was waiting. Tonight was the Evening with Santa event at the children's home, and he had insisted on accompanying her, despite the fact that she had to be there early. The rest of the royal family would arrive later.

Even Nicolas's mother, Queen Eleanor, had reluctantly approved of Alandra's efforts to aid the local orphanage. She hadn't come right out and complimented her on all of her hard work, or changed her attitude, but the few remarks she'd made about tonight's event had been mainly positive.

Alandra didn't let it go to her head. She knew the queen still disapproved of her.

As soon as she drew close, Nicolas took her elbow, offering a small smile. He was dressed in his princely finery, complete with a red sash running from shoulder to hip, and a number of important-looking medals pinned to his chest.

Alandra's dress was a sumptuous red velvet gown that hugged her curves and left her shoulders and arms bare. She wore classic, understated diamonds at her ears and throat.

"Shall we go?" Nicolas asked, and escorted her out of the palace into the slightly chilly evening air. It wasn't yet dark, but the sun was setting and dusk was well under way.

She had purposely scheduled tonight's affair so

that it could be both a fun party for the children and an opportunity for the adult guests to mingle. Especially since she had invited some very wealthy, influential individuals, whom she hoped would make generous donations.

When Alandra and Nicolas arrived, a crowd of photographers was already gathered outside the orphanage, snapping pictures. Inside, the home was decorated festively. There was a tree in the main entranceway, covered with ornaments handmade by the children. Holiday music filled the air.

After Alandra settled a few last-minute issues, she started mingling with the arriving guests.

The appearance of the rest of the royal family caused quite a stir. Voices hushed, heads turned and people stood frozen as they watched the king and queen.

Leaving Nicolas with his family, Alandra made her way to the other rooms. She began wandering around, double-checking that everything was running properly.

All in all, it looked as though the evening was progressing perfectly. She released a sigh, praying no accidents or crises cropped up to mar an otherwise successful occasion.

Turning back to survey the reception area, she immediately spotted Nicolas striding toward her. Tall and imposing, he seemed to tower over the crowd.

The air caught in her chest. She would have liked to blame her sudden inability to breathe on the tightness of her form-fitting dress, but knew it was all due to Nicolas.

Nicolas, who could stop her heart with a glance.

Nicolas, who made her palms damp and her stomach quiver.

Nicolas, who made her want to rethink her decision not to get any closer to him than necessary during her stay.

Be strong, she told herself, swallowing hard and making a concerted effort to keep her knees from quaking as he came closer.

When he reached her, he gave a small bow and took her hand, his eyes holding hers the entire time.

"Dance with me," he murmured softly.

His tone and princely manner made it more of a command than a request, but she did her best to argue. "I don't think Christmas music is exactly conducive to dancing," she said, glancing about the room. Although there were several couples taking the floor.

"Of course it is."

He tipped his head, as though paying extra attention to the slow strains of a holiday classic. Tightening his grasp, he tugged her behind him as he headed to the clear space at the center.

"Besides, it's my royal duty to set a good example for others, and we want everyone to enjoy themselves, don't we? Isn't that your goal, so that guests will feel more generous when it comes time to start writing checks?"

She could tell from his expression that he was taking pleasure in teasing her, tossing her own ambition back at her in an attempt to get what he wanted. His lips twitched and the corners of his eyes crinkled as he tried to keep his amusement in check.

She might have continued protesting, but it was too late. They had reached a small empty stretch of the hardwood floor, and Nicolas had his arm around her waist, pulling her against him.

He splayed his fingers at the small of her back, holding her in place and guiding her as they swayed in small circles. And just as he'd predicted, others began to follow their lead and joined them, dancing to the holiday carols being piped through the building.

This hadn't been part of her plans for the evening, but it did seem to be having a positive effect. Alandra hoped Nicolas didn't notice, or she might have to swallow her pride and tell him he'd been right.

The song came to an end and they stopped moving, but instead of releasing her, he continued to hold her, staring down into her eyes until her mouth went dry and butterflies decided to take up tap dancing in her belly. Her chest was too tight to draw a full breath, which made her head begin to spin.

She thought, for a brief moment, that he was going to kiss her. Right there, in the middle of a roomful of people.

And she was chagrined to realize that her mouth had opened slightly, that she was both anticipating the kiss and looking forward to it. Yearning for it, even.

With his gaze still locked on hers, he leaned in another inch, until she could feel his warm breath dancing across her skin.

"I can't kiss you here and now, the way I'd like, but I promise to rectify that before the night is through." His voice was low and mesmerizing, washing over her.

Dropping his hand from her waist, he smiled, gave a small bow and then turned and walked away, as though he hadn't just set every nerve ending in her body on high alert.

She watched him go, trying to regain control of her senses. And control of her limbs, which seemed incapable of movement, even as she struggled to get her brain to send the correct signals.

It wasn't until she noticed people beginning to stare that she shook off whatever spell had overtaken her, and was able to take step after measured step to the refreshment table. She poured herself a glass of punch and drank it down in nearly a single gulp.

This was bad, so very bad. He was wearing her down, eroding the last of her defenses.

She was very much afraid that she wouldn't be able to evade him for much longer.

Eight

It was late by the time the evening wound to a close, but as Alandra watched the guests filing out, she was delighted to see that the majority of them had smiles on their faces. Better yet, Mrs. Vincenza had happily reported that she'd received several generous contributions throughout the night, with promises of more to come.

Watching Santa Claus hand out presents to the children had obviously turned a number of hearts—exactly what Alandra had been hoping for. She'd seen more than a few eyes turn misty during the gift-giving ceremony, and many follow the children out of the room and up the stairs at bedtime.

While it hadn't been her main goal, Alandra hoped that tonight's event would result in some much-needed adoptions, as well as added donations.

Stifling a yawn behind her small clutch purse, she watched the door close behind the last guest a moment before she felt Nicolas come to stand beside her.

Although she wasn't surprised that she could sense his presence even before she saw him, it did disturb her. She didn't *want* to sense him. Didn't want to believe that they might be growing that close in such a short time, especially when she'd spent most of the last three weeks avoiding him.

Not that she'd been terribly successful. Nicolas, she was learning, had a way of being everywhere she was, whether she wanted him there or not.

She had to admit, though, that he'd been a definite asset this evening. Not only had he gotten everyone in the room to relax enough to dance to Christmas music, but he'd spent the rest of the night circulating through the crowd to shake hands, kiss cheeks and talk up the orphanage as an extremely worthy charity—or write-off, depending on who he was conversing with.

And she admired him for it. For caring about the children's home and about what he could do to make the fund-raiser a success.

Glendovia was his country, and she had been hired to do a job for it. But he seemed to know that she took her work of organizing charitable events and raising funds for worthy causes very, very seriously. Seemed to know…and in his own way, care.

That touched Alandra more than a dozen roses, a hundred glasses of champagne or a thousand romantic dates ever could have.

He might have taken a wrong first step with her by inviting her into his bed before even getting to know her, but he had taken a few right steps since. Redeeming right steps.

When he took her elbow now, she felt a familiar tingle in every millimeter of skin his fingers came in contact with.

"Ready to go?" he asked.

She nodded and let Nicolas adjust her wrap

around her shoulders before guiding her outside and into the waiting limousine.

Despite the late hour, there were still plenty of paparazzi gathered to snap more pictures upon the royal family's departure. The camera flashes burned her eyes and blinded her vision. She was only too happy to have the car door slam behind her, blocking out the pesky photographers.

When they arrived home, the family said their good-nights before heading for their respective bed-chambers. Alandra wished them all a good night, as well, before turning toward her own rooms.

"I'll walk with you," Nicolas said, catching up with her and once again slipping her arm through his.

She started to tell him it wasn't necessary, but thought better of it with his parents and siblings still within earshot. Instead, she inclined her head, tightened her hold on his arm and murmured, "Thank you."

They walked to her suite without speaking, and she was surprised to find it a comfortable silence. Perhaps because it had been such a long and busy day, and she was too tired to worry about what she should be saying or doing. She couldn't find it in

her to be concerned about what Nicolas might say
or do, either.

When they arrived, he opened the door, then
stood back for her to enter. Crossing the dark sitting room, she turned on a small table lamp, which
bathed the space in a yellow-gold light.

Alandra straightened and turned, and nearly
bumped into Nicolas, who had followed her silently and was standing mere inches away. For a
moment, her mind went blank. Her breath hitched
and her heart leaped at finding him so near.

She swallowed nervously and opened her
mouth to speak, though she didn't have a clue what
she planned to say.

Not that it mattered. Before she could utter a
sound or get her brain to function properly, Nicolas had lifted a hand to the back of her neck and
threaded his fingers into the loose hair at her nape.
He tugged her forward, and she went easily, willingly, like a puppet on a string.

Their eyes met, and in that brief second, she saw
passion and fire and desire. Those same emotions
caused her stomach to tumble to her toes, and
made her feel suddenly light-headed.

Then he bent and lowered his mouth to hers.

The minute their lips met the earth seemed to rock on its axis. Alandra had never felt such heat, such electricity, such an amazing and overwhelming need.

Nicolas's fingers at her nape tightened, while his other hand grasped her hip. Her own hands were on his shoulders, gripping and clawing. She couldn't seem to get close enough.

His scent filled her nostrils, spicy and masculine. As his tongue swept through her mouth, he tasted the same.

She kissed him back with equal fervor, delighting in the way contact with him flooded her senses.

Just when she thought she might expire from pleasure, Nicolas broke the kiss. "Say no," he whispered raggedly against her lips. "Tell me to go. Tell me you don't want this."

He kissed her again, hard and swiftly. "Go ahead, Alandra," he taunted softly, "tell me."

She knew what he was doing. He was challenging her to stick to her declaration that she wouldn't sleep with him during her visit. That she wouldn't allow herself to be seduced.

But, God help her, she couldn't. She wanted him too much to deny it any longer.

To deny him.

Wrapping her arms around his neck, she pressed her mouth to his. The same smoldering heat washed over her again and, with a sigh, she whispered, "Don't stop. Don't go. I do want this."

She expected him to smile—a cocky, self-important response to show her he'd known all along he would win their little cat-and-mouse game.

But he didn't smile. Instead, his eyes flashed with fire, a second before narrowing dangerously.

Bending slightly, he scooped her up, ball gown, high heels and all. His determined strides carried them to her bedroom, where he kicked the door closed and crossed to the wide, four-poster bed.

The room was dark, with only a hint of moonlight shining through the diaphanous curtains on the French doors. It took a moment for her eyes to adjust, but as Nicolas deposited her on the mattress, then stood back to unbutton his jacket, she decided it didn't matter. She could see him just well enough, and in a few minutes she would be touching him everywhere. Feeling him everywhere.

He stripped off his jacket and kicked off his shoes, then loosened the first few buttons of his shirt, keeping his gaze locked on her the entire time.

Not wanting to be a mere bystander, Alandra rose to her knees and pulled off her strappy heels, tossing them aside. She reached behind her for the zipper of her dress.

"No."

Nicolas's low, stern voice stopped her. He took two steps forward to the edge of the bed and ran his hands seductively down her bare arms.

"Let me."

Her stomach muscles clenched as his fingers ran over her abdomen and around her sides, to her lower back. Slowly, he slid his palms up the line of her spine.

His touch burned through the velvet of her gown as his hands trailed upward, and then drew the zipper down. The quiet rasp of the tiny metal teeth parting accompanied their harsh breathing.

When the zipper was lowered, her dress fell open, helped along by Nicolas's large, strong hands. She shrugged and shifted slightly; he pulled it away and dropped it unceremoniously at his feet.

Alandra knelt at the edge of the king-size mattress in her cherry-red bra and panties, and a pair of sheer, thigh-high stockings. Her heart was racing out of control, her nerves skittering like a million angry ants. Licking her dry lips, she remained perfectly still, watching Nicolas and waiting.

He stood equally still, his blue eyes riveted on her face. And then he reached for his shirt, undoing the buttons and pulling the tail from his slacks.

His movements weren't hurried, but they weren't patient, either. He made short work of removing the garment, letting it flutter to the floor while he reached for the front of his pants. There was no belt to slow him down, and with a flick of his wrist, he released both the catch and zipper.

Half-naked, he was impressive enough. But fully naked, he was the stuff of dreams and naughty female fantasies. His arms and chest were beautifully sculpted. A tight, flat abdomen flowed to narrow hips and long legs corded with muscle.

Alandra's pulse skittered and her mouth went dry as she focused her gaze to the area between his thighs. He was impressive there, too.

She didn't know what to say or how to act, so

merely sat where she was and waited for him to make the first move.

It didn't take long. With a single stride, he was with her, cradling her in his arms, while his mouth devoured hers.

Their lips meshed. Their tongues tangled. And everywhere their skin touched, she sizzled.

Alandra curled her fingers into his shoulders, her nails gently scraping. Behind her, she felt him fiddling with the clasp of her bra, and then it came free. She released him long enough to allow him to remove the garment.

Rather than wrapping his arms around her again, Nicolas reached for her breasts, cupping them in his palms, toying with the tight, beaded nipples. All without breaking their kiss.

She moaned into his mouth, pressing even closer. Her own hands roamed over every inch of hot, hard flesh she could reach—his arms, his back, his pectorals and the slim, sensitive sides of his waist.

It was his turn to make a ragged sound of longing when she ran her fingertips over the taut twin globes of his rear, then raked her nails back up to the base of his spine.

She almost smiled. She could feel the desperation rippling through him as he tightened his grasp on her breasts, deepening their kiss, pressing himself against her belly.

Without warning, he tugged her legs out from under her, so that she fell flat on her back on the bed. He followed her down, covering her completely as he trailed his lips across her cheeks, over her eyelids, along her jaw and behind her ear.

At the same time, his hands worked to remove her stockings, rolling them slowly down her thighs and calves, and over her feet. Next went her panties, and she lifted her hips to help him, until she was blessedly naked, rubbing against him in all the best places.

His mouth was at her throat now, licking and sucking and humming, sending little trills of sensation straight to her core. He cupped her buttocks, bringing her flush with his arousal and turning her insides liquid with longing.

"You're so beautiful," he murmured, still kissing everywhere he could reach. "Lovelier than I imagined. And much better than anything I've dreamed of these past weeks."

She smiled, running her fingers through his hair and enjoying his husky declaration, even if he'd said it to a million other women before. This wasn't about commitment or honesty. It was about lust and desire and untold pleasures, fleeting though they might be.

"You're not so bad yourself," she replied, remembering the multitude of erotic dreams that had revolved around him since she'd moved into the palace.

Grinning, he raised his head to gaze down at her. He leaned in to kiss her, hard and fast, then pulled back, his expression serious. "Tell me you want me," he demanded.

She studied him for a long moment, her eyes locked with his. He was more handsome than any man deserved to be, and when he focused his attentions on her, she felt like the only woman in the world. The only woman he was interested in, at any rate.

And right now, that was all that mattered.

"I want you," she whispered, wrapping her arms and legs around him and holding him tight. "Make love to me, Prince Stephan Nicolas Braedon."

No one had called him by his first name in years, not since he decided to go by Nicolas, after years of his sister referring to him as Nico. He held her gaze for another split second, then pressed his lips to hers. The kiss was hot enough to suck all the air from her lungs and from the room, and she kissed him back with equal enthusiasm.

His hands raked her sides. Then he was caressing her thighs, both outside and in.

His knuckles brushed the triangle of curls between her legs as he began to explore. He stroked and teased, groaning when he found her already damp.

She writhed beneath him as he used two fingers to plumb her depths. She was panting now, and her breathing grew more shallow as he traced his fingertips over the tiny nub of pleasure hidden within her folds.

He touched her there, and she exploded. The orgasm washed over her like a wave of heat.

His smug, satisfied smile greeted her when she opened her eyes. Her cheeks heated at his close scrutiny, and she felt suddenly self-conscious about her wanton response to his touch.

"You blush beautifully," he told her, kissing the corner of her mouth.

He didn't give her a chance to respond, but immediately began caressing her again, his hands filled with magic as they danced across her flesh, leaving no part of her unsatisfied.

The tip of his erection pressed against her opening, and she spread her legs wider, inviting him in. Little by little, he entered her, his heat and hardness filling her. The deeper he went, the more she responded, any signs of discomfort overpowered by the delight shivering through her.

But when he thrust forward in one powerful motion, what had been a minor tenderness turned to a sharp stab of pain that had her gasping aloud.

Nicolas jerked back, brows knit and eyes narrowed as he scowled down at her.

"Alandra," he said, his breathing slightly labored as he held himself perfectly still. "You're a *virgin?*"

Nine

She was a *virgin?*

How in the name of all that was holy could she be inexperienced?

Nicolas's mind raced back over everything he knew about Alandra. All the times he'd been with her, spoken with her, observed her from across a room without her knowledge. Nothing in her demeanor so much as *hinted* that she was an innocent.

And what about the scandal she'd been involved in back in the States? His mother had been only

too pleased to share the details of Alandra's indiscretion—a love affair with a married man.

A love affair with a married man that had left
her a *virgin?* Nicolas could feel his brow furrow-
ing, the skin of his face tightening as he continued to study her. And all the while he was
powerfully aware of their physical connection,
of the fact that he still ached and throbbed inside
of her.

"How can you be a virgin?" he demanded, his
tone brittle and more accusing than he'd intended.

Alandra's eyes grew wider, but passion still
filled them. "Forget about my virginity and finish
what you started."

To drive home her point, she wrapped her arms
around his neck and tilted her hips just enough to
send lightning bolts of sensation through his rigid
length. He sucked in a harsh breath, using every
ounce of willpower he possessed not to start moving, and thrust himself to a glorious but premature end.

His nostrils flared as he took several measured
breaths, counting to ten, then twenty. When he could
finally speak without groaning or sweating too pro-

fusely, he said, "I'm all for carrying on, but as soon as we're done, I *will* want to talk about this."

She rolled her eyes. "Fine. I fully expect you to make my first time memorable, though."

A grin flashed across his face and the mood in the room instantly shifted to a less intense level. There must be traces of royal blood somewhere in Alandra's ancestry. She had the imperial air down pat.

"Oh, darling," he murmured, leaning in to cover her mouth with his, "you can rely on it."

He occupied her with kisses and featherlight touches on her breasts and abdomen. And at the same time, he began to move his hips, slowly and carefully.

By now, her body had adjusted to his size and invasion. Her muscles were relaxed, warm and silky smooth with arousal.

He used long, gentle strokes to start, not wanting to do anything that would hurt or startle her. He hadn't been with a virgin since he himself had been one, and he wasn't sure exactly how to act. How fast might be too fast. How much might be too much.

But Alandra seemed far from intimidated. Her arms and legs were in constant motion, shamelessly exploring his naked body. And she wiggled beneath him, making it difficult for him to hold on to his resolve.

He locked his jaw and concentrated on breathing. His body was alive with sensation, his nerve endings electrified with need and lust and desperation.

"Can't you move any faster?" she panted at last, her back arching and nails raking his damp flesh.

He raised his head to look down at her. Her face was flushed, her hair spread out in a gleaming mass on the pale satin sheets.

"Is that an order?" he retorted, torn between amusement and disbelief.

Her lips curved slightly. "A request. You're treating me like I'm made of glass," she told him, "and I most certainly am not. I may be inexperienced at this sort of thing, but I'm not fragile."

"I don't want to hurt you," he admitted.

She lifted up from the mattress long enough to give him a quick, hard kiss. "You won't. I can take whatever you have to give and then some."

There was only one way to respond. "My pleasure."

His tongue flicked out to tease a ripe pink nipple, and he was smugly satisfied to feel a shudder ripple through her long, lithe form. He kept at it, wetting both tips, suckling them into stiff, rigid peaks.

When he had her shivering in his arms, grasping at his hair and whispering his name, he began to scoot her back, sliding her naked, pliant body across the silky coverlet. Then he grasped her hips and rolled, bringing her over him while he lay flat on his back.

"They say a woman is responsible for her own pleasure. Show me what you want."

Alandra stared down at him, her heart fluttering as she went from being startled by the sudden change of position to feeling empowered by his sensual declaration. His low voice rumbled through her, bringing goose bumps out along her flesh, and he held her hips when she straddled him.

A dozen sultry images of being in the lead and having Nicolas at her mercy played through her mind, and she loved every one.

Spreading her fingers, she pressed her palms on his chest and leaned forward. Her hair fell around her shoulders, the ends tickling his skin. She saw his impressive pectoral muscles jerk, and felt him swell inside of her.

Biting back a grin, she brushed her lips across the line of his jaw. "This is nice," she murmured, kissing her way to his ear. "Having you beneath me, defenseless."

His fingers flexed where he gripped her. "I only hope I have the strength to withstand your torture."

"So do I."

Taking the soft lobe of his ear between her teeth, she tugged gently. At the same time, she rose up on her knees, just an inch, then slowly lowered herself back down. Nicolas groaned deep in his throat, and heat burst in her center.

"Do you know what I really want?" she asked, watching her breath flutter the strands of his brown hair.

"What?" The word came out harsh and strangled as he tried to hold back his base desires.

"I want you to touch me. Everywhere. I love the feel of your hands on my body."

Immediately, he began to explore. His palms drifted to her buttocks, where he gave a little squeeze before sweeping back up the length of her torso to her breasts. Again his thumbs wreaked havoc with her nipples, and with a moan of her own, she kissed him.

Sensations swamped her, raising her blood pressure and making her insides vibrate like the strings of a well-played violin. As good as she'd always thought sex might be, she'd never expected it could be *this* good. That a man—any man—could make her feel both hot and cold at the same time. Make her pant and purr, shiver and shake.

Instinct kicked in and she began to move, her body seeming to have a mind of its own. Her hips canted back and forth, and she rose and fell on his rigid length.

He filled her completely, pressing deep and rubbing with a glorious friction along her hidden folds. Pleasure wound inside her like a spring, from her lips all the way to the apex of her thighs, growing tighter and tighter as the two of them picked up speed.

Feeling as though she were about to explode, she sat up, gasping for air. Her eyes drifted shut and she dragged her nails across his chest.

Beneath her, Nicolas seemed possessed of the same frantic need to plunge and writhe and buck to completion. He met her thrust for thrust, pounding into her on every downward slide. And when that coil of delicious tension building up inside her finally sprang loose, he was right there with her, gripping her even harder and giving a guttural shout of completion.

Alandra's own body shook with climax, rocking her to her very soul before melting into a pile of boneless limbs and damp, exhausted flesh on top of him. His arms slipped around her waist, and where her head rested on his chest, she could hear his heart thudding beneath her ear.

Her last thought before slipping into sleep was that she was glad she'd waited all these years to be with a man. And that when she'd finally taken the plunge, she was glad that man had been Nicolas.

"Now tell me how it is that you got to the age of twenty-nine with your virginity intact," Nicolas demanded.

It was late, the sky darker than before. They were lying in bed, half-asleep after another bout of strenuous, passionate lovemaking.

He'd protested that twice in one night was too much for her, that she would be sore in the morn-

ing. But she was having none of it, and had proceeded to convince him otherwise.

Now that she knew the pleasures that awaited
her, she had no intention of sleeping the night
away. In fact, she was already anticipating the third
time being especially charming.

At the moment, however, she was content to lie
in his arms, blissfully sated and tucked between
cool satin sheets.

"Don't you think my high moral fiber is reason
enough?" she replied sleepily.

"It might be, if you weren't more beautiful than a
supermodel, and hadn't recently been accused quite
publicly of having an affair with a married man."

With a sigh, she pushed herself up on one arm,
using her other hand to press the sheet to her breasts.
If he wasn't going to let the topic go, she might as
well tell him everything and get it over with.

"For the record, it wasn't an affair. Except perhaps in Blake's mind. Blake Winters," she clarified. "That was his name. I met him almost two
years ago at a fund-raising event. He's charming
and good-looking, and I admit I was attracted to
him. He started calling, sending flowers and gifts.

We went out a few times, and he was nice enough, but I didn't think we hit it off quite as well as he apparently did. And I *didn't* know he was married and had a family," she stressed, finally finding the courage to meet Nicolas's gaze.

"Even after I decided not to see him anymore, he wouldn't leave me alone. He kept calling, kept sending presents. He attended my functions and did his best to get me alone. Just about the time his attention started to border on frightening, he stopped trying to contact me."

She shifted uncomfortably, readjusting the sheet around her torso as she went back to looking anywhere but into Nicolas's eyes. "I thought that was the end of it, and then suddenly photographs of the two of us showed up in the press. They were probably taken at the charity events, but they were just suggestive enough to get tongues wagging—especially when a so-called 'source' leaked the information that we *had* been intimately involved. I think it was Blake himself. I think he *wanted* people to believe we were having an affair, maybe even thought, in some sick way, that it would make me go back to him."

She shook her head and took a deep breath, shrugging off the bad memories and any lingering remnants of the shame she'd felt when the story—however incorrect—had broken.

The hair on her nape rose when Nicolas reached out to run the back of his hand over her bare arm. His knuckles rasped along her skin, drawing gooseflesh everywhere he touched.

"Poor Alandra, working so hard to take care of everyone else, but having no one stand up for you when you most needed it."

His words, as well as his tone, surprised her, and for a moment she let herself believe them. A second later, though, self-pity transformed into her usual streak of independence, and she gave an unladylike snort.

"I had plenty of people to defend me," she told him. "Unfortunately, my family is no match for all of Texas high society. In situations like that, the only thing you can do is lie low and try not to do anything even more newsworthy until it all blows over."

His hand moved from her arm to her back. The light stroking lulled her and made her want to curl up beside him once again.

"Is that what you're doing here, in Glendovia?" Nicolas asked softly. "Lying low?"

She snuggled down again, draping herself cozily along his hard length. Resting her head on the curve of his shoulder, she asked, "Is this low enough for you?"

He gave a chuckle, then shifted slightly and pulled her tighter against him, readjusting the cool sheets so that they were both covered from the waist down.

Silence surrounded them, heavy but comfortable. It gave her the chance to listen to Nicolas's breathing and the sound of his heart pumping rhythmically beneath her ear.

"That explains the scandal that surrounds you back in the States," he said at last, his fingers drawing random circles on her upper body. "It doesn't, however, tell me how you managed to remain untouched for so long."

Her mouth twisted wryly, even though she knew he couldn't see her expression. "I'm a good girl. What do you think?"

"I think you're a very good girl," he murmured, his words edged with innuendo. "But no one who looks at you would ever believe you were a virgin."

She cocked her head back to glower at him. "Why? Because I forgot to wear my sweater with the big red *V* on the front?"

"No," he responded calmly. "Because you're one of the most beautiful women I've ever met, and sexuality trickles from your every pore. No heterosexual man could be in the same room with you without wanting you, and I find it hard to believe that one hadn't convinced you to sleep with him before now."

Sighing, she relaxed and settled back against Nicolas. "I don't know how to explain it, except to say that no man has truly enticed me enough. I've dated a lot of men, yes. Wealthy, attractive men. And there were a few times I came close, a few I thought I might be falling in love with. But something always stopped me."

"Until now."

Beneath her ear, his heart seemed to jump against his rib cage and double its beat. Her eyelids, already half-closed, drifted all the way shut, his pulse acting like a lullaby.

"Until now," she agreed, her voice growing faint as sleep began to tug at her. "I guess you could say that your invitation came at a very beneficial time. For a number of reasons."

"One of those reasons being that it gave me a chance to finally get you exactly where I wanted you." With one sinewy arm around her waist, he dragged her up so he could see her face, jarring her into full wakefulness.

Alandra wanted to argue the point or chastise herself for falling so effortlessly into his trap. But right now, in the darkest part of the night, with him lying warm and solid beneath her, she couldn't find it in her to be angry.

Later, maybe, but not now.

Ten

Rays of warm sunlight slanted through the French doors, crossing the carpeted floor and part of the bed, and pulling Alandra slowly awake.

She stretched and yawned and reached out an arm, expecting to find Nicolas asleep beside her. When her hand met nothing but cool, bare sheets, she opened her eyes and blinked until her vision focused.

She was naked and alone in a tangle of pale, wrinkled bedclothes.

Sitting up, she glanced around the room, but didn't find him there.

A sliver of disappointment snaked through her belly. Maybe it had been too much to hope that she'd be able to wake up in his arms. It wouldn't do, after all, for him to be caught sleeping with the hired help.

With a sigh, she rolled out of bed and reached for her robe. Knotting the belt at her waist, she glanced at the clock, her heart pitching when she saw that it was well past 10:00 a.m.

Good Lord, how could she have slept so late?

Not looking forward to the greeting she would receive when she finally made her way downstairs, Alandra showered and brushed her teeth, then started to dress. She wore a simple white sheath with a silver-bangle belt, and white platform sandals. Nothing too provocative, but nothing too dowdy, either.

She wanted to appear cool and confident when she next ran into Nicolas.

Sleeping with Nicolas—a prince, her employer and the man who had propositioned her at their first meeting—wasn't the smartest move she'd ever made. She should have been stronger, more resilient.

Because there was no way she was about to become his mistress for the rest of her time in Glendovia.

Resolve firmly in place, she strolled along the palace corridors and down the wide, curved, marble staircase. There was no one around, not even a servant, making her feel even more awkward about sleeping in so late.

She made her way to the dining room, where she'd spent the majority of her time with the royal family thus far, but the room was empty, long ago cleared of any traces of breakfast. From there, she drifted back across the foyer and down the opposite hallway toward Nicolas's office. She wasn't in a particular hurry to run into him, but he was her primary employer and she was already late getting to work.

The door was closed and she rapped softly, half hoping he wouldn't be there. But he called for her to enter after the first knock.

She schooled her breathing and stepped inside, closing the door at her back. He was seated behind his desk, working, but raised his head to greet her.

Scorching familiarity flashed in his eyes. The look made her heart hitch in her chest.

"Good morning," he murmured, setting down his pen and rising to his feet. "I trust you slept well."

His tone was formal, more formal than she would have expected from the man who'd shared her bed only hours before, with no hint of teasing or double entendre. Yet his gaze consumed her, sliding over her like warm honey, and making her want to do nothing more than relax into it, surrendering her body and her will to him once again.

"Very well, thank you." If he could be this decorous, then so could she. "I'm sorry to be running late this morning. Just because the children's Christmas event was a success doesn't mean I should be allowed to dawdle on the other causes you brought me here to deal with."

She purposely avoided any mention of how they'd spent their time after the Santa gift giveaway, sticking to a professional mode. It was better that way and would help her remain on an even keel.

One side of his mouth lifted, as though he knew exactly what she was trying to do. "I don't think sleeping in a few hours can be considered shirking your duties. However, if you have ideas for other fund-raising events, I'd love to hear them."

He waved a hand at one of the chairs in front of his desk, motioning for her to sit down. As soon as she did, he returned to his seat.

"Actually, I do have another idea," she said, feeling some of the tension seep from her body. Talking business was much better than discussing last night. "Not for a fund-raiser per se, but for the development of an organization."

"Really?" His brows rose and he leaned back in his chair, propping his fingertips together as he listened intently.

"Yes. Back in the States, we have a nationwide organization that works to fulfill the wishes of terminally ill children. I've noticed that you don't have anything like that set up here in Glendovia, and I think it would be a wonderful project for the royal family to undertake. It would bring you some outstanding press, and also fill a very real need for kids who are sick in the hospital or even at home, with no hope of recovery. I thought we could call it Dream a Little Dream."

After considering her proposal for several long

seconds, he asked, "And what kind of dreams would we be fulfilling for these children?"

"Whatever they wanted. Their dearest wish, if it's at all feasible. At home, the organization arranges for children to meet their favorite celebrities, spend an entire day at an amusement park that's been rented out just for them and their friends, go for a hot-air-balloon ride or learn to fly a plane. Things that the kids have always wanted to do, but otherwise wouldn't get the chance to because of their condition."

Nicolas returned her grin. "I suppose that could be arranged."

"So it's something you'd consider?" She leaned forward eagerly. "There would be much more involved than simply planning a fund-raising event. We're talking about renting office space, hiring employees, enormous national and possibly international publicity, probably even a press conference or two. And the organization would need continued support long after I return to America."

She thought she saw a flicker of unease cross his face at the mention of her leaving, but it was gone in an instant.

"It's a noble endeavor," he said, shifting so that his elbows once again rested on the desktop. "A good cause, and something that would bolster Glendovia's reputation and its citizens' esteem. I'll have to discuss it with the rest of the family, of course, but I would certainly be in favor of getting the ball rolling."

"Excellent." She grinned broadly, pleased that he was in favor of a project she'd begun to feel very passionate about.

"You have only a little over a week left of your stay," he pointed out.

His mouth was a flat line and his words were curt, as though he found that fact distasteful. The ripple of unease low in her belly told her that she wasn't entirely comfortable with it, either.

When she'd first arrived and discovered exactly who Prince Nicolas Braedon was, she'd threatened to turn around and fly back to Texas, even if it meant breaking her employment contract with the royal family. But now that she'd been here for a while and had really begun to dig into the work, she was enjoying her visit. Enjoying the palace and the country and its people.

She missed her family and was eager to return

to Texas to be with them again, but she was no longer looking forward to leaving, as she had been only a couple of weeks before.

"Do you think that's enough time to establish this organization and get it to the point where it can be turned over to others and still run smoothly?" Nicolas asked.

"I do."

"Even with Christmas coming up?"

"I'll work through the holiday. I was planning to do that, anyway."

Without her family to share in the festivities, and with a multitude of servants who had already decorated the palace from top to bottom, she suspected Christmas this year would end up passing much like any other day.

She'd been prepared all along to spend that time alone in her room rather than intruding upon the royal family's celebrations. At least this way she would have a nice, meaty project to work on and keep herself occupied.

She thought she heard him mutter, "We'll see about that" beneath his breath. But then he pushed himself away from his desk and stood, and in a firmer voice said, "All right. I'll bring it up with the family and see how they feel about it, then get back to you with a decision."

Nodding, she rose to her feet as he crossed the office to hold the door for her. She took a couple of steps in his direction, then stopped.

"Is there anything else?" he asked, noticing her hesitation.

She curled her fingers into fists at her sides, then released them, fidgeting anxiously while she tried to decide whether or not to voice the concerns circling through her brain.

"Alandra," he murmured softly, and started in her direction.

Straightening her shoulders, she met his eyes, stopping him in his tracks. "About last night…" she began, steeling her nerves for a conversation that filled her with dread.

"Yes?" he asked without inflection of any kind.

Obviously, he was in no mood to make this easier on her.

"It can't happen again," she told him quickly and succinctly, as if pulling off a bandage before the pain or aftereffects sank in.

"Oh?" Again his voice lacked inflection, but this time he raised an eyebrow, the only hint that he had any interest in what she was saying.

"No. I realize it's exactly what you wanted, your whole reason for inviting me here to begin with, but it was a mistake and it's not going to happen again."

For a long minute, Nicolas studied Alandra, taking in her rigid stance and stern countenance. He wondered how annoyed she would be if he told her how attractive she looked when she tried to be authoritative.

Deciding not to risk her wrath over that, when he was about to commit a much worse offense to her sensibilities, he pushed the door shut with a quiet click and slowly closed the short distance between them.

"I'm afraid that's unacceptable to me," he replied, raising a hand to touch her hair, which hung straight and silky around her shoulders.

He watched her head tip just a bit away from his hand, as though trying to move away from his touch. And then the tendons of her throat tightened and released as she swallowed, her gaze not quite meeting his.

"It doesn't matter whether you agree or not," she said. "I'm simply telling you the way things are going to be. What happened last night isn't going to happen again."

She sounded resolute. So much so that he couldn't help smiling.

Not that he could hold her response against her. She hadn't known him long enough to realize that he was a man who got what he wanted. He had no intention of giving up so easily or letting her go purely because she claimed their lovemaking last night was a mistake.

He disagreed. Strongly.

Still grinning, he let his hand graze her soft cheek and tuck a strand of hair behind one ear. "I beg to differ. Last night was magnificent."

Her gaze flitted away and a pale pink blush started to creep across her face.

"You have less than two weeks left in Glendovia, and I fully intend to enjoy them. To enjoy you. I know that you'll need to spend your days working, especially if you undertake this new project you've proposed. But your evenings will be free, and I want you to spend them with me, in my bed."

"Absolutely not." She shook her head and took a step back, breaking away from his touch.

As much as he wanted to close the distance between them and grab her up, kissing the quarrel from her luscious, red-tinged lips, he remained where he was, allowing her to believe a few inches of space would keep her safe from him.

A wry smile lifted the corner of his mouth. "You think that I lured you here, created a position for you within my country, to sleep with you for only one night? Alandra," he breathed softly, almost teasingly, "even if you didn't know me well enough by now, you have to realize that no prince would go to such lengths for a single night of sex, no matter how spectacular that sex might be."

Determination straightened his spine and pushed his shoulders back. "I am a bit more dedicated than that," he added, slowly stepping forward. He was encouraged to note that her wide eyes remained locked with his, and she barely seemed to register his approach.

"And now that I've had you, I have no intention of letting you slip away. I wanted to make love to you, and I've done that, but I'm far from sated."

Even as his voice fell, becoming low and rich and seductive, his finger lifted to gently brush against her body. First the curve of her waist and the underside of her breast, then the tender flesh of her upper arm. He kept the contact brief and featherlight, just the tips of his fingers grazing the material of her dress and her bare skin.

And even though he was scarcely touching her, he still felt the shiver of awareness that rippled through her. It sent a jolt of white-hot sensation through his system, gathering and pooling in his groin. He went hard and heavy in an instant, nearly desperate enough to throw her to the floor and make love to her right then and there.

He wouldn't, of course, though it wasn't his royal blood keeping him from doing anything so crass. When it came to being alone in a room with Alandra Sanchez, his royal blood be damned.

No, it was Alandra herself who kept his more base instincts in check. She was already nervous and shy and regretful about what had passed between them last night, and jumping at her now would only cause her to crawl deeper into her shell, to move further away from him.

Instead, he knew he would have to go slowly again, returning to his original plan of smooth, flawless seduction.

Oh, he would have her in his bed again—tonight, if he had anything to say about it. But it would require a bit of persuasion to get her there.

Alandra's chest rose as she inhaled, and her bright, expressive brown eyes drifted closed for a moment, her head tipping down in defeat.

"Please don't do this," she breathed raggedly. "Don't make me do something that I'll hate myself for later."

Her eyes fluttered open and she raised her head to meet his gaze. Her expression was resolute, if somewhat sad.

"I don't want to be Prince Nicolas's secret mistress. A temporary entertainment to be enjoyed while I'm here, then sent away when you're finished with me, never to be thought of again."

Something about her words twisted his heart painfully, and for a second he reconsidered his single-minded determination to have her, regardless of the consequences.

He didn't want to hurt her, didn't want to bring that look of misery to her face.

He wanted to hold her, kiss her, savor her like a glass of expensive brandy.

Why should it be more complicated than that? They were both mature adults, able to make their own decisions and spend time with whomever they chose.

Leaning in slightly, he let his warm breath fan her cheeks as he hovered a scant inch from her lush, kissable lips.

"I don't want you to hate yourself," he murmured quietly. "I just want to be with you. And though I can't change who I am or the prudence my role in this family requires, I don't think it needs to have any impact on our time together. What we do when we're alone, away from the public eye, is no one's business but ours."

He threaded his fingers through her hair, holding her tight and tipping her head back so he could better reach her mouth. He brushed his lips across hers, tasting her, feeling her, absorbing her energy and spirit into himself.

"I only want to be with you," he said without

breaking contact. "And after last night, I believe you want the same thing. You'll have to work very hard to convince me that isn't true."

She didn't answer, didn't pull way. He wasn't even sure she was still breathing. Pressing his advantage, he kissed her again, deeper this time, until her spine bowed against his body and her nails dug into the material of his jacket.

When he finally raised his head, they were both breathing heavily. A shaft of satisfaction rolled through him at the cloudy, unfocused look in her eyes.

"Very hard," he whispered.

Eleven

It was beyond difficult to convince Nicolas that she didn't want him. So impossible, in fact, that she'd given up trying.

How could she claim she wanted nothing to do with him when one touch of his hands or mouth melted her insides like a pot of chocolate fondue?

He'd discussed the idea for the Dream a Little Dream Foundation with his family, even asking Alandra to draw up an official proposal he could take to them. He'd also done a bit of research on his own into its American counterpart, so he could show them what the end product of such an endeavor might be like.

Reaction so far had been positive, and she and Nicolas had been working together on a daily basis to plan things in more detail, crossing all the t's and dotting all the i's. Once the king and queen approved, as well as the board of Glendovian officials who oversaw this type of thing, she would be given the freedom to get the ball rolling on establishing the foundation.

Daylight hours were not her problem. She had plenty to do to keep her busy, and managed to make sure she wasn't alone with Nicolas any more than necessary.

The door of his office stayed open while they were working, and if for some reason it was closed, she found a way to get it open again. If they were alone and things began to feel too tense, too dangerous, she'd make an excuse to get someone else into the room with them.

It was nighttime that caused her the most anxiety. After dinner, when Nicolas would walk her back to her rooms…holding her hand, standing too close, leaning into her at the door.

He kissed her cheek or sometimes her lips. Stroked her hand or shoulder. And always, *always* his eyes blazed with the clear desire to sweep her up in his arms and cart her off to bed.

She prayed he'd never figure out how very often she wished he would do just that.

Obviously, she wasn't safe around him, and she didn't know how she was going to make it another ten days without either giving in or going crazy.

Ten more long, arduous days and she could fly home, fly away to safety.

For some reason, though, that knowledge didn't comfort her as much as she would have hoped. In fact, it almost saddened her.

But that was an emotion she refused to examine. Her entire existence had been turned upside down, and as soon as she arrived home, life would begin to right itself and return to normal.

She hoped.

For now, though, it was late, and she'd thankfully managed to survive another day, another dinner, another long, excruciating walk back to her suite.

She'd changed into a pair of comfortable black satin pajamas and was ready to climb into bed when a soft knock sounded on the sitting room door.

A petite young woman in the uniform of the palace's household staff stood on the other side.

"Miss," she said, bobbing a slight curtsy. "Prince Nicolas sends this message and requests an immediate response." She held out a square envelope.

It was Nicolas's official stationery, Alandra saw, with her name scrawled in his expansive script across the front, and a dab of wax sealant pressed to the back.

Whatever was inside, she suspected, was either very important or very private.

Running a finger under the flap of the envelope, she broke the seal and removed the folded sheet of paper.

Alandra—
Your presence is required at a very important meeting concerning Dream a Little Dream. We fly to the other side of the island tomorrow morning. Pack for at least one night. Be ready to leave at 7:00 a.m.
Nicolas

She wasn't sure exactly what response he was awaiting, since he didn't seem to be giving her much choice in the matter. He hadn't asked if she wanted to go or would be willing to go, or was even able to go…he'd simply told her to be ready.

Refolding the note, she stuffed it back in the envelope before returning her attention to the servant. "Tell the prince I'll be in the main foyer by seven o'clock. Thank you."

The woman nodded and hurried off, ostensibly to deliver the message. More like announce Alandra's compliance, she thought crossly as she shut the door and headed back to the bedroom.

Though she wasn't particularly happy about this new development, she dragged an overnight bag from one of the closets and began to pack.

By the time she'd finished, she was truly exhausted. Climbing into bed, she hoped for a good night's sleep.

She would need all the rest she could get if she was going to be alone with Nicolas—away from the palace. Overnight.

She met Nicolas outside the palace at exactly 7:00 a.m. The entire place, inside and out, was decorated to the nines in anticipation of the Christmas Eve party the royal family was hosting in only two days' time.

"Good morning," he said.

"Good morning."

"I'm glad you were able to accompany me to this meeting," he told her once they were inside the car and heading down the driveway.

"I didn't have much choice in the matter, did I?" she replied, avoiding his gaze by staring out the window.

"You always have a choice."

She turned her head, meeting his blue eyes. "Well, your note didn't seem to *ask* if I'd like to go with you."

"I was afraid that if I did ask, you would have said no," he confessed.

"Of course I wouldn't have said no. As long as this meeting actually does concern the Dream a Little Dream Foundation. Or did you just say that to get me alone and away from the palace for a few days?" she asked quietly.

A moment passed before he responded. "This trip *is* about the foundation, and though I could probably handle things well enough on my own, I think it's important that you're there. I think you'll be glad you came."

He paused again, letting the silence fill with tension as his sharp gaze bored into hers. "But I'm also quite happy to get you away from the palace and to myself. I think you'll be glad for that, too—eventually."

His voice lowered to a warm, honeyed tone, and it took all of Alandra's willpower not to suck in a deep breath of air to replace what had gotten stuck in her throat.

She should be angry. He was manipulating her again, moving her how and where he wanted her in an effort to change her mind about sleeping with him.

One thing could be said for Nicolas Braedon— he knew what he wanted and didn't take no for an answer.

She didn't want to admit it, not even to herself, but the truth was his single-minded determination to seduce her made her feel...special.

It wasn't her intention to play with him, to turn this...whatever it was between them...into a game, but she suddenly realized she was enjoying herself. She enjoyed knowing that he wanted her.

Instead of arguing or giving in too soon, she merely shrugged and said, "I guess we'll have to wait and see."

The flight to the other side of the island was a short one, and they went straight from the small private airstrip to the office where the meeting was scheduled.

Alandra was stunned to learn that they weren't simply meeting with a few people *about* establishing the new foundation, but were meeting with many people to actually get the organization up and running.

As the morning meetings progressed, she realized Nicolas had been right. She was glad she'd come along.

She was also thrilled with the amount of progress they were making in such a short time. Over a working lunch she met wonderfully enthusiastic people raring to get started. She had no doubt they would do an excellent job of running the organization, whether she was there or not.

She and the prince said goodbye to the future Dream a Little Dream staff at five, and Nicolas instructed his driver to take them to a hotel where the royal family kept a suite of rooms.

Alandra wasn't taken aback, and she wasn't upset. In fact, she belatedly realized she'd expected as much. After her little revelation in the car on the way to the airport that morning, she even found herself looking forward to what the evening might bring.

The royal suite was gorgeous. Nicer, even, than her rooms at the palace.

The walls, carpeting and drapes were all done in varying shades of blue, with touches of white and tan. A set of dark mahogany French doors opened onto a small lanai overlooking the city and the coastline beyond. One of the doors was open, allowing a cool breeze to ruffle the long, diaphanous curtains, bringing in the salty scent of the sea.

"Are you hungry?" Nicolas asked, stepping to a desk that held a thick, black binder of hotel amenities.

She nodded, moving slowly in his direction as she continued to take in her surroundings. She wondered if she should bother unpacking, or simply live out of her overnight bag.

"I'll have something brought up," he said, flipping through the room service menu and then calling down to order what sounded like a veritable buffet of appetizers and entrées. Before hanging up, he asked for a bottle of their best wine, and strawberries with fresh whipped cream for dessert.

"We have about thirty minutes before the food arrives." Loosening his tie and shrugging out of his suit jacket, he draped both over the back of a chair as he crossed the room. "Would you care to change into something a bit more comfortable before it gets here?"

His gaze raked her from head to toe, raising gooseflesh every inch of the way.

She knew when to admit defeat—and when to enjoy a very handsome man who was more than willing to pleasure and worship her, if only for a short while.

"Do you have any special requests?" she asked, slowly removing her watch, and then her earrings.

Next she raised a hand to the top button of her blouse, slipping it through its hole.

His eyes followed her actions intently, glittering with longing and sending sparks of awareness through her.

"Naked works for me," he murmured, his voice gravelly with desire.

She chuckled, feeling a thrill of empowerment swelling in her veins. "Not just yet, I don't think," she said, turning on her heel and heading for the bedroom. "I wouldn't want to shock the waiter when he arrives."

"If he sees you naked, I could have him killed."

She laughed again, facing him with her hands on the knobs of the double bedroom doors.

"Let's not turn this trip into a crime spree just yet. Not if we can help it," she told him as she swung the doors closed. "I'll see what I can come up with on my own."

She stayed in the bedroom until she'd heard the room service waiter deliver dinner and leave again.

Opening one door a crack, she saw Nicolas standing before the round table on one side of the sitting area. It had been set with an array of dishes and stemware.

Stepping the rest of the way into the room, she paused and waited for him to notice her. When he did, his hand froze on the silver serving lid he'd been about to raise, and his gaze zeroed in on her like a heat-seeking missile.

She'd changed into a long black nightgown with spaghetti straps and lace-lined slits running from ankle to midthigh on each side. Her feet were bare, her red-tipped toes peeking out from beneath the hem of the nightie, and she'd combed her hair out to fall in a straight, silky curtain around her shoulders. The look on Nicolas's face told her how completely he appreciated her efforts.

"It's not naked, but I hope you approve."

He swallowed hard. "Very much so. I didn't think it was possible, but that gown may just be better than full nudity."

An amused smile tugged at her lips. "I'm glad you said something. Now I know not to take it off, no matter how much you beg."

"Princes don't beg," he informed her, stalking slowly toward her.

"No?" she asked, her mouth going suddenly dry.

"No."

He was standing in front of her now, close enough to touch, but keeping his arms at his sides. Her heart was pounding in her chest and she had to fight the urge to wiggle nervously.

"What do princes do, then?" she asked, her voice husky with growing pleasure.

Reaching out, he stroked the back of his fingers across her cheek. "It would be better if I showed you."

"Won't dinner get cold?"

"Do you care?"

Twelve

Late that night, Alandra lay in bed, wrapped snugly in Nicolas's arms. She couldn't have been more physically comfortable and sated...but her emotions were in an uproar.

She had done the very thing she'd sworn not to—she'd become Nicolas's lover.

As disturbing as that was, as much as it made her question her own character, it wasn't what had her teetering on the edge.

She'd realized not an hour before—while

Nicolas was kissing her, stroking her and making her sigh—that she was falling in love with him.

She swallowed hard, blinking to keep the moisture collecting at the corners of her eyes from spilling over. Beneath her cheek, Nicolas's chest rose and fell with his easy breathing.

This was bad. So bad. An affair was one thing. But how was she supposed to leave for home with a smile on her face if her heart was left behind, broken and bleeding?

How was she supposed to pretend that what had passed between them was just a holiday fling, when it had become so much more than that to her?

Nicolas shifted slightly in his sleep, causing her breath to catch. When he didn't wake up, she relaxed, feeling a bit steadier.

Since she knew she was merely a temporary distraction for him, and that he didn't share her newfound sentiments in the least, she would simply have to deal with the situation as best she could. Hide her feelings. And then, when the time came, she would walk away.

Closing her eyes, she began to drift off, telling

herself to get used to the pain squeezing her heart. It was going to be with her for a long time to come.

They returned to the other side of the island the following morning, Christmas Eve, with many hours to spare before the family's annual holiday party. Nicolas had made certain Alandra knew she was to attend, though she wasn't entirely looking forward to it.

Stepping off the plane, they were accosted by a large group of reporters, all snapping pictures and screaming out questions. She had trouble making out the exact words, and Nicolas bustled her into the back of the waiting limousine before she could decipher them.

"What was that about?" she asked breathlessly as the car shifted into gear and headed toward the palace.

He shook his head. "The press probably caught wind of our travels and are trying to see if it's worthy of front page news."

The media attention still seemed odd to her, since the trip had been business-related and the palace likely would have already delivered a press release outlining the prince's plans. But she pushed aside her misgivings and relaxed in the comfortable, stuffed leather seat.

When they arrived at the palace, the queen was waiting for them in the main foyer. Her face was pinched, her mouth set in a flat, angry line. Though she didn't raise her voice, the disapproval in her tone was clear as glass.

"In the library," she snapped. "Now."

Nicolas and Alandra exchanged a questioning glance, then slowly followed in the queen's rapid-fire footsteps.

As soon as they stepped into the library and closed the door behind them, Eleanor spun back around, holding a newspaper in her shaking hands. *"What,"* she demanded through clenched teeth, "is the meaning of this?"

Alandra stood perfectly still, stunned by the queen's obvious displeasure, but unsure of the cause. As hard as she tried, she couldn't make out the headline of the article being waved between them.

Seemingly unfazed by his mother's mood, Nicolas reached for the paper. There, taking up nearly all of the top half of the front page was a close-up photo of Nicolas and Alandra. They were standing on the balcony of the hotel suite, caught in an unmistakable embrace.

The photo had to have been taken after they had made love, then gone out on the balcony for a breath of fresh air...only to end up kissing for long, stolen moments before drifting back inside to make love again.

Alandra's cheeks flamed at both the memory and the knowledge that someone had been out there, snapping pictures of a very private moment.

Above the photo, sending a wave of nausea through her stomach, was a bold, glaring headline that declared her Prince Nicolas's American Tart.

Nicolas muttered a dark curse beneath his breath and lowered the newspaper.

Still vibrating with anger, the queen said, "You and your little...*American* are on the front page of every newspaper in Glendovia. I told you, Nicolas. I *told* you not to get involved with her, that she would only bring shame and embarrassment to our family."

The sick sensation clawing at Alandra's insides grew worse. She'd come to Glendovia to get away from one scandal, only to find herself smack in the middle of another.

And this one was even worse, because now it was true. She hadn't had an affair with Blake Winters, as the American press had claimed, but she *had* been sleeping with Nicolas.

"Mother," Nicolas growled.

His jaw was clenched, and the single word was clearly a warning. One the queen chose to ignore.

"Princess Lisette arrived less than an hour ago—in tears. She's crushed, and her parents are furious. Do you have any idea how this indignity will affect your upcoming nuptials? If she backs out of the engagement, our family's ties with hers will be fractured. The political future of Glendovia could be in peril."

"I think you're overreacting," Nicolas remarked, but it was obvious from his expression that the entire situation had him concerned.

Alandra's brain had gotten stuck on two words that made her heart feel as though it were being squeezed in a vise.

She turned her head toward Nicolas. "You're engaged?" she asked.

"It's not what you think," he said shortly. "I can explain."

But she didn't want to hear explanations, excuses, lies or more of the persuasive and creative arguments he seemed only too talented at spinning.

It was her turn to shake her head as she backed away.

"I'm sorry," she murmured shakily, directing her apology to the queen, not Nicolas. She had nothing to apologize to him for.

"I'm sorry," she said again, "I didn't know he was betrothed. I certainly didn't come here with the intention of getting involved with Nicolas. I would never have knowingly brought any embarrassment or undue attention to your family. I hope you can believe that."

The queen's pinched expression did not change as she turned to look at her son. "I'll expect the two of you to keep your distance from now on. You will conduct yourselves with the utmost decorum and stay as far from each other as possible while we rectify this situation. Is that understood?"

Nicolas looked as though he wanted to argue, but Alandra was already nodding. She blinked to hold back tears of humiliation, even as she licked her dry, parched lips.

"You may go," Eleanor told her, clearly dismissing her. "And you," she said to Nicolas, "will speak with Lisette immediately, and do your best to repair whatever damage has been done. Is that understood?"

Alandra slipped out of the office, closing the doors behind her without waiting to hear Nicolas's reply, and hurried across the parquet floor for the stairs. All she wanted was to get away, get back to her rooms, where she could be alone. What a fool she'd been. Again.

Standing in the doorway of her suite, Alandra took one last look around to be sure she hadn't left anything behind. All had been erased.

Closing the door quietly behind her, she walked down the hall, pulling her wheeled carry-on behind her. Instead of heading for the front of the palace, where guests would be arriving for the Christmas Eve party, she slipped toward the back, where a car was waiting to take her to the airport.

Leaving now meant giving up the hefty bonus

Nicolas had promised for the charity of her choice, but she simply couldn't stay. She wanted to go home, where she would be surrounded by family. Where she could hopefully hide and start to heal.

At the moment, the pain in her heart didn't feel as though it would ever go away, but she was hopeful. Hopeful that the sooner she left Glendovia, the sooner she could put this entire incident behind her. That the farther she could get from Nicolas, the faster she would begin to forget that she'd let herself fall in love with him—and that he'd been lying to her the entire time.

"Thank you for all of your help," she said to the woman who had helped her arrange for the car and a flight back to the United States.

Alandra handed her a stack of thick files and paperwork, with a separate sheet of stationery clipped to the outside. Despite her eagerness to leave, she had taken the time this afternoon to make certain the foundation wouldn't be left in the lurch.

"Please see that Prince Nicolas gets this. It should be everything he needs to continue with the Dream a Little Dream project."

The woman nodded and offered a small curtsy. "Yes, miss. It was a pleasure to meet you."

"Thank you," Alandra said, swallowing back tears. In only a few short weeks she had grown unaccountably close to the palace staff and was sincerely going to miss them.

With her throat too clogged to speak another word, she walked to the waiting vehicle and climbed in the back. It was dark outside, and too dark to see much of anything through the tinted rear windows. But even so, as the car rolled slowly away from the palace, Alandra kept her gaze focused straight ahead, not wanting to catch even one final glimpse of the site where she'd experienced both an incredible amount of happiness and an incredible amount of heartache.

Nicolas kept his expression impassive throughout the night, giving no hint of his dark, foul mood. He was only too relieved when the Christmas party drew to an end and he was able to slip away from his family and their guests.

He muttered a curse through gritted teeth as he made his way down the long hallway to Alandra's rooms. This was *not* the way he'd hoped things would turn out between them, or how he'd intended her visit to Glendovia to draw to a close.

When he reached her suite, he knocked lightly, then opened the door and entered without waiting for her response.

The lights were on and he heard noises coming from the bedroom, but something seemed oddly out of place.

"Alandra?" he called, striding in that direction.

He pushed open the door, immediately taking in the stripped bed and the lack of Alandra's personal items, which had been scattered about the first night he'd spent with her. A second later, a maid appeared in the bathroom doorway and gave a little squeak of surprise.

"Your Highness," she said, bowing her head.

"Where is Miss Sanchez?" he asked, frowning in consternation.

"I'm sorry, sir, but she's gone. Left just before the party began."

"She's gone?" he repeated, feeling as though his feet had been swept out from under him.

"Yes, sir. I believe she left something for you, though, with Delores. Shall I get her for you?"

"Yes, thank you. Have her bring it to my office, if you would, please."

"Yes, Your Highness."

The maid rushed around him and out of the room. Nicolas trailed behind at a much slower pace, taking a back stairwell to the first floor and heading for his private office. Ten minutes later, Delores arrived. She had a stack of folders in her arms.

"Miss Sanchez left these for you, sir," she said, handing them across the desk to him.

He thanked her, waiting until the servant had gone before opening the note on top of the pile. Alandra's letter was oddly lacking in emotion, simply explaining that she couldn't stay any longer, regardless of the requirements of her contract, now that she knew he was engaged to be married and those pictures had become public. The files, he discovered, held pages upon pages about the Dream a Little Dream Foundation.

He should have expected that she wouldn't want to leave unless she was sure all of the project details were in his hands, and that the establishment of the organization would move forward as planned.

The problem was, he hadn't expected her to leave at all. Not without talking with him, letting him explain.

He should have told her about Lisette in the beginning. Should have let her know that it was an arrangement made by his parents and not necessarily his choice. That even though he was betrothed to the princess, they had never been physically involved.

Lisette and his mother would be delighted to learn of Alandra's departure. Without her presence in Glendovia, the scandal of their affair would die a quick death, and life as they knew it could move on, including plans for his upcoming wedding.

He only wished he felt the same. Instead, he found himself wanting to charge down the hall and be driven to the airport, follow Alandra all the way back to Texas.

If only she'd given him a chance to explain.

With a sigh of regret, he crumpled her note.

It was better this way, he told himself as he left his office and strolled slowly to his rooms on the second floor. Now that Alandra was gone, things could return to normal. He could get back to the matters at hand without being preoccupied with thoughts of making love to her just one more time.

Yes, it was better this way. Better for everyone.

Thirteen

The noise from the back of the room buzzed in Alandra's ears. She really didn't want to do this.

After arriving home from Glendovia in the middle of the night—Christmas night, no less—she'd done her best to get her life back on track. News of her affair with Nicolas had yet to trickle back to the States. But if anyone in her immediate circle had heard about the affair they'd wisely chosen to ignore the gossip.

Everyone except her sister. Elena had waited

until they'd gotten home from the airport to say anything, but she'd known instinctively that something had sent Alandra running back to Texas.

The minute they were alone, Alandra had broken down and told her sister everything, pouring her heart out about the situation and how she'd unwisely fallen in love with a man she could never have. And as always, her sister had understood. She'd listened and offered appropriate responses at appropriate times, but never acted as though she thought Alandra had been a fool to get involved with Nicolas in the first place.

Elena was also the one who'd encouraged her most strongly to throw herself back into her work, when Alandra had wanted nothing more than to curl up in a ball and hide under the covers for the next month or two.

Which was how she'd ended up backstage at the Gabriel's Crossing Country Club. Long before she'd left for Glendovia, she had not only helped finalize the evening's New Year's Eve bachelorette auction, but she'd somehow allowed herself to be roped into being one of the bachelorettes, as well, and now they were holding her to her promise.

The event was in full swing. Six other women had already pranced down the runway to a smattering of applause and generous, good-hearted bidding by the interested bachelors in the audience. Two more ladies were set to take their walks, and then she would be next.

She swallowed hard, taking deep breaths to keep from drowning in panic. This wasn't her idea of a good time. She far preferred to remain behind the scenes at these events. Being the center of attention—especially with all of the publicity that had surrounded her lately—made her knees shake and her teeth rattle.

One bachelorette down, one to go.

"Alandra," a woman who was helping out backstage called in a loud whisper. "Get ready, you're next."

Oh, God, oh, God, oh, God.

For a brief second, she wondered how far she would be able to run in four-inch heels. She probably wouldn't get far, but it was still worth a try.

Inhaling deeply and praying she wouldn't trip over the hem of her gown, she started slowly down the makeshift runway to the sound of scattered clapping and the voice of the master of ceremonies, who extolled her many feminine virtues and outlined the details of the date she'd agreed upon beforehand.

She felt like an animal at a zoo, on display for the whole world to gawk at and appraise. And as she neared the end of the runway, her stomach plunged when she realized that not a single bid had been called out yet.

Oh, Lord, please let the floor open up and swallow me whole, she thought.

At the end of the runway, she stopped and posed, more from embarrassment than any wish to act like a supermodel. Except for the MC asking if there were any bids, any bids at all, the room had fallen into utter silence. The scandals, it seemed, hadn't quite died down, after all.

Alandra blinked, feeling the stares of a hundred people boring into her like laser beams. She was just about to turn in disgrace and walk back to the curtain when a voice rang out from the rear of the room.

"Two hundred and fifty thousand dollars."

Her heart stopped, and she strained to see who had made such an outrageously extreme offer. The rest of the crowd did the same, twisting in their seats for a glimpse of the mystery bidder.

Elated, the MC quickly declared Alandra "sold!" to the gentleman at the rear of the room. At that announcement, the bidder started forward.

As the bachelor walked toward her, he moved into better light, and Alandra's heart stopped again, but for a much different reason this time.

Nicolas, in all his royal finery, stepped through the crowd. A couple of hulking, black-suited bodyguards trailed behind, making his presence stand out all the more.

She opened her mouth to breathe his name, but no sound emerged.

At the end of the raised walkway, Nicolas stopped to gaze up at her. He stretched out a hand, his face showing nothing as he reached toward her.

"May I?" he asked in that rich, deep voice that sent shivers down her spine.

Without conscious thought, she put her hand in his and let him lift her bodily from the runway, then lead her back through the crowded room to the rear of the building. She let him take her away from her own event, away from the gawking stares and curious onlookers, to the limousine that waited just outside, on the paved country club driveway.

Nicolas handed her inside and climbed in behind her, allowing the driver to close the door. A second later, she heard the driver's door slam shut, but the partition was up, and she knew that for all intents and purposes, she and Nicolas were alone.

"What are you doing here?" she asked when she finally regained her senses and found her voice.

"I bought you," he replied easily, purposely ignoring the seriousness of her question.

The look in her eyes must have warned him he was skating on thin ice, because he sighed and shifted lightly on the leather seat.

"There have been some developments back in Glendovia since you left. Positive ones, in my estimation. For one, plans for the Dream a Little Dream Foundation are moving forward. We're estimating a March first start date for having everything up and running."

"I'm glad," she said softly. She was happy that things were moving smoothly with the plans she'd put into effect before leaving. But she doubted

Nicolas had flown all the way to America just to deliver an update.

"For another, I've reconsidered my original desire to have you as my mistress." His eyes met hers then, hard and unyielding. "It was short-sighted of me to believe that having you only temporarily would ever be enough."

Sliding across the seat, he wrapped his arms around her and tugged her against his chest. She went willingly.

"I've missed you, Alandra," he whispered against her hair. "I tried to forget you, tried to put you out of my mind and move on with what I knew I had to do."

His hands stroked her back, her neck, the side of her face. "But I couldn't go through with my engagement to Lisette when only one woman filled my heart. You're the one that I want, Alandra. Not as my lover or mistress, but as my wife."

Tipping her head back, she met his gaze, searching his startling blue eyes for the truthfulness in his words. And still she was afraid it was all a dream, that she would wake up to find herself alone, in her bed, with Nicolas nowhere around.

"I broke my engagement to Princess Lisette. It's caused a few hurt feelings and political problems between our two countries, but nothing that won't heal in time. And I've informed my family—my mother, especially—that I was coming to get you and wouldn't return unless you were at my side."

He slid his fingers through her hair, tugging loose the elaborate knot at the crown of her head and dislodging the tiny diamond clips holding it in place.

"Tell me you love me, Alandra, as much as I love you. Tell me you'll come to Glendovia with me, marry me and be my princess. My wife."

Her lashes fluttered as she struggled to absorb everything that Nicolas was saying. His determination and declaration of love, his willingness to put her before his responsibilities to the royal family and his country.

There were so many questions spinning through her brain, but when she opened her mouth, only one thing came out.

"I love you," she murmured, her own arms lifting to curl around his shoulders and hold him as tightly as he was holding her. "It wouldn't have hurt so much to leave if I didn't."

His mouth curved in a gentle smile. "I'm very glad to hear that. Does this mean you'll be my bride?"

A thrill of happiness squeezed her heart. She wanted nothing more than to say, "Yes, yes, yes!" and cover his face with kisses. But fear had her tugging away, watching his expression to be sure everything really was okay and that she could accept his proposal without making matters in both their lives so much worse.

"What about your mother?" she asked. "I don't need to tell you how much she dislikes me, and she was horribly upset about those photographs showing up in the papers. I can't imagine she'll be very pleased to hear you've asked me to marry you."

"Whatever problems my mother has with you are her own, and she'll have to learn to live with them. *My* feelings for you are what matter, and I can tell you quite unequivocally that I adore you." The corners of his mouth curved up in a grin, and he paused a brief moment to press a kiss to her lips. "And I'll have you know that the rest of my family is equally fond of you. They supported me one hundred percent when I told them of my plans to come here and try to win you back. My father included, and you can bet that he'll do his best to bring my mother around."

"You're sure about this?" Alandra asked softly. "I don't want to do anything that could hurt you or bring trouble to your family and country."

"I couldn't be more certain," he told her, and the conviction in his tone filled her with relief. "I would give up my title for you, and if you ask it, I will. You're all that I want, and I'll do whatever it takes to have you."

She couldn't decide whether to laugh or cry as pure delight poured through her clear to her soul. "Would you take me to a hotel—one without balconies, thank you very much—and make love to me?"

His eyes glittered dangerously, his hold around her waist tightening enough to have her gasping for breath.

"A prince's job is never done," he murmured a split second before his mouth touched hers.

* * * * *

ROYAL HOLIDAY BRIDE

BRENDA HARLEN

To Sharon & Ken May~

When I created the fictional island of Tesoro del Mar for the Reigning Men series, I was looking for a make-believe paradise. When you invited me to Exuma, I discovered that paradise is real—and it's in the Bahamas.

Thank you both so much for sharing it with me!

Chapter One

Princess Marissa Leandres of Tesoro del Mar had a plan.

If her plan seemed a little desperate, well, that was probably because she *was* desperate. For too many years, she'd been a good princess, behaving as was expected of her, careful not to make waves in the family or do anything that might result in a scandal. After all, her brother, Cameron, had created more than enough of those.

But time was running out and if she had any hope of taking control of her life and her future, she had to make a move. And she knew she would never have a better opportunity than tonight's masquerade ball.

What better way for a princess to shed the restrictions inherent to her title and all of her own personal inhibitions than to be someone else—at least for one night?

Still, she couldn't deny that she was nervous. Actually, she was more than nervous—she was terrified. But she was also determined.

She hadn't planned to be a twenty-eight-year-old virgin. As a teenager experiencing the first stirrings of physical attraction, she'd been cautious. Not that she'd thought of her virginity as any great prize, but she hadn't been anxious to throw it away, either—especially not with the possibility of a reporter or photographer lurking around every corner.

While a lot of her friends boasted about going "all the way," she'd been content to wait, at least until she met someone really special. Unfortunately, that special someone never did cross her path, and now her mother was ready to offer her as a virgin sacrifice to Anthony Volpini, the Duke of Bellemoro.

Marissa shuddered at the thought. No way was she going to let that happen. She'd shared one brief kiss with Anthony a few years back, and the memory of that lip-lock was not a pleasant one. The prospect of experiencing anything more intimate with the lecherous duke made her skin crawl. So tonight, she was dressed as Juno. And the goddess knew what she wanted.

As she made her way toward the ballroom, the elegantly engraved invitation trembled in her fingers. Her first test would be at the door, where her cousin and his wife, Prince Rowan and Princess Lara, would be greeting each and every guest. If she could get past them—

No, she wouldn't let herself think *if.* She had to be confident. She had to ignore the butterflies frantically winging around inside her tummy and refuse to think about all the reasons she should abort her plan—and she knew there were many. She couldn't have second thoughts about what she was doing, because if she didn't go through with it tonight, she would forever be a helpless pawn in her mother's unending games.

Drawing in a slow, deep breath, she took a step forward as the line of guests advanced. She couldn't help but smile when she caught a glimpse of herself in one of the antique mirrors that lined the halls. She'd worried that her plan would fail, that she would somehow be recognized, but as she curtsied to the prince regent and his wife and neither of them showed so much as a flicker of recognition, her butterflies began to settle.

Really, she had nothing to worry about. With the auburn wig, emerald-colored contacts and elaborate mask covering half of her face, her own mother wouldn't be able to identify her. Not to mention that the gold sandals on her feet added a full four inches to her usually petite five-foot-four-inch frame.

The one-shoulder toga-style gown hugged her breasts, nipped in at her waist and flowed to the floor with a slit halfway up her thigh on one side. It was more suggestive than revealing, but it made her feel sexy and daring—and nothing at all like the demure and conservative Princess Marissa.

She liked sensual fabrics and bright colors, but she didn't often wear them in public. She preferred to blend into the background, unnoticed by the paparazzi that had always shadowed her brother's every move. She'd certainly never worn anything so vibrant and bold, and she knew there was no way she could hide in the background in this outfit. But tonight she didn't want to hide—she wanted to be noticed. She wanted to be wanted.

Tonight, "the prim princess" was finally going to lose her virginity.

Dante Romero hated costume balls. He felt ridiculous enough in the finery he was required to wear for state functions without having to dress up and pretend to be someone else. As if being born a prince hadn't required him to do enough role-playing on a daily basis, he was now trapped in the role of King of Ardena.

It was his birthright and his burden, and one he hadn't expected to assume so early. Unfortunately, his father's health had rapidly deteriorated over the past few years to the point that King Benedicto and his advisers—and especially his doctors—had agreed it would be best for the country if he passed the throne to his son. It was a position Dante had been groomed for throughout his entire life, his inescapable destiny.

Not that he was looking to escape. He acknowledged and understood his responsibilities to his family, his people and his country. But he was barely thirty-two years old and he'd always thought he'd have more time before he had to accept those responsibilities—more time to be free before he gave his people a queen.

But his father had been unrelenting. He hadn't worried too much about his reputation as a playboy prince, but he was the king now and his country needed a queen. He needed a partner to share his life and a mother for his children—the future heirs to the throne.

That was one of the primary reasons he was in Tesoro del Mar now—not just to shake a few hands and smile for some photo ops, but to meet Princess Marissa Leandres, the only daughter of the Princess Royal and a cousin of the prince regent. His father was optimistic that he would find the princess "acceptable enough" to consider issuing a proposal of marriage, which would go a long way toward strengthening the ties between their respective countries.

It was, Dante understood, as good a reason as any for a king to choose a bride. Unlike the childhood song that claimed "first comes love, then comes marriage," Dante knew that it was more likely "first comes coronation, then comes marriage." The official ceremony had taken place only a few weeks earlier, and now the clock was ticking.

And so, at his father's insistence, he'd paid a thousand dollars for a ticket to this masquerade ball to benefit the

Port Augustine Children's Hospital and dressed himself up like Jupiter, just because Benedicto was certain that Princess Marissa would be in attendance and because he had yet to figure out how to refuse anything his ailing father asked of him.

"She's not unattractive," his mother had informed him, although she'd seemed slightly less enthusiastic than her husband about the idea of the Tesorian princess as her son's bride. "Just a little more conservative than the women you usually date, but she is always stylish and well put together."

Unwilling to rely on his mother's description, he'd done some research on his own. Finding pictures of the princess hadn't been very difficult—though she wasn't frequently on the covers of the tabloids, she did make public appearances for noteworthy causes. It seemed that the Port Augustine Children's Hospital was one of her favorites.

He would agree that she wasn't unattractive. In fact, when he studied her face more closely, he realized that she was actually quite beautiful, if not the type of woman who would ordinarily catch his eye. Medium height, average build, dark hair usually tied back in a braid or secured in a knot at the base of her neck. Her eyes were also dark, her smile as unobtrusive as the rest of her.

It shouldn't have been too difficult to pick her out of a crowd, except when the crowd was attired in fancy costumes and elaborate masks. As Dante looked around the ballroom of the royal palace, he realized that he was surrounded by gods and goddesses and various mythological creatures, some that he recognized but many more than he did not. Even the staff were in costume: the waiters as slaves and the security guards as gladiators.

It was as if he'd stepped into another world, and he had to give credit to the decorators for their efforts. The boundary of the dance floor was marked by tall Roman-style columns wrapped in green ivy and twinkling lights. Beyond the dance floor were round tables covered in white linen with laurel wreath centerpieces. Marble pedestals topped with busts of ancient philosophers had been placed around the perimeter of the room.

Some of the guests were in formal attire and carried simple stick masks as a nod to the theme; others had elaborate costumes and face decorations that ensured they remained anonymous. For Dante, the one benefit of being unrecognizable in his costume was that he'd been able to forgo having bodyguards flanking him as he moved through the crowd.

He stepped out of Medusa's path and fought against a smile as she turned to give a blatant once-over to a centaur. He decided that even if he didn't manage to locate Princess Marissa, it wouldn't be a boring night. But he wasn't willing to give up on his mission just yet. He scanned the crowd again, looking for someone who was trying to blend into the background—an observer rather than a participant. The harder he looked, the more convinced he became that his task was futile.

And then he saw her.

The dress was of the richest emerald where it was gathered at one shoulder, with the color gradually transitioning from green to blue until it became a vivid sapphire at her ankles. Her hair spilled down her back, a luxurious cascade of silky red curls. Enormous hammered-gold earrings dangled from her ears and wide bracelets of the same style glinted at both wrists.

Her mask was an elaborate design studded with blue-and-green jewels with a fan of peacock feathers on one side; behind it, her brilliant green eyes sparkled. Her glossy lips were lush and full and curved in a tempting smile. Her skin was pale and dusted with gold. The slope of her shoulders was graceful and sexy.

Lust shot through his veins, as strong and fierce as any bolt of lightning his namesake might have thrown down from the heavens. He forgot about his mission to find the Tesorian princess and made his way across the room to her.

He bowed; she curtsied.

"Juno," he acknowledged with a nod.

Those luscious lips curved. "Jupiter?"

"Isn't it obvious?"

She gave him a slow once-over, her emerald eyes skimming over the gold-trimmed purple toga, gold breastplate, down to the sandals on his feet. "The ruler of the gods is customarily depicted with a beard."

"I'm a man for whom practicality trumps convention," he told her.

"The facial hair was itchy," she guessed.

"And you are a woman who is obviously as smart as she is beautiful."

"I know that Jupiter had a lightning bolt. I didn't know that he had such a glib tongue."

"There's probably a lot about me that you don't know," he told her. "But if you would do me the honor of sharing a dance, we could start to fill in some of the blanks."

"I'd like that," she said.

She placed her hand in his, and he felt the jolt again.

Her gaze flew to his, and he saw the same awareness— the same desire—in her eyes that was coursing through his blood.

He lifted her hand, touched his lips to the back of it.

Her breath caught in her throat and her eyes widened.

He drew her closer, dropped his voice. "Or we could skip the dance."

She shook her head. "A tempting offer, but I want to dance…at least for now."

"And later?" he queried, leading her onto the dance floor.

Her lips curved in a slow, sexy smile that made his heart pound. "We'll figure that out as we go."

He was a good dancer, Marissa noted. He moved easily, naturally, and it felt so good to be held in his arms, close to his body. Her heart was pounding and her blood was humming. For the first time since she'd set her plan in motion, she started to believe that she could go through with it.

If she could be with Jupiter.

That this man had chosen to come to the ball dressed as her mythological mate was nothing more than a coincidence, she knew that. And yet, in her heart, she believed it was a sign that she was doing the right thing.

Or maybe it was just her hormones, because she honestly couldn't ever remember responding to a man as immediately and intensely as she'd responded to this one.

She tipped her head back, smiled when she met his gaze. She'd danced with a lot of men whose eyes had roamed the dance floor, looking for their next partner, their next conquest. But Jupiter seemed interested only in her, and for a woman who was used to standing on the sidelines, being the center of such focused attention was absolutely exhilarating.

Though his face was half-covered by a gold-colored mask, there was no disguising the strength or masculinity of his features. His eyes were as dark as espresso and surrounded by thick lashes, his jaw was strong and square, his lips exquisitely shaped and quick to curve.

"So why Jupiter?" she asked him now.

"Why would I choose the identity of any one god when I could be the ruler of the gods?" he countered.

"Lofty ambitions," she mused.

For just a second, she thought she saw a shadow cross his eyes. But then he smiled, and everything inside of her quivered.

"I would expect the consort of the king to have similarly grand desires," he noted.

She didn't think his use of the word *desires* was either inadvertent or inappropriate. She had very specific plans for this night, and while she didn't think they were particularly grand, she was determined to see them through.

"You don't honestly expect me to confess my grandest desires to a stranger on the dance floor, do you?" she challenged.

"But I'm not a stranger," he pointed out, leading her away from the crowd as the song ended. "I'm your mythological mate."

He plucked two glasses of champagne from the tray of a waiter and passed one to her.

She murmured her thanks and lifted the glass to her lips to soothe her suddenly parched throat. It was easy to flirt with him on the dance floor when they were surrounded by other dancers. But now, even though there were probably five hundred people in the ballroom, she felt as if they were alone. And the nerves tying knots in her stomach were equal parts anticipation and apprehension.

She had barely finished half of her champagne when she was approached by a Minotaur. Ballroom protocol dictated that an invitation not be refused, so she let him lead her back to the dance floor. After the Minotaur, she danced with Apollo, then with a senator. Each time she made her way around the dance floor past the table where she'd left Jupiter, she saw him watching her.

She felt like the belle of the ball and she had a wonderful time dancing and chatting with all of them, more comfortable in her anonymity than she'd ever been as Princess Marissa. But all the while, she was anxious to return to Jupiter.

"I was beginning to feel neglected," he said when she

finally escaped the dance floor and made her way back to him again.

"My apologies," she said sincerely, accepting the fresh glass of champagne he offered.

"No need to apologize," he assured her, leading her away from the crowd and onto the balcony. "It's understandable that every man in attendance would want a turn on the dance floor with the most beautiful woman here."

"There's that glib tongue again," she noted.

He maneuvered her into the shadows. "Do you believe in destiny?"

"I believe we make our own destiny," she said, and reminded herself that this was the destiny she had chosen. To take control of her life and her future.

"And I believe our paths were meant to cross tonight."

She wanted to think that he sounded sincere, but even if it was nothing more than a well-worn line, even if he was just looking for a quick hookup, wasn't that what she wanted, too? Wasn't that what she *needed* to prove that she was capable of controlling her own destiny?

"And now that our paths have crossed," she said, "where do we go from here?"

Dante wasn't entirely sure how to answer her question, except that he knew he wasn't going to walk away from the lovely goddess. Not just yet.

He knew nothing about her and she knew nothing about him, and maybe the anonymity was part of the attraction. He'd been born in a castle and raised from the cradle to understand that he would rule his country one day. It was a birthright that carried with it tremendous responsibility— and relentless public scrutiny. Everything he did was fodder for the tabloids. Every decision he made was documented and analyzed. Every woman he dated was subjected to background checks and media attention.

For the first time in as long as he could remember, he wasn't a royal representative of Ardena. It was as if he'd completely shed that identity when he'd donned the costume of the Roman god. And then he'd spotted his goddess.

He didn't know if he believed in destiny, but he did believe that she'd felt that same instantaneous tug of attraction he'd experienced when their eyes met across the room. And he hoped they would have a chance to explore that attraction.

So he replied to her question with one of his own. "Where do you want to go?"

She tilted her head, studying him with steady green eyes as she considered her response. "Are you married?"

"No." His response was quick, vehement.

Her lips twitched, as if she was trying not to smile. "Engaged?"

"No," he said again. "There's no one."

She continued to hold his gaze as she finished off her champagne. When the glass was empty, he set it aside and took her hands in his, noting the absence of any rings on the third finger of her left hand. "How about you? Boyfriend? Lover?"

She shook her head and her earrings glinted in the moonlight. "Completely unattached," she assured him.

"I'm very glad to hear that," he said, and lowered his head to kiss her.

Her lips were as soft as he'd suspected, and sweetly yielding. And the flavor of her lips buzzed through his veins, more potent than the champagne he'd drunk and more addictive than anything he'd ever tasted.

She neither pulled away nor moved closer, and he sensed a certain amount of both caution and curiosity in her response. He couldn't blame her for being wary—he was a stranger and they were alone in the shadows—but he didn't want her to be afraid. So he held his escalating desire firmly in check and forced himself to move slowly.

He touched his tongue tentatively to the seam of her lips, once, twice. The second time, her lips parted for him. When he dipped inside, she brushed his tongue with her own.

He wanted to pull her into his arms, to hold her tight against his body. He wanted to feel the soft press of her breasts against his chest, to let her feel the hard proof of his desire for her. He knew what he wanted—he wanted *her.* But he sensed that she was still undecided, and he was more than happy to take whatever time was needed to convince her that she wanted him, too.

Thankfully, she seemed willing to be convinced. When he released her hands and inched closer to her, she didn't protest. When he slid his hands from her waist to her breasts, she only sighed and pressed closer to him. It was all the encouragement he needed. The fabric of her costume was almost gossamer thin, and he could clearly feel the pattern of the lace on her bra. Through the lace, he traced circles around the peaks of her nipples, felt them pucker in response to his touch.

She gasped and shuddered, but didn't pull away. He eased his lips from hers and skimmed them along her jaw, down her throat, over the curve of her collarbone. The soft, sexy noises that sounded in her throat made his blood pound and his body ache.

Maybe this was crazy. It was certainly beyond scandalous. Anyone could wander out from the ballroom as easily as they had done, but he didn't care. He experienced a heady sense of freedom that he'd never known before, trusting that even if someone did venture out onto the balcony, they wouldn't catch the king of Ardena in a compromising position. Because he wasn't the king of Ardena right now—he was Jupiter, and making love with Juno seemed like the most natural thing in the world.

He tore his mouth from hers and drew in a deep, shuddering breath to say, "Come upstairs with me."

It was a plea as much as a demand, and there was only one answer Marissa wanted to give. She would follow him to the ends of the earth if he would keep doing what he'd been doing, if he could make those exquisite sensations ricocheting through her body never stop. But even with lust clouding her mind, something in his words gave her pause.

She'd been on the verge of saying "yes." She'd been on the verge of letting him take her right there on the balcony. Because she'd thought he was an anonymous stranger. But he hadn't said *come home with me* or *come back to my hotel.* He'd said *come upstairs with me.* And if he was staying at the palace, he had to have some kind of connection to the prince regent.

She drew back, tried to catch her breath and focus her thoughts. "You have a room…here at the palace?"

He hesitated, as if only now understanding the implications of his words. But then he said, "I'm visiting with a friend who is well acquainted with the minister of foreign affairs. He arranged for our accommodations."

It was a logical explanation and not one that would concern most women. Of course, most other women weren't closely related to the minister of foreign affairs.

She exhaled slowly, reconsidering his invitation. But if the connection to her brother was only through a friend of his, then this…interlude, she decided for lack of a better term, could remain anonymous. Which meant that his revelation didn't require her to abort her plan. At least not yet.

"That seems rather convenient," she said lightly.

He brushed his lips against hers again. "Or maybe it's destiny."

She smiled and splayed her palms on his breastplate. She could feel the ridges of the storm-cloud design beneath her fingertips, but what she wanted to feel was the warmth of his bare flesh. She wanted to explore every inch of him, with her hands and her lips. It was a shockingly bold desire for a woman with zero sexual experience, and a desire that she didn't want to deny any longer.

For the first time in her life, she wanted a man without hesitation. Maybe it was foolish, maybe it was irrefutable proof that she had set upon a desperate course, but it was true. She wanted to be with *this* man. She wanted him to kiss her again, she wanted to feel his lips on hers, his hands on her body, his naked flesh against hers.

She whispered against his lips, "Lead the way."

Chapter Two

As they made their way through the maze of hallways to the third floor of the north wing, Marissa's apprehension increased.

Could she do this? Could she really make love with a stranger? She wanted to—and not just because she was determined to finally lose her virginity, but because she wanted this man as she'd never wanted anyone before. Because he'd made her feel things she'd never felt before.

But what if she got scared? What if she stepped into his room and he pressed her up against the wall and shoved his tongue down her throat and—

She jolted when he took her hand.

Behind the gold mask that covered half of his face, his gaze was hot and intense, but when he spoke, his voice was carefully neutral. "If this isn't what you want—"

"No," she interrupted quickly, shoving aside the unpleasant memory of the Duke of Bellemoro. "It is."

"Good," he said, and slipped his arms around her waist to draw her close. He lowered his head and kissed her again.

He truly was an exceptional kisser, teasing her lips, coaxing her response. As their tongues danced and mated, she felt as if she could be content to continue kissing him forever. But contentment quickly gave way to desire, and desire to need.

"Maybe we should take this inside," he suggested against her lips.

She hadn't even realized they were still in the hall. What was it about this man that he could make her lose all concept of time and place? And not even care that she'd done so?

He kept one arm around her as he slipped the old-fashioned key into the lock and pushed open the door, and he was kissing her again when he steered her inside.

She was too busy enjoying the sensation of his hands on her body to wonder how he'd scored the corner suite that was usually reserved for state visitors of the highest rank. Too preoccupied to appreciate that the thick rug on the floor of the formal sitting room was an antique Savonnerie, or that the mullioned windows were draped with heavy velvet curtains. But she did notice the massive Chippendale four-poster bed with its pale blue silk cover and mountain of pillows when he steered her into the bedroom.

"One moment," he said, and released her long enough to light the trio of candles on the rosewood bedside table.

"I wouldn't have taken you for a romantic," she admitted.

"There are times when romantic gestures are called for." He took her hand again, brought it to his lips. "I would say this is one of them."

"You've already succeeded in luring me to your room," she reminded him.

"So I have." His quick grin was sexy and satisfied as he drew her into his arms again. "And now that I have you here…how about some champagne?"

She blinked. "Champagne?"

"Sure, I could call downstairs and ask them to send up a bottle—or we could get something to eat, if you're hungry."

She shook her head. "I don't want anything but you."

"And here I was trying to show some self-restraint."

"Why?"

"Because if I didn't, we'd already be naked and in the middle of that big bed right now."

"I want to see you naked," she said and reached for the hooks that held his breastplate in place. It was heavier than she'd expected, and it nearly slipped out of her grasp before he took the armor from her and set it aside.

"Same goes." He unfastened the braided gold rope at her waist, let it fall to the floor, then turned his attention to the twisted fabric at her shoulder. As he worked the knot, his fingertips brushed her bare skin and yearning flooded through her.

When the fastening was untied, the silky gown slid down the length of her body to pool at her feet so that she stood before him in only her mask, lacy sapphire bra, matching bikini panties and the gold-colored sandals.

His gaze skimmed over her, from her shoulders to her toes and back again, slowly, hungrily. "You're even more beautiful than I anticipated."

"And you're still mostly dressed," she noted.

He unclipped his leg guards, kicked off his sandals and tugged the tunic over his head. As she watched him strip away the various pieces of his costume, she couldn't help but think that he looked even more like a god without the period enhancements.

His skin was darkly tanned—apparently all over—and stretched taut over glorious muscles. His chest was broad and smooth, and she instinctively reached out to lay her palms against the warm flesh. She felt the sizzle spread through her veins and reverberate low in her belly.

He reached for the tie at the side of her mask, but she turned her head away. Above the top of his, she saw his brows lift.

"I'm more comfortable being Juno," she explained.

His smile was tinged with amusement and desire. "Then you won't mind if I keep mine on, too?"

She suspected it was going to be a little awkward, making love while both of them were wearing masks. But she knew it was the only way she would be able to follow through with her plan. She had no objection to removing all of her clothes so long as her face remained covered, because as much as she wanted to be naked with him, she couldn't risk her identity being exposed.

"No," she responded to his question. "In fact, I'd prefer it."

"Okay," he agreed.

She exhaled slowly as her hands slid downward. Her fingertips traced over the rippling muscles of his abdomen to the top of his fitted briefs, then dipped inside. He groaned when her fingers wrapped around him, and she had a moment of worry when she registered the size and strength of him. He was huge and rock hard, and the thought of his body joining with hers made her shiver with anticipation.

"You're going to obliterate what's left of my self-restraint," he warned her.

She tipped her head back to brush her lips against his. "Good."

He cupped his hands beneath her buttocks and lifted her off the ground in a move that was so quick and unexpected, her breath whooshed out of her lungs. He tumbled her back onto the bed, the full length of his body pressing against hers, and she gasped with shock and pleasure.

Then his mouth was on hers again, hot and hungry. He

wasn't coaxing so much as demanding now, and she was more than happy to give him what he wanted, what they both needed. She ran her hands over his shoulders, down his arms, relishing the feel of his flesh beneath her fingertips. She arched beneath him, eager for more, for everything. He nibbled on her bottom lip, and she sighed again as pleasure drowned out caution and reason and everything else. She had no thoughts of anything but this man and this moment, no need for anything more. And then she had no thoughts at all as her mind gave way to the bliss of sensation.

She was everything Dante had imagined...and more. Beautiful and passionate and so incredibly responsive. And she was his—if only for this one night.

He stroked his hands slowly down her torso, a careful study of delectable feminine curves. From the sexy slope of her shoulders...to the lushness of her breasts...to the indent of her waist...the flare of her hips...then down those long, shapely legs to the laces of her sandals.

He broke the kiss and reluctantly levered himself off of her. Her eyelids flickered, opened, and she propped herself up on her elbows. He touched a fingertip to her lips, to silence any questions or protests. She said nothing, but watched him curiously.

He tugged on the lace that was tied just below her knee, then slowly unwrapped the cord. His fingers traced lightly over her skin as he unwound it, and he heard the catch of her breath. He took his time removing the first sandal, but when he dropped it to the floor, he still held on to her foot. It was narrow and slender and incredibly sexy. He stroked a finger along the arch and felt her shiver. He lifted her foot higher, kissed her ankle, then let his lips skim up her calf to her knee.

He repeated the same process with her other sandal, her other leg. Then he propped her feet on the edge of the mattress so that her knees were bent and lowered his head between her thighs to kiss her through the thin barrier of lace. She gasped, as if shocked by the intimacy of his mouth on her. But she made no protest when he slid his hands beneath her buttocks, tilting her hips forward to remove her panties.

He used his thumbs to part the slick folds that protected her womanly core and flicked his tongue over her. Once. Twice. She sucked in a breath, then let it out in a rush. He teased her mercilessly, alternating quick strokes with slow circles until she was whimpering. Then he teased her some more, relentlessly driving her toward the ultimate pinnacle of pleasure and leisurely easing back again. When he was certain that she could take no more—when her heels were digging into the mattress and her hands were fisted in the covers and her breath was coming in short, shallow gasps—he pushed her over the edge.

She was still shuddering with the aftereffects of her climax as he made his way up her body. He unfastened the clasp at the front of her bra and pushed the lacy cups aside. He paused, taking a moment to enjoy the glorious nakedness of her long, lean body stretched out on his bed.

Her breasts were perfectly shaped and centered with rosy-pink nipples that he ached to touch, taste, savor. He dipped his head and swirled his tongue around one turgid peak, while his thumb traced the same path around the other. She cried out when a second climax racked her body.

She was incredible. And he wanted her more than he'd wanted any woman in a very long time. As he drew away only long enough to shed his briefs and don protection, he thanked the gods that had allowed their paths to cross and cursed the fates that had decreed they would only have this night.

When he lowered himself over her, his whole body was trembling with the anticipation of finally joining with hers.

She reached for him, her hands linking behind his head, drawing him down for another kiss.

His hands stroked over her again, arousing her, arousing himself. He could feel the blood pounding in his veins, hot and demanding. He could hear the beat of his heart, fast and fierce. Did she know how desperately he wanted her? How he ached for her?

Maybe she did, because her eyes—those gorgeous green eyes—met his and her hips lifted, and the silent urging snapped the last of his self-restraint. He guided himself into the slick heat between her thighs. But despite her apparent readiness, his entry wasn't easy. He gritted his teeth and fisted his hands in the quilt, forcing himself to go slow, to give her time to adjust to his size. His muscles ached with the effort of holding back and his heart pounded against his ribs as he inched a little farther, swallowing her soft sighs of acceptance, of pleasure.

He frowned when he felt an unexpected resistance, but before he could begin to comprehend what it might mean, her legs lifted to lock behind his hips, pulling him deeper so that he pushed through the barrier of her innocence.

He held himself completely still over her, his arms locked in position, his brows drawn together behind his mask.

How was this possible? How could he not have known? And what was he supposed to do now?

But she seemed oblivious to his inner turmoil. Her legs were still hooked around his hips and her hands clutched at his shoulders as she instinctively moved against him, until his control finally snapped and there was nothing left to hold him back.

He drove into her, hard and deep. She cried out, but he recognized that the sound wasn't one of shock or fear but pleasure. She met his rhythm, thrust for thrust, in a primitive and almost desperate race toward the release they both craved.

When the next climax took her to the edge and finally over, he could do nothing but surrender with her.

It was a long time before Marissa managed to catch her breath. She felt stunned, overwhelmed and exhilarated. She'd never even imagined that so many emotions and sensations could rocket through her system at the same time.

She'd felt desire before, subtle tugs that had piqued her curiosity and made her wonder. But there had been absolutely nothing subtle about what she'd experienced in Jupiter's arms. It had been so much more than she'd anticipated, so much more than she ever could have hoped for, and she would always be grateful to him for this night.

Unfortunately, she could tell that he wasn't feeling grateful. He was angry, and she was afraid that she knew why.

"You were a virgin," he said.

The accusation in his tone confirmed her fears and took some of the shine off of the experience for her. She shifted away from him, pulling up the corner of the quilt to cover herself.

"And you wanted someone with more experience?" she guessed, her cheeks flushed with embarrassment.

"I wanted to know." He rose from the bed and paced across the carpet, apparently unconcerned by his own nakedness. When he faced her again, his anger was visible despite the mask he still wore. "I had a right to know."

She pushed herself off of the bed, dragging the cover with her. "I'm sorry you were disappointed."

She started to gather up her costume, but it was hard to see through the tears that blurred her eyes. She'd had the most amazing, exhilarating sexual experience of her life, and her partner wished it had never happened.

He crossed the room in three quick strides and caught her arms. "I wasn't disappointed."

She couldn't read his mood. He'd sounded furious, but now he was looking at her with such tenderness in the depths of those beautiful dark eyes. She wished, for just a moment, that she could push the mask off of his face, to really see this man for who he was. But that wasn't just a futile wish, it was a dangerous one. It was the assurance of anonymity that had given her the courage to follow through with her plan. She couldn't let him discover her identity now.

"But you're angry," she said again.

"At myself."

"I don't understand," she admitted.

"I should have realized." Sighing, he thrust a hand through his hair. "If I'd known, I would have been more careful."

"You didn't hurt me."

But Dante knew that he had. Every muscle in her body had tensed when he'd pushed through the barrier of her virginity. He'd been stunned by the knowledge, and appalled that even when his brain had finally registered that she'd been an innocent, he hadn't been able to stop.

He'd wanted her with such desperation that even knowing she'd been untouched hadn't tempered his desire. In fact, discovering that he was her first had somehow stoked the burning need to take, to claim, to possess. One thought had echoed in his mind: *mine.*

Of course, she couldn't be. Not for more than this one night.

It was something they both knew, though neither had spoken aloud of the fact. The anonymity had served his own purposes—he'd thought this night would be one final fling without the heavy cloak of royal responsibilities that had settled around his shoulders. But now he was ashamed, knowing that he'd taken the innocence of a woman and he didn't even know her name.

He brushed his knuckles gently down her cheek. "Actually, if I'd known you were untouched, I would have made sure you stayed that way."

"Why?"

"Because your first time shouldn't have been with a stranger."

"It was what I wanted," she insisted.

"You deserved better. You deserved more. And I can't give you anything more than this night." His words were heavy with genuine regret.

She lifted her chin. "All of this night?"

It was more of a challenge than a question, and he fought against a smile. She had spirit and spunk and a willingness to go after what she wanted, and he felt both honored and humbled that she'd wanted him.

"Did you think I was going to turn you out of my room now that I've had my way with you?" he asked lightly.

"How would I know? This is new territory for me," she reminded him.

He took the gown that she'd twisted into a ball and set it aside. "I would very much like you to stay."

Marissa thought those words meant that he wanted to take her back to bed. Instead, he excused himself and disappeared into the adjoining bathroom. A few minutes later, he was leading her toward a deep tub filled with fragrant bubbles and surrounded by dozens of flickering candles.

"I thought a bath might help ease some of the soreness in your muscles," he told her.

"I won't be sorry to have aches to remind me of this night," she said, and meant it. "But how can I refuse when you went to so much trouble?"

He smiled and brushed a soft kiss over her lips. "Take as much time as you want."

She didn't plan to be long. She didn't want to waste a

single minute of the short time they would have together, but the bath was too tempting to resist. There was a robe on the back of the door, and she used the belt from it to tie the heavy length of hair up off of her neck. She didn't dare take off the wig or her mask. Though she kept a fairly low profile, there was always the possibility that she might be recognized, and that was a chance she couldn't take. Not tonight.

Pushing the worry aside, she stepped into the tub, sighing as she sank into the warm, scented water. She hadn't realized she was tense until she felt the stiffness seep out of her muscles. But while her body relaxed, her mind raced.

She'd lucked out tonight, she realized that. In retrospect, she could appreciate that her plan to go to bed with a stranger had been not just desperate but reckless. And she had absolutely no regrets. Maybe she did wish that she knew something about the man who had been such an attentive and considerate lover, but there was no point in getting to know a man whose presence in her life couldn't be anything more than temporary.

Pushing those thoughts from her mind, she rose from the tub and briskly rubbed a thick towel over her body. Then she released the tie that was holding her hair, tucked it through the loops of the robe she'd wrapped around herself and stepped back into the bedroom.

He'd lit more candles in here, too, she realized, and folded back the covers on the bed. An antique serving cart had been rolled into the room, on top of which sat an assortment of bowls and platters offering fresh fruits and an assortment of crackers and meats and cheeses. There was also a bottle of champagne in a silver bucket filled with ice beside two crystal flutes waiting to be filled.

"I thought we might have that champagne now," he said.

She was as surprised as she was flattered that he'd gone to so much trouble, but the wild pounding of her heart made her wary. Was she a complete sucker for romantic gestures? Or was it somehow possible that she could be falling in love with a man she didn't even know—a man that she wouldn't ever see again after this night?

She wasn't sure she could answer those questions, or that she wanted to, so she responded to his suggestion instead.

"Champagne sounds wonderful." Then she went to him and linked her hands behind his neck, urging his head down so that she could meet his lips with her own. "Later."

Her heart gave another sigh when he lifted her into his arms and carried her to the bed. She had never dreamed that such romance could be found anywhere outside of the pages of a Victorian novel, and knowing that she was unlikely to experience anything like it again, she savored every moment.

She promised herself that she would remember each stroke of his hands, every touch of his lips, and she knew that she would treasure the memories forever. Whatever happened tomorrow, whatever trials and tribulations she might face in the future, she would always have her recollection of this incredible night. No one could ever take that from her.

He lowered her gently onto the mattress and sank down beside her. He'd shown her pleasure already—so much more than she'd expected. But now, with every brush of his fingertips, there was even more. With every caress, he showed her that she wasn't just desired but revered. With every kiss, he proved that she wasn't just wanted but cherished. And when he finally joined his body with hers again, she felt not just connected but complete.

It was hours later before Marissa finally slipped from his bed.

She hadn't intended to stay so long. Truthfully, her plan for the evening had been remarkably sparse on details beyond finding a willing lover. She knew that she'd been fortunate to find one not just willing but eager to please, and she'd been reluctant to leave the warm comfort of his arms. But she did so, anyway, understanding that she had no other choice.

If anyone was to see her leaving his room—well, she didn't even want to imagine what kind of scandal that would cause. Definitely enough of a scandal that Anthony Volpini would have to accept she would never be his virgin bride. That thought made her smile, and for a brief moment she actually considered stomping her feet as she made her way down the hall so that she would be discovered.

But aside from an arranged marriage to the Duke of Bellemoro, there was nothing Marissa dreaded more than the possibility of finding herself at the center of a media circus. So instead of stomping, she carried her sandals in her hand to ensure a quiet escape as she slipped away from Jupiter's room.

Although she'd stayed longer than she'd intended, it was still early enough that Marissa didn't expect to encounter any servants moving through the halls just yet. So she didn't notice the shadow behind the curtains across the hall or hear the barely audible click of the shutter as her clandestine departure was captured by the camera's lens.

She was gone when Dante awoke. The only proof he had that she'd even been there was a lingering trace of her scent on his pillow and a broken peacock feather that he picked up off of the carpet near the bed.

He sat on the edge of the mattress with the feather in his hand and thought about the woman he knew only as Juno. They'd shared intimacies but not names, and while he didn't regret a minute of the time they'd spent together, he did regret that she'd disappeared from his bed and his life without even saying goodbye.

It wasn't impossible to imagine that their paths might

someday cross again, but the possibility did nothing to ease the unexpected emptiness inside of him. Because he knew that, in the unlikely event that they did meet again, he wouldn't recognize her. If he really wanted to ascertain her identity, he could probably finagle a copy of the guest list from one of the palace staff. But then what?

Was he really prepared to track down every female guest until he found a green-eyed redhead with a sexy little mole on her right hip? Of course not, because even if he had the time or the energy for such an endeavor, the discovery of Juno's true identity would change nothing. He'd known when he invited her back to his room that they could never be anything more than strangers in the night.

So why was he wishing for something different now? Why was he fantasizing about an impossible reunion with a woman he didn't even know?

His future was already laid out for him and last night had been only a temporary and forbidden deviation from the path that had been set for him at birth. It was time to set himself back on that path and be the king his country needed.

It was time to meet his bride.

Chapter Three

Marissa slapped a hand on her alarm to silence the incessant buzzing. She wasn't ready to get out of bed. Her reluctance had nothing to do with the fact that she'd crawled between the sheets less than four hours earlier and everything to do with the incredible sensual dreams from which she never wanted to awaken.

Dreams of a mouthwateringly sexy god with fathomless dark eyes behind a gold mask, a strong jaw with just a hint of shadow and a mouth that was both elegantly shaped and infinitely talented. She could almost taste his kiss, dark and potent and thoroughly intoxicating.

She snuggled deeper under the covers, certain she could feel the heat of his skin beneath her palms as she explored the planes and angles of all those glorious muscles. Broad shoulders, strong pecs, rippling abs and a very impressive—

She slapped at the alarm again.

Then, with a sigh that was equal parts resignation and

regret, she hit the off button and eased herself into sitting position.

Pushing back the covers, she swung her legs over the edge of the mattress. She winced a little as she made her way to the bathroom, feeling the tug of strained muscles in her thighs, the ache in her shoulders and an unfamiliar tenderness in her breasts.

Not a dream, after all, she realized, smiling as she turned on the shower and stripped away the silk boxers and cami that she slept in. Memories of the previous night played through her mind as she stepped beneath the spray.

A fantasy come true, but definitely not a dream.

As she'd donned her costume in preparation of the ball the previous evening, she'd worried that she might regret embarking on her course of action, but she'd been more worried about what her future might hold if she chose a course of inaction.

She'd taken control of her life and her future—as much as she could, anyway. Because according to the outdated but still valid laws of the principality, Marissa *could* be forced to marry the duke, but at least she wouldn't go to his bed a virgin on her wedding night.

She'd evaluated her options and she'd made a choice, and she didn't regret it now. How could she regret what had been the most incredible experience of her entire life?

If she felt any disappointment, it was only because she might never again know the kind of pleasure Jupiter had given to her. He'd been an incredibly attentive lover. He'd not just touched but tantalized every inch of her body with his hands and his lips and his tongue—

She turned her face into the spray and nudged the temperature dial downward to help cool her heated skin and resolved to stop fantasizing about what was past.

After she'd stepped out of the shower and toweled off, she

opened her closet in search of an appropriate outfit for brunch with her mother. In the midst of various shades of ivory and cream and beige, the stunningly vibrant dress she'd worn the night before shone like a beacon. Instinctively her hand reached out, her fingers caressing the shimmery fabric, and she made a mental note to send a heartfelt thank-you card to her dressmaker.

Then she purposely moved Juno's dress to the back of the closet because she was no longer a Roman goddess. She was just an ordinary princess again and she had to look the part for her meeting with the Princess Royal.

She selected a simple beige-and-white sheath-style dress, slipped her feet into a pair of matching kitten heels, then brushed her hair away from her face and secured it in a knot at the back of her head. She added simple gold hoop earrings and a couple of gold bangles on her wrist and decided the overall look was stylish if rather bland—and perfectly suited to Princess Marissa.

You're even more beautiful than I anticipated.

The echo of Jupiter's reverent whisper made her heart sigh. He'd made her feel beautiful. Desirable. *Desired.* But there was no hint of that woman in the reflection that looked back at her now.

She turned away from the mirror, refusing to admit that she longed to feel that way again. She knew that she could be beautiful. Elena had been—and still was—a stunning woman, and many people had remarked upon the similarities between mother and daughter. But while the Princess Royal always took care to highlight her best features, Marissa chose to downplay her own. Beautiful women did not go unnoticed, and she preferred the freedom to live her life as she chose rather than under a microscope.

Of course, she was a princess, so a certain amount of media attention was unavoidable. She even courted that attention when it served her purposes. But most of the time, she was happy to let the paparazzi chase after those who were much more bold and beautiful.

A knock at the door jolted her out of her reverie. She set down the cup of coffee she'd just poured and went to answer the summons.

There were few people who could gain access to the private elevator leading to her tenth-floor condo, so she wasn't surprised to open the door and find both of her sisters-in-law on the other side. She was disappointed that they didn't have her nieces with them, as she absolutely doted on Michael's five-year-old Riley and Cameron's eleven-month-old Jaedyn.

"What are you doing here?" she asked, because she knew they didn't have any plans to get together this morning.

Michael's wife, Hannah, was the first to respond. "We were worried about you."

Marissa led the way to the kitchen, where she filled another mug with coffee and a third with only milk. "Why would you be worried?"

"Because you had a migraine severe enough to keep you at home last night. It's not like you to miss an event benefiting the Children's Hospital," Gabriella—Cameron's very expectant wife—explained, accepting the milk with more resignation than enthusiasm.

She'd forgotten the excuse she'd made to both of them to explain her supposed absence from the event the night before. Though she didn't lie easily or well, the fib had been necessary to ensure that they weren't looking for her in the crowd.

Hannah stirred a spoonful of sugar into her coffee. "I called last night to see if you needed anything, but when there was no answer, I figured you turned off the ringer because of the headache."

Gabby's gaze narrowed suspiciously. "But when Hannah

told me that she'd called and didn't get an answer, I began to suspect that maybe you didn't miss the ball at all."

She sipped her coffee. "You're right. I was there," Marissa admitted. "But I left early."

"With the sexy guy in the purple toga?"

Marissa didn't bother to deny it. She'd already proven that she couldn't lie to them—at least not very well—and she didn't want to, anyway. They weren't just her sisters-in-law, they were her best friends, and she desperately needed friends to confide in right now.

"With Jupiter," she confirmed.

Gabby grinned. "Good for you."

Hannah's head swiveled toward her. "Are you kidding? It's not good—it's crazy."

"Was it good?" Gabby asked, not the least bit chastened by Hannah's outrage.

Marissa couldn't help but smile. "It was…fabulous."

"Details," Gabby immediately demanded.

Hannah only sighed.

"I'm sorry if you're disappointed in me," Marissa said to Michael's wife, and meant it.

"I'm not disappointed in you, just surprised," Hannah told her. "I've never known you to be reckless or impulsive, and leaving the ball with a stranger—"

"Was necessary," she interjected.

Even Gabriella seemed surprised by that revelation. "Why?"

Marissa lifted her chin. "Because I'd decided it was finally time to lose my virginity."

Her brothers' wives exchanged another look. Obviously neither of them had been aware of her lack of sexual experience, and why would they be?

"Okay, back up a minute and put this in context for us," Hannah suggested. "Why, having made it to this point in your life without losing your virginity, was it suddenly so urgent to do so?"

"Because there are rumors floating around that the Duke of Bellemoro is in the market for his second wife and, based on several appointments that he's had with the Princess Royal over the past few weeks, I figured out that Elena was preparing to offer me as a virgin sacrifice."

"There aren't a lot of suitable marriage prospects for a bona fide princess," Hannah noted. "So I can see why your mother might consider a match with someone holding such a high hereditary title to be a coup."

"But the Duke of Bellemoro?" Gabby winced sympathetically. She, too, had obviously heard the rumors of the duke's sexual proclivities. And despite his appreciation for women with a multitude of experience in his bedroom, he'd let it be known that he was seeking a more innocent type for his bride.

"Which is why I decided that I wasn't going to be manipulated," Marissa said firmly. "Not anymore."

"So don't be," Gabby said. "It's not as if Elena can force you to marry against your will."

"Actually, she can," Hannah interjected, sounding almost apologetic. "Archaic as it may be, the laws of this country still allow the parents of a princess to enter into a legal contract of marriage on her behalf."

"But not the parents of a prince?" Gabriella was as incensed by the inequality of its application as the law itself.

"I said it was archaic," Hannah reminded her.

"It's an old and acceptable tradition," Marissa said. "And my mother knows that I would honor such a contract because it's my duty as a member of the royal family to respect our history and uphold our customs."

"Because you'd never do anything that might create a scandal," Gabby noted.

"Losing your virginity to a stranger seems pretty scandalous to me," Hannah said.

"If the Princess Royal's daughter lost her virginity to a stranger, it would be scandalous," Marissa acknowledged, which was why she'd been so worried about the possibility that someone might recognize her. And during one turn around the dance floor, she'd spotted her sisters-in-law on the perimeter and had felt the weight of Gabriella's gaze on her. But her brother's wife had shown no hint of recognition, which reassured Marissa that her true identity would not be discovered. "Which is why I made sure that no one would know that I was Juno."

"Gabby recognized you," Hannah pointed out.

"I suspected," she clarified. "And I should say now that you looked absolutely stunning."

Before Marissa could respond, Hannah forged ahead again.

"It was still a crazy idea. No, not just crazy but dangerous," she said. "Do you have any idea how many things could have gone wrong?"

"Nothing went wrong," Marissa told her.

"Nothing except that you slept with a man you don't even know," Hannah countered.

"Actually, I didn't sleep at all until I got home around three this morning."

Gabby grinned. "You're actually bragging."

Marissa lifted her chin. Maybe she was bragging, and she wasn't going to apologize for it. If a wedding to the Duke of Bellemoro was in her future, at least she would have the memories of one fabulous night to help get her through it.

Hannah looked at her, the furrow in her brow easing. "It really was good?"

"It really was fabulous," she said again.

"Well, I guess that's something," she relented. "But you should have at least asked his name."

"I couldn't," Marissa said. "Because I had no intention of telling him mine. I wanted to be anonymous so that, for the first time in my life, I could feel confident that a man was interested in me and not my title or political connections."

"Still, I would think you'd at least be curious about his true identity," Gabriella mused.

"Of course I am. But the whole point of putting my plan into action last night was to ensure that no one would know who I was—it would hardly be fair if I changed the rules now."

"It would be easy enough to track him down," Hannah told her. "All you'd have to do is contact the palace's master of the household and find out who was staying in…whatever room he was staying in."

"It was the corner suite," Marissa answered automatically, "but I'm not going to do it."

"Why not?" Gabby demanded, clearly disappointed.

"Because he obviously had his own reasons for wanting to remain anonymous."

"Which only makes me more curious."

"Maybe he's married," Hannah suggested.

"He's not," Marissa assured her. "I did ask about that."

"Glad to know you did exercise some moral judgment before you gave your virginity to a stranger," Hannah noted, tongue-in-cheek.

"Thank you," Marissa said. "Now, if you two are finished with your interrogation, I'm going to kick you out so that I can stop at the hospital before I have to meet my mother and potential suitor for brunch."

Gabriella paused in the act of pushing back her chair. "Why did you say 'potential suitor'?"

"Just repeating Elena's words," Marissa explained. "You know my mother thrives on mystery and drama."

"So she never actually said it was the Duke of Bellemoro?" Hannah asked.

"No," she admitted, still not following the direction of their parallel thinking.

"What if it's not the duke?" Gabby pressed.

Marissa dismissed the possibility with a shake of her head. "Who else could it be?"

Dante had first met the Princess Royal about half a dozen years earlier when he'd accompanied his father on an official visit to Tesoro del Mar. His initial impression had been of a woman whose beauty was surpassed only by her ambition— an impression that was confirmed when, a few weeks after he'd taken the throne, she contacted him with a proposal to strengthen the bond between their respective countries.

At the time, he'd had more pressing issues to contend with, and she'd graciously agreed to defer the matter to another time. But when the invitation to the Mythos Ball arrived in the mail, he'd accepted that this meeting was one that could be put off no longer.

Since assuming his new role, Dante had been the recipient of more marriage proposals than he wanted to count. The majority of them were personal entreaties sent by hopeful future queens, though some were sent on behalf of the potential brides-to-be by a mother or sister or grandmother. Dante had delegated the task of responding to these offers to the palace's junior secretaries.

Elena's letter had been the exception. He was all too aware that Ardena's relationship with Tesoro del Mar—her closest neighbor, naval ally and trading partner—had become strained in recent years. Just as he was aware that it was his responsibility to do whatever he could to rectify the situation.

A marriage between Ardena's king and a Tesorian princess would go a long way toward doing that.

When he arrived at Elena's estate, Dante was prepared for the Princess Royal to do or say almost anything to convince him that he should marry her daughter, and he was willing to let himself be convinced. As his father had pointed out to him, there weren't a lot of single women of appropriate genealogy—and even fewer still with whom he didn't already have some kind of history.

"Your Majesty." The Princess Royal curtsied. "I'm so pleased you were able to take this time to meet with me while you're visiting Tesoro del Mar."

He bowed to her in turn. "The pleasure is mine, Your Highness."

"I trust you had a good time at the ball last evening," she said when they were seated in the parlor.

"I did," he agreed, though the remark caused his mind to flash back not to the charity event but to the pleasures he'd enjoyed after leaving the ballroom.

"Marissa will be pleased to hear it." Elena passed him a delicate gold-rimmed cup. "Unfortunately, she wasn't able to be there last night, but she tries to ensure that the annual ball isn't just successful but also enjoyable."

"I've heard that she's very committed to her work at the hospital." He sipped his coffee.

"She has experience with numerous charitable endeavors—an essential attribute for the wife of a king."

Dante had always found it easier to negotiate with people who were forthright about their demands rather than those who tiptoed around them. It was clear that the Princess Royal didn't believe in tiptoeing.

"I don't disagree," he told her. "But there are many other factors to consider."

"You won't find another candidate more suitable than Princess Marissa," Elena promised. "She has lived her whole life with the demands and duties of royal life, she is educated, well mannered, kindhearted and still innocent."

Definitely no tiptoeing going on here.

Dante set down his cup and cleared his throat. "I do think that the criteria for suitability have changed somewhat with the times."

"But your country's Marriage Act still enumerates some very specific criteria," Elena pointed out. "Including that the bride of a king must be of noble birth and pure virtue."

Technically, she was correct. But since a king was entitled to privacy on his wedding night, he wasn't concerned about the latter stipulation. "I'm not sure that's a realistic expectation in this day and age," he acknowledged, refusing to think about his mysterious virgin lover of the previous evening. "I'm more concerned that my future bride is untouched by scandal."

"I assure you that my daughter is untouched in every way that matters."

He forced a smile, though the calculation in her eyes made him uneasy. It was obvious that the Princess Royal wanted a union between their families and would do everything in her power to make it happen, and he couldn't help but feel a tug of sympathy for the princess whose mother so clearly viewed her as a commodity to be bartered.

"You don't think she would be reluctant to leave her friends and family here to live in another country?"

"Ardena is not so far," Elena said dismissively. "And a marriage between its king and a Tesorian princess would only strengthen the historically close ties between our two countries. It might even help our people forget the unnecessary stir created by your father on his last visit."

"Whether the stir was or was not necessary is a matter of perspective," Dante retorted, not even attempting to disguise the edge in his tone. "And he had reason to be concerned about your son's relationship with my sister."

"Well, that's past history, anyway," she said, conveniently forgetting that she'd been the one to bring up the subject. "What matters now is the future."

"Agreed," he said, only because he knew that the relationship between Prince Cameron and Princess Leticia alleged in the newspaper headlines had been predicated on nothing more than one dance in a nightclub.

Of course, the relationship Elena was advocating for her daughter would be based on even less, and Dante couldn't help wondering if the princess in question might not want more than a marriage founded solely on politics. And he was both baffled and infuriated that her mother didn't seem to want more for her.

Or maybe he was angry that he wasn't allowed to want more for himself. His parents' marriage had been "suggested" rather than arranged, and they'd been lucky enough to fall in love so that they wanted to honor the wishes of their respective families. When Dante had protested that he should be given the opportunity to find love, too, his parents had bluntly pointed out that he'd managed to find enough lovers without worrying about emotional attachments, and now it was time for him to accept that he had a responsibility to his country and its people. And that responsibility took precedence over all else.

"How does Princess Marissa feel about a potential wedding to the king of Ardena?"

"You don't need to worry about her feelings," she assured him. "She understands very well that duty must come before desire."

"You seem certain of that," he noted.

"Marissa understands the demands and responsibilities of

your position. She will stand by your side when you need her there and remain in the background when you don't."

He wasn't sure he wanted a wife who would be so docile and unassuming. He'd always admired women who had their own thoughts and ambitions, who challenged him to consider different ideas and perspectives, who were intelligent and strong and passionate. He wanted passion.

He wanted Juno.

He pushed the haunting memories of the previous night from his mind. He'd acted impulsively and recklessly, and he knew it couldn't ever happen again. He was the king of Ardena now, and he needed to find a wife.

He, too, knew that duty must come before desire, and he accepted that there could be no more stolen moments with sexy strangers. So he directed his attention back to his hostess.

"When can I meet your daughter?" he asked.

The Princess Royal's smile was smug. "She will join us for brunch."

Chapter Four

When her mother scheduled brunch for one o'clock, Marissa knew that the meal would be on the table at one o'clock—the Princess Royal was absolutely unyielding when it came to maintaining her schedule. Marissa also knew that Elena would not be pleased by her daughter's arrival at 1:08.

It wouldn't matter that she had called as she was leaving the hospital to advise that she was running late. The Princess Royal was as intolerant of excuses as she was of tardiness.

Marissa realized her lateness wouldn't score any points with the duke, either, but she was less concerned about him. Or maybe she was hoping that Anthony Volpini would be so annoyed by her delay that he would abandon all thoughts of marrying her. Buoyed by this thought, she practically skipped up the steps to her mother's front door.

Edmond, her mother's butler, had obviously been watching for her, because he opened the door before Marissa even had a chance to ring the bell.

"The Princess Royal and the king are in the dining room."

She started to nod, accepting that her mother wouldn't wait even eight minutes for an expected guest, then froze when the import of his words registered. "The king?"

"His Majesty, Dante Romero, King of Ardena," Edmond announced formally.

"But I thought…"

It didn't matter what she'd thought. Certainly her mother's butler wasn't interested in hearing about her mistaken assumptions. Marissa drew in a deep breath as she tried to consider the implications of this revelation, but she could only think, *I'm going to meet the king of Ardena*—a thought that made her heart beat hard and fast.

With excitement? Or apprehension? She honestly didn't know because she didn't know a lot about him. Although Dante Romero had been a favorite subject of many tabloids for a lot of years, Marissa had never paid much attention to those reports. But when he'd assumed the throne in February—after health issues forced his father to step down—it had become all but impossible to open up a newspaper or turn on a television and not see a photo or a video clip. And she had to admit, it was never a hardship to look at his picture.

But while the tabloids had loved him because the escapades of a playboy prince always generated good headlines, the legitimate press had been much more critical. Especially since he'd transitioned from "the Crown Prince of Ardena" to "His Majesty the King." They criticized his experience, challenged his knowledge of laws and customs, and questioned his ability to relate to his subjects. But he'd apparently put in a lot of long hours and made a concerted effort to alleviate the concerns of his detractors, and if he'd made a few mistakes along the way, Marissa thought those mistakes only proved that even a king was human.

That thought helped steady her erratically beating heart.

Still, she wished her mother had given her some warning. But the Princess Royal always liked to have the upper hand, and she obviously had it now since she'd somehow convinced the king to come to Tesoro del Mar to meet her daughter.

Elena had commented often enough that a princess's options for a good marriage were limited, and Marissa didn't doubt that she would have happily given her consent to any noble who requested her daughter's hand. But if Marissa somehow managed to snag the interest of a king...

Unfortunately, she knew that the king wasn't really interested in her. How could he be when he'd never even met her? Besides, she wasn't a cover model or a famous opera singer or a Hollywood starlet—and yes, the king had dated each of those and a lot more famous and beautiful women—but she *was* of noble birth. No, the reason for the king's presence in Tesoro del Mar had nothing to do with her personally and everything to do with politics.

"Are you all right, Your Highness?"

"Actually, I'm famished," she responded to the butler's question.

He smiled. "Cook has kept your plate warm. I'll make sure it's brought in right away."

"Thank you, Edmond." Marissa smiled back, then hurried to the dining room, now twelve minutes late.

Dante recognized her the moment she walked through the door.

Although they'd never met, she looked just like she did in the photos he'd uncovered—and very much a princess.

She wasn't the type of woman who would ordinarily attract his attention, even in a crowd of one, but he reminded himself that he wasn't just looking for a wife for himself but a queen for his country. And there was no doubt that Princess Marissa had all the grace and poise required of a woman in that position. She also had excellent bone structure, flawless skin and long, dark hair that he thought might be more flattering if it was left loose to frame her face rather than scraped back into a tight knot at the base of her neck.

And though he would never claim to be an expert on fashion, he felt her wardrobe could use some work, too. In every picture he'd seen of her, she was wearing some shade of beige. The dress she was wearing today was no different. It was stylish enough, he imagined, but the boxy cut gave no hint of any feminine curves and the beige-and-white combination was beyond bland, making him wonder if she had some kind of moral objection to color.

He tucked away the thought and pushed back his chair when she stepped into the room. The movement caught her attention, and her gaze shifted in his direction.

Their eyes locked, and Dante was surprised to realize that her eyes weren't brown, as he'd believed, but the color of amber, fringed by long, dark lashes.

The second surprise was the tightening in his gut, raw and purely sexual, and an inexplicable sense of recognition.

"Your Majesty," she said, dipping into an elegant curtsy. "I apologize if I've kept you waiting."

He bowed. "No apology is necessary," he assured her, though the disapproval in Elena's gaze warned that she did not agree. "I'm just pleased that you are able to join us."

The princess lowered herself into the chair that the butler held for her. As soon as she was seated, a server appeared with her plate.

"The king was telling me about the sights he'd like to see while he's in Tesoro del Mar," Elena said to her daughter.

Her intention might have been to simply make the princess aware of the topic of conversation, but the subtle edge in her voice gave Dante the impression that Elena was making a point about her daughter's tardiness rather than the current discussion.

Marissa's only response was to ask him, "Are you here on vacation, Your Majesty?"

"This trip is a combination of business and pleasure," he told her. "Although I'm hoping it will be less of the former and more of the latter."

"And are you enjoying yourself so far?" She picked up her knife and fork and sliced off the end of a crepe.

"Always," he assured her. "It is a beautiful country—in many ways so much like my own, and in many ways different."

"I've never been to Ardena," the princess admitted.

"Then you should definitely visit," he said. "And when you do, I'd be honored to have you stay at the palace as my guest."

"That sounds like a marvelous idea," the Princess Royal declared.

Marissa's smile was much more tentative than her mother's response.

"In the meantime," Dante continued, "I was hoping you might have some time tomorrow afternoon to attend the hot-air-balloon festival at Falcon Ridge with me."

"I appreciate the invitation," the princess said graciously, "but I have plans with my niece tomorrow."

Elena's eyes were frigid when she looked across the table at her daughter. "King Dante has invited you to spend the day with him," she admonished.

Marissa met her mother's gaze evenly, suggesting to Dante that she might not be as docile and dutiful as the Princess Royal had implied—a possibility that intrigued him.

He'd never felt the need to surround himself with people who would agree with his every word and deed, and he'd never enjoyed being with a woman who couldn't express her own thoughts and feelings. He was pleased by this evidence that the Princess Royal's daughter would not be one of them.

"And I have a previous commitment," Marissa pointed out to her mother.

"Which I wouldn't expect you to break," he assured her. "But maybe your niece would enjoy attending the festival with us."

Marissa's attention shifted back to him, revealing both surprise and suspicion. But when she spoke, her voice was carefully neutral. "That sounds like fun—if you're sure you wouldn't mind spending the afternoon with a five-year-old."

"I'm sure it will be my pleasure," he countered.

Apparently satisfied with the progress that had been made, the Princess Royal monopolized the rest of the conversation as they finished brunch. Marissa managed to eat a few bites of crepe and a couple of pieces of fruit, but her stomach was too tied up in knots to attempt any more than that. She didn't doubt for a minute that her mother had been the one to set up this meeting with the sole purpose of putting Marissa on display in front of the king, but the fact that he was here, having brunch in Elena's dining room, proved that he was at least considering the potential benefits of a union between their families.

And while the possibility of marrying the king of Ardena didn't fill her with the same kind of panic she'd experienced at the thought of spending the rest of her life with the Duke of Bellemoro, it didn't fill her with joy, either. Because whether she was compelled to marry the duke or the king or anyone else, it was the obligation aspect that made her uneasy. She wanted to fall in love and get married for all the right reasons, but she was a princess, and she understood her duty.

She was relieved when her mother stood up, signaling an end to the brunch. The king graciously thanked Elena for "the exquisite meal and delightful company" and formally bowed over her hand as an indication that he was taking his leave. He then turned to Marissa and bowed again as he raised her hand to brush his lips to the back of it.

Marissa held herself still, refusing to give any outward indication of the shocks and jolts that ricocheted through her body. She recognized the kiss for what it was—nothing more than an habitual gesture. She'd had her hand kissed before and the king had, no doubt, kissed countless women's hands in a similar fashion. There was certainly nothing provocative or even flirtatious about the gesture, and yet the brief touch of his mouth on her skin made her feel all hot and tingly.

She'd had the same kind of visceral reaction only once before, and that had been as recently as last night. The realization made her uneasy. Was it possible that having sex once—well, actually, three times over the course of one night—could turn her into a wanton? She was ashamed to think it might be true, but what other explanation could there be for her immediate physical response to a man she didn't even know?

Or maybe she was just shallow enough to be turned on by a handsome face. Because there was no denying that Dante Romero was far more handsome than any other man she'd ever met, and even more than she'd expected. He had a strong jaw, bedroom eyes and a sexy mouth—any one of those features alone would have snagged a woman's attention, but put them all together and the effect was irresistible.

As if the gods hadn't blessed him enough with that face, they'd also given him more than six feet in height and filled all of those inches with long, lean muscles. He was, without a doubt, the complete package—and judging from the glint in those dark eyes, the hint of a smile that played at the corners of those sexy lips, and too many headlines to count, he knew it.

"I'm already looking forward to tomorrow," he told her.

And since he knew it, she didn't see any need to cater to his undoubtedly oversize ego. She ensured that her response was polite but cool, giving no hint of the heat that was running through her veins. "As am I, Your Majesty."

Elena waited until the king had exited the room before facing her. "What was that about?" she demanded.

For a minute, Marissa thought the Princess Royal had somehow been privy to the lustful desires pulsing in her blood. But when her mother spoke again, Marissa realized that she hadn't picked up on any undercurrents between her daughter and the king.

"I went to great lengths to bring the king here to meet you—the least you could have done was show some genuine interest and appreciation."

"If you wanted me to be gracious and charming, you might have given me some warning," Marissa told her.

"I didn't want to get your hopes up, in case the arrangements for his trip fell through."

"That was thoughtful," Marissa said, "but unnecessary, because I don't have any hopes."

"Don't you even think about sabotaging this," Elena warned in an icy tone.

"Why would I? If you don't manage to finalize an agreement with the king, I'll just become a pawn in your negotiations with someone else."

"You should be flattered that the king of Ardena is interested."

"And I would be, if his interest was based on anything more than strengthening ties between two countries."

"Dante Romero is one of the most sought-after bachelors in the world."

"Who probably has a mistress in every major city around the globe," Marissa noted.

Elena shrugged as if the possibility was of no concern. "But he'll only have one wife, and that wife could be you."

"I've agreed to go to Falcon Ridge with him tomorrow and I will, but you're deluding yourself if you think that there will be a proposal at the end of the day," she warned her mother. "The king of Ardena has dated some of the most famous women in the world—models and movie stars and musicians. They're not just beautiful and glamorous, but savvy and sophisticated. Women who can not only handle living in the spotlight, but seek it out. Women who are absolutely nothing like me."

"Those are the women he dated," her mother agreed. "And not a single one of them would make an appropriate queen. You, on the other hand, are exactly what the king is looking for in a bride."

"He told you what he's looking for?"

"The requirements of a royal bride in Ardena aren't a matter of choice but of custom—and your blood is blue and your virtue unquestionable."

Marissa didn't dare correct her misconception. Instead, she only said, "It's still possible that the king might decide we're simply not compatible."

"That's his decision to make, of course." Elena narrowed her gaze. "But I trust you will do everything you can to help him see that you are."

"Why does this matter so much to you? Why do you care who I marry or even if I do?"

"I care because you're my daughter, and because it would be nice if at least one of my children exceeded my expectations."

Finally, Marissa got it. The Princess Royal had once envisioned grand futures for each of her sons. After Prince Julian was killed and his brother, Rowan, had taken the throne, Elena had attempted to undermine the prince regent and install Cameron in the palace. She'd been bitterly disappointed when her efforts failed. She'd been even more frustrated with Michael, because her oldest son had never shown any interest in following any path but his own. But all she'd ever expected of her daughter was that Marissa would marry well—as Elena's own father had expected of her.

Of course, the Princess Royal had defied her father by running off to marry a farmer. Unfortunately, Marissa had no similar prospects. And, in any event, she figured giving her virginity away to a stranger was probably enough defiance for one week. Besides, she didn't think there was any real danger of Ardena's new king actually wanting to marry her, and if keeping him company while he was in Tesoro del Mar kept her mother off of her back, it was a price she was willing to pay.

"I'll do my best to ensure the king has a wonderful time tomorrow," she promised.

"It would be better if you could spend the day alone with him. The presence of a child is hardly conducive to romance."

The "child" in question being Elena's granddaughter and the firstborn child of Marissa's brother Michael. And while there were many responses that sprang to mind, she reminded herself of the dangers of antagonizing her mother and only said, "The king didn't seem to have any objections to including Riley."

"That doesn't make it okay."

"If he wants to see me again after tomorrow, I'll make sure that I'm available," she said, trusting the offer would placate her mother.

"Where are you going now?" Elena demanded as Marissa started for the door.

"Back to the hospital."

"Weren't you already there today? Isn't that why you kept us waiting?"

"Yes," she admitted, though she could have pointed out that no one had, in fact, waited for her. "And I'm truly sorry that I was late but Devon was in respiratory distress and I couldn't leave until I knew that his condition was stabilized."

Of course, her mother didn't know who Devon was, nor did she care enough to ask. She'd never understood Marissa's commitment to Juno's Touch and the babies who passed through its doors.

Her colleagues at the hospital liked to tease that Juno's Touch was Marissa's baby, and in many ways that was true. She'd nurtured the idea from start to finish—an endeavor that had taken a lot more than the nine months of most babies. But it had been, and continued to be, a labor of love.

Of course, she wanted real babies someday. She wanted to experience the awe of growing a child in her womb, the satisfaction of nourishing a baby from her own breast, the completion of knowing she had someone to love forever. But until that time came, she had Juno's Touch, and she happily gave it her heart and soul.

"I'm not sure your continued involvement at the hospital is wise. You get far too attached to babies that aren't even yours," Elena admonished.

Unlike the Princess Royal, who hadn't even tried to form an attachment with her own three children, Marissa thought, though she didn't dare speak the words aloud.

"I can't spend all of my time at spa appointments and social events," she said lightly.

"Speaking of which, you might take some time to have your hair styled and get your nails done before tomorrow."

Marissa touched her lips to her mother's cheek. "I'll see if I can fit that in," she lied and made her escape.

Dante didn't have any specific plans when he left the Princess Royal's house. He only knew that he wasn't ready to go back to the palace and the suite of rooms that haunted him with memories of the hours he'd spent making love with the mysterious Juno the night before. So he instructed the chauffeur to take a drive along the waterfront, and he let his mind wander as he enjoyed the view out of his window.

Tesoro del Mar really was a beautiful country, but as much as he always enjoyed visiting, he always looked forward to going home. This time, he was less eager. Even though he wasn't scheduled to return to Ardena until the end of the following week, he knew that his parents would expect he would be ready to announce that he'd chosen a bride by then. And Dante's reluctance to settle down was exceeded only by his determination not to disappoint them again.

Thinking of home now, he reached inside the pocket of his jacket for his cell phone. Hearing his mother's voice on the other end of the line brought an immediate smile to his lips.

They spoke briefly for a few minutes before he ventured to ask, "How's Dad?"

"Well enough to be in the pool flirting with another woman."

The lightness of her tone eased some of his worry. "How is the physiotherapy going?"

"I thought he should be coming to the end of his treatment schedule, but Rita assures me that he's continuing to make progress. Personally, I think she enjoys the flirting as much as your father does."

"Whatever works," Dante said, echoing the doctor who had forced the king to face some hard truths about his future if he didn't take immediate action to improve his health.

It was the same doctor's advice that had finally convinced Benedicto to step down from the throne. Since then, the former king's blood pressure had leveled out, decreasing the likelihood of any more strokes and increasing the doctor's optimism for his recovery.

"How was the ball?" his mother asked now. "Did you meet Princess Marissa?"

"Good and yes," he responded to her questions in turn.

"And?" she prompted.

"We have a date tomorrow."

"I knew she wouldn't be able to resist you," Arianna said.

"I'm not sure that's the case at all," he confided. "Her mother seems more interested in a potential union than the princess herself."

"I can't say that surprises me," she admitted.

"You know the Princess Royal?"

"Our paths have crossed on a few occasions over the years."

"Why do I get the feeling there's something you're not telling me?"

"There's lots of things I don't tell you," she said without apology. "Because you have more important things to worry about. Including the fact that Dr. Geffen gave the board her resignation today."

Dante swore under his breath.

"She's not the only one we're going to lose if we don't get the hospital redevelopment plan back on schedule," Arianna warned.

"Tell me what I can do to help."

"The fundraising committee has some great ideas for drawing people and money to the auction." There was a momentary pause before she continued. "It was suggested that Princess Marissa's endorsement—and ideally her attendance—would succeed in focusing more attention on the cause."

Because Princess Marissa was famous not just for being royal but for her dedication to ensuring access to quality medical care for all children.

"Then make sure they know that Princess Marissa will be there."

There was another pause as his mother absorbed this information. Then she said, "Don't you think you should talk to Marissa about that first?"

A sign on the edge of the road caught his attention. Beside the familiar blue *H* were the words Port Augustine Children's Hospital.

"I'm on it," Dante promised her and disconnected the call.

Dante didn't actually expect the princess would be at the hospital on a Saturday afternoon, but he thought that if he could find a young female nurse or orderly on a break, he might be able to charm her into giving him a cursory tour of the facility. Except that instead of heading directly to the cafeteria, he followed the signs to the pediatric intensive-care unit first.

Siobhan Breslin had been airlifted from Mercy Medical Center in Ardena to PACH for surgery to repair an atrial septal defect. He'd been informed that the operation was a success, but since Dante was at the hospital, anyway, he thought he would check her status himself.

He found the neonatal intensive care but wasn't sure where to go from there. He thought about asking a nurse to direct him, but recognized that doing so could lead to questions he wasn't prepared to answer. When he caught a glimpse of Fiona, the baby's mom, he decided that Siobhan's condition was being monitored by enough people without his interference.

Making his way down another corridor, he found himself in front of a nursery. The words Juno's Touch were etched in the glass.

His mind automatically shifted from babies to red-haired, green-eyed goddesses and wondered at the irony of fate that the harder he tried to put the mysterious woman out of his mind, the more impossible it seemed. He didn't even know her real name—he didn't know anything about her. It was supposed to have been an interlude, one night in which he forgot about the obligations and responsibilities inherent to his title. One night to make love with a woman who made no demands and had no expectations of him.

His meeting with the Princess Royal and the recent conversation with his mother had clearly reminded him of those expectations, and he resolved to forget about the goddess and focus on the princess.

The sound of heels clicking on the tile floor drew his attention away from the nursery. When he turned, he found himself face-to-face with his future queen.

Chapter Five

The princess dropped into a curtsy, the gesture as elegant as it was automatic.

"I didn't realize you were visiting the hospital today, Your Majesty."

"It was an impulse," he admitted. And though he was just as surprised to see her here, he also recognized that this chance meeting might be the perfect opportunity to gain some insights into her role at the hospital. "But PACH is one of the most renowned children's hospitals in the Mediterranean and I was curious to see what you've done here before we finalize plans for expansion of our pediatric wing."

She scanned the ID tag that was pinned to her dress, releasing the locks on the door that controlled entry and exit to the nursery. "I'd heard that the expansion plans had been put on hold indefinitely."

"Some unexpected budget shortfalls have caused delays, but the plans remain unchanged," he assured her, deliberately downplaying what was yet another unfortunate situation attributed to his rule.

"Then you should definitely take a closer look around," she said. He accepted the invitation by following her through the door.

She went to one of the sinks along the back wall and soaped up her hands. "If you have specific questions, you should talk to Dr. Marotta," she advised. "I don't think he's here today, but I'd be happy to set up an appointment if you wanted to meet with him at another time."

Her offer sounded both genuine and heartfelt, and he was grateful. "Thank you."

She smiled as she rinsed and dried her hands. "We have a wonderful facility here and I'm always happy to show it off."

The princess then took a sterile gown from the cupboard and slipped it on over her dress before moving to one of the bassinets. She said something else, but her voice was pitched so low that he knew her words were intended only for the impossibly tiny baby she lifted into her arms.

"He's a little guy, isn't he?"

"You should have seen him when he was born," Marissa said. "He was just over three pounds then, but he's almost five now and getting bigger and stronger every day."

She scanned her ID tag at another door and Dante followed her into a room decorated in muted tones of blue and green with thick sage-colored carpet. There were prints on the walls—copies of famous works by Sisley and Pissarro and Monet—and classical music playing softly in the background. About a dozen rocking chairs were set up around the perimeter of the room, interspersed with tables offering books and magazines.

The princess then settled into a chair near the door and gestured for him to take the one beside her.

On the far side of the room, he saw a white-haired grandmother rocking a baby wrapped in a pink blanket. Beside her was a younger woman in a nurse's uniform holding another pink bundle. "Is it okay for me to be in here?"

Marissa settled the infant against her shoulder and set the chair in motion. "This is a community room for volunteer cuddlers of both genders to spend time with the premature babies."

"Volunteer cuddlers?"

She smiled and he felt that strange tug again—an inexplicable combination of attraction and recognition.

"There have been numerous studies done that confirm the benefits of human contact on every aspect of a preemie's development—cognitive, social and emotional," she explained. "That's the foundation of Juno's Touch."

"Juno's Touch?" he echoed again, his blood stirring in a way that reminded him how very much he'd enjoyed the goddess's touch the night before, until he firmly banished the memories from his mind.

"The Roman goddess Juno was the embodiment of the traditional female roles of wife and mother," the princess explained. "She was also the protector of the state, so it seemed appropriate—since our children are the future of not just the state but our world—to name the program after her."

It was a logical explanation, but still he wondered, "Who came up with the title?"

She seemed surprised by his question and maybe a little wary. "The board of directors approved it."

"But who proposed the name?"

"Does it matter?"

"Of course not. I was just curious," he said, trying to convince himself as much as her. Then, in an effort to change the subject, he asked, "So that's all you do here—just cuddle the babies?"

She smiled and he realized that he had underestimated the

princess again. Her demeanor might be reserved and her style somewhat bland, but she truly was a beautiful woman. And her beauty had nothing to do with her aristocratic bone structure or flawless ivory skin. Instead, it was revealed through the natural grace of her every movement, the easy curve of her temptingly shaped lips, the unexpected glint of amusement in the depths of her golden eyes. It was a beauty that came from deep within, from the honesty and integrity and compassion that were as much a part of her as the royal blood running through her veins.

"I know it doesn't seem like much," she acknowledged. "But it's a simple program that renders enormous benefits."

"But why do you need volunteers? Why don't the mothers cuddle their own babies?"

"A lot of them do," she told him. "Some of them spend twelve to eighteen hours a day at the hospital with their children. But that's not an option for everyone.

"There are so many causes of premature birth, and often the new mothers need to focus on healing themselves before they can take care of their babies. Or their babies might be in the hospital for weeks or months and they have other children at home who need their attention. For those mothers, the existence of this program gives them a much-needed break while still giving their babies much-needed attention."

"You really enjoy being part of it, don't you?"

Her smile was a little wistful this time. "There's nothing in the world like cuddling a baby. Maybe it's not rocket science, but this little guy needs me more than he needs an aerospace engineer, at least at this point in his life."

"It's obvious that you've found your calling," he said. "So why aren't you married with a dozen kids of your own already?"

"If I was, I'd hardly have any free time to spend here," she responded lightly.

"Which doesn't answer my question."

She lifted one shoulder—careful not to jostle the sleeping baby. "As old-fashioned as it may seem, I was hoping to fall in love and get married before I started having babies."

"I wouldn't say that it was old-fashioned so much as naive, especially for a woman in your position."

Her eyes flashed with fire. "You mean that a twenty-eight-year-old spinster should have given up such romantic dreams?"

He held up his hands in a gesture of surrender. "I wasn't referring to either your age or marital status but your royal title."

And as quickly as her ire had risen, it faded again. But the brief flare of temper was further proof that the princess wasn't nearly as unassuming and obedient as her mother wanted to believe.

"In that case, I apologize for jumping to conclusions."

"I apologize for being ambiguous."

She smiled again, her forgiveness coming easily in the wake of her frustration. "It wasn't your fault. I'm probably a little overly sensitive about the subject."

"If it helps, I'm no more thrilled than you are about the prospect of getting married for all the wrong reasons," he confided.

"At least you get to choose who you will marry," she said.

He frowned at that. "Are you saying that you don't?"

"Tesorian law provides for the parents of a princess to enter into a contract for marriage on her behalf, so my mother has the right to choose my husband."

"But she wouldn't force you to marry someone if you were truly opposed."

Even as he spoke the words that he hoped—for her sake—were true, he realized his error. During his brief acquaintance with the Princess Royal, he'd realized that she was a woman who liked to be in control, who would wield any power she possessed just to prove that she could.

"I hope that's an issue I won't ever have to face," she said sincerely.

"Does that mean you're not opposed to marrying me?" he asked her. When her brows lifted, he hastened to clarify. "Hypothetically, of course."

"I couldn't say for sure one way or the other, even hypothetically, because I don't know you."

Dante smiled. "Then we'll have to change that."

Marissa didn't stay at the hospital for very long after the king had gone. Usually there was nothing that soothed her soul as easily or completely as spending time with the babies, but tonight, there were thoughts and questions swirling through her mind that no amount of rocking and humming could quiet. One of those questions needed to be answered before she saw the king again the next day, so she detoured by Michael and Hannah's new home on the way to her own.

"Aunt Marissa!" Riley threw her arms around her waist and hugged her tight.

Marissa dropped a kiss on the little girl's head, then touched her lips to her brother's cheek. He looked a little unsettled, she thought, and realized that she might have come at a bad time.

"I should have called first," she apologized as Riley grabbed her hand and dragged her toward the living room.

"Of course not," he denied automatically. "We're always happy to see you."

The sentiment was confirmed by Hannah's quick smile when she saw Marissa enter the room. "This is an unexpected surprise," she said, abandoning the books she'd been sorting to give her sister-in-law a quick hug.

"We've got a surprise, too," Riley informed her.

Marissa looked from her niece, who was positively beaming, to her brother, whose expression reflected joy and terror in equal measures, to his wife, who seemed happy, if a little bit nervous, and thought she knew what that surprise was. But she didn't want to spoil Riley's fun, so she said, "What kind of surprise?"

"A really big surprise. Well, it's not really big yet. Actually, it's really, really tiny, but it's going to get really big," Riley explained. "Can you guess?"

"Hmm," Marissa said, tapping a finger against her chin. "Is it a color or a number?"

Riley giggled and shook her head, causing her pigtails to swing from side to side. "No—it's a baby! Mommy's having a baby and I'm going to be a big sister!"

Though the joy and terror in Michael's eyes had been a clear giveaway to Marissa—a man who had lost his first wife shortly after childbirth was entitled to be a little bit unnerved when his new wife announced her pregnancy—hearing the words filled Marissa's heart with a happiness that eclipsed everything else.

"That is a really big surprise," she assured Riley. Then to Hannah, "When did you find out?"

"Just now," her sister-in-law confessed, showing Marissa the stick with the plus sign in the window.

"Then this is a bad time," Marissa concluded. "You must want to celebrate—"

"We'll celebrate later," Michael said, giving his wife a meaningful look and a secret smile. "Because right now, it's Riley's bath time."

"I don't want a bath—I want to celebrate," Riley protested.

"We've got about eight months to celebrate and make plans," Hannah told the little girl. "But you've only got half an hour until your bedtime, so if you want to read the next chapter in your new book, you better get into the bath ASAP."

"Okay." Riley tugged on her father's hand. "Come on, Daddy—ASAP."

"Yes, Your Highness," Michael said, and let his daughter drag him out of the room.

Marissa smiled as she absorbed the news. She already had three beautiful nieces: Sierra, Gabriella and Cameron's now eighteen-year-old daughter, who was about to start her first year at the university in San Pedro; Jaedyn, Sierra's eleven-month-old baby sister; and Michael's five-year-old bundle of energy and inquisition known as Riley; but she was thrilled to learn that there wasn't just one but now two more babies on the way.

She was genuinely thrilled for both of her brothers and their families, and just the teensiest bit envious. "A baby," she said again.

"I know." Hannah grinned. "I've been hoping…but I was afraid to hope. And then, on my way home today, I decided just to pick up the test. Now we can stop wondering and start planning."

"You're going to be a fabulous mother—you *are* a fabulous mother."

"Thanks, but Riley makes it easy. Or maybe it was the fact that I didn't come into her life until she was almost four. This one—" she instinctively laid a hand on her still flat belly "—isn't likely to come out walking and talking, so I've got a lot to learn over the next eight months."

"Well, since you are going to have another child," Marissa began, thinking the news of her sister-in-law's pregnancy was an appropriate segue into the reason for her visit, "I was wondering if I could borrow Riley."

"Okay. As long as you return her when you're done."

Marissa had to smile at Hannah's easy response. "Aren't you even curious as to when and why?"

"When and why?" Hannah asked.

"Tomorrow for the hot-air-balloon festival at Falcon Ridge," Marissa told her. "Because I fibbed and said that I already had plans with Riley in order to avoid being alone with the man my mother wants me to marry."

"You want Riley to chaperone your date with the Duke of Bellemoro?" Hannah asked, trying to pick out the relevant details from the explanation her sister-in-law had blurted out.

"No, I want Riley to chaperone my date with the king of Ardena."

Hannah picked up the phone from the table beside her and began dialing.

Marissa frowned. "Who are you calling?"

"Gabriella. She has to hear about this."

Since Marissa figured it would be easier to tell the story to both of her sisters-in-law at the same time rather than in two separate installments, she didn't dissuade her. But she did wonder why she put the call on speakerphone.

"You need to come over," Hannah said, as soon as Gabby answered.

"Now?" The very pregnant princess sounded weary. "I just got into my pajamas—"

"So come in your pajamas," the newly pregnant princess told her. "I have big news."

"News that can't wait until tomorrow?"

"I'm pregnant and Marissa's engaged to the king of Ardena."

There was half a beat of silence before Gabby said, "I'll be there in five minutes."

The picture on the screen was fuzzy, and the more she increased the magnification of the photo, the fuzzier it got. That's what she got for working with cheap equipment. Unfortunately, since she wasn't a professional photographer, it was all she could afford. But now she worried that her efforts to pinch a few pennies might end up costing her big.

She turned her attention from the screen to the list of names beside the laptop. It was a copy of the final guest list for the masquerade ball, but even after reviewing it numerous times, she was no closer to ascertaining the identity of the mystery woman who had spent the night in Dante Romero's room at the palace.

Not that her identity really mattered, except insofar as it might add fuel to the fire of the scandal. An unmarried heiress looking for a good time? No big deal. But the devoted wife of a Tesorian cabinet member? Very big deal.

She clicked on the next photo, then the one after that. When the woman left his room in the early hours of the morning after, she carried her shoes in her left hand. Zooming in, she confirmed that the hand was bare.

With another click of the mouse, she restored the original image, looking for something—anything—that might provide a positive clue. Of course, it was hard to see anything with the damn mask covering half of the woman's face.

She clicked back through the images until she found the ones of the woman and the king locked together in a passionate embrace. She knew it was the king because she'd wheedled the location of his room out of a housekeeper, but without that knowledge, she could understand how someone might question that identification.

She rubbed the heels of her hands over eyes that were gritty from lack of sleep and too much time staring at the damn computer screen. When a familiar beep indicated an incoming text message, she snatched up her phone, her hands shaking and her heart pounding as she read her sister's message.

doctor confirmed shes doing great, should be ready 2 go home shortly, will keep u posted xoxoxo

She blew out a long breath, then replied simply:

thnx 4 update, c u soon

The message echoed in her mind and eased the ache in her heart. Tears of gratitude and relief filled her eyes, and she gave herself a moment to send up a brief but fervent prayer to express her appreciation to the big guy upstairs.

Then she turned back to the computer and the images of the king again, because she didn't owe him any thanks.

She didn't owe him anything but payback.

It was closer to twenty minutes by the time Gabriella arrived—not in her pajamas.

"I keep forgetting that I can't move as fast as I used to," she said by way of apology.

She hugged Hannah first. "Congratulations, Mommy."

Then she turned to Marissa and demanded, "Let me see the ring."

"There is no ring," she denied, shooting a look at Hannah. "I am *not* engaged. But I did have brunch with Dante Romero today."

"And she's got a date with him tomorrow," Hannah interjected.

"Well, I guess this means you were wrong about the duke," Gabby noted.

"But not wrong about my mother's plan to marry me off to a groom of her choosing."

"For once, I can't fault her choice," Hannah said.

"Ditto that," Gabby agreed.

"I feel compelled to point out that countless women around the world have reason to share your enthusiasm," Marissa said drily.

"Okay, so he hasn't exactly been…circumspect with respect to past relationships," Hannah acknowledged. "But I don't think he's been involved with anyone since he took the throne."

"Or maybe he's just learned to be discreet," Marissa suggested.

"The king does have a reputation," Gabriella acknowledged. "But it hardly rivals the one your brother built up over the years. If Cameron could change his ways, it's not impossible that Dante Romero could, too."

"Cameron changed his ways because he fell in love with you," Marissa pointed out. "Any interest the king of Ardena has in me is fueled by politics, not affection."

"It doesn't matter how something starts, only how it ends," said Hannah, who had met Prince Michael when she accepted the position as temporary nanny for his young daughter the previous summer.

"Trust me—the king is not going to propose, and I wouldn't accept his proposal if he did."

"Never say never," Gabby cautioned. "He's incredibly handsome and unbelievably charming."

"Says the woman happily married to my brother," Marissa remarked drily.

Cameron's wife only smiled. "Being married to your brother should have immunized me against other handsome and charming men, but not even I was immune to Dante Romero. And if he sets his sights on you, you won't have a chance."

"You're forgetting one important fact," Marissa reminded her sisters-in-law. "The king of Ardena will be expected to marry a virgin bride—and I no longer qualify."

Chapter Six

Security was always a concern whenever the king of Ardena attended any kind of public event, so the plan was for Dante's chauffeur to drive over to Marissa's condo first, and from there they would go together to pick up Riley. They were halfway to Riley's house when the princess's cell phone rang.

She glanced at the display. "It's my sister-in-law," she said apologetically before connecting the call.

Dante had no compunction about eavesdropping. After all, it wasn't as if he could leave the moving vehicle to give her some privacy. And while he could only hear Marissa's half of the conversation, it quickly became clear that there was a change of plans for the day. A change that, judging by the furrow between her brows and the nervous glances she sent in his direction, the princess wasn't happy about.

"Apparently Riley's running a fever," Marissa told him.

"Why do you say 'apparently'?" he asked curiously.

"Because I saw her last night and she was fine."

"Even I know kids can get sick without any notice."

"You're right," she admitted.

"But you suspect she isn't really ill," he guessed.

"I think if she was, Hannah would have sounded more worried."

"Do you think your mother somehow orchestrated the last-minute cancellation?"

"No," the princess responded without hesitation. "I can assure you that Hannah wouldn't do my mother any favors. This is entirely her own doing—her attempt to give us some time alone together."

"So I have an ally in your sister-in-law, do I?" he asked as Thomas pulled into a gravel parking lot.

"For today, anyway," Marissa grumbled. "Who can predict what she might do tomorrow?"

He couldn't help but grin in response to the obvious pique in her tone.

The chauffeur parked at the far end of the lot, away from all of the other vehicles. Several minutes passed before the door was opened and they were allowed to exit the car. Marissa knew the delay had been necessary to allow the security detail assigned to the king to survey the area and ensure there were no threats to his safety.

Her cousin, the prince regent, endured the same procedures whenever he went out. She understood that it was a way of life for a ruler and, to a lesser extent, for any royal. It was one of the reasons she preferred to keep a low profile. Unfortunately, a low profile wasn't possible in the company of the king of Ardena.

When he was satisfied that the area was secure, the chauffeur—whom Marissa suspected was likely a high-ranking member of the security team—carried a wicker basket and led the way. He guided them toward a table that had been moved some distance from the usual picnic area at the base of the nature trails—again, for security rather than privacy—while another guard followed behind.

Thomas spread a cloth over the table, then laid out the place settings and various containers of food before he bowed to the king and retraced his steps to return to the car. But Marissa knew they were not alone. So long as they remained in this public setting, there would be an invisible circle of security guards around them—and probably camera-wielding vultures in the trees.

"I was told that the best vantage point for the launch was the observation deck at the top of the trail. I was also warned that it would be impossible to secure that area because of its popularity and numerous access points, so I hope this is okay."

"This is fine," she assured him, surprised that he would even ask.

"We still have about half an hour until the launch," he noted. "Did you want to eat or walk or just relax?"

"Relaxing sounds good," she said, even as she wondered if it was possible to relax in the presence of a man who made all of her nerve endings hum.

He picked up the blanket Thomas had left on the bench and unfolded it on the grass in the center of the clearing and gestured for her to sit. She lowered herself onto the blanket, close to the edge to ensure that he had plenty of space on the other side.

He stretched out in the middle, on his back with his hands tucked behind his head and his feet crossed at the ankles.

"Is this how you like to relax?" he asked her. "By communing with nature?"

"I do enjoy being here—it's so beautiful and peaceful. In fact, I used to be a member of the Falcon Ridge Trail Walkers," she admitted. "But I stopped participating in the scheduled walks because the other members complained about the paparazzi scaring away the wildlife."

"Just one of the perks of being born royal," he noted in a dry tone.

A gust of air swept through the clearing, fluttering the leaves on the trees. Marissa tucked her knees up and wrapped her arms around them.

"Are you warm enough?" he asked her.

"I'm fine."

"You don't seem to be relaxing," he noted.

She wasn't. How could she possibly relax when he was so close? Close enough that she inhaled his tantalizing masculine scent whenever she took a breath. Close enough—

"Take off your shoes," he suggested.

"No, thank you."

"It's easier to relax when your feet are bare." He kicked off his own, then sat up to remove his socks.

She'd never thought feet were sexy. Of course, she should have realized that his would be. There didn't seem to be any part of Dante Romero that wasn't above average.

"Your turn."

"I don't…"

Her protest faltered when he reached over and picked up her foot. Suddenly her mind spun back to the night of the masquerade ball, when Jupiter removed her sandals. She remembered the way he'd unwound the lace, the slow and sensual brush of his fingers over her skin. Just the memory made her heart pound faster.

But this wasn't Jupiter, it was Dante, and he simply took hold of one shoe and tugged it off, then did the same with the other and carelessly tossed them aside.

Then he returned his attention to her now-bare feet, stroking his thumbs leisurely over the hot-pink lacquer on her toenails.

"Well, this answers one question," he murmured.

She swallowed. "What question is that?"

His gaze skimmed over her, from the ivory cowl-necked blouse to the sand-colored slacks. "Whether you disliked color."

"Neutrals are easier to coordinate," she informed him.

"But a lot less fun." He picked up one of her feet and stroked his thumb along the arch of her foot.

She didn't disagree. In fact, she didn't say anything because he was massaging her foot and she'd apparently lost the ability to form coherent thought. His thumb slid along the inside arch, circled the heel and traced the same path back again. She sighed with pleasure.

He smiled. "It feels good, doesn't it?"

"It does," she admitted. "But I'm not sure it would look good if there was a snapshot of this particular scene on the front page of tomorrow's paper."

"The area has been secured and no one knows we're even here," he told her, continuing to work his magic on her instep.

"You mean aside from the half-dozen guards patrolling the perimeter?"

"Aside from them," he agreed.

"How do you know?" she wondered.

"Because I made a point of stopping at the little café by the waterfront and asking about the beaches in San Pedro."

"Clever," she admitted.

He reached up and plucked the pins out of her hair, his movements so quick and deft that Marissa didn't even realize what he was doing until her hair was tumbling over her shoulders.

"If I'd wanted my hair down, I wouldn't have put it up," she told him, not bothering to disguise her annoyance.

"You always wear it up," he noted. "I wanted to see it down."

"And you're used to getting what you want, aren't you, Your Majesty?"

"Usually," he admitted.

She automatically scooped up her hair, but he smiled and held up the pins. With a sigh that was equal parts resignation and frustration, she released the tresses again.

"Much better," he told her and tucked the pins into his pocket. "Are you feeling more relaxed now?"

She was definitely feeling "more" something, but it wasn't relaxed. "Sure."

He shook his head, as if he knew she was lying. "It's the chemistry."

She swallowed, wondering if he was somehow able to read her thoughts. "Chemistry?"

"A physical attraction evidenced by the sparks sizzling in the air." He shifted closer, spreading his legs so that they straddled her hips while her feet were almost in his lap. "It's an elemental human response that occurs when a man and woman who are attracted to one another are in close proximity."

"You can't be attracted to me."

"It surprised me, too. Not that you're not an attractive woman," he hastened to clarify. "Just that you're not my usual type."

"Based on the extensive lineup of women you've dated, I wouldn't have guessed that you had a type."

"You might be right," he agreed. "Either way, the fact is that I like looking at you and being with you, and I can't help wondering if the attraction between us might grow into something more."

"I'm sure it's not a concern that keeps you up at night."

He was undaunted by her dismissive tone. "Of course, there's only one surefire way to answer that question."

"Maybe I don't want it answered."

"I think you do. Not consciously, perhaps," he allowed. "But subconsciously, it's preoccupying your thoughts. You're wondering when that first kiss might happen, whether you'll enjoy it, whether it will end with just one kiss or lead into something more."

If she hadn't been thinking about it before, she definitely was now. Not just thinking about it, but wanting it.

The sexy glint in his eyes warned her that he knew it.

"Instead of both of us wondering, why don't we just get it out of the way?" he suggested.

Before Marissa's frazzled brain could decipher his words, his lips were on hers.

Her first thought was that the man definitely knew how to kiss. Of course, his abundance of experience had no doubt allowed him to perfect his technique.

His mouth pressed against hers with just the right amount of pressure—enough to demonstrate that he was confident in her response but not so much that she felt his kiss was being forced upon her. He cradled her face in his hands, not to hold her immobile but only to adjust the angle of contact as he slowly deepened the kiss.

He touched the center of her upper lip with his tongue, a gentle stroke that sent waves of pulsing desire coursing through her system. Her lips parted and he slipped inside.

He continued to kiss her, continued to spin a seductive web around her, so that she was enveloped in layer after layer of sensation. Heat. Hunger. Need.

She wasn't accustomed to feeling like this, to wanting like this. But there was no denying that she did want him. She wanted him to kiss and touch her all over. She wanted to feel his lips and his hands on every part of her body. Mostly, she wanted to once again experience all those glorious sensations that had rocketed through her system when she'd made love with Jupiter.

Except that Dante wasn't Jupiter and this wasn't an anonymous encounter.

She pulled away from him and forced a smile. "Well, now that we got that out of the way, we should eat."

"I wouldn't say that we got anything out of the way," he denied. "In fact, I'd say that what we did was put the attraction between us front and center."

It was the promise in his eyes more than the words that made everything inside her quiver, but she refused to let him see it. "It was just an elemental human response to proximity," she said, turning his words back on him.

"Then I'll just have to ensure we maintain close proximity."

She ignored the heat that filled her cheeks.

"Lunch?" she prompted.

"Good idea." He grinned wickedly. "I'm starving."

Marissa couldn't help but be impressed by the selection of food. There were French breads and savory crackers, gourmet cheeses, thin slices of smoked salmon, duck foie gras with port wine and black Ardenan olives. They watched the balloons overhead as they leisurely sampled the various offerings, sipped on a crisp, chilled Chardonnay, and then nibbled on fresh fruit and dark chocolate truffles for dessert.

When they were finished, Marissa began packing up the leftovers in the basket Thomas had left. She found an unopened plastic container.

"What's this?" She didn't wait for a response but opened the lid, lifting a brow when she recognized the contents. "A peanut-butter-and-jelly sandwich?"

"I didn't know if Riley would be fond of pâtés and cheeses," he explained.

"That was very thoughtful," she said, noting that there

were also chocolate-chip cookies and a bottle of apple juice for the little girl.

"Well, I didn't actually pack it myself," he admitted. "But I'm not so self-absorbed that I wouldn't realize a five-year-old might prefer a simpler meal."

"There was a time when Riley didn't want to eat anything but chicken nuggets," Marissa admitted. "And while her eating habits are a little more expansive these days, she would definitely have gone for the peanut butter and jelly."

"You seem very close to her," he noted.

"I spent a lot of time with her when she was a baby, after Michael lost his wife," Marissa explained.

"He's remarried now, isn't he?"

"Yes, just this past spring," she confirmed. "And he and Hannah have another baby on the way, which Riley is absolutely thrilled about."

"I get the impression you're pretty thrilled, too."

She shrugged. "It's no secret that I'm a sucker for babies."

"My mother's going to love that about you."

"Be careful," she warned. "A woman could get ideas when a man talks about her meeting his parents."

"Well, it is traditional for a man to introduce his future bride to his family."

"So all those headlines about the king of Ardena searching for a queen aren't just rumor?"

"No, they're all true." He popped an olive in his mouth. "Well, all except the one about my alien bride."

She smiled at that. "Does your constitution require that a king be married?"

"It's not a requirement so much as an expectation, and the constitution provides far more latitude than do my parents."

Marissa was familiar with the weight of parental expectations. Although Elena had always demanded far more of her sons than her daughter, with both Michael and Cameron happily married now, the focus had shifted. She understood that her mother's determination to see her married to Dante Romero had nothing to do with wanting a suitable match for her daughter and everything to do with the stature she herself would gain as the king of Ardena's mother-in-law.

"But my parents are anxious for me to marry, not only because they believe our country needs a queen but because they're both eager for a grandchild."

"An heir for the next generation," she noted.

His brows lifted. "Actually, I'm not sure either of them is thinking about the future of the throne so much as their desire to have a baby around to spoil."

"What are your thoughts on that?"

"I like kids," he said easily. "And my dad was a great dad, so I'd hope I could do a decent job following in his footsteps."

"I met your father once," she told him.

"He didn't tell me that."

"He probably doesn't remember."

Dante's brows drew together. "Why would you say that?"

"Because it was more than twenty years ago."

"Really?"

"King Benedicto was in Tesoro del Mar for meetings with my uncle, and I was visiting the palace with my brothers. Of course, my brothers were running through the halls at full speed, as desperate to leave me behind as I was to keep up, and as I was racing up the stairs, I tripped and scraped the skin off of both of my knees."

Dante winced sympathetically. "That must have hurt."

She nodded. "And I screamed so that everyone would know it. Your dad was the first on the scene.

"He immediately scooped me up off the floor and carried me over to the wing chairs by the windows overlooking the rose garden. He cuddled me until my sobs subsided, then he sat me on the edge of one of the chairs and squatted down, carefully inspecting first one knee and then the next. The nanny hurried over with antiseptic cream and bandages and tried to send the king away so that she could tend to my injuries, but he insisted on cleaning and bandaging the scrapes himself. Then he took a handkerchief out of his pocket, wiped away the last of my tears, kissed my forehead and pronounced me good to go."

"That's quite a detailed memory," he remarked, sounding more than a little skeptical.

Marissa just smiled. "Every girl remembers the first time she falls in love."

"You fell in love with my father?"

"He was the first man—aside from my own father, who had passed away six months earlier—to hold me while I cried."

"That's your criteria for giving your heart?"

Her smile widened. "He was also very handsome."

"I've been told I'm the spitting image of King Benedicto when he was crowned, thirty-five years ago," he said, the devilish twinkle in those dark eyes assuring her that he was teasing.

She narrowed her gaze, as if struggling to see the resemblance. "You do have his ears," she finally acknowledged.

"And his charm?" he prompted hopefully.

"There's definite potential."

As Thomas drove back toward Marissa's condo later that afternoon, Dante found that he was genuinely reluctant for the day to end. He'd had a good time with the princess—she was easy to talk to and didn't hesitate to speak her mind on any number of topics, nor was she the least bit shy about letting him know when her ideas and opinions differed from his own.

He'd accepted the fact that he was attracted to her. What

surprised him was to realize how much he actually liked her. And that he could imagine himself spending the rest of his life with her.

Not that he was anxious to exchange vows, but he'd resigned himself to the necessity of it. And since he figured she had a right to know what his intentions were, he said, "I think we should get married."

Her brow lifted, but she replied in a similarly casual tone. "I think you're insane."

He grinned, because her response proved that his instincts about her were exactly right. He needed a wife who would stand up to him and say what was on her mind. "I realize that a marriage between us might seem impulsive—"

"Might?"

"But if you think about it," he continued as if she hadn't interrupted, "there are several valid reasons for us to marry and really no reason for us not to."

"How about the fact that I don't want to marry you?"

"Putting aside for now the fact that you acknowledged your wishes might not be a factor," he said, "why wouldn't you want to marry me?"

"Do you want a list?"

His brows rose. "Do you have one?"

"I could make one," she assured him. "And right at the top would be the fact that I don't even know you."

"I'm not suggesting we get married tomorrow."

"Well, in that case…" She paused as if reconsidering his offer, then shook her head. "The answer would still be no."

He cocked his head. "You really don't want to marry me?"

"Did you think I was being coy?"

The possibility had crossed his mind, and he realized that was his mistake. She wasn't the type of woman who played those kind of games, which was just one more thing he liked about her.

"No," he admitted. "But I do think your rejection was as impulsive as my proposal."

She didn't dispute the possibility.

"I have no desire to marry a woman against her will, but another man might not feel the same way," he cautioned.

"So you're saying that I should marry you because it's probably going to be the best offer I get?"

"No, I'm saying that you should give me—give *us*—a chance," he clarified.

"Isn't that what today was about?"

"Today was a first date. I'm asking for a second."

"Why?" she asked warily.

"Because I think your refusal to consider a relationship between us is more about resenting your mother's manipulations than any personal feelings toward me."

"I would think you would resist being manipulated as much as I do."

"I would," he agreed, "if I felt I was being manipulated."

"We both know you're not really interested in me."

"I'd say that kiss we shared in the park proves otherwise."

"You're making a big deal out of one little kiss," she warned him.

He just smiled, confident that their next kiss would prove otherwise. "I'm not asking you to run away to Ardena with me yet," he continued. "I just want a chance to get to know you."

"Because marrying a princess from Tesoro del Mar would be a strategic political move," she guessed.

"It would be foolish of me to deny that's true. However, the woman I choose as my bride—as my country's future queen—will be my wife for the rest of my life, and I have no intention of making that decision solely on the basis of political considerations."

"What other factors are there when you're responsible for the future of your country?" she challenged.

"Attraction. Affection. Intelligence. Compassion. Common interests. I don't want to stare into my coffee cup every morning because I can't carry on a conversation with the woman seated across the table from me."

"Sounds like you've given this some thought," she noted.

"Aside from international trade relations, the domestic economy, rising unemployment, health care and funding for education, I've hardly been able to think about anything else."

Her lips curved, just a little. Just enough to distract him with thoughts of how sweet those lips had tasted and how passionately she'd responded to his kiss.

"Well, that list certainly puts the matter of marriage into perspective," she said.

"Except that it is important. My parents' relationship taught me that having a true partner in life can make dealing with all of the other issues if not easier, at least manageable."

"You were lucky to have that kind of example."

"I know," he admitted. "And although I may not know you very well, the one thing I can say with absolute certainty is that you don't bore me."

"I'm so pleased to hear that, Your Majesty."

He grinned in response to her dry tone. "I imagine you'd be more pleased if I went back to Ardena and never bothered you again."

"As if spending time with the king of Ardena could ever be considered a bother."

"I'm having dinner with your cousin and his wife Tuesday night," he told her. "It will just be a small group, including the French ambassador and his spouse, and Prince Harry and his current companion. I'd be pleased if you could join us."

"I don't know how anyone could refuse such a gracious invitation."

He chuckled. "But no doubt if you did, you would."

Chapter Seven

There were three messages on her machine when Marissa got home after her outing with Dante. She predicted, even before she listened to them, that there would be one each from Elena, Gabriella and Hannah. Each one, of course, wanting to hear the details of her date with the king of Ardena.

She didn't return any of the calls because she hadn't yet decided how many of those details she was willing to share. Except that she absolutely would *not* tell her mother that he'd ever brought up the idea of marriage, because she knew that if she did, Elena would somehow manage to have the church booked before she even hung up the phone.

Except that the king of Ardena would be expected to marry in his own country so that his people could share in the celebration. The date would probably even be declared a national holiday, so that men, women and children could line the streets and wave flags. And if she was to make the list that Dante had asked her about, that would be the number-one reason why she didn't want to marry him.

I think your refusal to consider a relationship between us is more about resenting your mother's manipulations than any personal feelings toward me.

Number two: he was arrogant and smug.

Except that he was right, dammit.

Number three: he was far too insightful for her peace of mind.

She sank down on the edge of her sofa and reached for the remote. She didn't usually watch a lot of television, but she was in the mood for some mindless entertainment—or maybe desperate for any distraction that might push thoughts of Dante Romero out of her mind.

The knock at the door was a welcome reprieve. Even more welcome than her sisters-in-law was the plate of frosted brownies Gabriella carried.

"My mother baked today," she said, passing the plate to Marissa. "And since I've already gained a gazillion pounds with this baby, I thought I would bring these over to you."

"And as a heartfelt thank-you, I'll put on a pot of decaf."

While Marissa ground the beans, Hannah got out the cream and sugar and Gabby set out plates and napkins.

"Marissa?"

She looked up to see both of her friends watching her with concern.

"Sorry, I guess my mind wandered."

Gabby gestured to the plate of brownies. "I asked if you wanted one with or without nuts."

"Actually, I don't want either one right now."

"Are you feeling ill?" Hannah teased, because it wasn't like Marissa to ever turn down chocolate.

She carried the pot of coffee to the table. "Maybe I am,"

she said, looking directly at Hannah. "Maybe I picked up whatever bug it was that kept Riley home in bed today."

Michael's wife met her gaze evenly. "It was a headache that miraculously cured itself."

Gabby picked up quickly on the pointed reference to Marissa's own excuse for allegedly missing the ball.

"Riley was supposed to chaperone Marissa's date with the king," she remembered.

"Speaking of your date," Hannah said, anxious to get to the point of their visit. "How was it?"

"The balloons were spectacular," Marissa said. "It must have been a record launch, because I don't remember ever seeing so many before."

"We don't want to hear about the balloons," Gabby told her.

"What do you want to hear—details about how we did it in the back of his car?"

"Only if it's true."

Marissa had to sigh. "Only in my dreams."

"Oooh." Hannah reached for a second brownie. "Now this is getting good."

"It's not good," Marissa denied. "I'm not the kind of woman who indulges in sexual fantasies—"

"First of all," Gabby interrupted, "every woman should have fantasies. And if you've never had them before, it's probably only because you've never known anyone like Dante Romero."

"You're saying this is normal—to lust after a man I've only just met?"

"It is when that man looks like the king of Ardena," Hannah assured her.

"Wanting someone based on a purely physical attraction seems rather…shallow," she worried.

"Shallow, absolutely. Abnormal, no," Gabriella assured

her. "I fell in lust with your brother the first time I laid eyes on him."

"Me, too," Hannah said, then hastened to clarify, "but with your other brother."

"Seriously in lust?" Marissa pressed. "As in heart pounding and knees quivering?"

"And your blood pulsing in your veins so that you feel hot and tingly all over," Gabby added.

"And your body aching so desperately that you think you'll die if he doesn't touch you," Hannah finished.

"That about sums it up," Marissa agreed.

Gabby nodded. "Perfectly normal."

Even if it was normal, it was completely outside of Marissa's realm of experience. Because aside from the single night she'd spent with Jupiter, she had no experience.

"So what am I supposed to do about it?" she wanted to know.

"What do you want to do?" Hannah asked.

"I want to get naked with him." She pressed her hands to her cheeks. "And I can't believe I just said that out loud."

"Your secret is safe with us," Gabby promised her.

"I've never wanted to get naked with anyone before. Well, except for the night of the ball, and then it was for a specific purpose and not just because I'd met some guy who turned me inside out with lust." She worried her bottom lip. "Do you think losing my virginity turned me into a slut?"

Gabby snorted. "Not likely."

"How do you know?"

"Because I know *you*. And if you were easy, you *would* have had sex with him in the back of his car."

"Except that he doesn't want to have sex with me—he wants to marry me. Or he thinks he does."

"There are worse things than marrying a man who makes your blood hum," Hannah noted. "Not that sexual attraction alone is a good foundation for a lasting relationship, but it's a definite plus."

"Attraction aside for a minute," Gabriella said. "What else do you know about the guy?"

"He takes his responsibilities seriously. He wants to do what's best for his people, even when that means making unpopular decisions. When he talks about his family, you can hear the genuine affection in his voice. And when he asks a question, he actually listens to the answer. He's attentive and charming—maybe too charming. And he's considerate. When he thought that Riley was going to be with us today—" she slanted another look at Hannah "—he had a special lunch prepared for her."

"It sounds like you actually like him," Gabby noted, surprise in her voice.

She sighed. "I think I do."

"Why is that a problem?" Hannah wanted to know.

"Because it's not something I can put on my list of reasons not to marry him."

Marissa had been taught, at a very early age, that a princess had to have standards. So she never went out in public unless her outfit was coordinated, a minimum amount of makeup was applied and her hair was neatly groomed. But she didn't believe in spending an inordinate amount of time on her appearance, and she'd never been the type to primp in an effort to impress a man.

But as she dressed for dinner at the palace Monday night, she was conscious of the king's comment about the lack of color in her wardrobe. Though he hadn't said anything that wasn't true, the criticism had still stung. So she took extra care with her makeup, adding a touch of smoky shadow to her eyelids, an extra coat of mascara and a slick of gloss just a little bit darker than her usual shade.

Assessing the results in the mirror, she decided that the differences were noticeable but not drastic. The biggest change, and thankfully not one that anyone else could see, was the unexpected tangle of knots in her stomach. A tangle of knots that had nothing to do with going to dinner at the palace and everything to do with the identity of her date.

She'd offered to drive herself so that she could leave whenever she was ready, but he insisted on sending a car, refusing to listen to her argument that it was impractical for his chauffeur to drive from the palace to pick her up and take her back to the palace. Not that she minded having someone else do the driving for her—it was simply a luxury to which she wasn't accustomed.

A quick glance at the clock revealed that she had three minutes before Thomas was expected to arrive. She used those minutes to spray a quick spritz of perfume, double-check the contents of her jeweled clutch (ID, emergency cash, cell phone, lip gloss) and slip her feet into her shoes.

As if on cue, a knock sounded at the door.

"You're punctual," she said, opening the door.

The smile she had ready for Thomas faltered when she saw the king standing in the foyer, wearing formal evening dress—a black dinner jacket and trousers with a white collared shirt and black bow tie—and looking even more handsome than any man had a right to look.

"So are you," he noted, appreciation glinting in his eyes as they skimmed over her.

"Your Majesty." She curtsied automatically. "I wasn't expecting you."

"Is it not customary for a man to pick up his date?"

"Customary but not necessary," she said.

"I decided that I wanted to walk into the dining room with you, so that everyone knows we're together."

"What do you mean 'everyone'?"

"Well, Harry, specifically."

"Sounds like there's a story there," she mused.

"Not a very interesting one," he assured her.

"Perhaps I'll have to ask the prince for his interpretation of events."

"Okay, if you must know, I invited a lady friend to attend a gala event in London last year. As we were coming from different directions, we agreed to meet at the venue. Unfortunately, I got tied up on a conference call and arrived just as she was leaving."

"With Prince Harry," she guessed.

He acknowledged this with a short nod.

"Did her defection break your heart or bruise your ego?"

"Neither, really," he admitted. "But it was a lesson learned."

"Do you really think I'm the type of woman who would go home with someone other than the man who invited her?"

"I didn't think you were the type of woman who would go home even *with* the man who invited her, at least not on a second date," he teased. "But now you've given me hope for the evening."

Marissa felt her cheeks flush. *If only he knew...*

Dante had invited Marissa to be his date for dinner because her presence would round out the table and because he wanted to spend time with her. His reasons were no more complicated than that. But as he watched her across the table, chatting comfortably with the French ambassador—in French, of course—and flirting casually with Prince Harry, he realized that he was seeing yet another side of the multi-faceted princess.

For the most part, she chose to downplay her royal status. She had come into a substantial trust fund on her twenty-fifth birthday, but she maintained a modest lifestyle. Her condo was in a secure building in an exclusive neighborhood, but she lived alone, without any staff to attend to her. She drove her own car—a late-model Japanese compact—and even shopped for her own groceries.

And yet, as much as she might try to pretend she wasn't royal, when the occasion warranted, she slipped into the princess role as gracefully and effortlessly as any other woman might slip into a cloak. He found it fascinating to watch the transition, and realized her adaptability was just one more reason that she would fit easily into his world.

The only question, as far as he could tell, was whether or not she wanted to. Not that he was going to make the mistake of bringing up that topic of conversation again. At least not just yet.

For now, he was simply going to enjoy being with her.

After dessert and coffee in the parlor, when the guests started to take their leave, Dante turned to Marissa.

"Shall we take a walk in the garden?"

She had seemed comfortable and relaxed through most of the evening, chatting easily with the other guests, but the prospect of leaving the group to be alone with him gave her pause.

"It's late," she said. "I really should be getting home."

"Not so late," he assured her.

"I have an early meeting at the school board tomorrow."

"A short walk," he cajoled. "It's too beautiful a night to waste."

"All right." She relented and followed him out to the terrace.

She paused at the top of the wide stone steps, and he offered his arm to help her navigate the descent. She smiled as she tucked her hand into the crook of his elbow.

"A king and a gentleman," she noted.

"When the occasion warrants," he told her.

But the feelings that stirred in his belly weren't very gentlemanly when he caught a glimpse of the long, lean leg revealed by the slit up the front of her dress.

The dress itself had been a pleasant surprise to Dante. It was a strapless column of pale lavender silk that lightly skimmed the length of her body. It was feminine and elegant, and she truly looked beautiful in it.

On her feet she wore silver slingbacks that showed just a hint of her hot-pink toes and matched the silver clutch she carried. Her hair was swept up in some kind of twist, and the diamonds at her ears and looped around her wrist winked in the moonlight.

"Did I tell you how beautiful you look tonight?" he asked when they'd reached the bottom of the steps and he managed to tear his gaze away from her legs. "You look good in color."

"Well, there isn't a great selection of formal wear in beige," she said, tongue-in-cheek, as they started along the flagstone path.

"And I'll bet you bought this dress because you thought the color was understated."

"It is."

"No," he denied. "It's intriguing. Just a hint of purple— and maybe a hint of the woman who's wearing it."

"You're reading a lot into the color of a dress," she mused.

"I just can't help wondering why you try so hard not to draw attention to yourself."

"Maybe because I got far too much attention growing up simply by virtue of the fact that I was Prince Cameron's younger sister. He liked to party and he liked women, and the paparazzi loved him for it. And when I entered the social scene, they automatically gravitated toward me, assuming I would generate the same kind of headlines. I lost friends and boyfriends because there's no privacy or intimacy in a crowd. So I made a point of dropping off of the radar, and the paparazzi got bored and moved on."

Sadly, he could understand what she'd been through and why she'd made the choices she'd made. "And yet," he mused, "the media always seems to know when you're at a cultural event or charitable function."

She smiled, just a little. "I have no objection to putting myself in front of the camera for a good cause, but I'm not interested in peddling some designer's fashions for the style pages."

"Smart and savvy," he mused.

She led him into a private garden with fountains and columns and the scent of roses in the air.

"The first time Rowan proposed to Lara, it was in this garden," she told him.

"The first time?"

"They had an interesting—and quite public—courtship."

"I don't remember hearing about that."

"It was a lot of years ago now," she told him. "But it was a very big deal at the time—the prince regent of Tesoro del Mar falling in love with a nanny from Ireland."

"I didn't think a royal was allowed to marry a commoner without relinquishing his position in line to the throne."

"Not then, although Rowan has since changed the law. At the time, he had to hold a referendum to ensure the public approved before he could marry her."

"What if he'd lost the referendum?"

"I think he would have given up his title before he would have given up Lara." She sighed, perhaps just a little wistfully.

"Why didn't your cousin revoke the provision that allows your mother to arrange your marriage?"

"Because it's one of those laws that has been on the books

but unused for so long that no one even thinks about it anymore."

"What if you refused to go through with a marriage your mother arranged?"

"I wouldn't," Marissa admitted.

"Because the controversy would put you right in the center of the media spotlight," he guessed.

She didn't deny it.

"That's your biggest objection to getting involved with me, isn't it?"

"It's a factor," she admitted.

He stopped in the middle of the path and turned to face her. He tipped her chin up, saw the wariness battling with desire in the golden depths of her eyes.

She thought he was going to kiss her again. She *wanted* him to kiss her again, maybe as much as he wanted to kiss her. But while he might be eager to indulge in the sweet flavor of her lips, he didn't like to be predictable.

So instead of lowering his head to kiss her, he stroked his finger along the line of her jaw…to the full curve of her lower lip…across her cheek…to trace the outer shell of her ear.

She held herself still, but didn't manage to suppress the instinctive shiver that proved to Dante she was not immune to his touch.

"I'm going back to Ardena at the end of the week," he told her.

She nodded, but he thought he caught a flicker of disappointment in her eyes—or maybe that was just wishful thinking.

"I'd like you to come with me," he told her.

"Why?"

"Because I want the citizens of Ardena to get to know you before you are introduced to them as their new queen."

For about three seconds, she was absolutely speechless.

And then she said, "If that's your idea of a proposal, it could use some work."

He grinned. "I promise you, I'll do better when I'm ready to put the ring on your finger. For now, I was only trying to reassure you that my intentions are honorable."

She frowned. "You hardly even know me. How do you know you want to marry me?"

"Because you don't want to marry me."

"Are you really that perverse?"

He chuckled at the obvious bafflement in her tone. "If you think about it, it makes perfect sense."

"Sorry, but I don't see it."

"I haven't had a serious or exclusive relationship with anyone in the past several years, so in my efforts to find a wife, I'm having to start at square one. There are a lot of women who would willingly line up to be my bride, but most of them are more interested in my title and my wealth than me. But you're already a princess and you have your own income, so I don't have to wonder about your agenda."

"Then maybe the question shouldn't be 'why would you want to marry me?' but 'why would I want to marry you?'"

"Apparently I'm quite a catch," he told her.

"That whole 'ruler of your own country' thing doesn't really impress me," she warned.

"So tell me what does."

"Well, I did notice that you made an effort to keep the ambassador's wife entertained during dinner," she admitted. "You realized that she wasn't comfortable joining in the discussion about international politics, so you engaged her in a conversation about books and movies."

"I wasn't really enjoying the discussion about politics, either," he said lightly.

She tilted her head, studying him.

"Why are you looking at me like that?"

"I'm trying to figure you out."

"I'm not that complicated."

"I wouldn't have thought so," she admitted. "My first impression was of arrogance and entitlement, which was what I expected. After all, you're royal and rich and charismatic. But during the time that I've spent with you, I've realized that you're also insightful, charming and surprisingly self-effacing."

"So you do like me?"

She smiled. "I have enjoyed your company over the past couple of days."

"But?"

"But I think you're shortchanging yourself by seeking a marriage with political benefits rather than pursuing a romantic relationship."

"I'm not opposed to romance," he told her.

"I'm sure you've been responsible for some grand romantic gestures over the years."

His gaze narrowed. "And yet you still sound skeptical."

She shrugged. "It's easy when you've got a secretary who can order favorite flowers for your companion du jour, or make all the necessary reservations for a romantic candlelit dinner in Venice or Paris or Beijing, depending on the cuisine you crave, of course."

He didn't let his gaze shift away, knew that doing so would be an admission of complicity and provide the princess with yet another round of ammunition to use against him. Instead, he only said, "I would take you not to Paris but Bretagne—there's a little café on Rue Vieille du Temple that serves the most exquisite crepes."

"Okay, I'm impressed that you remember what I ate at brunch the other day," she admitted. "But I'm still not going to pack my bags and hop on a plane."

"I bet your mother would approve of your decision to take a trip with me," he said.

She narrowed her gaze on him. "Except that I haven't decided to take a trip with you."

He didn't know what else he could do or say to change her mind; he only knew that he had to because he'd promised his mother that he would find a way to get the princess to Ardena. Kidnapping seemed a little extreme and not likely to win him any points. Putting a bug in her mother's ear might be less criminal, but would undoubtedly win him even fewer points.

Now that he knew the origin of her distrust of the media, he understood why she would be reluctant to accompany him when he went home. Because the moment she stepped off the plane in the company of the king of Ardena, the press would be all over her.

But, as he suddenly recalled, she had no objection to putting herself in front of the camera for a good cause, and he just happened to have a good cause that needed some attention.

"Okay, I've tried bribery and blackmail," he acknowledged, "which leaves me only with begging."

"Why would you be begging?"

"Because I need your help."

She still looked wary. "My help with what?"

"With the upcoming charity auction for the pediatric wing at Mercy."

"What can I do?"

"Attend the event as my guest."

She turned away. "I don't think so."

He stepped in front of her again. "Why not?"

"Because I can't see how my attendance would be the least bit helpful."

"You underestimate your appeal, Princess."

She shook her head. "I don't think so."

"We're two years behind schedule on this project," he admitted. "But if this auction brings in the kind of money that I think it can, we could finally push forward with our plans."

"I'd be happy to make a donation—"

"I don't want your money. I just want a few hours of your time."

Her hesitation gave him hope. And while his invitation had been borne of desperation, he was pleased he'd followed the impulse, confident that her desire to remain in the background would succumb to her genuine desire to help a truly worthwhile cause.

"When is the auction?"

"October fifteenth."

She nibbled on her bottom lip. "I'm sure you know a lot of women—beautiful and famous women—whose presence would bring the media out in droves."

"I don't know anyone who advocates as passionately for the needs of children as you do."

"I'm flattered, really," she told him.

"But?" he prompted.

"But I'm also worried that my attendance might be misinterpreted," she admitted.

He'd considered the same issue—albeit with less concern—because he knew that being seen in the company of the princess could help repair some of the damage that too many years of indiscretion had done to his reputation.

"I'm surprised that you would weigh the nuisance of potential rumors against the benefits of a successful event," he mused, injecting just a hint of disappointment into his tone.

Her lips curved, just a little. "I'll give you an A for effort, Your Majesty, but I'm not that easily manipulated."

"Forget the A and give me a 'yes' in response to my invitation."

"Maybe."

"Well, that's better than a 'no,'" he acknowledged.

Chapter Eight

Marissa thought about Dante's request for a long time. She wanted to say yes because the hospital auction was exactly the sort of event she was happy to endorse. And she wanted to say no because she was worried that being with Dante could jeopardize her heart. Gabriella was right—she did like him. A lot. And the more time she spent with him, the more she liked him.

But in the end, she decided it wasn't fair to turn down his request for such decidedly personal reasons. Her only remaining concern was the advanced state of Gabriella's pregnancy.

She hated to think that she might be out of the country when her sister-in-law went into labor. Despite Gabriella's reminder that she still had more than two months until her scheduled due date, Marissa didn't give Dante her final answer about the auction until she had exacted a promise from the mother-to-be that she wouldn't have the baby until Marissa was home.

After she confirmed her plans with the king, she told Elena. Although her mother wasn't happy that her daughter was going to Ardena without a ring on her finger, she was thrilled that she was going. She was certain the trip was a prelude to a proposal, and she took Marissa aside to impress upon her the importance of being properly chaperoned whenever she was with the king to avoid even the suggestion of impropriety.

Marissa was tempted to tell her mother that it was too late to worry about her virtue, just to see how Elena might respond to that snag in her plans. But, of course, she didn't. And with as much trepidation as anticipation, Marissa began to prepare for her trip to Ardena.

In the last few days before her scheduled departure, she spent a lot of time at the hospital. She double- and triple-checked the volunteer schedule until Dr. Marotta took it away from her, promising her that they would somehow manage to take care of the babies and ensure the hospital walls didn't fall down during the few weeks that she would be gone.

Banished from the nursery, Marissa went down to the cafeteria for a muffin and a cup of coffee. She had just settled at a table when she sensed someone approaching.

"Excuse me, Your Highness."

She looked up to see a young woman standing beside her. Actually, she looked more like a teenager in her faded jeans and T-shirt with a backpack slung over one shoulder. A pretty teenager, with dark blond hair, mossy-green eyes and fingernails that had been bitten to the quick.

Marissa was aware that reporters came in all sorts of disguises, but she quickly decided that this girl was harmless enough and gestured for her to sit.

"I'm Naomi," she said.

"What can I do for you, Naomi?"

The girl shook her head. "I don't want anything from you. I just wanted to warn you."

"About what?" Marissa asked, more curious than alarmed.

"The king of Ardena."

Now her curiosity was definitely piqued. "Why do you think I need to be warned about the king of Ardena?"

"Because I heard that you're going out with him."

The girl might not be a reporter, but that didn't mean Marissa could trust her not to sell to the tabloids any information she might disclose. Experience had taught her that "a source close to the princess" was sometimes a stranger who had stood next to her in an elevator or taken her order from behind the deli counter at the supermarket.

"You shouldn't believe everything you hear," she advised.

Naomi, obviously expecting a confirmation or denial, seemed startled by the reply. But then she nodded. "You don't know me, so you have no reason to trust that what I'm telling you is true. But you need to know that the king has secrets."

"That's a rather vague allegation," Marissa said gently.

She didn't want to sound dismissive, but she didn't want to encourage the continuation of this conversation, either. Whatever the girl's grudge against Dante—and it seemed apparent that she had one—it wasn't any business of hers.

"If you don't believe me, ask him about Siobhan."

"Who is Siobhan?"

Naomi shook her head as she pushed back her chair. "It's not my story to tell."

Well, that was…bizarre, Marissa decided, as she watched the girl walk away.

And yet, it was hardly the most bizarre conversation she'd ever had with a stranger. For some reason, people seemed compelled to share the oddest information with her, as if it helped them feel that they'd made a personal connection with a member of the royal family. Marissa didn't usually mind, but there was something about the conviction in Naomi's eyes that unnerved her.

Then Dr. Marotta brought his coffee to her table and Marissa forced herself to put the girl and their strange conversation out of her mind.

The flight from Tesoro del Mar to Ardena was both short and uneventful. So short, in fact, that Marissa had little time to second-guess her decision or work herself into a panic about the media that would be waiting, in full force, to document the return of their king.

There had been no fanfare when they'd departed from the private airstrip in Tesoro del Mar, no one to see that Princess Marissa had boarded the plane with King Dante, and therefore no one to alert the royal press corps in Ardena to her presence. Marissa wasn't sure if the surprise element of her arrival would help her slip through unrecognized or if her unexpected appearance would focus more attention in her direction.

She took a deep breath as she paused by the door. Protocol dictated that she wait until the king reached the bottom of the stairs before she began her descent, but Dante surprised her—and everyone watching—by pausing on the first step to wait for her.

Now she was sure that everyone was looking at her. She forced herself to smile as she descended the portable staircase behind him. When she reached the bottom, he took her hand and gave her fingers a reassuring squeeze.

While she appreciated the gesture of support, she knew that the media would try to turn it into something more. But the king seemed unconcerned, smiling and waving as he led her across the tarmac to the waiting limo.

"That wasn't so bad, was it?" he asked when they were settled in the back and on their way to the palace.

"I'll let you know when I see the papers tomorrow."

Of course, in an era of instant communication, she didn't even have to wait that long. By the time they arrived at the palace, news of her arrival in Ardena had been tweeted around the world, captivating royal watchers in all parts of the globe with headlines ranging from Princess Bride-to-Be? and The New King's Newest Conquest? to Has the Prim Princess Tamed the Former Playboy Prince?

A statement was immediately released through the royal household's media liaison explaining that the princess was a friend of the king's who was visiting Ardena and would be in attendance at the Third Annual Dinner, Dance and Auction to benefit Mercy Medical Center. Marissa appreciated the effort, but she knew it wouldn't help. No amount of truth or fact would dissuade the media from generating the sensational headlines the public craved.

She also knew the media wouldn't be the only ones eager to scrutinize the Tesorian princess and her relationship with the king. A fact that was confirmed when she sat down to dinner with Dante's family a short while later.

On the plane, the king had given her the basic rundown on each of his family members. At twenty-nine, Jovanni—or Van, as he was called by his family and friends—was the next eldest and next in line to the throne. He was a scholar and a traveler who had studied at various and numerous institutions around the world, apparently acquiring degrees the way a tourist might pick up souvenir key chains, and now taught history and political science at the local university.

His twenty-five-year-old sister Francesca had an art history degree and a job as junior curator at the National Gallery of Art and Artifacts. And although Dante didn't mention it, a few years back, Princess Francesca had been briefly linked—at least in the press—with Marissa's cousin, Marcus Santiago.

Twenty-two-year-old Matteo had played semipro baseball in California for a couple of years, until he was caught in a compromising position with the wife of the team's owner. After that, he traveled from Las Vegas to Atlantic City, then on to Monte Carlo and Macao, somehow always managing to win greater fortunes than he lost and breaking all kinds of hearts along the way.

But it was nineteen-year-old Leticia who was considered the wild child of the Romero family. And it was she who had visited Tesoro del Mar with her father almost three years earlier, creating quite a scandal when photos of her dirty dancing with Prince Cameron were published in the local papers.

Despite being armed with this basic information, Marissa was still a little overwhelmed when she came face-to-face with the Romeros en masse. Benedicto may have given up the throne but he was still the head of the family, so he sat at the head of the table, with Arianna at the opposite end. As guest of honor, Marissa was seated to the queen's right, across from Dante. To her right was Jovanni, and next to him sat Francesa. Across from Francesca was Matteo, and beside him was Leticia.

Marissa had little experience with family meals. As children, she and her brothers had mostly been kept out of sight when their mother was entertaining, and even when she wasn't, Elena preferred to take her meals alone. But the Romeros were obviously accustomed to such gatherings, and no one seemed to worry about reaching in front of someone else or interrupting a conversation on the opposite side of the table. Marissa did her best to keep up with everything, but a couple of times throughout the meal, Dante gave her a gentle nudge with his foot under the table, followed by a pointed look in the direction of her plate to remind her to eat.

The meal was delicious, but it was the family dynamics that captivated Marissa.

Her conversations with Van confirmed that he was smart and unassuming—less expected were the quick smile and natural charm that immediately put Marissa at ease. Matt was as cocky and self-assured as she'd anticipated, a man to whom flirting was as natural as breathing. Francesca was mostly quiet and introspective, but she showed evidence of a surprising sense of humor. Leticia was the hardest to read. Despite her penchant for getting herself into sticky situations, Marissa got an impression of a sweet and surprisingly innocent young woman who was simply chafing against the limits and restrictions placed upon her by her status.

In addition to these individual impressions and the widely differing personalities of the siblings, Marissa got the sense that they were a tight-knit group. Certainly there didn't seem to be any obvious rivalries or jealousies, and especially not over the fact that Dante was now king.

They were all welcoming and gracious to Marissa, but she wasn't unaware of the looks that passed between them. And if she'd had any doubts before that she wasn't Dante's type, the curious glances and subtle inquisitions of his brothers and sisters put them firmly to rest.

After dinner, everyone went in different directions. Dante excused himself with an apology to Marissa, explaining that he had some political matters to discuss with his father; Van went to his suite to prepare a surprise quiz he planned to give to his students on Monday; and Matt headed out to meet some friends in town. Arianna went to her own quarters to attend to some correspondence; Francesca retreated to her studio to finish a painting.

"I don't have anywhere I need to be," Leticia confided to

Marissa. "But I am going to take the rest of this bottle of wine out to the terrace, if you want to join me."

"I would love to," Marissa agreed, pleased by the invitation.

She followed Dante's sister out to the back courtyard.

"Actually, I was hoping we'd have a minute to chat," Marissa said, accepting the glass of wine Leticia handed to her. "Because I wanted to thank you."

"I can't begin to imagine what for."

"For making headlines with my brother Cameron when you were in Tesoro del Mar a few years back."

"Oh." The young princess grinned. "I'd like to say we had a good time together, but the truth is, he brushed me off. He was very sweet about it, but very clear. I told my father the same thing, but he still freaked out."

Marissa sipped her wine. "Cameron freaked, too, when he saw the papers—which is, indirectly, how he and Gabriella hooked up again after sixteen years apart."

Leticia laughed. "Always glad to help. If you ever want to create a stir—or just stir up some gossip—I'm your girl."

"Just think of all that you could accomplish if you used your powers for good," Marissa teased.

"But it's more fun to be bad."

"Or at least pretend that you are."

The younger woman's gaze narrowed thoughtfully. "My big brother always did appreciate a woman who was more than just a pretty face."

"I'm flattered, I think," she said drily.

"You should be," Leticia said. "Dante has pretty high standards, and it's obvious that he really likes you."

"I can't imagine that he would have invited me to help out with the auction if he didn't."

"He actually told you that he wanted help with the auction?"

She nodded. "In fact, I have a meeting with the fundraising committee on Tuesday."

"Well, your association with the event will definitely combat some of the negative publicity that has befallen the hospital expansion."

Dante hadn't said anything to Marissa about negative publicity. He'd only commented that he believed her involvement could help raise the profile of the event and, consequently, attract more money to the cause.

Leticia topped up Marissa's glass, then her own. "Not to mention how much showing up as Dante's date will bolster his reputation after the hits he's taken."

Tingles of apprehension danced up Marissa's spine. "What kind of hits?"

Leticia winced. "You said he'd told you."

"He told me about the auction," she repeated.

"Well, then—" the princess lifted her glass "—let me wash down my foot with some pinot noir."

"What kind of hits?" Marissa asked again.

She sighed. "The press has been gunning for Dante since my father announced that he was stepping down. They've been claiming that the new king is out of touch with the needs of his people, socially unaware and fiscally irresponsible."

"That all sounds rather vague and, truthfully, not much different than the criticisms about any other form of government."

"You're right. But more specifically, there was an error made with respect to the allocation of funds in the national budget shortly after Dante took office. Somehow, money that had been earmarked for the hospital—for the purchase of equipment for the neonatal intensive-care unit—was instead diverted to the naval-defense fund."

"Why the naval-defense fund?"

"Where the money went isn't as important as the fact that

the hospital didn't get it," Leticia said. "And when a newborn's near-fatal medical condition wasn't diagnosed because Mercy didn't have the right equipment, Dante was blamed. The media alleged that he didn't care about the nation's health care or its children."

"And I've been vocal in my support of both," Marissa realized.

"I didn't mean to imply that your reputation is the only reason he's interested in you," Leticia said, sounding apologetic.

But for Marissa, the information certainly answered a lot of questions.

Dante was relieved to be home.

He was even more relieved that he'd succeeded in convincing Marissa to come back with him for the auction, which was exactly what he wanted. Or at least the first step in getting him what he wanted.

"I like your princess."

Dante couldn't help but smile in response to his father's typically blunt statement. "At this stage, I think she might object to being referred to as mine."

"Isn't she the one you're going to marry?"

"As soon as I can get her on board with that plan."

"I can't imagine that will take too long." Benedicto lowered himself into a vacant chair. "I've never known you not to get what you want."

"I'd say that the citizens of Ardena are probably more eager for a royal wedding than I am."

"You don't have to be eager but you do have to be committed," his father warned. "Marriage should be forever. If you're not sure, or if you don't think she's the right one, or if you have any doubts at all about whether she can handle the expectations and demands that will be placed upon her, then you should wait."

"I am committed," Dante assured him. He might not have been thrilled about the sudden pressure to marry, but he understood it. And he knew that he had an obligation to choose a bride who would not only make a suitable wife but an able representative of Ardena, and he was convinced that Marissa Leandres was the most appropriate choice.

Having been born a princess, she was accustomed to the intrusiveness of the media. Yet despite having lived much of her life under public scrutiny, she'd managed a mostly quiet existence without any scandals in her past or obvious skeletons in her closet. Not just a quiet but chaste existence, if her mother was to be believed. As he'd told Elena, he didn't expect a virgin bride, but he definitely didn't want an ex-boyfriend posting naked pictures of her on the internet after their engagement was announced.

Marissa was beautiful and if she'd chosen to play up her looks and dress the part, she could have coasted through life on the power of her celebrity. But she was smarter than that. Not just intelligent and well educated, but possessing a sharp mind that probed and challenged. She had ideas and opinions that she expressed articulately, and he genuinely enjoyed just talking with her.

She was kind and compassionate and was respected around the world for her charitable works. A lot of high-profile people had specific causes they endorsed or programs they funded. Marissa didn't lend her name to events for the publicity or write checks for the tax deduction. She was truly committed to bettering the lives of women and children around the globe, with a specific push toward doing so through access to better health care and education.

"What are you committed to?" his father asked now. "The concept of marriage in general or the princess in particular?"

"Both."

"Good, because you have to remember that the woman you choose as your queen will also be your wife. There will be times when it's just the two of you behind closed doors, and it's important that you can look forward to those times."

"We had the talk about the birds and the bees a long time ago," Dante reminded his dad.

"Unfortunately, we didn't also talk about good judgment. If we had, when I'd stepped down, the people wouldn't have been so concerned about a playboy running the palace."

It was only years of experience and training that ensured he didn't flinch beneath his father's steely gaze.

"But youthful indiscretions can be forgiven," Benedicto continued, "maybe even forgotten. And your behavior since taking the throne has been circumspect."

Dante felt no pride in response to his father's words. How could he when the image of the red-haired, green-eyed goddess—naked on his bed, save for the mask that concealed her face—nudged at the back of his mind? However, he could, and did, feel relief that at least he had shown *some* discretion that night. No one, not even Juno, knew that Jupiter was really the king of Ardena.

But as much as he'd enjoyed the hours he'd spent making love with Juno, he'd had an unexpected revelation when he'd woken up alone. He was tired of one-night stands. He wanted a partner. Someone not just to share his bed but to share his life.

And then he'd met Marissa, and he'd felt a surprising sense of rightness, as if everything was falling into place. Almost as if it was…destiny.

"You've had to make a lot of adjustments since February," Benedicto continued. "And you've done so without complaint."

"As much as the whole firstborn thing wasn't really my

choice, none of this is—aside from the timing—unexpected. Both you and Mom spent a lot of years not just prepping me to take the throne, but providing an example of what it takes to make a marriage succeed."

"I hope we have, because finding a comfortable balance between your duties and your desires is important in life." Benedicto smiled. "We didn't have five kids together out of a sense of obligation, you know."

"Please." Dante held up a hand. "There are certain details a son doesn't need to know about his parents' marriage."

"Fair enough," his father said. "But you should think about those details before embarking on your own."

Oh, he'd thought about those...details. And even though he'd kissed Marissa only once, that single kiss had been enough to hint at the passion within her, a passion he was eager to explore.

One step at a time, he reminded himself.

Marissa never slept easily in an unfamiliar bed, so before she returned to her room, she decided to find something to read. Upon their arrival, Dante had given her a quick tour of the palace, and she was fairly confident that she could navigate the route to the library and back to her suite.

She only took one wrong turn on the way and was happily perusing the shelves when Dante's father entered the room.

She curtsied. "Good evening again, Your Majesty."

He seemed startled to see her, as if they hadn't shared a meal at the same table a few hours earlier. And when he did address her, he said, "It's good to see you again, Elena."

Marissa was taken aback, not just to hear him speak her mother's name but by the warmth in his tone. "I'm not Elena, Your Majesty. I'm her daughter, Marissa."

He frowned, as if what she was saying didn't make any sense to him. Then the bewilderment in his eyes cleared and he smiled at her. "Forgive my confusion," he said. "I didn't realize before how very much you look like her."

"Do you know my mother?"

"I did, a very long time ago."

Which surprised Marissa, but not nearly as much as his next statement.

"In fact, we were supposed to be married."

She frowned, thinking it likely that he had the Princess Royal confused with someone. Because if Dante's father had been engaged to Marissa's mother, she was sure that detail would have come up at least once during the numerous conversations in which Elena had pushed her daughter to consider marriage to Benedicto's son.

"I'd only met her a few times," the king's father continued, "but every time, her beauty quite simply took my breath away. She thought I was quite handsome, too. At least she said that she did.

"But she was stubborn and headstrong, and regardless of her feelings for me, she refused to be forced into an arranged marriage. So while my father and her father were discussing the details of our betrothal, she ran off and married another man."

"Gaetan Leandres," Marissa murmured, familiar with at least that part of the story. "My father."

His eyes clouded again. "That might be right. It was a long time ago."

"At least forty years," she guessed, since her brother Michael was almost that age.

He nodded.

Marissa had thought she was familiar with the story of her parents' whirlwind romance, but in the version she knew, there had never been any mention of Benedicto Romero. If what Dante's father was telling her now was true, and she had no reason to suspect that it wasn't, then there was obviously a lot more to the tale than she'd ever suspected.

And she couldn't help but wonder if that "more" was somehow motivating Elena's efforts to push her daughter and the present king of Ardena together.

Chapter Nine

On Wednesday, Marissa was invited to take tea with Dante's mother in her sitting room.

After the petits fours were set out and tea had been poured, Arianna said, "I understand you don't often travel outside of Tesoro del Mar, so I wanted to express how pleased we all are that you've chosen to visit Ardena."

"His Majesty was very persuasive when he issued the invitation," Marissa told her.

The queen mother smiled. "My son inherited more than his fair share of his father's charm. As a result, it is a rare occasion when he doesn't get his own way."

"I'm sure it is."

"But I didn't invite you here to talk about Dante. I invited you here so that we could get to know one another." Arianna sipped her tea. "Considering your royal status, there's limited information readily available about you aside from your charitable endeavors."

"Have you been looking for information?"

The queen selected a pretty pink cake from a platter. "You can't blame a mother for being curious about the woman who has snagged her son's attention."

"No," Marissa agreed. "But if you're trying to determine if I'm good enough for your son, why don't we just agree that I'm not?"

Arianna seemed to puzzle over this as she sipped her tea. "Are you saying that you don't want to marry Dante?"

His mother sounded so incredulous, Marissa had to smile.

"I think he's a good man, and I've enjoyed spending time with him, but I have no interest in being his queen."

"So your only reason for coming to Ardena was to *not* have a relationship with my son?" the queen asked skeptically.

"Well, that wasn't my only reason," Marissa conceded. "I also came because Dante suggested that my attendance could help promote the auction for Mercy Medical Center."

"I'm sure it will," Arianna agreed. "But I didn't realize that was the enticement he used to bring you here."

Now it was Marissa's turn to be puzzled by her choice of words. "Are you suggesting that he had another reason?"

"Well, according to all of the newspapers, the king is courting his queen."

"The newspapers are wrong."

"Are you sure?"

"Yes, I'm sure. Dante knows I don't want to marry him."

"You've told him this?" his mother asked, amusement evident in her tone.

"Yes."

Arianna smiled. "That could be precisely why he's chosen you."

"He hasn't chosen me," Marissa said, though she was aware that the protest sounded weak.

"Perhaps not," the queen allowed. "But if he has, remember that it's rare for Dante not to get what he wants."

The queen's warning echoed in the back of Marissa's mind for the next few days. She was certain that a single conversation with Dante would answer all of her questions. Unfortunately, the king remained elusive.

After more than a week away, she could understand that he had a lot of work to catch up on. She could hardly blame him for being tied up with appointments and conferences or away from the palace for various state functions.

And she managed to keep herself busy, too. She had meetings with the fundraising committee to review and revise all manner of details for the upcoming auction. She walked in the garden and swam in the pool, and she spent a lot of time at her computer, emailing her friends and family back in Tesoro del Mar. Hannah was ecstatic in the early stages of her pregnancy; Gabriella was cranky in the last trimester of hers. And Dr. Marotta insisted that everything was running so smoothly at the hospital, no one even noticed that she was gone.

She was pouting over that one when she ventured outside to enjoy the sun on Monday afternoon and found her attention caught by some trees in the distance. As much time as she'd spent wandering the grounds, she'd never noticed them before and she couldn't resist exploring.

She tipped her head back and jolted when she saw movement out of the corner of her eye. With a self-conscious laugh, she pressed her hand to her furiously beating heart. "You scared me, Your Majesty."

"My apologies," Benedicto said. "I couldn't resist the lure of a beautiful woman in my olive grove."

"I should be the one to apologize if I've wandered where

I shouldn't have. I didn't expect to find an orchard on the grounds, and my curiosity was piqued."

"Guests are free to wander wherever they wish," Benedicto assured her. "And it has been a long time since anyone has shown an interest in my trees."

"They're beautiful," she said truthfully, letting her fingers trace a deep ridge in the gnarled trunk of the tree closest to her. "So unique and full of character."

"There's a lot of history in those twisted branches," the former king agreed. "And a lot of generations have harvested their bounty."

She noted the clusters of green fruit. "When will you pick these?"

"Actually, we don't pick them. We shake the branches," he told her. "And we usually start around the end of November, finishing in late January or early February. You're welcome to help, if you're interested. We can always use an extra pair of hands."

"I am interested," she said. But she wondered if she would still be in the country then or if, having satisfied her obligations in Ardena, she would have gone back to Tesoro del Mar.

...it's rare for Dante not to get what he wants.

But what did he want? Did he want her help with the auction or did he want something more?

Arianna's words teased Marissa's mind with possibilities. To marry the king of Ardena would mean many things. For Marissa, the biggest negative would be the complete lack of privacy. As queen, everything she said and did would be scrutinized and criticized, analyzed and interpreted. But she wondered now if there might not be enough positives to more than balance the scales. And one undeniable positive was the attraction she'd felt for the king almost from the start, an attraction that continued to grow.

"What are you interested in?"

The tantalizingly familiar voice skimmed over her like a caress, making her think of all kinds of answers to the question that had absolutely nothing to do with olive trees.

"The princess was asking about the harvest," Benedicto explained to his son.

"And mother was asking where her husband had run away to," Dante said.

Though his tone was light, Marissa heard the undercurrent of worry.

"She should have guessed I'd run away with a pretty lady," he said and winked at Marissa.

"Obviously your son comes by his charm honestly enough," she noted.

Benedicto grinned. "But be careful—he's as stubborn as he is charming," he warned. "He needs a woman with a strong backbone, someone who will not only stand up to him, but stand behind him."

"Dad—"

"I'm only trying to help your cause," Benedicto explained.

"It would be a bigger help to give us some time alone," Dante said pointedly.

"Okay," his father relented, squeezing Marissa's hand before he released it. "But don't try any hanky-panky. This one isn't just a princess. She's a real lady."

"I know."

Marissa watched Benedicto make his way back toward the palace. When Arianna met him in the courtyard, something her husband said caused her to throw her head back and laugh. Then Benedicto caught her around the waist and drew her into his arms for a kiss that made Marissa sigh.

"Your father is a wonderful man," she said to Dante now.

"He obviously thinks just as highly of you," he noted.

"I didn't realize we'd wandered out of sight. I'm sorry you were worried."

"Why would I be worried?"

"Maybe because his memory has started slipping a little," she suggested.

"Why would you say that?" he challenged.

"Am I wrong?"

Dante glanced away, back toward the house, but not before she saw the flash of pain in his eyes. "No," he admitted.

She waited for him to continue. After his father and mother went inside, he did so.

"The official diagnosis is vascular cognitive impairment," he explained. "Likely precipitated by a series of minor and undiagnosed strokes he suffered over the past two years."

She touched a hand to his arm. "I'm sorry."

"There are moments of obvious confusion, and my mother doesn't like him to wander off on his own. But his good days outnumber the bad, so we've managed to keep his condition under wraps."

"I'm not going to tell anyone," she assured him.

"I know." He caught her hand as she started to draw it away and linked their fingers together. "Thank you."

"For what?"

"For being so warm and generous, kind and compassionate, smart and strong."

She lifted a brow. "That's a pretty thorough character assessment considering you met me hardly more than a week ago."

"In that brief amount of time, I've had the opportunity to observe you in various situations," he told her. "I've witnessed your interactions with your mother—who is an undeniably strong and unyielding woman. But you don't let her push you around. You decide when to stand firm and when to give way. And I've seen you as a volunteer at the hospital, and I've watched your eyes go soft when you hold one of those tiny babies in your arms."

"You're very observant, Your Majesty."

"You're a fascinating woman, Your Highness. But aside from all of that," he continued, "I know my dad likes you. And while his mind might drift to the past occasionally, he's always been a great judge of character."

"Well, he did warn me about *you*," she said lightly.

He tugged her toward him. "You don't look very worried."

"Why would I be? You assured me your intentions are honorable."

"But 'honorable' is not synonymous with 'innocent,'" he cautioned as he reached up to tuck a loose strand of hair behind her ear, his fingertip brushing the sensitive shell as he did so.

She shivered in response to the light caress. He smiled.

"That's something else I've observed—the way your pulse races when I touch you."

She swallowed, as disconcerted by the accuracy of his insight as she was by his nearness.

"Considering your legendary exploits, I would expect you to be accustomed to the effect you have on women."

"Right now I'm only interested in the effect I have on *you*," he said, stroking a finger down the curve of her cheek.

She pushed his hand away. "Well, I'm not interested in your meaningless flirtations."

"Why do you refuse to believe that I'm attracted to you?"

It wasn't that she *refused* to believe it so much as she *couldn't* believe it. She knew she wasn't his type. She wasn't as beautiful or sexy or sophisticated as the women he usually dated, which was why she'd assumed his interest was predicated upon her title and nationality, and his belief—albeit mistaken—that she was an innocent.

"Why are you so intent on denying what's between us?"

His hands stroked up her arms, his fingertips following the ridge of her collarbone, then dipping to trace the deep V of her jacket. Heat swept through her body, making her heart pound and her body yearn, making her nipples ache for the touch of his hands. A soft sigh escaped through parted lips.

"We would be good together, Marissa. I have no doubts at all about that."

"I'm not going to fall into your bed," she told him.

"I'd be happy to carry you."

She shook her head. "I'm not the type of woman to be swept away by promises or passion."

"I don't think you know what type of woman you really are," he countered.

"But I'll bet you could show me," she said drily.

"I'd prefer for us to figure it out together." His voice was as tantalizing as his hands. "I want to watch your face when I touch you, to watch the hesitation in your eyes change to awareness and desire. I want to hear your breath catch and feel your muscles quiver. I want to kiss you, long and slow and deep."

He was seducing her with nothing more than his words, without even touching her. And if her body had felt hot and tingly before, that was nothing compared to what she was feeling now.

She had to moisten her lips before she could speak, but when she managed to respond, she was pleased to note that her voice was level, giving no hint of the desire churning in her veins. "You want a lot of things," she noted. "And if you got them, I'm sure you'd be disappointed."

"I'm sure I wouldn't be," he said. "And neither would you."

Though her experience was extremely limited, the intensity of her physical response to him warned that it wasn't an idle promise. And she knew that if he touched her again right now, she would melt into a puddle at his feet.

But he didn't.

Because Dante was afraid that if he touched her now, he

wouldn't be able to stop. And as much as he wanted her—and believed she wanted him, too—he could tell she wasn't ready to take their relationship to the next step.

So instead he only said, "Take a walk with me."

"Is that a personal request or a royal command?"

He grinned at the pique in her tone. "Whatever will get you to say yes."

He led her to the stone gazebo at the top of the hill. From there, they could see the ocean. He breathed deeply, inhaling the familiar tang of salty air that he always missed when he was away from home. But beneath the scent of the ocean, he caught a hint of Marissa's perfume, and he noticed that the breeze had caught a few more strands of her hair and tugged them free of the loose knot at the back of her head.

He gestured for her to sit, and she lowered herself onto the edge of a bench, crossing her feet at the ankles and folding her hands in her lap. Her pale yellow skirt and boxy jacket were unappealing, but there was an inexplicable something about Marissa that drew him. And he suspected that if he ever got her out of those boring clothes, he would find the Tesorian princess wasn't nearly as dull as she wanted everyone to believe, that the carefully cultivated image was nothing more than a facade, and that beneath the cool and prim shell beat a warm and passionate heart.

He sat beside her and picked up the thread of their earlier conversation. "There is a powerful chemistry between us, Your Highness. An undeniable attraction that I believe could provide a solid foundation for marriage."

"I thought you'd given up on the idea of marrying me."

"A king doesn't surrender at the first sign of opposition," he told her.

"I thought you were searching for a bride, not outlining a military campaign."

"Apparently both require careful and strategic planning in order to overcome the enemy's opposition."

Her lips curved, just a little. "Am I the enemy?"

"No," he denied. "But you need to understand that I'm not the enemy, either. I didn't write the law that gives your mother the authority to choose your husband, Marissa."

"I'm aware of that."

"And I don't blame you for feeling trapped."

Which was exactly how Marissa felt.

Trapped between the proverbial rock and hard place.

But since her mind was churning out idioms, wasn't it better to be trapped with the devil she knew? Maybe she didn't know Dante Romero very well, but she at least had an idea of what he wanted from her. If she didn't marry the king of Ardena, there was still the possibility—more likely the inevitability—that Elena would simply choose a different husband for her daughter. Maybe even the Duke of Bellemoro.

Of course, that possibility was what had driven Marisa to take such drastic action the night of the ball. At the time, she'd been confident that she was doing the right thing. In retrospect, she had to accept that giving her virginity to a stranger rather than having it taken by the duke hadn't been such a brilliant scheme since it meant she was no longer suitable to marry the one suitor she might not have objected to marrying.

But the truth was that even if she decided to marry Dante—disregarding for a moment the fact that she was no longer "pure of virtue" and therefore probably unsuitable to be the king's bride—it wouldn't really be her choice. If it was up to Marissa, she wouldn't be choosing to get married at this point in her life. She would wait until she'd fallen in love—and until the man she loved had fallen in love with her, too. Unfortunately, since the Princess Royal had decided to seek a husband for her daughter, Marissa's only choice was whether to accept her mother's decision willingly or not.

"I'm not expecting an answer right now," he told her. "I just want you to consider the possibilities. And while I'm not unaware of what you would be giving up if you were to leave Tesoro del Mar to make a life with me here, I'm confident that the trade-offs would make it worth your while."

"Such as?"

"No longer being subjected to your mother's arbitrary exercise of power."

On the surface, that sounded tempting, but she said, "Instead, I would be subjected to yours."

He shook his head. "Equal partners, Marissa. That's what I'm offering you. As my wife, you would be queen, and as the queen of Ardena you would have the opportunity and freedom to pursue your own interests. You could even continue the work you were doing at PACH in the soon-to-be-expanded pediatric wing at Mercy."

He had to know that she would be tempted by this offer. The work she'd done at the hospital in Port Augustine had been incredibly fulfilling and rewarding.

"And, at the end of the day," he continued, "when you'd finished taking care of everyone else's babies, you could come home to your own."

Her eyes lifted to his. "When you embark on a military campaign, you take the big guns, don't you?"

"The key to a successful negotiation is to know what the other party wants," he told her.

"What do *you* want?"

"I told you—a queen for Ardena, a wife to share my life, a mother for my children." He smiled as his gaze skimmed over her. "And the pleasure of taking the woman who is my wife and the mother of my children to bed every night."

She was undeniably tempted by his offer. And tempted by

the tantalizing thought of making love with him. She couldn't help but wonder what kind of lover he would be, if he could make her feel the way she'd felt when she was with Jupiter—

She banished the thought to the back of her mind. She couldn't think about him now, she wouldn't let herself consider that the most incredible night of her life might have been the biggest mistake she'd ever made.

"That's a lot to consider."

He shifted closer to her, so that his thigh pressed against hers. "Or you could trust what's in your heart and take a leap of faith."

"I trust my heart." She rose to her feet, needing to put some distance between them. "I don't trust *your* motives."

He followed her to the other side of the gazebo. "I've been completely honest about what I want."

She studied him for a minute. "Okay, but I want you to be honest about something else."

"Anything," he said automatically.

"Why did money intended for the hospital end up in the defense fund?"

He wasn't so quick to respond to that question. And when he finally did, his answer didn't make a lot of sense to Marissa.

"Because in 1982 there was a very real threat of invasion by a Greek drug cartel that wanted control of the underwater caves on the northern shores of the island."

"You would have been a child in 1982."

He just nodded.

"It wasn't your signature on the budget," she realized. "It was your father's."

He didn't confirm or deny it. He only said, "My father had already stepped down."

But Marissa wasn't fooled, and she found herself wondering what kind of man would willingly subject himself to the criticism and ridicule of his people in order to protect and preserve the reputation of his father. The answer was suddenly as clear as it was simple: a man whose love for his family was as steadfast as his loyalty to them. And she suspected that any woman lucky enough to win Dante's heart would experience the same unwavering affection and devotion.

She just didn't know if that woman could ever be her.

Chapter Ten

Marissa didn't believe that the way to a man's heart was through his stomach, but she did believe that the way to a benefactor's wallet was. In her experience, the rich were always more generous after they'd been well fed, and one of the first things she'd done when she met with the catering company in charge of the meal for the Dinner, Dance and Auction was to reconfigure the menu. If this event was to garner special attention, she argued, it needed to offer something a little more special than the typical rubber-chicken plate.

The caterers grumbled about clients wanting changes made at the eleventh hour, and insisted that her "special" menu would require "special" payment. Marissa slapped down a quote from a competitor, which outlined exactly what she wanted for the meal at a cost commensurate with what the committee had agreed to pay for the original.

But she understood that successful negotiations required

give-and-take on both sides, and while she refused to pay anything more than the contract price, she did offer to include the revised menu in the auction program, with the catering company's logo and contact information. The benefit was obvious: impress the guests with the meal, and the referral business from the high-end clientele was potentially unlimited.

So the guests who attended the event in the Grand Ballroom of the Castalia Hotel in downtown Saint Georgios were presented with baskets of artisan breads instead of dinner rolls, served tomato and bocconcini salad rather than mixed greens, and offered their choice of succulent Chateaubriand with roasted red potatoes and glazed baby carrots or grilled sea bass with wild rice and peppers and mushrooms.

Throughout the meal, diners were encouraged to browse the auction tables and make an offer on favorite items, and Marissa was pleased to note that the bidding had become quite competitive even before dessert—a delectable walnut-date torte—was served. And by nine o'clock, she was certain that the Third Annual Dinner, Dance and Auction to benefit Mercy Medical Center was going to be an unqualified success.

If she'd been nervous about anything aside from the revenues generated by the event, it was the seating plan. She was attending the auction as the king's guest, and she knew that a lot of eyes would be focused on their table throughout the evening. Thankfully, all of Dante's family was in attendance, as well, and since Van had invited a fellow professor from the university and Francesca was accompanied by her on-again, off-again boyfriend of the past three years, their table of ten was filled with people she could trust not to spend the entire meal staring at her and Dante.

Away from the table, it was a different story, of course. But Marissa was prepared for that, and since she understood that this curiosity had probably sold a lot of tickets to the event, she tried to be gracious.

About halfway through the meal, Dr. Nikolas Stamos, chairman of the board of directors of Mercy Foundation, took the podium to welcome everyone and thank them for their generous and ongoing support of the hospital and its programs. Then he spoke briefly about the history of the facility, touched on recent advances in medical science and outlined plans for the future of Mercy. He was passionate and eloquent but, most importantly, he was concise.

He'd been a little disgruntled when Marissa nixed his suggestion of a PowerPoint presentation outlining the projected costs of the expansion. But whereas she'd strong-armed the caterer, she'd sweet-talked the chairman, gently pointing out that people who had paid to walk through the door should have an opportunity to enjoy their meal without the weight of moral obligation or social responsibility being forced upon them.

The chairman had been skeptical, but in the end, he'd deferred to her expertise. And when Dr. Stamos had taken his seat again, Marissa and Dante began to work the room.

This was Marissa's specialty. She tended to steer away from crowds, but she was good with people in more intimate situations. And she was content to circulate here, taking the time to speak with anyone who wanted a word, happily discussing what she knew about the proposed hospital expansion and politely deflecting inquiries about her relationship with the king.

Dante stayed close by and proved willing to respond to whatever subjects were directed his way. He was knowledgeable and articulate, and he had a knack for connecting with people. He was charming and sincere. When he asked a question of someone else, he actually listened to the response.

And when a question was asked of him, he considered his reply rather than reciting a stock answer.

He was the king—ruling wasn't just his responsibility, but his birthright. He didn't need the approval of anyone in this room, but she realized that he wanted to at least earn their respect. He was showing them that he was accessible, willing to listen to their concerns in order to better respond to them. And Marissa was forced to acknowledge that she'd made a mistake in assuming that the new king wasn't anything more than his reputation.

She wasn't in the habit of making premature judgments about other people. As a princess, she was often subjected to stereotyping, and she should have known better than to accept the king as a particular "type." Just as she wasn't as sweet and docile and empty-headed as many believed a princess should be, she should have recognized that Dante wasn't one-dimensional.

Of course, he'd done nothing to contradict the media's image of him. From the moment they'd met, he'd flirted with and teased her relentlessly. But now she knew that the carefree playboy image he'd so carefully cultivated was just an image—the sexy charmer was undoubtedly an aspect of his personality, but it wasn't the complete definition of the man.

By the time they'd finished their circuit of the room, the band had started to play and several couples were on the dance floor. She glanced back at the table, looking for Dante's parents, and noted that the seats they'd occupied at dinner were empty.

"You're looking for someone," Dante guessed.

"Your dad," she said. "I promised him a dance."

"My parents decided to have an early night."

"Oh," she said, genuinely disappointed.

"Of course, I'd be happy to take his place," Dante said to her.

Her brows lifted. "Haven't you already done that?"

"I meant as your dance partner," he clarified, offering his hand.

She hesitated.

"Didn't the instructors at your finishing school teach you that it's impolite to decline a gentleman's request to dance?"

"They did," she acknowledged. "I just figured there was enough talk going around about our relationship without giving the crowd more reason to speculate."

"They're speculating already," he warned. "Wondering why Princess Marissa is refusing the king's gallant invitation. Doesn't she know that he's considered quite the catch—that women around the world are vying for the opportunity to be his queen, and that half of the women in this country would give almost anything for the opportunity to be held in his arms?"

"That would be the half that haven't already been in his arms?" she guessed, even as she placed her hand in his.

"Ouch."

But he was smiling as he led her into the waltz, and while Marissa had some reservations about agreeing to this dance, she couldn't fault his style. He executed the steps smoothly, so that they moved in sync with the other couples. And as they spun around the dance floor, she couldn't hold back the images that spun through her mind.

Images of the Mythos Ball and the man she knew only as Jupiter.

Maybe it wasn't surprising that the memories would be triggered by this dance. After all, she hadn't danced with anyone else since she'd danced with Jupiter that night.

Not that Dante reminded her of Jupiter in any specific way. The king was taller than the god—or maybe it was just that the shoes she was wearing tonight didn't add a full four inches to her own height. And the king's chest wasn't as broad. Of course, he wasn't wearing a breastplate, either. But there was one real and disturbing similarity, and that was the quivering excitement that originated low in her belly and slowly spread through her body.

Lust.

She recognized it now for what it was and saw no reason to romanticize the feeling. The king was an undoubtedly handsome and charismatic man and she was hardly the first woman to have lustful feelings for him. But she was likely the first who had made any effort to resist them.

"You're an excellent dancer, Your Majesty," she noted, hoping that the effort of making conversation would distract her from the blood pulsing in her veins.

"It's easy with an excellent partner," he told her. "And a sincere pleasure with a beautiful one. Have I told you how stunning you look tonight?"

She felt her cheeks flush. Though she hadn't strayed too far from her usual color palette, the slim strapless gown of chocolate-colored silk was more eye-catching than her usual attire. And while she'd promised herself that she wasn't dressing to catch the king's eye, she was pleased that he'd noticed.

"You aren't accustomed to compliments," he noted.

"I'm not accustomed to anyone looking at me the way you do," she admitted.

"And you're smart to be wary," he admitted. "Because while a man can't help but look at what he admires, he is rarely content to simply look."

And then he shifted topics as deftly as he transitioned through the steps of the waltz. "I saw you talking to the chief of pediatric medicine earlier."

"Dr. Kalidindi was interested in learning more about the volunteer-cuddler program at PACH."

"Juno's Touch."

She was surprised that he'd remembered the name—and

she was frustrated by her own inability to forget about the one night in which she'd experienced the power and freedom of being the goddess Juno.

"He's interested in launching a similar program here, and he asked if I would be willing to help get things started."

"What was your answer?"

He sounded more curious than concerned, as if her response was of no consequence to him.

"I told him I would have to think about it. I have a life and responsibilities in Tesoro del Mar that I've already neglected for more than three weeks. Not to mention that you must be anxious to get rid of me so that your life can go back to normal."

"You have to know I don't want to get rid of you, Your Highness. In fact, I'd very much like you to stay."

"Our agreement was that I would come to Ardena to help with the auction," she reminded him.

"So let's make a new agreement."

"I'm not sure it would be wise for me to stay any longer."

"Playing it safe, Princess? Or running scared?"

Both, she acknowledged, if only to herself. Aloud she said, "The song is over, Your Majesty."

"But I'm not ready to let you go."

"People are watching."

"I don't care."

"I do." She curtsied and stepped back. "I told you when I agreed to come here that I didn't want my photo splashed across the newspapers under headlines speculating about the nature of our relationship."

He fell into step beside her as she moved away from the dance floor and back to their table. "Then let's stop the speculation."

She picked up her water glass, sipped. "How?"

"By announcing our engagement."

Her heart actually stuttered, and she realized that at some point over the past few weeks, the idea of marrying the king had become less daunting and more enticing. She wasn't entirely sure when her feelings toward him had changed, but she suspected it was around the time she'd stopped thinking about him as His Majesty the King of Ardena and started seeing him as Dante Romero.

Because she knew now that he wasn't just a ruler, he was a man. And while he was undoubtedly handsome and charming and smart and sexy, he was more than that. He was a man she liked and admired. She enjoyed spending time with him, she respected the sharpness of his mind and the warmth of his heart and she seriously lusted after his body.

Okay, so there could be some definite benefits to letting the king put a ring on her finger. But would he want to put a ring on her finger if he knew about her one-night love affair?

"Not tonight," she finally responded to his suggestion.

"You didn't say no this time," he mused. "Maybe next time you'll actually say yes."

Marissa danced with several other people after that, including Dr. Kalidindi, who used the excuse of a fox-trot to press his case. He was as charming as he was persistent, and at the end of their three minutes on the dance floor she found herself agreeing to at least stay another week so that she could tour the pediatric wing of the hospital and meet with him.

When she finally made her way off of the dance floor, she decided to steal a quiet moment alone and catch a breath of fresh air. As guests had been coming and going through the main doors, she opted to slip out of the side entrance for a little privacy.

Apparently she wasn't the only one with that idea, as she saw that Dante had gone out this way, too. Well, she figured it was as good a time as any to tell him that she was staying in Ardena—at least for another week.

It wasn't until he turned to speak to someone that she realized he wasn't alone. She paused with her hand on the glass, her heart hammering in her chest.

She couldn't see who he was with, but he looked angry. Furious. Then his companion stepped into the light, and Marissa sucked in a breath as she recognized the girl who had introduced herself as Naomi when she met her at the hospital in Port Augustine.

She pushed open the door, just a little, unashamedly eavesdropping. They were too far away for her to hear their words, but Dante's tone was harsh, the girl's softer, almost taunting.

Maybe Naomi did know some of the king's secrets—or maybe she *was* one of his secrets. The possibility made Marissa's stomach churn.

No—if Naomi had been sleeping with the king, she would have said so. She'd only told Marissa to ask him about Siobhan, and then she'd refused to say anything more.

It's not my story to tell.

Then whose story was it?

Marissa decided it was time she got an answer to that question.

After their dance, Dante and Marissa went in opposite directions. As much as he wished he could spend all of his time with her, he understood the expectations and protocols of his position. But by midnight, the crowd had thinned considerably and they were finally able to head back to the palace.

He was going to suggest opening a bottle of champagne to toast to the success of the evening, but noticed that she was rubbing her forehead.

"Ready to call it a night?" he asked.

She surprised him by shaking her head. "Actually, I think I'm going to go out back to get some air."

"Do you want company?"

"It's your palace," she reminded him.

Not the most gracious invitation he'd ever received, but he was willing to take it.

She settled in one of the chairs facing the pool, and he chose the one beside her.

"I figured you'd be exhausted after all the work you did— not just today and tonight, but over the past few weeks."

"I am exhausted," she admitted. "But too wired to sleep just yet."

"Anything in particular on your mind?"

"A few things."

He wondered if one of those things was his proposal—or at least the offer from Dr. Kalidindi. "Which one is responsible for that little crease between your brows?"

She shifted her chair so that she was facing him more directly before she responded. "Siobhan."

He looked startled. "What do you know about her?" he asked cautiously.

"I don't know anything," she admitted. "I was hoping you would tell me."

If it was true that she didn't know anything, he could keep the details sparse, giving her enough information to satisfy her curiosity and nothing more. Except that she was looking at him with such unguarded faith that he knew no half-truths would suffice. She was trusting him to tell her the truth; he could only hope that she would believe him when he did.

"Siobhan is the six-month-old daughter of Fiona Breslin, a part-time assistant events coordinator here at the palace. When she was born, she seemed to be a normal, healthy baby, but after a few weeks, Fiona noticed that the infant was struggling to catch her breath and her skin had a slightly bluish tinge."

"She had a hole in her heart," Marissa guessed.

"You obviously spend *a lot* of time at the hospital."

She shook her head. "Gabriella's daughter, Sierra, was born with an atrial septal defect."

"Well, an echocardiogram confirmed that it was an ASD, and while Siobhan's doctor kept promising Fiona that the hole would close on its own, her condition continued to worsen. She finally took her to the hospital, where it was determined that she needed emergency surgery. Unfortunately, there wasn't a surgeon at Mercy qualified to perform that kind of surgery on an infant."

"You sent her to PACH," Marissa realized. "I remember when she was brought in—just a few weeks ago. Dr. Nardone did the surgery."

"And now Siobhan is recovering on schedule."

"There has to be more to the story," she guessed.

He nodded. "As a part-time employee, Fiona had limited medical insurance that didn't cover the cost of transportation to, or any kind of procedure in, a foreign country. It was Fiona's sister, Naomi, who came to me. She said that I had to help, because if I didn't, my baby was going to die."

Marissa's gaze never flickered, never wavered.

"You're not going to ask if it's true—if the baby is mine?" She shook her head. "I know it's not."

He was as surprised as he was touched by her unquestioning support. "While I appreciate your vote of confidence, how can you be so sure?"

"Because you date supermodels and movie stars—women who, while not of equivalent rank to a king, would be able to relate to you on somewhat equal terms. You would never sleep with someone who worked for you, however indirectly, because of the disparity in your positions. And if I'm wrong about that and you did get involved with an employee, you would never abdicate your responsibilities."

"Well, Fiona didn't know that about me, and apparently—though our paths only crossed on an infrequent basis—she developed something of an infatuation with me."

"She would be one of the half of the women in this country who would give almost anything for the opportunity to be held in your arms?" she teased.

He smiled, appreciating her attempt to lighten the conversation.

"But since that wasn't happening, she hooked up with someone else. And when she found out she was pregnant, she was too ashamed to admit to her sister that the father of her baby abandoned her, so she told her that I was the father."

"An allegation easy enough to disprove," Marissa reminded him.

"But not without a whole lot of publicity and fanfare. And it wasn't just that I didn't want the press speculating that I might have fathered a child out of wedlock and all the issues that went along with that. I didn't want to refocus attention on the funding problem at the hospital, which may or may not have resulted in the baby's condition not being diagnosed properly and treated sooner."

"You covered the cost of Siobhan's medical care, didn't you?"

He nodded. "And maybe that was a mistake, because Naomi interpreted that as proof I felt responsible for the baby and assumed it meant the baby was mine."

"But if you hadn't stepped in, she would have died."

And that was all he'd thought about at the time. He hadn't considered the implications of his actions beyond the fact that they were necessary to save the life of a child.

"So what does she want from you now?" Marissa asked.

"Who?"

"Naomi. I saw her with you at the hotel."

"She doesn't want anything from me. It seems her sole purpose in life, now that her sister's baby is home, is to expose my true character to the people of Ardena, to prove I'm unworthy of wearing the crown."

Marissa reached across the space that separated them and took his hands. "Then you shouldn't worry—because if the people of Ardena see you for who you really are, they'll know how lucky they are to have you as their king."

Her words were a balm to his bruised confidence. "They'd be more likely to believe that if they had a queen who believed it, too."

She only smiled as she released his hands. "Good night, Your Majesty."

He stood with her. "Am I wrong in thinking that we've become friends over the past few weeks, Your Highness?"

"I don't think so," she replied.

"Then maybe you could call me Dante instead of using my title all of the time?"

She nodded. "Good night, Dante."

Nearly a week had passed since the auction and Marissa had yet to make definite plans for her return to Tesoro del Mar. She'd thought she would be eager to get back, and she did miss her family and her friends and the routines at PACH that had become so much a part of her life over the past several years. But whenever she thought about saying goodbye to Dante, she felt an unexpected pang deep inside her heart.

So for now, she was content to maintain the status quo and keep in touch with her family through phone calls and emails. She was at the computer now, and smiling as she read the latest update from Sierra, who was having the time of her life at the University of San Pedro. Marissa finished reading and had just clicked Reply when a quick knock sounded on the door.

Before she had a chance to say anything, the handle turned and Dante walked in. In the six days that had passed since the auction, she'd hardly seen him at all. But suddenly he was here and, without any explanation or apology for his intrusion, he crossed the room to where she was seated at the desk and closed the lid on her laptop.

She lifted her brows. "What are you doing?"

"I'm breaking you out of here," he told her.

"I didn't realize I was being held prisoner."

"Well, I assumed you must be, since you haven't stepped foot outside of the gates of the palace in the past six days, except to visit Dr. Kalidindi."

"Maybe because I haven't wanted to step foot outside of the gates," she suggested.

"I know you don't like being hounded by the media—that's why I brought these." He tossed a neatly folded bundle of clothes on the settee.

"Where did you get those?"

"I pilfered them from Leticia's wardrobe," he explained. "We're going incognito."

She sorted through the items. "How are a pair of jeans, a sweatshirt and a baseball cap going to help me blend in?"

"They're not going to help you blend. Princess Marissa blends. Your disguise is *not* to blend."

"You're kidding."

"Nope." He started toward the door. "I'm giving you five minutes to change, then we're out of here."

"But I was—"

"Four minutes and fifty-five seconds."

She scowled at the back of the door.

After six days of almost no communication, what gave him the right to barge in and start issuing orders? Okay, maybe he was the king of Ardena, but he wasn't the boss of her. And even if she was admittedly curious about his plans, she wasn't going to jump just because he told her to. Not until she was ready.

She opened the lid of her computer again and typed her response to Sierra. When she'd finished her message, she surveyed the borrowed outfit again.

Leticia was of similar height and build to Marissa, but her taste in clothes was very different. Marissa eyed the boldly printed T-shirt, cherry-red hoodie and low-cut dark wash jeans with skepticism. Although she didn't wear them often, she did have jeans of her own—softly faded and conservatively cut—and she was more than a little tempted to dig them out of her drawer instead of wearing Leticia's. But she knew the bundle of clothes Dante had borrowed from his sister wasn't just a commentary on her wardrobe but a challenge, and Marissa never liked to back down from a challenge.

She carried the bundle into the adjoining bedroom and stripped off her skirt and blouse.

Dante paused in the open doorway of Marissa's bedroom, his jaw on the carpet.

He'd counted down the promised five minutes and, assuming that she'd had plenty of time to perform a simple change of clothes, knocked on the door of her sitting room and walked in. But she wasn't in the sitting room—and she hadn't closed the door that separated it from the bedroom.

And she was naked—well, naked except for a couple of scraps of very sexy red lace.

She had her back to him, presenting him with a spectacular view of strong shoulders, slender torso, deliciously curved buttocks and mile-long legs. He swallowed, trying to unstick his tongue from the roof of his mouth to say something. Not that he would be able to speak any coherent words, because the only thought going through his mind was *ohmylordthere-isagodinheaven.*

She bent over to pick up the jeans that she'd laid out on the foot of the bed and his blood roared in his head. She put one foot in, then the other, then she wriggled her hips as she slid the denim up those long, lean legs.

"I know I didn't get those undergarments from my sister's closet."

Marissa yelped and spun around, her eyes wide.

Dante grabbed hold of the doorjamb for support, because as glorious as the view had been of her backside, the front—where delicate cups of scarlet lace cradled unexpectedly lush breasts—was even better.

She grabbed for the T-shirt on the bed, holding it in front of her like a shield. But it was too late—the image of her gorgeous, mostly naked body was already imprinted on his brain forever.

"Don't you knock?" she demanded.

"I told you I would give you five minutes, and your five minutes are up."

"That doesn't give you the right to barge in here!"

"You're right," he admitted.

"Could you please stop staring?" she snapped.

He managed to clear his throat, though he couldn't tear his gaze away. "I honestly don't think I can."

"Dante…"

"Yes?"

"Get out!"

Marissa sank onto the edge of the mattress when he was gone, her heart pounding, her knees weak. She might have succeeded in banishing Dante from her room, but cooling the heat in her veins proved to be a much more challenging task.

With a groan of purely sexual frustration, she yanked the T-shirt over her head, shoved her arms in the sleeves of the sweater and slapped the ball cap on top of her head.

She didn't feel any better when she was done, but at least she was dressed.

He hadn't made a move toward her. He'd just stood in the doorway, more than three feet away. But she'd felt the hunger in his gaze as it raked over her—as tangible as a caress. All it had taken was a look, and everything inside of her had trembled. With awareness. Desire. Need.

It made her wonder what might have happened if he'd actually touched her—just the lightest touch of his fingertips on her skin. Or kissed her—the barest brush of his mouth against hers. No doubt her body would have gone up in flames.

And no way would she be alone on this big, soft bed right now.

Chapter Eleven

Marissa laughed when she saw the beat-up old Volkswagen parked in the underground garage. "We're going out in that?"

"This was my very first car," Dante told her. "And the only one in the garage guaranteed to attract no attention from the paparazzi."

"I can't imagine why."

"But as further insurance that we won't be followed, Thomas just drove through the front gates, headed toward the art gallery. It's a popular tourist destination and the type of cultural experience a visiting princess would certainly enjoy."

"I take it we're not going to the art gallery."

"No, we're not," he confirmed.

But he didn't tell her where they were going.

It was only because she was watching the scenery outside of the window and noticed the recurring signs that she realized he was taking her to Messini National Park.

When she decided to make the trip to Ardena, she'd done some research on the country and had been fascinated by the descriptions of the rocky terrain and the abundance of flora and fauna that existed there.

"We are going to commune with nature," he finally said as he pulled into a completely empty parking lot.

"Hiking the gorge," she guessed. She glanced down at the tennis shoes on her feet with some trepidation.

"It's more of a walk than a hike," he told her, seeming to anticipate her concern. "Other than the first half a kilometer, which is steep, the rest is relatively flat and fairly easy to navigate, so your footwear should be fine."

"How long is this walk?" she wondered.

"It shouldn't take more than a couple of hours, to go through and back again. Maybe less, since we shouldn't have any crowds to contend with."

"I thought I read that this was a popular sightseeing destination. Did you issue some kind of royal decree to get rid of all the tourists?"

"I wish that was an option," he said. "But the truth is, it's only ever really busy during the height of tourist season— between early June and late September," he told her. "Which is why I've always preferred to come early in the spring or late in the fall. Not just to avoid the crowds of visitors scaring away the wildlife, but because the temperature is more moderate."

He opened the hatchback and pulled out a backpack. "Water, power bars, blanket, flashlight, first-aid kit," he explained. "Just in case."

There was only one other vehicle near the start of the trail, so Marissa figured it was a safe bet that they had eluded the paparazzi and let herself relax and enjoy the fresh air and stunning view. He was right about the beginning of the trail—it was steep and comprised mostly of loose rocks, causing her to almost lose her footing once or twice. The first time, Dante grabbed her elbow to steady her. After the second time, he took her hand. And even when the trail leveled out, he kept hold of it.

Their conversation was mostly casual and sporadic, and Marissa found she genuinely enjoyed just being with him, walking along and holding his hand. After an hour, they were almost at the end of the gorge, so Dante suggested they pause to catch their breath. He shrugged the backpack off of his shoulder and took out two bottles of water, passing one to her.

"What do you think?"

"It's incredible," she said, and meant it.

He smiled. "I thought you would like it out here."

"I didn't realize you would," she admitted. "You don't strike me as the outdoorsy type."

"Why's that?"

"Because you look really good in a suit."

He grinned. "You think so?"

"As if you haven't been told that a thousand times before," she remarked drily.

"But never by you."

"I didn't figure your ego needed the stroking." A glimpse of movement caught the corner of her eye and her breath stalled.

"Maybe not my ego," he was saying, "but—"

She reached out and grabbed his arm.

"That's not actually the body part I was thinking about, either."

She glared at him and dropped her voice to a whisper. "What is that?"

He followed the direction of her finger, smiling when he saw what she was pointing at. "A wild goat."

Her hand dropped from his arm. "Those horns are huge."

"You can tell his age by the number of knobs that run up

the length of the horn," he explained. "If you want to get close enough."

"I'll pass."

He chuckled. "It's not likely he'd let you get that close, anyway."

Marissa kept her eyes on the goat—partly because she was fascinated by it but mostly to ensure it maintained a safe distance—until it scampered away.

"This is one of the greatest perks of my job," he said to her.

"Wild goats?"

"Being the boss," he amended. "And being able to sneak out early on a Friday afternoon to spend a few hours in the company of a beautiful woman."

Though her cheeks warmed with pleasure at the compliment, she knew it was a line he'd probably spoken to a lot of women before her. "Well, you are the expert on women."

He gave her a reproachful look as he reached for her hand again. "How are we ever going to make plans for our future if you keep throwing the past in my face?"

"Is it the past?"

"Absolutely," he assured her. "The citizens of Ardena might tolerate a playboy prince but they would never approve of a philandering king."

"But if that king is seen in the company of the 'Prim Princess,' it would go a long way toward restoring his approval rating, wouldn't it?"

"I've never understood that nickname," he said. "Now that I've seen your underwear, I understand it even less. And I find it curious that a woman whose wardrobe is so deliberately bland would favor lingerie that is anything but."

"If you must know, I'm usually a white-cotton kind of girl," she said, her cheeks a bit flushed. "But that set was on sale the last time I was in London."

"I think you're lying."

"Fifty percent off," she said.

"I meant about the white cotton."

Maybe she was lying, but it was a little unnerving that he could read her so easily. She blew out a frustrated breath. "Could we forget about my underwear for five minutes?"

He grinned. "Absolutely not."

She used her free hand to smack him in the chest.

"Assaulting the king is a capital offense," he warned.

"Ardena doesn't have capital punishment."

"I could change that."

"But you wouldn't."

"How do you know?"

"Because you have too much respect for your people to wield your power arbitrarily."

"That's quite the vote of confidence from someone who's only known me a few weeks."

"You're right," she acknowledged. "But I haven't seen any evidence that would contradict it."

"I threatened to fire the chef this morning because he gave me turkey bacon instead of regular bacon with my eggs."

"It's not really a threat if the person on the receiving end knows there's no possibility of follow-through."

"Why are you so sure that I wouldn't fire him?"

"Because he's been cooking your eggs since the days when you ate them soft-boiled with toasted soldiers."

He scowled. "How do you know this stuff?"

She smiled. "I talk to people."

"You mean you use your charm to wheedle secrets out of people."

"I hardly think your breakfast menu is a matter of national security."

"Maybe not," he allowed. "But do you draw a line in your questioning? Is anything off-limits?"

"For now, that will remain *my* secret."

"Do you have many secrets, Your Highness?"

"Not many," she denied. "Although there is something… I don't know if it's really a secret so much as something you should know."

"What's that?"

She stopped and turned so that she was facing him. She worried that it might be a mistake to tell him the truth, but knew it was a bigger mistake not to. She couldn't continue with this charade, allowing the king to think they might have a future together. So she blurted out. "I'm not a virgin."

He seemed to mull over her statement for a minute, then he nodded and resumed walking. "Neither am I."

She fell into step beside him again. "I can't say I'm absolutely shocked by that revelation."

"Did you think I would be shocked by yours?"

"I thought you probably had certain expectations."

"Because a king is expected to marry a woman of noble birth and pure virtue?"

She nodded.

"Expectations have changed since that law was written in the eighteenth century," he told her.

"It really doesn't matter to you?"

"It would be hypocritical of me if it did," he said. "Although I do have one question."

She looked up at him.

"Why are we having this conversation here and now?"

"I figured the middle of the gorge was a safer venue than in my bedroom when I was only half-dressed."

His eyes darkened; his lips curved. "Good point. Because if I'd known then what I know now, we might not have left the palace."

She didn't doubt that was a distinct possibility, and part of the reason that she'd felt compelled to make her confession.

Because as much as she wanted to experience making love with Dante, she was also terrified of that experience. He'd been with a lot of women, women undoubtedly much more knowledgeable and skilled in the bedroom than she, and if and when they did take that next step, she wanted to ensure that his expectations weren't too high.

"I'm not a virgin," she said again. "But I don't have a lot of sexual experience, and—"

"I don't need to hear about your past lovers."

"Lover—singular." She felt her cheeks flush as she made the confession. "There's only been one."

"It doesn't matter," he said. "Because when we make love, you won't think about anyone but me, and you won't remember anyone's touch but mine."

His tone was filled with arrogance, his eyes dark with promise, and Marissa wanted him to prove those words more than she'd ever wanted anything. But as much as her body yearned, her heart was wary.

When she'd been with Jupiter, she hadn't known enough about what to expect to worry. She hadn't realized that sharing herself with a man could be such an incredible experience. She certainly hadn't expected to feel a real and deep connection when their bodies were joined together. Or a profound sense of loss when she slipped away from his room. He'd been a stranger to her, a man whose face she hadn't seen and whose name she didn't know, and still, in the few hours that they'd been together, he'd somehow managed to steal a little piece of her heart.

She knew Dante, not just the kind of man he was but the type of king he wanted to be. Over the past few weeks, she'd talked with him and laughed with him. She'd listened to his hopes and dreams and ambitions, and she'd shared her own with him in turn. She'd watched him with his parents and siblings, noting the obvious affection and close bond the family shared. She'd seen him in front of the cameras, smiling easily and charming the crowd as he cut ceremonial ribbons or shook hands with visiting diplomats. And she'd seen him when the cameras were gone, with a furrow between his brows because being a king wasn't just about photo ops but hard decisions and tough choices.

During that time, she'd realized one undeniable truth: she didn't just like him, she was starting to fall in love with him. And she was very much afraid that she wouldn't be able to make love with him without falling the rest of the way.

As they made their way back through the gorge, Dante couldn't stop thinking about Marissa's revelation.

Her words had surprised him, partly due to the unexpected timing and bluntness of their delivery, but he wouldn't have said he was shocked by her confession. Although the Princess Royal had been confident that Marissa was "still innocent," he hadn't honestly expected that she was untouched. After all, she was twenty-eight years old and, regardless of the efforts she made to hide it, a beautiful woman.

But the Princess Royal's statement hadn't been inaccurate. Because while Marissa might not be a virgin, she was still, in many ways, an innocent. And it was his awareness of that innocence—conscious or not—that had held his growing desire for her in check over the past few weeks.

The first time he'd kissed her, he'd sensed the initial hesitation in her response. He'd admittedly moved in fast and realized that she might prefer to take things at a slightly slower pace. Unfortunately, patience wasn't one of his virtues. When he saw something he wanted, he tended to go after it—and maybe he'd been surprised to realize that he wanted Marissa, but the desire he felt when he was with her was undeniable.

With her mouth moving so softly and sweetly beneath his, that desire had quickly escalated. He'd deepened the kiss and she'd responded, and the flavor of her passion had shot through his veins like a drug.

When he'd finally ended the kiss, he'd seen the reflection of his own wants and needs in the depths of those golden eyes. But hovering beyond the edges of her arousal were hints of something that suggested she was just a little bit afraid.

So he'd ordered himself to take a step back, to give her the time he sensed she needed, to let her set the pace. He'd deliberately kept his touch casual, his flirtation light. And he'd refused to give in to the urge to kiss her again.

But right now, he really wanted to kiss her again.

Thankfully, they were now navigating the steeper part of the trail, and that forced him to focus on something other than his desire for the princess.

"Thank you," she said as they approached the parking lot. "For breaking me out of the palace for a few hours."

"It was my pleasure," he assured her.

"I just hope you don't feel it's your obligation to keep me entertained while I'm here."

He wanted to ask how much longer she planned to stay in Ardena, but he was afraid that if he did, she might get the impression he was anxious for her to go. And nothing could be further from the truth. Instead, he responded teasingly, "Actually, today was about you entertaining me."

"In that case, you're welcome," she said.

"And tomorrow, you get to entertain the whole family."

She halted in midstep. "What does that mean?"

He put his hand on the small of her back, nudging her forward. "It means that my mother has some big meet-the-family dinner planned for tomorrow night."

"I've met your family," she reminded him.

"You met my parents and my siblings. Tomorrow night you'll meet everyone else."

"Who is 'everyone else'?" she wanted to know.

"My grandmothers from both sides, my father's sisters and their husbands and children, my mother's brother, his wife and their daughter."

"Why do I need to meet all of these people?"

"Because you are Princess Marissa of Tesoro del Mar and as soon as they learned you were visiting, they insisted upon an invitation to the palace to meet you."

"What did you tell them about our relationship?" she asked warily, following him back to the car.

"I didn't tell them anything," he assured her. "But I can't vouch for anything my mother may or may not have said."

"I knew coming to Ardena was a bad idea."

"It's dinner with my family, not a press conference."

"I'd rather face a crowd of rabid reporters than a table filled with aunts and uncles and cousins assessing my suitability as a potential royal bride."

"You could put an end to a lot of their questions by letting me put a ring on your finger." He tossed the pack into the back, closed it again.

"I thought you'd given up on that."

"Why would you think that?"

"Well, it wasn't really anything you said or did," she said as he came around to open the passenger door for her. "More like all the things you didn't say or do."

"Such as not kissing you?"

"That's one," she admitted, a hint of pique in her tone.

If only she knew how difficult it had been to keep his distance from her. To resist the urge to kiss her and do all the other things he wanted to do.

"And not leaning close—" he shifted so that his body was angled toward her "—so that I could breathe in your scent when I'm talking to you?"

"I didn't actually think of that one." Her voice was a little softer now, huskier.

"And not touching you—" he traced a fingertip lightly over the line of her collarbone, above the low neckline of her T-shirt "—just for the pleasure of feeling the silky texture of your skin?"

Her eyes drifted shut and her throat moved as she swallowed.

He dipped his head, whispering close to her ear. "And not easing you down onto the middle of your bed to strip those scraps of lace from your body? Tell me, did you think about that one?"

He eased away from her and smiled. The verbal seduction had aroused him unbearably, but he got a little bit of satisfaction from realizing that she was just as aroused as he was.

She blew out a long, slow breath. "I am sooo out of my league with you."

"You wouldn't say that if you knew how twisted up inside I am with wanting you."

Her lips curved. "Really?"

"I promise you, Marissa, my reasons for not doing any or all of those things has absolutely nothing to do with a lack of desire."

"Then...why?"

"Because I don't just want you in my bed—I want you in my life. And I've realized it's not fair to use the attraction between us to put pressure you. So I'm backing off until you decide to give me an answer to my proposal."

"Are you actually refusing to have sex with me until I agree to marry you?"

"Let's just say I'm giving you time."

"What if I don't want time?"

"What do you want?"

She tipped her head back to meet his gaze. "For starters, I want a proper proposal."

His heart actually missed a beat. "Are you going to say yes?"

"It's not a proper proposal if you're not sweating the answer to the question," she informed him.

So he reached into his pocket and then, right there in the middle of the parking lot, he got down on one knee—and watched the princess's jaw drop. He took her hand, felt her fingers tremble in his.

"Marissa Leandres, will you do me the honor of becoming my wife and the queen of Ardena?"

"You have a ring." She said it in the same slightly terrified tone of voice that she might have used to say "you have a gun" if she'd found one was pointed at her.

"Of course I have a ring," he told her. "It's a little difficult to propose without one."

"I can't believe you had a ring. In your pocket. The whole time we were hiking the gorge."

"Actually, I've been carrying it around with me for about a week now, trusting that you would eventually come to your senses."

Her brows lifted. "I wouldn't make any assumptions about my senses, considering that I haven't yet answered your question."

"Well, maybe you could get around to that," he prompted. "These stones are tough on the knees."

She reached for his other hand and drew him to his feet. "Yes, Dante Romero, king of Ardena, I will marry you."

He slid the ring on her finger.

She slid her arms around his neck and lifted her mouth to his. "Now take me home and take me to bed."

He grinned. "Your wish is my command, Your Highness."

Chapter Twelve

Unfortunately, their plans hit a snag when they got back to the palace and found the driveway was crowded with vehicles and the parlor filled with people.

"You told me the party was tomorrow." Marissa's voice was a frantic whisper.

"Because my mother told me the party was tomorrow." Dante also kept his voice low as they hurried through the foyer, hoping to avoid being seen by any of the guests.

But they didn't avoid his mother.

"There you are." Arianna caught them at the foot of the stairs. "I thought I might have to call to summon you home."

If she was surprised by the princess's casual—and borrowed—attire, she didn't show it. She only smiled at Marissa. "The guest of honor shouldn't be late for her own party."

"You said the party was tomorrow," Dante reminded her.

"Because I wanted to surprise you both," the queen said,

unaffected by the reproach in his tone. Because while he might be the king of Ardena, he was still her son.

"Well, as it turns out, I have a surprise, too."

"Oh?" Arianna's gaze automatically dropped to Marissa's left hand, but Dante held it in his own so that the ring on her finger remained out of sight—at least for the moment.

"But we're both sweaty and dusty after a trek through the gorge, so we'd like some time to freshen up."

"Of course," his mother agreed. "But don't take too long. Hors d'oeuvres will be served in less than an hour."

Dante and Marissa started up the stairs as Arianna went back to the party.

"So much for my plan to ignore the crowd and sneak you up to my room," he lamented.

She wasn't entirely sure if he was joking. "Would you really have taken me up to your room with all these people here?"

He paused at the top of the landing and slid his arm around her waist to draw her close. "Princess, I would have taken you in the backseat of that beat-up old car if I'd known we'd be coming back to a full house." His lips twisted in a wry smile. "My own fault, I guess, for wanting something more memorable and comfortable than cracked vinyl upholstery."

"It would have been memorable for me," she said. "I've never done it in the back of a car."

"Neither have I," he admitted. "But it wasn't how I envisioned celebrating our engagement."

"Well—" she slid her palms up his chest and over his shoulders to link them behind his neck "—your mom did give us almost an hour."

"Trust me, Princess, the first time I make love with you, it's going to take a lot more time than that."

"You keep making these promises and I have yet to see any evidence of follow-through."

The glint in his eyes was sexy, determined and just a little bit dangerous, and it sent shivers of anticipation dancing down her spine.

"Screw the party," he decided, reaching for the handle of her door.

Then muttered a curse when the sound of a throat being cleared, deliberately and loudly, came from down the hall.

Marissa had to laugh, though she really wanted to scream in expression of her own frustration. "Does it feel as if the world is conspiring against us?"

"Not the world, just my family," he grumbled as Francesca drew nearer.

"Mother sent me up on the pretext of checking to see if Marissa needed any help getting ready."

"And the real reason?" Dante asked.

His sister grinned. "I think she's afraid that the king will try to sneak some alone time with the princess." Her eyes went wide as she caught sight of the ring. "Or should I say his bride-to-be?"

"Oh. Um." Marissa looked at Dante, not quite sure what to say and afraid she'd broken some sort of protocol by letting his sister see the ring before he'd told his parents of their engagement.

"It's great-grandmother's ring," Francesca murmured, then looked to her brother for confirmation.

Dante only gave a brief nod.

"But you said—"

"That I couldn't take great-grandmother's ring until I'd found the right woman to give it to," he concluded for her.

His sister turned her attention back to Marissa. "Has my mother seen it?"

"We haven't told anyone yet," she said.

"I won't let on that I was the first to know," Francesca promised. Then she kissed both of Marissa's cheeks before turning to kiss her brother's cheeks, too. "I'm so happy for both of you."

"We'd be happy, too, if you'd get lost for a while," Dante told her.

His sister shook her head, almost regretfully. "If I go back downstairs, she'll just send Leticia or maybe even come up herself."

"You're right," he acknowledged. Then he turned his back on her and kissed Marissa softly, deeply. "Later."

Later seemed to be a very long time in coming.

What Arianna had promised would be a simple dinner party to introduce Marissa to the rest of the family turned into an impromptu celebration of their engagement, and it seemed as if none of the guests ever intended to go home.

And then, to the collective surprise of everyone gathered, the butler entered the room to announce the arrival of another guest.

"Her Royal Highness, the Princess Royal Elena Leandres of Tesoro del Mar."

Three hours later, Marissa still wasn't sure what had precipitated her mother's impromptu trip to Ardena. But at least the Princess Royal seemed to be behaving herself—sipping brandy and chatting amiably with the other guests.

"It's my fault," Dante admitted when she confessed she was at a complete loss to explain her mother's sudden and unexpected arrival.

"What did you do?"

"I called and told her that we were engaged because I didn't want her to read about it in the paper."

Which was both a sweet and thoughtful gesture, but she had to ask, "Couldn't you have at least waited until morning?"

"I could and should have," he agreed. "And I would have

if I'd known she had some weird kind of maternal radar that made her show up before you could sacrifice your virtue outside of wedlock."

She laughed at the thought. "My mother doesn't have a motherly bone—never mind anything else maternal—in her body."

"But maybe she's right," he said.

The quiet resignation in his tone made her wary. "About what?"

"Wanting you to wait."

"She wants me to wait because she thinks I'm a virgin," Marissa reminded him.

"And you're not," he acknowledged.

"Right, so there's no reason for us to wait."

"Except that you've only ever been with one man."

She was completely baffled by his response. "So?"

"So he must have been someone you really cared about."

He was wrong. In fact, he was so far off base she might have laughed if she didn't feel so much like crying. Hannah was right—Marissa never should have given her virginity to a stranger. She should have waited, not necessarily to fall in love but at least to be with someone she liked, someone she truly cared about. Someone like Dante.

She could tell him the truth—that her lover had been a stranger, a man whose name—and face—she didn't even know, a one-night stand. But if she told him that, would he look at her with censure instead of respect? Would he decide that a woman who could give her virginity away so easily wasn't a suitable bride, after all?

"First you didn't want to sleep with me until I'd made a decision about your proposal, now you want to wait until we're married?"

"I just can't see it happening with your mother looking over my shoulder—figuratively speaking."

"I'll make sure she's on a plane back to Tesoro del Mar by tomorrow."

"But just in case she isn't that easy to get rid of, let's set a date."

"For sex?"

"And I thought I had a one-track mind," he said, shaking his head. "No, I meant for the wedding."

"June," she said, because she'd always imagined that she would one day be a June bride.

"I was thinking December."

She stared at him. "As in two months from now?"

"Sure. Two months from today," he agreed.

"Are you kidding? We can't possibly plan a wedding in two months."

"Probably not," he agreed. "Which is why we'll delegate."

And so their wedding date was set for December twenty-first, because Dante thought their wedding would be a perfect way to start the holiday celebrations.

Arianna and Benedicto weren't surprised that Dante and Marissa wanted a short engagement, but they were surprised by how very short it would be. Elena, on the other hand, didn't seem at all bothered by the narrow time frame. No doubt she knew that the wedding, and consequently all of the planning, would take place in Ardena, so all that would be expected of her was to greet the guests as the mother of the bride.

Still, Marissa thought she would want to be involved in making the arrangements, and when she went to her mother's room Monday morning, she didn't expect to see the Princess Royal's suitcases packed and ready to go. "You're leaving already?"

"There's really no reason for me to stay any longer," Elena said. "You're going to be busy deciding on flowers and menus and cakes—all the kind of details that you always handle so well—and I've got appointments and meetings to attend to at home."

Marissa wasn't disappointed that her mother wasn't staying, but she was disappointed that Elena didn't seem more interested in her only daughter's wedding. And then she recognized a truth that had been nudging at the back of her mind since the Princess Royal had shown up the night of her engagement to Dante.

"You didn't really come here for me," she said to her mother. "You just used the engagement as an excuse to see Benedicto."

For a moment—maybe just half a second—Marissa thought she caught a glimpse of genuine emotion flicker in her mother's eyes. But it was just a glimpse, and it was gone before she could begin to decipher what it might have been.

"I was…curious," Elena admitted. "I hadn't seen him in a very long time."

"Why didn't you ever tell me that you knew him?"

"It didn't seem relevant."

"The father of my fiancé was almost your fiancé, and you didn't think that piece of information was relevant?"

"As I said, it was a long time ago."

"He said that he was going to marry you."

"No formal arrangements had been made."

The confirmation wasn't unexpected, and still Marissa couldn't seem to put all of the pieces together. At least not in any way that made sense to her.

"You could have been the queen of Ardena."

And she couldn't imagine anything that would have made her mother happier. She'd had a chance to step into the spotlight—to marry the man who would be king, to stand beside him as his queen—and she'd turned it down.

"Yes, I could have been," Elena agreed, but offered no further information or explanation.

Marissa found herself thinking of Arianna, the woman who had married Benedicto, become his wife and his queen and the mother of his children. A woman who loved her family and enjoyed spending time with them, who smiled frequently and laughed easily, who was not just content but truly happy with her life. A woman who was undoubtedly aware of the history between her husband and her future daughter-in-law's mother and had still graciously opened up her home to the other woman.

Elena, by contrast, never seemed content. No matter what she had, it was never what she wanted; no matter how much she had, it was never enough. Marissa had never stopped hoping that her mother would find happiness somewhere, but she was beginning to despair of that ever happening.

"Did you love him?" she asked her mother now.

Elena considered her answer for a moment before replying, "I loved the idea of marrying a man who would someday be king."

Which was, Marissa realized with a combination of acceptance and disappointment, exactly the response she should have expected from her mother. And yet, it didn't explain why Elena had refused a marriage that would have given her everything she wanted.

"But even more than I wanted to be queen," she continued, "I wanted my father to know that I could make my own choices."

"And yet, you had no reservation about making mine for me," Marissa noted.

"Because I wanted you to make a better choice than the one I had made."

"How did you end up with my father?"

"A chance meeting, a physical attraction." Elena's lips

curved, just a little, in response to the memory. "He was big and strong and so incredibly, ruggedly handsome. Just looking at him made my heart pound and my knees weak.

"But reality has a way of dulling the brilliant shine of a new romance, and when I discovered I was pregnant with Michael and he insisted that we should get married, I panicked."

"You were pregnant before you got married?" Marissa had never been privy to that little detail, and she was shocked that Elena would reveal it now.

"Disgraceful, isn't it?" Her mother actually smiled, as if pleased to have been involved in such a scandal. "But as thrilling as it was to have a passionate affair with a farmer, I knew it wouldn't be nearly as exciting to be the wife of a commoner. So I planned to seduce Benedicto and tell him that the baby was his."

Marissa couldn't hold back her shocked gasp.

"But before I could put my plan into action, Gaetan showed up at the palace," Elena continued. "He told my father that I was pregnant and that he wanted to marry me. Prince Emmanuel was furious."

Elena blinked and Marissa thought she caught a glimpse of moisture in her eyes, but when the Princess Royal looked at her daughter again, her face was composed.

"He kicked me out," she said matter-of-factly. "And he told me that if I married the father of my baby, I would keep my title and my inheritance. But if I refused, he would disown me."

Marissa winced, imagining how those cruel words would have stabbed through Elena's fragile heart. Maybe she'd been impulsive and reckless, but she'd been young and desperately seeking her father's attention, and Marissa couldn't help but think that the seeds of her mother's present unhappiness might have been sown by her father's rejection on that long-ago day.

"So I married Gaetan," Elena concluded. "And the country priest was persuaded, by a sizable donation to the church coffers, to backdate the certificate so that no one would raise an eyebrow when a child was born less than eight months after our wedding.

"And then Cameron was born two years after that and, as far as I was concerned, I'd fulfilled my wifely obligations to my husband," Elena said. "I'd borne him two sons and had no intention of going through pregnancy and childbirth again.

"But he persuaded me to try once more, because he wanted a little girl. And from the moment you were born, you were his princess. Even if you hadn't been one by blood, you would have been one in his eyes."

Marissa felt the sting of tears in her eyes. "I barely even remember him," she admitted softly.

"He was a good man," Elena told her. "And a great father."

"But you didn't love him," she realized.

Her mother shook her head. "Not the way he deserved to be loved," she admitted. "And not the way he loved me."

"But you stayed with him."

"I'd made my choice, and if my life wasn't everything I'd hoped it might be, I had no one to blame but myself," she explained. "I still don't know if it was right or wrong, but I can't deny that I've often wondered how different things might have been if I'd walked away from Gaetan instead of toward him. And if it seems as if I pushed you into Dante's arms, it's because I didn't want you to make the same mistakes I did.

"Maybe an arranged marriage to the king of Ardena isn't the fairy-tale romance you've dreamed of, but the reality is that, regardless of whom you marry, you will be stuck under the same roof with him for the rest of your life. And I guarantee you that the roof of a palace will afford you much more freedom than that of a three-bedroom farmhouse in the middle of nowhere."

Marissa didn't doubt that was true. But she'd gladly live in a farmhouse in the middle of nowhere if she knew that she was loved. Instead, she was preparing for her holiday wedding to the man she loved with no idea if he would ever fall in love with her, too.

The King Finally Chooses His Queen!

That headline—and countless variations of it—was everywhere she turned. The attention Dante and Marissa were getting was ridiculous. Part of that was a result of the world being in love with love, especially when there was a royal romance involved. Since all of the pomp and circumstance surrounding Prince William's wedding to Catherine Middleton, everyone was clamoring for more.

There was no doubt that Ardena's king and the Tesorian princess made a beautiful couple. It would only make it that much more tragic when the esteemed ruler fell from grace. And he would fall—of that she had no doubt.

If His Majesty's conduct was deemed "unbecoming," the King's Council could demand that he abdicate. The provision was one that had never actually been used in Ardena's history, but it was legal and valid, and she was determined to compile all the evidence the council needed to take away Dante Romero's crown.

The presence of Marissa Leandres was a complication she hadn't anticipated. She had no grudge against the Tesorian princess, but she wasn't going to feel guilty if the king's bride-to-be got caught in the crossfire.

After all, she'd been warned.

Chapter Thirteen

Marissa had kept in regular contact with both of her sisters-in-law, via email and telephone, since she'd left Tesoro del Mar. That contact had gone from frequent to daily in the almost two weeks that had passed since Marissa and Dante announced their engagement and the date of their Christmas wedding. So she was neither surprised nor alarmed when her cell rang and she recognized Hannah's number on the display.

The panic didn't start until she heard her say, "You have to get on a plane and get your butt back here now."

"Why? What's wrong?"

"What's wrong is that you made Gabriella promise not to have the baby until you got home, but no one checked to make sure the baby was in agreement with the deal."

Excitement pushed aside the panic. "Gabby's in labor?"

"Her water broke ten minutes ago. The contractions haven't started yet, but—"

"I have to call the airline. I have to get home." While Dante had access to a private jet for business and personal use, she didn't feel comfortable asking for a free ride back to Tesoro del Mar. In any event, commercial flights between the two island nations were frequent enough that she wouldn't have to wait long to get on a plane for the trip home.

"Michael just finished booking your ticket. He's sending the details to your cell phone."

"In that case, I'll see you soon."

She disconnected that call, then dialed Thomas to request a ride to the airport. She figured she would call Dante when she was en route but remembered that he was at a planning meeting. Instead, she grabbed her passport and hurried to the king's private office to write a quick note for him.

Reaching across the desk for a pen, she accidentally knocked his leather-bound agenda off the edge. As she bent to retrieve it, a flash of color caught her eye and her heart jolted.

Between the pages, where the book had fallen open, was a single peacock feather.

She lifted it by the broken end and stroked a finger over the silky face, tracing the outer edge of the eye as questions pounded in her brain.

Could this be the same feather that had broken off of her mask? She didn't know where or when she'd lost the feather, not having discovered that the decoration was missing until she got home in the early hours of the morning after the masquerade ball.

Was it possible that Dante was the man she'd made love with that night? Holding that feather in her hand, she knew it wasn't only possible but true. Dante *was* Jupiter.

Now that she'd put the pieces together, she wondered that she hadn't recognized the truth sooner. The unexpected attraction she'd felt when she first met the king was so eerily similar to the feelings she'd experienced with Jupiter. Not

similar—the same. She hadn't been attracted to two different men, because they were the same man.

Bits and pieces of their conversation from that first night
filtered through her mind:

*Why would I choose the identity of any one god when I
could be the ruler of the gods?* A logical perspective, now
that she understood he was the ruler of his country.

I can't give you anything more than this night. Because he
was a king in search of a queen, but distracted from his quest
by the magical seduction of the night.

And it explained why he'd been as careful as she to ensure
that their encounter remained anonymous. Had he intended
it to be one last fling before he found a bride? Or was it his
modus operandi? Was he the kind of man who would take any
willing woman to his bed? Certainly the tabloids had given
him that reputation, and maybe if Marissa had learned of the
Jupiter connection a few weeks earlier, she might have been
more inclined to believe it.

Or maybe not. Because even that night, when she knew
nothing about him and had no clue as to his real identity, he'd
been an attentive and considerate lover. Not a man who used
women for his own purposes, but one who respected and appreciated them. And when he'd realized that he'd taken her
innocence, he'd seemed genuinely remorseful.

*...if I'd known you were untouched, I would have made
sure you stayed that way.*

Why?

Because your first time shouldn't be with a stranger.

Jupiter had asked her if she believed in destiny—she'd told
him that she was in control of her destiny. But now, realizing
that her lover that night was the man she was going to marry,
she acknowledged that there might have been a stronger force
at work than her own determination. Maybe she and Dante
really were fated to be together.

She'd fallen halfway in love with him that night, without even knowing who he was. And now, knowing everything else that she knew about him, she couldn't help but tumble the rest of the way.

Through the window, she saw Thomas's car coming down the drive. Quickly tucking the feather between the pages again, she closed the book and returned it to its place on his desk.

She left Dante's office, forgetting to write a note.

After almost nine months in office, the new king felt as if he was finally getting the hang of things. Of course, it helped that the men and women who had been his father's most trusted advisers were now his advisers. Under their tutelage, he was making real progress, and even the press was reporting a significant improvement in his approval rating. Or maybe it was just the holidays on the horizon that were responsible for his critics being in a more charitable mood. But the biggest change, from Dante's perspective, was having Marissa in his life.

If he thought about it, it might surprise him how much he looked forward to seeing her at the end of every day. So he tried not to think about it and just enjoy the happiness and contentment he felt when he was with her. Not that he was entirely content, but he knew he only had himself to blame for the status quo.

It had been his decision to wait to consummate their relationship, and it wasn't a decision his fiancée had acceded to willingly. As she continued to remind him by doing everything possible to elevate the level of his frustration. Sliding her hand along his thigh whenever she sat beside him at dinner, rubbing her breast against his arm when she reached for the remote control if they were watching television, letting her lips brush his ear when she whispered to him. And when he kissed her—because he wasn't masochistic enough to cut off all physical contact—she did things with her tongue that nearly made his eyes cross.

She might be an admitted novice at lovemaking, but she was a definite pro at seduction. And with each day that passed, his resistance was waning in direct proportion to his escalating desire. Until he began to wonder why he was fighting against something that he wanted as badly as she did.

By the time he was heading back to his suite Wednesday night, he'd decided to stop fighting and start planning. After all, he wasn't without his own skills when it came to setting a scene for seduction.

He had a definite spring in his step when he set off to find his future queen.

While another office was being renovated for Marissa's future use, he'd suggested that she could work in the office that adjoined his suite, and she often did. But when he peeked in there today, it was empty. He checked her suite next—ensuring that he knocked before he entered, because a man could only handle so much temptation—but she wasn't there, either. He glanced in the library, conservatory, kitchen and pool area, and though there were plenty of staff bustling around as preparations were being made not just for the wedding reception that would be held on-site but for the upcoming holiday season, there was no sign of Marissa.

He went back to his office, only now noticing the large, flat envelope on his desk. There was a neatly printed label on the front with his name and Personal & Confidential in bold print. But there was no postmark, and he instinctively suspected that Naomi was behind whatever was in the envelope.

He was growing tired of her threats. He'd tried to see things from her perspective: she truly believed that he'd seduced her sister then abandoned her when she got pregnant, denying paternity of the baby simply because he was embarrassed to have fathered a child out of wedlock with a commoner. If any part of that scenario had been true, she would have been entitled to her anger and her frustration. But it was all a fabrication, a lie Fiona had made up rather than admit the truth to the little sister who adored her.

He'd been honest with Naomi, but loyalty to her sister had closed her mind to the truth. She'd refused to listen to any version of events that didn't correspond with the story that was set in her mind. His offer to have a paternity test didn't sway her—"the lab techs would say whatever the king wanted them to say." His willingness to cover the costs of not just Siobhan's medical bills but Fiona's travel and living expenses while in Tesoro del Mar didn't soften her—"that's the least you can do for your own child."

He'd confronted Fiona. She'd been embarrassed and ashamed, but she'd owned up to her lies. Unfortunately, her confession to her sister had fallen on deaf ears and Naomi remained convinced that he'd somehow bribed or blackmailed Fiona into changing her story, burying the truth.

If there was one bright light in the whole dark mess, it was that Marissa believed in him. Even before she'd heard the whole story, she'd trusted that he was too honorable and decent to do what Naomi had accused him of doing. And because she believed in him, she made him want to be a better person.

He'd spent his whole life in the spotlight. He was accustomed to attention and adoration. But no one had ever made him feel the way he felt when he was with Marissa.

He opened the flap, then tipped the package so the document would slide out. He almost hoped it was a court application for child support—he'd almost rather go public to clear up the story than continue to live with the cloud of suspicion over his head.

Except that it wasn't a document—it was a collection of photos that spilled out.

Glossy, full-color, eight-by-ten photos.

He sifted through the pictures, his heart pounding hard and fast inside his chest.

The pictures had been taken the night of the Mythos Ball, outside of his room at the palace. Pictures of a man and a woman in period costume and elaborate masks. Jupiter and Juno.

He sifted through the photos. The one on top was a full-body shot. More specifically, Jupiter's body pressing Juno's against the door, their mouths locked together. There were several photos of them kissing. And then the photographer had creatively zoomed and cropped to show a close-up of his tongue touching the bow of her top lip and his hand on her breast.

Naomi had made it her mission to destroy him, and he realized that these pictures might finally do it. He didn't think he would lose the throne. While the publication of the images—if that was what Naomi intended—would hardly be a shining moment for the crown, what had happened that night was nothing more complicated than two consenting adults hooking up for a few hours of mutual pleasure. There was no one who could claim it was anything more nefarious than that.

Unless Naomi had somehow discovered Juno's true identity. Or if—the thought made his blood run cold—she had always known the truth about who Juno was and the whole interlude had been a setup from the beginning.

He buried his face in his hands. Okay, so maybe he was being paranoid. After all, it wasn't as if Juno had approached him—he'd been the one who spotted her, and he'd been the one to invite her back to his room.

Juno had been a fantasy. And for one glorious night, she'd

been his fantasy. Then he'd met Marissa. And he'd discovered that she was better than any fantasy, because she was generous and compassionate and real.

Truthfully, he didn't even care if the people of Ardena wanted to take away his crown as a result of this indiscretion. The only thing that mattered to him was Marissa. He couldn't lose her now. If he did—

He felt as if there was a clamp around his chest, squeezing tight.

No, he wouldn't even consider the possibility.

But what if she'd seen these pictures?

Marissa went straight to the hospital from the airport and managed to arrive a full twenty minutes before Talisa Jaime Leandres entered the world.

Hannah and Michael were already at the hospital when she arrived. While they waited, they talked about weddings and babies and all manner of subjects in between. Or maybe it would be more accurate to say that Marissa and Hannah talked while Michael paced.

And then, finally, Cameron stepped out of the delivery room. He looked bone-tired but was wearing a mile-wide grin. "Who wants to see our beautiful new baby girl?"

Of course they all did, but Marissa let Hannah and Michael lead the way because she knew that they had to be home for Riley when she finished school. After they'd congratulated the parents and oohed and aahed over the baby and promised to come back later with Riley, they slipped out of the room, allowing Marissa her first unobstructed view of the newborn.

"Oh, wow." She felt the sting of tears and a sharp pang of longing as her gaze landed on the perfect little girl swaddled in a pink blanket in her sister-in-law's arms. "She's absolutely gorgeous."

The proud daddy smiled. "She is, isn't she?"

He sounded so smug that Marissa couldn't resist teasing, "Because she looks like her mother."

"I think she has her daddy's nose," Gabby said loyally.

Marissa studied the baby for a minute, then shook her head. "Nope—no sign of her daddy at all."

"And I'm okay with that," Cameron said as he leaned in to kiss his wife. "Because I happen to be married to the most beautiful woman in the world."

"And the fact that you can say that with a straight face so soon after I've given birth proves that you really do love me."

"With all my heart," he promised and brushed his lips against hers again.

Marissa's heart sighed as she watched them.

There had been a time when her brother was one of the most notorious playboys around and she didn't think he would ever change. But from the moment he'd met up with Gabriella again, after almost sixteen years apart, everything had changed. Marissa had been surprised by his apparent transformation, and then she'd realized it wasn't that Cameron had changed, but that he'd finally found the woman he loved.

She wondered if she was foolish to hope that Dante would ever look at her with the same obvious love and devotion she saw in her brother's eyes when he looked at his wife. She knew that Dante's proposal was based on practical and political reasons. Emotion wasn't a factor in the equation, at least not on his side. But she was optimistic that the attraction and affection between them would help them to build a strong and solid marriage. And she did believe that the holidays were a time of miracles, maybe even enough to hope that their Christmas wedding would truly lead to a happily-ever-after.

* * *

Dante had already checked his phone, and while the record showed several missed calls from Marissa, there were no messages. And when he'd dialed her number, his call went directly to voice mail.

Where the heck could she have gone that she would have turned off her phone?

He had picked up the phone to try her number again when it began to ring.

"Marissa?"

"It's a girl," she said, and she sounded so blissfully happy that, for a moment, his mind went blank. "Nearly eight pounds and twenty inches, and absolutely gorgeous."

"You're in Tesoro del Mar," he realized.

"Of course. That's where Gabby was having the baby." And then, as if she'd just realized that he might have been worried to arrive home and find his fiancée had disappeared, she said, "Oh, Dante, I'm so sorry. I went into your office to leave a note, but…I got distracted, and then the car was there to take me to the airport and I completely forgot."

He exhaled a breath he hadn't realized he was holding. She'd been in his office but she hadn't seen the pictures. She hadn't left the palace because she was angry or upset—she left because her sister-in-law was in labor. The knowledge didn't entirely alleviate his concerns, but Marissa's explanation reassured him that there wasn't an immediate crisis.

"It's the baby thing," she said, and he could hear the smile in her voice.

"It's okay," he said, willing to forget his momentary panic now that the vise around his chest had finally eased. But the sticky note scrawled with the words "You will pay" attached to the back of one of the photos continued to worry his mind and weight on his heart.

"I really want a baby, Dante."

"That's hardly a revelation."

"I don't mean that I want a baby at some vague point in the future," she clarified. "I want us to make a baby. Soon."

The idea of procreating had always seemed to Dante like just another of those royal expectations he was required to fulfill. But a baby with Marissa—yeah, he really wanted that.

"It's kind of hard to do long-distance," he warned.

"It's kind of hard to do without making love," she pointed out.

"Then I guess I'll have to let you have your way with me."

"Really?" She sounded as dubious as she did hopeful. "Because so help me, Dante, if you're not serious—"

"I am very serious," he promised her.

"What changed your mind?"

"I looked at the calendar and saw that December twenty-first is too damn far away."

She laughed. "I'll be back at two o'clock on Friday."

"I have meetings all day Friday," he told her, even as he mentally reviewed his schedule to figure out if there were some things that could be moved around.

"Then I guess we'll have to wait until Friday night."

"We could get started sooner if you came back tonight," he suggested, hoping to tempt her, wanting—almost desperately—to hold her in his arms. Because as soon as she got home, he would tell her about the photos, and then he could finally put that night behind him and look forward to his future with Marissa.

"I've got some things to do here tomorrow," she told him.

"They're going to put up the Christmas tree in the foyer tomorrow," he said, hoping her desire to participate in the holiday preparations would convince her to change her plans.

"I'm sorry I'll have to miss that," she said.

He took some solace from the fact that she sounded sincerely regretful and crossed his fingers that Naomi wouldn't make another move until he had a chance to talk to Marissa. Maybe when Naomi threatened to make him pay she was hoping for money, and he would get some kind of blackmail demand before she went public with the photos. And though it chafed to think of giving her anything, he knew he would pay whatever she wanted to keep the pictures out of the media and his fiancée out of the spotlight.

"I miss you already," he told her.

"I've only been gone a few hours."

And he'd been to hell and back in those few hours, trying to figure out where she'd gone and why she'd left him. Of course, he didn't admit any of that to her now. He only said, "I guess I've just become accustomed to having you around."

"Then maybe it's a good thing that I'll be away for a few days. I wouldn't want you to start taking me for granted."

"Never again," he promised and knew that it was true.

If she would only come home, he would spend every day of the rest of their lives showing her how very much she meant to him.

Marissa was eager to get back to Ardena—to get back to Dante. Unlike the first trip she'd taken on the king's private plane, this time she experienced absolutely no apprehension about leaving her home. This time, she felt as if she was going home.

In the almost five weeks that she'd spent in Ardena, she'd quickly grown to appreciate the rugged country and its resilient people. She knew she would miss the staff and her routines at PACH, but she'd found new direction and purpose working with Dr. Kalidindi at Mercy. The entire Romero family had welcomed her from the start—Arianna a little more hesitantly than the rest, but now that Marissa knew of her mother's past with the other woman's husband, she could understand her reservations—and she'd been honored and humbled by their acceptance. She was looking forward to being part of their family, to sharing the holidays and participating in local traditions with them—including the upcoming olive harvest and the Christmas parade. But the most unexpected and thrilling discovery for Marissa was that she'd fallen in love with the man she was going to marry.

She wasn't ready to believe that Dante had fallen in love with her, too, but she was hopeful that it might happen. Someday.

When she exited into the arrivals lounge, she was so intent on searching for the chauffeur that her gaze skipped right past her fiancé. It was actually the two broad-shouldered guards flanking him that she spotted first, and when she realized that Dante was there to meet her, her heart skipped a beat.

She hadn't expected to see him and she was suddenly nervous. She'd only been away three days, but those three days had seemed interminable. She smoothed a hand down the front of her sapphire-colored dress, wondering if he would look at her any differently today and how she would feel if he did.

His gaze skimmed over her slowly, appreciatively, and his lips curved as he made his way toward her.

She curtsied; he bowed; cameras flashed.

"I thought you had meetings all day," she said.

"I managed to clear my schedule so that I could be here to meet you."

His gaze dropped to her mouth, and she knew that he wanted to kiss her. She also knew that he was as conscious of the crowd of onlookers as she, so he only lifted her hand to his lips.

"I didn't expect you to be here," she said, torn between pleasure and guilt. "But it was a thoughtful gesture."

"Not a grand gesture?" he teased, referencing a comment she'd made once before.

"That will depend on the vehicle your chauffeur is driving."

He laughed and offered his arm.

Marissa placed her hand in the crook of his elbow and pretended she didn't notice all of the heads that turned in their direction. There would be more photos in the paper tomorrow and new headlines, but she refused to let it bother her. She might not have completely overcome her wariness of the media, but she'd accepted that there would be very little privacy in her life with the king of Ardena—and she knew that a few stolen moments with Dante would make everything worthwhile.

She smiled when she saw the glossy stretch Bentley waiting for them. "Okay, I'll give you *grand*."

Thomas greeted her with a formal bow and a quick wink as he reached for the handle of the door. Marissa stepped up into the back of the car—and into a veritable greenhouse.

The back of the limo was absolutely filled with flowers. Buckets and buckets overflowing with colorful, fragrant blooms. She had a moment to think it was a good thing the king's bodyguards rode in a separate vehicle because there was no room for them back here.

She skimmed a finger over the velvety-soft petal of a lavender calla lily as Dante settled beside her. "A *very* grand gesture," she amended.

"Flowers are a common element in many courtship rituals," he told her.

"Are you courting me, Your Majesty?"

"Considering that our wedding is only a few weeks away, it seemed like I should fit that in somewhere."

"I appreciate the effort," she assured him, "but you don't have to wine—"

She broke off, laughing as he popped the cork on a bottle of champagne.

"You were saying?" he prompted.

"That you don't need to wine and dine me," she finished, even as she accepted the glass of wine he passed to her.

"Good, because I haven't planned as far ahead as dinner." He tapped the rim of his glass against hers. "Welcome home, Marissa."

And then, finally, he kissed her.

It was a long while later before he said, "I like your dress."

She smiled, pleased that he had noticed. "Hannah and Gabby convinced me that all the beige in the world wouldn't insulate the king's fiancée from public scrutiny, so I decided to show my true colors."

"I like those true colors—just as long as this isn't some kind of wardrobe reversal and now your underwear is white cotton," he said.

She shook her head and whispered, close to his ear, "Purple satin demi-cup bra."

His lips curved. "Matching bikinis?"

She shook her head again and saw the spark of hope fade. "Matching thong."

His eyes glittered with heat and hunger. "You really enjoy torturing me, don't you?"

"Maybe." She shifted so that her lips hovered just a breath away from his. "Just a little."

The limo drew to a stop.

Dante took her hand.

She asked no questions and made no protest as he ushered her toward the double front doors on which hung twin wreaths decorated with gold bows. Inside the foyer was the Christmas tree he'd told her about—it was at least fifteen feet tall and elegantly decorated with gold-and-silver balls and bows. But he didn't give her any time to admire the holiday decor, instead leading her directly upstairs and into his suite.

She held his gaze as he closed the door, her eyes filled with passion and promise as she reached for the tie at the side of her dress. He caught her hands, knowing there was no way he would be able to get a single word out if she unfastened that knot.

"We need to talk."

Marissa's hands dropped to her sides as she looked at him, her expression one of both disappointment and disbelief. "You're telling me that you cleared your schedule this afternoon because you want to talk?"

He let his gaze skim over her again, admiring the way the silky blue fabric of the wrap-style dress molded to her feminine curves and wanting her with a desperation he'd never known before.

"No," he said honestly, his voice husky with desire. "What I want to do is strip you naked and take you to bed and spend hours showing you how much I missed you."

Her lips started to curve.

"But I need to be honest with you about something first."

The smile faded. "That sounds ominous."

He took her hands, squeezed gently. "I hope not."

"Then just say it fast and get it over with."

But somehow he didn't think blurting out that he'd had sex with another woman the night before they met was going to score him any points. So he decided to start his explanation a little closer to the beginning.

"When I went to Tesoro del Mar in September, it was with the intention of asking you to marry me."

"But you didn't even know me then."

"I knew enough," he said. "You once asked if it was one of my assistant's jobs to research the likes and dislikes of my dates. I never went to such lengths for a casual acquaintance, but my advisers felt it was necessary for me to have some basic information about the women who were on the bride list."

Her brows rose. "The bride list?"

"Sorry—that's what my brother Matt dubbed it. But it was a list of women that my advisers decided were the most suitable candidates for marriage."

"And I was on that list because I was a Tesorian princess."

"You were at the top of the list. And I decided that as long as we were reasonably compatible, I wouldn't bother to look any further."

"I'm flattered," she said, though her tone suggested otherwise.

The phone on his desk rang, but Dante ignored it. He wasn't going to allow anything to interrupt his confession, because he knew that Marissa needed to know the truth about the secret in his past before they could look to their future together. And she had to know now. Though he couldn't be certain that the text message he'd received while waiting for Marissa's plane at the airport had been from Naomi, the brief tick tock was clearly a warning that his time was running out.

"I was prepared to marry for duty rather than desire," he admitted. "So I was very pleasantly surprised to discover that there was something more between us, right from the beginning."

He took her left hand, rubbed his thumb over the ring on her third finger. "Do you remember how surprised Francesca was when she realized I'd given you my great-grandmother's ring?"

She nodded.

"My father had offered it to me before I made that trip and I wouldn't take it. Because I couldn't imagine giving a ring that my great-grandfather had given to my great-grandmother, as an expression of his love and affection, to a woman I was marrying only out of obligation."

The cell phone in his pocket vibrated and a trickle of unease worked its way down his spine. But he forged ahead, desperate to tell her the truth, to make her understand.

"I chose to give you that ring because my feelings for you changed, because I fell in love with you. And when I put that ring on your finger, I did so knowing that I would always be faithful to the woman who wore it."

"You...love me?" She sounded so bewildered and she looked up at him with so much love and hope shimmering in her eyes it nearly broke his heart—because he knew that what he was about to tell her might break hers.

"I do love you," he said again.

A knock sounded on the door. Not a polite tap but an impatient summons.

Marissa's gaze moved from the door to the phone, which had started to ring again. The cell in his pocket was also vibrating, though she couldn't know that.

"So far none of this is what I feared," she said. "So why don't you tell me what I'm missing?"

Before he could respond, the door opened.

"Dante—" Matt visibly winced when he saw that Marissa was in the room. "I'm sorry to interrupt," he said to the princess. "But I need to speak with my brother. It's extremely important."

But Dante didn't need Matteo to tell him what he already knew.

The urgency of the ringing phones and his brother's appearance at his door within days of receiving that package from Naomi could only mean that she'd followed through on her threat. And that somehow, in the short span of time between when Dante met Marissa at the airport and now, the photos had gone viral.

Chapter Fourteen

Marissa didn't think she'd ever seen Dante sweat. But she could see it now, the light sheen of perspiration on his brow, the tension in his tightly clenched jaw, the pleading in his eyes. And the warmth that had flooded her system when he'd told her he loved her suddenly turned to ice.

"What's going on, Dante?"

The phone in her purse was ringing now, too, but she didn't reach for it. She somehow knew that her call was connected to the ringing of his phone and his brother's presence, but she didn't want to hear the answer from anyone but Dante.

She glanced at the prince, who was still hovering in the doorway and looking at her with pity and apology in his eyes.

"Photos?" It was the only word Dante spoke to Matt.

His brother nodded.

"I need some time with my fiancée," the king said.

"Of course," Matt agreed and backed out, closing the door behind him.

The phone on the desk had stopped ringing again, but her cell continued to chime. She pulled it out of her purse and turned it off. The sudden silence in the room was ominous.

"Photos?" she asked, her voice little more than a whisper.

He swallowed. "It was before I met you."

"What was before you met me?"

"It was a fling. A one-night stand."

Her eyes filled with tears.

"I'm sorry," he said. "I didn't want you to find out this way."

"If it was before you met me, why does it matter?" she asked, even though she knew that it did. Dante's past exploits were hardly a secret, but she was his fiancée now—

She looked down at the ring on her finger.

I chose to give you that ring...because I fell in love with you.

"It doesn't," he said, as if he could make her believe it. "Not to me. But there will be talk, speculation that I was with her when I was engaged to you, that I cheated on you."

"Who is she?"

He ran his hands through his hair. "I don't know."

"How can you not..." The question trailed off as a sudden, startling thought came to her.

Was it possible that he was talking about the night of the Mythos Ball? The night she was almost certain that they had spent together?

"Who took the photos?"

"I don't know," he said again. "I'd guess Naomi or someone she knows, because copies were delivered to me a few days ago."

"I want to see them."

He winced. "Marissa—"

"Aren't they all over the internet by now, anyway?"

"Probably," he admitted reluctantly.

She waited while he went over to his desk, unlocked the bottom drawer and pulled out a large envelope.

Her fingers were trembling as she took the package from him. If she was right, the pictures inside would be of Juno and Jupiter. If she was wrong...

Her stomach churned at the thought. If she was wrong, she would find herself looking at pictures of Dante and another woman, maybe touching that other woman, kissing her and even making love with her.

She'd rather know than speculate.

She opened the flap and tipped out the photos.

And her heart started beating again.

Dante didn't want to see the shock and hurt and betrayal on her face when she looked at the pictures, but he couldn't seem to look away.

He heard the sharp intake of her breath as the photos spilled out of the envelope. Yep, there was the shock. She sifted through the images, scrutinizing each one closely enough that her study made him uneasy.

He waited for her to rage, to cry, to throw something at him. But after she'd looked at all of the photos, she put them back in the envelope and said, "I know who she is."

"Whoever she is, you have to believe that I didn't go to the ball looking to hook up with someone," he said, desperate for her to trust him. "In fact, I only went because I thought you would be there."

"Instead you met Juno."

He should have realized that she would recognize the peacock feathers in the mask as one of the goddess's trademarks because of her association with the Juno's Touch project at PACH.

"The mythos theme for the ball was my idea," she told him now. "The costumes were my idea. And I was Juno."

He stared at her, stunned. He wanted to believe what she said was true, but it seemed too incredible.

"She had red hair and green eyes—" he shook his head, startled by what was so patently obvious to him now "—easy enough to fake with a wig and colored contacts."

She nodded.

"You knew," he said, startled anew by this realization. "You knew that I was Jupiter, that I was the man you made love with that night, and you didn't tell me?"

"I only figured it out a few days ago," she told him, clearly on the defensive now. "Before I left for Tesoro del Mar, when I went into your office to write a note, I knocked your agenda off of the desk and found a peacock feather in it."

He didn't know how he was supposed to respond or even how he was supposed to feel. Was it appropriate to feel relief that he hadn't been with someone else? To feel shock that the woman he had been with was the woman he loved? But he had to set aside the shock, and he knew that any sense of relief was premature because discovering the real identity of Juno wasn't going to make the scandal of the photos go away.

"What are we going to do now?" Marissa asked, apparently having tracked the direction of his thoughts. "How are we supposed to respond to something like this?"

"I'm sure my advisers are already meeting with the palace's media liaison to figure out all the potential angles," he told her. "Right now, I see a couple of possibilities. We can ignore the photos and trust that something bigger and juicier will take over the headlines by the end of the week. Or I can make an official statement acknowledging that those are photos of me taken the night of the masquerade ball and asserting that there has been no one else in my life since I met you."

"Or we could call a press conference where I show up in

Juno's costume to put an end to the speculation once and for all."

"No way." His response was as definite as it was immediate.

"Why not?"

"Because I know how much you hate being the center of any kind of media attention and this will be the worst possible kind." In fact, knowing how strongly she felt about avoiding publicity, he was shocked that she would ever come up with such a plan.

"I wouldn't have chosen to go public with the information," she admitted. "But you can't honestly expect me to remain in the shadows now that those photos are everywhere."

"Those photos were taken because Naomi was targeting *me*. There's no reason to drag you into the middle of this."

"No reason except that I'm already in the middle of it."

He shook his head. "I can't completely isolate you from the fallout, but I can—and will—ensure you're protected as much as possible. And there is absolutely no way I'm involving you in a sex scandal."

"They're sexy pictures," she said. "But not *sex* pictures."

"The distinction isn't going to mean much to the reporters shouting questions at you and photographers blinding you with flashbulbs."

"I don't need you to protect me, Dante. I need you to let me stand by your side, to show the world that we are united."

"But why would you want to? I know this whole scenario is a nightmare for you."

"Because I love you," she said simply.

The words rocked him to the core. Stunned him. Humbled him.

He touched his forehead to hers. "I don't deserve you," he said. "But I am so incredibly grateful for you."

She wrapped her arms around his waist, holding him tight. "And I will stand by your side, for now and forever," she vowed. "But I won't be tucked away and then taken out when it suits your purposes. I need to be your partner. I need you to know that I will always be there for you."

"I want you by my side," he said. "But you can't blame me for wanting to protect you."

"I don't blame you," she assured him. "I'm just telling you that I won't accept it."

"I guess that means we're going to do a press conference— together."

Less than twenty-four hours after Matteo knocked on the door of Dante's suite, Dante and Marissa stood together outside the front gates of the palace to issue their joint statement to the media.

Marissa knew the ripple effects would continue for a while, but they'd done what they could and from this point on, they just had to ride out the waves. Dante took her hand, guiding her away from the crowd. The festively decorated gates closed behind them, shutting out the reporters and photographers. But cameras continued to flash, capturing every step as they made their way, hand in hand, back to the palace.

"Well, that's done," Dante said, careful to keep his voice low.

Marissa could only breathe a slow and shaky sigh of relief. She didn't want him to know how absolutely terrified she'd been, or that she was still shaking on the inside. But she'd faced down the reporters without batting an eyelash—and without throwing up. She figured if she could face that rabid pack of reporters with such a meaty story, anything else she would encounter would be a piece of cake.

Of course, Dante had done all the talking, reading a joint statement that had been carefully prepared and meticulously proofed. They were advised not to take any questions, since they weren't prepared to lie about the events of that night and the king's advisers didn't want either of them to admit they hadn't even exchanged names before they'd gotten naked together.

Dante squeezed her hand. "You survived your first trial by fire," he said reassuringly.

"Hopefully my first and last," she said.

Waiting at the top of the steps behind the balustrade draped with an evergreen garland, were all of Dante's family. Benedicto stood tall, clasping Arianna's hand in his own. They were flanked by their other four children, with Jovanni and Leticia on one side and Francesca and Matteo on the other. The decorated evergreen trees lined up in the background made it appear as if they were posing for a Christmas greeting card, reminding Marissa that—despite everything else that had happened over the past few days—the holidays were rapidly approaching.

But it wasn't the decor that had snagged her attention— it was the Romero family's unexpected show of support. Marissa hadn't realized they were there—truthfully, she wished they hadn't had to witness any of what had been revealed in the past twenty-four hours. Seeing them now, her eyes filled with tears.

Her own family was, by virtue of being in Tesoro del Mar, more removed from the situation. But for the citizens of Ardena, there was no distance or objectivity. Dante was their king—the head of their government, ambassador of their nation and supposed role model for future generations. And the effects of his behavior were real and immediate.

Marissa feared that for Benedicto and Arianna and their children the situation was even more personal. To them, Dante wasn't just the king of Ardena; he was their son and their brother. Despite the public show of support, she couldn't help but fear that they were privately disappointed.

It was Arianna who broke the silence when they reached the top of the steps, but only to say, "Come, Marissa. The dressmaker is here for final approval on your wedding gown design."

It was exactly the distraction she needed to push the press conference out of her mind, if only for a little while. She reviewed the sketches, suggested a few minor changes. Her measurements were double-checked, the designer clucking her disapproval about brides unnecessarily dropping pounds and dresses requiring last-minute adjustments.

"I'm sorry," Marissa said to Arianna when the designer had gone.

Dante's mother looked genuinely puzzled. "Whatever are you apologizing for?"

"For my selfish and reckless behavior."

Arianna perched on the edge of the stool in front of Marissa and took both of her hands. "You are one of the most selfless and considerate people I've ever known," she said sincerely. "But no one goes through life without making mistakes. Fortunately, most people don't have to worry that those mistakes will be broadcast to the world and judged by those who have no right to judge. Unfortunately for you, as a princess and soon-to-be queen, you don't fall into the category of 'most people.'"

"I thought you'd be angry."

"I'm furious," the queen promised. "But not with you, and not even with Dante, although this admittedly isn't his first... indiscretion."

Marissa managed a smile at that.

"And I'm grateful that you were there with my son today."

"Where else would I have been?"

"I imagine, if Dante had been given a choice, you would

have been safely tucked inside the palace, away from the cameras and questions."

"Obviously you know your son well."

"He is a lot like his father, sometimes frustratingly so." Arianna released her hands abruptly and stood up. "Your designer was asking about the jewelry you planned to wear with your dress."

"I haven't given it much thought."

The queen moved to the dresser and picked up a burgundy velvet box. "Well, perhaps you'd like to think about these."

She opened the lid, revealing a pair of stunning chandelier-style diamond earrings.

"My mother-in-law gave them to me on my wedding day," Arianna told her. "For me, they were 'something new.' If you'd like to wear them, they could be your 'something borrowed.'"

Marissa's eyes blurred. "I would very much like to wear them. Thank you."

When Marissa left the queen's rooms, she was advised by one of Dante's assistants that the king wished to see her in his private office. She hadn't planned to seek him out, assuming that he'd be in strategy meetings for the rest of the day, but she was glad he'd asked for her. As difficult as it had been for Marissa to face the hoard of reporters, she knew it had been even harder for the king, who felt he had disappointed his people, and she wanted to make sure he was okay.

She knocked on the door.

"Come in."

He was at his desk, but he didn't seem to be focused on the papers spread out in front of him. When she stepped through the door, his gaze zeroed in on her and the weight on his shoulders seemed to lift a little.

"I didn't think it would take that long to measure you for one wedding dress," he said, rising from his chair.

"I spent a few minutes with your mother when the fitting was done."

"Are you okay?"

"Don't I look relatively unscathed?"

His smile was wry as he reached for her hands. "I didn't mean after your chat with my mother but after the press conference."

"I'm okay." She tipped her head back to meet his gaze. "How about you?"

"I'm much better now," he said and touched his lips gently to hers.

"Is that why I'm here—because you felt the need to check up on me?"

"No, you're here because, after bleeding out the most personal details of my life to the public, I wanted some time alone with you," he told her.

"To talk?" she asked lightly.

He smiled as he turned the handle of the door that separated his office from his bedroom. "I know there are still things to be said, and I want you to know that I'm sorry for all of this and grateful that you were there with me today, but no. Right now, I don't want to talk. I just want to hold you."

She turned willingly into his embrace.

Dante held on tight, breathing in her scent, relishing the warm softness of her body pressed against him.

But eventually the need to both take and offer comfort turned into something stronger, deeper and more demanding. Desire stirred in his belly, pulsed in his veins. With Marissa's body tucked so closely against his, she couldn't fail to notice that he was aroused. Which she proved when she asked, "Are you sure you just want to hold me?"

He chuckled softly. "Maybe I want more than that."

"I want you to make love with me, Dante." She tipped her head back to look at him, those beautiful gold eyes swirling with emotion. "I want to be with you more than anything else in the world. And after everything that's happened in the past twenty-four hours, I think we should cherish every minute we have together."

He cupped her face gently in his palms, stroked his thumbs gently over her cheeks. "I'm not going to argue with that."

"But I'm scared," she admitted. "The first night we made love, I was scared because I didn't know what to expect. The next day, I was scared because I was certain that I would never see you again, and I knew that no one else could ever make me feel the way I felt when I was in your arms. Now I'm scared because what I feel for you is so much more than I ever expected."

"We're on equal ground there," he promised her. "I've been with other women, but I've never felt about anyone else the way I feel about you."

"I've only ever been with you," she reminded him softly.

With everything else that had been going on, his brain had somehow failed to make that connection.

"I was your first lover," he said and felt a surge of what could only be described as primal satisfaction. She was his, had always been his and would always be his.

"My only lover."

He touched his lips to hers. "The only one you're ever going to know."

"The only one I want," she promised him.

"For the past several weeks, I've been thinking about our first time together, wanting to make sure it was perfect for you, without realizing we've already had our first time together."

"And it was perfect," she assured him.

"I can do better."

She smiled at the eagerness of his claim. "Do you think so?"

"I know so."

"Then take me to bed, Dante, and show me."

"Is that a personal request or a royal command?"

She smiled again and he knew she was remembering the day she'd asked that same question of him—albeit in a different context—and his response.

"Whatever gets you naked with me," she told him.

He scooped her into his arms.

Chapter Fifteen

Dante lowered Marissa gently onto the mattress, then he slowly and methodically began to remove her clothes.

He started with the plum-colored jacket. He held her gaze as he undid the first and then the second gold button, then tossed it aside. There were a lot more buttons down the front of her ivory-colored blouse. Tiny pearl buttons that he slipped out of the little loops of satin that held them secure, one by one. He spread the two sides apart to reveal a bronze-colored lace fantasy that barely covered the soft swell of her breasts. With a groan of pure male appreciation, he lowered his head to press his lips to her collarbone, to the hollow between her breasts, to the pale, tender skin just above her belly button.

He reached beneath her for the zipper at the back of her skirt, slowly slid it downward, then tugged the skirt over her hips, down the length of her legs. He'd expected that her underwear would match the bra—he hadn't expected a coordinating garter belt, too. He tossed the skirt aside with her jacket, his attention riveted by the contrast of bronze lace and ivory skin and barely there silk stockings. His fingertips traced the scalloped band at the top of her stockings, carefully following the contours, and she quivered. He reached around to the back of her thighs to release the clips there, then returned to the front and undid those, as well. Then he rolled her stockings, one by one, down her legs and discarded them with the suit.

"You are..." For a moment, words actually failed him. And though he didn't think the description did her justice, he finally settled on "spectacular."

She smiled, pleased by his compliment, but he could see the lingering hint of nerves in her eyes.

He discarded his jacket, pants, shirt and socks, but decided it wasn't just smart but necessary to keep his briefs on for the moment. She watched as he stripped away his clothes, her gaze roaming avidly over his body. When he joined her on the bed again, she reached for him, her hands stroking over his chest, his shoulders, his back.

"I've dreamed of touching you like this," she told him. "Of feeling the warmth of your skin beneath my palms. Of your body pressed against mine. Moving inside me."

Her words lit a fire in his veins. He captured her mouth, kissing her deeply, hungrily. She moaned in pleasure and arched against him so that her breasts brushed against his chest, her pelvis against his groin. He gritted his teeth, trying to control his body's instinctive reaction to her sensual movements. Two more minutes of her body rubbing against his and he would go off like a novice inside his briefs.

He captured those eager hands, cuffing her wrists and holding them over her head. She pouted, just a little, and he couldn't resist nipping at the sexy fullness of her bottom lip. She moaned softly, her eyes closing as her back arched, pressing her torso more fully against his.

"You are dangerous, woman."

Her lips curved now, the slow, sexy smile of a woman who knew she was in control.

He was determined to change that.

He shifted so that his knees were straddling her thighs, then lowered his head to her breast. He rubbed his lips over the peak of her nipple straining against the lace, and her breath hitched. He let his teeth scrape along the same path and felt the air shudder out of her lungs. Then her took the turgid peak in his mouth and suckled her through the delicate fabric, and her whole body shuddered.

He shifted his attention to the other breast and repeated the pattern until she was breathless and trembling. Then he released the clasp at her back and slowly drew the straps down her arms, uncovering just a hint of her pale skin, then a little bit more and a little bit more again, until her breasts were completely bared to his hungry gaze.

And then he used his lips and his tongue and his teeth again, to sample and savor the flavor of her naked flesh. While his mouth was busy with her breasts, his hands skimmed down her torso, following her curves and contours. Her quick, shallow breaths warned that she was close to the edge as he stripped away the garter, then slid a hand down the front of her bikinis. She gasped at the intimacy of the contact as his fingers sifted through the soft curls and flew apart when he found her center.

He shifted away from her only long enough to yank off his briefs and tug her bikinis down over her hips. He didn't wait for the aftershocks to fade, but eased into her while her body was still shuddering. Her second orgasm followed immediately on the heels of the first, her inner muscles clamping around him like a vice, and the rhythmic pulsing nearly pulled him over the edge with her.

He fisted his hands in the sheet, waiting for the waves of

her release to subside, as he was swamped by emotions far deeper than any he'd ever imagined.

He'd already told her he loved her, because he knew that he did. But when he sank into her, when she opened up and took him inside, he felt a soul-deep connection he'd never known before.

Because no one had ever bothered to look into his heart as Marissa had done. She'd taken the time to know him and understand him, and despite all of his flaws and faults, she'd accepted him and loved him. And because she did, the experience of making love with her was all the more intimate.

It wasn't just the physical joining of two bodies, but the mating of two hearts, the merging of two souls.

It was a long time after before Marissa could move, not that she wanted to go anywhere. She was more than happy to be right where she was, tucked close to Dante's body. Her head was on his shoulder and her hand was over his heart, absorbing the rhythm of each steady beat.

"You were right," she said when she finally summoned the energy to speak.

He touched his lips to her forehead. "About?"

"That was better."

"Told you."

She heard the smugness in his tone and suspected he was wearing the familiar cocky grin she'd come to know so well, but she was too lazy to tip her head back to confirm her suspicion.

"Do me a favor?" she asked.

"What's that?"

"Remind me never to challenge you to prove something again—I don't think I could survive it."

"I bet you could."

Her breath caught in her throat when his hand closed over her breast.

She'd honestly thought she was sated. Not just satisfied but completely spent. But all it had taken was one touch and desire coursed through her system anew.

"Dante." She wasn't sure if it was a plea or a warning.

His only response was to shift so that she was once again beneath him. Then he rubbed his lips against hers, nibbling, teasing.

"I bet you could," he repeated.

And, once again, he was right.

The headlines weren't quite what she expected.

Not just unexpected but disappointing. The people of Ardena should have been clamoring for the Casanova king to step down; instead, they were suddenly fascinated by the "obvious passion" between their ruler and his soon-to-be bride, turning the tawdry events of that night into a chapter in some great love story.

Tears burned the back of her eyes.

It wasn't fair. He was supposed to pay for what he'd done to Fiona, for abandoning her and walking away from his own child.

Her phone beeped. She opened the message:

r u there? on my way home, big news 2 share

She texted back: im here

And waited to see what news her sister had now.

Almost a month after the photos were first posted online, interest in the sexy pictures of the king and his fiancée had faded but not completely died. But there had been other scandals around the world and more important issues to deal with at home.

Dante's timely intervention had helped negotiate an agreement between the Minister of the Environment and the Fisheries Union that kept the fishermen on the water and had them singing their praises of the king. Dr. Kalidindi had been vocal in his appreciation of the princess's help with the new volunteer-cuddler program at Mercy Medical Center, and the general consensus was that the king had made a good choice in his soon-to-be queen.

Overall, Marissa felt confident that the storm had been weathered. And now the country was gearing up for the royal wedding, just two weeks away, and the Christmas holiday after that. As she waited for Dante, admiring the effect of the twinkling lights wrapped around the hedges that bordered the courtyard, the absolute last person on her mind was Naomi Breslin. She certainly didn't think there was any possibility the girl would have the nerve to seek her out. Nor did she think there was any way Naomi would ever get past the front gates of the property. So she was both shocked and distressed to see her in the courtyard.

"I sometimes worked as a server when extra help was needed for big events," Naomi explained before Marissa could even ask, then voluntarily handed over her security pass.

Marissa tucked it in her pocket. "What are you doing here?"

"I wanted to apologize."

"An apology can't undo what you did," she told her.

"I know, but—" The rest of the words seemed to get stuck in her throat when she saw Dante coming toward them.

"I've called security," he told Naomi. "You're lucky I didn't call the police."

She just nodded, her eyes filling with tears. "I needed to see you, to tell you how sorry I am." Then she reached into the pocket of her jeans and pulled out a folded piece of paper. "And I wanted you to see this."

"If this is another photo—" Dante warned, taking the page from her.

Her cheeks flushed. "No. It's a copy of Siobhan's paternity test."

He handed it back without even looking at it.

"You don't want to know who her father is?"

"It has nothing to do with me, because there was never any possibility that she was mine."

"I know that now," Naomi admitted. "My sister told me everything when Rico came back."

Marissa assumed Rico must be the baby's father, and while the revelation of this information couldn't change anything, it did give her hope that she and Dante might be able to move forward with their lives without always worrying that Naomi might be lurking around the next corner, trying to cause trouble for them.

"I tried to ruin your life because I thought you'd ruined hers." She glanced down at Dante's and Marissa's joined hands. "I'm glad I didn't succeed."

Then she curtsied to the king and his fiancée and turned to meet the guards who had arrived to escort her off of the property.

"Well, that was…surprising," Marissa said.

"And surprisingly insightful," Dante said.

"You could have her arrested."

"I could," he agreed. "But it wouldn't accomplish anything. Besides, she was right."

"About the fact that she tried to ruin your life?"

He shook his head. "About the fact that she didn't succeed. She wanted to create a scandal so huge, I would lose the throne. But when I saw those pictures, the only possibility that scared me was the possibility of losing you."

Marissa kissed him lightly. "That's never going to happen."

"And that's why she didn't succeed. Because as long as I have you, I have everything that matters."

For Marissa, the final days leading up to the wedding were a frantic carousel of fittings and Christmas shopping and packing for the honeymoon and double-checking all the details for the big day. The nights in Dante's arm were her respite—a chance for her to finally pause long enough to catch her breath and revel in the exquisite lovemaking of the man who would soon be her husband.

But she spent the night of December twentieth alone in her own room, to uphold the tradition that the groom should not see his bride before the wedding. But she wasn't completely alone. Dante's sisters rounded up the girls—their mother, Marissa's mother, Gabby and Hannah—who had come to Ardena with their families for the occasion and were also staying at the palace—and stopped by with a couple of bottles of champagne.

Actually, they had two bottles of champagne and a bottle of sparkling grape juice, the nonalcoholic version intended for Hannah, who was in her fifth month of pregnancy, and Gabby, who was nursing seven-week-old Talisa. The children were also in attendance, of course, but Sierra was keeping an eye on the little ones in the guest wing.

Francesca claimed the wine was part of a traditional celebration of a bride-to-be's last night as a single woman. Leticia said she didn't care about the tradition—any night was a good night for bubbly. Marissa discreetly tipped her champagne into the pot of the poinsettia tree in her sitting room and refilled her glass from the other bottle. Though she didn't yet know for sure, she thought it was possible that the recent tenderness in her breasts and increased fatigue might be early signs of pregnancy and she didn't want to take any chances if she was lucky enough to already have a new life growing inside of her.

But even if she wasn't yet pregnant, Marissa couldn't help but feel as if she was the luckiest woman in the world. It was the night before her wedding to the man she loved with all of her heart, and she was fortunate enough to spend it with four friends who would all be her sisters by virtue of marriage, the soon-to-be mother-in-law who had graciously welcomed her into the family and her own mother. And if Elena's presence wasn't the highlight of her night, at least her mother did nothing to spoil the occasion.

While Marissa faked drinking champagne with the girls, Dante was sipping brandy with the men—his father, his brothers and Marissa's brothers. He'd had some apprehension about meeting Michael and Cameron—after all, he was indirectly responsible for scandalous pictures of their little sister being posted on the internet—but they'd reassured him that they wouldn't put any visible bruises on him before the wedding since he was doing the honorable thing by marrying Marissa. Dante thought he scored some points, and saved himself some grief, by telling them that he wasn't marrying Marissa because it was the right thing to do, but because he loved her with his whole heart.

Before the brandy decanter was empty, Cameron excused himself for the night, eager to get back to his own room and check on his children. Michael followed his brother.

"I remember what it was like to be a new father," Benedicto mused. "The excitement, the nervousness and the indescribable joy of having a child who is the best parts of both parents."

"He's talking about when I was born," Matt teased his brothers. "Because I'm the only one who is a combination of all the best parts."

Van, because he was closest, cuffed the side of his brother's head. Dante just chuckled.

"You all inherited different characteristics and traits," Benedicto said. "But when each of you is lucky enough to hold your own child in your arms, and hopefully that won't be too far in the future—" he sent a pointed luck in Dante's direction "—you'll appreciate how a parent's love for a child never falters, even when that child is exhibiting some of the not-so-good parts."

Dante didn't say anything to encourage his father's hopes, but he suspected that his parents weren't going to have to wait much more than nine months for the grandchild they both coveted, if even that.

And with those last words, the old king hugged his son and wished him a good-night. Van walked out with his father, leaving only Matt with the groom-to-be.

"Last chance to make a break for it," his little brother said, only half teasing. "If you go now, you've got quite a few hours before anyone would even notice you were gone."

Dante just shook his head, because he knew that a life with Marissa was his best chance for the happily-ever-after he never thought he would have.

The morning of December twenty-first dawned clear and bright and unseasonably cold.

But Marissa didn't worry about the weather. She didn't care about anything except that today was the day she was going to become Dante's wife. Of course, their marriage would also elevate her status from that of princess to queen, but she decided she had enough butterflies in her stomach without thinking about that. Or maybe the slight queasiness was something more than butterflies.

She was afraid to hope. Afraid to want anything more when she was already so incredibly blessed.

But a baby...Dante's baby. It was impossible to even think those words without a smile spreading across her face.

She was still smiling when Gabriella snuck into her room and tucked a flat, narrow box into the pocket of her robe. Marissa didn't ask why and her sister-in-law didn't say. She just kissed the bride's cheek and slipped out again.

Marissa was grateful they'd opted for an early-afternoon ceremony, so that she didn't have any time to sit around and wait. In fact, she barely had time to nibble on a piece of toast and sip a cup of tea before she was surrounded by people fussing over her hair and touching up her makeup.

When she was finally groomed and polished and dressed, her mother came into her room. Her gaze moved from the pile of curls on top of Marissa's head to the peep-toe sandals on her feet, and Marissa instinctively braced herself. But she was completely unprepared when Elena, her eyes shimmering with moisture, said, "You truly are the most beautiful bride I've ever seen."

It was the sincerity in her tone even more than the unexpected compliment that made Marissa's throat tight. She managed a shaky smile. "And you're the most beautiful mother of the bride."

Elena picked up Marissa's bouquet of white calla lilies tied with a wide satin ribbon and handed it to her daughter. "I do want you to be happy."

Of course, the words sounded more like a royal command than a wish, but Marissa appreciated them nonetheless.

"I already am," she said and meant it.

Her mother gave her a quick hug, the impulsive gesture of affection even more unexpected than the kind words.

"In that case, we better get to the church. We don't want to keep your groom waiting."

The church was decorated in royal fashion for the holiday wedding of Ardena's king and the Tesorian princess. In addition to the enormous wreath over the arched entranceway, there were evergreen garlands wrapped around the balcony railings. Gold bows marked the ends of the pews and a mountain of Christmas flowers bordered the steps to the alter. But Dante had barely noticed any of the decorations. He was waiting for his bride, and not very patiently.

Now that the day was finally here, he wanted it to be done. He wanted Marissa as his wife so they could officially start their life together.

Then, finally, she was there. The first glimpse of his bride at the back of the church simply took his breath away.

He didn't know enough about bridal fashions to recognize that the Roman-inspired asymmetrical dress was made of layers of snowy chiffon with a wide band of beading at the empire-style waist. He just knew that she was absolutely stunning. And with every step she took toward him, the joy in his heart continued to swell until it overflowed and filled every part of him.

She was his bride. His goddess. His heart.

And when he spoke his vows, he didn't hesitate or falter. Although the words had been spoken by countless grooms before him, he felt as if they'd been written from his heart. And when it was Marissa's turn, her gaze was just as steady, her voice as clear.

Church bells were ringing in celebration of the union of Ardena's king and his new queen as they exited the church... just in time to see the first flakes of snow begin to fall from the sky.

"You told me it wouldn't snow," the bride said.

"What I said was that the forecasters were probably wrong when they predicted snow because it hasn't snowed in this part of the country in more than fifteen years," her groom reminded her.

"It's snowing now."

"Which proves that today is a day of miracles."

"More than you probably know," she murmured, a smile playing at the corners of her mouth.

His gaze dipped to her belly as anticipation jumped in his own. "Baby?" He barely mouthed the word, wanting to ensure his question couldn't possibly be overheard.

She nodded, her eyes filled with both joy and uncertainty.

He knew how eager she was to start a family, so he guessed that any hesitation she was experiencing was a result of not knowing how he would respond to the news. He was more than happy to reassure her. "That is absolutely the best Christmas present you could give me."

Her lips curved. "In that case, Merry Christmas, Your Majesty."

And then, right there at the top of the steps and with thousands of jubilant Ardenans watching, the king kissed his queen.

Epilogue

KING DANTE WEDS TESORIAN PRINCESS
by Alex Girard

Snow is an extremely rare occurrence in Saint Georgios. Such a rare occurrence, in fact, that any amount of snowfall would usually be front-page news. But on the first official day of winter, not even a blizzard could have upstaged the pre-Christmas nuptials of His Majesty the King Dante Romero of Ardena to Her Highness Princess Marissa Leandres of Tesoro del Mar.

Just as the bells of Sacred Heart began to toll in celebration of their marriage, the people who had braved the unseasonably cold weather to line the streets in the hopes of catching a glimpse of the king and his new queen were treated to a lovely display of fluffy white flakes swirling in the sky—and then, the lovelier image of the bride as she exited the church with her groom.

It was a picture-perfect moment, made even more perfect when the royal couple shared their first kiss as husband and wife and the crowd roared its approval.

The royal wedding was a celebration for the whole nation, but it was also very much a family affair. The bride was attended by both of the groom's sisters, Princesses Francesca and Leticia, and her niece Princess Sierra, with another niece, Princess Riley, as her flower girl. The groom's best man was his father, and his brothers, Princes Jovanni and Matteo, performed ushering duties.

In the midst of all of the carefully orchestrated pageantry, there were moments of spontaneity (the flower girl climbing the cake table to see the decorations at the very top), and possibly some hints of romance on the horizon (the groom's youngest brother danced mostly with the bride's eldest niece). And by the time the cake was cut and the dancing was done, the snow had stopped falling.

But it was evident to anyone who witnessed the exchange of vows that the newlyweds weren't worried about the weather...they were just looking forward to their holiday honeymoon.

* * * * *

YULETIDE BABY SURPRISE

CATHERINE MANN

To Savannah

One

Dr. Mariama Mandara had always been the last picked for a team in gym class. With good reason. Athletics? Not her thing. But when it came to spelling bees, debate squads and math competitions, she'd racked up requests by the dozens.

Too bad her academic skills couldn't help her sprint faster down the posh hotel corridor.

More than ever, she needed speed to escape the royal watchers tracking her at the Cape Verde beachside resort off the coast of West Africa, which was like a North Atlantic Hawaii, a horseshoe grouping of ten islands. They were staying on the largest island, Santiago.

No matter where she hid, determined legions were all too eager for a photo with a princess. Why couldn't they accept she was here for a business conference, not socializing?

Panting, Mari braced a hand against the wall as she

stumbled past a potted areca silk palm strung with twinkling Christmas lights. Evading relentless pursuers wasn't as easy as it appeared in the movies, especially if you weren't inclined to blow things up or leap from windows. The nearest stairwell door was blocked by two tourists poring over some sightseeing pamphlet. A cleaning cart blocked another escape route. She could only keep moving forward.

Regaining her balance, she power-walked, since running would draw even more attention or send her tripping over her own feet. Her low-heeled pumps thud-thud-thudded along the plush carpet in time with a polyrhythmic version of "Hark! The Herald Angels Sing" wafting from the sound system. She just wanted to finish this medical conference and return to her research lab, where she could ride out the holiday madness in peace, crunching data rather than candy canes.

For most people, Christmas meant love, joy and family. But for her, the "season to be jolly" brought epic family battles even twenty years after her parents' divorce. If her mom and dad had lived next door to each other—or even on the same continent—the holidays would not have been so painful. But they'd played transcontinental tug-of-war over their only child for decades. Growing up, she'd spent more time in the Atlanta airport and on planes with her nanny than actually celebrating by a fireside with cocoa. She'd even spent one Christmas in a hotel, her connecting flight canceled for snow.

The occasional cart in the hall now reminded her of that year's room-service Christmas meal. Call her crazy, but once she had gained more control over her world, she preferred a simpler Christmas.

Although simple wasn't always possible for someone

born into royalty. Her mother had crumbled under the pressure of the constant spotlight, divorced her Prince Charming in Western Africa and returned to her Atlanta, Georgia, home. Mari, however, couldn't divorce herself from her heritage.

If only her father and his subjects understood she could best serve their small region through her research at the university lab using her clinical brain, rather than smiling endlessly through the status quo of ribbon-cutting ceremonies. She craved her comfy, shapeless clothes, instead of worrying about keeping herself neat as a pin for photo ops.

Finally, she spotted an unguarded stairwell. Peering inside, she found it empty but for the echo of "Hark! The Herald Angels Sing" segueing into "Away in a Manger." She just needed to make it from the ground level to her fifth-floor room, where she could hole up for the night before facing the rest of the week's symposiums. Exhausted from a fourteen-hour day of presentations about her research on antiviral medications, she was a rumpled mess and just didn't have it in her to smile pretty for the camera or field questions that would be captured on video phone. Especially since anything she said could gain a life of its own on the internet in seconds these days.

She grasped the rail and all but hauled herself up step after step. Urgency pumped her pulse in her ears. Gasping, she paused for a second at the third floor to catch her breath before trudging up the last flights. Shoving through the fifth-floor door, she almost slammed into a mother and teenage daughter leaving their room. The teen did a double take and Mari turned away quickly, adrenaline surging through her exhaustion and powering her down the hall. Except now she was going in the opposite direction, damn it.

Simply strolling back into the hall wasn't an option until she could be sure the path was clear. But she couldn't simply stand here indefinitely, either. If only she had a disguise, something to throw people off the scent. Head tucked down, she searched the hall through her eyelashes, taking in a brass luggage rack and monstrously big pots of African feather grass.

Her gaze landed on the perfect answer—a roomservice cart. Apparently abandoned. She scanned for anyone in a hotel uniform, but saw only the retreating back of a woman walking away quickly, a cell phone pressed to her ear. Mari chewed her lip for half a second then sprinted forward and stopped just short of the cloth-draped trolley.

She peeked under the silver tray. The mouth-watering scent of saffron-braised karoo lamb made her stomach rumble. And the tiramisu particularly tempted her to find the nearest closet and feast after a long day of talking without a break for more than coffee and water. She shook off indulgent thoughts. The sooner she worked her way back to her room, the sooner she could end this crazy day with a hot shower, her own tray of food and a soft bed.

Delivering the room-service cart now offered her best means of disguise. A hotel jacket was even draped over the handle and a slip of paper clearly listed Suite 5A as the recipient.

The sound of the elevator doors opening spurred her into action.

Mari shrugged the voluminous forest-green jacket over her rumpled black suit. A red Father Christmas hat slipped from underneath the hotel uniform. All the better for extra camouflaging. She yanked on the hat over her upswept hair and started pushing the heavily laden cart toward the suite at the end of the hall, just as voices swelled behind her.

"Do you see her?" a female teen asked in Portuguese, her squeaky tones drifting down the corridor. "I thought you said she ran up the stairs to the fifth floor."

"Are you sure it wasn't the fourth?" another high-pitched girl answered.

"I'm certain," a third voice snapped. "Get your phone ready. We can sell these for a fortune."

Not a chance.

Mari shoved the cart. China rattled and the wheels creaked. Damn, this thing was heavier than it looked. She dug her heels in deeper and pushed harder. Step by step, past carved masks and a pottery elephant planter, she walked closer to suite 5A.

The conspiring trio drew closer. "Maybe we can ask that lady with the cart if she's seen her...."

Apprehension lifted the hair on the back of Mari's neck. The photos would be all the more mortifying if they caught her in this disguise. She needed to get inside suite 5A. Now. The numbered brass plaque told her she was at the right place.

Mari jabbed the buzzer, twice, fast.

"Room service," she called, keeping her head low.

Seconds ticked by. The risk of stepping inside and hiding her identity from one person seemed far less daunting than hanging out here with the determined group and heaven only knew who else.

Just when she started to panic that time would run out, the door opened, thank God. She rushed past, her arms straining at the weight of the cart and her nose catching a whiff of manly soap. Her favorite scent—

clean and crisp rather than cloying and obvious. Her feet tangled for a second.

Tripping over her own feet as she shoved the cart was far from dignified. But she'd always been too gangly to be a glamour girl. She was more of a cerebral type, a proud nerd, much to the frustration of her family's press secretary, who expected her to present herself in a more dignified manner.

Still, even in her rush to get inside, curiosity nipped at her. What type of man would choose such a simple smell while staying in such opulence? But she didn't dare risk a peek at him.

She eyed the suite for other occupants, even though the room-service cart only held one meal. One very weighty meal. She shoved the rattling cart past a teak lion. The room appeared empty, the lighting low. Fat leather sofas and a thick wooden table filled the main space. Floor-to-ceiling shutters had been slid aside to reveal the moonlit beach outside a panoramic window. Lights from stars and yachts dotted the horizon. Palms and fruit trees with lanterns illuminated the shore. On a distant islet, a stone church perched on a hill.

She cleared her throat and started toward the table by the window. "I'll set everything up on the table for you."

"Thanks," rumbled a hauntingly familiar voice that froze her in her tracks. "But you can just leave it there by the fireplace."

Her brain needed less than a second to identify those deep bass tones. Ice trickled down her spine as if snow had hit her African Christmas after all.

She didn't have to turn around to confirm that fate was having a big laugh at her expense. She'd run from an irritation straight into a major frustration. Out of all the hotel suites she could have entered, somehow she'd landed in the room of Dr. Rowan Boothe.

Her professional nemesis.

A physician whose inventions she'd all but ridiculed in public.

What the hell was he doing here? She'd reviewed the entire program of speakers and she could have sworn he wasn't listed on the docket until the end of the week.

The door clicked shut behind her. The tread of his footsteps closed in, steady, deliberate, bringing the scent of him drifting her way. She kept her face down, studying his loafers and the well-washed hem of his faded jeans.

She held on to the hope that he wouldn't recognize her. "I'll leave your meal right here then," she said softly. "Have a nice evening."

His tall, solid body blocked her path. God, she was caught between a rock and a hard place. Her eyes skated to his chest.

A very hard, muscle-bound place encased in a white button-down with the sleeves rolled up and the tail untucked. She remembered well every muscular—annoying—inch of him.

She just prayed he wouldn't recognize her from their last encounter five months ago at a conference in London. Already the heat of embarrassment flamed over her.

Even with her face averted, she didn't need to look further to refresh her memory of that too handsome face of his. Weathered by the sun, his Brad Pitt–level good looks only increased. His sandy blond hair would have been too shaggy for any other medical professional to carry off. But somehow he simply appeared too im-

mersed in philanthropic deeds to be bothered with anything as mundane as a trip to the barber.

The world thought he was Dr. Hot Perfection but she
simply couldn't condone the way he circumvented rules.

"Ma'am," he said, ducking his head as if to catch her
attention, "is there a problem?"

Just keep calm. There was no way for him to identify her from the back. She would rather brave a few
pictures in the press than face this man while she wore
a flipping Santa Claus hat.

A broad hand slid into view with cash folded over
into a tip. "Merry Christmas."

If she didn't take the money, that would appear sus-
picious. She pinched the edge of the folded bills, doing
her best to avoid touching him. She plucked the cash
free and made a mental note to donate the tip to charity. "Thank you for your generosity."

"You're very welcome." His smooth bass was too appealing coming from such an obnoxiously perfect man.

Exhaling hard, she angled past him. Almost home
free. Her hand closed around the cool brass door handle.

"Dr. Mandara, are you really going so soon?" he
asked with unmistakable sarcasm. He'd recognized her.
Damn. He was probably smirking, too, the bastard.

He took a step closer, the heat of his breath caressing her cheek. "And here I thought you'd gone to all this
trouble to sneak into my room so you could seduce me."

Dr. Rowan Boothe waited for his words to sink
in, the possibility of sparring with the sexy princess/
research scientist already pumping excitement through
his veins. He didn't know what it was about Mariama
Mandara that turned him inside out, but he'd given up

analyzing the why of it long ago. His attraction to Mari was simply a fact of life now.

Her disdain for him was an equally undeniable fact, and to be honest, it was quite possibly part of her allure.

He grew weary with the whole notion of the world painting him as some kind of saint just because he'd rejected the offer of a lucrative practice in North Carolina and opened a clinic in Africa. These days, he had money to burn after his invention of a computerized medical diagnostics program—a program Mari missed no opportunity to dismiss as faux, shortcut medicine. Funding the clinic hadn't even put a dent in his portfolio so he didn't see it as worthy of hoopla. Real philanthropy involved sacrifice. And he wasn't particularly adept at denying himself things he wanted.

Right now, he wanted Mari.

Although from the look of horror on her face, his half-joking come-on line hadn't struck gold.

She opened and closed her mouth twice, for once at a loss for words. Fine by him. He was cool with just soaking up the sight of her. He leaned back against the wet bar, taking in her long, elegant lines. Others might miss the fine-boned grace beneath the bulky clothes she wore, but he'd studied her often enough to catch the brush of every subtle curve. He could almost feel her, ached to peel her clothes away and taste every inch of her café-au-lait skin.

Some of the heat must have shown on his face because she snapped out of her shock. "You have got to be joking. You can't honestly believe I would ever make a move on you, much less one so incredibly blatant."

Damn, but her indignation was so sexy and yeah, even cute with the incongruity of that Santa hat perched on her head. He couldn't stop himself from grinning.

She stomped her foot. "Don't you dare laugh at me."

He tapped his head lightly. "Nice hat."

Growling, she flung aside the hat and shrugged out of the hotel jacket. "Believe me, if I'd known you were in here, I wouldn't have chosen this room to hide out."

"Hide out?" he said absently, half following her words.

As she pulled her arms free of the jacket to review a rumpled black suit, the tug of her white business shirt against her breasts sent an unwelcome surge of arousal through him. He'd been fighting a damned inconvenient arousal around this woman for more than two years, ever since she'd stepped behind a podium in front of an auditorium full of people and proceeded to shoot holes in his work. She thought his computerized diagnostics tool was too simplistic. She'd accused him of taking the human element out of medicine. His jaw flexed, any urge to smile fading.

If anyone was too impersonal, it was her. And, God, how he ached to rattle her composure, to see her tawny eyes go sleepy with all-consuming passion.

Crap.

He was five seconds away from an obvious erection. He reined himself in and faced the problem at hand— the woman—as a more likely reason for her arrival smoked through his brain. "Is this some sort of professional espionage?"

"What in the hell are you talking about?" She fidgeted with the loose waistband on her tweedy skirt.

Who would have thought tweed would turn him inside out? Yet he found himself fantasizing about pulling those practical clunky shoes off her feet. He would kiss his way up under her skirt, discover the silken inside of her calf...

He cleared his throat and brought his focus up to her heart-shaped face. "Playing dumb does not suit you." He knew full well she had a genius IQ. "But if that's the way you want this to roll, then okay. Were you hoping to obtain insider information on the latest upgrade to my computerized diagnostics tool?"

"Not likely." She smoothed a hand over her swept-back hair. "I never would have pegged you as the conspiracy theorist sort since you're a man of science. Sort of."

He cocked an eyebrow. "So you're not here for information, Mari." If he'd wanted distance he should have called her Dr. Mandara, but too late to go back. "Then why are you sneaking into my suite?"

Sighing, she crossed her arms over her chest. "Fine. I'll tell you, but you have to promise not to laugh."

"Scout's honor." He crossed his heart.

"You were a Boy Scout? Figures."

Before he'd been sent to a military reform school, but he didn't like to talk about those days and the things he'd done. Things he could never atone for even if he opened free clinics on every continent, every year for the rest of his life. But he kept trying, by saving one life at a time, to make up for the past.

"You were going to tell me how you ended up in my suite."

She glanced at the door, then sat gingerly on the arm of the leather sofa. "Royal watchers have been trailing me with their phones to take photos and videos for their five seconds of fame. A group of them followed me out the back exit after my last seminar."

Protective instincts flamed to life inside him. "Doesn't your father provide you with bodyguards?"

"I choose not to use them," she said without explanation, her chin tipping regally in a way that shouted the subject wasn't open for discussion. "My attempt to slip away wasn't going well. The lady pushing this room-service cart was distracted by a phone call. I saw my chance to go incognito and I took it."

The thought of her alone out there had him biting back the urge to chew out someone—namely her father. So what if she rejected guards? Her dad should have insisted.

Mari continued, "I know I should probably just grin for the camera and move on, but the images they capture aren't…professional. I have serious work to do, a reputation to maintain." She tipped her head back, her mouth pursed tight in frustration for a telling moment before she rambled on with a weary shake of her head. "I didn't sign on for this."

Her exhaustion pulled at him, made him want to rest his hands on her drooping shoulders and ease those tense muscles. Except she would likely clobber him with the silver chafing dish on the serving cart. He opted for the surefire way to take her mind off the stress.

Shoving away from the bar, he strode past the cart toward her again. "Poor little rich princess."

Mari's cat eyes narrowed. "You're not very nice."

"You're the only one who seems to think so." He stopped twelve inches shy of touching her.

Slowly, she stood, facing him. "Well, pardon me for not being a member of *your* fan club."

"You genuinely didn't know this was my room?" he asked again, even though he could see the truth in her eyes.

"No. I didn't." She shook her head, the heartbeat throbbing faster in her elegant neck. "The cart only had your room number. Not your name."

"If you'd realized ahead of time that this was my room, my meal—" he scooped up the hotel jacket and Santa hat "—would you have surrendered yourself to the camera-toting brigade out there rather than ask me for help?"

Her lips quivered with the first hint of a smile. "I guess we'll never know the answer to that, will we?" She tugged at the jacket. "Enjoy your supper."

He didn't let go. "There's plenty of food here. You could join me, hide out for a while longer."

"Did you just invite me to dinner?" The light of humor in her eyes animated her face until the air damn near crackled between them. "Or are you secretly trying to poison me?"

She nibbled her bottom lip and he could have sworn she swayed toward him. If he hooked a finger in the vee of her shirt and pulled, she would be in his arms.

Instead, he simply reached out and skimmed back the stray lock of sleek black hair curving just under her chin. "Mari, there are a lot of things I would like to do to you, but I can assure you that poisoning you is nowhere on that list."

Confusion chased across her face, but she wasn't running from the room or laughing. In fact, he could swear he saw reluctant interest. Enough to make him wonder what might happen if...

A whimper snapped him out of his passion fog.

The sound wasn't coming from Mari. She looked over his shoulder and he turned toward the sound. The cry swelled louder, into a full-out wail, swelling from across the room.

From under the room-service cart?

He glanced at Mari. "What the hell?"

She shook her head, her hands up. "Don't look at me."

He charged across the room, sweeping aside the linen cloth covering the service cart to reveal a squalling infant.

Two

The infant's wail echoed in the hotel suite. Shock resounded just as loudly inside of Mari as she stared at the screaming baby in a plastic carrier wedged inside the room-service trolley. No wonder the cart had felt heavier than normal. If only she'd investigated she might have found the baby right away. Her brain had been tapping her with the logic that something was off, and she'd been too caught up in her own selfish fears about a few photos to notice.

To think that poor little one had been under there all this time. So tiny. So defenseless. The child, maybe two or three months old, wore a diaper and a plain white T-shirt, a green blanket tangled around its tiny, kicking feet.

Mari swallowed hard, her brain not making connections as she was too dumbstruck to think. "Oh, my God, is that a baby?"

"It's not a puppy." Rowan washed his hands at the wet-bar sink then knelt beside the lower rack holding the infant seat. He visibly went into doctor mode as he checked the squalling tyke over, sliding his hands under and scooping the child up in his large, confident hands. Chubby little mocha-brown arms and legs flailed before the baby settled against Rowan's chest with a hiccupping sigh.

"What in the world is it doing under there?" She stepped away, clearing a path for him to walk over to the sofa.

"I'm not the one who brought the room service in," he countered offhandedly, sliding a finger into the baby's tiny bow mouth. Checking for a cleft palate perhaps?

"Well, I didn't put the baby there."

A boy or girl? She couldn't tell. The wriggling bundle wore no distinguishing pink or blue. There wasn't even a hair bow in the cap of black curls.

Rowan elbowed aside an animal-print throw pillow and sat on the leather couch, resting the baby on his knees while he continued assessing.

She tucked her hands behind her back. "Is it okay? He or she?"

"Her," he said, closing the cloth diaper. "She's a girl, approximately three months old, but that's just a guess."

"We should call the authorities. What if whoever abandoned her is still in the building?" Unlikely given how long she'd hung out in here flirting with Rowan. "There was a woman walking away from the cart earlier. I assumed she was just taking a cell phone call, but maybe that was the baby's mother?"

"Definitely something to investigate. Hopefully there will be security footage of her. You need to think through what you're going to tell the authorities, review every detail in your mind while it's fresh." He sounded more like a detective than a doctor. "Did you see anyone else around the cart before you took it?"

"Are you blaming this on me?"

"Of course not."

Still, she couldn't help but feel guilty. "What if this is my fault for taking that cart? Maybe the baby wasn't abandoned at all. What if some mother was just trying to bring her child to work? She must be frantic looking for her daughter."

"Or frantic she's going to be in trouble," he replied dryly.

"Or he. The parent could be a father." She reached for the phone on the marble bar. "I really need to ring the front desk now."

"Before you call, could you pass over her seat? It may hold some clues to her family. Or at least some supplies to take care of her while we settle this."

"Sure, hold on."

She eased the battered plastic seat from under the cart, winging a quick prayer of thankfulness that the child hadn't come to some harm out there alone in the hall. The thought that someone would so recklessly care for a precious life made her grind her teeth in frustration. She set the gray carrier beside Rowan on the sofa, the green blanket trailing off the side.

Finally, she could call for help. Without taking her eyes off Rowan and the baby, she dialed the front desk.

The phone rang four times before someone picked up. "Could you hold, please? Thank you," a harried-sounding hotel operator said without giving Mari a chance to shout "No!" The line went straight to Christmas carols, "O Holy Night" lulling in her ear.

Sighing, she sagged a hip against the garland-draped wet bar. "They put me on hold."

Rowan glanced up, his pure blue eyes darkened with an answering frustration. "Whoever decided to schedule a conference at this time of year needs to have his head examined. The hotel was already jam-packed with holiday tourists, now conventioneers, too. Insane."

"For once, you and I agree on something one hundred percent." The music on the phone transitioned to "The Little Drummer Boy" as she watched Rowan cradle the infant in a way that made him even more handsome. Unwilling to get distracted by traveling down that mental path again, she shifted to look out the window at the scenic view. Multicolored lights blinked from the sailboats and ferries.

The Christmas spirit was definitely in full swing on the resort island. Back on the mainland, her father's country included more of a blend of religions than many realized. Christmas wasn't as elaborate as in the States, but still celebrated. Cape Verde had an especially deep-rooted Christmas tradition, having been originally settled by the Portuguese.

Since moving out on her own, she'd been more than happy to downplay the holiday mayhem personally, but she couldn't ignore the importance, the message of hope that should come this time of year. That a parent could abandon a child at the holidays seemed somehow especially tragic.

Her arms suddenly ached to scoop up the baby, but she had no experience and heaven forbid she did something wrong. The little girl was clearly in better hands with Rowan.

He cursed softly and she turned back to face him. He

held the baby in the crook of his arm while he searched the infant seat with the other.

"What?" she asked, covering the phone's mouthpiece. "Is something the matter with the baby?"

"No, something's the matter with the parents. You can stop worrying that some mom or dad brought their baby to work." He held up a slip of paper, baby cradled in the other arm. "I found this note tucked under the liner in the carrier."

He held up a piece of hotel stationary.

Mari rushed to sit beside him on the sofa, phone still in hand. "What does it say?"

"The baby's mother intended for her to be in this cart, in *my* room." He passed the note. "Read this."

Dr. Boothe, you are known for your charity and generosity. Please look over my baby girl, Issa. My husband died in a border battle and I cannot give Issa what she needs. Tell her I love her and will think of her always.

Mari reread the note in disbelief, barely able to process that someone could give away their child so easily, with no guarantees that she would be safe. "Do people dump babies on your doorstep on a regular basis?"

"It's happened a couple of times at my clinic, but never anything remotely like this." He held out the baby toward her. "Take Issa. I have some contacts I can reach out to with extra resources. They can look into this while we're waiting for the damn hotel operator to take you off hold."

Mari stepped back sharply. "I don't have much experience with babies. No experience actually, other than kissing them on the forehead in crowds during photo ops."

"Didn't you ever babysit in high school?" He cradled the infant in one arm while fishing out his cell phone with his other hand. "Or do princesses not babysit?"

"I skipped secondary education and went straight to college." As a result, her social skills sucked as much as her fashion sense, but that had never mattered much. Until now. Mari smoothed a hand down her wrinkled, baggy skirt. "Looks to me like you have Issa and your phone well in hand."

Competently—enticingly so. No wonder he'd been featured in magazines around the globe as one of the world's most eligible bachelors. Intellectually, she'd understood he was an attractive—albeit irritating—man. But until this moment, she hadn't comprehended the full impact of his appeal.

Her body flamed to life, her senses homing in on this moment, on *him*. Rowan. The last man on the planet she should be swept away by or attracted to.

This must be some sort of primal, hormonal thing. Her ticking biological clock was playing tricks on her mind because he held a baby. She could have felt this way about any man.

Right?

God, she hoped so. Because she couldn't wrap her brain around the notion that she could be this drawn to a man so totally wrong for her.

The music ended on the phone a second before the operator returned. "May I help you?"

Heaven yes, she wanted to shout. She needed Issa safe and settled. She also needed to put space between herself and the increasingly intriguing man in front of her.

She couldn't get out of this suite soon enough.

"Yes, you can help. There's been a baby abandoned just outside Suite 5A, the room of Dr. Rowan Boothe."

Rowan didn't foresee a speedy conclusion to the baby mystery. Not tonight, anyway. The kind of person who threw away their child and trusted her to a man based solely on his professional reputation was probably long gone by now.

Walking the floor with the infant, he patted her back for a burp after the bottle she'd downed. Mari was reading a formula can, her forehead furrowed, her shirt half-untucked. Fresh baby supplies had been sent up by the hotel's concierge since Rowan didn't trust anything in the diaper bag.

There were no reports from hotel security or authorities of a missing child that matched this baby's description. So far security hadn't found any helpful footage, just images of a woman's back as she walked away from the cart as Mari stepped up to take it. Mari had called the police next, but they hadn't seemed to be in any hurry since no one's life was in danger and even the fact that a princess was involved didn't have them moving faster. Delays like this only made it more probable the press would grab hold of information about the situation. He needed to keep this under control. His connections could help him with that, but they couldn't fix the entire system here.

Eventually, the police would make their way over with someone from child services. Thoughts of this baby getting lost in an overburdened, underfunded network tore at him. On a realistic level, he understood he couldn't save everyone who crossed his path, but something about this vulnerable child abandoned at Christmas tore at his heart all the more.

Had to be because the kid was a baby, his weak spot.

He shrugged off distracting thoughts of how badly he'd screwed up as a teenager and focused on the present. Issa burped, then cooed. But Rowan wasn't fooled into thinking she was full. As fast as the kid had downed that first small bottle, he suspected she still needed more. "Issa's ready for the extra couple of ounces if you're ready."

Mari shook the measured powder and distilled water together, her pretty face still stressed. "I think I have it right. But maybe you should double-check."

"Seriously, I'm certain you can handle a two-to-one mixture." He grinned at seeing her flustered for the first time ever. Did she have any idea how cute she looked? Not that she would be happy with the "cute" label. "Just think of it as a lab experiment."

She swiped a wrist over the beads of sweat on her forehead, a simple watch sliding down her slim arm. "If I got the proportions wrong—"

"You didn't." He held out a hand for the fresh bottle. "Trust me."

Reluctantly, she passed it over. "She just looks so fragile."

"Actually, she appears healthy, well fed and clean." Her mother may have dumped her off, but someone had taken good care of the baby before that. Was the woman already regretting her decision? God, he hoped so. There were already far too few homes for orphans here. "There are no signs she's been mistreated."

"She seems cuddly," Mari said with a wistful smile.

"Are you sure you wouldn't like to hold her while I make a call?"

She shook her head quickly, tucking a stray strand of hair back into the loose knot at her neck. "Your special contacts?"

He almost smiled at her weak attempt to distract him from passing over the baby. And he definitely wasn't in a position to share much of anything about his unorthodox contacts with her. "It would be easier if I didn't have to juggle the kid and the bottle while I talk."

"Okay, if you're sure I won't break her." She chewed her bottom lip. "But let me sit down first."

Seeing Mari unsure of herself was strange, to say the least. She always commanded the room with her confidence and knowledge, even when he didn't agree with her conclusions. There was something vulnerable, approachable even, about her now.

He set the baby into her arms, catching a whiff of Mari's perfume, something flowery and surprisingly whimsical for such a practical woman. "Just be careful to support her head and hold the bottle up enough that she isn't drinking air."

Mari eyed the bottle skeptically before popping it into Issa's mouth. "Someone really should invent a more precise way to do this. There's too much room for human error."

"But babies like the human touch. Notice how she's pressing her ear against your heart?" Still leaning in, he could see Mari's pulse throbbing in her neck. The steady throb made him burn to kiss her right there, to taste her, inhale her scent. "That heartbeat is a constant in a baby's life in utero. They find comfort in it after birth, as well."

Her deep golden gaze held his and he could swear something, an awareness, flashed in her eyes as they played out this little family tableau.

"Um, Rowan—" her voice came out a hint breathier than normal "—make your call, please."

Yeah, probably a good idea to retreat and regroup while he figured out what to do about the baby—and about having Mari show up unexpectedly in his suite.

He stepped into his bedroom and opened the French door onto the balcony. The night air was that perfect temperature—not too hot or cold. Decembers in Cape Verde usually maxed out at between seventy-five and eighty degrees Fahrenheit. A hint of salt clung to the air and on a normal night he would find sitting out here with a drink the closest thing to a vacation he'd had in... He'd lost count of the years.

But tonight he had other things on his mind.

Fishing out his phone, he leaned on the balcony rail so he could still see Mari through the picture window in the sitting area. His gaze roved over her lithe body, which was almost completely hidden under her ill-fitting suit. At least she wouldn't be able to hear him. His contacts were out of the normal scale and the fewer people who knew about them, the better. Those ties traced back far, all the way to high school.

After he'd derailed his life in a drunk-driving accident as a teen, he'd landed in a military reform school with a bunch of screwups like himself. He'd formed life-time friendships there with the group that had dubbed themselves the Alpha Brotherhood. Years later after college graduation, they'd all been stunned to learn their headmaster had connections with Interpol. He'd recruited a handful of them as freelance agents. Their troubled pasts—and large bank accounts—gave them a cover story to move freely in powerful and sometimes seedy circles.

Rowan was only tapped for missions maybe once

a year, but it felt damn good to help clean up underworld crime. He saw the fallout too often in the battles between warlords that erupted in regions neighboring his clinic.

The phone stopped ringing and a familiar voice said, "Speak to me, Boothe."

"Colonel, I need your help."

The Colonel laughed softly. "Tell me something new. Which one of your patients is in trouble? Or is it another cause you've taken on? Or—"

"Sir, it's a baby."

The sound of a chair squeaking echoed over the phone lines and Rowan could envision his old headmaster sitting up straighter, his full attention on the moment. "You have a baby?"

"Not *my* baby. *A* baby." He didn't expect to ever have children. His life was too consumed with his work, his mission. It wouldn't be fair to a child to have to compete with third-world problems for his father's attention. Still, Rowan's eyes locked in on Mari holding Issa so fiercely, as if still afraid she might drop her. "Someone abandoned an infant in my suite along with a note asking me to care for her."

"A little girl. I always wanted a little girl." The nostalgia in the Colonel's voice was at odds with the stern exterior he presented to the world. Even his clothes said stark long after he'd stopped wearing a uniform. These days, in his Interpol life, Salvatore wore nothing but gray suits with a red tie. "But back to your problem at hand. What do the authorities say?"

"No one has reported a child missing to the hotel security or to local authorities. Surveillance footage hasn't shown anything, but there are reports of a woman walking away from the cart where the baby was abandoned. The police are dragging their feet on showing up here to investigate further. So I need to get ahead of the curve here."

"In what way?"

"You and I both know the child welfare system here is overburdened to the crumbling point." Rowan found a plan forming in his mind, a crazy plan, but one that felt somehow right. Hell, there wasn't any option that sat completely right with his conscience. "I want to have temporary custody of the child while the authorities look into finding the mother or placing her in a home."

He might not be the best parental candidate for the baby, but he was a helluva lot better than an overflowing orphanage. If he had help...

His gaze zeroed in on the endearing tableau in his hotel sitting room. The plan came into sharper focus as he thought of spending more time with Mari.

Yet as soon as he considered the idea, obstacles piled in his path. How would he sell her on such an unconventional solution? She freaked out over feeding the kid a bottle.

"Excuse me for asking the obvious, Boothe, but how in the hell do you intend to play papa and save the world at the same time?"

"It's only temporary." He definitely couldn't see himself doing the family gig long-term. Even thinking of growing up with his own family sent his stomach roiling. Mari made it clear her work consumed her, as well. So a temporary arrangement could suit them both well. "And I'll have help...from someone."

"Ah, now I understand."

"How do you understand from a continent away?" Rowan hated to think he was that transparent.

"After my wife wised up and left me, when I had our

son for the weekend, I always had trouble matching up outfits for him to wear. So she would send everything paired up for me." He paused, the sound of clinking ice carrying over the phone line.

Where was Salvatore going with this story? Rowan wasn't sure, but he'd learned long ago that the man had more wisdom in one thumb that most people had in their entire brain. God knows, he'd saved and redirected dozens of misfit teenagers at the military high school.

Salvatore continued, "This one time, my son flipped his suitcase and mixed his clothes up. I did the best I could, but apparently, green plaid shorts, an orange striped shirt and cowboy boots don't match."

"You don't say." The image of Salvatore in his uniform or one of those generic suits of his, walking beside a mismatched kid, made Rowan grin. Salvatore didn't offer personal insights often. This was a golden moment and Rowan just let him keep talking.

"Sure, I knew the outfit didn't match, although I didn't know how to fix it. In the end, I learned a valuable lesson. When you're in the grocery store with the kid, that outfit shouts 'single dad' to a bevy of interested women."

"You used your son to pick up women?"

"Not intentionally. But that's what happened. Sounds to me like you may be partaking of the same strategy with this 'someone' who's helping you."

Busted. Although he felt compelled to defend himself. "I would be asking for help with the kid even if Mari wasn't here."

"Mariama Mandara?" Salvatore's stunned voice reverberated. "You have a thing for a local princess?"

Funny how Rowan sometimes forgot about the princess part. He thought of her as a research scientist. A professional colleague—and sometimes adversary. But most of all, he thought of her as a desirable woman, someone he suddenly didn't feel comfortable discussing with Salvatore. "Could we get back on topic here? Can you help me investigate the baby's parents or not?"

"Of course I can handle that." The Colonel's tone returned to all business, story time over.

"Thank you, sir. I can't tell you how much I appreciate this." Regardless of his attraction to Mari, Rowan couldn't lose sight of the fact that a defenseless child's future hung in the balance here.

"Just send me photos, fingerprints, footprints and any other data you've picked up."

"Roger. I know the drill."

"And good luck with the princess," Salvatore said, chuckling softly before he hung up.

Rowan drew in a deep breath of salty sea air before returning to the suite. He hated being confined. He missed his clinic, the wide-open spaces around it and the people he helped in a tangible way rather than by giving speeches.

Except once he returned home in a week to prepare for Christmas, his window of time with Mari would be done. Back to business.

He walked across the balcony and entered the door by the picture window, stepping into the sitting room. Mari didn't look up, her focus totally on the baby.

Seeing Mari in an unguarded moment was rare. The woman kept major walls up, giving off a prickly air. Right now, she sat on the sofa with her arms cradling the baby—even her body seemed to wrap inward protectively around this child. Mari might think she knew nothing about children, but her instincts were good. He'd watched enough new moms in his career to identify the ones who would have trouble versus the ones who sensed the kid's needs.

The tableau had a Madonna-and-child air. Maybe it was just the holidays messing with his head. If he wanted his half-baked plan to work, he needed to keep his head on straight and figure out how to get her on board with helping him.

"How's Issa doing?"

Mari looked up quickly, as if startled. She held up the empty bottle. "All done with her feeding."

"I'm surprised you're still sticking around. Your fans must have given up by now. The coast will be clear back to your room."

Saying that, he realized he should have mentioned those overzealous royal watchers to Salvatore. Perhaps some private security might be in order. There was a time he didn't have the funds for things like that, back in the days when he was buried in the debt of school loans, before he'd gone into partnership with a computer-whiz classmate of his.

"Mari? Are you going back to your room?" he repeated.

"I still feel responsible for her." Mari smoothed a finger along the baby's chubby cheek. "And the police will want to speak to me. If I'm here, it will move things along faster."

"You do realize the odds are low that her parents will be found tonight," he said, laying the groundwork for getting her to stick around.

"Of course, I understand." She thumbed aside a hint of milk in the corner of the infant's mouth. "That doesn't stop me from hoping she'll have good news soon."

"You sure seem like a natural with her. Earlier, you said you never babysat."

She shrugged self-consciously. "I was always busy studying."

"There were no children in your world at all?" He sat beside her, drawing in the scent of her flowery perfume. Curiosity consumed him, a desperate need to know exactly what flower she smelled like, what she preferred.

"My mother and father don't have siblings. I'm the only child of only children."

This was the closest to a real conversation they'd ever exchanged, talk that didn't involve work or bickering. He couldn't make a move on her, not with the baby right here in the room. But he could feel her relaxing around him. He wanted more of that, more of her, this exciting woman who kept him on his toes.

What would she do if he casually stretched his arm along the back of the sofa? Her eyes held his and instead of moving, he stayed stock-still, looking back at her, unwilling to risk breaking the connection—

The phone jangled harshly across the room.

Mari jolted. The baby squawked.

And Rowan smiled. This particular moment to get closer to Mari may have ended. But make no mistake, he wasn't giving up. He finally had a chance to explore the tenacious desire that had been dogging him since he'd first seen her.

Anticipation ramped through him at the thought of persuading her to see this connection through to its natural—and satisfying—conclusion.

Three

Pacing in front of the sitting room window, Mari cradled the baby against her shoulder as Rowan talked with the local police. Sure, the infant had seemed three months old when she'd looked at her, but holding her? Little Issa felt younger, more fragile.

Helpless.

So much about this evening didn't add up. The child had been abandoned yet she seemed well cared for. Beyond her chubby arms and legs, she had neatly trimmed fingernails and toenails. Her clothes were simple, but clean. She smelled freshly bathed. Could she have been kidnapped as revenge on someone? Growing up, Mari had been constantly warned of the dangers of people who would try to hurt her to get back at her father, as well as people would use her to get *close* to her father. Trusting anyone had been all but impossible.

She shook off the paranoid thoughts and focused on

the little life in her arms. Mari stroked the baby's impossibly soft cheeks, tapped the dimple in her chin. Did she look like her mother or father? Was she missed? Round chocolate-brown eyes blinked up at her trustingly.

Her heart squeezed tight in her chest in a totally illogical way. She'd only just met the child, for heaven's sake, and she ached to press a kiss to her forehead.

Mari glanced to the side to see if Rowan had observed her weak moment, but he was in the middle of finishing up his phone conversation with the police.

Did he practice looking so hot? Even in jeans, he owned the room. Her eyes were drawn to the breadth of his shoulders, the flex of muscles in his legs as he shuffled from foot to foot, his loafers expensive but well worn. He exuded power and wealth without waste or conspicuous consumption. How could he be such a good man and so annoying at the same time?

Rowan hung up the phone and turned, catching her studying him. He cocked an eyebrow. She forced herself to stare back innocently, her chin tipping even as her body tingled with awareness.

"What did the police say?" she asked casually, swaying from side to side in a way she'd found the baby liked.

"They're just arriving outside the hotel." He closed the three feet between them. "They're on their way up to take her."

"That's it?" Her arms tightened around Issa. "She'll be gone minutes from now? Did they say where they will be sending her? I have connections of my own. Maybe I can help."

His blue eyes were compassionate, weary. "You and I both already know what will happen to her. She will be sent to a local orphanage while the police use their limited resources to look into her past, along with all the other cases and other abandoned kids they have in their stacks of files to investigate. Tough to hear, I realize. But that's how it is. We do what we can, when we can."

"I understand." That didn't stop the frustration or the need to change things for this innocent child in her arms and all the children living in poverty in her country.

He scooped the baby from her before she could protest. "But that's not how it has to be today. We *can* do something this time."

"What do you mean?" She crossed her empty arms over her chest, hope niggling at her that Rowan had a reasonable solution.

"We only have a few more minutes before they arrive so I need to make this quick." He hefted the baby onto his shoulder and rubbed her back in small, hypnotic circles. "I think we should offer to watch Issa."

Thank heaven he was holding the child because he'd stunned Mari numb. She watched his hand smoothing along the baby's back and tried to gather her thoughts. "Um, what did you say?"

"We're both clearly qualified and capable adults." His voice reverberated in soothing waves. "It would be in the best interest of the child, a great Christmas message of goodwill, for us to keep her."

Keep her?

Mari's legs folded out from under her and she sank to the edge of the leather sofa. She couldn't have heard him right. She'd let her attraction to him distract her. "What did you say?"

He sat beside her, his thigh pressing warm and solid against hers. "We can have temporary custody of her, just for a couple of weeks to give the police a chance to find out if she has biological relatives able to care for her."

"Have you lost your mind?" Or maybe she had lost hers because she was actually tempted by his crazy plan.

"Not that I know of."

She pressed the back of her wrist to her forehead, stunned that he was serious. Concerns cycled through her head about work and the hoopla of a media circus. "This is a big decision for both of us, something that should be thought over carefully."

"In medicine I have to think fast. I don't always have the luxury of a slow and steady scientific exam," he said, with a wry twist to his lips. "Years of going with my gut have honed my instincts, and my instincts say this is the right thing to do."

Her mind settled on his words and while she never would have gotten to that point on her own, the thought of this baby staying with him rather than in some institution was appealing. "So you'll be her temporary guardian?"

"Our case is more powerful if we offer to do this as a partnership. Both of us." His deep bass and logic drew her in. "Think of the positive PR you'll receive. Your father's press corps will be all over this philanthropic act of yours, which should take some pressure off you at the holidays," he offered, so logically she could almost believe him.

"It isn't as simple as that. The press can twist things, rumors will start about both of us." What if they thought it was *her* baby? She squeezed her eyes closed and bolted off the sofa. "I need more time."

The buzzer rang at the door. Her heart went into her throat.

She heard Rowan follow her. Felt the heat of him at her back. Felt the urgency.

"Issa doesn't have time, Mari. You need to decide if you'll do this. Decide to commit now."

She turned sharply to find him standing so close the three of them made a little family circle. "But you could take her on your own—"

"Maybe the authorities would accept that. But maybe not. We should lead with our strongest case. For her." He cradled the baby's head. "We didn't ask for this, but we're here." Fine lines fanned from the corners of his eyes, attesting to years of worry and long hours in the sun. "We may disagree on a lot of things, but we're people who help."

"You're guilt-tripping me," she accused in the small space between them, her words crackling like small snaps of electricity. And the guilt was working. Her concerns about gossip felt absolutely pathetic in light of the plight of this baby.

As much as she gave Rowan hell about his computer inventions, she knew all about his humanitarian work at the charity clinic. He devoted his life to helping others. He had good qualities underneath that arrogant charm.

"Well, people like us who help in high-stakes situations learn to use whatever means are at our disposal." He half smiled, creasing the lines deeper. "Is it working?"

Those lines from worry and work were real. She might disapprove of his methods, but she couldn't question his motivations, his altruistic spirit. Seeing him deftly rock the baby to sleep ended any argument. For this one time at least, she was on his team.

For Issa.

"Open the door and you'll find out."

* * *

Three hours later, Mari watched Rowan close the hotel door after the police. Stacks of paperwork rested on the table, making it official. She and Rowan had temporary custody of the baby while the police investigated further and tried to track down the employee who'd walked away from the cart.

Issa slept in her infant seat, secure for now.

Mari sighed in relief, slumping in exhaustion back onto the sofa. She'd done it. She'd played the princess card and all but demanded the police obey her "request" to care for the baby until Christmas—less than two weeks away—or until more information could be found about Issa's parents. She'd agreed to care for the child with Rowan Boothe, a doctor who'd saved countless young lives. The police had seemed relieved to have the problem resolved so easily. They'd taken photos of the baby and prints. They would look into the matter, but their faces said they didn't hold out much hope of finding answers.

Maybe she should hire a private detective to look deeper than the police. Except it was almost midnight now. Any other plans would have to wait until morning.

Rowan rested a hand on Mari's shoulder. "Would you get my medical bag so I can do a more thorough checkup? It's in the bedroom by my shaving kit. I'd like to listen to her heart."

He squeezed her shoulder once, deliciously so, until her mouth dried right up from that simple touch.

"Medical bag." She shot to her feet. "Right, of course."

She was too tired and too unsettled to fight off the sensual allure of him right now. She stepped into Rowan's bedroom, her eyes drawn to the hints of him everywhere. A suit was draped over the back of a rattan rocker by sliding doors that led out to a balcony. She didn't consider herself a romantic by any stretch but the thought of sitting out there under the stars with someone...

God, what was the matter with her? This man had driven her bat crazy for years. Now she was daydreaming about an under-the-stars make-out session that would lead back into the bedroom. His bedroom.

Her eyes skated to the sprawling four-poster draped with gauzy netting, a dangerous place to look with his provocative glances still steaming up her memories. An e-reader rested on the bedside table, his computer laptop tucked underneath. Her mind filled with images of him sprawled in that massive bed—working, reading—details about a man she'd done her best to avoid. She pulled her eyes away.

The bathroom was only a few feet away. She charged across the plush carpet, pushing the door wide. The scent of him was stronger in here, and she couldn't resist breathing in the soapy aroma clinging to the air—patchouli, perhaps. She swallowed hard as goose bumps of awareness rose on her skin, her senses on overload.

A whimpering baby cry from the main room reminded her of her mission here. She shook off frivolous thoughts and snagged the medical bag from the marble vanity. She wrapped her hands around the well-worn leather with his name on a scratched brass plate. The dichotomy of a man this wealthy carrying such a battered bag added layers to her previously clear-cut image of him.

Clutching the bag to her stomach, she returned to the sitting room. Rowan set aside a bottle and settled the baby girl against his shoulder, his broad palm patting her back.

How exactly were they going to work this baby bargain? She had absolutely no idea.

For the first time in her life, she'd done something completely irrational. The notion that Rowan Boothe had that much power over her behavior rattled her to her toes.

She really was losing it. She needed to finish this day, get some sleep and find some clarity.

From this point forward, she would keep a firmer grip on herself. And that meant no more drooling over the sexy doc, and definitely no more sniffing his tempting aftershave.

Rowan tapped through the images on his laptop, reviewing the file on the baby, including the note he'd scanned in before passing it over to the police. He'd sent a copy of everything to Colonel Salvatore. Even though it was too early to expect results, he still hoped for some news, for the child's sake.

Meanwhile, though, he'd accomplished a freaking miracle in buying himself time with Mari. A week or so at the most, likely more, but possibly less since her staying rested solely on the child. If relatives were found quickly, she'd be headed home. He didn't doubt his decision, even if part of his motivation was selfish. This baby provided the perfect opportunity to spend more time with Mari, to learn more about her and figure out what made her tick. Then, hopefully, she would no longer be a thorn in his side—or a pain in his libido.

He tapped the screen back to the scanned image of the note that had been left with the baby.

Dr. Boothe, you are known for your charity and generosity. Please look over my baby girl, Issa.

My husband died in a border battle and I cannot give Issa what she needs. Tell her I love her and will think of her always.

His ears tuned in to the sound of Mari walking toward him, then the floral scent of her wrapped around him. She stood behind him without speaking and he realized she was reading over his shoulder, taking in the note.

"Loves her?" Mari sighed heavily. "The woman abandoned her to a stranger based on that person's reputation in the press."

"I take it your heart isn't tugged." He closed the laptop and turned to face her.

"My heart is broken for this child—" she waved toward the sleeping infant in the baby seat "—and what's in store for her if we don't find answers, along with a truly loving and responsible family."

"I'm hopeful that my contacts will have some information sooner than the police." A reminder that he needed to make the most of his time with Mari. What if Salvatore called with concrete news tomorrow? He looked over at Mari, imagining being with her, drawing her into his bedroom, so close to where they were now. "Let's talk about how we'll look after the baby here during the conference."

"Now?" She jolted in surprise. "It's past midnight."

"There are things to take care of, like ordering more baby gear, meeting with the hotel's babysitting service." He ticked off each point on his fingers. "Just trying to fill in the details on our plan."

"You actually want to plan?" Her kissable lips twitched with a smile.

"No need to be insulting," he bantered right back, enjoying the way she never treated him like some freaking saint just because of where he chose to work. He wasn't the good guy the press painted him to be just because he'd reformed. The past didn't simply go away. He still had debts that could never be made right.

"I'm being careful—finally. Like I should have been earlier." Mari fidgeted with the hem of her untucked shirt, weariness straining her face, dark circles under her eyes. "She's a child. A human being. We can't just fly by the seat of our pants."

He wanted to haul Mari into his arms and let her sleep against his chest, tell her she didn't have to be so serious, she didn't have to take the weight of the world on her shoulders. She could share the load with him.

Instead, he dragged a chair from the tiny teak table by the window and gestured for her to sit, to rest. "I'm not exactly without the means or ability to care for a child. It's only for a short time until we figure out more about her past so we don't have to fly by the seat of our pants." He dragged over a chair for himself as well and sat across from her.

"How is it so easy for you to disregard the rules?" She slumped back.

"You're free to go if you wish."

She shook her head. "I brought her in here. She's my responsibility."

Ah, so she wasn't in a rush to run out the door. "Do you intend to personally watch over her while details are sorted out?"

"I can hire someone."

"Ah, that's right. You're a princess with endless resources," he teased, taking her hands in his.

She pulled back. "Are you calling me spoiled?"

He squeezed her fingers, holding on, liking the feel

of her hands in his. "I would never dare insult you, Princess. You should know that well enough from the provocative things I said to you five minutes ago."

"Oh. Okay." She nibbled on her bottom lip, surprise flickering through her eyes.

"First things first." He thumbed the inside of her wrists.

"Your plan?" Her breathing seemed to hitch.

"We pretend to be dating and since we're dating, and we'd be spending this holiday time together anyway, we decided to help with the child. How does that work for a plan?"

"What?" She gasped in surprise. "Do you really think people are going to believe we went from professional adversaries to lovers in a heartbeat?"

He saw her pulse throb faster, ramping up his in response.

"Lovers, huh? I like the sound of that."

"You said—"

"I said dating." He squeezed her hands again. "But I like your plan better."

"This isn't a plan." She pulled free, inching her chair back. "It's insanity."

"A plan that will work. People will believe it. More than that, they will eat it up. Everyone will want to hear more about the aloof princess finding romance and playing Good Samaritan at Christmastime. If they have an actual human interest piece to write about you it will distract them from digging around to create a story."

Her eyes went wide with panic, but she stayed in her seat. She wasn't running. Yet. He'd pushed as far as he could for tonight. Tomorrow would offer up a whole new day for making his case.

He shoved to his feet. "Time for bed."

"Oh, um," she squeaked, standing, as well. "Bed?"

He could see in her eyes that she'd envisioned them sharing a bed before this moment. He didn't doubt for a second what he saw and it gave him a surge of victory. Definitely best to bide his time and wait for a moment when she wasn't skittish. A time when she would be all in, as fully committed as he was to exploring this crazy attraction.

"Yes, Mari, bed. I'll watch the baby tonight and if you're comfortable, we can alternate the night shift."

She blinked in surprise. "Right. The night schedule. Are you sure you can handle a baby at night and still participate in the conference?"

"I'm a doctor. I've pulled far longer shifts with no sleep in the hospital. I'll be fine."

"Of course. Then I'll call the front desk to move me to a larger suite so I'll have enough space for the baby and the daytime sitter."

"No need to do that. This suite is plenty large enough for all of us."

Her jaw dropped. "Excuse me?"

"All of us," he said calmly, holding her with his eyes as fully as he'd held her hand, gauging her every blink. Needing to win her over. "It makes sense if we're going to watch the baby, we should do it together for efficiency. The concierge already sent someone to pack your things."

Her chest rose faster and faster, the gentle curves of her breasts pressing against the wrinkled silk of her blouse. "You've actually made quite a few plans."

"Sometimes flying by the seat of your pants works quite well." Otherwise he never would have had this chance to win her over. "A bellhop will be delivering your luggage shortly along with more baby gear that I ordered."

"Here? The two—three—of us? In one suite?" she asked, although he noticed she didn't say no.

Victory was so close.

"There's plenty of space for the baby. You can have your own room. Unless you want to sleep in mine." He grinned. "You have to know I wouldn't object."

Four

Buttoning up her navy blue power suit the next morning, Mari couldn't believe she'd actually spent the night in Rowan Boothe's hotel suite. Not his room, but a mere wall away. He'd cared for the baby until morning as he'd promised. A good thing, since she needed to learn a lot more before she trusted herself to care for Issa.

She tucked pins into her swept-back hair, but the mirror showed her to be the same slightly rumpled academic she'd always been. While she wasn't a total innocent when it came to men, she wasn't the wild and reckless type who agreed to spend the night in the same suite as a guy she'd never actually dated. She'd expected to toss and turn all night after the confusing turn of events. She couldn't believe she'd agreed.

Yet in spite of all her doubts, she'd slept better than anytime she could remember. Perhaps because the odds of anyone finding her here were next to nil. Her longtime professional feud with him was well-known, and they hadn't yet gone public with this strange idea of joint custody of an abandoned baby. The hotel staff or someone on the police force would likely leak juicy tidbits about the royal family to the press, but it would all be gossip and conjecture until she and Rowan made their official statement verifying the situation.

Soon enough the world would know. Eventually the cameras would start snapping. Her gut clenched at the thought of all those stalkers and the press feeding on the tiniest of details, the least scrap of her life. What if they fed on the innocence of the baby?

Or what if they picked up on the attraction between her and Rowan?

There was still time to back out, write it all off as simple gossip. The urge was strong to put back on that Christmas hat and slip away, to hide in her lab, far, far from the stress of being on show and always falling short. She craved the peace of her laboratory and cubby-hole office, where she truly reigned supreme. Here, in Rowan's suite, she felt so off-kilter, so out of control.

A coo from the other room reminded her she needed to hurry. She stepped away from the mirror and slid her feet into her low, blue pumps. She pulled open her bed-room door, then sagged to rest against the doorjamb. The sight of the little one in a ruffled pink sleeper, rest-ing against Rowan's shoulder, looked like something straight off a greeting card. So perfect.

Except that perfection was an illusion.

Even though Rowan had the baby well in hand, the child was helpless outside their protection. Issa had no one to fight for her, not really, not if Mari and Rowan gave up on her. Even if Mari left and Rowan stayed, he couldn't offer the baby everything Mari could. Her fame—that fame she so resented—could be Issa's salvation.

The baby would get an exposure the police never could have provided. In these days of DNA testing, it wasn't as if fake relatives could step forward to claim a precious infant. So Mari wasn't going anywhere, except to give her presentation at the medical conference, then she'd take the baby for a walk with Rowan.

Looking around the suite strewn with baby paraphernalia, anyone would believe they were truly guardians of the child. Rowan had ordered a veritable nursery set up with top-of-the-line gear. A portable bassinet rested in the corner of the main room, a monitor perched beside it. He'd ordered a swing, a car seat, plus enough clothes, food and diapers for three babies for a month.

He knew what an infant needed, or at least he knew who to call.

Hopefully that call had included a sitter since he was dressed for work as well, in a black Savile Row suit with a Christmas-red tie. God, he was handsome, with his blond hair damp and combed back, his broad hand patting the baby's back. His face wore a perpetual five-o'clock shadow, just enough to be nighttime sexy without sliding over into scruffy.

He filled out the expensive suit with ease. Was there any realm that made this man uncomfortable? He'd taken care of the baby through the night and still looked totally put together.

His eyes searched hers and she shivered, wondering what he saw as he stood there holding Issa so easily. The man was a multitasker. He was also someone with an uncanny knack for getting into a person's mind. He'd found her vulnerable spot in one evening. After all of her tense and bicontinental Christmases, she simply couldn't bear for this child to spend the holidays confused and scared while the system figured out what to do with her—and the other thousands of orphans in their care.

She couldn't replace the child's mother, but she could make sure the child was held, cared for, secure. To do that, she needed to keep her mind off the charismatic man a few feet away.

He looked over at her as if he'd known she was there the whole time. "Good morning. Coffee's ready along with a tray of pastries."

And some sweet, sticky *bouili* dipping sauce.

Her mouth watered for the food almost as much as for the man. She walked to the granite countertop and poured herself a mug of coffee from the silver carafe. She inhaled the rich java fragrance steaming up from the dark roast with hints of fruity overtones. "Did she sleep well?"

"Well enough, just as I would expect from a baby who's experienced so much change," he said, tucking the baby into a swing with expert hands. "The hotel's sending up a sitter for the day. I verified her references and qualifications. They seem solid, so we should be covered through our lecture presentations. Tonight we can take Issa out for dinner and a stroll incognito, kill time while we let the cops finish their initial investigation. If they haven't found out anything by tomorrow, we can go public."

Dinner out? Revealing their plan to the world? Her heart pounded with nerves, but it was too late to go back now. The world would already be buzzing with leaked news. Best to make things official on their own terms.

If Issa's family wasn't found by tomorrow, she would have to call her parents and let them know about her strange partnership with Rowan. First, she had to decide how she wanted to spin it so her parents didn't jump to the wrong conclusions—or try to interfere. This needed to be a good thing for the baby, not just about positive press. She would play it by ear today and call them tonight once she had a firmer idea of what she'd gotten herself into.

Maybe Issa would be back with relatives before supper. A good thing, right?

Rowan started the baby swing in motion. The click-click-click mingled with a low nursery tune.

Mari cleared her throat. "I'll check on Issa during lunch and make sure all's going well with the sitter."

"That's a good idea. Thank you." He cradled a cup in strong hands that could so easily crush the fine china.

She shrugged dismissively. It was no hardship to skip the luncheon. She disliked the idle table chitchat at these sorts of functions anyway. "No big sacrifice. Nobody likes conference lunch food."

Laughing softly, he eyed her over his cup of coffee. "I appreciate your working with me on this."

"You didn't leave me much choice, Dr. Guilt Trip."

His smile creased dimples into his face. "Who'd have thought you'd have a sense of humor?"

"That's not nice." She traced the rim of her cup.

"Neither is saying I coerced you." He tapped the tip of her scrunched nose. "People always have a choice."

Of course he was right. She could always walk, but thinking overlong about her compulsion to stay made her edgy. She sat at the table, the morning sun glistening off the ocean waters outside. "Of course I'm doing this of my own free will, for Issa's sake. It has absolutely nothing to do with you."

"Hello? I thought we weren't going to play games."

She avoided his eyes and sipped her steaming java. "What do you mean, games?"

"Fine. I'll spell it out." He set down his cup on the table and sat beside her, their knees almost touching. "You have made it your life's mission to tear down my research and to keep me at arm's length. Yet you chose to stay here, for the baby, but you and I both know there's more to it than that. There's a chemistry between us, sparks."

"Those sparks—" she proceeded warily "—are just a part of our disagreements."

"Disagreements? You've publically denounced my work. That's a little more than a disagreement."

Of course he wouldn't forget that. "See, sparks. Just like I said."

His eyes narrowed. If only he could understand her point. She only wanted to get past his impulsive, pig-headed mindset and improve his programs.

"Mari, you're damn good at diverting from the topic."

"I'm right on point," she said primly. "This is about our work and you refused to consider that I see things from another angle. You've made it your life's mission to ignore any pertinent input I might have for your technological inventions. I am a scientist."

He scraped a hand over his drying hair. "Then why are you so against my computer program?"

"I thought we were talking about what's best for Issa." She glanced at the baby girl still snoozing in the swing with the lullaby playing.

"Princess, you are making my head spin." He sagged back. "We're here for Issa, but that doesn't mean we can't talk about other things, so quit changing the subject every three seconds. In the interest of getting along better during these next couple of weeks, let's discuss your public disdain for my life's work."

Was he serious? Did he really want to hash that out now? He certainly looked serious, drinking his coffee and downing bites of breakfast. Maybe he was one of those people who wanted to make peace at the holidays in spite of bickering all year round. She knew plenty about that. Which should have taught her well. Problems couldn't be avoided or the resolutions delayed. Best to confront them when given the opening.

"Your program is just too much of a snapshot of a diagnosis, too much of a quick fix. It's like fast-food medicine. It doesn't take into account enough variables." Now she waited for the explosion.

He inhaled a deep breath and tipped back in his chair before answering. "I can see your point. To a degree, I agree. I would welcome the chance to give every patient the hands-on medical treatment of the best clinic in the world. But I'm treating the masses with a skeleton team of medical professionals. That computer program helps us triage in half the time."

"What about people who use your program to cut corners?"

Rowan frowned. "What do you mean?"

"You can't truly believe the world is as altruistic as you? What about the clinics using that program to funnel more patients through just to make more money?"

His chair legs hit the floor, his jaw tightening. "I can't be the conscience for the world," he said in an even tone although a tic had started in the corner of his azure-blue eye. "I can only deal with the problems in front of me. I'm working my tail off to come up with help. Would I prefer more doctors and nurses, PAs and midwives, human hands? Hell, yes. But I make do with what I have and I do what I can so those of us who are here can be as efficient as possible under conditions they didn't come close to teaching us about during my residency."

"So you admit the program isn't optimal?" She couldn't believe he'd admitted to the program's short-comings.

"Really?" He threw up his hands. "That's your take-away from my whole rambling speech? I'm being prac-tical, and you're being idealistic in your ivory tower of research. I'm sorry if that makes you angry to hear."

"I'm not the volatile sort." She pursed her lips tightly to resist the temptation to snap at him for devaluing her work.

Slowly, he grinned, leaning closer. "That's too bad."

"Pardon me?" she asked, not following his logic at all.

"Because when you get all flustered, you're really hot."

Her eyes shot open wide, surprise skittering through her, followed by skepticism. "Does that line really work for you?"

"I've never tried it before." He angled closer until his mouth almost brushed hers. "You'll have to let me know."

Before she could gasp in half a breath of air, he brushed his mouth over hers. Shock quickly turned to something else entirely as delicious tingles shimmered through her. Her body warmed to the feel of him, the newness of his kiss, their first kiss, a moment already burning itself into her memory, searing through her with liquid heat.

Her hand fluttered to his chest, flattening, feeling the steady, strong beat of his heart under her palm matching the thrumming heartbeat in her ears. His kiss was nothing like she would have imagined. She'd expected him to be out of control, wild. Instead, he held her like spun glass. He touched her with deft, sensitive hands, surgeon's hands that knew just the right places to graze, stroke, tease for maximum payoff. Her body thrilled at the caress down her spine that cupped her bottom, bringing her closer.

Already she could feel herself sinking into a spiral of lush sensation. Her limbs went languid with desire. She wanted more of this, more of him, but they were a heartbeat away from tossing away their clothes and inhibitions. Too risky for a multitude of reasons, not the least of which was the possibility of someone discovering them.

Those sorts of exposé photos she absolutely did not want circulating on the internet or anywhere else.

Then, too soon he pulled away. How embarrassing that he was the one to stop since she already knew the kiss had to end. Never had she lost control this quickly.

Cool air and embarrassment washed over her as she sat stunned in her chair. He'd completely knocked the world out from under her with one simple kiss. Had he even been half as affected as she was by the moment? She looked quickly at him, but his back was to her already and she realized he was walking toward the door.

"Rowan?"

He glanced over his shoulder. "The buzzer—" Was that a hint of hoarseness in his voice? "The baby sitter has arrived."

Mari pressed her fingers to her still tingling lips, wondering if a day apart would be enough time to shore up her defenses again before their evening out.

* * *

That evening, Rowan pushed the baby stroller along the marketplace road. Vendors lined the street, and he eyed the place for potential trouble spots. Even with bodyguards trailing them, he kept watch. The baby in the stroller depended on him.

And so did the woman beside him. Mari wore her business suit, without the jacket, just the skirt and blouse, a scarf wrapped over her head and large sunglasses on for disguise, looking like a leggy 1940s movie star.

She strolled beside him, her hand trailing along stalls that overflowed with handwoven cloths and colorful beads. Bins of fresh fruits and vegetables sat out, the scent of roasting turkey and goat carrying on the salty beach breeze. Waves crashed in the distance, adding to the rhythmic percussion of a local band playing Christmas tunes while children danced. Locals and tourists angled past in a crush, multiple languages coming at him in stereo—Cape Verdean Creole, Portuguese, French, English…and heaven knew how many others.

Tonight, he finally had Mari out of the work world and alone with him. Okay, alone with him, a baby, bodyguards and a crush of shoppers.

The last rays of the day bathed Mari in a crimson glow. She hadn't referenced their kiss earlier, so he'd followed her lead on that, counting it a victory that she wasn't running. Clearly, she'd been as turned on as he was. But still, she hadn't run.

With the taste of her etched in his memory, there was not a chance in hell he was going anywhere. More than ever, he was determined to get closer to her, to sample a hell of a lot more than her lips.

But he was smart enough to take his time. This

woman was smart—and skittish. He made his living off reading subtle signs, deciphering puzzles, but this woman? She was the most complex individual he'd ever met.

Could that be a part of her appeal? The mysterious element? The puzzle?

The "why" of it didn't matter so much to him right now. He just wanted to make the most of this evening out and hopefully gain some traction in identifying Issa's family. While they'd gotten a few curious looks from people and a few surreptitiously snapped photos, so far, no one had openly approached them.

He checked left and right again, reconfirming their unobtrusive security detail, ensuring the men were close enough to intervene if needed. Colonel Salvatore had been very accommodating about rounding up the best in the business ASAP, although he still had no answers on the baby's identity. Issa's footprints hadn't come up in any databases, but then the child could have been a home birth, unregistered. Salvatore had insisted he hadn't come close to exhausting all their investigative options yet.

For now, their best lead would come from controlled press exposure, getting the child seen and praying some legit relative stepped up to claim her.

Meanwhile, Rowan finally had his chance to be with Mari, to romance her, and what better place than in this country he loved, with holiday festivities lightening the air. He would have cared for the baby even if Mari had opted out, so he didn't feel guilty about using the child to persuade Mari to stay. He was just surprised she'd agreed so easily.

That gave him pause—and encouragement.

She hesitated at a stall of clay bowls painted with

scenes of everyday life. She trailed her fingers along a piece before moving on to the jewelry, where she stopped for the longest time yet. He'd found her weakness. He wouldn't have pegged her as the type to enjoy those sorts of baubles, but her face lit up as she sifted through beads, necklaces. She seemed to lean more toward practical clothes and loose-fitting suits or dresses. Tonight she wore a long jean jumper and thick leather sandals.

Her hand lingered on the bracelets before she stepped back, the wistfulness disappearing from her golden eyes. "We should find somewhere to eat dinner. The conference food has left me starving for something substantial."

"Point the way. Ladies choice tonight," he said, curious to know what she would choose, what she liked, the way he'd just learned her preferences on the bracelets. Shoppers bustled past, cloth sacks bulging with purchases, everything from souvenirs to groceries.

Instinctively, she moved between the baby stroller and the hurrying masses. "How about we eat at a street-side café while we watch the performances?"

"Sounds good to me." He could keep watch better that way, but then he always kept his guard up. His work with Interpol showed him too well that crime didn't always lurk in the expected places.

He glanced down the street, taking in the carolers playing drums and pipes. Farther down, a group of children acted out the nativity in simple costumes. The sun hadn't gone down yet, so there was less worry about crime.

Rowan pointed to the nearby café with blue tables and fresh fish. "What about there?"

"Perfect, I'll be able to see royal watchers coming."

"Although your fan club seems to have taken a break." He wheeled the stroller toward the restaurant where the waitress instructed them to seat themselves. Issa still slept hard, sucking on a fist and looking too cute for words in a red Christmas sleeper.

Mari laughed, the scarf sliding down off her head, hanging loosely around her neck. "Funny how I couldn't escape photo-happy sorts at the hotel—" she tugged at either end of the silky scarf "—and yet now no one seems to notice me when some notoriety could serve some good."

"Issa's photo has already been released to law enforcement. If nothing comes of it by tomorrow morning, the story will break about our involvement and add an extra push. For now, anyway, the baby and I make good camouflage for you to savor your dinner."

"Mama-flage," she said as he held out her chair for her.

"Nice! I'm enjoying your sense of humor more and more." And he was enjoying a lot more about her as well this evening. He caught the sweet floral scent on her neck as he eased her chair into place.

His mind filled with images of her wearing only perfume and an assortment of the colorful beads from the marketplace. Damn, and now he would be awake all night thinking about the lithe figure she hid under her shapeless suits.

Mari glanced back at him, peering over her sunglasses, her amber eyes reflecting the setting sun. "Is something the matter?"

"Of course not." He took his seat across from her, his foot firmly on the stroller even knowing there were a half-dozen highly trained bodyguards stationed anonymously around them. She might not use them, but he'd made sure to hire a crew for the safety of both Mari and Issa.

The waitress brought glasses and a pitcher of fruit juice—guava and mango—not showing the least sign of recognizing the royal customer she served. This was a good dry run for when they would announce their joint custody publicly.

"What a cute baby," the waitress cooed without even looking at them. "I just love her little red Christmas outfit. She looks like an adorable elf." She toyed with toes in tiny green booties.

"Thank you," Mari said, then mouthed at Rowan, "Mama-flage."

After they'd placed their order for swordfish with *cachupa*—a mixture of corn and beans—Mari leaned back in her chair, appearing far more relaxed than the woman who'd taken refuge in his suite the night before. She eased the sunglasses up to rest on top of her head.

"You look like you've had a couple of servings of grogue." Grogue was a sugar cane liquor drunk with honey that flowed freely here.

"No alcohol for me tonight, thank you." She lifted a hand. "My turn to watch the baby."

"I don't mind taking the night shift if you're not comfortable."

She raised a delicately arched dark eyebrow. "Somewhere in the world, a couple dozen new moms just swooned and they don't know why."

"I'm just trying to be helpful. You have the heavier presentation load."

She stirred sugar into her coffee. "Are you trying to coerce me into kissing you again?"

"As I recall, I kissed you and you didn't object."

She set her spoon down with a decisive clink. "Well, you shouldn't count on doing it again."

"Request duly noted," he replied, not daunted in the least. He saw the speeding of her pulse, the flush of awareness along her dusky skin.

He started to reach for her, just to brush his knuckles along that pulse under the pretense of brushing something aside—except a movement just out of the corner of his eye snagged his attention. Alert, he turned to see an older touristy-looking couple moving toward them.

Mari sat back abruptly, her hand fluttering to her throat. Rowan assessed the pair. Trouble could come in any form, at any age. The bodyguards' attention ramped up as they stalked along the perimeter, closing the circle of protection. Mari reached for her sunglasses. Rowan didn't see any signs of concealed weapons, but he slid his hand inside his jacket, resting his palm on his 9 mm, just in case.

The elderly husband, wearing a camera and a manpurse over his shoulder, stopped beside Mari.

"Excuse us, but would you mind answering a question?" he asked with a thick New Jersey accent.

Was their cover busted? If so, did it really matter that they went public a few hours early? Not for him or the baby, but because he didn't want Mari upset, bolting away from the press, terrified, like the night before.

She tipped her head regally, her shoulders braced as she placed the sunglasses on the table. "Go ahead."

The wife angled in eagerly. "Are the two of you from around here?"

Rowan's mouth twitched. Not busted at all. "Not from the island, ma'am. We both live on the mainland."

"Oh, all right, I see." She furrowed her brow. "Maybe

you can still help me. Where's the Kwanzaa celebration?"

Mari's eyes went wide with surprise, then a hint of humor glinted before her face went politely neutral. "Ma'am, that's an American tradition."

"Oh, I didn't realize." Her forehead furrowed as she adjusted her fanny pack. "I just didn't expect so much Christmas celebration."

Mari glanced at the children finishing up their nativity play and accepting donations for their church. "Africa has a varied cultural and religious heritage. How much of each you find depends on which portion of the continent you're visiting. This area was settled by the Portuguese," she explained patiently, "which accounts for the larger influence of Christian traditions than you might find in other regions."

"Thank you for being so patient in explaining." The wife pulled out a travel guide and passed it to her husband, her eyes staying on Mari. "You look very familiar, dear. Have I seen you somewhere before?"

Pausing for a second, Mari eyed them, then said, "People say I look like the Princess Mariama Mandara. Sometimes I even let folks believe that."

She winked, grinning mischievously.

The older woman laughed. "What a wicked thing to do, young lady. But then I imagine people deserve what they get if they like to sneak photos for the internet."

"Would you like a photo of me with the baby on your phone?" Mari leaned closer to the stroller, sweeping back the cover so baby Issa's face was in clear view. "I'll put on my best princess smile."

"Oh, I wouldn't even know how to work the camera on that new phone our kids gave us for our fiftieth anniversary." She elbowed her husband. "We just use our old Polaroid, isn't that right, Nils?"

"I'm getting it out, Meg, hold on a minute." He fished around inside his man-purse.

Mari extended her arm. "Meg, why don't you get in the photo, too?"

"Oh, yes, thank you. The grandkids will love it." She fluffed her bobbed gray hair with her fingers then leaned in to smile while her husband's old Polaroid spit out picture after picture. "Now you and your husband lean in to pose for one with your daughter."

Daughter? Rowan jolted, the fun of the moment suddenly taking on a different spin. He liked kids and he sure as hell wanted Mari, but the notion of a pretend marriage? That threatened to give him hives. He swallowed down the bite of bile over the family he'd wrecked so many years ago and pretended for the moment life could be normal for him. He kneeled beside Mari and the baby, forcing his face into the requisite smile. He was a good actor.

He'd had lots of practice.

The couple finished their photo shoot, doling out thanks and leaving an extra Polaroid shot behind for them. The image developed in front of him, blurry shapes coming into focus, much like his thoughts, his need to have Mari.

Rowan sank back into his chair as the waitress brought their food. Once she left, he asked Mari, "Why didn't you tell that couple the truth about us, about yourself? It was the perfect opening."

"There were so many people around. If I had, they would have been mobbed out of the photo. When the official story about us fostering the baby hits the news in the morning, they'll realize their photo of a princess is real and they'll have a great story to tell their grand-children. We still get what we want and they get their cool story."

"That was nice of you to do for them." He draped a napkin over his knee. "I know how much you hate the notoriety of being royalty."

She twisted her napkin between her fingers before dropping it on her lap. "I'm not an awful person."

Had he hurt her feelings? He'd never imagined this boldly confident woman might be insecure. "I never said you were. I think your research is admirable."

"Really? I seem to recall a particular magazine interview where you accused me of trying to sabotage your work. In fact, when I came into your suite with the room-service cart, you accused me of espionage."

"My word choices may have been a bit harsh. The stakes were high." And yeah, he liked seeing her riled up with fire in her eyes. "My work world just doesn't give me the luxury of the time you have in yours."

"I simply prefer life to be on my terms when possible. So much in this world is beyond anyone's control."

Her eyes took on a faraway look that made him burn to reel her back into the moment, to finish the thought out loud so he could keep learning more about what made this woman tick. But she'd already distanced herself from him, deep in thought, looking off down the road at the musicians.

He needed those insights if he expected to get a second kiss—and more from her. But he was beginning to realize that if he wanted more, he was going to have to pony up some confidences of his own. An uncomfortable prospect.

As he looked at Mari swaying absently in time with the music, her lithe body at ease and graceful, he knew having her would be well worth any cost.

Five

Mari soaked in the sound of street music mellowing the warm evening air. The steady beat of the *bougarabou* drum with the players' jangling bracelets enriching the percussion reminded her of childhood days. Back when her parents were still together and she lived in Africa full-time, other than visits to the States to see her maternal grandparents.

Those first seven years of her life had been idyllic—or so she'd thought. She hadn't known anything about the painful undercurrents already rippling through her parents' marriage. She hadn't sensed the tension in their voices over royal pressures and her mother's homesickness.

For a genius, she'd missed all the obvious signs. But then, she'd never had the same skill reading people that she had for reading data. She'd barely registered that her mother was traveling to Atlanta more and more frequently. Her first clue had come near the end when she'd overheard her mom talking about buying a home in the States during their Christmas vacation. They wouldn't be staying with her grandparents any longer during U.S. visits. They would have their own place, not a room with family. Her parents had officially split up and filed for divorce over the holidays.

Christmas music never sounded quite the same to her again, on either continent.

The sway melted away from her shoulders and Mari stilled in her wrought-iron seat. The wind still wound around her as they sat at the patio dining area, but her senses moved on from the music to the air of roasting meat from the kitchen and the sound of laughing children. All of it was almost strong enough to distract her from the weight of Rowan's gaze.

Almost.

She glanced over at him self-consciously. "Why are you staring at me? I must be a mess." She touched her hair, tucking a stray strand back into the twist, then smoothed her rumpled suit shirt and adjusted the silver scarf draped around her neck. "It's been a long day and the breeze is strong tonight."

Since when had she cared about her appearance for more than the sake of photos? She forced her hands back to her lap.

Rowan's tanned face creased with his confident grin. "Your smile is radiant." He waved a broad hand to encompass the festivities playing out around them. "The way you're taking in everything, appreciating the joy of the smallest details, your pleasure in it all is... mesmerizing."

His blue eyes downright twinkled like the stars in the night sky.

Was he flirting with her? She studied him suspiciously. The restaurant window behind him filled with the movement of diners and waiters, the edges blurred by the spray of fake snow. She'd always been entranced by those pretend snowy displays in the middle of a warm island Christmas.

"Joy? It's December, Rowan. The Christmas season of *joy*. Of course I'm happy." She thought fast, desperate to defer conversation about her. Talking about Rowan's past felt a lot more comfortable than worrying about tucking in her shirt, for God's sake. "What kind of traditions did you enjoy with your family growing up?"

He leaned back in his chair, his gaze still homed in solely on Mari in spite of the festivities going on around them. "We did the regular holiday stuff like a tree, carols, lots of food."

"What kind of food?" she asked just as Issa squirmed in the stroller.

He shrugged, adjusting the baby's pacifier until the infant settled back to sleep. "Regular Christmas stuff."

His ease with the baby was admirable—and heart-tugging. "Come on," Mari persisted, "fill in the blanks for me. There are lots of ways to celebrate Christmas and regular food here isn't the same as regular food somewhere else. Besides, I grew up with chefs. Cooking is still a fascinating mystery to me."

He forked up a bite of swordfish. "It's just like following the steps in a chemistry experiment."

"Maybe in theory." She sipped her fruit juice, the blend bursting along her taste buds with a hint of coconut, her senses hyperaware since Rowan kissed her. "Suffice it to say I'm a better scientist than a cook. But back to you. What was your favorite Christmas treat?"

He set his fork aside, his foot gently tapping the

stroller back and forth. "My mom liked to decorate sugar cookies, but my brother, Dylan, and I weren't all that into it. We ate more of the frosting than went on the cookies."

The image wrapped around her like a comfortable blanket. "That sounds perfect. I always wanted a sibling to share moments like that with. Tell me more. Details... Trains or dump trucks? Bikes or ugly sweaters?"

"We didn't have a lot of money, so my folks saved and tucked away gifts all year long. They always seemed a bit embarrassed that they couldn't give us more, but we were happy. And God knows, it's more than most of the kids I work with will ever have."

"You sound like you had a close family. That's a priceless gift."

Something flickered through his eyes that she couldn't quite identify, like gray clouds over a blue sky, but then they cleared so fast she figured she must have been mistaken. She focused on his words, more curious about this man than any she'd ever known.

"At around three-thirty on Christmas morning, Dylan and I would slip out of our bunk beds and sneak downstairs to see what Santa brought." He shared the memory, but the gray had slipped into his tone of voice now, darkening the lightness of his story. "We would play with everything for about an hour, then put it back like we found it, even if the toy was in a box. We would tiptoe back into our room and wait for our parents to wake us up. We always pretended like we were completely surprised by the gifts."

What was she missing here? Setting aside her napkin, she leaned closer. "Sounds like you and your brother share a special bond."

"Shared," he said flatly. "Dylan's dead."

She couldn't hold back the gasp of shock or the empathetic stab of pain for his loss. For an awkward moment, the chorus of "Silver Bells" seemed to blare louder, the happy music at odds with this sudden revelation. "I'm so sorry, Rowan. I didn't know that."

"You had no reason to know. He died in a car accident when he was twenty."

She searched for something appropriate to say. Her lack of social skills had never bothered her before now. "How old were you when he died?"

"Eighteen." He fidgeted with her sunglasses on the table.

"That had to be so horrible for you and for your parents."

"It was," he said simply, still toying with her wide-rimmed shades.

An awkward silence fell, the echoes of Christmas ringing hollow now. She chewed her lip and pulled the first question from her brain that she could scavenge. "Were you still at the military reform school?"

"It was graduation week."

Her heart squeezed tightly at the thought of him losing so much, especially at a time when he should have been celebrating completing his sentence in that school.

Without thinking or hesitating, she pushed aside her sunglasses and covered Rowan's hand. "Rowan, I don't even know what to say."

"There's nothing to say." He flipped his hand, skimming his thumb along the inside of her wrist. "I just wanted you to know I'm trusting you with a part of my past here."

Heat seeped through her veins at each stroke of his thumb across her pulse. "You're telling me about yourself to...?"

His eyes were completely readable now, sensual and steaming over her. "To get closer to you. To let you know that kiss wasn't just an accident. I'm nowhere near the saint the press likes to paint me."

Heat warmed to full-out sparks of electricity arcing along her every nerve ending. She wasn't imagining or exaggerating anything. Rowan Boothe *wanted* her.

And she wanted to sleep with him.

The inescapable truth of that rocked the ground underneath her.

The noise of a backfiring truck snapped Rowan back into the moment. Mari jolted, blinking quickly before making a huge deal out of attacking her plate of swordfish and *cachupa,* gulping coffee between bites.

The sputtering engine still ringing in his ears, Rowan scanned the marketplace, checking the position of their bodyguards. He took in the honeymooners settling in at the next table. The elderly couple that had photographed them earlier was paying their bill. A family of vacationers filled a long stretch of table.

The place was as safe as anywhere out in public.

He knew he couldn't keep Mari and the baby under lock and key. He had the security detail and he hoped Mari would find peace in being out in public with the proper protection. The thought of her being chased down hallways for the rest of her life made him grind his teeth in frustration. She deserved better than to live in the shadows.

He owed little Issa a lot for how she'd brought them together. He was moved by the sensitive side of Mari he'd never known she had, the sweetly awkward humanity beneath the brilliant scientific brain and regal royal heritage.

Leaning toward the stroller, Rowan adjusted the baby's bib, reassured by the steady beat of her little heart. He'd given her a thorough physical and thank God she was healthy, but she was still a helpless, fragile infant. He needed to take care of her future. And he would. He felt confident he could, with the help of Salvatore either finding the baby's family or lining up a solid adoption.

The outcome of his situation with Mari, however, was less certain. There was no mistaking the desire in her golden eyes. Desire mixed with wariness.

A tactical retreat was in order while he waited for the appropriate moment to resume his advances. He hadn't meant to reveal Dylan's death to her, but their talk about the past had lulled him into old memories. He wouldn't let that happen again.

He poured coffee from the earthen pot into his mug and hers. "You must have seen some lavish Christmas celebrations with your father."

Her eyes were shielded, but her hand trembled slightly as she reached for her mug. "My father keeps things fairly scaled back. The country's economy is stabilizing thanks to an increase in cocoa export, but the national treasury isn't flush with cash, by any means. I was brought up to appreciate my responsibilities to my people."

"You don't have a sibling to share the responsibility."

The words fell out of his mouth before he thought them through, probably because of all those memories of his brother knocking around in his gut. All the ways he'd failed to save Dylan's life. If only he'd made different decisions... He forced his attention back into the present, on Mari.

"Both of my parents remarried other people, divorced again, no more kids, though." She spread her hands, sunglasses dangling from her fingers. "So I'm it. The future of my country."

"You don't sound enthusiastic."

"I just think there has to be someone better equipped." She tossed aside the glasses again and picked up her coffee. "What? Why the surprised look? You can't think I'm the best bet for my people. I would rather lock myself in a research lab with the coffeemaker maxed out than deal with the day-to-day events of leading people."

"I think you will succeed at anything life puts in your path." Who had torn down this woman's confidence? If only she saw—believed in—her magnificence. "When you walk in a room, you damn near light up the place. You own the space with your presence, lady."

She blew into her mug of coffee, eyeing him. "Thanks for the vote of confidence. But people and all their intangibles like 'magnificence' are beyond me. I like concrete facts."

"I would say some people would appreciate logic in a leader."

She looked away quickly, busying herself with adjusting the netting around the baby's stroller. "I wasn't always this way."

"What do you mean?"

"So precise." She darted a quick glance at him out of the corner of her eye. "I was actually a very scatterbrained child. I lost my hair ribbons in hotels, left my doll or book on the airplane. I was always oversleeping or sluggish in the morning, running late for important events. The staff was given instructions to wake me up a half hour ahead of time."

His mom had woken him and Dylan up through elementary school, then bought them an alarm clock—a really obnoxious clock that clanged like a cowbell. No one overslept. "Did this happen in your mother's or your father's home?"

"Both places. My internal clock just wasn't impressed by alarms or schedules."

She was a kid juggling a bicontinental lifestyle, the pressures of royal scrutiny along with the social awkwardness of being at least five grades ahead of her peers.

When did she ever get to relax? "Sounds to me like you traveled quite a bit in your life. I'm sure you know that losing things during travel is as common as jet lag, even for adults."

"You're kind to make excuses." She brushed aside his explanation. "I just learned to make lists and structure my world more carefully."

"Such as?" he asked, suddenly finding the need to learn more about what shaped her life every bit as important as tasting her lips again.

"Always sitting in the same seat on an airplane. Creating a routine for the transatlantic trips, traveling at the same time." She shrugged her elegant shoulders. "The world seemed less confusing that way."

"Confusing?" he repeated.

She chewed her bottom lip, which was still glistening from a sip of coffee. "Forget I said anything."

"Too late. I remember everything you say." And what a time to realize how true that was.

"Ah, you're one of those photographic-memory sorts. I imagine that helps with your work."

"Hmm…" Not a photographic memory, except when it came to her. But she didn't need to know that.

"I'm sure my routines sound a bit overboard to you. But my life feels crazy most of the time. I'm a princess.

There's no escaping that fact." She set her mug down carefully. "I have to accept that no matter how many lists I make, my world will never be predictable."

"Sometimes unpredictable has its advantages, as well." He ached to trace the lines of her heart-shaped face and finish with a tap to her chin.

Her throat moved in a long swallow. "Is this where you surprise me with another kiss?"

He leaned in, a breath away, and said, "I was thinking this time you could surprise me."

She stared back at him so long he was sure she would laugh at him for suggesting such a thing, especially out in public. Not that the public problem bothered the honeymooners at the next table. Just when Rowan was certain she would tell him to go to hell—

Mari kissed him. She closed those last two inches between them and pressed her lips to his. Closemouthed but steady. He felt drunk even though he hadn't had anything but coffee and fruit juice all evening. The same drinks he tasted on Mari's lips. Her hands, soft and smooth, covered his on the table. Need, hard and insistent, coursed through his body over an essentially simple kiss with a table between them.

And just that fast, she let go, pushing on his chest and dropping back into her chair.

A flush spread from her face down the vee of her blouse. "That was not... I didn't mean..."

"Shhh." He pressed a finger to her lips, confidence singing through him along with the hammering pulse of desire. "Some things don't need to be analyzed. Some things simply are. Let's finish supper so we can turn in early."

"Are you propositioning me?" Her lips moved under his finger.

Deliberately seductive? Either way, an extra jolt of want shot through him, a want he saw echoed in her eyes.

He spread his arms wide. "Why would you think that?" he asked with a hint of the devil in his voice. "I want to turn in early. It's your night with the baby."

The tension eased from her shoulders and she smiled back, an ease settling between them as they bantered. God, she was incredible, smart and lithe, earnest and exotic all at once. He covered her hand with his—

A squeal from the next table split the air. "Oh, my God, it's her." The honeymooner at the next table tapped her husband's arm insistently. "That princess... Mariama! I want a picture with her. Get me a photo, pretty please, pookie."

Apparently the mama-flage had stopped working. They didn't have until the morning for Mari to become comfortable with the renewed public attention. The story about them taking care of a baby—*together*— was about to leak.

Big-time.

Two hours later, Mari patted Issa's back in the bassinet to be sure she was deeply asleep then flopped onto the bed in the hotel suite she shared with Rowan.

Alone in her bedroom.

Once that woman shouted to the whole restaurant that a princess sat at the next table, the camera phones started snapping before her head could stop reeling from that impulsive kiss. A kiss that still tingled all the way to the roots of her hair.

Rowan had handled the curious masses with a simple explanation that they were watching a baby in foster care. More information would be forthcoming at a morning press conference. Easy as pie.

Although she was still curious as to where all the bodyguards had come from. She intended to confront her father about that later and find out why he'd decided to disregard her wishes now of all times.

Granted, she could see the wisdom in a bit more protection for Issa's sake and she liked to think she would have arranged for something tomorrow…on a smaller scale. The guards had discreetly escorted her from the restaurant, along with Rowan and the baby, and all the way back to the hotel. No ducking into bathrooms or racing down hallways. Just a wall of protection around her as Rowan continued to repeat with a smile and a firm tone, "No further comment tonight."

Without question, the papers would be buzzing by morning. That press conference would be packed. Her father's promo guru couldn't have planned it better.… Had Rowan known that when they kissed? Did he have an agenda? She couldn't help but wonder since most people in her life had their own agendas—with extras to spare.

This was not the first time the thought had come to her. By the time she'd exited the elevator, she was already second-guessing the kiss, the flirting, the whole crazy plan. She knew that Rowan wanted her. She just couldn't figure out why.

Until she had more answers, she couldn't even consider taking things further.

She sat up again, swinging her legs off the side of the bed. Besides, she had a baby to take care of and a phone call to make. Since Issa still slept blissfully in the lacy bassinet after her bottle, Mari could get to that other pressing concern.

Her father.

She swiped her cell phone off the teak end table and thumbed auto-dial...two rings later, a familiar voice answered and Mari blurted out, "Papa, we need to talk...."

Her father's booming laugh filled the earpiece. "About the boyfriend and the baby you've been hiding from me?"

Mari squeezed her eyes shut, envisioning her lanky father sprawled in his favorite leather chair on the lanai, where he preferred to work. He vowed he felt closer to nature out there, closer to his country, even though three barriers of walls and guards protected him.

Sighing, she pressed two fingers to her head and massaged her temples. "How did you hear about Rowan and Issa? Have you had spies watching me? And why did you assign bodyguards without consulting me?"

"One question at a time, daughter dear. First, I heard about your affiliation with Dr. Boothe and the baby on the internet. Second, I do not spy on my family—not often, anyway. And third, whatever bodyguards you're referring to, they're not mine. I assume they're on your boyfriend's payroll."

Her head throbbed over Rowan hiring bodyguards without consulting her. Her life was snowballing out of control.

"He's not my boyfriend—" even though they'd kissed and she'd enjoyed the hell out of it "—and Issa is not our baby. She's a foster child, just like Rowan said at the restaurant."

Even though her heart was already moved beyond measure by the chubby bundle sleeping in the frilly bassinet next to her bed.

"I know the baby's not yours, Mariama."

"The internet strikes again?" She flopped back, rolling to her side and holding a pillow to her stomach as she monitored the steady rise and fall of Issa's chest as she slept.

"I keep tabs on you, daughter dear. You haven't been pregnant and you've never been a fan of Rowan Boothe."

An image flashed in her mind of Rowan pacing the sitting room with Issa in his arms. "The baby was abandoned in Dr. Boothe's hotel room and we are both watching over her while the authorities try to find her relatives. You know how overburdened Africa is with orphans. We just couldn't let her go into the system when we had the power to help her."

"Hmm…" The sound of him clicking computer keys filtered through the phone line—her father never rested, always worked. He took his position as leader seriously, no puppet leadership role for him. "And why are you working with a man you can't stand to help a child you've never met? He could have taken care of this on his own."

"I'm a philanthropist?"

"True," her dad conceded. "But you're also a poor liar. How did the child become your responsibility?"

She'd never been able to get anything past her wily father. "I was trying to get away from a group of tourists trying to steal a photo of me at the end of a very long day. I grabbed a room-service tray and delivered it." The whole crazy night rolled through her mind again and she wondered what had possessed her to act so rashly. Never, though, could she have foreseen how it would end. "Turns out it was for Rowan Boothe and there was an abandoned baby inside. There's nothing going on between us."

A squawk from Issa sent her jolting upright again to

pat the baby's back. An instant later, a tap sounded on the door from the suite beyond. She covered the mouthpiece on the phone. "We're okay."

Still, the bedroom door opened, a quizzical look on Rowan's face. "Everything all right?"

"I've got it." She uncovered the phone. "Dad, I need to go."

Rowan lounged against the doorjamb, his eyes questioning. Pressing the phone against her shoulder to hold it to her ear, she tugged her skirt over her knees, curling her bare toes.

"Mari, dear," her father said, "I do believe you have gotten better at lying after all. Seems like there's a lot going on in your life I don't know about."

Her pulse sped up, affirming her father was indeed right. This wasn't just about Issa. She was lying to herself in thinking there was nothing more going on with Rowan. His eyes enticed her from across the room, like a blue-hot flame drawing a moth.

But her father waited on the other end of the line. Best to deflect the conversation, especially while the object of her current hormonal turmoil stood a few feet away. "You should be thrilled about this whole setup. It will make for great publicity, a wonderful story for your press people to spin over the holidays. Papa, for once I'm not a disappointment."

Rowan scowled and Mari wished she could call back the words that had somehow slipped free. But she felt the weight of the knowledge all the same. The frustration of never measuring up to her parents' expectations.

"Mari, dear," her father said, his voice hoarse, "you have never been a disappointment."

A bittersweet smile welled from the inside out.

"You're worse at lying than I am. But I love you anyway. Good night, Papa."

She thumped the off button and swung her bare feet to the floor. Her nerves were a jangled mess from the emotions stirred up by talking to her dad…not to mention the smoldering embers from kissing Rowan. The stroke of his eyes over her told her they were a simple step, a simple word away from far more than a kiss.

But those tangled nerves and mixed-up feelings also told her this was not the time to make such a momentous decision. Too much was at stake, the well-being of the infant in their care…

And Mari's peace of mind. Because it would be far too easy to lose complete control when it came to this man.

Six

Refusing to back down from Rowan's heated gaze, Mari stiffened her spine and her resolve, closing the last three feet between them. "Why did you order body-guards without consulting me?"

He frowned. "Where did you think they'd come from?"

"My father."

"I just did what he should have. I made sure to look after your safety," he said smoothly, arrogantly.

Her chin tipped defiantly. He might have been right about them needing bodyguards—for Issa's sake—but she wasn't backing down on everything. "Just because I kissed you at the restaurant does *not* mean I intend to invite you into my bed."

Grinning wickedly, he clamped a hand over his heart. "Damn. My spirit is crushed."

"You're joking, of course." She stopped just shy of

touching him, the banter sparkling through her like champagne bubbles.

"Possibly. But make no mistake, I do want to sleep with you and every day I wait is...torture." The barely restrained passion in his voice sent those intoxicating bubbles straight to her head. "I'm just reasonable enough to accept it isn't going to happen tonight."

"And if it never happens?" she asked, unwilling to let him know how deeply he affected her.

"Ah, you said 'if.'" He flicked a loose strand of hair over her shoulder, just barely skimming his knuckles across her skin. "Princess, that means we're already halfway to naked."

Before she could find air to breathe, he backed away, slowly, deliberately closing the door after him.

And she'd thought her nerves were a tangled, jangled mess before. Her legs folded under her as she dropped to sit on the edge of the bed.

A suddenly very cold and empty bed.

Rowan walked through the hotel sliding doors that led out to the sprawling shoreline. The cool night breeze did little to ease the heat pumping through his body. Leaving Mari alone in her hotel room had been one of the toughest things he'd ever done, but he'd had no choice for two reasons.

First, it was too soon to make his move. He didn't want to risk Mari changing her mind about staying with him. She had to be sure—very sure—when they made love.

Second reason he'd needed to put some distance between himself and her right now? He had an important meeting scheduled with an Interpol contact outside the hotel. An old school friend of his and the person responsible for their security detail tonight.

Rowan jogged down the long steps from the pool area to the beach. Late-night vacationers splashed under the fake waterfall, others floated, some sprawled in deck loungers with drinks, the party running deep into the night.

His appointment would take place in cabana number two, away from prying eyes and with the sound of the roaring surf to cover conversation. His loafers sank into the gritty sand, the teak shelter a dozen yards away, with a grassy roof and canvas walls flapping lightly in the wind. Ships bobbed on the horizon, lights echoing the stars overhead.

Rowan swept aside the fabric and stepped inside. "Sorry I'm late, my friend."

His old school pal Elliot Starc lounged in a recliner under the cabana in their designated meeting spot as planned, both loungers overlooking the endless stretch of ocean. "Nothing better to do."

Strictly speaking that couldn't be true. The freelance Interpol agent used his job as a world-renowned Formula One race-car driver to slip in and out of countries without question. He ran in high-powered circles. But then that very lifestyle was the sort their handler, Colonel Salvatore, capitalized on—using the tarnished reputations of his old students to gain access to underworld types.

Of course, Salvatore gave Rowan hell periodically for being a do-gooder. Rowan winced. The label pinched, a poor fit at best. "Well, thanks all the same for dropping everything to come to Cape Verde."

Elliot scratched his hand over his buzzed short hair. "I'm made of time since my fiancée dumped me."

"Sorry about that." Talk about headline news. Elliot's past—his vast past—with women, filled headlines across multiple continents. The world thought that's what had broken up the engagement, but Rowan suspected the truth. Elliot's fiancée had been freaked out by the Interpol work. The job had risked more than one relationship for the Brotherhood.

What would Mari think if she knew?

"Crap happens." Elliot tipped back a drink, draining half of the amber liquid before setting the cut crystal glass on the table between them. "I'd cleared my schedule for the honeymoon. When we split I gave her the tickets since the whole thing was my fault anyway. She and her 'BFF' are skiing in the Alps as we speak. I might as well be doing something productive with my time off."

Clearly, Elliot wouldn't want sympathy. Another drink maybe. He looked like hell, dark circles under his eyes. From lack of sleep most likely. But that didn't explain the nearly shaved head.

"Dude, what happened to you?" Rowan asked, pointing to the short cut.

Elliot's curly mop had become a signature with his fans who collected magazine covers. There were even billboards and posters.... All their pals from the military academy—the ones who'd dubbed themselves the Alpha Brotherhood—never passed up an opportunity to rib Elliot about the underwear ad.

Elliot scratched a hand over his shorn hair. "I had a wreck during a training run. Bit of a fire involved. Singed my hair."

Holy hell. "You caught on fire?"

Elliot grinned. "Just my hair."

"How did I miss hearing about that?"

"No need. It's not a big deal."

Rowan shook his head. "You are one seriously messed-up dude."

But then all his former classmates were messed up in some form. Came with the territory. The things that had landed them in that reform school left them with baggage long after graduation.

"You're the one who hangs out in war-torn villages passing out vaccinations and blankets for fun."

"I'm not trailed by groupies." He shuddered.

"They're harmless most of the time."

Except when they weren't. The very reason he'd consulted with Elliot about the best way to protect Mari and Issa. "I can't thank you enough, brother, for overseeing the security detail. They earned their pay tonight."

"Child's play. So to speak." Elliot lifted his glass again, draining the rest with a wince. "What's up with your papa-and-the-princess deal?"

"The kid needed my help. So I helped."

"You've always been the saint. But that doesn't explain the princess."

Rowan ignored the last part of Elliot's question. "What's so saintly about helping out a kid when I have unlimited funds and Interpol agents at my disposal? Saintly is when something's difficult to do."

"And the woman—the princess?" his half-drunk buddy persisted. "She had a reputation for being very difficult on the subject of Dr. Rowan Boothe."

Like the time she'd written an entire journal piece pointing out potential flaws in his diagnostics program. Sure, he'd made adjustments after reading the piece, but holy hell, it would have been nice—and more expedient—if she'd come to him first. "Mari needs my help, too. That's all it is."

Elliot laughed. "You are so damn delusional."

A truth. And an uncomfortable one.

Beyond their cabana tent, a couple strolled arm-in-arm along the shoreline, sidestepping as a jogger sprinted past with a loping dog.

"If you were a good friend you would let me continue with my denial."

"Maybe I'm wrong." Elliot lifted the decanter and refilled his glass. "It's not denial if you acknowledge said problem."

"I am aware of that fact." His unrelenting desire for Mari was a longtime, ongoing issue he was doing his damnedest to address.

"What do you intend to do about your crush on the princess?"

"Crush? Good God, man. I'm not in junior high."

"Glad you know that. What's your plan?"

"I'm figuring that out as I go." And even if he had one, he wasn't comfortable discussing details of his— feelings?—his attraction.

"What happens if this relationship goes south? Her father has a lot of influence. Even though you're not in his country, his region still neighbors your backyard. That could be…uncomfortable."

Rowan hadn't considered that angle and he should have. Which said a lot for how much Mari messed with his mind. "Let me get this straight, Starc. *You* are doling out relationship advice?"

"I'm a top-notch source when it comes to all the wrong things to do in a long-term relationship." He lifted his glass in toast. "Here's to three broken engagements and counting."

"Who said I'm looking for long-term?"

Elliot leveled an entirely sober stare his way, holding for three crashes of the waves before he said, "You truly are delusional, dude."

"That's not advice."

"It is if you really think about it."

He'd had enough of this discussion about Mari and the possibility of a train wreck of epic proportions. Rowan shoved off the lounger, his shoes sinking in the sand. "Good night."

"Hit a sore spot, did I?" Still, Starc pushed.

"I appreciate your...concern. And your help." He clapped Elliot on the shoulder before sweeping aside the canvas curtain. "I need to return to the hotel."

He'd been gone long enough. As much as he trusted Elliot's choice of guards, he still preferred to keep close.

Wind rolled in off the water, tearing at his open shirt collar as he made his way back up the beach toward the resort. Lights winked from trees. Fake snow speckled windows. Less than two weeks left until Christmas. He would spend the day at his house by the clinic, working any emergency-room walk-ins as he did every year. What plans did Mari have? Would she go to her family?

His parents holed up on Christmas, and frankly, he preferred it that way. Too many painful memories for all of them.

He shut off those thoughts as he entered the resort again. Better to focus on the present. One day at a time. That's the way he'd learned to deal with the crap that had gone down. And right now, his present was filled with Mari and Issa.

Potted palms, carved masks and mounted animal heads passed in a blur as he made his way back to his suite. He nodded to the pair of guards outside the door before stepping inside.

Dimmed lights from the wet bar bathed the sitting

area in an amber glow. Silence echoed as he padded his way to Mari's room. No sounds came from her room this time, no conversation with her royal dad.

The door to Mari's room was ajar and he nudged it open slowly, pushing back thoughts of invading her privacy. This was about safety and checking on the baby.

Not an insane desire to see what Mari looked like sleeping.

To appease his conscience, he checked the baby first and found the chubby infant sleeping, sucking on her tiny fist as she dreamed. Whatever came of his situation with Mari, they'd done right by this baby. They'd kept at least one child safe.

One day at a time. One life saved at a time. It's how he lived. How he atoned for the unforgivable in his past.

Did Issa's mother regret abandoning her child? The note said she wanted her baby in the care of someone like him. But there was no way she could have known the full extent of the resources he had at his disposal with Interpol. If so, she wouldn't have been as quick to abandon her child to him because he could and would find the mother. It wasn't a matter of if. Only a matter of when.

He wouldn't give up. This child's future depended on finding answers.

All the more reason to tread carefully with Mari. He knew what he wanted, but he'd failed to take into consideration how much of a help she would be. How much it would touch his soul seeing her care for the baby. From her initial reaction to the baby, he'd expected her to be awkward with the child, all technical and analytical. But she had an instinct for children, a tenderness in her heart that overcame any awkwardness. A softness that crept over her features.

Watching her sleep now, he could almost forget the way Mari had cut him down to size on more than one occasion in the past. Her hair was down and loose on her pillow, black satin against the white Egyptian cotton pillowcase. Moonlight kissed the curve of her neck, her chest rising and falling slowly.

He could see a strap of creamy satin along her shoulder. Her nightgown? His body tightened and he considered scooping her up and carrying her to his room. To hell with waiting. He could persuade her.

But just as he started to reach for her, his mind snagged on the memory of her talking about how she felt like she'd been a disappointment to her family. The notion that anyone would think this woman less than amazing floored him. He might not agree with her on everything, but he sure as hell saw her value.

Her brilliance of mind and spirit.

He definitely needed to stick to his original plan. He would wait. He couldn't stop thinking about that snippet of her phone conversation with her father. He understood that feeling of inadequacy all too well. She deserved better.

Rather than some half-assed seduction, he needed a plan. A magnificent plan to romance a magnificent woman. The work would be well worth the payoff for both of them.

He backed away from her bed and reached for his cell phone to check in with Salvatore. Pausing at the door, he took in the sight of her, imprinting on his brain the image of Mari sleeping even though that vision ensured *he* wouldn't be sleeping tonight.

Mari's dreams filled with Rowan, filled with his blue eyes stroking her. With his hands caressing her as they floated together in the surf, away from work and responsibilities. She'd never felt so free, so languid, his kisses and touches melting her bones. Her mind filled with his husky whispers of how much he wanted her. Even the sound of his voice stoked her passion higher, hotter, until she ached to wrap her legs around his waist and be filled with his strength.

She couldn't get enough of him. Years of sparring over their work, and even the weather if the subject came up... Now all those frustrating encounters exploded into a deep need, an explosive passion for a man she could have vowed she didn't even like.

Although like had nothing to do with this raw arousal—she felt a need that left her hot and moist between the legs until she squirmed in her bed.

Her bed.

Slowly, her dream world faded as reality interjected itself with tiny details, like the slither of sheets against her skin. The give of the pillow as her head thrashed back and forth. The sound of the ocean outside the window—and the faint rumble of Rowan's voice beyond her door.

She sat upright quickly.

Rowan.

No wonder she'd been dreaming of him. His voice had been filtering into her dream until he took it over. She clutched the puffy comforter to her chest and listened, although the words were indistinguishable. From the periodic silences, he must be talking to someone on the phone.

Mari eased from the bed, careful not to wake the baby. She pulled her robe from over a cane rocking chair and slipped her arms into the cool satin. Her one decadent pleasure—sexy peignoir sets. They made her feel like a silver-screen star from the forties, complete with furry kitten-heel slippers, not so high as to trip her up, but still ultrafeminine.

Would Rowan think them sexy or silly if he noticed them? God, he was filling up her mind and making her care about things—superficial things—that shouldn't matter. Even more distressing, he made her want to climb back into that dream world and forget about everything else.

Her entire focus should be on securing Issa's future. Mari leaned over the lace bassinet to check the infant's breathing. She pressed a kiss to two fingers and skimmed them over Issa's brow, affection clutching her heart. How could one little scrap of humanity become so precious so fast?

Rowan's voice filtered through the door again and piqued her curiosity. Who could he be talking with so late at night? Common sense said it had to be important, maybe even about the baby.

Her throat tightened at the thought of news about Issa's family, and she wasn't sure if the prospect made her happy or sad. She grasped the baby monitor receiver in her hand.

Quietly, she opened the door, careful not to disturb his phone conversation. And yes, she welcomed the opportunity to look at Rowan for a moment, a double-edged pleasure with the heat of her dream still so fresh in her mind. He stood with his back to her, phone pressed to his ear as he faced the picture window, shutters open to reveal the moonlit shoreline.

She couldn't have stopped herself if she tried. And she didn't try. Her gaze skated straight down to his butt. A fine butt, the kind that filled out jeans just right and begged a woman to tuck her hand into his back pocket.

Why hadn't she noticed that about him before? Perhaps because he usually wore his doctor's coat or a suit.

The rest of him, though, was wonderfully familiar. What a time to realize she'd stored so much more about him in her memory than just the sexy glide of his blond hair swept back from his face, his piercing blue eyes, his strong body.

Her fingers itched to scale the expanse of his chest, hard muscled in a way that spoke of real work more than gym time with a personal trainer. Her body responded with a will of its own, her breasts beading in response to just the sight of him, the promise of pleasure in that strong, big body of his.

Were the calluses on his hand imagined in her dream or real? Right now it seemed the most important thing in the world to know, to find out from the ultimate test— his hands on her bare flesh.

His back still to her, he nodded and hmmed at something in the conversation, the broad column of his neck exposed, then he disconnected his call.

Anticipation coursed through her, but she schooled her face to show nothing as he turned.

He showed no surprise at seeing her, his moves smooth and confident. He placed his phone on the wet bar, his eyes sweeping over all of her. His gaze lingered on her shoes and he smiled, then his gaze stroked back up to her face again. "Mari, how long have you been awake?"

"Only a few minutes. Just long enough to hear you 'hmm' and 'uh-huh' a couple of times." She wrapped her arms around her waist, hugging the robe closed and making sure her tingling breasts didn't advertise her arousal. "If I may ask, who were you talking to so late?"

"Checking on our security and following up a lead on the baby."

She stood up straighter and joined him by the window, her heart hammering in her ears. "Did you find her family?"

"Sorry." He cupped her shoulder in a warm grasp, squeezing comfortingly. "Not yet. But we're working on it."

She forced herself to swallow and moisten her suddenly dry mouth. "Who is this 'we' you keep mentioning?"

"I'm a wealthy man now. Wealthy people have connections. I'm using them." His hand slid away, calluses snagging on her satin robe.

Calluses.

The thought of those fingers rasping along her skin made her shiver with want. God, she wasn't used to being this controlled by her body. She was a cerebral person, a thinker, a scientist. She needed to find level ground again, although it was a struggle.

Reining herself in, she eyed Rowan, assessing him. Her instincts told her he was holding something back about his conversation, but she couldn't decipher what that might be. She searched his face, really searched, and what a time to realize she'd never looked deeper than the surface of Rowan before. She'd known his history—a reformed bad boy, the saintly doctor saving the world and soaking up glory like a halo, while she was a person who preferred the shadows.

She'd only stepped into the spotlight now for the baby. And that made her wonder if his halo time had another purpose for him—using that notoriety for his causes. The possibility that she could have been mistaken about his ego, his swagger, gave her pause.

Of course she could just be seeking justification for how his kisses turned her inside out.

Then his hand slid down her arm until he linked fingers with her and tugged her toward the sofa. Her stomach leaped into her throat, but she didn't stop him, curious to see where this would lead. And reluctant to let go of his hand.

He sat, drawing her to sit beside him. Silently. Just staring back at her, his thumb stroking across the inside of her wrist.

Did he expect her to jump him? She'd already told him she wouldn't make the leap into bed with him. Had a part of her secretly hoped he would argue?

Still, he didn't speak or move.

She searched for something to say, anything to fill the empty space between them—and take her mind off the tantalizing feel of his callused thumb rubbing along her speeding pulse. "Do you really think Issa's family will be found?"

"I believe that every possible resource is being devoted to finding out who she is and where she came from."

The clean fresh scent of his aftershave rode every breath she took. She needed to focus on Issa first and foremost.

"Tomorrow—or rather, later this morning—we need to get serious about going public with the press. No more playing at dinner, pretend photos and controlled press releases. I need to use my notoriety to help her."

He squeezed her wrist lightly. "You don't have to put yourself in the line of fire so aggressively."

"Isn't that why you asked me to help you? To add oomph to the search?" His answer became too important to her.

"I could have handled the baby alone." He held her gaze, with undeniable truthfulness in his eyes. "If we're honest here, I wanted to spend more time with you."

Her tummy flipped and another of those tempting Rowan-scented breaths filled her. "You used the baby for selfish reasons? To get closer to me?"

"When you put it like that, it sounds so harsh."

"What *did* you mean then?"

He linked their fingers again, lifting their twined grasp and resting it against his chest. "Having you here does help with the baby's care and with finding the baby's family. But it also helps me get to know you better."

"Do you want to know me better or kiss me?"

His heart thudded against her hand as he leaned even closer, just shy of their lips touching. "Is there a problem with my wanting both?"

"You do understand that nothing is simple with me." Her breath mingled with his.

"Because of who you are? Yes, I realize exactly who you are."

And just that fast, reality iced over her. She could never forget who she was...her father's daughter. A princess. The next in the royal line since she had no siblings, no aunts or uncles. As much as she wanted to believe Rowan's interest in her was genuine, she'd been used and misunderstood too many times in the past.

She angled away from him. "I know you think I'm a spoiled princess."

"Sometimes we say things in anger that we don't mean. I apologize for that." He stretched his arm along the back of the sofa without touching her this time.

"What *do* you think of me?" The opinion of others hadn't mattered to her before.... Okay, that was a lie.

Her parents' opinion mattered. She'd cared what her first lover thought of her only to find he'd used her to get into her father's inner circle.

"Mari, I think you're smart and beautiful."

She grinned. "Organized and uptight."

He smiled back. "Productive, with restrained passions."

"I *am* a spoiled princess," she admitted, unable to resist the draw of his smile, wanting to believe what she saw in his eyes. "I've had every luxury, security, opportunity imaginable. I've had all the things this baby needs, things her mother is so desperate to give her she would give her away to a stranger. I feel awful and guilty for just wanting to be normal."

"Normal life?" He shook his head, the leather sofa creaking as he leaned back and away. "I had that so-called normal life and I still screwed up."

She'd read the press about him, the way he'd turned his life around after a drunk-driving accident as a teen. He was the poster boy for second chances, devoting his life to making amends.

Her negative reports on his program weren't always popular. Some cynics in the medical community had even suggested she had an ax to grind, insinuating he might have spurned her at some point. That assumption stung her pride more than a little.

Still, she couldn't deny the good he'd done with his clinic. The world needed more people like Dr. Rowan Boothe.

"You screwed up as a teenager, but you set yourself on the right path again once you went to that military high school."

"That doesn't erase my mistake. Nothing can." He plowed a hand through his hair. "It frustrates the hell out of me that the press wants to spin it into some kind of feel-good story. So yeah, I get your irritation with the whole media spin."

"But your story gives people hope that they can turn their lives around."

He mumbled a curse.

"What? Don't just go Grinchy on me." She tapped his elbow. "Talk. Like you did at dinner."

"Go Grinchy?" He cocked an eyebrow. "Is that really a word?"

"Of course it is. I loved that movie as a child. I watched a lot of Christmas movies flying across the ocean to spend Christmas with one parent or the other. So, back to the whole Grinchy face. What gives?"

"If you want to change my mood, then let's talk about something else." His arm slid from the back of the sofa until his hand cupped her shoulder. "What else did you enjoy about Christmas when you were a kid?"

"You're not going to distract me." With his words or his touch.

"Says who?" Subtly but deliberately, he pulled her closer.

And angled his mouth over hers.

Seven

Stunned still, Mari froze for an instant. Then all the simmering passion from her dream earlier came roaring to the surface. She looped her arms around Rowan's neck and inched closer to him on the sofa. The satin of her peignoir set made her glide across the leather smoother, easier, until she melted against him, opened her mouth and took him as boldly as he took her.

The sweep of his tongue carried the minty taste of toothpaste, the intoxicating warmth of pure him. His hands roved along her back, up and down her spine in a hypnotizing seduction. He teased his fingers up into her hair, massaging her scalp until her body relaxed, muscle by tense muscle, releasing tensions she hadn't even realized existed. Then he stirred a different sort of tension, a coiling of desire in her belly that pulled tighter and tighter until she arched against him.

Her breasts pressed to his chest, the hard wall of him

putting delicious pressure against her tender, oversensitized flesh.

He reclined with her onto the couch, tucking her beneath him with a possessive growl. She nipped his bottom lip and purred right back. The contrast of cool butter-soft leather beneath her and hot, hard male over her sent her senses on overload.

The feel of his muscled body stretching out over her, blanketing her, made her blood pulse faster, thicker, through her veins. She plucked at the leather string holding back his hair, pulled it loose and glory, glory, his hair slipped free around her fingers. She combed her hands through the coarse strands, just long enough to tickle her face as he kissed.

And this man sure did know how to kiss.

Not just with his mouth and his bold tongue, but he used his hands to stroke her, his body molding to hers. His knee slid between her legs. The thick pressure of his thigh against the core of her sent delicious shivers sparkling upward. All those sensations circled and tightened in her belly with a new intensity.

Her hands learned the planes and lines of him, along his broad shoulders, down his back to the firm butt she'd been checking out not too long ago. Every nerve ending tingled to life, urging her to take more—more of him and more of the moment.

She wanted all of him. Now.

Hooking a leg around his calf, she linked them, bringing him closer still. Her hips rocked against his, the thick length of his arousal pressing against her stomach with delicious promise of what they could have together. Soon. Although not soon enough. Urgency throbbed through her, pulsing into a delicious ache between her legs.

He swept aside her hair and kissed along the sensitive curve of her neck, nipping ever so lightly against her pulse. She hummed her approval and scratched gently over his back, along his shoulders, then down again to yank at his shirt. She couldn't get rid of their clothes fast enough. If she gave herself too long to think, too many practical reasons to stop would start marching through her mind—

A cool whoosh of air swept over her. She opened her eyes to see Rowan standing beside the sofa. Well, not standing exactly, but halfway bent over, his hands on his legs as he hauled in ragged breath after breath. His arousal was unmistakable, so why was he pulling away?

"What? Where?" She tried again to form a coherent sentence. "Where are you going?"

He stared at her in the moonlight, his chest rising and falling hard, like he'd run for miles. His expression was closed. His eyes inscrutable.

"Good night, Mariama."

Her brain couldn't make his words match up with what she was feeling. Something didn't add up. "Good night? That's it?"

"I need to stop now." He tucked his shirt in as he backed away. "Things are getting too intense."

She refused to acknowledge the twinge of hurt she felt at his words. She wasn't opening her emotions to this man.

"Yeah, I noticed." She brazened it out, still committed to re-creating the amazing feelings from her dream. "That intensity we were experiencing about twenty seconds ago was a good thing."

"It will be good, Mari. When you're ready."

Damn, but he confused her. She hated feeling like

he student in need of remedial help. The one who didn't
'get" it.

"Um, hello, Rowan. I'm ready now."

"I just need for you to be sure." He backed away an-
other step, his hair tousled from her hungry fingers.
'See if you feel the same in the morning. Good night,
Mariama."

He pivoted into his room and closed the door behind him.

Mari sagged back on the sofa, befuddled as hell.
What was his game here? He bound her to him by en-
listing her help with the baby. He clearly wanted her.
Yet, he'd walked away.

She wasn't innocent. She'd been with men—two.
The first was a one-night stand that had her clamping
her legs shut for years to come after she'd learned he'd
only wanted access to her family. Then one long-term
deal with a man who'd been as introverted as her. Their
relationship had dissolved for lack of attention, fading
into nothing more than convenient sex. And then not
so convenient. Still, the breakup had been messy, her
former lover not taking well to having his ego stung
over being dumped. He'd been a real jerk.

Whereas Rowan was being a total gentleman. Not
pushing. Not taking advantage.

And he was driving her absolutely batty.

Holding back had threatened to drive Rowan over
the edge all night long.

At least now he could move forward with the day.
The salty morning breeze drifted through the open shutters as he tucked his polo shirt into his jeans, already
anticipating seeing Mari. Soon. He'd never wanted a
woman this much. Walking away from her last night

had been almost impossible. But he was making progress. She wanted him and he needed this to be very, very reciprocal.

So he needed to move on with his plan to romance her. Neither of them had a presentation at the conference today. He suspected it wouldn't take much persuasion to convince her to skip out on sitting through boring slide presentations and rubber chicken.

During his sleepless night, he'd racked his brain for the best way to sweep her off her feet. She wasn't the most conventional of women. He'd decided to hedge his bets by going all out. He'd started off with the traditional stuff, a flower left on her pillow while she'd been in the shower. He'd also ordered her favorite breakfast delivered to her room. He planned to end the day with a beachside dinner and concert.

All traditional "dating" fare.

The afternoon's agenda, however, was a bit of a long shot. But then he figured it was best to hedge his bets with her. She'd seemed surprised by the breakfast, and he could have sworn she was at least a little charmed by his invitation to spend the day together. Although he still detected a hint of wariness.

But reminding her of how they could appease the press into leaving her alone by feeding them a story persuaded her. For now, at least. He just prayed the press conference went smoothly.

Rowan opened his bedroom door and found Mari already waiting for him in the sitting area with Issa cradled in her arms. She stood by the stroller, cooing to the baby and adjusting a pink bootie, her face softening with affection.

Mari wore a long silky sheath dress that glided across subtle curves as she swayed back and forth. And the pink tropical flower he'd left on her pillow was now tucked behind her ear. He stood captivated by her grace as she soothed the infant to sleep. Minutes—or maybe more—later, she leaned to place the baby in the stroller.

She glanced to the side, meeting his gaze with a smile. "Where are we going?"

Had she known he was there the whole time? Did she also know how damn difficult it had been to walk away from her last night? "It's a surprise."

"That makes me a little nervous." She straightened, gripping the stroller. "I'm not good at pulling off anything impetuous."

"We have a baby with us." He rested a hand on top of hers. "How dangerous could my plan be?"

Her pupils widened in response before her gaze skittered away. "Okay, fair enough." She pulled her hand from his and touched the exotic bloom tucked in her hair. "And thank you for the flower."

Ducking his head, he kissed her ear, right beside the flower, breathing in the heady perfume of her, even more tantalizing than the petals. "I'll be thinking of how you taste all day long."

He sketched a quick kiss along her regally high cheekbone before pulling back. Gesturing toward the private elevator, he followed her, taking in the swish of her curls spiraling just past her shoulders. What a time to realize how rarely he saw her with her hair down. She usually kept it pulled back in a reserved bun.

Except for last night when she'd gone to bed. And now.

It was all he could do to keep himself from walking up behind her, sliding his arms around her and pulling her flush against him. The thought of her bottom nestled against him, his face in the sweet curve of her neck… damn. He swallowed hard. Just damn.

He followed her into the elevator and thankfully the glide down went quickly, before he had too much time in the cubicle breathing in the scent of her. The elevator doors opened with a whoosh as hefty as his exhale.

His relief was short-lived. A pack of reporters waited just outside the resort entrance, ready for them to give their first official press conference. He'd expected it, of course. He'd even set this particular one up. But having Mari and the baby here put him on edge. Even knowing Elliot Starc's detail of bodyguards were strategically placed didn't give him total peace. He wondered what would.

Mari pushed the stroller while he palmed her back, guiding her through the lobby. Camera phones snap-snap-snapped as he ushered Mari and Issa across the marble floor. Gawkers whispered as they watched from beside towering columns and sprawling potted ferns.

The doorman waved them through the electric doors and out into chaos. Rowan felt Mari's spine stiffen. Protectiveness pumped through him anew.

He ducked his head toward her. "Are you sure you're okay with this? We can go back to the suite, dine on the balcony, spend our day off in a decadent haze of food and sunshine."

She shook her head tightly. "We proceed as planned. For Issa, I will do anything to get the word out about her story, whatever it takes to be sure she has a real family who loves her and appreciates what a gift she is."

Her ferocity couldn't be denied—and it stirred the hell out of him. Before he did something crazy like kiss her until they both couldn't think, he turned to the reporters gathered on the resort's stone steps.

"No questions today, just a statement," he said firmly with a smile. "Dr. Mandara and I have had our disagreements in the past, but we share a common goal in our desire...to help people in need. This is the holiday season and a defenseless child landed in our radar, this little girl. How could we look away? We're working together to care for this baby until her family can be found. If even Mari and I can work together, then maybe there's hope...."

He winked wryly and laughter rippled through the crowd.

Once they quieted, he continued, "That's all for now. We have a baby, a conference agenda and holiday shopping to juggle. Thank you and Merry Christmas, everyone."

Their bodyguards emerged from the crowd on cue and created a circular wall around them as they walked from the resort to the shopping strip.

Mari glanced up at him, her sandals slapping the wooden boardwalk leading to the stores and stalls of the shoreline marketplace. "Are we truly going shopping? I thought men hated shopping."

"It's better than hanging out inside eating conference food. I hope you don't mind. If you'd rather go back..."

"Bite your tongue." She hip-bumped him as he strode beside her.

"Onward then." He slipped his arm around her shoulders, tucking her to him as they walked.

She glanced up at him. "Thank you."

If he dipped his head, he could kiss her, but even though he'd set up this press coverage, he balked at that much exposure. "Thanks for what?"

"For the press conference, and taking the weight of that worry off me. You handled the media so perfectly.

I'm envious of your ease, though." She scrunched her elegant nose. "I wish I had that skill. Running from them hasn't worked out that well for me."

"I just hope the statement and all of those photos will help Issa."

"Why wouldn't it?"

Helping Interpol gain access to crooks around the world had given him insights into just how selfish, how Machiavellian, people could be. "Think of all the crackpots who will call claiming to know something just to attach themselves to a high-profile happening or hoping to gain access to you even for a short while knowing that DNA tests will later prove them to be frauds."

"God, I never thought of that," she gasped, her eyes wide and horrified.

He squeezed her shoulder reassuringly, all too aware of how perfectly she fit to his side. "The police are going to be busy sifting through the false leads that come through."

"That's why you wanted to wait a day to officially announce we're fostering her...." she whispered softly to herself as they passed a cluster of street carolers.

"Why did you think I waited?" He saw a whisper of chagrin shimmer in her golden eyes. "Did you think I was buying time to hit on you?"

She lifted a dark eyebrow. "Were you?"

"Maybe." Definitely.

She looked away, sighing. "Honestly, I'm not sure what I thought. Since I stumbled into your suite with that room-service cart, things have been...crazy. I've barely had time to think, things are happening so fast. I just hate to believe anyone would take advantage of this precious baby's situation for attention or reward money."

The reality of just how far people would go made his

jaw flex. "We'll wade through them. No one gains access to this child or you until they've been completely vetted. We will weed through the false claims and selfish agendas. Meanwhile, she's safe with us. She turns toward your voice already."

"You're nice to say that, but she's probably just in search of her next bottle."

"Believe what you want. I know differently." He'd seen scores of mothers and children file through his clinic—biological and adoptive. Bonds formed with or without a blood connection.

"Are you arguing with me? I thought we were supposed to be getting along now. Isn't that what you said at the press conference?"

"I'm teasing you. Flirting. There's a difference." Unable to resist, he pressed a kiss to her forehead.

"Oh."

"Relax. I'm not going to hit on you here." There were far too many cameras for him to be too overt. "Although a longer kiss would certainly give the press something to go wild about. Feed them tidbits and they'll quit digging for other items."

Furrows dug into her forehead. "But it feels too much like letting them win."

"I consider it controlling the PR rather than letting it control me." He guided her by her shoulders, turning toward a reporter with a smile before walking on. "Think about all the positive publicity you're racking up for your father."

"This may have started out to be about keeping the press off my back, but now it's more about the baby."

He agreed with her on that account. But the worry on her face reminded him to stay on track with his plan.

"This conversation is getting entirely too serious for a day of fun and relaxation."

"Of course…" She swiped her hand over her forehead, squeezing her eyes closed for an instant before opening them again and smiling. "Who are you shopping for today? For your family?"

"In a sense."

He stopped in front of a toy store.

Her grin widened, her kissable lips glistening with a hint of gloss. "Are we shopping for Issa?"

"For the kids at my clinic."

Toy shopping with Rowan and Issa, like they were a family, tore at Mari's heart throughout the day. The man who'd left a flower on her pillow and chosen her favorite breakfast was charming. But the man who went shopping for the little patients at his free clinic?

That man was damn near irresistible.

Riding the elevator back up to their suite, she grabbed the brass bar for balance. Her unsteady feet had nothing to do with exhaustion or the jerk of the elevator—and everything to do with the man standing beside her.

Her mind swirled with memories of their utterly carefree day. The outing had been everything she could have hoped for and more. Sure, the paparazzi had followed them, lurking, but Rowan had controlled them, fielding their questions while feeding them enough tidbits to keep them from working themselves into a frenzy. Best of all, Issa had gotten her press coverage. Hopefully the right people would see it.

As much as Mari's stomach clenched at the thought of saying goodbye to the baby, she wanted what was best for the child. She wanted Issa to feel—and be—loved unreservedly. Every child deserved that. And

Rowan was doing everything possible to help this child he'd never met, just like he did the patients at his clinic, even down to the smallest detail.

Such as their shopping spree.

It would have been easier to write it off as a show for the press or a trick to win her over. But he had a list of children's names with notes beside them. Not that she could read his stereotypically wretched doctor's scrawl. But from the way he consulted the list and made choices, he'd clearly made a list of kids' names and preferences. The bodyguards had been kept busy stowing packages in the back of a limo trailing them from store to store.

And he hadn't left Issa off his list. The baby now had a new toy in her stroller, a plush zebra, the black-and-white stripes captivating the infant. The vendor had stitched the baby's name in pink on the toy.

Issa.

The one part of her prior life the little one carried with her—a name. Used for both boys and girls, meaning savior. Appropriate this time of year... Her feet kicked. Could the name be too coincidental? Could whoever left the baby have made up the name to go with the season—while leading authorities astray?

She leaned in to stroke the baby's impossibly soft cheek. Issa's lashes swept open and she stared up at Mari for a frozen moment, wide dark eyes looking up with such complete trust Mari melted. What happened if family came forward and they didn't love her as she deserved?

Those thoughts threatened to steal Mari's joy and she shoved them aside as the elevator doors whooshed open. She refused to let anything rob her of this perfect day and the promise of more. More time with Issa. More time with Rowan.

More kisses?

More of everything?

He'd walked away last night because he thought she wasn't ready. Maybe he was right. Although the fact that he cared about her needs, her well-being, made it all the more difficult to keep him at arm's length. And she couldn't even begin to imagine how his plans for seducing her fit into this whole charade with the baby.

Questions churned in her mind, threatening to steal the joy from the day. In a rare impulsive move, she decided to simply go with the flow. She would quit worrying about when or if they would sleep together and just enjoy being with Rowan. Enjoy the flirting.

Revel in the chemistry they shared rather than wearing herself out denying its existence.

Butterflies stirred in her stomach. She pushed the stroller into their suite just as Rowan's arm shot out to stop her.

"Someone's here," he warned a second before a woman shot up from the sofa.

A woman?

The butterflies slowed and something cold settled in her stomach. Dread?

A redhead with a freckled nose and chic clothes squealed, "Rowan!"

The farm-fresh bombshell sprinted across the room and wrapped her arms around Rowan's neck.

Dread quickly shifted to something darker.

Jealousy.

Eight

Rowan braced his feet as the auburn-haired whirlwind hit him full force. He'd spoken with his business partner and the partner's wife, Hillary, about the current situation. But he'd assured them Elliot Starc had things under control. Apparently his friends weren't taking him at his word.

Who else was waiting in the suite to blindside him? So much for romance tonight.

"Hillary." Rowan hugged his friend fast before pulling away. "Not that I'm unhappy to see you, but what are you doing here tonight?"

She patted his face. "You should know that word spreads fast among the Brotherhood and everyone available is eager to help." She glanced over her shoulder at Mari and the baby. "And of course, we're insanely curious about your new situation."

Mari looked back and forth between them, a look of confusion on her face. "The Brotherhood?"

"A nickname for some of my high school class-mates," Rowan explained. "We used to call ourselves the Alpha Brotherhood."

They still did, actually, after a few drinks over a game of cards. The name had started as a joke between them, a way of thumbing their noses at the frat-boy types, and after a while, the label stuck.

Hillary thrust a hand toward Mari. "Hi, I'm Hillary Donavan. I'm married to Rowan's former classmate and present business partner, Troy."

Mari's eyebrows arched upward. "Oh, your husband is the computer mogul."

Hillary took over pushing the stroller and preceded them into the suite as if it was her hotel penthouse. "You can go ahead and say it. My husband is the Robin Hood Hacker."

"I wasn't…" Mari stuttered, following the baby buggy deeper into the room. "I wouldn't…uh…"

"It's okay," Hillary said with a calm smile that had smoothed awkward moments in her days as an event planner for high-powered D.C. gatherings. "You can relax. Everyone knows my husband's history."

Mari smiled apologetically, leaning into the stroller to pull the sleeping baby out and cradle her protectively in her arms. "I'm not particularly good with chitchat."

"That's all right. I talk plenty for two people." She cupped the back of the infant's head. "What an ador-able baby. Issa, right?"

"Yes." Rowan pushed the stroller to a corner, light-weight gauzy pink blanket trailing out the side. "Did you see the gossip rags or did the Brotherhood tell you that, too?"

Hillary made herself at home on the leather sofa. "Actually, I'm here to help. Troy and Rowan are more than just business partners on that computer diagnostics project you so disapprove of—" Hillary winked to take the sting out the dig "—they're also longtime friends. I have some last-minute Christmas shopping to do for those tough-to-buy-for people in my life, and voilà. Coming here seemed the perfect thing to do."

The pieces came together in Rowan's mind, Hillary's appearance now making perfect sense. While the Brotherhood kept their Interpol work under wraps, Hillary knew about her husband's freelance agent work and Salvatore had even taken her into the fold for occasional missions. Now she was here. He should have thought of it himself, if his brain hadn't been scrambled by a certain sexy research scientist.

Hillary would make the perfect bodyguard for Mari and Issa. No one would question her presence and she added a layer of protection to this high-profile situation.

Although sometimes the whole Interpol connection also came with dangers. God, he was in the middle of an impossible juggling act.

The baby started fussing and Rowan extended his arms to take her. Mari hesitated, tucking the baby closer. Rowan lifted an eyebrow in surprise.

"Mari? I can take her." He lifted the baby from Mari's arms. "You two keep talking."

"Wow." Hillary laughed. "You sure handle that tiny tyke well. No wonder you're dubbed one of the world's hottest bachelors. Snap a photo of you now and you'll need your own bodyguard."

Mari's smile went tight and Rowan wondered... Holy hell, she couldn't be jealous. Could she? Was that the same look he'd seen drifting through her eyes when Hillary had hugged him earlier? He wanted her to desire him, but he also wanted—needed—for her to trust him.

"Enough, Hillary. You were talking about Troy's computer search...."

"Right—" she turned back to Mari "—and you're taking care of the baby, Rowan. So vamoose. Go fill out your list for Santa. I've got this."

Rowan cocked an eyebrow over being so summarily dismissed. And putting Issa in the bassinet in another room would give him the perfect excuse to slip away and call Troy.

Not to mention time to regroup for the next phase of winning over Mari. He'd made progress with her today.

Now he just had to figure out how to persuade his friends to give him enough space to take that romancing to the next level.

Mari sank to the edge of the sofa. Her head was spinning at how fast things were changing around her. Not to mention how fast this woman was talking.

"Hold on a moment, please." Mari raised a hand. "What were you saying about computer searches into Issa's past?"

Hillary dropped into the wide rattan chair beside her. "No worries. It's all totally legal computer work. I promise. Troy walks on the right side of the law these days. And yes, it's okay to talk about it. I know about my husband's past, and I assume you know about Rowan's. But they've both changed. They're genuinely trying to make amends in more ways than most could imagine."

Mari blinked in the wake of Hurricane Hillary, confused. Why would Rowan have needed to make amends for anything? Sure, he'd led a troubled life as a teen, but his entire adult life had been a walking advertisement for charity work. Even if she disputed some of his methods, she couldn't deny his philanthropic spirit. "I've read the stories of his good deeds."

"There's so much more to Rowan than those stories."

She knew that already. The press adored him and his work, and she had to admit his clinic had helped many. She just wished they could come to an agreement on how to make his work—the computerized side and even the personal side—more effective. If she could solve that problem, who knew how many more small clinics in stretched-thin outposts of the world would benefit from Rowan's model of aid?

"Hillary, why are you telling me this?"

"The competitive animosity between the two of you is not a secret." She tipped her head to the side, twirling a strand of red hair contemplatively. "So I find it strange that you're here."

"I'm here for the baby."

"Really?" Hillary crossed her legs, her eyes glimmering with humor and skepticism. No getting anything past this woman. "There are a million ways the two of you could care for this child other than sharing a suite."

Mari bristled, already feeling overwhelmed by this confident whirlwind who looked like a Ralph Lauren model in skinny jeans and a poet's shirt.

Smoothing her hands over her sack dress, Mari sat up stiffly, channeling every regal cell in her body. "This is quite a personal conversation to be having with someone I only just met."

"You're right. I apologize if I've overstepped." She held up a hand, diamond wedding band set winking in the sunlight. "I've become much more extroverted since marrying Troy. I just wanted you to know Rowan's a better man than people think. A better man than he knows."

Great. Someone else pointing out the perfection of Dr. Rowan Boothe. As if Mari didn't already know. God, how she resented the feelings of insecurity pumping through her. She wanted to be the siren in the peignoir, the confident woman certain that Rowan wanted her with every fiber of his soul. And yes, she knew that was melodramatic and totally unscientific.

Forcing her thoughts to slow and line up logically, she realized that Rowan's eyes had followed her all day long—no skinny jeans needed. And Hillary was right. He and Mari both could have figured out a dozen different ways to care for this baby and stir publicity without sharing a suite. She was here because she wanted to be and Rowan wanted her here, as well.

No more flirting. No more games. No more holding back. She burned to sleep with Rowan.

The next time she had him alone, she intended to see the seduction through to its full, satisfying conclusion.

Finally, Rowan closed his suite door after dinner with Hillary, Troy and Elliot. He plowed his hands through his hair as Mari settled the baby for the night in his room.

He appreciated the help of his friends—but by the end of supper he had never been happier to see them all head to their own suites. Troy and Hillary were staying in the suite across the hall. Elliot Starc was a floor below, monitoring the surveillance vans outside the resort.

Rowan was more than a little surprised that his friends felt such a need to rally around him just because another orphan had landed on his doorstep. Issa wasn't the first—and she certainly wouldn't be the last—child in need of his patronage.

He suspected his friends' increased interest had something to do with Mari's involvement. No doubt he hadn't been as successful as he would have liked at hiding his attraction to her all these years. They were here out of curiosity as well as genuine caring, stepping up on a personal level, even if Mari didn't know the full weight of what they brought to the table for security and he wasn't in a position to tell her.

Now that a story had broken about an orphan at Christmastime, the attention was swelling by the second. Holiday mayhem made it tougher than ever to record all the comings and goings at the resort. Bogus leads were also coming in by the hundreds. So far no sign of a valid tip. Hillary and Troy were rechecking the police work through computer traces, using Interpol databases.

Intellectually, he understood these things took time and persistence, but thinking about the kid's future, worrying about her, made this more personal than analytical.

Somewhere out there, the baby's family had to be seeing the news reports. Even if they didn't want to claim her, surely someone would step forward with information. Even if the answer came in the form of official surrender of parental rights, at least they would know.

He understood full well how family ties didn't always turn out to be as ideal as one would hope. Memories of his brother's death, of his parents' grief and denial burned through him. He charged across the sitting area to the bar. He started to reach for the scotch and stopped himself. After the way his brother died...

Hell, no.

He opted for a mug of fresh local ginger tea and

one of the Christmas sugar cookies instead and leaned against the bar, staring out over the water as he bit the frosted tree cookie in half. Tomorrow, he and Mari both had conference presentations, then this weekend, the closing dinner and ball. Time was ticking away for all of them. He had to make the most of every moment. Tomorrow, he'd arranged for a spa appointment for Mari after her last presentation. Surely she would appreciate some privacy after all the scrutiny....

The door from Rowan's room opened. Mari slid through and closed it quietly after her. "Baby's sleeping soundly. I would have taken her tonight, you know."

"Fair is fair," he said. "We struck a bargain."

"You're a stubborn man. But then I understand that trait well."

Walking toward him, her silvery-gray sheath dress gliding over her sleek figure, she set the nursery monitor on the edge of the bar. Christmas tunes played softly over the airwaves—jazz versions, soft and soothing. Mari had fallen into the habit of setting her iPhone beside the monitor and using the music to reassure herself the listening device was still on.

She poured herself a mug of steaming ginger tea as well, adding milk and honey. Cupping the thick pottery in both hands, she drank half then cradled the mug to her with a sigh.

He skimmed his knuckles along her patrician cheekbones. "Are you okay?"

Nodding, she set aside her glass. "I just didn't expect the press coverage to be so...comprehensive."

Was it his imagination or did she lean into his touch.

"You're a princess. What you do makes the news." Although even he was surprised at just how intense the media attention had become.

The hotel staff had closed off access to their floor aside from them and the Donavans, a measure taken after a reporter was injured on a window-washing unit trying to get a bonus photo. Rowan rubbed at a kink in the back of his neck, stress-induced from worrying his tail off about all the possible holes in the security. He wasn't sure he felt comfortable taking Mari and Issa out of the hotel again, even with guards.

"But I wanted to bring positive coverage for Issa. Not all of these cranks…"

And she didn't know the half of it. Troy had informed him about a handful of the more colorful leads the police hadn't bothered mentioning. A woman claiming to be Mari's illegitimate half sister had called to say the baby belonged to her. Another call had come from an area prison with someone saying their infant daughter resembled Issa and she thought it was her twin, whom they'd thought died at birth.

All of which turned out to be false, but there was no need to make Mari more upset by sharing the details. "My contacts will sift through them."

"Who are these contacts you keep talking about? Like Hillary and her husband?" She picked up the glass again and sipped carefully.

His glass.

His body tightened as her lips pressed to the edge.

He cleared his throat. "I went to a military high school. Makes sense that some of them would end up in law enforcement positions."

"It was a military *reform* school." She eyed him over the rim of the tumbler through long lashes.

"Actually, about half were there because they wanted a future in the military or law enforcement." He rattled off the details, anything to keep from thinking about how badly he wanted to take that glass from her and kiss her until they both forgot about talking and press conferences. "The rest of us were there because we got into trouble."

"Your Alpha Brotherhood group—you trust these friends with Issa's future?"

"Implicitly."

Shaking her head, she looked away. "I wish I could be as sure about whom to trust."

"You're worried."

"Of course."

"Because you care." Visions of her caring for the baby, insisting Issa stay in her room tonight even though it was his turn, taunted him with how attached she was becoming to the little one already. There was so much more to this woman than he'd known or guessed. She was more emotional than she'd ever let on. Which brought him back to the strange notion that she'd been jealous of Hillary.

A notion he needed to dispel. "What did you think of Hillary?"

"She's outspoken and she's a huge fan of yours." She folded her arms over her chest.

"You can't be jealous."

"At first, when she hugged you…I wondered if she was a girlfriend," she admitted. "Then I realized it might not be my right to ask."

"I kissed you. You have a right to question." He met her gaze full-on, no games or hidden agendas. Just pure honesty. "For the record, I'm the monogamous type. When I'm with a woman, I'm sure as hell not kissing other women."

Her eyes flashed with quick relief before she tipped

her head to the side and touched his chest lightly. "What happened last night—"

"What almost happened—"

"Okay, almost happened, along with the parts that did—"

"I understand." He pressed a hand over hers, wanting to reassure her before she had a chance to start second-guessing things and bolting away. "You want to say it can't happen. Not again."

"Hmm…" She frowned, toying with the simple watch on her wrist. "Have you added mind reader to your list of accomplishments now? If so, please do tell me why I would insist on pushing you away."

"Because we have to take care of the baby." He folded her hand in his and kissed her knuckles, then her wrist. "Your devotion to her is a beautiful thing."

"That's a lovely compliment. Thank you. I would say the same about you."

"A compliment?" he bantered back. "I did *not* expect that."

"Why ever not?" She stepped closer until her breasts almost brushed his chest.

The unmistakably seductive move wasn't lost on him. His pulse kicked up a notch as he wondered just how far she would take this.

And how far he should let it go.

"There is the fact that you haven't missed an opportunity to make it clear how much you don't like me or my work."

"That could be a compelling reason to keep my distance from you." She placed her other hand on his chest, tipping her face up to him until their lips were a whisper apart.

"Be on notice…" He took in the deep amber of her

eyes, the flush spreading across her latte-colored, creamy skin. "I plan to romance you, sweep you off your feet even."

"You are—" she paused, leaning into him, returning his intense gaze "—a confusing man. I thought I knew you but now I'm finding I don't understand you at all. But you need to realize that after last night's kiss…"

"It was more than a kiss," he said hoarsely.

"You're absolutely right on that." Her fingers crawled up his chest until she tapped his bottom lip.

He captured her wrist again just over the thin watch. He thought of the bracelets he'd surreptitiously picked up for her at the marketplace, looking forward to the right moment to give them to her. "But I will not make love to you until you ask me. You have to know that."

"You're mighty confident." Her breath carried heat and a hint of the ginger tea.

Who knew tea could be far more intoxicating than any liquor? "Hopeful."

"Good." Her lips moved against his. "Because I'm asking."

And damn straight he didn't intend to walk away from her again.

Nine

Mari arched up onto her toes to meet Rowan's mouth sealing over hers. Pure want flooded through her. Each minute had felt like an hour from the moment she'd decided to act on her desire tonight until the second he'd kissed her.

Finally, she would be with him, see this crazy attraction through. Whether they were arguing or working together, the tension crackled between them. She recognized that now. They'd been moving toward this moment for years.

She nipped his bottom lip. "We have to be quiet so we don't wake the baby."

"Hmm…" His growl rumbled his chest against her. "Sounds challenging."

"Just how challenging can we make it?" She grazed her nails down his back, the fabric of his shirt carrying the warmth and scent of him.

"Is that a dare?"

She tucked her hands into the back pockets of his jeans as she'd dreamed of doing more than once. "Most definitely."

Angling his head to the side, he stared into her eyes. "And you're sure you're ready for this?"

She dug her fingers into his amazing tush. "Could you quit being so damn admirable? I'm very clearly propositioning you. I am an adult, a very smart adult, totally sober, and completely turned on by you. If that's not clear enough for you, then how about this? Take me to bed or to the couch, but take me now."

A slow and sexy smile creased dimples into his sun-bronzed face. "How convenient you feel that way since you absolutely mesmerize me."

Her stomach fluttered at the obvious appreciation in his eyes, his voice. His *touch*. He made her feel like the sensuous woman who wore peignoirs. He made her feel sexy. Sexier than any man ever had, and yes, that was a part of his appeal.

But she couldn't deny she'd always found him attractive. Who wouldn't? He took handsome to a whole new level, in a totally unselfconscious way. The blond streaks in his hair came from the sun—his muscles from hard work.

And those magnificent callused hands... She could lose herself in the pure sensation of his caress.

He inched aside the strap of her silvery-gray dress. She'd chosen the silky fabric for the decadent glide along her skin—yes, she usually preferred shapeless clothes, but the appreciation in Rowan's eyes relayed loud and clear he'd never judged her by what she wore. He saw her. The woman. And he wanted her.

That knowledge sent a fresh thrill up her spine.

He kissed along her bared neck, to her shoulder, his teeth lightly snapping her champagne-colored satin bra strap—another of her hidden decadences, beautiful underwear. Her head fell back, giving him fuller access. But she didn't intend to be passive in this encounter. Not by a long shot. Her hands soaked up the play of his muscles flexing in his arms as she stroked down, down, farther still to his waistband.

She tugged his polo shirt free and her fingers crawled up under the warm cotton to find even hotter skin. She palmed his back, scaled the hard planes of his shoulder blades as a jazz rendering of "The First Noel" piped through the satellite radio. He was her latest fantasies come to life.

Unable to wait a second longer, she yanked the shirt over his head even if that meant he had to draw his mouth away from her neck. She flung aside his polo, the red shirt floating to rest on the leather sofa. Fire heated his eyes to the hottest blue flame. He skimmed off the other strap of her dress until the silk slithered down her body, hooking briefly on her hips before she shimmied it the rest of the way off to pool at her feet. She kicked aside her sandals as she stepped out of the dress.

His gaze swept over her as fully as she took in the bared expanse of his broad chest, the swirls of hair, the sun-bronzed skin. He traced down the strap of her bra, along the lace edging the cups of her bra, slowly, deliberately outlining each breast. Her nipples beaded against the satin, tight and needy. She burned to be closer to him, as close as possible.

Her breath hitched in her throat and she stepped into his arms. The heat of his skin seared her as if he'd stored up the African sun inside him and shared it with her now.

"Here," she insisted, "on the sofa or the floor. I don't care. Just hurry."

"Princess, I have waited too damn long to rush this. I intend to have you completely and fully, in a real bed. I would prefer it was my bed, but there's a baby snoozing in the bassinet in my room. So let's go to yours."

"Fine," she agreed frantically. "Anywhere, the sooner the better." She slipped a finger into the waistband of his jeans and tugged.

"I like a lady who knows what she wants. Hell, I just like you."

His hands went to the front clasp of her bra and plucked it open and away with deft hands. She gasped as the overhead fan swooshed air over her bared flesh. Then he palmed both curves, warming her with a heat that spread into a tingling fire.

Through the haze of passion she realized her hand was still on his buckle. She fumbled with his belt, then the snap of his jeans, his zipper, until she found his arousal hard and straining against her hand. A growl rumbled low in his throat and she reveled in the sound. Drew in the scent of his soap and his sweat, perspiration already beading his brow from his restraint as she learned the feel of him. She stroked the steely length down, up and again.

"We have to be quiet," she reminded him.

"Both of us," he said with a promise in his voice and in his narrowed eyes.

One of his hands slid from her breast down to her panties, dipping inside, gliding between her legs. She was moist and ready for him. If she'd had her way they would be naked and together on the sofa. He was the one who'd insisted on drawing this out, but then they'd always been competitive.

Although right now that competition was delivering a tense and delicious result rather than the frustration of the past. She bit her bottom lip to hold back a whimper of pleasure. He slipped two fingers inside, deeper, stroking and coaxing her into a moist readiness. She gripped his shoulders, her fingernails digging half-moons into his tanned skin. Each glide took her higher until her legs went weak and he locked an arm around her back.

She gasped against his neck, so close to fulfillment. Aching for completion. "Let's take this to the bed."

"Soon, I promise." His late-day beard rasped against her cheek and he whispered in her ear, "But first, I need to protect you."

She gritted her teeth in frustration over the delay. "Rowan, there are guards stationed inside and outside of the hotel. Can we talk about security forces later?"

Cupping her face in his broad palms, he kissed the tip of her nose. "I mean I need to get birth control."

"Oh..." She gasped, surprised that she hadn't thought of it herself. She'd come in here with the intention of seducing him and she hadn't given a thought to the most important element of that union. So much for her genius IQ in the heat of the moment.

"I'll take care of it." He stepped away and disappeared from her room, his jeans slung low on his hips. Lean muscles rippled with every step.

She was an intelligent, modern woman. A scientist. A woman of logic. She liked to believe she would have realized before it was too late.... Before she could complete the thought, Rowan returned. He tossed a box of condoms on the bed.

"My goodness," she said, smiling, "you're an ambitious man."

"I'll take that as another challenge."

"Sounds like one where we're both winners. Now how about getting rid of those jeans."

"Your wish is my command, Princess." He toed off his shoes, no socks on, and peeled down his jeans without once taking his eyes off her.

His erection strained against his boxers and she opened her arms for him to join her. Then he was kissing her again and, oh, my, but that man knew how to kiss. The intensity of him, the way he was so completely focused on her and the moment fulfilled a long-ignored need to be first with a man. How amazing that the man who would view her this way—see only her—would be Rowan.

He reclined with her on the bed, into the thick comforter and stack of tapestry pillows, the crash and recede of the waves outside echoing the throb of her pulse. The sound of the shore, the luxurious suite, the hard-bodied man stretched over her was like a fantasy come true.

Only one thing kept it from being complete—something easily taken care of. She hooked her thumbs into the band of his boxers and inched them down. He smiled against her mouth as his underwear landed on the floor. Finally—thank heavens—finally, they met bare body to bare body, flesh-to-flesh. The rigid length of him pressed against her stomach, heating her with the promise of pleasure to come.

She dragged her foot up the back of his calf, hooking her leg around him, rocking her hips against him. He shifted his attention from her lips to her neck, licking along her collarbone before reaching her breasts—his mouth on one, his hand on the other. He touched and tasted her with an intuition for what she craved and more, finding nuances of sensitive patches of skin she hadn't realized were favored spots.

And she wanted to give him the same bliss.

Her fingers slid between them until her hand found his erection, exploring the length and feel of him. His forehead fell to rest against her collarbone. His husky growl puffed along oversensitized skin as she continued to stroke. Her thumb glided along the tip, smoothing a damp pearl, slickening her caress. Her mind filled with images of all the ways she wanted to love him through the night, with her hands and her mouth, here and in the shower. She whispered those fantasies in his ear and he throbbed in response in her hand.

Groaning, he reached out to snatch up the box of condoms. Rolling to his side, he clasped her wrist and moved her hand away, then sheathed himself. She watched, vowing next time she would do that for him.

Next time? Definitely a next time. And a next night.

Already she was thinking into the future and that was a scary proposition. Better to live in the now and savor this incredible moment. She clasped Rowan's shoulders as he shifted back over her again.

He balanced on his elbows, holding his weight off her. The thick pressure of him between her legs had her wriggling to get closer, draw him in deeper. She swept her other leg up until her ankles hooked around his waist. Her world filled with the sight of his handsome face and broad shoulders blocking out the rest of the world.

He hooked a hand behind her knee. "Your legs drive me crazy. Do you know that?"

"I do now. I also know you're driving me crazy waiting. I want all of you. Now." She dug her heels into his buttocks and urged him to…

Fill her.

Stretch her.

Thrill her.

Her back bowed up to meet him thrust for thrust, hushed sigh for sigh. Perspiration sealed them together, cool sheets slipping and bunching under them. In a smooth sweep, he kicked the comforter and tapestry pillows to the floor.

Tension gathered inside her, tightening in her belly. Her head dug back into the mattress, the scent of them mingling and filling every gasping breath. He touched her with reverence and perception, but she didn't want gentle or reverent. She needed edgy; she needed completion.

She pushed at his shoulder and flipped him to his back, straddling him, taking him faster and harder, his heated gaze and smile of approval all the encouragement she needed. His hands sketched up her stomach to her breasts, circling and plucking at her nipples as she came, intensifying waves of pleasure, harder, straight to the core of her. She rode the sensations, rode him, taking them both to the edge…and into a climax. Mutual. She bit her bottom lip to hold back the sounds swelling inside her as she stayed true to their vow to keep quiet. Rowan's jaw flexed, his groans mingling with her sighs.

Each rolling wave of bliss drew her, pulling her into a whirlpool of total muscle-melting satisfaction. Her arms gave way and she floated to rest on top of him. Rowan's chest pumped beneath her with labored breaths. His arms locked around her, anchoring her to him and to the moment.

Her body trembled in the wake of each aftershock rippling through her.

Exhaustion pulled at her but she knew if she slept, morning would come too fast with too many questions and possibilities that could take this away. So she blinked back sleep, focusing on multicolored lights beyond the window. Yachts, a sailboat, a ferry. She took in the details to stay awake so once her languid body regained strength, she could play out all those fantasies with Rowan.

She wanted everything she could wring from this stolen moment in case this night was all they could have before she retreated to the safety and order of her cold, clinical world.

"Are you asleep?" Mari's soft voice whispered through Rowan's haze as he sprawled beside her.

He'd wanted Mari for years. He'd known they would be good together. But no way in hell could he have predicted just how mind-blowingly incredible making love to this woman would be.

Sleep wasn't even an option with every fiber of him saturated with the satiny feel of her, the floral scent of her, the driving need to have her again and again until...

His mind stopped short of thoughts of the end. "I'm awake. Do you need something?"

Was she about to boot him out of her bed? Out of her life? He knew too well how fast the loyalties of even good people could shift. He grabbed the rumpled sheet free from around his feet and whipped it out until it fanned to rest over them.

She rolled toward him, her fingers toying with the hair on his chest. "I'm good. *This* is good, staying right here, like this. The past couple of days have been so frenzied, it's a relief to be in the moment."

"I hear ya." He kissed the top of her head, thinking of the bracelets he'd bought for her from the market and planning the right time to place them on her elegant arm.

Her fingers slowed and she looked up at him through long sweeping eyelashes. "You're very good with Issa. Have you ever thought about having kids of your own?"

His voice froze in his throat for a second. He'd given up on perfect family life a long time ago when he'd woken in the hospital to learn he and his brother were responsible for a woman losing her baby. Any hope of resurrecting those dreams died the day his brother crashed his truck into the side of a house.

Rowan sketched his fingers along Mari's stomach. He'd built a new kind of family with the Brotherhood and his patients. "I have my kids at the clinic, children that need me and depend on me."

"So you know that it's possible to love children that aren't your blood relation."

Where was she going with this? And then holy hell, it became all too clear. She was thinking about the possibility of keeping Issa beyond this week. "Are you saying that you're becoming attached to the little rug rat?"

"How could I not?" She leaned over him, resting her chin on her folded hands as she looked into his eyes. "I wonder if Issa landed with me for a reason. I've always planned not to get married. I thought that meant no kids for me—I never considered myself very good with them. But with Issa, I know what to do. She even responds to my voice already."

She was right about that. They shared a special bond that had to be reassuring to an infant whose world had been turned upside down by abandonment. But questions about the baby's past *would* be answered soon. He thought of Hillary and Troy working their tails off to find the baby's family. He hated to think of Mari setting herself up for heartache.

She shook her head before he could think of how

to remind her. "I know it's only been a couple of days and she could well have family out there who wants her. Or her mother might change her mind. I just hate the limbo."

He swept her hair from her face and kissed her, hard. "You won't be in limbo for long, I can promise you that." Guilt pinched over how he'd brought her into this, all but forced her to stay with him. "My friends and I won't rest until we find the truth about Issa's past. That's a good thing, you know."

"Of course I do. Let's change the subject." She pulled a wobbly smile. "I think it's amazing the way your friends all came to help you at the drop of a hat."

"It's what we do for each other." Just as he'd done his best to help his buddy Conrad reconcile with his wife earlier this year. He owed Conrad for helping him start the clinic, but he would have helped regardless.

"In spite of your rocky teenage years, you and your friends have all turned into incredible success stories. I may not always agree with some of your projects, but your philanthropic work is undeniable. It's no secret that your other friend, the casino owner—Conrad Hughes— has poured a lot of money into your clinic, as well."

He tensed at her mention of one of his Alpha Brotherhood buddies, wishing he could share more about the other side of his life. Needing to warn her, to ensure she didn't get too close. There weren't many women who could live with the double life he and his friends led with their Interpol work. Mari had enough complicating her life with her heritage. Better to keep the conversation on well-known facts and off anything that could lead to speculation.

"Conrad invested the start-up cash for my clinic. He

deserves the credit. My financial good fortune came later."

"No need to be so modest. Even before your invention of the diagnostics program, you could have had a lucrative practice anywhere and you chose to be here in Africa, earning a fraction of the salary."

He grunted, tunneling his hand under the sheet to cup her butt and hopefully distract her. "I got by then and I get by even better now."

She smiled against his chest. "Right, the billions you made off that diagnostics program we keep arguing about. I could help you make it better."

He smacked her bottom lightly. "Is that really what you want to talk about and risk a heated debate?"

"Why are you so quick to deflect accolades? The press is totally in love with you. You could really spin that, if you wanted."

He grimaced. "No, thanks."

She elbowed up on his chest. "I do understand your reticence. But think about it. You could inspire other kids. Sure you went to a military reform school, but you studied your butt off for scholarships to become a doctor, made a fortune and seem to be doing your level best to give it all away."

"I'm not giving it *all* away," he said gruffly, a sick feeling churning in his gut at the detour this conversation was taking. He avoided that damn press corps for just this reason. He didn't want anyone digging too deeply and he sure as hell didn't want credit for some noble character he didn't possess. "If I donate everything, I'll be broke and no good to anyone. I'm investing wisely."

"While donating heavily of your money and time."

Throwing all his resources into the black hole of guilt

that he'd never fill. Ever. He took a deep breath to keep that dark cavern at bay.

"Stop, okay?" He kissed her to halt her words. "I do what I do because it's the right thing. I have to give back, to make up for my mistakes."

Her forehead furrowed. "For your drunk-driving accident in high school? I would say you've more than made restitution. You could hire other doctors to help you carry the load."

"How can a person ever make restitution for lives lost?" he barked out, more sharply than he'd intended. But now that he'd started, there was no going back. "Do you know why I was sentenced to the military reform school for my last two years of high school?"

"Because you got in a drunk-driving accident and a woman was injured. You made a horrible, horrible mistake, Rowan. No one's denying that. But it's clear to anyone looking that you've turned your life around."

"You've done your homework where my diagnostics model is concerned, but you've obviously never researched the man behind the medicine." He eased Mari off him and sat up, his elbows on his knees as he hung his head, the weight of the memories too damn much. "The woman driving the other car was pregnant. She lost the baby."

"Oh, no, Rowan how tragic for her." Mari's voice filled with sadness and a hint of horror, but her hand fluttered to rest on his back. "And what a heavy burden for you to carry as the driver of the car."

She didn't know the half of it. No one did. To let the full extent of his guilt out would stain his brother's memory. Yet, for some reason he couldn't pinpoint, he found himself confessing all for the first time. To Mari. "But I wasn't driving."

Her hand slid up to rub the back of his neck and she sat up beside him, sheet clasped to her chest. "The news reports all say you were."

"That's what we told the police." He glanced over at her. "My brother and I both filled out formal statements saying I was the driver."

She stared back at him for two crashes of the waves before her eyes went wide with realization. "Your brother was actually the one behind the wheel that night? And he was drunk?"

Rowan nodded tightly. "We were both injured in the car accident, knocked out and rushed to the nearest hospital. When I woke up from surgery for a punctured lung, my mother was with me. My dad was with my brother, who'd broken his nose and fractured his jaw. They wanted us to get our stories straight before we talked to the police."

That night came roaring back to him, the confusion, the pain. The guilt that never went away no matter how many lives he saved at the clinic.

"Did your parents actually tell you to lie for your brother?" Her eyes went wider with horror. Clearly her parents would have never considered such a thing.

Most never would. He understood that, not that it made him feel one bit better about his own role in what had happened. She needed to understand the position they'd all been in, how he'd tried to salvage his brother's life only to make an even bigger mistake. One that cost him…too much.

"We were both drunk that night, but my brother was eighteen years old. I was only sixteen, a minor. The penalty would be less for me, but Dylan could serve hard time in jail. If I confessed to driving the car, Dylan could still have a future, a chance to turn his life around while he was still young."

"So you took the blame for your brother. You allowed yourself to be sentenced to a military reform school because your family pressured you, oh, Rowan…" She swept back his hair, her hands cool against his skin. "I am so sorry."

But he didn't want or deserve her comfort or sympathy. Rather than reject it outright, he linked fingers with her and lowered her arms.

"There was plenty of blame to go around that night. I could have made so many different choices. I could have called a cab at the party or asked someone else to drive us home." The flashing lights outside reminded him of the flash of headlights before the wreck, the blurred cop cars before he'd blacked out, then finally the arrival of the police to arrest him. "I wasn't behind the wheel, but I was guilty of letting my brother have those keys."

His brother had been a charismatic character, everyone believed him when he said he would change, and Rowan had gotten used to following his lead. When Dylan told him he was doing great in rehab, making his meetings, laying off the bottle, Rowan had believed him.

"What about your brother's guilt for what happened that night? Didn't Dylan deserve to pay for what happened to that woman, for you giving up your high school years?"

Trust Mari to see this analytically, to analyze it in clear-cut terms of rights and wrongs. Life didn't work that way. The world was too full of blurred gray territory.

"My brother paid plenty for that night and the decisions I made." If Rowan had made the right choices in the beginning, his brother would still be alive today. "Two years later, Dylan was in another drunk-driving accident. He drove his truck into the side of a house. He died." Rowan drew in a ragged breath, struggling like hell not to shrug off her touch that left him feeling too raw right now. "So you see, my decisions that night cost two lives."

Mari scooted to kneel in front of him, the sheet still clasped to her chest. Her dark hair spiraled around her shoulders in a wild sexy mess, but her amber eyes were no-nonsense. "You were sixteen years old and your parents pressured you to make the wrong decision. They sacrificed you to save your brother. They were wrong to do that."

Memories grated his insides, every word pouring acid on freshly opened wounds. He left the bed, left her, needing to put distance between himself and Mari's insistence.

He stepped over the tapestry pillows and yanked on his boxers. "You're not hearing me, Mari." He snagged his jeans from the floor and jerked them on one leg at a time. "I accept responsibility for my own actions. I wasn't a little kid. Blaming other people for our mistakes is a cop-out."

And the irony of it all, the more he tried to make amends, the more people painted him as some kind of freaking saint. He needed air. Now.

A ringing phone pierced the silence between them.

Not her ringtone. His, piping through the nursery monitor. Damn it. He'd left his cell phone in his room. "I should get that before it wakes the baby."

He hotfooted it out of her room, grateful for the excuse to escape more of her questions. Why the hell couldn't they just make love until the rest of the world faded away?

With each step out the door, he felt the weight of her gaze following him. He would have to give her some kind of closure to her questions, and he would. Once he had himself under control again.

He opened the door leading into his bedroom. His phone rang on the bamboo dresser near the bassinet. He grabbed the cell and took it back into the sitting area, reading the name scrolling across the screen.

Troy Donavan?

Premonition burned over him. His computer pal had to have found something big in order to warrant a call in the middle of the night.

Mari filled the doorway, tan satin sheet wrapped around her, toga-style. "Is something wrong?"

"I don't know yet." He thumbed the talk button on the cell phone. "Yes?"

"Hi, Rowan." Hillary's voice filled his ear. "It's me. Troy's found a trail connecting a worker at the hotel to a hospital record on one of the outlying islands— he's still working the data. But he's certain he's found Issa's mother."

Ten

Mari cradled sleeping Issa in her arms, rocking her for what would be the last time. She stared past the garland-draped minibar to the midday sun marking the passage of the day, sweeping away precious final minutes with this sweet child she'd already grown to love.

Her heart was breaking in two.

She couldn't believe her time with Issa was coming to an end. Before she'd even been able to fully process the fact that she'd actually followed through on the decision to sleep with Rowan, her world had been tossed into utter chaos with one phone call that swept Issa from them forever.

Troy Donavan had tracked various reflections of reflections in surveillance videos, piecing them together with some maze of other cameras in everything from banks to cops' radar to follow a path to a hint of a clue. They'd found the woman who'd walked away from the room-service trolley where Issa had been hidden. They'd gone a step further in the process to be sure. At some point, Mari had lost the thread of how he'd traced the trail back to a midwife on the mainland who'd delivered Issa. She'd been able to identify the mother, proving the baby's identity with footprint records.

The young mother had made her plan meticulously and worked to cover her tracks. She'd uncovered Rowan's schedule to speak at this conference then managed to get hired as a temp in the extra staff brought on for the holiday crowd. That's why she hadn't been on the employee manifest.

It appeared she'd had a mental breakdown shortly after leaving her child and was currently in a hospital. Issa had no grandparents, but she had a great aunt and uncle who wanted her. Deeply. In their fifties, their four sons were all grown but they hadn't hesitated in stepping up to care for their great niece. They owned a small coastal art gallery on the mainland and had plenty of parenting knowledge. They weren't wealthy, but their business and lives were stable.

All signs indicated they could give Issa a wonderful life full of love. Mari should be turning cartwheels over the news. So many orphans in Africa had no one to call their own and here Issa had a great family ready and eager to care for her.

Still, Mari could barely breathe at the prospect of handing over the baby, even though she knew this was the best thing for Issa.

The main door opened and Mari flinched, clutching the tiny girl closer. Rowan entered, lines fanning from his eyes attesting to the sleepless night they'd both endured after the fateful phone call about Issa's identity.

Rowan had scraped his hair back with a thin leather tie, his jeans and button-down shirt still sporting the wrinkles from when she'd tossed them aside in an effort to get him naked. That seemed eons ago now. Those moments after the call when they'd hastily gotten dressed again had passed in a frenzied haze.

"Any news?" she asked, feeling like a wretched person for hoping somehow she could keep Issa. She wasn't in any position to care for a baby. She'd never even given much thought to being a mother. But right now, it was the only thing she could think about. Who knew that a baby could fill a void in her life that she would have never guessed needed filling?

He shook his head and sat on the arm of the sofa near her, his blue eyes locked on the two of them. "Just more verification of what we learned last night. The mother's note was honest. Her husband was a soldier killed in a border dispute. And just more confirmation to what we already knew—she picked up a job doing temp work here, which is why she didn't show up on the initial employee search. The woman you saw that night running from the cart was, in fact, Issa's mother. She has family support back on the mainland. But it appears her husband's death hit her especially hard when she was already suffering from postpartum depression."

That last part hadn't been in the early reports. The whole issue became muddier now that the baby hadn't been left out of selfishness, but rather out of a deep mental illness. "Issa ended up in a room-service cart because of postpartum depression?"

"Approximately one in eight new mothers suffer from it in the States." He pinched the bridge of his nose as if battling a headache. "Even more so here with the rampant poverty and lack of medical care."

Mari's arms twitched protectively around the bundled infant. Would it have made a difference for Issa's mother if the family had been more supportive? Or had they been shut out? So many questions piled on top of each other until she realized she was simply looking for someone to blame, a reason why it would be okay to keep Issa. The scent of baby detergent—specially bought so she could wash the tiny clothes herself—mingled with sweet baby breath. Such a tender, dear bundle...

When Issa squirmed, Mari forced herself to relax—at least outwardly. "I guess I should be grateful she didn't harm her child. What happens now?"

Mari's eyes dropped to the child as Issa fought off sleep, her tiny fingers clenching and unclenching.

"She goes to her family," he said flatly.

"Where were they when Issa's mother felt so desperate?" The question fell from Mari's heart as much as her mouth, the objective scientist part of her nowhere to be found. She had to be certain before she could let go.

Rowan's hand fell to a tiny baby foot encased in a Christmas plaid sleeper. "The aunt and uncle insist they offered help, and that they didn't know how badly their niece was coping."

"Do you believe them?"

"They don't live nearby so it's entirely possible they missed the signs. Issa's only three months old." He patted the baby's chest once before shoving to his feet again, pacing restlessly. "They came for the funeral six weeks ago, left some money, followed up with calls, but she told them she was managing all right."

"And they believed her." How awful did it make her that she was still desperately searching for something to fault them for, some reason why they couldn't be the right people to raise the little angel in her arms.

"From everything our sources can tell, they're good people. Solid income from their tourist shop." He stopped at the window, palming the glass and leaning forward with a weary sigh. "They want custody of Issa and there's no legal or moral reason I can see why they shouldn't have her."

"What about what we want?" she asked quickly, in case she might have second thoughts and hold back the words.

"We don't have any rights to her." He glanced back over his shoulder. "This is the best scenario we could have hoped would play out. That first night when we spoke to the cops, we both never really dreamed this good of a solution could be found for her."

"I realize that… It's just…"

He turned to face her, leaning back and crossing his arms over his chest. "You already love her."

"Of course I care about her."

A sad half smile tipped his mouth. "That's not what I said."

"I've only known her a few days." Mari rolled out the logic as if somehow she could convince herself.

"I've watched enough new mothers in my line of work to know how fast the heart engages."

What did he hope to achieve by this? By stabbing her with his words? "I'm not her mother."

"You have been, though. You've done everything a mother would do to protect her child. It's not surprising you want to keep her."

Mari's throat clogged with emotion. "I'm in no position to take care of a baby. She has relatives who want her and can care for her. I know what I have to do."

"You're giving her the best chance, like a good mother." He cupped the back of her head, comfort in his gaze and in his touch.

She soaked up his supporting strength. "Are you trying to soften me up again?"

"I'm wounded you would think I'm that manipulative." He winked.

"Ha," she choked on a half laugh. "Now you're trying to make me smile so I won't cry."

He massaged her scalp lightly. "It's okay to cry if you need to."

She shook her head. "I think I'll just keep rocking her, maybe sing some Christmas carols until her family arrives. I know she won't remember me, but..."

A buzzer sounded at their suite door a second before Hillary walked in, followed by Troy. Mari sighed in relief over the brief reprieve. The aunt and uncle weren't here yet.

Hillary smiled gently. "The family is on their way up. I thought you would want the warning."

"Thank you for your help tracking them down." Mari could hardly believe she managed to keep her voice flat and unemotional in light of the caldron churning inside her.

Troy sat on the sofa beside his wife, the wiry computer mogul sliding an arm around Hillary's shoulders. "I'm glad we were able to resolve the issue so quickly."

Yet it felt like she'd spent a lifetime with Rowan and the baby.

Hillary settled into her husband's arm. "Mari, did Rowan tell you the tip that helped us put the pieces together came from the press coverage you brought in?"

"No, not that I remember." Although he might have

said something and she missed it. Since she'd heard Issa was leaving, Mari had been in a fog.

"Thanks to the huge interest your name inspired, we were contacted by a nurse whose story sounded legit. We showed her the composite sketch we'd pieced together from the different camera angles." Hillary rambled on, filling the tense silence. "She identified the woman as a patient she'd helped through delivery. From there, the rest of the pieces came together. She never would have heard about this if not for you and Rowan. You orchestrated this perfectly, Mari."

"With your help. Rowan is lucky to have such great friends."

And with those words she realized she didn't have people to reach out to in a crisis. She had work acquaintances, and she had family members she kept at arm's length. She spent her life focused on her lab. She'd sealed herself off from the world, running from meaningful relationships as surely as she ran from the press. Shutting herself away from her parents' disapproval—her father wanting her to assume her role of princess, her mother encouraging her to be a rebellious child embracing a universe beyond. Ultimately she'd disappointed them both. Rowan and this baby were her first deep connections in so long....

And it was tearing her apart to say goodbye to them.

She didn't want this pain. She wanted her safe world back. The quiet and order of her research lab, where she could quantify results and predict outcomes.

The buzzer sounded again and Mari bit her lip to keep from shouting in denial. Damn it, she would stay in control. She would see this through in a calm manner, do nothing to upset Issa.

Even though every cell in her cried out in denial.

* * *

Rowan watched helplessly as Mari passed the baby over to her relatives—a couple he'd made damn sure to investigate to the fullest. He'd relocated orphans countless times in his life and he'd always been careful, felt the weight of responsibility.

Never had that weight felt this heavy on his shoulders.

He studied the couple, in their fifties, the husband in a crisp linen suit, the wife in a colorful dress with a matching headscarf. The aunt took Issa from Mari's arms while the uncle held a diaper bag.

Mari twisted her hands in front of her, clearly resisting the temptation to yank the baby back. "She likes to be held close, but facing outward so she can see what's going on. And you have to burp her after every ounce of formula or she spits up. She likes music—"

Her voice cracked.

The aunt placed a hand on her arm. "Thank you for taking such good care of little Issa, Princess. If we had known about our niece's intentions, we would have volunteered to take Issa immediately. But when a young mother assures you she is fine, who would ever think to step in and offer to take her child? Trust us though, we will shower her with love. We will make sure she always knows you have been her guardian angel...."

With teary eyes, Mari nodded, but said nothing.

Troy stepped into the awkward silence. "My wife and I will escort you to your car through a back entrance to be sure the press doesn't overrun you."

Thank God, Troy quickly ushered them out before this hellish farewell tore them all in half. Rowan stole one last look at the baby's sweet chubby-cheeked face, swallowed hard and turned to Mari. No doubt she needed him more now.

The second the door closed behind the Donavans, Mari's legs folded.

She sank into the rocking chair again, nearly doubled over as she gulped in air. Her lovely face tensed with pain as she bit her lower lip. "Rowan, I don't think," she gasped, "I can't...I can't give my presentation this afternoon."

He understood the feeling. Rowan hooked his arm around her shoulders. "I'll call the conference coordinator. I'll tell them you're sick."

"But I'm never sick." She looked up at him with bemused eyes, bright with unshed tears. "I never bow out at work. What's wrong with me?"

"You're grieving." So was he. Something about this child was different, maybe because of the role she'd played in bringing Mari to him. Maybe because of the Christmas season. Or perhaps simply because the little tyke had slipped past the defenses he worked so hard to keep in place as he faced year after year of treating bone-crushing poverty and sickness. "You're human."

"I only knew her a few days. She's not my child...." Mari pressed a hand to her chest, rubbing a wound no less deep for not being visible. "I shouldn't be this upset."

"You loved her—you still do." He shifted around to kneel in front of her, stroking her face, giving Mari comfort—a welcome distraction when he needed it most. "That's clear to anyone who saw you with her."

"I know, damn it." She blinked back tears. "I don't want to think about it. I don't want to feel any of this. I just need...this."

Mari grabbed his shirt front, twisted her fist in the

fabric and yanked him toward her as she fell into him. Rowan absorbed their fall with his body, his shoulders meeting the thick carpet. Mari blanketed him, her mouth meeting his with a frenzy and intensity there was no denying. She'd found an outlet for her grief and he was damn well ready to help her with that. They both needed this.

Needed an outlet for all the frustrated emotions roaring through the room.

She wriggled her hips erotically against his ready arousal. A moan of pleasure slipped from her lips as she nipped his ear. There was no need to be silent any longer. Their suite was empty. Too empty. Their first encounter had been focused on staying quiet, in control as they discovered each other for the first time.

Tonight, control didn't exist.

He pushed those thoughts away and focused on Mari, on making sure she was every bit as turned on as he was. He gathered the hem of her dress and bunched it until he found the sweet curve of her bottom. He guided her against him, met her with a rolling rhythm of his own, a synchronicity they'd discovered together last night.

Sitting up, increasing the pressure against his erection, she yanked his shirt open, buttons popping free and flying onto the carpet. Her ragged breathing mingled with his. He swept her dress off and away until she wore only a pale green satin bra and underwear. He was quickly realizing her preference for soft, feminine lingerie and he enjoyed peeling it from her. He flung the bra to rest on the bar. Then twisted his fist in her panties until the thin strap along her hip snapped. The last scrap of fabric fell away.

She clasped his head in her hands and drew his face

to her breasts. Her guidance, her demands, made him even harder. He took her in his mouth, enjoying the giving as much as the taking. Her moans and sighs were driving him wild. And yes, he had his own pent-up frustrations to work out, his own regret over seeing Issa leave… He shut down those thoughts, grounding himself in the now.

Arching onto her heels, Mari fumbled with the fly of his pants.

"Condom," he groaned. "In my pocket."

He lifted his butt off the floor and she stroked behind him to pluck the packet free. Thank heaven he'd thought to keep one on him even in a crisis. Because he couldn't stomach the thought of stopping, not even for an instant.

Then he felt her hands on him, soft, stroking. He throbbed at her touch as she sheathed him in the condom, then took him inside her. His head dug back as he linked fingers with her, following the ride where she took him, hard and fast, noisy and needy. The fallout would have to take care of itself, because right now, they were both locked in a desperate drive to block out the pain of loss.

Already, he could feel the building power of his release rolling through him. He gritted his teeth, grinding back the need to come. Reaching between them to ease her over the edge with him. One look at her face, the crescendo of her sweet cries, told him she was meeting him there now. He thrust, again and again until his orgasm throbbed free while hers pulsed around him.

He caught her as she collapsed into his arms. He soaked in the warmth of her skin, the pounding of her heart—hell, everything about her.

The cooling air brought hints of reality slithering

back, the world expanding around them. The roaring in his ears grew louder, threatening this pocket of peace. It was too soon for him to take her again, but that didn't rule out other pleasurable possibilities.

Rowan eased Mari from him and onto her back. He kissed her mouth, her jaw, along her neck, inhaling the floral essence of her. Her hands skimmed up and down his spine as she reclined languidly. Smiling against her skin, he nipped his way lower, nuzzling and stroking one breast then the other.

"Rowan?"

"Shhh…" He blew across her damp nipple. The damp brown tip pebbled even tighter for him and he took her in his mouth, flicking with his tongue.

He sprinkled kisses along the soft underside, then traveled lower, lower still until he parted her legs and stroked between her thighs, drawing a deep sigh from her. He dipped his head and breathed in the essence of her, tasted her. Teased at the tight bundle of nerves until she rambled a litany of need for more. He was more than happy to comply.

A primitive rush of possession surged through him. She was his. He cupped the soft globes of her bottom and brought her closer to him, circled and laved, worked her until her fingers knotted restlessly in his hair. He took her to the edge of completion again, then held back, taking her to the precipice again and again, knowing her orgasm would be all the more powerful with the build.

Her head thrashed against the carpet and she cried out his name as her release gripped her. Her hands flung out, knocking over an end table, sending a lamp crashing to the floor.

He watched the flush of completion spread over her

as he slid back up to lay beside her. The evening breeze drifted over them, threatening to bring reality with it.

There was only one way to make it through the rest of this night. Make love to Mari until they both collapsed with exhaustion. Rolling to his knees, he slid his arms under her, lifting as he stood. He secured her against his chest, the soft give of her body against his stirring him.

Her arm draped around his neck, her head lolling against him as she still breathed heavily in the aftermath of her release. He strode across the suite toward his bedroom, his jeans open and riding low on his hips. Hell, he'd never even gotten his pants off.

He lowered Mari to his bed, the sight of her naked body, long legs and subtle curves stirring him impossibly hard again. Shadows played along her dusky skin, inviting him to explore. To lose himself in the oblivion of her body. To forget for a few hours that the emptiness of their suite was so damn tangible… No baby sighs. No iPhone of Christmas lullabies. Gone.

Just like Issa. Their reason for staying together.

Eleven

Mari had spent a restless night in Rowan's arms. As the morning light pierced through the shutters, he'd suggested they get away from the resort and all the memories of Issa that lurked in their suite. She hadn't even hesitated at jumping on board with his plan.

Literally.

Mari stretched out on the bow of the sailboat and stared up at the cloudless sky, frigate birds gliding overhead with their wide wings extended full-out. Waves slapped against the hull, and lines pinged against the mast. Rowan had leased the thirty-three-foot luxury sailboat for the two of them to escape for the day to a deserted shore. No worries about the press spying on them and no reminders of the baby. Nothing to do but to stare into the azure waters, watching fish and loggerhead turtles.

God, how she needed to get away from the reminders. Her time with the baby had touched her heart and made her realize so many things were missing in her life. Love. Family. She'd buried herself in work, retreating into a world that made sense to her after a lifetime of feeling awkward in her own skin. But holding that sweet little girl had made Mari accept she'd turned her back on far too much.

That didn't mean she had any idea how to fix it. Or herself. She watched Rowan guiding the sailboat, open shirt flapping behind him, sun burnishing his blond hair.

Rowan had made love to her—and she to him— until they'd both fallen into an exhausted sleep. They'd slept, woken only long enough to order room service and made love again. She had the feeling Rowan was as confused and empty as she, but she couldn't quite put her finger on why.

For that matter, maybe she was just too lost in her own hurt to understand his.

In the morning, he'd told her to dress for a day on a boat. She hadn't questioned him, grateful for the distraction. Mari had tossed on a sarong, adding dark glasses and an old-school Greta Garbo scarf to make her escape. He'd surprised her with a gift, bracelets she'd admired at the marketplace their first night out with Issa. She stretched her arm out, watching the sun refract off the silver bangles and colorful beads.

Rowan sailed the boat, handling the lines with ease as the hull chopped through the water toward an empty cove, lush mountains jutting in the distance. They'd followed the coast all morning toward a neighboring island with a private harbor. If only the ache in her heart was as easy to leave behind.

She rolled to her tummy and stretched out along her

towel, her well-loved body languid and a bit stiff. Chin on her hands, she gazed out at the rocks jutting from the water along the secluded coastline. She watched the gannets and petrels swoop and dive for fish. Palm trees clustered along the empty shoreline, creating a thick wall of foliage just beyond the white sandy beaches. Peaceful perfection, all familiar and full of childhood memories of vacationing along similar shores with her parents.

A shadow stretched across her, a broad-shouldered shadow. She flipped to her back again, shading her eyes to look up at Rowan. "Shouldn't you be at the helm?"

"We've dropped anchor." He crouched beside her, too handsome for his own good in swim trunks and an open shirt, ocean breeze pulling at his loose hair. "Come with me and have something to drink?"

She clasped his outstretched hand and stood, walking with him, careful to duck and weave past the boom and riggings. The warm hardwood deck heated her bare feet. "You didn't have to be so secretive about our destination."

"I wanted to surprise you." He jumped down to the deck level, grasping her waist and lowering her to join him. He gestured to where he'd poured them two glasses of mango juice secured in the molded surface between the seat cushions, the pitcher tucked securely in an open cooler at his bare feet.

"That's your only reason?"

"I wasn't sure you would agree, and we both needed to get away from the resort." He passed her a glass, nudging her toward the captain's chair behind the wheel. "Besides, my gorgeous, uptight scientist, you need to have fun."

"I have fun." Sitting, she sipped her drink. The sweet

natural sugars sent a jolt of energy through her, his words putting her on the defensive. "My work is fun."

He cocked an eyebrow, shooting just above his sunglasses.

"Okay, my work is rewarding. And I don't recall being all that uptight when I was sitting on the bar last night." She eyed him over the glass.

"Fair enough. I'm taking you out because I want you mellow and softened up so when I try to seduce you later you completely succumb to my charm." He thudded the heel of his palm to his forehead, clearly doing his best to take her mind off things. "Oh, wait, I already seduced you."

"Maybe I seduced you." She tossed aside her sunglasses and pulled off his aviator shades, her bracelets chiming with each movement. She leaned in to kiss him, more than willing to be distracted from the questions piling up in her mind.

Like where they would go from here once the conference was over. Since she didn't have any suggestions in mind, she sure wasn't going to ask for his opinion.

"Whose turn is it, then, to take the initiative?" He pulled her drink from her and stepped closer.

"I've lost count." She let her eyes sweep over him seductively, immersing herself in this game they both played, delaying the inevitable.

"Princess, you do pay the nicest compliments." He stroked her face, along the scarf holding back her hair, tugging it free.

"You say the strangest things." She traced his mouth, the lips that had brought her such pleasure last night.

"We're here to play, not psychoanalyze."

Her own lips twitched with a self-deprecating smile. "Glad to know it, because I stink at reading people."

"Why do you assume that?" His question mingled with the call of birds in the trees and the plop of fish.

"Call it a geek thing."

"You make geek sexy." He nipped her tracing finger, then sucked lightly.

She rolled her eyes. "You are such a…"

"A what?"

"I don't even have words for you."

His eyes went serious for the first time this morning. "Glad to know I mystify you as much as you bemuse me."

"I've always thought of myself as a straightforward person. Some call that boring." She flinched, hating the feeling that word brought, knowing she couldn't—wouldn't—change. "For me, there's comfort in routine."

Those magnificently blue eyes narrowed and darkened. "Tell me who called you boring and I'll—"

She clapped a hand over his mouth, bracelets dangling. "It's okay. But thanks." She pulled her hand away, a rogue wave bobbing the boat beneath her. "I had trouble making friends in school. I didn't fit in for so many reasons—everything from my ridiculous IQ to the whole princess thing. I was either much younger than my classmates or they were sucking up because of my family. There was no sisterhood for me. It was tough for people to see the real me behind all that clutter."

"I wasn't an instant fit at school, either." He shifted to stand beside her, looping an arm around her shoulders bared by the sarong.

She leaned against him, looking out over the azure blue waters. The continent of her birth was such a mixture of lush magnificence and stark poverty. "You don't need to change your history to make me feel better. I'm okay with myself."

"God's honest truth here." He rested his chin on top of her head. "My academy brothers and I were all misfits. The headmaster there did a good job at redirecting us, channeling us, helping us figure out ways to put our lives on the right path again."

"All of you? That's quite a track record."

He went still against her. "Not all of us. Some of us were too far gone to be rehabilitated." His sigh whispered over her, warmer than the sun. "You may have read in the news about Malcolm Douglas's business manager—he was a schoolmate of ours. He lost his way, forgot about rules and integrity. He did some shady stuff to try and wrangle publicity for his client."

"Your friend. Malcolm. Another of your Brotherhood?"

"Malcolm and I aren't as close as I am to the others. But yes, he's a friend." He turned her by her shoulders and stared into her eyes. "We're not perfect, any of us, but the core group of us, we can call on each other for anything, anytime."

"Like how the casino owner friend provided the start-up money for your clinic…"

Rowan had built an incredible support system for himself after his parents failed him. While she'd cut herself off from the world.

"That he did. You wouldn't recognize Conrad from the high school photos. He was gangly and wore glasses back then, but he was a brilliant guy and he knew it. Folks called him Mr. Wall Street, because of his dad and how Conrad used his trust fund to manipulate the stock market to punish sweatshop businesses."

"You all may have been misfits, but it appears you share a need for justice."

"We didn't all get along at first. I was different

from them, though, or so I liked to tell myself. I didn't come from money like most of the guys there—or like you—and I wasn't inordinately talented like Douglas. I thought I was better than those overprivileged brats."

"Yet, Conrad must respect you to have invested so much money to start the clinic."

"If we're going to be honest—" he laughed softly "—I'm where I am today because of a cookie."

"A cookie?" She tipped her head back to the warm sunshine, soaking in the heat of the day and the strength of the man beside her.

"My mom used to send me these care packages full of peanut-butter cookies with M&M's baked into them." His eyes took on a faraway look and a fond smile.

Mari could only think that same mother had sent him to that school in his brother's place. Those cookies must have tasted like dust in light of such a betrayal from the woman who should have protected him. She bit back the urge to call his mother an unflattering name and just listened, ocean wind rustling her hair.

"One day, I was in my bunk, knocking back a couple of those cookies while doing my macro biology homework." He toyed with the end of her scarf. "I looked up to find Conrad staring at those cookies like they were caviar. I knew better than to offer him one. His pride would have made him toss it back in my face."

She linked fingers with him and squeezed as he continued, her cheek against the warm cotton of his shirt, her ear taking in the steady thrum of his heart.

"We were all pretty angry at life in those days. But I had my cookies and letters from Mom to get me through the days when I didn't think I could live with the guilt of what I'd done."

What his family had done. His mother, father and his brother. Why couldn't he see how they'd sacrificed him?

"But back to Conrad. About a week later, I was on my way to the cafeteria and I saw him in the visitation area with his dad. I was jealous as hell since my folks couldn't afford to fly out to visit me—and then I realized he and his dad were fighting."

"About what?" She couldn't help but ask, desperate for this unfiltered look into the teenage Rowan, hungry for insights about what had shaped him into the man he'd become.

"From what Conrad shouted, it was clear his father wanted him to run a scam on Troy's parents and convince them to invest in some bogus company or another. Conrad decked his dad. It took two security guards to pull him off."

Hearing the things that Rowan and his friends had been through as teens, she felt petty for her anger over her own childhood. The grief Rowan and his friends had faced, the storms in their worlds, felt so massive in comparison to her own. She had two parents that loved her, two homes, and yes, she was shuttled back and forth, but in complete luxury.

"And the cookie?"

"I'm getting there." He sketched his fingers up and down her bare arm. "Conrad spent a couple of days in the infirmary—his dad hit him back and dislocated Conrad's shoulder. The cops didn't press charges on the old man because the son threw the first punch. Anyhow, Conrad's first day out of the infirmary, I felt bad for him so I wrapped a cookie in a napkin and put it on his bunk. He didn't say anything, but he didn't toss it back in my face, either." He threw his hands wide. "And here I am today."

Her heart hurt so badly she could barely push words out. "Why are you telling me this?"

"I don't know. I just want you to understand why my work is so important to me, so much so that I couldn't have kept Issa even if her family didn't come through. Because if I start keeping every orphan that tugs at my emotions, I won't be able to sustain all I've fought so hard to build. The clinic…it's everything to me. It helps me fill the hole left by Dylan's death, helps me make up for the lives lost."

She heard him, heard an isolation in his words in spite of all those friends. He'd committed himself to a life of service that left him on a constant, lonely quest. And right then and there, her soul ached for him.

She slid her hand up into his hair, guiding his mouth to hers. He stepped between her knees, and she locked her arms around his neck. Tight. Demanding and taking.

"Now," she whispered against his mouth, fishing in his back pocket for a condom.

He palmed her knees apart and she purred her approval. Her fingers made fast work of his swim trunks, freeing his erection and sheathing him swiftly, surely.

She locked her legs around his waist and drew him in deeper. He drove into her again and again. She angled back, gripping the bar, bracelets sliding down to collect along her hand. He took in the beauty of her, her smooth skin, pert breasts, her head thrown back and hair swaying with every thrust. The boat rocked in a rhythm that matched theirs as his shouts of completion twined and mingled with hers, carried on the breeze.

In that moment she felt connected to him more than physically. She identified with him, overwhelmed by an understanding of him being as alone in the world as her. But also hammered by a powerlessness to change that. His vision and walls were as strong as hers, always had been. Maybe more so.

What a time to figure out she might have sacrificed too much for her work—only realizing that now, as she fell for a man who would sacrifice anything for *his*.

The taste of the sea, sweat and Mari still clinging to his skin, Rowan opened the door to their suite the next morning, praying the return to land and real life wouldn't bring on the crushing sense of loss. He'd hoped to distract her from Issa—and also find some way to carve out a future for them. They were both dedicated to their work. They could share that, even in their disagreements. They could use that as a springboard to work out solutions. Together. His time with her overnight on the sailboat had only affirmed that for him.

He just hoped he'd made a good start in persuading Mari of the same thing.

Guiding her into the suite with a hand low on her spine, he stepped deeper into the room. Only to stop short. His senses went on alert. There was someone here.

Damn it, there was more traffic through this supposedly secure room than through the lobby. Which of course meant it was one of his friends.

Elliot Starc rose from the sofa and from Mari's gasp beside him, clearly she recognized the world-famous race-car driver…and underwear model.

Rowan swallowed a curse. "Good morning, Elliot. Did you get booted out of your own room?"

Laughing, Elliot took Mari's hand lightly and ignored Rowan's question. "Princess, it's an honor to meet you."

"Mr. Starc, you're one of Rowan's Brotherhood friends, I assume."

Elliot's eyebrows shot up. "You told her?"

"We talk." Among other things.

"Well, color me stunned. That baby was lucky to have landed in Rowan's room. Our Interpol connections kept all of you safe while bringing this to a speedy conclusion."

Crap. The mention of Interpol hung in the air, Mari's eyes darting to his.

Oblivious to the gaffe, Elliot continued, "Which brings me to my reason for being here. I've emailed a summary of the existing security detail, but I need to get back to training, get my mind back in the game so I don't set more than my hair on fire."

Rowan pulled a tight smile. "Thanks, buddy."

Mari frowned. "Interpol?"

Elliot turned sharply to Rowan. "You said you told her about the Brotherhood."

"Classmates. I told her we're classmates." He didn't doubt she would keep his secret safe, but knowing wouldn't help her and anything that didn't help was harmful. "You, my friend, made a mighty big assumption for someone who should know better."

"She's a princess. You've been guarding her." Elliot scratched his sheared hair. "I thought… Ah, hell. Just…" Throwing his hands out and swiping the air as if that explained it all, Elliot spun on his heel and walked out the door.

Mari sat hard, sinking like a stone on the edge of the sofa. "You're with Interpol?" She huffed on a long sigh. "Of course you're with Interpol."

"I'm a physician. That's my primary goal, my mission in life." He paused, unable to dodge the truth as he kneeled in front of her. "But yes, I help out Interpol on occasion with freelance work in the area. No one thinks twice about someone like me wandering around wealthy fundraisers or traveling to remote countries."

He could see her closing down, pulling away.

"Mari?"

"It's your job. I understand."

"Are you angry with me for not telling you?"

"Why would you? It's not my secret to know. Your friend…he assumed more about us than he should. But you know I won't say a word. I understand well what it's like to be married to your work."

Her words came out measured and even, her body still, her spine taking on that regal "back off" air that shouted of generations of royalty. "Mari, this doesn't have to mean things change between us. If anything we can work together."

"Work, right…" Her amber eyes flickered with something he couldn't quite pin down.

"Are you all right?"

"I'll be fine. It's all just a lot to process, this today. Issa yesterday."

He cradled her shoulders in his hands. She eased away.

"Mari, it's okay to shout at me if you're mad. Or to cry about Issa. I'm here for you," he said, searching for the right way to approach her.

"Fine. You want me to talk? To yell? You've got it. I would appreciate your acting like we're equal rather than stepping into your benevolent physician shoes because no one would dare to contradict the man who does so much for the world." She shrugged free of his grip.

"Excuse me for trying to be a nice guy." He held up his hands.

"You're always the nice guy." She shot to her feet. "The saint. Giving out comfort, saving the world, using that as a wall between you and other people."

"What the hell are you talking about?" He stood warily, watching her pace.

"There you go. Get mad at me." She stopped in front of him, crossing her arms over her chest. "At least real emotions put us on an even footing. Oh, wait, we're not even. You're the suave doctor/secret agent. I'm the awkward genius who locks herself away in a lab."

"Are we really returning to the old antagonistic back-and-forth way of communicating?" he asked. Her words felt damn unfair when he was working his tail off to help her through a rough time. "I thought we'd moved past that."

"That's not what I'm talking about and you know it. You're a smart man."

"Actually, you're the certified genius here. How about you explain it to me."

"You want me to cry and grieve and open myself up to you." She jabbed his chest with one finger, her voice rising with every word. "But what about you? When do you open up to me? When are you going to give me something besides the saintly work side of your life?"

"I've told you things about my past," he answered defensively.

"To be fair, yes you have," she conceded without backing down. "Some things. Certainly not everything. And when have you let me in? You're fine with things as long as you're the one doling out comfort. But accepting it? No way. Like now. You have every reason to grieve for Issa."

"She's in good hands, well cared for," he said through gritted teeth.

"See? There you go doing just what I said. You want me to cry and be emotional, but you—" she waved a hand "—you're just fine. Did you even allow yourself to grieve for your brother?"

His head snapped back, her words smacking him even as she kept her hands fisted at her sides. "Don't you dare use my brother against me. That has nothing to do with what we're discussing now."

"It has everything to do with what we're talking about. But if I'm mistaken, then explain it to me. Explain what you're feeling."

She waited while he searched for the right words, but everything he'd offered her so far hadn't worked. He didn't have a clue what to say to reassure her. And apparently he waited too long.

"That's what I thought." She shook her head sadly, backing away from him step by step. "I'm returning to my old room. There's no reason for me to be here anymore."

She spun away, the hem of her sarong fluttering as she raced into her room and slammed the door. He could hear her tossing her suitcase on the bed. Heard her muffled sobs. And heard the click of the lock that spoke loud and clear.

He'd blown it. Royally, so to speak. He might be confused about a lot of things. But one was crystal clear.

He was no longer welcome in Mari's life.

Twelve

The conference was over. Her week with Rowan was done.

Mari stood in front of the mirrored vanity and tucked the final pin into her hair, which was swept back in a sleek bun. Tonight's ball signified an official end to their time together. There was no dodging the event without being conspicuous and stirring up more talk in the press.

As if there wasn't enough talk already. At least all reports from the media—and from Rowan's Interpol friends—indicated that Issa was adapting well in her new home after only a couple of days. Something to be eternally grateful for. A blessing in this heartbreaking week.

Her pride demanded she finish with her head held high.

After her confrontation with Rowan, she'd waited the

remainder of her stay, hoping he would fight for her as hard as he fought for his work, for every person who walked through those clinic doors. But she hadn't heard a word from him since she'd stormed from his room and she'd gone back to her simple room a floor below. How easily he'd let her go, and in doing so, broken her heart.

But his ability to disconnect with her also filled her with resolve.

She wouldn't be like him anymore, hiding from the world. She was through staying in the shadows for fear of disappointing people.

Mari smoothed her hands down the shimmering red strapless dress, black swirls through the fabric giving the impression of phantom roses. The dress hugged her upper body, fitted past her hips then swept to the ground with a short train. It was a magnificent gown. She'd never worn anything like it. She would have called it a Cinderella moment except she didn't want to be some delicate princess at the ball. She was a one-day queen, boldly stepping into her own.

Her hands fell to the small tiara, diamonds refracting the vanity lights. Carefully, she tucked the crown—symbolic of so much more—on her head.

Stepping from her room, she checked the halls and, how ironic, for once the corridor was empty. No fans to carefully maneuver. She could make her way to the brass-plated elevator in peace.

Jabbing the elevator button, she curled her toes in her silken ballet slippers. Her stomach churned with nerves over facing the crowd downstairs alone, even more than that, over facing Rowan again. But she powered on, one leather-clad foot at a time. While she was ready to meet the world head-on in her red Vera Wang, she wasn't prepared to do so wearing high heels that would likely send her stumbling down the stairs.

She was bold, but practical.

Finally, the elevator doors slid open, except the elevator wasn't empty. Her stomach dropped in shock faster than a cart on a roller-coaster ride.

"Papa?" She stared at her father, her royal father.

But even more surprising, her mother stood beside him. "Going down, dear?"

Stunned numb, she stepped into the elevator car, brass doors sliding closed behind her.

"Mother, why are you and Papa here? *Together?*" she squeaked as her mom hugged her fast and tight.

The familiar scent of her mom's perfume enveloped her, like a bower of gardenias. And her mom wasn't dressed for a simple visit. Susan Mandara was decked out for the ball in a Christmas-green gown, her blond hair piled on top of her head. Familiar, yet so unusual, since Mari couldn't remember the last time she'd seen Adeen and Susan Mandara standing side by side in anything other than old pictures.

Her father kissed her on the forehead. "Happy Christmas, little princess."

She clutched her daddy's forearms, the same arms that used to toss her high in the air as a child. Always catching her.

Tonight, her father wore a tuxedo with a crimson tribal robe over it, trimmed in gold. As a child, she used to sneak his robes out to wear for dress-up with her parents laughing, her mother affectionately calling him Deen, her nickname for him. She'd forgotten that happy memory until just now.

Her mother smoothed cool hands over her daughter's face. "Your father and I have a child together." She gave

Mari's face a final pat. "Deen and I are bonded for life, *by* life, through you. We came to offer support and help you with all the press scrutiny."

Did they expect her to fail? She couldn't resist saying, "Some of this togetherness would have been welcome when I was younger."

"We've mellowed with age." Susan stroked her daughter's forehead. "I wish we could have given you a simpler path. We certainly wanted to."

If her mother had wanted to keep things simple, marrying a prince was surely a weird way to go about it.

Her father nodded his head. "You look magnificent. You are everything I wanted my princess to grow up to be."

"You're just saying that because I'm decked out in something other than a sack," she teased him, even though her heart ached with the cost of her newfound confidence. "But I can assure you, I still detest ribbon cuttings and state dinners."

"And you still care about the people. You'll make your mark in a different manner than I did. That's good." He held out both elbows as the elevator doors slid open on the ground floor. "Ladies? Shall we?"

Decorations in the hallway had doubled since she went upstairs to change after the final presentation of the day. Mari strode past oil palm trees decorated with bells. Music drifted from the ballroom, a live band played carols on flutes, harps and drums.

The sounds of Christmas. The sounds of home. Tables laden with food. She could almost taste the sweet cookies and the meats marinated in *chakalaka*.

A few steps later, she stood on the marble threshold of the grand ballroom. All eyes turned to her and for a moment her feet stayed rooted to the floor. Cameras clicked and she didn't so much as flinch or cringe. She wasn't sure what to do next as she swept the room with her eyes, taking in the ballroom full of medical professionals decked out in all their finery, with local bigwigs in attendance, as well.

Then her gaze hitched on Rowan, wearing a traditional tuxedo, so handsome he took her breath away.

His hair was swept back, just brushing his collar, his eyes blue flames that singed her even from across the room. She expected him to continue ignoring her. But he surprised her by striding straight toward her. All eyes followed him, and her heart leaped into her throat.

Rowan stopped in front of them and nodded to her father. "Sir, I believe your daughter and I owe the media a dance."

Owe the media?

What about what they owed each other?

And how could he just stand there as if nothing had happened between them, as if they hadn't bared their bodies and souls to each other? She had a gloriously undignified moment of wanting to kick him. But this was her time to shine and she refused to let him wreck it. She stepped into his arms, and he gestured to the band. They segued into a rendition of "Ave Maria," with a soloist singing.

Her heart took hope that he'd chosen the piece for her. He led her to the middle of the dance floor. Other couples melted away and into the crowd, leaving them alone, at the mercy of curious eyes and cameras.

As she allowed herself to be swept into his arms— into the music—she searched for something to say. "I appreciate the lovely song choice."

"It fits," he answered, but his face was still creased in a scowl, his eyes roving over her.

"Don't you like the dress?"

"I like the woman in the dress," he said hoarsely. "If you'd been paying attention, you would have realized my eyes have been saying that for a long time before you changed up your wardrobe."

"So why are you scowling?"

"Because I want this whole farce of a week to be over."

"Oh," she said simply, too aware of his hand on her waist, his other clasping her fingers.

"Do you believe me? About the dress, I mean." His feet moved in synch with hers, their bodies as fluid on the dance floor as they'd been making love.

"We've exchanged jabs in the past, insults even, but you've always been honest."

"Then why are you still sleeping on another floor of the hotel?"

"Oh, Rowan," she said bittersweetly. "Sex isn't the problem between us."

"Remind me what is?"

"The way you close people—me—out. It took me a long time to realize I'm deserving of everything. And so are you."

"I guess there's nothing left to say then."

The music faded away, and with a final sweep across the floor he stopped in front of her parents.

Rowan passed her hand back to her father. "With all due respect, sir, take better care of her."

Her mother smothered a laugh.

Her father arched a royal eyebrow. "I beg your pardon."

"More security detail. She's a princess. She deserves to be cared for and protected like one."

With a final nod, Rowan turned away and melted into the crowd and out of her life.

Five hours later, Mari hugged her pillow to her chest, watching her mom settle into the other double bed in the darkened room. "Mother, aren't we wealthy enough for you to have a suite or at least a room of your own?"

Susan rolled to her side, facing her daughter in the shadowy room lit only by moonlight streaming in. "I honestly thought you would be staying with Dr. Boothe even though this room was still booked in your name. And even with the show of good faith your father and I have given, we're not back to sharing a room."

Curtains rustled with the night ocean breeze and sounds of a steel-drum band playing on the beach for some late-night partiers.

"Rowan and I aren't a couple anymore." Although the haunting beauty of that dance still whispered through her, making her wonder what more she could have done. "It was just a...fling."

The most incredible few days of her life.

"Mari dear, you are not the fling sort," her mother reminded her affectionately. "So why are you walking away from him?"

Tears clogged her throat. "I'm honestly too upset to talk about this." She flipped onto her back, clenching her fists against the memory of his tuxedoed shoulders under her hands.

The covers rustled across the room as her mother sat up. "I made the biggest mistake of my life when I was about your age."

"Marrying my father. Yeah, I got that." Was it in her DNA to fail at relationships? Her parents had both been divorced twice.

"No, marrying the man I loved—your father—was the right move. Thinking I could change him? I screwed up there." She hugged her knees to her chest, her graying blond hair trailing down her back. "Before you think I'm taking all the blame here, he thought I would change, as well. So the divorce truly was a fifty-fifty screw-up on our part. He should have realized my free spirit is what he fell in love with and I should have recognized how drawn I was to his devotion to his country."

What was her mother trying to tell her? She wanted to understand, to step outside of the awkwardness in more ways than just being comfortable in a killer red dress. Except her mom was talking about not changing at all.

"You're going to have to spell it out for me more clearly."

"Your father and I weren't a good couple. We weren't even particularly good at being parents. But, God, you sure turned out amazing," her mother said with an unmistakable pride, soothing years of feeling like a disappointment. "Deen and I did some things right, and maybe if we'd focused more on the things we did right, we might have lasted."

Mari ached to pour out all the details of her fight with Rowan, how she needed him to open up. And how ironic was it that he accused her of not venting her emotions? Her thoughts jumbled together until she blurted out in frustration, "Do you know how difficult it is to love a saint?"

Her mother reached out in the dark, across the divide between their beds. "You love him?"

Mari reached back and clasped her mother's hand.

"Of course I do. I just don't know how to get through to him."

"You two have been a couple for—what?—a week? Seems to me like you're giving up awful fast."

Mari bristled defensively. "I've known him for years. And it's been an intense week."

"And you're giving that up? I'd so hoped you would be smarter than I was." Her mom gave her hand a final squeeze. "Think about it. Good night, Mari."

Long into the night, Mari stared out the window at the shoreline twinkling with lighted palm trees. The rolling waves crashed a steady reminder of her day sailing with Rowan. He'd done so much to comfort her. Not just with words, but with actions, by planning the day away from the hotel and painful memories.

What had she done for him?

Nothing.

She'd simply demanded her expectations for him rather than accepting him as he was. He'd accepted and appreciated her long before a ball gown. Even when he disagreed with her, he'd respected her opinion.

Damn it all, she *was* smarter than this. Of course Rowan had built walls around himself. Every person in his family had let him down—his parents and his brother. None of them had ever put him or his well-being first. Sure, he'd made friends with his schoolmates, but he'd even admitted to feeling different from them.

Now she'd let him down, as well. He'd reached out to her as best he could and she'd told him what he offered wasn't good enough, maybe because she'd been scared of not being enough for him.

But she knew better than that now. A confidence flowed through her like a calming breeze blowing in off the ocean. With that calm came the surety of what to do next.

It was time to fight for the man she loved, a man she loved for his every saintly imperfection.

Rowan had always been glad to return to his clinic on the mainland. He'd spent every Christmas here in surgical scrubs taking care of patients since moving to Africa. He welcomed the work, leaving holiday celebrations to people with families.

Yet, for some reason, the CD of Christmas carols and a pre-lit tree in the corner didn't stir much in the way of festive feelings this year. A few gifts remained for the patients still in the hospital, the other presents having been passed out earlier, each box a reminder of shopping with Mari.

So he buried himself in work.

Phone tucked under his chin, he listened to Elliot's positive update on Issa, followed by a rambling recounting of his Australian Christmas vacation. Rowan cranked back in a chair behind his desk, scanning a computer file record on a new mother and infant due to be discharged first thing in the morning.

One wing of the facility held a thirty-bed hospital unit and the other wing housed a clinic. Not overly large, but all top-of-the-line and designed for efficiency. They doled out anything from vaccinations to prenatal care to HIV/AIDS treatment.

The most gut-wrenching of all? The patients who came for both prenatal care and HIV treatment. There was a desperate need here and he couldn't help everyone, but one at a time, he was doing his damnedest.

The antibacterial scent saturated each breath he took. Two nurses chatted with another doctor at the station across the hall. Other than that, the place was quiet as a church mouse this late at night.

"Elliot, if you've got a point here, make it. I've got a Christmas Eve dinner to eat."

Really, just a plate to warm in the microwave but he wasn't particularly hungry anyhow. Visions of Mari in that red gown, cloaked in total confidence, still haunted his every waking and sleeping thought. He'd meant what he'd said when he told her it didn't matter to him what clothes she wore. But he was damn proud of the peace she seemed to have found with being in the spotlight. Too bad he couldn't really be a part of it.

"Ah, Rowan, I really thought you were smarter than me, brother," Elliot teased over the phone from his Australian holiday. The background echoed with drunken carolers belting out a raucous version of "The Twelve Days of Christmas."

"As I recall, our grades were fairly on par with each other back in the day."

"Sure, but I've had about four concussions since then, not to mention getting set on fire."

A reluctant smile tugged at Rowan. "Your point?"

"Why in the hell did you let that woman go?" Elliot asked, the sounds of laughter and splashing behind him. "You're clearly crazy about her and she's nuts about you. And the chemistry... Every time you looked at each other, it was all I could do not to shout at you two to get a room."

"She doesn't want me in her life." The slice of her rejection still cut so much deeper than any other.

"Did she tell you that?"

"Very clearly," he said tightly, not enjoying in the least reliving the moment. "I think her words were along the lines of 'have a nice life.'"

"You've never been particularly self-aware."

He winced, closing down the computer file on his new maternity patient. "That's what she said."

"So are you going to continue to be a miserable ass or are you going to go out and meet Mari at the clinic gate?"

At the gate? He creaked upright in his chair, swinging his feet to the floor. "What the hell are you talking about? You're in Australia."

But he stormed over to look out his office window anyway.

"Sure, but you tasked me with her security and I figured some follow-up was in order. I've been keeping track of her with a combo of guards and a good old-fashioned GPS on her rental car. If my satellite connection is any good, she should be arriving right about… now."

Rowan spotted an SUV rounding the corner into sight, headlights sweeping the road as the vehicle drove toward the clinic. Could it really be Mari? Here? Suddenly, Elliot's call made perfect sense. He'd been stringing Rowan along on the line until just the right moment.

"And Rowan," Elliot continued, "be sure you're the one to say the whole 'love you' part first since she came to you. Merry Christmas, brother."

Love her?

Of course he loved her. Wanted her. Admired her. Desired her. Always had, and why he hadn't thought to tell her before now was incomprehensible to him. Thank God for his friends, who knew him well enough to boot him in the tail when he needed that nudge most.

Thank God for Mari, who hadn't given up on him. She challenged him. Disagreed with him. But yet here she was, for him.

The line disconnected as he was already out the door and sprinting down the hall, hand over his pager to keep it from dislodging from his scrubs in his haste. His gym shoes squeaked against the tiles as he turned the corner and burst out through the front door, into the starlit night. The brisk wind rippled his surgical scrubs.

The tan SUV parked beside the clinic's ambulance under a sprawling shea butter tree. The vehicle's dome light flicked on, and Merry Christmas to him, he saw Mari's beautiful face inside. She stepped out, one incredibly long leg at a time, wearing flowing silk pants and a tunic. The fabric glided along her skin the way his hands ached to do again.

Her appearance here gave him the first hope in nearly a week that he would get to do just that.

"You came," he said simply.

"Of course. It's Christmas." She walked toward him, the African night sky almost as magnificent as his princess. She wore the bracelets he'd given her, the bangles chiming against each other. Toe-to-toe, she stopped in front of him, the sweet scent and heat of her reaching out to him. "Where else would I be but with the man I l—"

He pressed a finger against her lips. "Wait, hold that thought. I have something I need to say first. I love you, Mariama Mandara. I've wanted you and yes, loved you, for longer than I can remember. And I will do whatever it takes to be worthy of your love in return."

"Ah, Rowan, don't you know? You're already exactly what I need and everything I want. God knows, if you get any more saintly you're likely to be raptured and I would miss you so very much. I love you, too."

Relief flooded him, his heart soaking up every word like the parched ground around him absorbing a rain shower. Unable to wait another second, he hauled her to his chest and kissed her, deeply, intensely, hoping she really understood just how much he meant those words. He loved her. The truth of that sang through him as tangibly as the carols carrying gently through an open window.

Ending the kiss with a nip to his bottom lip, Mari smiled up at him. "I had a far more eloquent speech planned. I even practiced saying it on the way over because I wanted the words to be as special as what we've shared together."

"I hope you trust I love you, too." He only wished he had a more romantic way of telling her.

"I do. You showed me." She tugged the ends of the stethoscope draped around his neck, her bracelets sliding along her arm. "I just needed to stop long enough to listen with my heart. And my heart says we're perfect for each other. That we're meant to be together."

"Then why did we give each other such a hard time all these years?"

"We are both smart, dedicated people with a lot to offer, but we should be challenged. It makes us better at what we do." She tugged his face closer, punctuating the words with a quick kiss. "And if I have my way, I'm going to challenge you every day for the rest of my life."

"You have mesmerized me since the moment I first saw you." Desire and love interlocked inside him, each spiking the other to a higher level.

"That's one of the things I love most about you." She toyed with his hair, which just brushed the collar of his scrubs.

"What would that be?" He looped his arms low around her waist.

"You think my baggy, wrinkled wardrobe is sexy."

"Actually, I think peeling the clothes off of you is life's most perfect pleasure." He brought them closer together, grateful to have her in his arms, determined never to let this woman slip away from him again.

"Well, then, Dr. Boothe, let's find somewhere private to go so you can unwrap your Christmas present."

* * * * *

 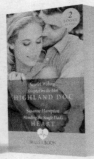 

LET'S TALK
Romance

For exclusive extracts, competitions
and special offers, find us online:

 facebook.com/millsandboon

 @MillsandBoon

 @MillsandBoonUK

Get in touch on 01413 063232

For all the latest titles coming soon, visit
millsandboon.co.uk/nextmonth